**Every Dead Thing**
**Dark Hollow**

*About the author*

John Connolly was born in Dublin in 1968 and
is a regular contributor to the *Irish Times*.

John Connolly

# Every Dead Thing
## and
# Dark Hollow

CORONET BOOKS
Hodder & Stoughton

First published as two separate volumes:
*Every Dead Thing* © 1999 John Connolly
First published in Great Britain in 1999 by Hodder & Stoughton
First published in paperback in 1999 by Hodder & Stoughton
A division of Hodder Headline
A Coronet paperback

*Dark Hollow* © 2000 John Connolly
First published in Great Britain in 2000 by Hodder & Stoughton
First published in paperback in 2000 by Hodder & Stoughton
A division of Hodder Headline
A Coronet paperback
This paperback omnibus edition 2003

The right of John Connolly to be identified as the Author of
the Work has been asserted by him in accordance with the
Copyright, Designs and Patents Act 1988.

All characters in this publication are fictitious
and any resemblance to real persons, living or dead,
is purely coincidental.

A CIP catalogue record for this title
is available from the British Library

ISBN 0 340 83081 6

Typeset by Hewer Text Ltd, Edinburgh
Printed and bound in Great Britain by
Clays Ltd, St Ives plc

Hodder & Stoughton
A division of Hodder Headline
338 Euston Road
London NW1 3BH

# Every Dead Thing

John Connolly

# Part One

I am every dead thing . . . I am re-begot
Of absence, darknesse, death; things which are not.

*John Donne,* 'A Nocturnall Upon S. Lucies Day'

# Prologue

*It is cold in the car, cold as the grave. I prefer to leave the a/c on full, to let the falling temperature keep me alert. The volume on the radio is low but I can still hear a tune, vaguely insistent over the sound of the engine. It's early REM, something about shoulders and rain. I've left Cornwall Bridge about eight miles behind and soon I'll be entering South Canaan, then Canaan itself, before crossing the state line into Massachusetts. Ahead of me, the bright sun is fading as day bleeds slowly into night.*

The patrol car arrived first on the night they died, shedding red light into the darkness. Two patrolmen entered the house, quickly yet cautiously, aware that they were responding to a call from one of their own, a policeman who had become a victim instead of the resort of victims.

I sat in the hallway with my head in my hands as they entered the kitchen of our Brooklyn home and glimpsed the remains of my wife and child. I watched as one conducted a brief search of the upstairs rooms while the other checked the living room, the dining room, all the time the kitchen calling them back, demanding that they bear witness.

I listened as they radioed for the Major Crime Scene Unit, informing them of a probable double homicide. I could hear the shock in their voices, yet they tried to communicate what

3

they had seen as dispassionately as they could, like good cops should. Maybe, even then, they suspected me. They were policemen and they, more than anyone else, knew what people were capable of doing, even one of their own.

And so they remained silent, one by the car and the other in the hallway beside me, until the detectives pulled up outside, the ambulance following, and they entered our home, the neighbours already gathering on their stoops, at their gates, some moving closer to find out what had happened, what could have been visited on the young couple beyond, the couple with the little blonde girl.

'Bird?' I ran my hands over my eyes as I recognised the voice. A sob shuddered through my system. Walter Cole stood over me, McGee further back, his face bathed by the flashes of the patrol-car lights but still pale, shaken by what he had seen. Outside there was the sound of more cars pulling up. An EMT arrived at the door, distracting Cole's attention from me. 'The medical technician's here,' said one of the patrolmen, as the thin, whey-faced young man stood by. Cole nodded and gestured towards the kitchen.

'Birdman,' Cole repeated, this time with greater urgency and a harder tone to his voice. 'Do you want to tell me what happened here?'

*I pull into the parking lot in front of the flower shop. There is a light breeze blowing and my coat tails play at my legs like the hands of children. Inside, the store is cool, cooler than it should be, and redolent with the scent of roses. Roses never go out of style, or season.*

*A man is bending down, carefully checking the thick, waxy leaves of a small, green plant. He rises up slowly and painfully as I enter.*

*'Evening,' he says. 'Help you?'*

*'I'd like some of those roses. Give me a dozen. No, better make it two dozen.'*

*'Two dozen roses, yessir.' He is heavy-set and bald, maybe in his*

4

*early sixties. He walks stiffly, hardly bending his knees. The joints of his fingers are swollen with arthritis.*

'*Air-conditioning is playing up,*' *he says. As he passes by the ancient control unit on the wall, he adjusts a switch. Nothing happens.*

*The store is old, with a long, glass-fronted hot-house along the far wall. He opens the door and begins lifting roses carefully from a bucket inside. When he has counted twenty-four, he closes the door again and lays them on a sheet of plastic on the counter.*

'*Gift wrap 'em for ya?*'

'*No. Plastic is fine.*'

*He looks at me for a moment and I can almost hear the tumblers fall as the process of recognition begins.*

'*Do I know you from someplace?*'

*In the city, they have short memories. Further out, the memories last longer.*

## Supplemental Crime Report

**NYPD**       **Case Number:** 96-12-1806

**Offence:**   Homicide

**Victim:**    Susan Parker, W/F

               Jennifer Parker, W/F

**Location:**  1219 Hobart Street, kitchen

**Date:**      12 Dec 1996     **Time:** Around 2130 hrs

**Means:**     Stabbing

**Weapon:**    Edged weapon, possibly knife (not found)

**Reporting Officer:**  Walter Cole, Detective Sergeant

**Details:**

On 13 December 1996, I went to 1219 Hobart Street in response to a request by Officer Gerald Kersh for detectives to work a reported homicide.

Complainant Detective Second Grade Charles Parker stated he left house at 1900 hrs following argument with wife, Susan Parker. Went to Tom's Oak tavern and remained there until around 0130 hrs on December

13th. Entered house through front door and found furniture in hallway disturbed. Entered kitchen and found wife and daughter. Stated that wife was tied to kitchen chair but daughter's body appeared to have been moved from adjacent chair and arranged over mother's body. Called police at 0155 hrs and waited at scene.

Victims, identified to me by Charles Parker as Susan Parker (wife, 33 years old) and Jennifer Parker (daughter, 3 years old), were in kitchen. Susan Parker was tied to a kitchen chair in centre of floor facing door. A second chair was placed beside it, with some ropes still attached to rear struts. Jennifer Parker was lying across her mother, face up.

Susan Parker was barefoot and wearing blue jeans and white blouse. Blouse was ripped and had been pulled down to her waist, exposing breasts. Jeans and underwear had been pulled down to her calves. Jennifer Parker was barefoot, wearing a white nightdress with blue flower pattern.

I directed Crime Scene Technician Annie Minghella to make a full investigation. After victims were confirmed dead by Medical Examiner Clarence Hall and released, I accompanied bodies to hospital. I observed Dr Anthony Loeb as he used rape kit and turned it over to me. I collected following items of evidence:

> 96-12-1806-M1: white blouse from body of Susan
>    Parker (Victim No. 1)
> 96-12-1806-M2: blue denim jeans from body of
>    Victim 1
> 96-12-1806-M3: blue cotton underwear from body
>    of Victim 1

96-12-1806-M4: combings from pubic hair of
   Victim 1
96-12-1806-M5: washings from vagina of Victim 1
96-12-1806-M6: scrapings from under Victim 1's
   fingernails, right hand
96-12-1806-M7: scrapings from under Victim 1's
   fingernails, left hand
96-12-1806-M8: combings from Victim 1's hair,
   right front
96-12-1806-M9: combings from Victim 1's hair, left
   front
96-12-1806-M10: combings from Victim 1's hair,
   right rear
96-12-1806-M11: combings from Victim 1's hair,
   left rear.
96-12-1806-M12: white/blue cotton nightdress
   from body of Jennifer Parker (Victim No. 2)
96-12-1806-M13: washings from vagina of Victim 2
96-12-1806-M14: scrapings from under Victim 2's
   fingernails, right hand
96-12-1806-M15: scrapings from under Victim 2's
   fingernails, left hand
96-12-1806-M16: combings from Victim 2's hair,
   right front
96-12-1806-M17: combings from Victim 2's hair,
   left front
96-12-1806-M18: combings from Victim 2's hair,
   right rear
96-12-1806-M19: combings from Victim 2's hair,
   left rear.

It had been another bitter argument, made worse by the fact
that it followed our lovemaking. The embers of previous fights
were stoked back into glowing life: my drinking, my neglect of

Jenny, my bouts of bitterness and self-pity. When I stormed from the house, Susan's cries followed me into the cold night air.

It was a twenty-minute walk to the bar. When the first shot of Wild Turkey hit my stomach the tension dissipated from my body and I relaxed into the familiar routine of the drunk: angry, then maudlin, sorrowful, remorseful, resentful. By the time I left the bar only the hard-core remained, a chorus of drunks and sots battling with Van Halen on the juke-box. I stumbled at the door and fell down the steps outside, barking my knees painfully on the gravel at their base.

And then I stumbled home, sick and nauseous, cars swerving wildly to avoid me as I swayed on to the road, the faces of the drivers wide with alarm and anger.

I fumbled for my keys as I arrived at the door and scraped the white paint beneath the lock as I struggled to insert the key. There were a lot of scrapes beneath the lock.

I knew something was wrong as soon as I opened the front door and stepped into the hall. When I had left, the house had been warm, the heating on full blast because Jennifer especially felt the winter cold. She was a beautiful but fragile child, as delicate as a china vase. Now the house was as cold as the night outside, as cold as the grave. A mahogany flower-stand lay fallen on the carpet, the flower-pot broken in two pieces amid its own soil. The roots of the poinsettia it had contained were exposed and ugly.

I called Susan's name once, then again, louder this time. Already the drunken haze was clearing and I had my foot on the first step of the stairs to the bedrooms when I heard the back door bang against the sink unit in the kitchen. Instinctively I reached for my Colt DE but it lay upstairs on my desk, upstairs where I had discarded it before facing Susan and another chapter in the story of our dying marriage. I cursed myself then. Later, it would come to symbolise all of my failure, all of my regrets.

I moved cautiously towards the kitchen, the tips of my fingers glancing against the cold wall on my left. The kitchen door was almost closed and I edged it open slowly with my hand. 'Susie?' I called as I stepped into the kitchen. My foot slid gently on something sticky and wet. I looked down and I was in Hell.

*In the florist's, the old man's eyes are narrowed in puzzlement. He shakes his finger good-naturedly in front of me.*

*'I'm sure I know you from someplace.'*

*'I don't think so.'*

*'You from around here? Canaan, maybe? Monterey? Otis?'*

*'No. Someplace else.' I give him a look that tells him this is a line of inquiry he doesn't want to pursue and I can see him backing off. I am about to use my credit card but decide not to. Instead, I count out the cash from my wallet and lay it on the counter.*

*'Someplace else,' he says, nodding as if it has some deep, inner meaning for him. 'Must be a big place. I meet a lot of fellers from there.'*

*But I am already leaving the store. As I pull away, I can see him at the window, staring after me. Behind me, water drips gently from the rose stems and pools on the floor.*

## Supplemental Crime Report Contd.
### Case Number: 96-12-1806

Susan Parker was seated in a pine kitchen chair, facing north towards the kitchen door. Top of the head was ten feet, seven inches from north wall and six feet three inches from east wall. Her arms were pulled behind her back and . . .

tied to the bars at the back of the chair with thin cord. Each foot was in turn tied to a leg of the chair, and I thought her face, mostly concealed by her hair, seemed so awash with blood that no skin could be seen. Her head hung back so that her throat gaped open like a second mouth caught in a silent, dark-red scream. Our daughter lay splayed across Susan, one arm hanging between her mother's legs.

The room was red around them, like the stage of some terrible revenger's tragedy where blood was echoed with blood. It stained the ceiling and the walls as if the house itself had been mortally wounded. It lay thick and heavy on the floor and seemed to swallow my reflection in a scarlet darkness.

Susan Parker's nose had been broken. Injury was consistent with impact against wall or floor. Bloodstain on wall near kitchen door contained fragments of bone, nasal hair and mucus . . .

Susan had tried to run, to get help for our daughter and herself, but she had made it no further than the door. Then he had caught her, had grabbed her by the hair and smashed her against the wall before dragging her, bleeding and in pain, back to the chair and to her death.

Jennifer Parker was stretched, facing upwards, across her mother's thighs, and a second pine kitchen chair was positioned beside that of her mother. Cord wrapped around the back of the chair matched marks on Jennifer Parker's wrists and ankles.

There was not so much blood around Jenny, but her night-dress was stained by the flow from the deep cut in her throat. She faced the door, her hair hanging forward, obscuring her face, some strands sticking to the blood on her chest, the toes of her naked feet dangling above the tiled floor. I could only look at her for a moment because Susan drew my eyes towards her in death as she had in life, even amid the wreckage of our time together.

And as I looked upon her I felt myself slide down the wall and a wail, half animal, half child, erupted from deep inside me. I gazed at the beautiful woman who had been my wife, and her bloody, empty sockets seemed to draw me in and envelop me in darkness.

The eyes of both victims had been mutilated, probably with a sharp, scalpel-like blade. There was partial flensing of the chest of Susan Parker. The skin from the clavicle to the navel had been partially removed, pulled back over the right breast and stretched over the right arm.

The moonlight shone through the window behind them, casting a cold glow over the gleaming countertops, the tiled walls, the steel faucets on the sink. It caught Susan's hair, coated her bare shoulders in silver and shone through parts of the thin membrane of her skin pulled back over her arm like a cloak, a cloak too frail to ward off the cold.

There was considerable mutilation of the genital areas of both victims and

And then he had cut off their faces.

*It is darkening rapidly now and the headlights catch the bare branches of trees, the ends of trimmed lawns, clean white mailboxes, a child's bicycle lying in front of a garage. The wind is stronger now and when I leave the shelter of the trees I can feel it buffeting the car. Now I am*

*heading towards Becket, Washington, the Berkshire Hills. Almost there.*

There was no sign of forcible entry. Complete measurements and a sketch of the entire room were noted. Bodies were then released.

Dusting for fingerprints gave the following results:

Kitchen/hall/living room - usable prints later identified as those of Susan Parker (96-12-1806-7), Jennifer Parker (96-12-1806-8) and Charles Parker (96-12-1806-9).

Rear door of house from kitchen - no usable prints; watermarks on surface indicate that door was wiped down. No indication of robbery.

No prints were developed from tests on victims' skin.

Charles Parker was taken to Homicide and gave statement (attached).

I knew what they were doing as I sat in the interrogation room: I had done it so many times myself. They questioned me as I had questioned others before, using the strange, formal locutions of the police interrogation. 'What is your recollection as to your next move?' 'Do you recall in relation to the bar the disposition of the other drinkers?' 'Did you notice the condition as to the lock on the rear door?' It is an obscure, convoluted jargon, an anticipation of the legalese that clouds any criminal proceedings like smoke in a bar.

When I gave my statement Cole checked with Tom's and confirmed that I was there when I said I was, that I could not have killed my own wife and child.

Even then, there were whispers. I was questioned again and again about my marriage, about my relations with Susan, about my movements in the weeks coming up to the killings.

I stood to gain a considerable sum in insurance from Susan, and I was questioned about that as well.

According to the ME, Susan and Jennifer had been dead for about four hours when I found them. Rigor mortis had already taken hold at their necks and lower jaws, indicating that they had died at around 21.30, maybe a little earlier.

Susan had died from severing of the carotid artery, but Jenny . . . Jenny had died from what was described as a massive release of epinephrine into her system, causing ventricular fibrillation of the heart, and death. Jenny, always a gentle, sensitive child, a child with a traitor-weak heart, had literally died of fright before her killer had a chance to cut her throat. She was dead when her face was taken, said the ME. He could not say the same for Susan. Neither could he tell why Jennifer's body had been moved after death.

Further reports to follow.
                    Walter Cole, Detective Sergeant.

I had a drunk's alibi: while someone stole away my wife and my child I downed bourbon in a bar. But they still come to me in my dreams, sometimes smiling and beautiful as they were in life and sometimes faceless and bloodied as death left them, beckoning me further into a darkness where love has no place and evil hides, adorned with thousands of unseeing eyes and the flayed faces of the dead.

*It is dark when I arrive and the gate is closed and locked. The wall is low and I climb it easily. I walk carefully, so as not to tread on memorial stones or flowers, until I stand before them. Even in the darkness, I know where to find them and they, in their turn, can find me.*

*They come to me sometimes, in the margin between sleeping and waking, when the streets are silent in the dark or as dawn seeps through the gap in the curtains, bathing the room in a dim, slow-growing light. They come to me and I see their shapes in the gloom, my wife and child together, watching me silently, ensanguined in unquiet death. They come to me, their breath in the night breezes that brush my cheek and their fingers in the tree branches tapping on my window. They come to me and I am no longer alone.*

# Chapter One

The waitress was in her fifties, dressed in a tight black mini-skirt, a white blouse and black high heels. Parts of her spilled out of every item of clothing she wore, making her look as if she had swollen mysteriously some time between dressing and arriving for work. She called me 'darlin'' each time she filled my coffee cup. She didn't say anything else, which was fine by me.

I had been sitting at the window for over ninety minutes now, watching the brownstone across the street, and the waitress must have been wondering exactly how long I was planning to stay and if I was ever going to pay the check. Outside, the streets of Astoria buzzed with bargain-hunters. I had even read *The New York Times* from start to finish without nodding off in-between as I passed the time waiting for Fat Ollie Watts to emerge from hiding. My patience was wearing thin.

In moments of weakness, I sometimes considered ditching the *New York Times* on weekdays and limiting my purchase to the Sunday edition, when I could at least justify buying it on the grounds of bulk. The other option was to begin reading the *Post*, although then I'd have to start clipping coupons and walking to the store in my bedroom slippers.

I remembered a story I heard about the media tycoon Rupert Murdoch and how he approached Bloomingdale's in the hope of getting its management to advertise in the *Post* after he took it over in the 1980s. In response, the head of Bloomingdale's had arched an eyebrow and told him: 'The problem, Mr Murdoch, is that your readers are our shoplifters.' I wasn't a big fan of Bloomingdale's, but it was a persuasive argument against a subscription to the *Post*.

Maybe in reacting so badly to the *Times* that morning I was simply killing the messenger. It had been announced that Hansel McGee, a state Supreme Court judge and, according to some, one of the worst judges in New York, was retiring in December and might be nominated to the board of the city's Health and Hospitals Corporation.

Even seeing McGee's name in print made me ill. In the 1980s, he had presided over the case of a woman who had been raped when she was nine years old by a fifty-four-year-old man named James Johnson, an attendant in Pelham Bay Park who had convictions for robbery, assault and rape.

McGee overturned a jury award of $3.5 million to the woman with the following words: 'An innocent child was heinously raped for no reason at all; yet that is one of the risks of living in a modern society.' At the time, his judgment had seemed callous and an absurd justification for overturning the ruling. Now, seeing his name before me again after what had happened to my family, his views seemed so much more abhorrent, a symptom of the collapse of goodness in the face of evil.

Erasing McGee from my mind, I folded the newspaper neatly, tapped a number on my cellphone and turned my eyes to an upper window of the slightly run-down apartment building opposite. The phone was picked up after three rings and a woman's voice whispered a cautious hello. It had a sound of cigarettes and booze to it, like a bar door scraping across a dusty floor.

'Tell your fat asshole boyfriend that I'm on my way to pick

him up and he'd better not make me chase him,' I told her. 'I'm real tired and I don't plan on running around in this heat.' Succinct, that was me. I hung up, left five dollars on the table and stepped out on to the street to wait for Fat Ollie Watts to panic.

The city was in the middle of a hot, humid summer spell, which was due to end the following day with the arrival of thunderstorms and rain. Currently, it was hot enough to allow for T-shirts, chinos and overpriced sunglasses or, if you were unlucky enough to be holding down a responsible job, hot enough to make you sweat like a pig under your suit as soon as you left the a/c behind. There wasn't even a gust of wind to rearrange the heat.

Two days earlier, a solitary desk fan had struggled to make an impact on the sluggish warmth in the Brooklyn Heights office of Benny Low. Through an open window I could hear Arabic being spoken on Atlantic Avenue and I could smell the cooking scents coming from the Moroccan Star half a block away. Benny was a minor-league bail bondsman who had banked on Fat Ollie staying put until his trial. The fact that he had misjudged Fat Ollie's faith in the justice system was one reason why Benny continued to be a minor-league bondsman.

The money being offered on Fat Ollie Watts was reasonable and there were things living on the bottom of ponds that were smarter than most bail jumpers. There was a $50,000 bond on Fat Ollie, the result of a misunderstanding between Ollie and the forces of law and order over the precise ownership of a 1993 Chevy Beretta, a 1990 Mercedes 300 SE and a number of well-appointed sports vehicles, all of which had come into Ollie's possession by illegal means.

Fat Ollie's day started to go downhill when an eagle-eyed patrolman, familiar with Ollie's reputation as something less than a shining light in the darkness of a lawless world, spotted the Chevy under a tarpaulin and called for a check on the plates.

They were false and Ollie was raided, arrested and questioned. He kept his mouth shut but packed a bag and headed for the hills as soon as he made bail in an effort to avoid further questions about who had placed the cars in his care. That source was reputed to be Salvatore 'Sonny' Ferrera, the son of a prominent *capo*. There had been rumours lately that relations between father and son had deteriorated in recent weeks, but nobody was saying why.

'Fuckin' goomba stuff,' as Benny Low had put it that day in his office.

'Anything to do with Fat Ollie?'

'Fuck do I know? You want to call Ferrera and ask?'

I looked at Benny Low. He was completely bald and had been since his early twenties, as far as I knew. His glabrous skull glistened with tiny beads of perspiration. His cheeks were ruddy and flesh hung from his chin and jowls like melted wax. His tiny office, located above a halal store, smelt of sweat and mould. I wasn't even sure why I had said I would take the job. I had money: insurance money, money from the sale of the house, money from what had once been a shared account, even some cash from my retirement fund, and Benny Low's money wasn't going to make me happier. Maybe it was just something to do.

Benny Low swallowed once, loudly. 'What? Why are you lookin' at me like that?'

'You know me, Benny, don't you?'

'Fuck does that mean? Course I know you. You want a reference? What?' He laughed half-heartedly, spreading his pudgy hands wide as if in supplication. 'What?' he said, again. His voice faltered and, for the first time, he looked scared. I knew that people had been talking about me in the months since the deaths, talking about things I had done, things I might have done. The look in Benny Low's eyes told me that he had heard about them, too, and believed that they could be true.

Something about Fat Ollie's flight just didn't sit right. It wouldn't be the first time that Ollie had faced a judge on a stolen vehicles rap, although the suspected connection to the Ferreras had forced the bond up on this occasion. Ollie had a good lawyer to rely on, otherwise his only connection to the automobile industry would have come from making license plates on Rikers Island. There was no particular reason for Ollie to run, and no reason why he would risk his life by fingering Sonny over something like this.

'Nothing, Benny. It's nothing. You hear anything else, you tell me.'

'Sure, sure,' said Benny, relaxing again. 'You'll be the first to know.'

As I left his office, I heard him mutter under his breath. I couldn't be sure what he said but I knew what it sounded like. It sounded like Benny Low had just called me a killer like my father.

It had taken me most of the next day to locate Ollie's current squeeze through some judicious questioning, and another fifty minutes that morning to determine if Ollie was with her through the simple expedient of calling the local Thai food joints and asking them if they had made any deliveries to the address in the last week.

Ollie was a Thai food freak and, like most skips, stuck to his habits even while on the run. People don't change very much, which usually makes the dumb ones easy to find. They take out subscriptions to the same magazines, eat in the same places, drink the same beers, call the same women, sleep with the same men. After I threatened to call the health inspectors, an Oriental roach motel called the Bangkok Sun House confirmed deliveries to one Monica Mulrane at an address in Astoria, leading to coffee, *The New York Times* and a phone-call to wake Ollie up.

True to form and dim as a ten-watt bulb, Ollie opened the door of 2317 about four minutes after my call, stuck his head out and then commenced an awkward shambling run down the steps towards the sidewalk. He was an absurd figure, strands of hair slicked across his bald pate, the elasticated waistband of his tan pants stretched across a stomach of awesome size. Monica Mulrane must have loved him a whole lot to stay with him, because he didn't have money and he sure as hell didn't have looks. It was strange, but I kind of liked Fat Ollie Watts.

He had just set foot on the sidewalk when a jogger wearing a grey sweatsuit with the hood pulled up appeared at the corner, ran up to Ollie and pumped three shots into him from a silenced pistol. Ollie's white shirt was suddenly polka-dotted with red and he folded to the ground. The jogger, left-handed, stood over him and shot him once more in the head.

Someone screamed and I saw a brunette, presumably the by now recently bereaved Monica Mulrane, pause at the door of her apartment block before she ran to the sidewalk to kneel beside Ollie, passing her hands over his bald, bloodied head and crying. The jogger was already backing off, bouncing on the balls of his feet like a fighter waiting for the bell. Then he stopped, returned and fired a single shot into the top of the woman's head. She folded over the body of Ollie Watts, her back shielding his head. Bystanders were already running for cover behind cars, into stores, and the cars on the street ground to a halt.

I was almost across the street, my Smith & Wesson in my hand, when the jogger ran. He kept his head down and moved fast, the gun still held in his left hand. Even though he wore black gloves, he hadn't dropped the gun at the scene. Either the gun was distinctive or the shooter was dumb. I was banking on the second option.

I was gaining on him when a black Chevy Caprice with

tinted windows screeched out from a side-street and stood waiting for him. If I didn't shoot, he was going to get away. If I did shoot, there would be hell to pay with the cops. I made my choice. He had almost reached the Chevy when I squeezed off two shots, one hitting the door of the car and the second tearing a bloody hole in the right arm of the jogger's top. He spun, firing two wild shots in my direction as he did so, and I could see his eyes were wide and ultra-bright. The killer was wired.

As he turned towards the Chevy it sped away, the driver spooked by my shots, leaving Fat Ollie Watts's killer stranded. He fired off another shot, which shattered the window of the car to my left. I could hear people screaming and, in the distance, the wail of approaching sirens.

The jogger sprinted towards an alley, glancing over his shoulder at the sound of my shoes hammering on the road behind him. As I made the corner a bullet whined off the wall above me, peppering me with pieces of concrete. I looked up to see the jogger moving beyond the mid-point of the alley, staying close to the wall. If he got around the corner at the end, I would lose him in the crowds.

The gap at the end of the alley was, briefly, clear of people. I decided to risk the shot. The sun was behind me as I straightened, firing twice in quick succession. I was vaguely aware of people at either side of me scattering like pigeons from a stone as the jogger's right shoulder arched back with the impact of one of my shots. I shouted at him to drop the piece but he turned awkwardly, his left hand bringing the gun up. Slightly off balance, I fired two more shots from around twenty feet. His left knee exploded as one of the hollow points connected and he collapsed against the wall of the alley, his pistol skidding harmlessly away towards some trash cans and black sacks.

As I closed on him I could see he was ashen-faced, his mouth twisted in pain and his left hand gripping the air around his shattered knee without actually touching the wound. Yet his eyes were still bright and I thought I heard him giggle as he pushed himself from the wall and tried to hop away on his good leg. I was maybe fifteen feet from him when his giggles were drowned by the sound of brakes squealing behind him. I looked up to see the black Chevy blocking the end of the alley, the window on its passenger side down, and then the darkness within was broken by a single muzzle flash.

The gunman bucked and fell forward on the ground. He spasmed once and I could see a red stain spreading across the back of his sweatsuit top. There was a second shot, the back of his head blew a geyser of blood in the air and his face banged once on the filthy concrete of the alley. I was already making for the cover of the trash cans when a bullet whacked into the brickwork above my head, showering me with dust and literally boring a hole through the wall. Then the window of the Chevy rolled up and the car shot off to the east.

I ran to where the jogger lay. Blood flowed from the wounds in his body, creating a dark red shadow on the ground. The sirens were close now and I could see onlookers gathered in the sunlight, watching me as I stood over the body.

The patrol car pulled up minutes later. I already had my hands in the air and my gun on the ground before me, my permit beside it. Fat Ollie Watts's killer was lying at my feet, blood now pooled around his head and linked to the red tide that was congealing slowly in the alley's central gutter. One patrolman kept me covered while his partner patted me down, with more force than was strictly necessary, against the wall. The cop patting me down was young, no more than twenty-three or twenty-four, and cocky as hell.

'Shit, we got Wyatt Earp here, Sam,' he said. 'Shootin' it out like it was *High Noon*.'

'Wyatt Earp wasn't in *High Noon*,' I corrected him, as his partner checked my ID. The cop punched me hard in the kidneys in response and I fell to my knees. I heard more sirens near by, including the tell-tale whine of an ambulance.

'You're a funny guy, hot shot,' said the young cop. 'Why'd you shoot him?'

'You weren't around,' I replied, my teeth gritted in pain. 'If you'd been here I'd have shot you instead.'

He was just about to cuff me when a voice I recognised said, 'Put it away, Harley.' I looked over my shoulder at his partner, Sam Rees. I recognised him from my days on the force and he recognised me. I don't think he liked what he saw.

'He used to be a cop. Leave him be.'

And then the three of us waited in silence until the others arrived.

Two more blue and whites arrived before a mud-brown Nova dumped a figure in plain clothes on the kerb. I looked up to see Walter Cole walking towards me. I hadn't seen him in almost six months, not since his promotion to lieutenant. He was wearing a long brown leather coat, incongruous in the heat. 'Ollie Watts?' he said, indicating the shooter with an inclination of his head. I nodded.

He left me alone for a time as he spoke with uniformed cops and detectives from the local precinct. I noticed that he was sweating heavily in his coat.

'You can come in my car,' he said, when he eventually returned, eyeing the cop called Harley with ill-concealed distaste. He motioned some more detectives towards him and made some final comments in quiet, measured tones before waving me in the direction of the Nova.

'Nice coat,' I said appreciatively, as we walked to his car. 'How many girls you got in your stable?'

Walter's eyes glinted briefly. 'Lee gave me this coat for my birthday. Why do you think I'm wearing it in this goddamned heat? You fire any shots?'

'A couple.'

'You do know that there are laws against discharging fire-arms in public places, don't you?'

'I know that but I'm not sure about the guy dead on the ground back there. I don't think the guy who shot him knows either. Maybe you could try a poster campaign.'

'Very funny. Now get in the car.'

I did as he said and we pulled away from the kerb, the onlookers gaping curiously at us as we headed off through the crowded streets.

# Chapter Two

Five hours had elapsed since the death of Fat Ollie Watts, his girlfriend, Monica Mulrane, and the shooter, as yet unidentified. I had been interviewed by a pair of detectives from Homicide, neither of whom I knew. Walter Cole did not participate. I was brought coffee twice but otherwise I was left alone after the questionings. Once, when one of the detectives left the room to consult with someone, I caught a glimpse of a tall, thin man in a dark linen suit, the ends of his shirt collar sharp as razors, his red silk tie unwrinkled. He looked like a fed, a vain fed.

The wooden table in the interrogation room was pitted and worn, caffeine-stamped by the edges of hundreds, maybe thousands, of coffee cups. At the left-hand side of the table, near the corner, someone had carved a broken heart into the wood, probably with a nail. And I remembered that heart from another time, from the last time I sat in this room . . .

'Shit, Walter . . .'

'Walt, it ain't a good idea for him to be here.'

Cole looked at the detectives ranged around the walls, slouched on chairs around the table.

'He's not here,' he said. 'As far as everyone in this room is concerned, you never saw him.'

The interrogation room was crowded with chairs and an

additional table had been brought in. I was still on compassionate leave and, as it happened, two weeks away from quitting the force. My family had been dead for two weeks and the investigation had so far yielded nothing. With the agreement of Lieutenant Cafferty, soon to retire, Cole had called a meeting of detectives involved in the case and one or two others who were regarded as among the best homicide detectives in the city. It was to be a combination of brainstorm and lecture, the lecture coming from Rachel Wolfe.

Wolfe had a reputation as a fine criminal psychologist, yet the Department steadfastly refused to consult her. It had its own deep thinker, Dr Russell Windgate, but, as Cole once put it: 'Windgate couldn't profile a fart.' He was a sanctimonious, patronising bastard but he was also the Commissioner's brother, which made him a sanctimonious, patronising, influential bastard.

Windgate was attending a conference of committed Freudians in Tulsa, and Cole had taken the opportunity to consult Wolfe. She sat at the head of the table, a stern but not unattractive woman in her early thirties, with long, dark-red hair which rested on the shoulders of her dark blue business suit. Her legs were crossed and a blue pump hung from the end of her right foot.

'You all know why Bird wants to be here,' continued Cole. 'You'd all want the same thing, if you were in his place.' I had bullied and cajoled him to let me sit in on the briefing. I had called in favours I didn't even have the right to call in, and Walter had relented. I didn't regret doing what I did.

The others in the room remained unconvinced. I could see it in their faces, in the way they shifted their gaze from us, in the shrug of a shoulder and the unhappy twist of a mouth. I didn't care. I wanted to hear what Wolfe had to say. Cole and I took seats and waited for her to begin.

Wolfe lifted a pair of glasses from the table-top and put them on. Beside her left hand, a newly carved heart shone wood-bright. She glanced through some notes, pulled out two sheets from the sheaf and began.

'Right, I don't know how familiar you are with all this, so I'll take it slowly.' She paused for a moment. 'Detective Parker, you may find some of this difficult.' There was no apology in her voice, it was a simple statement of fact. I nodded and she continued. 'What we're dealing with here appears to be sexual homicide, sadistic sexual homicide.'

I traced the carved heart with the tip of my finger, the texture of the wood briefly returning me to the present. The door of the interrogation room opened and, through the gap, I saw the fed pass by. A clerk entered with a white 'I Love NY' cup. The coffee smelt as if it had been brewing since that morning. When I put in the creamer it created only the slightest difference in the colour of the liquid. I sipped it and grimaced.

'A sexual homicide generally involves some element of sexual activity as the basis for the sequence of events leading to death,' continued Wolfe, sipping at her coffee. 'The stripping of the victims and the mutilation of the breasts and genitals indicate a sexual element to the crime, yet we have no evidence of penetration in either victim by either penis, fingers or foreign objects. The child's hymen was undamaged and there was no evidence of vaginal trauma in the adult victim.

'We also have evidence of a sadistic element to the homicides. The adult victim was tortured prior to death. Flensing took place, specifically on the front of the torso and the face. Combined with the sexual elements, you're dealing with a sexual sadist who obtains gratification from excessive physical and, I would think, mental torture.

'I think he – and I'm assuming it's a male, for reasons I'll go into later – wanted the mother to watch the torture and killing of her child before she herself was tortured and killed. A sexual sadist gets his kicks from the victim's response to torture: in this case, he had two victims, a mother and child, to play off against each other. He's translating sexual fantasies into violent acts, torture and, eventually, death.'

Outside the door of the interrogation room I heard voices suddenly raised. One of them was Walter Cole's. I didn't recognise the other. The voices subsided again, but I knew that they were talking about me. I would find out what they wanted soon enough.

'Okay. The largest focus group for sexual sadists consists of white female adults who are strangers to the killer, although they may also target males and, as in this case, children. There is also sometimes a correspondence between the victim and someone in the offender's own life.

'Victims are chosen through systematic stalking and surveillance. The killer had probably been watching the family for some time. He knew the husband's habits, knew that if he went to the bar then he would be missing for long enough to allow him to complete what he wanted to do. In this case, I don't think the killer managed that completion.

'The crime scene is unusual in this case. Firstly, the nature of the crime means that it requires somewhere solitary to give the offender time with his victim. In some cases, the offender's residence may have been modified to accommodate his victim, or he may use a converted car or van for the killing. In this case, the killer chose not to do this. I think he may like the element of risk involved. I also think he wanted to make, for want of a better term, an "impression".'

An impression, like wearing a bright tie to a funeral.

'The crime was carefully staged to impact in the most traumatic way on the husband when he returned home.'

Maybe Walter had been right. Maybe I shouldn't have come to the briefing. Wolfe's matter-of-factness reduced my wife and child to the level of another gruesome statistic in a violent city, but I hoped that she would say something which would resonate inside me and provide some clue to drive the investigation forward. Two weeks is a long time in a murder case. After two weeks with no progress, unless you get very, very lucky, the investigation starts to grind to a halt.

'This seems to indicate a killer of above-average intelligence, one who likes playing games and gambling,' said Wolfe. 'The fact that he appeared to want the element of shock to play a part could lead us to conclude that there was a personal element to what he did, directed against the husband, but that's just speculation and the general pattern of this type of crime is impersonal.

'Generally, crime scenes can be classified as organised, disorganised or some mix of the two. An organised killer plans the murder and targets the victim carefully, and the crime scene will reflect this element of control. The victims will meet certain criteria which the killer has set: age, hair colour maybe, occupation, lifestyle. The use of restraints, as we have in this case, is typical. It reflects the elements of control and planning, since the killer will usually have to bring them to the scene.

'In cases of sexual sadism, the act of killing is generally eroticised. There's a ritual involved, it's usually slow, and every effort is made to ensure that the victim remains conscious and aware up to the point of death. In other words, the killer doesn't want to end the lives of his victims or victims prematurely.

'Now in this case he didn't succeed, because Jennifer Parker, the child, had a weak heart and it failed following the release of epinephrine into her system. Combined with her mother's attempted escape and the damage caused to her face by striking it against the wall, which may have resulted in temporary loss of consciousness, I believe the killer felt he was losing control of the situation. The crime scene moved from organised to disorganised and, shortly after he commenced flensing, his anger and frustration got the better of him and he mutilated the bodies.'

I wanted to leave then. I had made a mistake. Nothing could come of this, nothing good.

'As I said earlier, mutilation of the genitals and breasts is a feature of this type of crime but this case doesn't conform to the general pattern in a number of crucial ways. I think the mutilation in this case was either a result of anger and loss of control, or it was an attempt to disguise something else, some other element of the ritual which had already commenced and from which the killer was trying to divert attention. In all likelihood, the partial flensing is the key. There's a strong element of display – it's incomplete, but it's there.'

'Why are you so sure it's a white male?' asked Joiner, a black homicide detective with whom I'd worked once or twice.

'The most frequent perpetrators of sexual sadism are white males. Not women, not black males. White males.'

'You're off the hook, Joiner,' someone said. There was a burst of laughter, an easing of the tension that had built up in the room. One or two of the others glanced at me but for the most part they acted as if I wasn't there. They were professionals, concentrating on amassing any information that might lead to a greater understanding of the killer.

Wolfe let the laughter fade. 'Research indicates that as many as forty-three per cent of sexual murderers are married. Fifty per cent have children. Don't make the mistake of thinking that you're looking for some crazy loner. This guy may be the hero of his local PTA meetings, the coach of the Little League team.

'He could be engaged in a profession that brings him into contact with the public, so he's probably socially adept and he may use that to target his victims. He may have engaged in antisocial behaviour in the past, although not necessarily something serious enough to have gotten him a police record.

'Sexual sadists are often police buffs or weapons freaks. He may try to stay in touch with the progress of the investigation, so watch out for individuals who ring in with leads or who try to trade off information. He also owns a clean, well-maintained car: clean so it doesn't attract attention, well maintained because he has to be sure he doesn't get stranded at or near the crime scene. The car could have been modified to allow him to transport victims: the door and window handles in the rear will have been removed, the trunk may have been soundproofed. If you think you have a possible suspect, check the trunk for extra fuel, water, ropes, cuffs, ligatures.

'If you go for a search warrant, you'll be looking for any items relating to sexual or violent behaviour: pornographic magazines, videos, low-end true crime stuff, vibrators, clamps, women's clothing, particularly undergarments. Some of these may have belonged to victims or he may have taken other personal items from them. Look out also for diaries and manuscripts: they may contain details of victims, fantasies, even the crimes themselves. This guy may also have a collection of police equipment and almost certainly has a knowledge of police procedures.' Wolfe took a deep breath and sat back in her chair.

'Is he going to do it again?' asked Cole. There was silence in the room for a moment.

'Yes, but you're making one assumption,' said Wolfe. Cole looked puzzled.

'You're assuming this is the first. I take it a VICAP has been done?'

VICAP, operational since 1985, was the FBI's Violent

31

Criminal Apprehension Program. Under VICAP, a report was completed on solved or unsolved homicides or attempted homicides, particularly those involving abductions, or which were apparently random or motiveless or sexually orientated; missing persons cases, where foul play was suspected; and unidentified dead bodies where the manner of death was known, or suspected to be, homicide. These were then submitted to the National Center for the Analysis of Violent Crime at the FBI's academy in Quantico, in an effort to determine if similar pattern characteristics existed elsewhere in the VICAP system.

'It was submitted.'

'Have you requested a profile?'

'Yes, but no profile as yet. Unofficially, the MO doesn't match. The removal of the faces marks it out.'

'Yeah, what about the faces?' It was Joiner again.

'I'm still trying to find out more,' said Wolfe. 'Some killers take souvenirs from their victims. There may be some kind of pseudo-religious or sacrificial element to this case. I'm sorry, I'm really not sure yet.'

'You think he could have done something like this before?' said Cole.

Wolfe nodded. 'He may have. If he has killed before, then he may have hidden the bodies and these killings could represent an alteration in a previous pattern of behaviour. Maybe, after killing quietly and unobtrusively, he wanted to bring himself to a more public arena. He may have wanted to draw attention to his work. The unsatisfactory nature of these killings, from his point of view, may now cause him to go back to his old pattern. Alternatively, he could recede into a period of dormancy, that's another possibility.

'But if I was to gamble, I'd say that he's been planning his next move carefully. He made mistakes the last time and I don't think he achieved the effect he was looking for. The next time, he won't make any mistakes. The next time, unless you catch him first, he's really going to make an impact.'

The door of the interrogation room opened and Cole entered with two other men.

'This is Special Agent Ross, FBI, and Detective Barth from Robbery,' said Cole. 'Barth was working the Watts case. Agent Ross here deals with organised crime.'

Close up, Ross's linen suit looked expensive and tailored. Barth, in his JC Penney jacket, looked like a slob by comparison. The two men stood against opposite walls and nodded. When Cole sat, Barth sat as well. Ross remained standing against the wall.

'Anything you're not telling us here?' Cole asked.

'No,' I said. 'You know as much as I do.'

'Agent Ross believes that Sonny Ferrera was behind the killing of Watts and his girlfriend and that you know more than you're saying.' Ross picked at something on the sleeve of his shirt and dropped it to the floor with a look of distaste. I think it was meant to represent me.

'There was no reason for Sonny to kill Ollie Watts,' I replied. 'We're talking stolen cars and false number plates here. Ollie wasn't in a position to scam anything worthwhile from Sonny and he didn't know enough about Sonny's activities to take up ten minutes of a jury's time.'

Ross stirred and moved forward to sit on the edge of the table. 'Strange that you should turn up after all this time – what is it? Six, seven months? – and suddenly we're knee deep in corpses,' he said, as if he hadn't heard a word I'd said. He was forty, maybe forty-five, but he looked to be in good condition. His face was heavily lined with wrinkles, which didn't seem as if they came from a life of laughter. I'd heard a little about him from Woolrich, after Woolrich left New York to become the feds' Assistant Special Agent in Charge in the New Orleans field office.

There was silence then. Ross tried to stare me out, then looked away in boredom.

'Agent Ross here thinks that you're holding out on us,' said Cole. 'He'd like to sweat you for a while, just in case.' His expression was neutral, his eyes bland. Ross had returned to staring at me.

'Agent Ross is a scary guy. He tries to sweat me, there's no telling what I'll confess to.'

'This is not getting us anywhere,' said Ross. 'Mr Parker is obviously not co-operating in any way and I—'

Cole held up a hand, interrupting him. 'Maybe you'd both leave us alone for a time, get some coffee or something,' he suggested. Barth shrugged and left. Ross remained seated on the table and looked as if he was going to say more, then he stood up abruptly and quickly walked out, closing the door firmly behind him. Cole exhaled deeply, loosened his tie and opened the top button of his shirt. 'Don't dump on Ross. He'll bring a ton of shit down on your head. And on mine.'

'I've told you all I know on this,' I said. 'Benny Low may know more, but I doubt it.'

'We talked to Benny Low. The way Benny tells it, he didn't know who the President was until we told him.' He twisted a pen in his hand. ' "Hey, it's just bidness", that's what he said.' It was a pretty fair imitation of one of Benny Low's verbal quirks. I smiled thinly and the tension in the air dissipated slightly.

'How long you been back?'

'Couple of weeks.'

'What have you been doing?'

What could I tell him? That I wandered the streets, that I visited places where Jennifer, Susan and I used to go together, that I stared out of the window of my apartment and thought about the man who had killed them and where he might be, that I had taken on the job for Benny Low because I was afraid

34

that, if I did not find some outlet, I would eat the barrel of my gun?

'Not a lot. I plan to look up some old stoolies, see if there's anything new.'

'There isn't, not at this end. You got anything?'

'No.'

'I can't ask you to let it go, but . . .'

'No, you can't. Get to it, Walter.'

'This isn't a good place for you to be right now. You know why.'

'Do I?'

Cole tossed the pen hard on the table. It bounced to the edge and hung there briefly before dropping to the floor. For a moment I thought he was going to take a swing at me but then the anger went from his eyes.

'We'll talk about this again.'

'Okay. You going to give me anything?' Among the papers on the table, I could see reports from Ballistics and Firearms. Five hours was a pretty short time in which to get a report. Agent Ross was obviously a man who got what he wanted.

I nodded at the papers. 'What did Ballistics say about the bullet that took out the shooter?'

'That's not your concern.'

'Walter, I watched the kid die. The shooter took a pop at me and the bullet went clean through the wall. Someone's got distinctive taste in weaponry.'

Cole stayed silent.

'No one picks up hardware like that without someone knowing,' I said. 'You give me something to go on, maybe I might find out more than you can.'

Cole thought for a minute and then flicked through the papers for the Ballistics report. 'We got sub-machine bullets, 5.7mm weighing less than one-tenth of an ounce.'

I whistled. 'That's a scaled-down rifle round, but fired from a handgun?'

'The bullet is mainly plastic but has a full-metal jacket, so it doesn't deform on impact. When it met the shooter's body, it transferred most of its force so there was almost no energy when it exited.'

'And the one that hit the wall?'

'Ballistics reckons a muzzle velocity of over two thousand feet per second.'

That was an incredibly fast bullet. A Browning 9-millimetre fires bullets of a quarter of an ounce at about eleven hundred feet per second.

'They also reckon that this thing could blow through Kevlar body armour like it was rice paper. At six hundred feet, the thing could penetrate almost fifty layers.' Even a .44 Magnum will only penetrate body armour at very close range.

'But once it hits a soft target . . .'

'It stops.'

'Is it domestic?'

'No, Ballistics say European. Belgian. They're talking about something called a "Five-seveN" – that's big F, big N, after the manufacturers. It's a prototype made by FN Herstal for anti-terrorist and hostage rescue operations, but this is the first time one has turned up outside national security forces.'

'You contacting the maker?'

'We'll try, but my guess is we'll lose it in the middle men.'

I stood up. 'I'll ask around.'

Cole retrieved his pen and waved it at me like an unhappy schoolteacher lecturing the class wise-guy. 'Ross still wants your ass.'

I took out a pen and scribbed my cellphone number on the back of Cole's legal pad.

'It's always on. Can I go now?'

'One condition.'

'Go on.'

'I want you to come over to the house tonight.'

'I'm sorry, Walter, I don't make social calls any more.'

He looked hurt. 'Don't be an asshole. This isn't social. Be there, or Ross can lock you in a cell till Doomsday for all I care.'

I stood up to leave.

'You sure you've told us everything?' asked Cole to my back.

I didn't turn around. 'I've told you all I can, Walter.'

Which was true, technically at least.

Twenty-four hours earlier, I had found Emo Ellison.

Emo lived in a dump of a hotel on the edge of East Harlem, the kind where the only guests allowed in the rooms are whores, cops or criminals. A Plexiglass screen covered the front of the super's office and no one was inside. I walked up the stairs and knocked on Emo's door. There was no reply but I thought I heard the sound of a hammer cocking on a pistol.

'Emo, it's Bird. I need to talk.'

I heard footsteps approach the door.

'I don't know nothin' about it,' said Emo, through the wood. 'I ain't got nothin' to say.'

'I haven't asked you anything yet. C'mon, Emo, open up. Fat Ollie's in trouble. Maybe I can do something. Let me in.'

There was silence for a moment and then the rattle of a chain. The door opened and I stepped inside. Emo had retreated to the window but he still had the gun in his hand. I closed the door behind me.

'You don't need that,' I said. Emo hefted the gun once in his hand then put it on a bedside locker. He looked more comfortable without it. Guns weren't Emo's style. I noticed that the fingers of his left hand were bandaged. I could see yellow stains on the tips of the bandages.

Emo Ellison was a thin, pale-faced, middle-aged man who had worked on and off for Fat Ollie for five years or so. He was an average mechanic but he was loyal and knew when to keep his mouth shut.

'Do you know where he is?'

'He ain't been in touch.'

He sat down heavily on the edge of the neatly made bed. The room was clean and smelt of air-freshener. There were one or two prints on the walls, and books, magazines and some personal items were neatly arrayed on a set of Home Depot shelves. 'I hear you're workin' for Benny Low. Why you doin' that?'

'It's work,' I replied.

'You hand Ollie over and he's dead, that's your work,' said Emo.

I leaned against the door. 'I may not hand him over. Benny Low can take the loss. But I'd need a good reason not to.'

The conflict inside him played itself out on Emo's face. His hands twisted and writhed over each other and he looked once or twice at the gun. Emo Ellison was scared.

'Why did he run, Emo?' I asked softly.

'He used to say you were a good guy, a stand-up guy,' said Emo. 'That true?'

'I don't know. I don't want to see Ollie hurt, though.'

Emo looked at me for a time and then seemed to make a decision.

'It was Pili, Pili Pilar. You know him?'

'I know him.' Pili Pilar was Sonny Ferrara's right-hand man.

'He used to come once, twice a month, never more than that, and take a car. He'd keep it for a couple of hours, then bring it back. Different car each time. It was a deal Ollie made, so he wouldn't have to pay off Sonny. He'd fit the car with false plates and have it ready for Pili when he arrived.

'Last week, Pili comes, collects a car and drives off. I came in late that night, 'cos I was sick. I got ulcers. Pili was gone before I got there.

'Anyway, after midnight I'm sittin' up with Ollie, talkin' and stuff, waitin' for Pili to bring back the car, when there's this bang outside. When we get out there, Pili's wrapped the car around the gate and he's lying on the wheel. There's a dent in the front, too, so we figure maybe Pili was in a smash and didn't want to wait around after.

'Pili's head is cut up bad where he smacked the windscreen and there's a lot of blood in the car. Ollie and me push it into the yard and then Ollie calls this doc he knows and the guy tells him to bring Pili around. Pili ain't movin' and he's real pale, so Ollie drops him off at the doc's in his own car and the doc insists on packing him off to the hospital 'cos he thinks Pili's skull is busted.'

It was all flowing out of Emo now. Once he began the tale he wanted to finish it, as if he could diminish the burden of knowing by telling it out loud. 'Anyway, they argue for a while but the doc knows this private clinic where they won't ask too many questions and Ollie agrees. The doc calls the clinic and Ollie comes back to the lot to sort out the car.

'He has a number for Sonny but there's no answer. He's got the car in back but he doesn't want to leave it there in case, y'know, it's a cop thing. So he calls the old man and lets him know what happened. So the old man tells him to sit tight, he'll send a guy around to take care of it.

'Ollie goes out to move the car out of sight but when he comes back in, he looks worse than Pili. He looks sick and his hands are shakin'. I say to him, "What's wrong?", but he just tells me to get out and not to tell no one I was there. He won't say nothin' else, just tells me to get goin'.

'Next thing I hear, the cops have raided the place and then Ollie gets bail and disappears. I swear, that's the last I heard.'

'Then why the gun?'

'One of the old man's guys came by here a day or two back.'
He gulped. 'Bobby Sciorra. He wanted to know about Ollie,
wanted to know if I'd been there the day of Pili's accident. I said
to him, "No," but it wasn't enough for him.'

Emo Ellison started to cry. He lifted up his bandaged fingers
and slowly, carefully, began to unwrap one of them.

'He took me for a ride.' He held up the finger and I could see
a ring-shaped mark crowned with a huge blister that seemed to
throb even as I looked at it. 'The cigarette lighter. He burned
me with the car cigarette lighter.'

Twenty-four hours later, Fat Ollie Watts was dead.

# Chapter Three

Walter Cole lived in Richmond Hill, the oldest of the Seven Sisters neighbourhoods in Queens. Begun in the 1880s, it had a village centre and town common and must have seemed like Middle America re-created on Manhattan's doorstep when Walter's parents first moved there from Jefferson City shortly before the Second World War. Walter had kept the house, north of Myrtle Avenue on 113th Street, after his parents retired to Florida. He and Lee ate almost every Friday in Triangle Hafbrau, an old German restaurant on Jamaica Avenue, and walked in the dense woods of Forest Park during the summer.

I arrived at Walter's home shortly after nine. He answered the door himself and showed me into what, for a less educated man, would have been called his den, although den didn't do justice to the miniature library he had assembled over half a century of avid reading: biographies of Keats and Saint-Exupéry shared shelf space with works on forensics, sex crimes and criminal psychology. Fenimore Cooper stood back to back with Borges; Barthelme looked uneasy surrounded by various Hemingways.

A Macintosh PowerBook sat on a leather-topped desk beside three filing cabinets. Pictures by local artists adorned the walls and a small glass-fronted case in the corner displayed shooting trophies, haphazardly thrown together as if Walter was simultaneously proud of his ability yet embarrassed by his pride. The top half of the window was open and I could smell freshly mown grass and hear the sound of kids playing street hockey in the warm evening air.

The door to the den opened and Lee entered. She and Walter had been together for twenty-four years and they shared each other's lives with an ease and grace that Susan and I had never approached, even at the best of times. Lee's black jeans and white blouse hugged a figure that had survived the rigours of two children and Walter's love of Oriental cuisine. Her ink-black hair, through which strands of grey wove like moonlight on dark water, was pulled back in a ponytail. When she reached up to kiss me lightly on the cheek, her arms around my shoulders, the scent of lavender enfolded me like a veil and I realised, not for the first time, that I had always been a little in love with Lee Cole.

'It's good to see you, Bird,' she said, her right hand resting lightly on my cheek, lines of anxiety on her brow giving the lie to the smile on her lips. She glanced at Walter and something passed between them. 'I'll be back later with some coffee.' She closed the door softly behind her on the way out.

'How are the kids doing?' I asked, as Walter poured himself a glass of Redbreast Irish whiskey – the old stuff with the screw top.

'Good,' he replied. 'Lauren still hates high school. Ellen's going to study law in Georgetown in the fall so at least one member of the family will understand the way it works.' He inhaled deeply as he raised the glass to his mouth and sipped. I gulped involuntarily and a sudden thirst gripped me. Walter noticed my discomfiture and reddened.

'Shit, I'm sorry,' he said.

'It's all right,' I responded. 'It's good therapy. I notice you're still swearing in the house.' Lee hated swearing, routinely telling her husband that only oafs resorted to profanity in speech. Walter usually countered by pointing out that Wittgenstein once brandished a poker in the course of a philosophical argument, proof positive in his eyes that erudite discourse sometimes wasn't sufficiently expressive for even the greatest of men.

He moved to a leather armchair at one side of the empty fireplace and motioned me to its opposite number. Lee entered with a silver coffee pot, creamer and two cups on a tray and then left, glancing anxiously at Walter as she did. I knew they had been talking before I arrived: they kept no secrets from each other and their unease seemed to indicate that they had discussed more than their concerns about my well-being.

'Do you want me to sit under a light?' I asked. A small smile moved across Walter's face with the swiftness of a breeze and then was gone.

'I heard things over the last few months,' he began, looking into his glass like a mystic examining a crystal ball. I stayed silent. 'I know you talked to the Feds, pulled in some favours so you could take a look at files. I know you were trying to find the man who killed Susan and Jenny.' He looked at me for the first time since he had begun talking.

I had nothing to say, so I poured some coffee for both of us, then picked up my own cup and sipped. It was Javan, strong and dark. I breathed deeply. 'Why are you asking me this?'

'Because I want to know why you're here, why you're back. I don't know what you've become if some of the things I've heard are true.' He swallowed, and I felt sorry for him, for what he had to say and the questions he had to ask. If I had answers to some of them I wasn't sure that I wanted to give them, or that Walter really wanted to hear them. Outside, the kids had finished their game as darkness drew in and there was a stillness in the air that made Walter's words sound like a portent.

'They say you found the guy who did it,' he said, and this

time there was no hesitation, as if he had steeled himself to say what he had to say. 'That you found him and killed him. Is that true?'

The past was like a snare. It allowed me to move a little, to circle, to turn, but, in the end, it always dragged me back. More and more, I found things in the city – favourite restaurants, bookshops, tree-shaded parks, even hearts carved bone-white into the wood of an old table – that reminded me of what I had lost, as if even a moment of forgetfulness was a crime against their memories. I slipped from present to past, sliding down the snake-heads of memory into what was and what would never be again.

And so, with Walter's question, I fell, back to late April, back to New Orleans. They had been dead for almost four months.

Woolrich sat at a table at the rear of the Café du Monde, beside a bubblegum machine with his back against the wall of the main building. On the table before him stood a steaming cup of *café au lait* and a plate of hot *beignets* covered in powdered sugar. Outside, people bustled down Decatur, past the green and white pavilion of the café, heading for the cathedral or Jackson Square.

He wore a tan suit, cheaply made, and his silk tie was stretched and faded so that he didn't even bother to button his shirt at the collar, preferring instead to let the tie hang mournfully at half mast. The floor around him was white with sugar, as was the only visible part of the green vinyl chair upon which he sat.

Woolrich was an Assistant SAC of the local FBI field office over at 1250 Poydras. He was also one of the few people from my police past with whom I'd stayed in touch in some small way and one of the only Feds I had ever met who didn't make me curse the day Hoover was born. More than that, he was my friend. He had stood by me in the days following the killings, never questioning, never doubting. I remember him standing rain-soaked by the grave, water dripping from the rim of his outsized fedora. He had been transferred to New Orleans soon after, a promotion that reflected a successful apprenticeship in at least three other field offices and his ability to keep his head in the turbulent environment of the New York field office in downtown Manhattan.

He was messily divorced, the marriage over for maybe twelve years. His wife had reverted to her maiden name, Karen Stott, and lived in Miami with an interior decorator whom she had recently married. Woolrich's only daughter Lisa – now, thanks to her mother's efforts, Lisa Stott – had joined some religious group in Mexico, he said. She was just eighteen. Her mother and her new husband didn't seem to care about her, unlike Woolrich, who cared but couldn't get his act together sufficiently to transfer his feelings into supportive actions. The disintegration of his family pained him in a very particular way, I knew. He came from a broken family himself, a white-trash mother and a father who was well meaning but inconsequential, too inconsequential to hold on to his hellcat wife. Woolrich had always wanted to do better, I think. More than the rest, I believed he shared my sense of loss when Susan and Jennifer were taken.

He had put on more weight since I last saw him and the hair on his chest was visible through his sweat-soaked shirt. Rivulets rolled down from a dense thatch of rapidly greying hair and into the folds of flesh at his neck. For such a big man, the Louisiana summers would be a form of torture. Woolrich may have looked like a clown, may even have acted that way when it suited him, but no one in New Orleans who knew him ever underestimated him. Those who had in the past were either already rotting in Angola penitentiary or, if you believed some of the rumours, rotting in the ground.

'I like the tie,' I said. It was bright red and decorated with lambs and angels.

'I call it my metaphysical tie,' Woolrich replied. 'My George Herbert tie.'

We shook hands, Woolrich wiping *beignet* crumbs from his shirtfront as he stood. 'Damn things get everywhere,' he said. 'When I die, they'll find *beignet* crumbs up the crack of my ass.'

'Thanks, I'll hold that thought.'

An Asian waiter in a white paper cap bustled up and I ordered coffee. 'Bring you *beignets*, suh?' he asked. Woolrich grinned. I told the waiter I'd skip the *beignets*.

'How you doin'?' asked Woolrich, taking a huge gulp of hot coffee that would have scarified the throat of a lesser man.

'I'm okay. How's life?'

'Same as it ever was: gift-wrapped, tied with a red bow and handed to someone else.'

'You still with . . . what was her name? Judy? Judy the nurse?'

Woolrich's face creased unhappily, as if he'd just encountered a hair in his *beignet*.

'Judy the nut, you mean. We split up. She's gone to work in La Jolla for a year, maybe more. I tell you, I decide to take her away for a romantic vacation a couple of months back, rent us a room in a two-hundred-dollar-a-night inn near Stowe, take in the country air if we left the window of the bedroom open, you know the deal. Anyway, we arrive at this place and it's older than Moses's dick, all dark wood and antique furniture and a bed you could lose a team of cheerleaders in. But Judy, she turns whiter than a polar bear's ass and backs away from me. You know what she says?'

I waited for him to continue.

'She says that I murdered her in the very same room in a previous life. She's backed up against the door, reaching for the handle and looking at me like she's expecting me to turn into the Son of Sam. Takes me two hours to calm her down and even then she refuses to sleep with me. I end up sleeping on a couch in the corner, and let me tell you, those goddamn antique couches may look like a million bucks and cost more but they're about as comfortable to sleep on as a concrete slab.'

He finished off the last bite of *beignet* and dabbed at himself with a napkin.

'Then I get up in the middle of the night to take a leak and she's sitting up in bed, wide awake, with the bedside lamp upside down in her hand, waiting to knock my head off if I come near her. Needless to say, this put an end to our five days of passion. We checked out the next morning, with me over a thousand dollars in the hole.

'But you know what the really funny thing is? Her regression therapist has told her to sue me for injuries in a past life. I'm about to become a test case for all those donut-heads who watch a documentary on PBS and think they were once Cleopatra or William the Conqueror.'

His eyes misted over at the thought of his lost thousand dollars and the games Fate plays on those who go to Vermont looking for uncomplicated sex.

'You heard from Lisa lately?'

His face clouded over and he waved a hand at me. 'Still with the Jesus huggers. Last time she rang me, it was to say that her leg was fine and to ask for more money. If Jesus saves, he must have had all his cash tied up with the Savings and Loan.' Lisa had broken her leg in a roller-skating accident the previous year, shortly before she found God. Woolrich was convinced that she was still concussed.

He stared at me for a time, his eyes narrowed. 'You're not okay, are you?'

'I'm alive and I'm here. Just tell me what you've got.'

He puffed his cheeks and then blew out slowly, marshalling his thoughts as he did so.

'There's a woman, down in St Martin Parish, an old Creole. She's got the gift, the locals say. She keeps away the gris-gris. You know, bad spirits, all that shit. Offers cures for sick kids, brings lovers together. Has visions.' He stopped and rolled his tongue around his mouth, and squinted at me.

'She's a psychic?'

'She's a witch, you believe the locals.'

'And do you?'

'She's been . . . helpful, once or twice in the past, according to the local cops. I've had nothing to do with her before.'

'And now?'

My coffee arrived and Woolrich asked for a refill. We didn't speak again until the waiter had departed and Woolrich had drained half of his coffee in a steaming mouthful.

'She's got about ten children and thousands of goddamn grandchildren and great-grandchildren. Some of them live with her or near her, so she's never alone. She's got a bigger extended family than Abraham.' He smiled but it was a fleeting thing, a brief release before what was to come.

'She says a young girl was killed in the bayou a while back, in the marshlands where the Barataria pirates used to roam. She told the sheriff's office but they didn't pay much attention. She didn't have a location, just said a young girl had been murdered in the bayou. Said she had seen it in a dream.

'Sheriff didn't do nothing about it. Well, that's not entirely true. He told the local boys to keep an eye out and then pretty much forgot all about it.'

'What brings it up again now?'

'The old woman says she hears the girl crying at night.'

I couldn't tell if Woolrich was just embarrassed by what he was saying, or whether he was spooked, but he looked towards the window and wiped his face with a giant grubby hand-kerchief.

'There's something else, though.' He folded the hand-kerchief and stuffed it back in his trouser pocket.

'She says the girl's face was cut off.' He breathed in deeply. 'And that she was blinded before she died.'

We drove north on 1–10 for a time, past the outlet mall and on towards West Baton Rouge with its truck stops and gambling joints, its bars full of oil workers and, elsewhere, blacks, all drinking the same rotgut whiskey and cheap, watery Dixie beer. A hot wind, heavy with the dense, decayed smell of the bayou, pulled at the trees along the highway, whipping their branches back and forth. Then we crossed on to the raised Atchafalaya highway, its supports embedded beneath the waters as we entered the Atchafalaya swamp and Cajun country.

I had only been here once before, when Susan and I were younger and happier. Along the Henderson Levee Road we passed the sign for McGee's Landing, where I'd eaten tasteless chicken and Susan had picked at lumps of deep-fried alligator so tough even other alligators would have had trouble digesting it. Then a Cajun fisherman had taken us on a boat trip into the swamps, through a semi-submerged cypress forest. The sun sank low and bloody over the water, turning the tree stumps into dark silhouettes like the fingers of dead men pointing accusingly at the heavens. It was another world, as far removed from the city as the moon was from the earth, and it seemed to create an erotic charge between us as the heat made our shirts cling to our bodies and the sweat drip from our brows. When we returned to our hotel in Lafayette we made love urgently and with a passion that superseded love, our drenched bodies moving together, the heat in the room as thick as water.

Woolrich and I did not go as far as Lafayette this time, with its motels and gas stations and the promise of the food in Prejeans, better than Randol's but with less atmosphere, where the Cajun bands played while locals and tourists mixed, drinking cold beers from Abita Springs and picking at catfish.

Woolrich left the highway for a two-lane road that wove through the bayou country for a time before turning into little more than a rutted track, pitted by holes filled with dank, foul-smelling swamp water around which insects buzzed in thick swarms. Cypress and willow lined the road and, through them, the stumps of trees were visible in the waters of the swamp, relics of the harvestings of the last century. Lily-pads clustered at the banks and, when the car slowed and the light was right, I could see bass moving languidly in their shadows, breaking the water occasionally.

I had heard that Jean Lafitte's brigands had made their home here. Now others had taken their place, killers and smugglers who used the canals and marshes as hiding places for heroin and marijuana, and as dark, green graves for the butchered, their bodies adding to the riotous growth of nature, their decay masked by the rich stench of vegetation.

We took one further turn, and here the cypress overhung the road. We rattled over a wooden bridge, the wood gradually returning to its original colour as the paint flaked and disintegrated. In the shadows at its far end I thought I saw a giant shadow watching us as we passed, his eyes white as eggs in the darkness beneath the trees.

'You see him?' said Woolrich.

'Who is he?'

'The old woman's youngest son. Tee Jean, she calls him. Petit Jean. He's kinda slow, but he looks out for her. They all do.'

'All?'

'There's six of 'em in all in the house. The old woman, her son, three kids from her second eldest's marriage – he's dead, died with his wife in a car crash three years back – and a daughter. She has five more sons and three daughters all living within a few miles of here. Then the local folks, they look after her too. She's kind of the matriarch around these parts, I guess. Big magic.'

I looked to see if he was being ironic. He wasn't.

We left the trees and arrived in a clearing before a long, single-storey house raised above the ground on stripped stumps of trees. It looked old but lovingly built, the wood on the front unwarped and carefully overlapped, the shingles on the roof undamaged but, here and there, darker where they had been replaced. The door stood open, blocked only by a wire screen, and chairs and children's toys littered the porch, which ran the length of the front of the house and disappeared around the side. From behind, I could hear the sound of children and the splashing of water.

The screen door was opened and a small, slim woman appeared at the top of the steps. She was about thirty, with delicate features and lush, dark hair drawn back in a ponytail from her light coffee-coloured skin. Yet as we stepped from the car and drew nearer, I could see her skin was pitted with scars, probably from childhood acne. She seemed to recognise Woolrich for, before we said anything, she held the door open so I could step inside. Woolrich didn't follow. I turned back towards him.

'You coming in?'

'I didn't bring you here, if anyone asks, and I don't even want to see her,' he said. He took a seat on the porch and rested his feet on the rail, watching the water gleam in the sunlight.

Inside, the wood was dark and the air cool. Doors at either side opened into bedrooms and a formal-looking living room with old, obviously hand-carved furniture, simple but carefully and skilfully crafted. An ancient radio with an illuminated dial and a band dotted with the names of far-flung places played a Chopin nocturne, which flowed through the house and into the last bedroom where the old woman waited.

She was blind. Her pupils were white, set in a huge moon face from which rolls of fat hung to her breastbone. Her arms, visible through the gauze sleeves of her multicoloured dress, were bigger than mine, and her swollen legs were like the trunks of small trees ending in surprisingly small, almost dainty, feet. She sat, supported by a mountain of pillows, on a giant bed in a room lit only by a hurricane lamp, the drapes closed against the sunlight. She was at least three hundred and fifty pounds, I guessed, probably more.

'Sit down, chile,' she said, taking one of my hands in her own and running her fingers lightly over mine. Her eyes stared straight ahead, not looking at me, as her fingers traced the lines on my palm.

'I know why you here,' she said. Her voice was high, girlish, as if she were a huge speaking doll whose tapes had been mixed up with a smaller model. 'You hurtin'. You burnin' inside. Little girl, you woman, they gone.' In the dim light, the old woman seemed to crackle with hidden energy.

'Tante, tell me about the girl in the swamp, the girl with no eyes.'

'Poor chile,' said the old woman, her brow furrowing in sorrow. 'She the fu'st here. She was runnin' from sumpin' and she loss her way. Took a ride wi' him and she never came back. Hurt her so, so bad. Didn't touch her, though, 'cept with the knife.'

She turned her eyes towards me for the first time and I realised she was not blind, not in any way that mattered. As her hands traced the lines of my palm, my eyes closed and I felt that she had been there with the girl in her final moments, that she might even have brought her some comfort as the blade went about its business. 'Hush, chile, you come with Tante now. Hush, chile, take my hand, you. He done hurtin' you now.'

And I heard and felt, deep within myself, the blade cutting, grating, separating muscle from joint, flesh from bone, soul from body, the artist working on his canvas, and I felt pain dancing through me, arcing through a fading life like a lightning flash, welling like the notes of a hellish song through the unknown girl in the Louisiana swamp. And in her agony I felt the agony of my own child, my own wife, and I felt certain that this was the same man. Even as the pain faded to its last for the girl in the swamp, she was in darkness and I knew he had blinded her before he killed her.

'Who is he?' I said.

She spoke, and in her voice there were four voices: the voices of a wife and a daughter, the voice of an old obese woman on a bed in a wine-dark room, and the voice of a nameless girl who died a brutal, lonely death in the mud and water of a Louisiana swamp.

'He the Travellin' Man.'

Walter shifted in his chair and the sound of his spoon against the china cup was like the ringing of chimes.

'No,' I said. 'I didn't find him.'

# Chapter Four

Walter had been silent for a time, the whiskey now almost drained from his glass. 'I need a favour, not for me but for someone else.'

I waited.

'It's to do with the Barton Trust.'

The Barton Trust had been founded in his will by old Jack Barton, an industrialist who made his fortune by supplying parts for the aeronautical industry after the war. The Trust provided money for research into child-related issues, supported paediatric clinics and generally provided childcare money that the state would not. Its nominal head was Isobel Barton, old Jack's widow, although the day-to-day running of the business was the responsibility of an attorney named Andrew Bruce and the Trust's chairman, Philip Kooper.

I knew all this because Walter did some fund-raising for the Trust on occasion – prize draws, bowling competitions – and also because, some weeks before, the Trust had entered the news for all the wrong reasons. During a charity fête held in the grounds of the Barton house on Staten Island a young boy, Evan Baines, had disappeared. In the end, no trace of the boy had been found and the cops had pretty much given up hope. They believed he had somehow strayed from the grounds and been abducted. It merited some mention in the newspapers for a time and then was gone.

'Evan Baines?'

'No, at least I don't think so, but it may be a missing person. A young woman, friend of Isobel Barton, seems to have gone missing. It's been a few days and Mrs Barton's worried. Her name's Catherine Demeter. Nothing to link her with the Baines disappearance; she hadn't even met the Bartons at that point.'

'Bartons plural?'

'Seems she was dating Stephen Barton. You know anything about him?'

'He's an asshole. Apart from that, he's a minor drug pusher for Sonny Ferrera, grew up near the Ferreras on Staten Island and fell in with Sonny as a teenager. He's into steroids, also coke, I think, but it's minor league stuff.'

Walter's brow furrowed. 'How long have you known about this?' he asked.

'Can't remember,' I replied. 'Gym gossip.'

'Jesus, don't tell us anything we might find useful. I've only known since Tuesday.'

'You're not supposed to know,' I said. 'You're the police. Nobody tells you things you're supposed to know.'

'You used to be a cop too,' Walter muttered. 'You've picked up some bad habits.'

'Gimme a break, Walter. How do I know who you're checking up on? What am I supposed to do, go to confession to you once a week?' I poured some hot coffee into my cup. 'Anyway, you think there might be a connection between this disappearance and Sonny Ferrera?' I continued.

'It's possible,' said Walter. 'The Feds were tracking Stephen Barton for a time, maybe a year ago, long before he was supposed to have started seeing Catherine Demeter. They were chasing their tails with that kid, so they let it go. According to the Narcotics file she doesn't seem to have been involved, at

55

least not openly, but what do they know? Some of them still think a crack pipe is something a plumber fixes. Maybe she could have seen something she wasn't supposed to see.'

His face betrayed how lame he thought the link was, but he left me to voice it. 'C'mon, Walter, steroids and minor coke? There's money in it but, like I said, it's strictly minor league compared to the rest of Ferrera's business. If he knocked off someone over musclehead drugs then he's even more stupid than we know he is. Even his old man thinks he's the result of a defective gene.'

Ferrera Senior, sick and decrepit but still a respected figure, had been known to refer to his only son as 'that little prick' on occasion. 'Is that all you've got?'

'As you say, we're the police. No one tells us anything useful,' he replied drily.

'Did you know Sonny is impotent?' I offered.

Walter stood up, waving his empty glass in front of his face and smiling for the first time that evening. 'No, no, I didn't. I'm not sure I wanted to know, either. What the hell are you, his urologist?' He glanced over at me as he reached for the Redbreast. I waved my fingers in a gesture of disregard that went no further than my wrist.

'Pili Pilar still with him?' I asked, testing the waters.

'Far as I know. I hear he pushed Nicky Glasses out of a window a few weeks back because he fell behind on the vig.'

'Tough on Nicky. Another hundred years and he'd have had the loan paid off. Pili'd better ease up on his temper or he's gonna run out of people to push through windows.'

Walter didn't smile.

'Will you talk to her?' he asked as he resumed his seat.

'MPs, Walter . . .' I sighed. Fourteen thousand people disappeared in New York every year. It wasn't even clear if this woman was missing – in which case she didn't want to be found or someone else didn't want her found – or simply misplaced, which meant that she had merely upped sticks and moved off to another town without breaking the news to her good friend Isobel Barton, or to her lovely boyfriend Stephen Barton.

Those are the kinds of issues PIs have to consider when faced with missing-persons cases. Tracing missing persons is bread and butter for PIs, but I wasn't a PI. I had taken on Fat Ollie's skip because it was easy work, or seemed to be at the time. I didn't want to file for a PI license with the State Licensing Services in Albany. I didn't want to get involved in missing-persons work. Maybe I was afraid it would distract me too much. Maybe I just didn't care enough, not then.

'She won't go to the cops,' said Walter. 'The woman isn't even officially missing yet, since no one has reported her.'

'So how come you know about it?'

'You know Tony Loo-Loo?' I nodded. Tony Loomax was a small-time PI with a stammer who had never graduated beyond skips and white-trash divorces.

'Loomax is an unusual candidate for Isobel Barton's custom,' I said.

'It seems he did some work for one of the household staff a year or two back. Traced her husband who'd run off with their savings. Mrs Barton told him she wanted something similar done, but wanted it done on the QT.'

'Still doesn't explain your involvement.'

'I have some stuff on Tony, mild overstepping of legal boundaries, which he would prefer I didn't act on. Tony figured I might like to know that Isobel Barton had been making low-key approaches. I spoke to Kooper. He believes the Trust doesn't need any more bad publicity. I figured maybe I could do him a favour.'

'If Tony has the call, then why are you approaching me?'

'We've encouraged Tony to pass it on. He's told Isobel Barton that he's passing her on to someone she can trust because he can't take the case. Seems his mother just died and he has to go to the funeral.'

'Tony Loo-Loo doesn't have a mother. He was brought up in an orphanage.'

'Well, *someone*'s mother must have died,' said Walter testily. 'He can go to that funeral.'

He stopped and I could see the doubt in his eyes as the rumours he had heard flicked a fin in the depths of his mind. 'And that's why I'm approaching you. Even if I tried to do this quietly through the usual channels someone would know. Christ, you take a drink of water at headquarters and ten guys piss it out.'

'What about the girl's family?'

He shrugged. 'I don't know much more but I don't think there is one. Look, Bird, I'm asking you because you're good. You were a smart cop. If you'd stayed on the force the rest of us would have been cleaning your shoes and polishing your shield. Your instincts were good. I reckon they still are. Plus you owe me one: people who go shooting up the boroughs don't usually walk away quite so easily.'

I was silent for a time. I could hear Lee banging around in the kitchen while a TV show played in the background. Perhaps it was a remnant of what had taken place earlier, the apparently senseless killing of Fat Ollie Watts and his girl-friend, the death of the shooter, but it felt as if the world had shifted out of joint and that nothing was fitting as it should. Even this felt wrong. I believed Walter was holding back on me.

I heard the doorbell ring and then there was a muffled exchange of voices, one of them Lee's and the other a deep male voice. Seconds later there was a knock on the door and Lee showed in a tall, grey-haired man in his fifties. He wore a dark blue double-breasted suit – it looked like Boss – and a red Christian Dior tie with an interlocking gold CD pattern. His shoes sparkled like they'd been shined with spit although, since this was Philip Kooper, it was probably someone else's spit.

Kooper was an unlikely figure to act as chairman and spokesman of a children's charity. He was thin and pale, and his mouth managed the unique trick of being simultaneously slim and pursed. His fingers were long and tapering, almost like claws. Kooper looked like he had been disinterred for the express purpose of making people uneasy. If he had turned up at one of the Trust's kids' parties, all of the children would have cried.

'This him?' he asked Walter, after declining a drink. He flicked his head at me like a frog swallowing a fly. I played with the sugar bowl and tried to look offended.

'This is Parker,' nodded Walter. I waited to see if Kooper would offer to shake hands. He didn't. His hands remained clasped in front of him like a professional mourner at a particularly uninvolving funeral.

'Have you explained the situation to him?'

Walter nodded again but looked embarrassed. Kooper's manners were worse than a bad child's. I stayed seated and didn't say anything. Kooper sniffed and then stood in silence while he looked down on me. He gave the impression that it was a position with which he was entirely familiar.

'This is a delicate situation, Mr Parker, as I'm sure you'll appreciate. Any communication in this matter will be made to me in the first instance before you impart any information to Mrs Barton. Is that clear?'

I wondered if Kooper was worth the effort of annoying and decided, after looking at Walter's look of discomfort, that he probably wasn't, at least not yet. But I was starting to feel sorry for Isobel Barton and I hadn't even met her.

'My understanding was that Mrs Barton was hiring me,' I said eventually.

'That's correct, but you will be answerable to me.'

'I don't think so. There's a small matter of confidentiality. I'll look into it but, if it's unconnected with the Baines kid or the Ferreras, I reserve the right to keep what I learn between Isobel Barton and myself.'

'That is not satisfactory, Mr Parker,' said Kooper. A faint blush of colour rose in his cheeks and hung there for a moment, looking lost in the tundra of his complexion. 'Perhaps I am not making myself clear: in this matter, you will report to me first. I have powerful friends, Mr Parker. If you do not co-operate I can ensure that your license is revoked.'

'They must be very powerful friends because I don't have a license,' I said. I stood up and Kooper's fists tightened slightly. 'You should consider yoga,' I said. 'You're too tense.'

I thanked Walter for the coffee and moved to the door.

'Wait,' he said. I turned back to see him staring at Kooper. After a few moments, Kooper gave a barely perceptible shrug of his shoulders and moved to the window. He didn't look at me again. Kooper's attitude and Walter's expression conspired against my better judgement, and I decided to talk to Isobel Barton.

'I take it she's expecting me?' I asked Walter.

'I told Tony to tell her you were good, that if the girl was alive you'd find her.'

There was another brief moment of silence.

'And if she's dead?'

'Mr Kooper asked that question as well,' said Walter.

'What did you say?'

He swallowed the last of his whiskey, the ice cubes rattling against the glass like old bones. Behind him, Kooper was a dark silhouette against the window, like a promise of bad news.

'I told him you'd bring back the body.'

★   ★   ★

In the end, that's what it all came down to: bodies – bodies found and bodies yet to be found. And I recalled how Woolrich and I stood outside the old woman's house and looked out over the bayou on that April day. I could hear the water lapping gently at the shore and, further out, I watched a small fishing boat bobbing on the water, two figures casting out from either side. But both Woolrich and I were looking deeper than the surface, as if, by staring hard enough, we could penetrate to the depths and find the body of a nameless girl in the dark waters.

'Do you believe her?' he said at last.

'I don't know. I really don't know.'

'There's no way we're gonna find that body, if it exists, without more than we've got. We start trawling for bodies in bayous and pretty soon we're gonna be knee deep in bones. People been dumping bodies in these swamps for centuries. Be a miracle if we didn't find something.'

I walked away from him. He was right, of course. Assuming there was a body, we needed more from the old woman than she had given us. I felt like I was trying to grip smoke, but what the old woman had said was the closest thing yet to a lead on the man who had killed Jennifer and Susan.

I wondered if I was crazy, taking the word of a blind woman who heard voices in her sleep. I probably was.

'Do you know what he looks like, Tante?' I had asked her, watching as her head moved ponderously from side to side in response.

'Only see him when he comes for you,' she replied. 'Then you know him.'

I reached the car and looked back to see a figure on the porch with Woolrich. It was the girl with the scarred face, standing gracefully on the tips of her toes as she leaned towards the taller man. I saw Woolrich run his finger tenderly across her cheek and then softly speak her name: 'Florence.' He kissed her lightly on the lips, then turned and walked towards me without looking back at her. Neither of us said anything about it on the journey back to New Orleans.

# Chapter Five

It rained throughout that night, breaking the shell of heat that had surrounded the city, and the streets of Manhattan seemed to breathe easier the next morning. It was almost cool as I ran. The pavement was hard on my knees but large areas of grass were sparse in this part of the city. I bought a newspaper on the way back to my apartment then showered, changed and read over breakfast. Shortly after 11.00 a.m. I called a cab and headed out to the Barton house.

Isobel Barton lived in the secluded house her late husband had built in the seventies near Todt Hill, an admirable if unsuccessful attempt to replicate the antebellum houses of his native Georgia in an east-coast setting and on a smaller scale. Old Jack Barton, an amiable soul by all accounts, had apparently made up with money and determination for what he lacked in good taste.

The gate to the drive was open as I arrived and the exhaust fumes of another car hung in the air. The cab turned in just as the electronic gates were about to rumble closed, and we followed the lead car, a white BMW 320i with tinted windows, to the small courtyard in front of the house. The cab looked out of place in that setting, although how the Barton household might have felt about my own battered Mustang, currently undergoing repairs, I wasn't so sure.

As I pulled up a slim woman dressed conservatively in a grey suit emerged from the BMW and watched me curiously as I paid the cab driver. Her grey hair was tied back in a bun, which did nothing to soften her severe features. A large black man wearing a chauffeur's uniform appeared at the door of the house and moved quickly to intercept me as I walked from the departing cab.

'Parker. I believe I'm expected.'

The chauffeur gave me a look that told me if I was lying he'd make me wish I'd stayed in bed. He asked me to wait before turning back to the woman in grey. She glanced at me briefly but nastily before exchanging a few words with the chauffeur, who moved off to the back of the house as she approached me.

'Mr Parker, I'm Ms Christie, Mrs Barton's personal assistant. You should have stayed at the gate until we were sure who you were.' In a window above the door, a curtain twitched slightly and then was still.

'If you have a staff entrance I'll use that in future.' I got the impression from Ms Christie that she hoped that eventuality wouldn't arise. She eyed me coldly for a moment then turned on her heel. 'If you'll come with me, please,' she said over her shoulder, as she moved towards the door. The grey suit was threadbare at the edges. I wondered if Mrs Barton would haggle over my rates.

If Isobel Barton was short of cash she could simply have sold off some of the antiques that furnished the house because the interior was an auctioneer's wet dream. Two large rooms opened out at either side of a hallway filled with furniture that looked like it was only used when presidents died. A wide staircase curved up to the right; a closed door lay straight ahead while another nestled under the stairs. I followed Ms Christie through the latter and into a small but surprisingly bright and modern office with a computer in a corner and a TV and video unit built into the bookshelves. Maybe Mrs Barton wouldn't haggle about the rates after all.

Ms Christie sat down behind a pine desk, removed some papers from her valise and shuffled through them in obvious irritation before finding what she wanted.

'This is a standard confidentiality agreement drawn up by the Trust's legal advisers,' she began, pushing it towards me with one hand while clicking a pen simultaneously with the other. 'It is an undertaking on your behalf to keep all communication relating to the matter in hand between Mrs Barton, myself and yourself.' She used the pen to point to the relevant sections on the agreement, like an insurance salesman trying to slip a bum contract past a sucker. 'I'd like you to sign it before we proceed any further,' she concluded.

It seemed like nobody involved with the Barton Trust had a particularly trusting nature. 'I don't think so,' I said. 'If you're concerned about possible breaches of confidentiality then hire a priest to do your work. Otherwise you'll have to take my word that what passes between us will go no further.' Perhaps I should have felt guilty about lying to her. I didn't. I was a good liar. It's one of the gifts God gives alcoholics.

'That's not acceptable. I am already unconvinced about the necessity of hiring you and I certainly feel it is inappropriate to do so without—'

She was interrupted by the sound of the office door opening. I turned to see a tall, attractive woman enter, her age indeterminable through a combination of the gentleness of nature and the magic of cosmetics. At a glance I would have guessed she was in her late forties but if this was Isobel Barton, then I knew she was closer to fifty-five, maybe older. She wore a pale blue dress, which was too subtly simple to be anything but expensive and displayed a figure that was either surgically enhanced or extremely well preserved.

As she drew closer and the tiny wrinkles in her face became clearer I guessed it was the latter: Isobel Barton did not look like the sort of woman who resorted to plastic surgery. Around her neck, gold and diamonds glittered and a pair of matching earrings sparkled as she walked. Her hair, too, was grey, but she let it hang long and loose on her shoulders. She was still an attractive woman and she walked like she knew it.

Philip Kooper had borne the brunt of the media attention following the disappearance of the Baines boy, but that attention had not been significant. The Baines boy was from a family of dopers and no-hopers. His disappearance merited a mention only because of the Trust and even then the Trust's lawyers and patrons had called in enough favours to ensure that speculation was kept to a minimum. The boy's mother was separated from his father and they hadn't been getting along any better since he left.

The police were still trying to trace the father in case of a possible snatch, even though every indication was that the father, a petty criminal, hated his child. In some cases, that might be enough to justify taking the child and killing him to get at his estranged wife. When I was a rookie patrolman, I once arrived at a tenement to find a man had abducted his baby daughter and drowned her in the bath because his ex-wife wouldn't let him have the TV after they separated.

Only one piece of coverage of the Baines disappearance stuck in my mind: a picture of Mrs Barton snapped head-bowed as she visited the mother of Evan Baines in a run-down project. It was supposed to have been a private visit. The photographer, returning from the scene of a drug-killing, just happened to be passing. One or two papers took the picture, but they ran it small.

'Thank you, Caroline. I'll talk to Mr Parker alone for a time.' She smiled as she said it but the tone brooked no argument. Her assistant affected a lack of concern at the dismissal but her eyes flashed fire. When she had left the room, Mrs Barton seated herself on a stiff-backed chair away from the desk and motioned me towards a black leather couch, then turned her smile on me.

'I'm sorry about that. I didn't authorise any such agreement but Caroline can be over-protective of me at times. Can we offer you coffee, or would you prefer a drink?'

'Neither, thank you. Before you go any further, Mrs Barton, I should tell you that I don't really do missing-persons work.' In my experience, searching for missing persons was best left to specialist agencies with the manpower to chase up leads and possible sightings. Some solo investigators who took on that kind of work were at best ill equipped and at worst little better than parasites who preyed on the hopes of those who remained to keep funding minimal efforts for even smaller returns.

'Mr Loomax said you might say that, but only out of modesty. He told me to say he would regard it as a personal favour.'

I smiled, despite myself. The only favour I would give Tony Loo-Loo would be not to piss on his grave when he died.

According to Mrs Barton, she had met Catherine Demeter through her son, who had seen the girl working at DeVries's department store and had pestered her for a date. Mrs Barton and her son – her stepson, to be accurate, since Jack Barton had been married once before to a Southern woman who had divorced him after eight years and moved to Hawaii with a singer – were not close. She was aware that her son was engaged in activities that were, as she put it, 'unsavoury', and had tried to get him to change his ways, 'both for his own sake and the sake of the Trust'. I nodded sympathetically. Sympathy was the only possible emotion to feel for anyone involved with Stephen Barton.

When she heard he was seeing a new girlfriend she asked if they could all meet together, she said, and a date had been arranged. In the end her son had failed to appear but Catherine had turned up and, after an initial awkwardness, the two quickly struck up a friendship far more amicable than the relationship that existed between the girl and Stephen Barton. The two had continued to meet occasionally for coffee and lunch. Despite invitations, the girl had politely refused offers from Mrs Barton to come out to the house and Stephen Barton had never brought her.

Then Catherine Demeter had simply dropped out of sight. She had left work early on Saturday and had failed to keep an early dinner appointment on Sunday with Mrs Barton. That was the last anyone had heard of Catherine Demeter, said Mrs Barton. Two days had now passed and she had heard nothing from her.

'Because of, well, the publicity that the Trust has received recently over the disappearance of that poor child I was reluctant to cause a fuss or draw any further adverse attention down on us,' she said. 'I rang Mr Loomax and he seemed to think that Catherine may simply have drifted on somewhere else. It happens a lot, I believe.'

'Do you think there's something more to it than that?'

'I really don't know, but she was so happy with her job and she appeared to be getting on well with Stephen.' She stopped for a moment at this mention of her son's name, as if considering whether or not to proceed. Then: 'Stephen has been running wild for some time – since before his father's death, in fact. Do you know the Ferrera family, Mr Parker?'

'I'm aware of them.'

'Stephen fell in with their youngest son, despite all of our efforts. I know he keeps bad company and I know he's involved with drugs. I'm afraid he may have dragged Catherine into something. And . . .' She paused again, briefly. 'I enjoyed her company. There was something gentle about her and she seemed so sad sometimes. She said that she was anxious to settle down here, after moving around for so long.'

'Did she say where she had been?'

'All over. I gather that she had worked in a number of states.'

'Did she say anything about her past, give any indication that something might be troubling her?'

'I think something may have happened to her family when she was young. She told me that she had a sister who died. She didn't say any more. She said she couldn't talk about it and I didn't press her on it.'

'Mr Loomax may be right. She may simply have moved on again.'

Mrs Barton shook her head insistently. 'No, she would have told me, I'm sure of it. Stephen hasn't heard from her and neither have I. I'm afraid for her and I want to know that she is safe. That's all. She doesn't even have to know that I hired you, or that I was concerned for her. Will you take the case?'

I was still reluctant to do Walter Cole's dirty work and to take advantage of Isobel Barton but I had little else on my plate, except an appearance in court the following day on behalf of an insurance firm, another case I had taken for the exercise.

If there was a connection between the disappearance of Catherine Demeter and Sonny Ferrera, then she was almost certainly in trouble. If Sonny had been involved in the killing of Fat Ollie Watts, it was clear that he was going off the rails.

'I'll give it a few days,' I said. 'As a favour,' I added. 'Do you want to know my rates?'

She was already writing a cheque, drawn on her private account and not that of the Trust. 'Here's three thousand dollars in advance and this is my card. My private number is on the back.'

She moved her chair forward. 'Now, what else do you need to know?'

That evening, I had dinner in River on Amsterdam Avenue, close to 70th Street, where the classic beef made it the best Vietnamese in town and where the staff moved by so softly that it was like being waited on by shadows or passing breezes. I watched a young couple at a nearby table intertwining their hands, running their fingers over each other's knuckles and fingertips, tracing delicate circles in their palms, then gripping their hands together and pressing the heel of each hand forcefully against the other. And as they simulated their lovemaking, a waitress drifted by and smiled knowingly at me as I watched.

# Chapter Six

The day after I visited Isobel Barton, I made a brief visit to court in connection with the insurance case. A claim had been made against a phone company by a contracted electrician who said he had fallen down a hole in the road while examining underground cables and was no longer able to work as a result.

He may not have been able to work but he had still been able to power-lift five hundred pounds in a cash contest in a Boston gymnasium. I had used a palm-size Panasonic video camera to capture his moment of glory. The insurance company presented the evidence to a judge, who suspended any further decision on the matter for one week. I didn't even have to give evidence. Afterwards I had coffee in a diner and read the paper before heading over to Pete Hayes's old gym in TriBeCa.

I knew Stephen Barton worked out there sometimes. If his girlfriend had disappeared then there was a strong possibility that Barton might know where she had gone or, equally importantly, why. I remembered him vaguely as a strong, Nordic-looking type, his body obscenely pumped from steroid use. He was in his late twenties but the combination of training and sunbeds had worn his face to the consistency of old leather, adding at least ten years to his age.

As artists and Wall Street lawyers had started moving into the TriBeCa area, attracted by loft-space in the cast-iron and masonry buildings, Pete's gym had moved upmarket, filling what used to be a spit and sawdust place with mirrors and potted palms and, sacrilege upon sacrilege, a juice bar. Now heavyweight boneheads and serious power-lifters worked out alongside accountants with paunches and female executives with power-dress business suits and cellphones. The notice-board at the door advertised something called 'spinning', which involved sitting on a bike for an hour and sweating yourself into a red agony. Ten years ago, even the suggestion that the gym might be used for such a purpose would have caused Pete's regular clientele to bust the place up.

A wholesome-looking blonde in a red leotard buzzed me into Pete's office, the last bastion of what the gym had once been. Old posters advertising power-lifting competitions and Mr Universe shows shared wall space with pictures of Pete alongside Steve Reeves, Joe Weider and, oddly, the wrestler Hulk Hogan. Body-building trophies sat in a glass-fronted cabinet while behind a battered pine desk sat Pete himself, his muscles slackening in old age but still a powerful, impressive figure, his salt and pepper hair cut in a short military style. I had trained in the gym for almost six years, until I was promoted to detective and started to destroy myself.

Pete stood and nodded, his hands in his pockets and his loose-fitting top doing nothing to conceal the size of his shoulders and arms.

'Long time,' he said. 'Sorry about what happened to . . .' He trailed off and moved his chin and shoulders in a kind of combination shrug, a gesture to the past and what it con-tained.

I nodded back and leaned against an old gunmetal-grey filing cabinet adorned with decals advertising health supplements and lifting magazines.

'Spinning, Pete?'

He grimaced. 'Yeah, I know. Still, spinning makes me two hundred dollars an hour. I got forty exercise bikes on the floor above us and I couldn't make more money with a printing press and green ink.'

'Stephen Barton around?'

Pete kicked at some imaginary obstacle on the worn wooden floor. 'Not for a week or so. He in trouble?'

'I don't know,' I replied. 'Is he?'

Pete sat down slowly and, wincing, stretched his legs out in front of him. Years of squatting had taken their toll on his knees, leaving them weak and arthritic. 'You're not the first person to come here asking about him this week. Couple of guys in cheap suits were in here yesterday trying to find him. Recognised one of them as Sal Inzerillo, used to be a good light-middleweight until he started taking falls.'

'I remember him.' I paused. 'Works for old man Ferrera now, I hear.'

'Might do,' nodded Pete. 'Might do. Might have worked for the old man in the ring too, if you believe the stories. This about drugs?'

'I don't know,' I replied. Pete glanced at me quickly to see if I was lying, decided I wasn't and went back to examining the tops of his sneakers. 'You hear of any trouble between Sonny and the old man, anything that might have involved Stephen Barton?'

'There's trouble between them, sure, otherwise what's Inzerillo doing damaging my floor with his black rubber soles? Don't know that it involves Barton, though.'

I moved on to the subject of Catherine Demeter. 'Do you remember a girl with Barton recently? She may have been around here sometimes. Short dark hair, slight overbite, maybe in her early thirties.'

'Barton has lots of girls but I don't remember that one. Don't notice, mostly, unless they're smarter than Barton, which makes me wonder.'

'Not difficult,' I said. 'This one probably was smarter. Is Barton a hitter?'

'He's mean, sure. Popping pills frazzled his brain, gave him bad 'roid rage. It's fight or fuck with him. Fuck mainly. My old lady could take him in a fight.' He looked at me intently. 'I know what he was into, but he didn't sell here. I'd have force-fed his shit to him till he burst if he tried it.' I didn't believe Pete but I let it go. Steroids was part of the game now and there was nothing Pete could do except bluster.

He pursed his lips and pulled his legs slowly in. 'A lot of women were attracted to him by his size. Barton was a big guy and he sure talked big. Some women just want the protection someone like him seems to offer. Some just want to fuck a big guy and some want to be protected. They believe if they give the guy what he wants he'll look out for them.'

'Pity she chose Stephen Barton, then,' I said.

'Yeah,' agreed Pete. 'Maybe she wasn't so smart after all.'

I had brought my training gear with me and did ninety minutes in the gym. It had been some time since I trained properly. To avoid embarrassment I skipped the bench and stuck to shoulders, back and light arm work, enjoying the sensation of strength and movement in the bent-over rows and the pressure on my biceps during the curls.

I still looked pretty good, I thought, although the assessment was a result of insecurity instead of vanity. At just under six feet, I still retained some of my lifter's build – the wide shoulders, definition in the biceps and triceps and a chest which was at least bigger than two eggs frying on the sidewalk – and I hadn't regained much of the fat I had lost during the year. I still had my hair, although there was grey creeping back from the temples and sprinkling the fringe. My eyes were clear enough to be recognisably grey-blue, set in a slightly long face now deeply etched at the eyes and mouth with the marks of remembered grief. Clean-shaven, with a decent haircut, a good suit and some flattering light, I could look almost respectable. In the right light, I could even have claimed to be thirty-two without making people snigger too loudly. It was only two years less than my age on my driver's licence, but these little things become more important as you get older.

When I was finished, I packed my gear, declined Pete's offer of a protein shake – it smelt like rotten bananas – and stopped off for a coffee instead. I felt relaxed for the first time in weeks, the endorphins pumping through my system and a pleasant tightness developing across my shoulders and back.

The next call I made was to DeVries's department store. The personnel manager called himself a human resources manager and, like personnel managers the world over, was one of the least personable people one could meet. Sitting opposite him, it was difficult not to feel that anyone who could happily reduce individuals to resources, to the same level as oil, bricks and canaries in coal mines, probably shouldn't be allowed to have any human relations that didn't involve locks and prison bars. In other words, Timothy Cary was a first-degree prick from the tip of his close-cropped dyed hair to the toes of his patent leather shoes.

I had contacted his secretary earlier that afternoon to make the appointment, telling her that I was acting for an attorney in the matter of an inheritance coming to Ms Demeter. Cary and his secretary deserved each other. A wild dog on a chain would have been more helpful than Cary's secretary, and easier to get past.

'My client is anxious that Ms Demeter be contacted as soon as possible,' I told him, as we sat in his small, prissy office. 'The will is extremely detailed and there are a lot of forms to be filled out.'

'And your client would be . . .?'

'I'm afraid I can't tell you that. I'm sure you understand.'

Cary looked like he understood but didn't want to. He

leaned back in his chair and gently rubbed his expensive silk tie between his fingers. It had to be expensive. It was too tasteless to be anything else. Crisp lines showed along his shirt as if it had just been removed from its packet, assuming Timothy Cary would have anything to do with something so plebeian as a plastic wrapper. If he ever visited the shop floor it must have been like an angel descending, albeit an angel who looked like he'd just encountered a bad smell.

'Miss Demeter was due in work yesterday.' Cary glanced down at a file on his desk. 'She had Monday off and we haven't seen her since.'

'Is that usual, to have Monday off?' I wasn't anxious to know but the question distracted Cary from the file. Isobel Barton didn't have Catherine Demeter's new address. Catherine would usually contact her or Mrs Barton would have her assistant leave a message at DeVries's. As Cary brightened slightly at the opportunity to discuss a subject close to his heart and started mouthing off about work schedules, I memorised her address and SSN. I eventually managed to interrupt him for long enough to ask if Catherine Demeter had been ill on her last day in work, or had complained of being disturbed in any way.

'I'm not aware of any such communication. Miss Demeter's position with DeVries is currently under review as a result of her absence,' he concluded smugly. 'I hope, for her sake, that her inheritance is considerable.' I don't think he meant it.

After some routine delaying tactics, Cary gave me permission to speak with the woman who had worked with Catherine on her last shift in the store. I met her in a supervisor's office off the sales floor. Martha Friedman was in her early sixties. She was plump with dyed-red hair and a face so caked with cosmetics that the floor of the Amazon jungle probably saw more natural light, but she tried to be helpful. She had been working with Catherine Demeter in the china department on

Saturday. It was her first time to work with her, since Mrs Friedman's usual assistant had been taken ill and someone was needed to cover for her in the last hour before closing.

'Did you notice anything unusual about her behaviour?' I asked, as Mrs Friedman took the opportunity afforded by some time in the supervisor's office to discreetly examine the papers on his desk. 'Did she seem distressed or anxious in any way?'

Mrs Friedman furrowed her brow slightly. 'She broke a piece of china, an Aynsley vase. She had just arrived and was showing it to a customer when she dropped it. Then, when I looked around, she was running across the shop floor, heading for the escalators. Most unprofessional, I thought, even if she was sick.'

'And was she sick?'

'She *said* she felt sick, but why run for the escalators? We have a staff washroom on each level.'

I got the feeling that Mrs Friedman knew more than she was saying. She was enjoying the attention and wanted to draw it out. I leaned towards her confidentially.

'But what do *you* think, Mrs Friedman?'

She preened a little and leaned forward in turn, touching my hand lightly to emphasise her point.

'She saw someone, someone she was trying to reach before they left the store. Tom, the security guard on the east door, told me she ran out by him and stood looking around the street. We're supposed to get permission to leave the store when on duty. He should have reported her, but he just told me instead. Tom's a *schvartze*, but he's okay.'

'Do you have any idea who she might have seen?'

'No. She just refused to discuss it. She doesn't have any friends among the staff, far as I can tell, and now I can see why.'

I spoke to the security guard and the supervisor, but they couldn't add anything to what Mrs Friedman had told me. I stopped at a diner for coffee and a sandwich, returned to my apartment to pick up a small black bag my friend Angel had given me and then took another cab to Catherine Demeter's apartment.

# Chapter Seven

The apartment was in a converted four-storey redstone in Greenpoint, a part of Brooklyn populated mainly by Italians, Irish and Poles, the latter counting a large number of former Solidarity activists among them. It was from the Greenpoint Continental Ironworks that the ironclad *Monitor* had emerged to fight the Confederate ship *Merrimac*, when Greenpoint was Brooklyn's industrial centre.

The cast-iron manufacturers, the potters and printers were all gone now, but many of the descendants of the original workers still remained. Small clothing boutiques and Polish bakeries shared frontage with established kosher delis and stores selling used electrical goods.

Catherine Demeter's block was still a little run down, and kids wearing sneakers and low-slung jeans sat on the steps of most of the buildings, smoking and whistling and calling at passing women. She lived in apartment fourteen, probably near the top. I tried the bell but wasn't surprised when there was no answer from the intercom. Instead I tried twenty and, when an elderly woman's voice responded, I told her I was from the gas company and had a report of a leak but the supervisor's apartment was empty. She was silent for a moment then buzzed me in.

I guessed she'd probably check with the super so time was limited, although if the apartment didn't reveal anything about where Catherine Demeter might have gone, I'd have to talk to the super anyway, or approach the neighbours or maybe even talk to the mailman. As I passed into the lobby I flipped open the mailbox for apartment fourteen and shone my flashlight inside, finding only a copy of the most recent *New York* magazine and what looked like two junk mail drops. I let the box close and took the stairs up to the third floor.

It was silent, with six newly varnished apartment doors along the hall, three on each side. I walked quietly to number fourteen and took the black bag from under my coat. I knocked once more on the door, just to be sure, and removed the power rake from the bag. Angel was the best B&E man I knew and even as a cop I'd had reasons to use him. In return, I'd never hassled Angel and he'd stayed out of my way professionally. When he did go down, I'd done my best to make things a little easier for him inside. The rake had been a thank-you of sorts. An illegal thank-you.

It looked like an electric drill but was smaller and slimmer, with a prong at its tip that acted as a pick and tension tool. I stuck the prong in the lock and squeezed the trigger. The rake clattered noisily for a couple of seconds and then the lock turned. I slipped in quietly and closed the door behind me, seconds before another door down the hall opened. I stayed still and waited until it closed again, then put the rake back in the bag, reopened the door and took a toothpick from my pocket. I snapped it into four pieces and jammed them into the lock. It would give me time to get to the fire-escape if someone tried to enter the apartment while I was there. Then I closed the door and turned on the lights.

A short hallway with a threadbare rug led to a clean living room, cheaply furnished with a battered TV and a mismatched sofa and chairs. To one side was a small kitchen and to the other a bedroom.

I checked the bedroom first. Some paperback novels stood on a small shelf beside the bed. The only other furniture consisted of a wardrobe and dressing table, both of which appeared to have been made up from IKEA kits. I checked under the bed and found an empty suitcase. There were no cosmetics on the dressing table, which meant that she had probably packed a small overnight bag when she left and taken them with her. She probably hadn't intended to stay away for long and she certainly didn't appear to have left for good.

I checked the wardrobe but there were only clothes and a few pairs of shoes inside. The first two drawers in the dressing table also contained only clothes but the last one was filled with papers, the accumulated documents, tax forms and employment records of a life spent moving from city to city, from job to job.

Catherine Demeter had spent a long time in the waitressing game, moving from New Hampshire to Florida and back again with the social season. She had also spent some time in Chicago, Las Vegas and Phoenix as well as numerous small towns, judging by the collection of wage slips and tax documents in her drawer. There were also various bank statements. She had about $39,000 in a savings account in a city bank, as well as some shares bound carefully with a thick blue ribbon. Finally, there was a passport, updated recently, and within it three extra passport-size photos of herself.

Catherine Demeter, true to Isobel Barton's description, was a small attractive woman in her mid-thirties, five-two, with dark hair cut short in a bob, pale blue eyes and a fair complexion. I took the extra photos and put them in my wallet, then turned to examine the only item of a very personal nature in the drawer.

It was a photo album, thick and worn at the corners.

Within it was what I assumed to be a history of the Demeter family, from sepia-tinted photos of grandparents, through the wedding of what I guessed were her parents and on through the photos of two girls growing up, sometimes with parents and friends, sometimes together, sometimes alone. Pictures from the beach, from family holidays, from birthdays and Christmas and Thanksgiving, the memories of two sisters starting off in life. The resemblance between the two was clear. Catherine was the younger, the overbite visible even then. The girl I took to be her sister was perhaps two or three years older, with sandy-coloured hair, a beautiful girl even at eleven or twelve.

There were no more pictures of her after that age. The rest consisted of Catherine alone or with her parents and the record of her growth was more periodic, the sense of celebration and joyfulness gone. Eventually, they dwindled away to nothing with a final picture of Catherine on the day of her high-school graduation, a solemn-looking young woman with dark rings beneath eyes that seemed close to tears. The testimonial attached came from the principal of Haven High School, Virginia.

Something had been removed from the final pages of the album. Small pieces of what appeared to be newspaper rested at the base of the album pages, most merely tiny fragments as thin as threads but one about an inch square. The paper was yellowing with age, with a fragment of a weather report on one side and part of a photo on the other, the tip of some sand-blonde hair visible in one corner. Tucked into the last page were two birth certificates, one for Catherine Louise Demeter dated 5 March 1962 and the other for Amy Ellen Demeter, dated 3 December 1959.

I returned the album to the drawer and went into the bathroom next door. It was clean and neat, like the rest of the apartment, with soap, shower gels and foam bath arranged neatly on the white tile by the bath and towels stored on a small shelf under the sink. I opened one side of the medicine cabinet on the wall. It contained toothpaste, floss and mouthwash, as well as some non-prescription medicines for cold relief, water retention and evening primrose capsules. There were no birth-control pills or other contraceptives. Maybe Stephen Barton took care of that, although I doubted it. Stephen didn't seem like the new-age type.

The other side of the cabinet contained a miniature pharmacy with enough uppers and downers to keep Catherine moving like a roller-coaster. There was Librium, for mood swings, Ativan to combat agitation, and Valium, Thorazine and Lorazepam for anxiety. Some were empty, others half empty. The most recent came from a prescription from Dr Frank Forbes, a psychiatrist. I knew the name. 'Fucking Frank' Forbes had screwed or attempted to screw so many of his patients that it was sometimes suggested that they should charge him. He had been on the verge of losing his license on a number of occasions, but the complaints were either with-drawn, never got to court or were suppressed through the judicious application of some of Fucking Frank's funds. I heard he had been unusually quiet lately after one of his patients had contracted a dose of the clap after an encounter with Frank and then had promptly slapped a lawsuit on him. This one, I gathered, was proving difficult for Fucking Frank to bury.

Catherine Demeter was clearly a very unhappy woman and was unlikely to get any happier if she was seeing Frank Forbes. I wasn't too keen on visiting him. He had once tried to come on to Elizabeth Gordon, the daughter of one of Susan's divorced friends, and I'd paid him a visit to remind him of his duties as a doctor and to threaten to throw him from his office window if it ever happened again. After that, I tried to take a semi-professional interest in Frank Forbes's activities.

There was nothing else of note in Catherine's bathroom, or in the rest of her apartment. As I was leaving I stopped at her telephone, picked it up and pressed the re-dial button. After the beeps subsided a voice answered.

'Haven County Sheriff's Office, hello?'

I hung up and dialled a guy I knew in the telephone company. Five minutes later he came back with a list of local numbers called from Friday to Sunday. There were only three and they were all mundane – a Chinese takeaway, a local laundry and a movie-information line.

The local company couldn't give me details of any long-distance calls made, so I dialled a second number. This one connected me with one of the many agencies that offer PIs and those with a deep and abiding interest in other people's business the opportunity to purchase confidential information illegally. The agency was able to tell me within twenty minutes that fifteen calls had been made to Haven, Virginia, numbers on Saturday evening through Sprint, seven to the sheriff's office and eight to a private residence in the town. I was given both numbers and I dialled the second. The message on the answering-machine was terse: 'This is Earl Lee Granger. I'm not here right now. Leave a message after the beep or, if it relates to police business, contact the sheriff's office at . . .'

I dialled the number, got the Haven County sheriff's office again and asked to speak to the sheriff.

I was told that Sheriff Granger wasn't available, so I asked to speak to whoever was in charge in his absence. The ranking deputy was Alvin Martin, I learned, but he was out on a case. The deputy on the phone didn't know when the sheriff would be back. From his tone, I guessed the sheriff hadn't simply gone out to buy cigarettes. He asked me my name and I thanked him and hung up.

It seemed that something had caused Catherine Demeter to

get in touch with the sheriff in her home town, but not with the NYPD. If there was nothing else, I'd have to pay a visit to Haven. First, though, I decided to pay a visit to Fucking Frank Forbes.

# Chapter Eight

I stopped off at Azure on Third Avenue and bought myself some expensive fresh strawberries and pineapple from the deli, then took them around to the Citicorp Building to eat in the public space. I liked the building's simple lines and its strange, angled top. It was also one of the few new developments where a similar imagination had been applied to its interior: its seven-storey atrium was still green with trees and shrubs, its shops and restaurants were packed with people, and a handful of worshippers sat silently in its simple, sunken church.

Two blocks away, Fucking Frank Forbes had a swish office in a seventies smoked-glass development, at least for the present. I took the elevator up and entered the reception area, where a young and pretty brunette was typing something on the computer. She looked up as I entered and smiled brightly. I tried not to let my jaw hang as I smiled back.

'Is Dr Forbes available?' I asked.

'Do you have an appointment?'

'I'm not a patient, thankfully, but Frank and I go way back. Tell him Charlie Parker wants to see him.'

Her smile faltered a little but she dialled through to Frank's office and gave him the message. Her face paled slightly as she listened to his response but she held herself together remarkably well, all things considered.

'I'm afraid Dr Forbes can't see you,' she said, the smile now fading rapidly.

'Is that really what he said?'

She blushed slightly. 'No, not quite.'

'Are you new here?'

'This is my first week.'

'Frank select you personally?'

She looked puzzled. 'Ye-es.'

'Get another job. He's a deviant and he's on his way out of business.'

I walked past her and entered Frank's office while she took all this in. There was no patient in Frank's consulting room, just the good doctor himself leafing through some notes on his desk. He didn't look pleased to see me. His thin moustache curled in distaste like a black worm and a red bloom spread from his neck to his high, domed forehead before disappearing into his brush of wiry black hair. He was tall, over six feet, and he worked out. He looked real good, but looks were as far as it went. There was nothing good about Fucking Frank Forbes. If he handed you a dollar, the ink would be running before it got to your wallet.

'Get the fuck out, Parker. In case you've forgotten, you can't come barging in here any more. You're not a cop now and the force is probably all the richer for your absence.' He leaned towards the intercom button but his receptionist had already entered behind me.

'Call the police, Marcie. Better still, call my lawyer. Tell him I'm about to file for harassment.'

'Hear you're giving him a lot of business at the moment, Frank,' I said, taking a seat in a leather upright opposite his desk. 'I also hear Maibaum and Locke are handling the lawsuit for that unfortunate woman with the social disease. I've done some business with them in the past and they're real hot. Maybe I could put them on to Elizabeth Gordon. You remember Elizabeth, don't you, Frank?'

Frank cast an instinctive glance over his shoulder at the window and twisted his chair away from it.

'It's okay, Marcie,' he said, nodding uneasily to the receptionist. I heard the door close softly behind me. 'What do you want?'

'You have a patient called Catherine Demeter.'

'Come on, Parker, you know I can't discuss my patients. Even if I could, I wouldn't share shit with you.'

'Frank, you're the worst shrink I know. I wouldn't let a dog be treated by you because you'd probably try to fuck it, so save the ethics for the judge. I think she may be in trouble and I want to find her. If you don't help me I'll be in touch with Maibaum and Locke so fast you'll think I'm telepathic.'

Frank tried to look like he was wrestling with his conscience, although he couldn't have found his conscience without the aid of a shovel and an exhumation order.

'She missed an appointment yesterday. She didn't give any notice.'

'Why was she seeing you?'

'Involutional melancholia, mainly. That's depression to you, characteristic of middle to later stages of life. At least that's what it seemed like, initially.'

'But . . .?'

'Parker, this is confidential. Even I have standards.'

'You're joking. Go on.'

Frank sighed and fiddled with a pencil on his blotter, then moved to a cabinet, removed a file and sat back down. He opened it, leafed through it, and began to talk.

'Her sister died when Catherine was eight, or rather her sister was killed: she was one of a number of children murdered in a town called Haven in Virginia in the late sixties, early seventies. The children, males and females, were abducted, tortured and their remains dumped in the cellar of an empty house outside the town.' Frank was detached now, a doctor running through a case history which might have been as distant as a fairy story to him for all the emotion he put into the telling.

'Her sister was the fourth child to die, but the first white child. After she disappeared the police began to take a real interest. A local woman, a wealthy local woman, was suspected – her car had been seen near the house after one of the children disappeared and then she tried an unsuccessful snatch on a kid from another town about twenty miles away. The kid, a boy, raked her face with his nails, then gave a description to the cops.

'They went after her but the locals heard and got to the house first. Her brother was there. He was a homosexual, according to locals, and the cops believed she had an accomplice, a male who might have driven the car while she made the snatches. The locals figured the brother was a likely suspect. He was found hanged in the basement.'

'And the woman?'

'Burned to death in another of the old houses. The case simply . . . faded away.'

'But not for Catherine?'

'No, not for her. She left the town after graduating from high school, but her parents stayed. The mother died about ten years ago, father shortly after. And Catherine Demeter just kept moving.'

'Did she ever go back to Haven?'

'No, not after the funerals. She said everything was dead to her there. And that's it, pretty much. It all comes back to Haven.'

'Any boyfriends, or casuals?'

'None that she mentioned to me, and question time is over. Now get out. If you ever bring this up again, in public or in private, I'll sue your ass for assault, harassment and anything else my lawyer can come up with.'

I got up to leave.

'One more thing,' I said. 'For Elizabeth Gordon and her continued non-acquaintance with Maibaum and Locke.'

'What?'

'The name of the woman who burned to death.'

'Modine. Adelaide Modine and her brother William. Now please, get the fuck out of my life.'

# Chapter Nine

Willie Brew's auto shop looked run-down and unreliable, if not blatantly dishonest, from the outside. Inside it wasn't a whole lot better but Willie, a Pole whose name was unpronounceable and had been shortened to Brew by generations of customers, was just about the best mechanic I knew.

I had never liked this area of Queen's, only a short distance north from the roar of the cars on the Long Island Expressway. Ever since I was a boy, I seemed to associate it with used-car lots, old warehouses and cemeteries. Willie's garage, close by Kissena Park, had been a good source of information over the years, since every deadbeat friend of Willie's with nothing better to do than listen in on other people's business tended to congregate there at some time or another, but the whole area still made me uneasy. Even as an adult, I hated the drive from JFK to Manhattan as it skirted these neighbourhoods, hated the sight of the run-down houses and liquor stores.

After my father's death, my mother had moved us back to Maine, to her hometown of Scarborough, where treelines replaced cityscapes and only the racing enthusiasts, travelling from Boston and New York to the races at Scarborough Downs, brought with them the sights and smells of the big cities. Maybe that was why I always felt like a visitor when I looked at Manhattan: I always seemed to be seeing the city through new eyes.

Willie's place was situated in a neighbourhood that was fighting gentrification tooth and nail. Willie's block had been bought by the owner of the Japanese noodle house next door – he had other interests in downtown Flushing's Little Asia and seemed to want to extend his reach further south – and Willie was involved in a partially legal battle to ensure that he wasn't shut down. The Japanese responded by sending fish smells through the vents into Willie's garage. Willie sometimes got his own back by getting Arno, his chief mechanic, to drink some beers and eat a Chinese, then stumble outside, stick his fingers down his throat and vomit outside the noodle house. 'Chinese, Vietnamese, Japanese – all that shit looks the same when it comes out,' Willie used to say.

Inside, Arno, small, wiry and dark, was working on the engine of a beat-up Dodge. The air was thick with the smell of fish and noodles. My '69 Mustang was raised up on a platform, unrecognisable bits and pieces of its internal workings strewn around on the floor. It looked no more likely to be on the road again in the near future than James Dean. I'd called earlier to tell Willie I'd be dropping by. The least he could have done was pretend to be doing something with it when I arrived.

The sound of loud swearing came from inside Willie's office, which was up a set of wooden stairs to the right of the garage floor. The door flew open and Willie rumbled down the steps, grease on his bald head and his blue mechanic's overalls open to the waist to show a dirty white T-shirt straining over his huge belly. He climbed arduously up a set of boxes placed beneath the vent in a step pattern and put his mouth to the grille.

'You slant-eyed sons of bitches,' he shrieked. 'Quit stinkin' my garage out with fish or I'm gonna get nuclear on your ass.' There was the sound of something shouted in Japanese from the other end of the vent and then a burst of Oriental laughter. Willie thumped the grille with the heel of his hand and climbed down. He squinted at me in the semi-darkness before recognising me.

'Bird, how you doin'? You want a coffee?'

'I want a car. My car. The car you've had for over a week now.'

Willie looked crestfallen. 'You're angry with me,' he said, in mock-soothing tones. 'I understand your anger. Anger is good. Your car, on the other hand, is not good. Your car is bad. The engine's shot to shit. What have you been running it on, nuts and old nails?'

'Willie, I need my car. The taxi drivers are treating me like an old friend. Some of them have even stopped trying to rip me off. I've considered hiring a rental car to save myself embarrassment. In fact, the only reason I haven't hit you for a car is that you said the repairs would take a day or two at most.'

Willie slouched over to the car and nudged a cylindrical piece of metal with the toe of his boot.

'Arno, what's the story on Bird's Mustang?'

'It's shit,' said Arno. 'Tell him we'll give him five hundred dollars to scrap it.'

'Arno says to give you five hundred dollars to scrap it.'

'I heard him. Tell Arno I'll burn his house down if he doesn't fix my car.'

'Day after tomorrow,' came a voice from under the hood. 'Sorry for the delay.'

Willie clapped me on the shoulder with a greasy hand.

'Come up for a coffee, listen to the local gossip.' Then, quietly: 'Angel wants to see you. I told him you'd be around.'

I nodded and followed him up the stairs. Inside the office, which was surprisingly neat, four men sat around a desk drinking coffee and whiskey from tin mugs. I nodded to Tommy Q, who I'd busted once for handling pirated video-cassettes, and a thickly moustached hot-wire guy known, unsurprisingly, as Groucho. Beside him sat Willie's other assistant, Jay, who, at sixty-five, was ten years older than Willie but looked at least ten years older than that again. Beside him sat Coffin Ed Harris.

'You know Coffin Ed?' said Willie.

I nodded. 'Still boosting dead guys, Ed?'

'Naw, man,' said Coffin Ed. 'I gave all that up a long time ago. I got a bad back.'

Coffin Ed Harris had been the kidnapper to beat all kidnappers. Coffin Ed figured that live hostages were too much like hard work, since there was no telling what they might do or who might come looking for them. Dead targets were easier to handle, so Coffin Ed took to robbing mortuaries.

He would watch the death notices, pick a decedent who came from a reasonably wealthy family and then steal the corpse from the mortuary or the funeral home. Until Coffin Ed came along and bucked the system, funeral homes weren't usually well guarded. Coffin Ed would store the corpses in an industrial freezer he kept in his basement and then ask for a ransom, usually nothing too heavy. Most of the relatives were quite happy to pay to get their loved ones back before they started to rot.

He did well until some old Polish aristocrat took offence at his wife's remains being held to ransom and hired a private army to go looking for Coffin Ed. They found him, although Coffin Ed just about got away through a bolt-hole in his basement, which led to his neighbour's yard. He got the last laugh, too. The power company had cut off Ed's electricity three days before because he hadn't been paying his bills. The old Pole's wife stank like a dead possum by the time they found her. Since then, things had gone downhill for Coffin Ed and he now presented a down-at-heel figure in the back of Willie Brew's garage.

There was an uneasy silence for a moment, which was broken by Willie.

'You remember Vinnie No-Nose?' said Willie, handing me a steaming cup of black coffee, which was already turning the tin mug red hot but still couldn't hide the smell of gasoline from its interior. 'Wait'll you hear Tommy Q's story. You ain't missed nothing yet.'

Vinnie No-Nose was a B&E guy out of Newark who had taken one fall too many and had decided to reform, or at least to reform as far as any guy can who has made a living for forty years by ripping off other people's apartments. He got his nickname from a long unsuccessful involvement with amateur boxing. Vinnie, small and a potential victim for any New Jersey low-life with a penchant for inflicting violence, saw an ability to use his fists as his potential salvation, like lots of other short guys from rough neighbourhoods. Sadly, Vinnie's defence was about as good as the Son of Sam's and his nose was eventually reduced to a mush of cartilage with two semi-closed nostrils like raisins in a pudding.

Tommy Q proceeded to tell a story involving Vinnie, a decorating company and a dead gay client which could have put him in court if he'd told it in a respectable place of employment. 'So the fruit ends up dead, in a bathroom, with this chair up his ass and Vinnie ends up back in jail for peddling the pics and stealing the dead guy's video,' he concluded, shaking his head at the strange ways of non-heterosexual males.

He was still laughing his ass off at the story when the smile died on his face and the laugh turned into a kind of choking sound in his throat. I looked behind me to see Angel in the shadows, with curly black hair spilling out from under his blue watch-cap and a sparse growth of beard that would have made a thirteen-year-old laugh. A dark blue longshoreman's jacket hung open over a black T-shirt and his blue jeans ended in dirty, well-worn Timberlands.

Angel was no more than five-six and, to the casual onlooker, it was difficult to see why he should have struck fear into Tommy Q. There were two reasons. The first was that Angel was a far better boxer than Vinnie No-Nose and could have pummelled Tommy Q to horsemeat if he wanted to, which might well have been the case since Angel was gay and might have found the source of Tommy's humour less than amusing.

The second and probably more compelling reason for Tommy Q's fear was that Angel's boyfriend was a man known only as Louis. Like Angel, Louis had no visible means of support, although it was widely known that Angel, now semi-retired at the age of forty, was one of the best thieves in the business, capable of stealing the fluff from the President's navel if the money was good enough.

Less widely known was the fact that Louis, tall, black and sophisticated in his dress sense, was a hitman almost without equal, a killer who had been reformed somewhat by his relationship with Angel and who now chose his rare targets with what might be termed a social conscience.

Rumour had it that the killing of a German computer expert named Gunther Bloch in Chicago the previous year had been the work of Louis. Bloch was a serial rapist and torturer, who preyed on young, sometimes very young, women in the sex resorts of South East Asia where much of his business was transacted. Money usually covered all ills, money paid to pimps, to parents, to police, to politicians.

Unfortunately for Bloch, someone in the upper reaches of the government in one of his nations of choice couldn't be bought, especially after Bloch strangled an eleven-year-old girl and dumped her body in a trash can. Bloch fled the country, money was redirected to a 'special project' and Louis drowned Gunther Bloch in the bathroom of a $1,000-a-night hotel suite in Chicago.

Or so rumour had it. Whatever the truth of the matter, Louis was regarded as very bad news and Tommy Q wanted in future to be able to take a bath, however rarely, without fear of drowning.

'Nice story, Tommy,' said Angel.

'It's just a story, Angel. I didn't mean anything by it. No offence meant.'

'None taken,' said Angel. 'At least, not by me.'

Behind him, there was a movement in the darkness and Louis appeared. His bald head gleamed in the dim light and his muscular neck emerged from a black silk shirt within an immaculately cut grey suit. He towered over Angel by more than a foot and, as he did so, he eyed Tommy Q intently for a moment.

'Fruit,' he said. 'That's a . . . *quaint* term, Mr Q. To what does it refer, exactly?'

The blood had drained from Tommy Q's face and it seemed to take him a very long time to find enough saliva to enable him to gulp. When he did eventually manage, it sounded like he was swallowing a golf ball. He opened his mouth but nothing came out, so he closed it again and looked at the floor in the vain hope that it would open up and swallow him.

'It's okay, Mr Q, it was a good story,' said Louis, in a voice as silky as his shirt. 'Just be careful how you tell it.' Then he smiled a bright smile at Tommy Q, the sort of smile a cat might give to a mouse to take to the grave with it. A drop of sweat ran down Tommy Q's nose, hung from the tip for a moment and then exploded on the floor. By then, Louis had gone.

'Don't forget my car, Willie,' I said, then followed Angel from the garage.

# Chapter Ten

We walked a block or two to a late-nite bar and diner Angel knew. Louis strolled a few yards ahead of us, the late-evening crowds parting before him like the Red Sea before Moses. Once or twice women glanced at him with interest. The men mostly kept their eyes on the ground, or found something suddenly interesting in the boarded-up shopfronts or the night sky.

From inside the bar came the sound of a vaguely folky singer performing open-guitar surgery on Neil Young's 'Only Love Can Break Your Heart'. It didn't sound like the song was going to pull through.

'He plays like he hates Neil Young,' said Angel, as we entered.

Ahead of us, Louis shrugged. 'Neil Young heard that shit, he'd probably hate himself.'

We took a booth. The owner, a fat, dyspeptic man named Ernest, shambled over to take our order. Usually, the waitresses in Ernest's took the orders but Angel and Louis commanded a degree of respect, even here.

'Hey, Ernest,' said Angel, 'how's business?'

'If I was an undertaker, people'd stop dying,' replied Ernest. 'And, before you ask, my old lady's still ugly.' It was a long-established exchange.

'Shit, you been married forty years,' said Angel. 'She ain't gonna get no better-lookin' now.'

Angel and Louis ordered club sandwiches and Ernest wandered away. 'I was a kid and looked like him I'd cut my dick off and make money singin' castrato, 'cos it ain't gonna be no use no other way.'

'Bein' ugly ain't done you no harm,' said Louis.

'I don't know,' grinned Angel. 'I was better-looking, I coulda screwed a white guy.'

They stopped bickering and we waited for the singer to put Neil Young out of his misery. It was strange meeting these two, now that I was no longer a cop. When we had encountered each other before – in Willie's garage, or over coffee, or in Central Park if Angel had some useful information to impart, or if he simply wanted to meet to talk, to ask after Susan and Jennifer – there had been an awkwardness, a tension between us, especially if Louis was near by. I knew what they had done, what Louis, I believed, still did, silent partnerships in assorted restaurants, dealerships and Willie Brew's garage notwithstanding.

On this occasion, that tension was no longer present. Instead, for the first time I felt the strength of the bond of friendship that had somehow grown between Angel and me. More than that, from both of them I felt a sense of concern, of regret, of humanity, of trust. They would not be here, I knew, if they felt otherwise.

But maybe there was something more, something I had only begun to perceive. I was a cop's nightmare. Cops, their families, their wives and children, are untouchables. You have to be crazy to go after a cop, crazier still to take out his loved ones. These are the assumptions we live by, the belief that after a day spent looking at the dead, questioning thieves and rapists, pushers and pimps, we can return to our own lives, knowing that our families are somehow apart from all this and that, through them, we can remain apart from it too.

But that belief system had been shaken by the deaths of

Jennifer and Susan. Someone wasn't respecting the rules and, when no easy answer was forthcoming, when no perp with a grudge could conveniently be apprehended, enabling all that had taken place to be explained away, another reason had to be found: I had somehow drawn it on myself, and on those closest to me. I was a good cop who was well on the way to becoming a drunk. I was falling apart and that made me weak, and someone had exploited that weakness. Other cops looked at me and they saw not a fellow officer in need, but a source of infection, of corruption. No one was sorry to see me go, maybe not even Walter.

And yet what had taken place had somehow brought me closer to both Angel and Louis. They had no illusions about the world in which they lived, no philosophical constructions which allowed them to be at once a part of, and apart from, that world. Louis was a killer: he couldn't afford delusions of that kind. Because of the closeness of the bond that existed between them, Angel couldn't afford those delusions either. Now they had also been taken away from me, like scales falling from my eyes, leaving me to re-establish myself, to find a new place in the world.

Angel picked up an abandoned paper from the booth next door and glanced at the headline.

'You see this?' I looked and nodded. A guy had tried to pull some heroic stunt during a bank raid in Flushing earlier in the day and ended up with both barrels of a sawn-off emptied into him. The papers and news bulletins were full of it.

'Here's some guys out doin' a job,' began Angel. 'They don't want to hurt nobody, they just want to go in, get the money – which is insured anyway so what does the bank care? – and get out again. They only got the guns 'cos no one's gonna take them seriously otherwise. What else they gonna use? Harsh words?

'But there's always gotta be some asshole who thinks he's

immortal 'cos he's not dead yet. The guy, he's young, keeps himself in good condition, thinks he's gonna get more pussy than Long Dong Silver if he busts up the bank raid and saves the day. Look at this guy: real estate agent, twenty-nine, single, pulling down one-fifty a year and he gets a hole blown in him bigger'n the Holland Tunnel. Lance Petersen.' He shook his head in wonderment. 'I never met anyone called Lance in my whole life.'

'That's 'cos they all dead,' said Louis, glancing seemingly idly around the room. 'Fuckers keep standing up in banks and getting shot. Guy was probably the last Lance left alive.'

The clubs arrived and Angel started eating. He was the only one who did.

'So how you doin'?'

'Okay,' I said. 'Why the ambush?'

'You don't write, you don't call.' He smiled wryly. Louis glanced at me with mild interest then returned his attention to the door, the other tables, the doors to the restrooms.

'You been doin' some work for Benny Low, I hear. What you doin' workin' for that fat piece of shit?'

'Passing time.'

'You want to pass time, stick pins in your eyes. Benny's just using up good air.'

'Come on, Angel, get to it. You're rattling away and Louis here is acting like he expects the Dillinger gang to walk in and spray the counter.'

Angel put down his half-eaten section of club and dabbed almost daintily at this mouth with a napkin. 'I hear you've been asking after some girlfriend of Stephen Barton's. Some people are very curious to know why that might be.'

'Such as?'

'Such as Bobby Sciorra, I hear.'

I didn't know if Bobby Sciorra was psychotic or not, but he was a man who liked killing and had found a willing employer in old man Ferrera. Emo Ellison could testify to the likely result of Bobby Sciorra taking an interest in one's activities. I had a suspicion that Ollie Watts, in his final moments, had found that out as well.

'Benny Low was talking about some kind of trouble between the old man and Sonny,' I said. ' "Fuckin' goombas fighting among themselves", was how he put it.'

'Benny always was a diplomat,' said Angel. 'Only surprise is the UN didn't pick up on him before now. There's something weird goin' on there. Sonny's gone to ground and taken Pili with him. No one's seen them, no one knows where they are, but Bobby Sciorra's looking real hard for both of them.' He took another huge bite of his sandwich. 'What about Barton?'

'I figure he's gone underground too but I don't know. He's minor league and wouldn't have much to do professionally with Sonny or the old man beyond some muling, though he may once have been close to Sonny. May be nothing to it. Barton may not be connected.'

'Maybe not, but you've got bigger problems than finding Barton or his girl.'

I waited.

'There's a hit out on you.'

'Who?'

'It's not local. It's out of town, Louis don't know who.'

'Is it over the Fat Ollie thing?'

'I don't know. Even Sonny isn't such a moron that he'd put a contract out over some hired gun who got himself wasted 'cos you stepped in. The kid didn't mean anything to anyone and Fat Ollie's dead. All I know is you're irritating two generations of the Ferrera family and that can't be good.'

Cole's favour was turning into something more complicated than a missing-persons case, if it was ever that simple.

'I've got one for you,' I said. 'Know anyone with a gun that can punch holes through masonry with a tenth of an ounce 5.7-millimetre bullet? Sub-machine rounds.'

'You gotta be fuckin' kidding. Last time I saw something like that it was hangin' on top of a tank turret.'

'Well, that's what killed the shooter. I saw him blown away and there was a hole knocked through the wall behind me. The gun's Belgian-made, designed for anti-terrorist police. Someone local picked up a piece of hardware like that and took it to the range, it's gotta get around.'

'I'll ask,' said Angel. 'Any guesses?'

'My guess would be Bobby Sciorra.'

'Mine too. So why would he be cleaning up after Sonny's mess?'

'The old man told him to.'

Angel nodded. 'Watch your back, Bird.'

He finished his sandwich and then stood to go. 'C'mon. We can give you a ride.'

'No, I want to walk for a while.'

Angel shrugged. 'You packing?'

I nodded. He said he'd be in touch. I left them at the door. As I walked, I was conscious of the weight of the gun beneath my arm, of every face I passed in the crowd and of the dark pulse of the city throbbing beneath my feet.

# Chapter Eleven

Bobby Sciorra: a malevolent demon, a vision of ferocity and sadism who had appeared before the old man, Stefano Ferrara, when he was on the verge of insanity and death. Sciorra seemed to have been conjured up from some bleak corner of Hell by the old man's anger and grief, a physical manifestation of the torture and destruction he wished to inflict on the world around him. In Bobby Sciorra he found the perfect instrument of pain and ugly death.

Stefano had watched his own father build a small empire from the family's modest house in Bensonhurst. In those days Bensonhurst, bordered by Gravesend Bay and the Atlantic Ocean, still had a small-town feel. The scent of deli food mingled with that of wood-burning ovens from the local pizza parlours. People lived in two-family homes with wrought-iron gates and, when the sun shone, they would sit out on their porches and watch their kids play in their tiny gardens.

Stefano's ambition would take him beyond his roots. When his time came to take over the operation, he built a big house on Staten Island; when he stood at his rear-facing windows, he could see the edge of Paul Castellano's mansion on Todt Hill, the $3.5 million White House and, probably from his topmost window, the grounds of the Barton Estate. If Staten Island was good enough for the head of the Gambino family and a benevolent millionaire, then it was good enough for Stefano.

When Castellano died after being shot six times at Sparks restaurant in Manhattan, Stefano was, briefly, the biggest boss on Staten Island.

Stefano married a woman from Bensonhurst named Louisa. She hadn't married him out of any kind of love familiar from romantic novels: she loved him for his power, his violence and, mainly, his money. Those who marry for money usually end up earning it. Louisa did. She was emotionally brutalised and died shortly after giving birth to her third son. Stefano didn't remarry. There was no grief there; he just didn't need the bother of another wife, especially after the first had produced his heirs.

The first child, Vincent, was intelligent and represented the best hope for the family's future. When he died in a swimming pool from a massive brain haemorrhage at twenty-three, his father didn't speak for a week. Instead, he shot Vincent's pair of Labradors and retired to his bedroom. By then Louisa had been dead for seventeen years.

Niccolo, or Nicky, two years younger than his brother, took his place at his father's right hand. As a rookie, I watched him roam the city in his huge, bullet-proofed Cadillac, surrounded by soldiers, carving himself a reputation as a thug to match his father. By the early 1980s, the family had overcome an initial distaste for the drugs trade and was flooding the city with every kind of drug it could lay its hands on. Most people stayed out of the way and any potential rivals were warned off or ended up as fish chum.

The Yardies were another matter. The Jamaican gangs had no respect for established institutions, for the old ways of doing business. They looked at the Italians and saw dead meat; a shipment of cocaine worth two million dollars was boosted from the Ferreras and two soldiers were left dead. Nicky responded by ordering a cull of the Yardies: their clubs were hit, their apartments, even their women. In a three-day period, twelve of them died, including most of those responsible for the cocaine theft.

Maybe Nicky imagined that would be the end of it and things would return to normal again. He still cruised the streets in his car, still ate in the same restaurants, still acted as if the threat of violence from the Jamaicans has dissipated in the face of this show of force.

His favourite haunt was Da Vincenzo, an upmarket Mom and Pop operation in his father's old Bensonhurst neighbourhood, which was smart enough not to forget its roots. Maybe Nicky also liked the echoes of his brother in the name but his paranoia led him to have the glass in the windows and doors replaced with some military-strength panes, the sort used by the President. Nicky could enjoy his fusilli in peace, undisturbed by the imminent threat of assassination.

He had only just ordered one Thursday evening in November when the black van pulled into the side-street opposite, its back facing towards the window. Nicky may have glanced at it as it stopped, may have noticed that its windscreen had been removed and replaced with a black wire grille, may even have frowned as the rear doors sprang open and something white flared briefly in the darkness of its interior, the back-blast rattling the grille.

He may even have had time to register the RPG-7 warhead as it powered towards the window at 600 feet per second, smoke trailing it from behind, its roar penetrating the thick panes before they exploded inwards, glass and hot metal fragments and the slug from the missile's copper liner tearing Nicky Ferrera into so many pieces that his coffin weighed less than sixty pounds when it was carried up the aisle of the church three days later.

The three Jamaicans responsible disappeared into the underworld and the old man vented his fury on his enemies and his friends in an orgy of abuse, of violence and of death. His business fell apart around him and his rivals closed in, recognising in his madness the opportunity to rid themselves of him once and for all.

Just as his world seemed about to implode on itself, a figure appeared at the gates of his mansion and asked to speak with the old man. He told the guard he had some news about the Yardies, the guard passed on the message and, after a search, Bobby Sciorra was admitted. The search was not a complete one: Sciorra held a black plastic sack which he refused to open. Guns were trained on him as he approached the house and he was told to halt on the lawn, about fifty feet from the steps of the house where the old man stood in wait.

'If you're wasting my time, I'll have you killed,' said the old man. Bobby Sciorra just smiled and tipped the contents of the bag on the illuminated lawn. The three heads rolled and bumped against each other, the dreadlocks coiled like dead snakes with Bobby Sciorra smiling above them like some obscene Perseus. Thick, fresh blood hung languorously from the edges of the sack before dripping slowly on to the grass.

Bobby Sciorra 'made his bones' that night. Within one year he was a made guy, an ascent up the family ladder made doubly unique by its speed and the relative obscurity of Sciorra's background. The feds had no file on him and Ferrera appeared able to add little more. I heard rumours that he had crossed the Colombos once, that he had operated out of Florida for a time on a freelance basis, but nothing more than that. Yet the killing of the linchpins of the Jamaican posse was enough to earn him the trust of Stefano Ferrera and a ceremony in the basement of the Staten Island house, which resulted in the pricking of Sciorra's trigger finger over a holy picture and his tie-in to Ferrera and his associates.

From that day on, Bobby Sciorra was the power behind the Ferrera throne. He guided the old man and his family through the trials and tribulations of post-RICO New York, when the

FBI's Racketeer Influenced Corruption Organisation statutes allowed the feds to prosecute organisations and conspirators that benefited from crime, instead of just the individuals who committed those crimes. The major New York families – Gambino, Luchese, Colombo, Genovese and Bonnano – numbering maybe four thousand made guys and associates, all took big hits, losing the heads of their families to jail or the reaper. But not the Ferreras. Bobby Sciorra took care of that, sacrificing some minor players along the way to ensure the survival of the family.

The old man might have preferred to take even more of a back seat in the family operation if it hadn't been for Sonny. Poor dumb, vicious Sonny, a man without the intelligence of either of his brothers but with at least their combined capacity for violence. Any operations he controlled degenerated into bloodshed, but none of it troubled Sonny. Corpulent and bloated even in his twenties, he enjoyed the mayhem and the killing. The deaths of the innocent in particular seemed to give him an almost sexual thrill.

Gradually, his father sidelined him and left him to his own devices of steroids, small-time drug deals, prostitution and occasional violence. Bobby Sciorra tried to keep him under some sort of control, but Sonny was beyond control or reason. Sonny was vicious and evil, and when his father died, a queue of men would form to ensure Sonny joined him as soon as possible.

# Chapter Twelve

I never expected to end up living in the Village. Susan, Jennifer and I had lived out on Park Slope in Brooklyn. On Sundays we could stroll down to Prospect Park and watch the kids playing ball, Jennifer kicking at the grass with her small, pink sneakers, before heading to Raintree's for a soda, the sound of the band in the band shell drifting in through the stained-glass windows.

On such days, life seemed as long and welcoming as the green vista of Long Meadow. We would walk Jenny between us, Susan and I, and exchange glances over her head as she burst forth with an endless stream of questions, observations, strange jokes that only a child could understand. I would hold her hand in mine and, through her, I could reach out to Susan and believe that things would work out for us, that we could somehow bridge the gap that was growing between us. If Jenny ran ahead, I would move close to Susan and take her hand and she would smile at me as I told her that I loved her. Then she would look away, or look to her feet, or call Jenny, because we both knew that telling her I loved her was not enough.

When I decided to return to New York at the start of the summer, after months of searching for some sign of their killer, I informed my lawyer and asked him to recommend a realtor. In New York, there are about three hundred million square feet of office space and not enough places to put the people who work in them. I couldn't say why I wanted to live in Manhattan. Maybe it was just because it wasn't Brooklyn.

Instead of a realtor, my lawyer produced a network of friends and business acquaintances, which eventually led to me renting an apartment in a red-brick house in the Village with white shutters on the windows and a stoop that led up to a fanlighted front door. It was a little closer to St Mark's Place than I might have preferred – since the days when W. H. Auden and Leon Trotsky had roomed there, St Mark's had become the Village with a Vengeance, full of bars, cafés and overpriced boutiques – but it was still a good deal.

The apartment was unfurnished and I pretty much left it that way, adding only a bed, a desk, some easy chairs, a stereo and small TV. I removed books, tapes, CDs and vinyl from storage, along with one or two personal belongings, and set up a living space to which I had only the minimum attachment.

It was dark outside as I lined the guns before me on the desk, stripped them down and cleaned each one carefully. If the Ferreras were coming after me, I wanted to be prepared.

In all my time on the force, I had been forced to draw my weapon to protect myself on only a handful of occasions. I had never killed a man while on duty and had only once fired at another human being, when I had shot a pimp in the stomach as he came at me with a long-bladed knife.

As a detective, I had spent most of my time in robbery and homicide. Unlike vice, which was a world in which the threat of violence and death to a cop was a real possibility, homicide involved a different type of police work. As Tommy Morrison, my first partner, used to say, anybody who's going to die in a homicide investigation is already dead by the time the cops arrive.

I had abandoned my Colt Delta Elite after the deaths of Susan and Jennifer. Now I had three guns in my possession. The .38 Colt Detective Special had belonged to my father, the only thing of his I had retained. The 'Prancing Pony' badge on the left side of the rounded butt was worn and the frame was scratched and pitted, but it remained a useful weapon, light at just over a pound in weight and easily concealed in an ankle holster or a belt. It was a simple, powerful revolver, and I kept it in a sleeve beneath the frame of my bed.

I had never used the Heckler & Koch VP70M outside a range. The 9mm semi-automatic had belonged to a pusher who had died after becoming hooked on his own product. I had found him dead in his apartment after a neighbour had complained about the smell. The VP70M, a semi-plastic military pistol holding eighteen rounds, lay, still unused, in its case, but I had taken the precaution of filing away the serial number.

Like the .38, it had no safety. The attraction of the gun lay in the accessory shoulder stock which the pusher had also acquired. When fitted, it made an internal adjustment to the firing mechanism which turned the weapon into a full-automatic submachine-gun that could fire twenty-two hundred rounds per minute. If the Chinese ever decided to invade, I could hold them off for at least ten seconds with all the ammunition I had. After that, I'd have to start throwing furniture at them. I had removed the H&K from the compartment in the Mustang's trunk where I usually stored it. I didn't want anyone stumbling across it while the car was being serviced.

The third-generation Smith & Wesson was the only gun I carried, a 10mm auto model specially developed for the FBI and acquired through the efforts of Woolrich. After cleaning it, I loaded it carefully and placed it in my shoulder holster. Outside, I could see the crowds making for the bars and restaurants of the Village. I was just about to join them when the cellphone buzzed beside me and thirty minutes later I was preparing to view the body of Stephen Barton.

Red lights flashed, bathing everything in the parking lot with the warm glow of law and order. A patch of darkness marked the nearby McCarren Park and, to the south-west, traffic passed over the Williamsburg Bridge heading for the Brooklyn-Queens Expressway. Patrolmen lounged by cars, keeping the curious and the ghoulish behind barriers. One reached out to block my way – 'Hey, gotta keep back' – when we recognised each other. Vecsey, who remembered my father and would never make it beyond sergeant, withdrew his hand.

'It's official, Jimmy. I'm with Cole.' He looked over his shoulder and Walter, who was talking with a patrolman, looked over and nodded. The arm went up like a traffic barrier and I passed through.

Even yards from the sewer I could smell the stench. A frame had been erected around the area and a lab technician in boots was climbing out of the manhole.

'Can I go down?' I asked. Two men in neatly cut suits and London Fog raincoats had joined Cole, who barely nodded. The FBI letters weren't visible on the backs of their coats so I assumed they were keeping a low profile. 'Uncanny,' I said as I passed, 'they could almost be regular people.' Walter scowled. They joined in.

I slipped on a pair of gloves and climbed down the ladder into the sewer. I gagged with my first breath, the river of filth that ran beneath the tree-lined avenues of the city forcing a taste of bile into the back of my throat. 'It's easier if you take shallow breaths,' said a sewer worker, who stood at the base of the ladder. He was lying.

I didn't step from the ladder. Instead, I pulled my Maglite

from my pocket and pointed it to where a small group of maintenance workers and cops stood around an arc-lit area, their feet sloshing through stuff about which I didn't even want to think. The cops gave me a brief glance then returned with bored looks to watching the med guys go about their business. Stephen Barton lay about five yards from the base of the ladder in a tide of shit and waste, his blond hair moving wildly with the current. It was obvious that he had simply been dumped through the manhole at street level, his body rolling slightly when it hit the bottom.

The ME stood up and pulled the rubber gloves from his hands. A plainclothes homicide detective, one I didn't recognise, directed a quizzical look at him. He returned one of frustration and annoyance. 'We'll need to look at him in the lab. I can't tell shit from shit down here.'

'Come on, give us a fucking break,' the detective whined lamely.

The ME hissed through his teeth in irritation. 'Strangled,' he said, as he elbowed his way through the small group. 'Knocked unconscious first with a blow to the back of the head, then strangled. Don't even ask for a time of death. He could have been down here for a day or so, probably no longer. The body's pretty flaccid.' Then the sound of his feet echoed through the sewer as he clacked up the ladder.

The detective shrugged. 'Ashes to ashes, shit to shit,' he said, then turned back towards the body.

I climbed up to street level, the ME behind me. I didn't need to look at Barton's body. The blow to the head was unusual, but not extraordinary. It can take as long as ten minutes to kill a man by strangulation, assuming he doesn't manage to break free in the process. I had heard of would-be assassins losing handfuls of hair, patches of skin and, in one case, an ear to a struggling victim. Far better, where possible, to tap him on the head first. Tap him hard enough and strangling him might not be necessary at all.

Walter was still talking to the feds so I moved as far away from the sewer as I could get while still remaining within the police cordon and drew deep breaths of night air. The smell of human waste underpinned everything, clinging to my clothes with the grim resolution of death itself. Eventually the feds returned to their car and Walter walked slowly towards me, hands stuck in his trouser pockets.

'They're going to bring Sonny Ferrera in,' he said.

I snorted. 'For what? His lawyer will have him out before he even has time to take a leak. That's assuming he was even involved, or that they can find him. This bunch couldn't find the ground if they fell over.'

Walter wasn't in the mood. 'What do you know? The kid was running shit for Ferrera, he fucks him over and ends up dead, strangled what's more.' Strangulation had become the Mob's preferred method of despatch in recent years: quiet and no mess. 'That's the feds' line and, anyway, they'd bring Sonny Ferrera in on suspicion of ignoring a no-smoking sign if they thought it would stick.'

'C'mon, Walter, this isn't a Ferrera job. Dumping a guy in a sewer . . .' But he was already walking away, a raised right hand indicating that he didn't want to hear any more. I followed him. 'What about the girl, Walter? Maybe she fits in somewhere?'

He turned back to me and put a hand on my shoulder. 'When I called you, I didn't think you were going to come running in like Dick Tracy.' He glanced back at the feds. 'Any sign of her?'

'I think she blew town. That's all I'm saying for the present.'

'The ME thinks Barton could have been killed early Tuesday. If the girl left town after that, it could tie her in.'

'Are you going to mention her to the feds?'

Walter shook his head. 'Let them go chasing after Sonny Ferrera. You stay on the girl.'

'Yassuh,' I said. 'I'ma keep lookin'.' I hailed a cab, conscious that the feds were looking at me even as I got in and we drove away into the night.

# Chapter Thirteen

It was common knowledge that the old man was having trouble keeping his only surviving son under control. Ferrera had watched the *cosa nostra* tear itself apart back in Italy as it tried, with increasing brutality, to intimidate and destroy the state's investigators. Instead, its methods had served to reinforce the determination of the braver ones to continue the fight; the families were now like one of their own victims bound in the *incaprettamento*, the method of execution known as 'the goat strangling'. Like a victim bound with ropes to his arms, legs and neck, the more the families struggled, the more the rope around them grew tighter. The old man was determined that this should not happen to his own organisation. By contrast, Sonny saw in the violence of the Sicilians a method of tyranny that suited his own aspirations for power.

Maybe that was the difference between father and son. Wherever possible old Ferrera had used the 'white *lupara*' when an assassination was necessary, the complete disappearance of the victim without even a trace of blood to give away the truth of what had taken place. The strangling of Barton was certainly a Mafia hallmark but the dumping was not. If the old man had been responsible for his death then his final resting place would probably have been the sewers all right, but not before he had been dissolved in acid and poured down a drain.

So I didn't believe the old man had ordered the killing of Isobel Barton's stepson. His death and the sudden disappearance of Catherine Demeter had come too close together to be mere coincidence. It was possible, of course, that Sonny had ordered them both to be killed for some reason, for if he was as crazy as he seemed then another corpse would be unlikely to trouble him. On the other hand, it was also possible that Demeter had killed her own boyfriend and then fled. Perhaps he hit her once too often, in which case Mrs Barton was now paying me to find someone who was not only a friend but, potentially, her son's killer.

The Ferrera house was set in tree-shrouded grounds. Entry was by a single iron gate, electronically operated. An intercom was set into the pillar on the left-hand side. I buzzed, gave my name and told the voice I wanted to see the old man. From the top of the pillar a remote camera was focused on the cab and, although no one was visible in the grounds, I guessed three to five guns were in my immediate vicinity.

Some one hundred yards from the house sat a dark Dodge sedan with two males sitting in the front seats. I could expect a visit from the feds as soon as I got back to my apartment, possibly sooner.

'Walk through. Wait inside the gate,' said the voice from the intercom. 'You'll be escorted to the house.' I did as I was told and the cab pulled away. A grey-haired man in a dark suit and standard-issue shades appeared from behind the trees, a Heckler & Koch MP5 held at port arms. Behind him was another younger man, similarly dressed. To my right I could see two more guards, also armed.

'Lean against the wall,' said the grey-haired man. He frisked me professionally while the others watched, removing the clip from my own Smith & Wesson along with the spare clip on my belt. He pulled back the slide to eject the round in the chamber and handed the gun back to me. Then he motioned me towards the house, walking to my right and slightly behind me so that he could keep an eye on my hands. One man shadowed us at either side of the road. It was hardly surprising that old man Ferrera had lived so long.

The house was surprisingly modest from the outside, a long two-storey dwelling with narrow windows at the front and a gallery running along the lower level. More men patrolled the meticulously kept garden and the gravelled driveway. A black Mercedes stood at the right of the house, its driver waiting near by if needed. The door was already open as we approached and Bobby Sciorra stood in the hallway, his right hand clasping his left wrist like a priest waiting for the offerings.

Sciorra was six feet five inches tall and probably weighed less than one-sixty, his long, thin limbs like blades beneath his grey single-breasted suit, his striated neck almost feminine in its length, its pallor enhanced by the pristine whiteness of the collarless shirt buttoned beneath it. Short dark hair surrounded a bald pate, which ended in a cone so sharp as to appear pointed. Sciorra was a knife made flesh, a human instrument of pain, both surgeon and scalpel. The FBI believed that he had personally committed more than thirty killings. Most of those who knew Bobby Sciorra believed the FBI was conservative in its estimate.

He smiled as I approached, revealing perfectly white teeth glistening behind narrow, slash lips, but the smile never reached his blue eyes. Instead it disappeared in the jagged scar that ran from his left ear, across the bridge of his nose and ended just below the right earlobe. The scar devoured his smile like a second mouth.

'You got some balls coming here,' he said, still smiling, his head shaking gently from side to side as he said it.

'That an admission of guilt, Bobby?' I asked.

The smile never faltered. 'Why do you want to see the boss?

He's got no time for shit like you.' The smile broadened perceptibly. 'By the way, how are your wife and kid? Kid must be – what? – four by now.'

A dull red throbbing began to pulse in my head but I held it back, my hands tightening at my sides. I knew I'd be dead before my hands closed on Sciorra's white skin.

'Stephen Barton turned up dead in a sewer this evening. The feds are looking for Sonny and probably for you as well. I'm concerned for your welfare. I wouldn't want anything bad to happen to either of you that I wasn't a part of.'

Sciorra's smile remained the same. He seemed about to answer when a voice, low but authoritative, sounded over the house intercom system. Age gave it a gravelly resonance in which the rattle of death was present, lurking in the background like the traces of Don Ferrera's Sicilian roots.

'Let him in, Bobby,' it said. Sciorra stepped back and opened a set of draught-excluding double doors half-way down the hall. The grey-haired guard walked behind me as I followed Sciorra, who waited until he had closed the draught doors before opening a second door at the end of the hall.

Don Ferrera sat in an old leather armchair behind a big office desk, not entirely dissimilar from Walter Cole's desk although its gilt inlay raised it into a different league from Walter's comparatively Spartan possession. The curtains were drawn, and wall lights and table lamps gave a dim yellow glow to the pictures and bookshelves that lined the walls. I guessed from their age and condition that the books were probably worth a lot and had never been read. Red leather chairs stood against the walls, complementing Don Ferrera's own chair and some sofas that surrounded a long low table at the far end of the room.

Even sitting down and stooped by age, the old man was an impressive figure. His hair was silver and greased back from his temples, but an unhealthy pallor seemed to underly his tanned complexion and his eyes appeared rheumy. Sciorra closed the door and once more assumed his priestlike stance, my escort remaining outside.

'Please, sit,' said the old man, motioning towards an armchair. He opened a silver box of Turkish cigarettes, each ringed with small gold bands. I thanked him but refused. He sighed. 'Pity. I like the scent but they are forbidden me. No cigarettes, no women, no alcohol.' He closed the box and looked longingly at it for a moment, then clasped his hands and rested them on the desk before him.

'You have no title now,' he said. Among 'men of honour', to be called Mr when you had a title was a calculated insult. Federal investigators sometimes used it to belittle Mob suspects, dispensing with the more formal Don or Tio.

'I understand no insult is intended, Don Ferrera,' I said. He nodded and was silent.

As a detective I had had some dealings with the men of honour and always approached them cautiously and without arrogance or presumption. Respect had to be met with respect and silences had to be read like signs. Among them, everything had meaning and they were as economical and efficient in their modes of communication as they were with their methods of violence.

Men of honour only spoke of what concerned them directly, only answered specific questions and would stay silent rather than tell a lie. A man of honour had an absolute obligation to tell the truth and only when the behaviour of others altered so far as to make it necessary to break these rules of behaviour would he do so. All of which assumed that you believed pimps and killers and drug-dealers were honourable in the first place, or that the code was anything more than the incongruous trapping of another age, pressed into service to provide a sheen of aristocracy for thugs and murderers.

I waited for him to break the silence.

He stood and moved slowly, almost painfully, around the room and stopped at a small side-table on which a gold plate gleamed dully.

'You know, Al Capone used to eat off gold plates? Did you know that?' he asked. I told him that I hadn't known.

'His men used to carry them in a violin case to the restaurant and lay them on the table for Capone and his guests and then they'd all eat off them. Why do you think a man would feel the need to eat off a gold plate?' He waited for an answer, trying to catch my reflection in the plate.

'When you have a lot of money, your tastes can become peculiar, eccentric,' I said. 'After a while, even your food doesn't taste right unless it's served on bone china, or gold. It's not fitting for someone with so much money and power to eat from the same plates as the little people.'

'It goes too far, I think,' he replied, but he no longer seemed to be talking to me and it was his own reflection he was examining in the plate. 'There's something wrong with it. There are some tastes that should not be indulged, because they are vulgar. They are obscene. They offend nature.'

'I take it that isn't one of Capone's plates.'

'No, my son gave it to me as a gift on my last birthday. I told him the story and he had the plate made.'

'Maybe he missed the point of the story,' I said. The old man's face looked weary. It was the face of a man who had not enjoyed his sleep for some time.

'The boy who was killed, you think my son was involved? You think this was a piece of work?' he asked eventually, moving back into my direct line of vision and staring away from me at something in the distance. I didn't look to see what it was.

'I don't know. The FBI appears to think so.'

He smiled, an empty, cruel smile which reminded me briefly of Bobby Sciorra. 'And your interest in this is the girl, no?'

I was surprised, although I should not have been. Barton's past would have been common knowledge to Sciorra at least and would have been passed on quickly when his body was discovered. I thought my visit to Pete Hayes might have played a part too. I wondered how much he knew and his next question gave me the answer: not much.

'Who are you working for?'

'I can't say.'

'We can find out. We found out enough from the old man at the gym.'

So that was it. I shrugged gently. He was silent again for a time.

'Do you think my son had the girl killed?'

'Did he?' I responded. Don Ferrera turned back towards me, the rheumy eyes narrowing.

'There is a story told about a man who believes he is being cuckolded by his wife. He approaches a friend, an old, trusted friend, and says, "I believe my wife is cheating on me but I don't know with whom. I have watched her closely but I cannot find out the identity of this man. What do I do?"

'Now his friend is the man who is cheating with his wife, but to divert the other's attention he says that he saw the wife with another man, a man with a reputation for dishonourable conduct with other men's wives. And so the cuckold turns his gaze on this other man and his wife continues to cheat on him with his best friend.' He finished and gazed intently at me.

Everything has to be interpreted, everything is codified. To live with signs is to understand the necessity of understanding meanings in seemingly irrelevant pieces of information. The old man had spent most of his life looking for the meanings in things and expected others to do likewise. In his cynical little anecdote lay his belief that his son was not responsible for Barton's death but that whoever was responsible stood to benefit from the concentration of the police and FBI on his son's assumed guilt. I glanced at Bobby Sciorra and wondered how much Don Ferrera really knew about what went on behind those eyes. Sciorra was capable of anything, even of undermining his boss for his own gains.

'I hear maybe Sonny has taken a sudden interest in my good health,' I said.

The old man smiled. 'What kind of interest in your health, Mr Parker?'

'The kind of interest which could result in my health suddenly ceasing to be good.'

'I don't know anything about that. Sonny is his own man.'

'That may be, but if anyone pulls anything on me I'll see Sonny in Hell.'

'I'll have Bobby look into it,' he said.

That didn't make me feel a whole lot better. I stood up to leave.

'A clever man would be looking for the girl,' said the old man, also standing up and moving towards a door in a corner of the room behind the desk. 'Alive or dead, the girl is the key.'

Maybe he was right, but the old man must have had his own reasons for pointing me towards her. And as Bobby Sciorra escorted me to the front door, I wondered if I was the only person looking for Catherine Demeter.

There was a cab waiting at the gates of the Ferrera house to take me back to the Village. As it turned out, I had enough time to shower and make a pot of coffee at my apartment before the FBI came knocking on my door. I had changed into jogging pants and a sweatshirt so I felt a little casual next to Special Agents Ross and Hernandez. The Blue Nile were playing in the background, causing Hernandez to wrinkle his nose in distaste. I didn't feel the need to apologise.

Ross did most of the talking while Hernandez ostentatiously examined the contents of my bookshelf, looking at covers and reading the dustjackets. He hadn't asked if he could and I didn't like it.

'There are some picture ones on the lower shelf,' I said. 'No Crayolas, though. I hope you brought your own.'

Hernandez scowled at me. He was in his late twenties and probably still believed everything he had been taught about the agency in Quantico. He reminded me of the tour guides in the Hoover Building, the ones who herd the Minnesota housewives around while dreaming of gunning down drug-dealers and international terrorists. Hernandez probably still refused to believe that Hoover had worn a dress.

Ross was a different matter. He had been involved with the Feds' Truck Hijack Squad in New York in the seventies and his name had been linked to a number of high-profile RICO cases since then. I believed he was probably a good agent, but a lousy human being. I had already decided what I was going to tell him: nothing.

'Why were you at the Ferrera house this evening?' he began, after declining an offer of coffee like a monkey refusing a nut.

'I've got a paper route. It's one of my drops.' Ross didn't even grin. Hernandez' scowl deepened. If I'd been of a nervous disposition, the strain might have proved too much for me.

'Don't be an asshole,' said Ross. 'I could arrest you on suspicion of involvement with organised crime, hold you for a while, let you go, but what good would that do either of us? I'll ask you again: why were you at the Ferrera house this evening?'

'I'm conducting an investigation. Ferrera might have been connected to it.'

'What are you investigating?'

'That's confidential.'

'Who hired you?'

'Confidential.' I was tempted to put on a sing-song voice, but I didn't think Ross was in the right frame of mind. Maybe he was right: maybe I was an asshole, but I was no nearer to finding Catherine Demeter than I had been twenty-four hours ago, and her boyfriend's death had opened up a range of possibilities, none of which was particularly appealing. If Ross was out to nail Sonny Ferrera or his father then that was his problem. I had enough of my own.

'What did you tell Ferrera about Barton's death?'

'Nothing he didn't know already, seeing as how Hansen was at the scene before you were,' I replied. Hansen was a reporter with the *Post*, a good one. There were flies that envied Hansen's ability to sniff out a corpse, but if someone had had time to tip Hansen off it was pretty certain that someone had informed Ferrera even earlier. Walter was right: parts of the police department leaked like a poor man's shoes.

'Look,' I said. 'I don't know any more than you do. I don't think Sonny was involved, or the old man. As for anyone else . . .'

Ross's eyes flicked upwards in frustration. After a pause, he asked if I'd met Bobby Sciorra. I told him I'd had that pleasure. Ross stood and picked at some microscopic speck on his tie. It looked like the sort you picked up in Filene's Basement after the good stuff had gone.

'Sciorra's being mouthing off about teaching you a lesson, I hear. He thinks you're an interfering prick. He's probably right.'

'I hope you'll do everything in your power to protect me.'

Ross smiled, a minute hitching of the lips that revealed small, pointed canines. He looked like a rat reacting to a stick poked in its face.

'Rest assured, we'll do everything in our power to find the culprit when something happens to you.' Hernandez smiled, too, as they headed for the door. Like father, like son.

I smiled back. 'You can let yourselves out. And, Hernandez . . .' He stopped and turned.

'I'm gonna count those books.'

Ross was right to be concentrating his energies on Sonny. He may have been strictly minor league in many ways – a few porn parlours near Port Authority, a social club on Mott with a handwritten notice taped above the phone reminding members that it was bugged, assorted petty drug deals, shylocking and running whores hardly made him Public Enemy Number One – but Sonny was also the weak link in the Ferrera chain. If he could be broken, then it might lead to Sciorra and to the old man himself.

I watched the two FBI men from my window as they climbed into their car. Ross paused at the passenger side and stared up at the window for a time. It didn't crack under the pressure. Neither did I, but I had a feeling that Agent Ross wasn't really trying, not yet.

# Chapter Fourteen

It was after ten the next morning when I arrived at the Barton house. An unidentified flunkey answered the door and showed me into the same office in which I had met Isobel Barton two days before, with the same desk and the same Ms Christie with what looked like the same grey suit on and the same unwelcoming look on her face.

She didn't offer me a seat so I stood with my hands in my pockets to stop my fingers getting numb in the chilly atmosphere. She busied herself with some papers on the desk, not sparing me a second look. I stood by the fireplace and admired a blue china dog that stood at the far end of the mantelpiece. It was part of what had probably once been a pair, since there was an empty space on the opposite side. He looked lonely without a friend.

'I thought these things usually came in twos?'

Ms Christie glanced up, her face crumpled in annoyance like an image on old newspaper.

'The dog,' I repeated. 'I thought china dogs like that came in matching pairs.' I wasn't particularly concerned about the dog but I was tired of Ms Christie ignoring me and I derived some petty pleasure from irritating her.

'It was once part of a pair,' she replied, after a moment. 'The other was . . . damaged some time ago.'

'That must have been upsetting,' I said, trying to look like I meant it while simultaneously failing to do so.

'It was. It had sentimental value.'

'For you, or Mrs Barton?'

'For both of us.' Ms Christie realised she had been forced to acknowledge my presence despite her best efforts, so she carefully put the cap on her pen, clasped her hands together and assumed a businesslike expression.

'How is Mrs Barton?' I asked. What might have been concern moved swiftly across Ms Christie's features and then disappeared, like a gull gliding over a cliff face.

'She has been under sedation since last night. As you can imagine, she took the news badly.'

'I didn't think she and her stepson were that close.'

Ms Christie tossed me a look of contempt. I probably deserved it.

'Mrs Barton loved Stephen as if he were her own son. Don't forget that you are merely an employee, Mr Parker. You do not have the right to impugn the reputation of the living or the dead.' She shook her head at my insensitivity. 'Why are you here? There's a great deal to be done before—'

She stopped and, for a moment, looked lost. I waited for her to resume. 'Before Stephen's funeral,' she finished, and I realised that there might be more to her apparent distress at the events of last night than simple concern for her employer. For a guy who had all the higher moral qualities of a hammer-head shark, Stephen Barton had certainly attracted his share of admirers.

'I have to go to Virginia,' I said. 'It may take more than the advance I was given. I wanted to let Mrs Barton know before I left.'

'Is this to do with the killing?'

'I don't know.' It was becoming a familiar refrain. 'There may be a connection between Catherine Demeter's disappearance and Mr Barton's death but we won't know unless the police find something or the girl turns up.'

'Well, I can't authorise that kind of spending at the present time,' began Ms Christie. 'You'll have to wait until after—'

I interrupted her. Frankly, I was getting tired of Ms Christie. I was used to people not liking me but most at least had the decency to get to know me first, however briefly. 'I'm not asking you to authorise it and, after my meeting with Mrs Barton, I don't think you have anything to do with it. But as a common courtesy I thought I'd offer my sympathies and tell her how far I've got.'

'And how far have you got, *Mr* Parker?' she hissed. She was standing now, her knuckles white against the desk. In her eyes something vicious and poisonous raised its head and flashed its fangs.

'I think the girl may have left the city. I think she went home, or back to what used to be home, but I don't know why. If she's there I'll find her, make sure she's okay and contact Mrs Barton.'

'And if she isn't?'

I let the question hang without a reply. There was no answer, for if Catherine Demeter wasn't in Haven then she might as well have dropped off the face of the earth until she did something that made her traceable, like using a credit card or making a telephone call to her worried friend.

I felt tired and frayed at the edges. The case seemed to be fragmenting, the pieces spinning away from me and glittering in the distance. There were too many elements involved to be merely coincidental and yet I was too experienced to try to force them all together into a picture that might be untrue to reality, an imposition of order upon the chaos of murder and killing. Still, it seemed to me that Catherine Demeter was one of those pieces and that she had to be found so that her place in the order of things could be determined.

'I'm leaving this afternoon. I'll call if I find anything.'

Ms Christie's eyes had lost their shine and the bitter thing that lived within her had curled back on itself to sleep for a time. I was not even sure that she heard me. I left her like that, her knuckles still resting on the desk, her eyes vacant, seemingly staring somewhere within herself, her face slick and pale as if troubled by what she saw.

As it turned out, I was delayed by further problems with my car and it was 4.00 p.m. before I drove the Mustang back to my apartment to pack my bag.

A welcome breeze blew as I walked up the steps, fumbling for my keys. It sent candy wrappers cartwheeling across the street and set soft-drink cans tolling like bells. A discarded newspaper skimmed the sidewalk with a sound like the whisperings of a dead lover.

I walked the four flights of stairs to my door, entered the apartment and turned on a table lamp. I prepared a brew of coffee and packed as it percolated. About thirty minutes later I was finishing my coffee, my overnight bag at my feet, when the cellphone rang.

'Hello, Mr Parker,' said a man's voice. The voice was neutral, almost artificial, and I could hear small clicks between the words as if they had been reassembled from a completely different conversation.

'Who is this?'

'Oh, we've never met, but we had some mutual acquaintances. Your wife and daughter. You might say I was with them in their final moments.' The voice alternated between sets of words: now high, then low, first male, then female. At one point, there appeared to be three voices speaking simultaneously, then they fell away to a single male voice once again.

The apartment seemed to drop in temperature and then fall away from me. There was only the phone, the tiny perforations of the mouthpiece and the silence at the other end of the line.

'I've had freak calls before,' I said, with more confidence

than I felt. 'You're just another lonely man looking for a house to haunt.'

'I cut their faces off. I broke your wife's nose by slamming her against the wall by your kitchen door. Don't doubt me. I am the one you've been looking for.' The last words were all spoken by a child's voice, high-pitched and joyous.

I felt a stabbing pain behind my eyes and my blood sounded loudly in my ears like waves crashing against a headland, bleak and grey. There was no saliva in my mouth, just a dry dusty sensation. When I swallowed, the feeling was that of dirt travelling down my throat. It was painful and I struggled to find my voice.

'Mr Parker, are you all right?' The words were calm, solicitous, almost tender, but spoken by what sounded like four different voices.

'I'll find you.'

He laughed. The synthesised nature of the sound was more obvious now. It seemed to break up into tiny units, just as a TV screen does when you get too close and the picture becomes merely a series of small dots.

'But I've found *you*,' he said. 'You wanted me to find you, just as you wanted me to find them and to do what I did. You brought me into your life. For you, I flamed into being.

'I had been waiting so long for your call. You wanted them to die. Didn't you hate your wife in the hours before I took her? And don't you sometimes, in the deep dark of the night, have to fight back your sense of guilt at the feeling of freedom it gave you knowing she was dead? I freed you. The least you could do is show some gratitude.'

'You're a sick man, but that isn't going to save you.' I pressed caller ID on the phone and a number came up, a number I recognised. It was the number of the call-box at the corner of the street. I moved towards the door and began making my way down the stairs.

'No, not man. In her final moments your wife knew that, your Susan, mouth to mouth's kiss, as I drew the life from her. Oh, I lusted for her in those last, bright-red minutes but, then, that has always been a weakness of our kind. Our sin was not pride, but lust for humanity. And I chose her, Mr Parker, and I loved her in my way.' The voice was now deep and male. It boomed in my ear like the voice of a god, or a devil.

'Fuck you,' I said, the bile rising in my throat as I felt sweat bead my brow and run in rivulets down my face, a sick, fearful sweat that defied the fury in my voice. I had come down three flights of stairs. There was one flight left to go.

'Don't go yet.' The voice became that of a female child, like my child, my Jennifer, and in that moment I had some inkling of the nature of this 'Travelling Man'. 'We'll talk again soon. By then, maybe my purpose will be clearer to you. Take what I give you as a gift. I hope it will ease your suffering. It should be coming to you right . . . about . . . *now.*'

I heard the buzzer sound in my apartment upstairs. I dropped the phone to the floor and drew the Smith & Wesson from my holster. I took the remaining steps two at a time, racing down the stairs with adrenaline pumping through my system. My neighbour Mrs D'Amato, startled by the noise, stood at her apartment door, the one nearest the front entrance, a housecoat held tight at her neck. I rushed past her, wrenched open the door and came out low, my thumb already clicking down the safety.

On the step stood a black child of no more than ten years, a cylindrical, gift-wrapped parcel in his hand and his eyes wide in fear and shock. I grabbed him by the collar and flung him inside, shouting for Mrs D'Amato to hold him, to get both of them away from the package, and ran down the steps of the brownstone and on to the street.

It was deserted except for the papers and the rolling cans. It was a strange desertion, as if the Village and its inhabitants had conspired with the Travelling Man against me. At the far end of the street, beneath the street-lamp, a telephone booth stood. There was no one there and the handset was hanging in its place. I ran towards it, moving away from the corner wall as I approached in case anyone was waiting at the other side. Here, the street was alive with passers-by, gay couples hand in hand, tourists, lovers. In the distance I saw the lights of traffic and I heard around me the sounds of a safer, more mundane world I seemed to have left behind.

I spun at the sound of footsteps behind me. A young woman was approaching the phone, fumbling in her purse for change. She looked up as she saw me approach and backed off at the sight of the gun.

'Find another,' I said. I took one last look around, clicked the safety and stuck the gun in the waistband of my pants. I braced my foot against the pillar of the booth and with both hands I wrenched the connecting cable from the phone with a strength that was not natural to me. Then I returned to my apartment house, carrying the receiver before me like a fish on the end of a line.

Inside her apartment Mrs D'Amato was holding the kid by his arms while he struggled and fought, with tears rolling down his cheeks. I held his shoulders and squatted down to his level.

'Hey, it's okay. Take it easy. You're not in any trouble, I just want to ask you some questions. What's your name?'

The boy quieted down a little, although he still shook with sobs. He glanced around nervously at Mrs D'Amato and then made an attempt to break for the door. He nearly made it, too, his jacket slipping from his body as he pulled out his arms, but the force of his efforts made him slip and fall and I was on him. I hauled him to a chair, sat him down and gave Mrs D'Amato Walter Cole's number. I told her to tell him it was urgent and to get over here fast.

'What's your name, kid?'

'Jake.'

'Okay, Jake. Who gave you this?' I nodded towards the parcel, which stood on the table beside us, wrapped in blue paper decorated with teddy bears and candy cane and topped with a bright blue ribbon.

Jake shook his head, the force sending tears flying off in both directions.

'It's all right, Jake. There's no need to be scared. Was it a man, Jake?' Jake, Jake. Keep using his name, calm him, get him to concentrate.

His face swivelled towards me, the eyes huge. He nodded.

'Did you see what he looked like, Jake?'

His chin crumpled and he started to cry in loud sobs, which brought Mrs D'Amato back to the kitchen door.

'He said he'd hurt me,' said Jake. 'He said he'd *cu-cut my face off.*'

Mrs D'Amato moved beside him and he buried his face in the folds of her housecoat, wrapping his small arms around her thick waist.

'Did you see him, Jake? Did you see what he looked like?'

He turned from the housecoat.

'He had a knife, like doctors use on TV.' The boy's mouth hung wide with terror. 'He showed it to me, touched me with it here.' He lifted a finger to his left cheek.

'Jake, did you see his face?'

'He was all dark,' said Jake, his voice rising in hysteria. 'There was nuh-nuhthin' there.' His voice rose to a scream: '*He didn't have no face.*'

I told Mrs D'Amato to take Jake into the kitchen until Walter Cole arrived then sat down to examine the gift from the Travelling Man. It was about ten inches high and eight inches in diameter and it felt like glass. I took out my pocket knife and gently prised back an edge of the wrapping, examining it for wires or pressure pads. There was nothing. I cut the two strips of tape holding the paper in place and gently removed the grinning bears, the dancing candy cane.

The surface of the jar was clean and I smelt the disinfectant he had used to erase any traces of himself. In the yellowing liquid it contained I saw my own face doubly reflected, first on the surface of the glass and then inside, on the face of my once-beautiful daughter. It rested gently against the side of the jar, now bleached and puffy like the face of a drowning victim, scraps of flesh like tendrils rising from the edges and the eyelids closed as if in repose. And I moaned in a rising tide of agony and fear, hatred and remorse. In the kitchen, I could hear the boy named Jake sobbing and, mingled with his cries, I suddenly heard my own.

I don't know how much time elapsed before Cole arrived. He stared ashen-faced at the thing in the jar and then called Forensics.

'Did you touch it?'

'No. There's a phone as well. The number matches the caller ID but there won't be any traces. I'm not even sure he was at that phone. His voice was synthesised in some way. I think he was running his words through some form of sophisticated software, something with voice recognition and tone manipulation, and maybe bouncing it off that number. I don't know. I'm guessing, that's all.' I was babbling, words tripping over each other. I was afraid of what might happen if I stopped talking.

'What did he say?'

'I think he's getting ready to start again.'

He sat down heavily and ran his hand over his face and through his hair. Then he picked up the paper by one edge with a gloved hand and almost gently used it to cover the front of the jar, like a veil.

'You know what we have to do,' he said. 'We'll need to know everything he said, anything at all that might help us to get a lead on him. We'll do the same with the kid.'

I kept my eyes on Cole, on the floor, anywhere but on the table and the remains of all that I had lost.

'He thinks he's a demon, Walter.'

Cole looked once again at the shape of the jar.

'Maybe he is.'

As we left for the station, cops milled around the front of the building, preparing to take statements from neighbours, passers-by, anyone who might possibly have witnessed the actions of the Travelling Man. The boy Jake came with us, his parents arriving shortly after with that frightened, sick look that poor, decent people get in the city when they hear that one of their children is with the police.

The Travelling Man must have been following me throughout the day, watching my movements so he could put into action what he had planned. I traced back my movements, trying to remember faces, strangers, anyone whose gaze might have lingered for just a moment too long. There was nothing.

At the station, Walter and I went through the conversation again and again, pulling out anything that might be useful, that might stamp some distinguishing feature on this killer.

'You say the voices changed?' he asked.

'Repeatedly. At one point, I even thought I heard Jennifer.'

'There may be something in that. Voice synthesis of that kind would have to be done using some sort of computer. Shit, he could simply have routed the call through that number, like you said. The kid says he was given the jar at four p.m. and told to deliver it at four thirty-five exactly. He waited in an alley, counting the seconds on his Power Rangers digital watch. That could have given this guy enough time to get to his home base and bounce the call. I don't know enough about these things.

Maybe he needed access to an exchange to do what he did. I'll have to get someone who knows to check it out.'

The mechanics of the voice synthesis were one thing, but the reasons for the synthesis were another. It might have been that the Travelling Man wanted to leave as few traces of himself as possible: a voice pattern could be recognised, stored, compared and even used against him at some point in the future.

'What about the kid's comment, that this guy with the scalpel had no face?' asked Walter.

'A mask of some kind, maybe, to avoid any possibility of identification. He could be marked in some way, that's another option. The third choice is that he is what he seems to be.'

'A demon?'

I didn't reply. I didn't know what a demon was, if an individual's inhumanity could cause him to 'cross over' in some way, to become something less than human; or if there were some things that seemed to defy any conventional notion of what it meant to be human, of what it meant to exist in the world.

When I returned to the apartment that night, Mrs D'Amato brought me up a plate of cold cuts and some Italian bread and sat with me for a time, fearful for me after what had taken place that afternoon.

When she left, I stood beneath the shower for a long time, the water as hot as I could take it, and I washed my hands again and again. I lay awake then for a long time, sick with anger and fear, watching the cellphone on my desk. My senses were so heightened that I could hear them hum.

# Chapter Fifteen

'Read me a story, Daddy.'
  'What story do you want to hear?'
  'A funny story. The three bears. The baby bear is funny.'
  'Okay, but then you have to go to sleep.'
  'Okay.'
  'One story.'
  'One story. Then I go to sleep.'

*In an autopsy, the body is first photographed, clothed and naked. Certain parts of the body may be X-rayed to determine the presence of bone fragments or foreign objects embedded in the flesh. Every external feature is noted: the hair colour, the height, the weight, the condition of the body, the colour of the eyes.*

'Baby Bear opened his eyes wide. "Somebody's been eating my porridge, and it's all gone!"'
  'All gone!'
  All gone.

*The internal examination is conducted from top to bottom, but the head is examined last. The chest is examined for any sign of rib fractures. A Y-shaped incision is made by cutting from shoulder to shoulder, crossing over the breasts, then moving down from the lower tip of the sternum to the pubic region. The heart and lungs are exposed. The pericardial sac is opened and a sample of blood is taken to determine the blood type of the victim. The heart, lungs, oesophagus and trachea are removed. Each organ is weighed, examined and sliced into sections. Fluid in the thoracic pleural cavity is removed for analysis. Slides of organ tissue are prepared for analysis under a microscope.*

'And then Goldilocks ran away and the three bears never saw her again.'

'Read it again.'

'No, we agreed. One story. That's all we have time for.'

'We have more time.'

'Not tonight. Another night.'

'No, tonight.'

'No, another night. There'll be other nights, and other stories.'

*The abdomen is examined and any injuries are noted before the removal of the organs. Fluids in the abdomen are analysed and each separate organ is weighed, examined and sectioned. The contents of the stomach are measured. Samples are taken for toxicological analysis. The order of removal is usually as follows: the liver, the spleen, the adrenals and kidneys, the stomach, pancreas and intestines.*

'What did you read?'

'*Goldilocks and the Three Bears.*'

'Again.'

'Again.'

'Are you going to tell me a story?'

'What story would you like to hear?'

'Something dirty.'

'Oh, I know lots of stories like that.'
'I know you do.'

*The genitalia are examined for injuries or foreign material. Vaginal and anal swabs are obtained and any foreign matter collected is sent to a DNA lab for analysis. The bladder is removed and a urine sample is sent to toxicology.*

'Kiss me.'
'Kiss you where?'
'Everywhere. On my lips, my eyes, my neck, my nose, my ears, my cheeks. Kiss me everywhere. I love your kisses on me.'
'Suppose I start with your eyes and move down from there.'
'Okay. I can live with that.'

*The skull is examined in an effort to find evidence of injury. The intermastoid incision is made from one ear to the other, across the top of the head. The scalp is peeled away and the skull exposed. A saw is used to cut through the skull. The brain is examined and removed.*

'Why can't we be like this more often?'
'I don't know. I want us to be, but I can't.'
'I love you like this.'
'Please, Susan . . .'
'No . . .'
'I could taste the booze on your breath.'
'Susan, I can't talk about this now. Not now.'
'When? When are we going to talk about it?'
'Some other time. I'm going out.'
'Stay, please.'
'No. I'll be back later.'
'Please . . .'

★   ★   ★

Rehoboth Beach in Delaware has a long boardwalk bordered on one side by the beach and on the other by the sort of amusement arcades you remember from your childhood: 25-cent games played with wooden balls which you roll into holes to score points; horse races with metal horses loping down a sloped track with a glass-eyed teddy bear for the winner; a frog-pond game played with magnets on the end of a child's fishing line.

They've been joined now by noisy computer games and space-flight simulators, but Rehoboth still retains more charm than, say, Dewey Beach further up the coast, or even Bethany. A ferry runs from Cape May in New Jersey to Lewes on the Delaware coast and, from there, it's maybe five or six miles south to Rehoboth. It's not really the best way to approach Rehoboth, since you run the gamut of burger joints, outlet stores and shopping malls on Highway One. The approach north through Dewey is better, running along the shore with its miles of dunes.

From that direction, Rehoboth benefits from the contrast with Dewey. You cross into the town proper over a kind of ornamental lake, past the church and then you're on Rehoboth's main street, with its bookstores, its T-shirt shops, its bars and restaurants set in big old wooden houses, where you can drink on the porch and watch people walk their dogs in the quiet evening air.

Four of us had decided on Rehoboth as the place to go for a weekend break to celebrate Tommy Morrison's promotion, despite its reputation as something of a gay hotspot. We ended up staying in the Lord Baltimore, with its comfortable, anti-quated rooms harking back to another era, less than a block away from the Blue Moon bar where crowds of well-tanned, expensively dressed men partied loudly into the night.

I had just become Walter Cole's partner. I suspected Walter had pulled strings to have me assigned as his partner, although nothing was ever said. With Lee's agreement, he travelled with me to Delaware, along with Tommy Morrison and a friend of mine from the Academy named Joseph Bonfiglioli, who was shot dead a year later while chasing a guy who had stolen eighty dollars from a liquor store. Each evening at 9.00 p.m., without fail, Walter would call Lee to check on her and the kids. He was a man acutely aware of the vulnerability of a parent.

Walter and I had known each other for some time – four years by then, I think. I met him first in one of the bars in which cops used to hold court. I was young, just out of uniform and still admiring my reflection in my new tin. Great things were expected of me. It was widely believed that I would get my name in the papers. I did that, although not in the way that anyone would have imagined. Walter was a stocky figure wearing slightly down-at-heel suits, a dark shadow of a beard on his cheeks and chin even when he had shaved only an hour before. He had a reputation as a dogged, concerned investigator, one who had occasional flashes of brilliance that could turn an investigation around when legwork had failed to produce a result and the necessary quota of luck upon which almost every investigation depends was not forthcoming.

Walter Cole was also an avid reader, a man who devoured knowledge in the same way that certain tribes devour their enemies' hearts in the hope that they will become braver as a result. We shared a love of Runyon and Wodehouse; of Tobias Wolff, Raymond Carver, Donald Barthelme; the poetry of e.e. cummings and, strangely, of the Earl of Rochester, the Restoration dandy tortured by his failings – his love of alcohol and women and his inability to be the husband that he believed his wife deserved.

I recall Walter wandering along the boardwalk at Rehoboth with a Popsicle in his hand, a garish shirt hanging over a pair of khaki shorts, his sandals slapping lightly on the sand-scattered wood and a straw hat protecting his already balding head. Even as he joked with us, examining menus and losing money on the slots, stealing fries from Tommy Morrison's big Thrasher's paper tub, paddling in the cool Atlantic surf, I knew that he was missing Lee.

And I knew, too, that to live a life like Walter Cole's – a life almost mundane in the pleasure it derived from small happinesses and the beauty of the familiar, but uncommon in the value it attached to them – was something to be envied.

I met Susan Lewis, as she then was, for the first time in Lingo's Market, an old-style general store which sold produce and cereals alongside expensive cheeses and boasted its own in-store bakery. It was still a family-run operation – a sister, a brother and their mother, a tiny, white-haired woman with the energy of a terrier.

On our first morning in the resort, I stumbled out to buy coffee and a newspaper in Lingo's, my mouth dry, my legs still unsteady from the night before. She stood at the deli counter, ordering coffee beans and pecans, her hair tied loosely in a ponytail. She wore a yellow summer dress, her eyes were a deep, dark blue and she was very, very beautiful.

I, on the other hand, was very much the worse for wear, but she smiled at me as I stood beside her at the counter, oozing alcohol from my pores. And then she was gone, trailing a hint of expensive scent behind her.

I saw her a second time that day, at the YMCA as she stepped from the pool and entered the dressing rooms, while I tried to sweat out the alcohol on a rowing machine. It seemed to me that, for the next day or two, I caught glimpses of her every-where: in a bookshop, examining the covers of glossy legal thrillers; passing the launderette, clutching a bag of donuts; peering in the window of the Irish Eyes bar with a girlfriend; and, finally, I came upon her one night as she stood on the boardwalk, the sound of the arcades behind her and the waves breaking before her.

She was alone, caught up in the sight of the surf gleaming white in the darkness. Few people strolled on the beach to obscure her view and, at the periphery, away from the arcades and the fast-food stalls, it was startlingly empty.

She looked over at me as I stood beside her. She smiled. 'Feeling better now?'

'A little. You caught me at a bad time.'

'I could *smell* your bad time,' she said, her nose wrinkling.

'I'm sorry. If I'd known you were going to be there, I'd have dressed up.' And I wasn't kidding.

'It's okay. I've had those times.'

And, from there, it began. She lived in New Jersey, commuted to Manhattan each day to work in a publisher's office and every second weekend she visited her parents in Massachusetts. We were married a year later and we had Jennifer one year after that. We had maybe three very good years together before things started to deteriorate. It was my fault, I think. When my parents married they both knew the toll a policeman's life could take on a marriage, he because he lived that life and saw its results reflected in the lives around him, she because her father had been a deputy in Maine and had resigned before the cost became too high. Susan had no such experience.

She was the youngest of four children, both of her parents were still alive and they all doted on her. When she died, they ceased to speak to me. Even at the graveside, no words passed between us. With Susan and Jennifer gone, it was as if I had been cut adrift from the tide of life and left to float in still, dark waters.

# Chapter Sixteen

The deaths of Susan and Jennifer attracted a great deal of attention, although it soon faded. The more intimate details of the killing — the skinning, the removal of the faces, the blindings — were kept from the public, but it didn't stop the freaks from coming out of the woodwork. For a time, murder tourists would drive up to the house and videotape each other standing in the yard. A local patrolman even caught one couple trying to break in through the back door in order to pose in the chairs where Susan and Jennifer had died. In the days after they had been found, the phone rang regularly with calls from people who claimed to be married to the killer, or who felt certain that they had met him in a past life or, on one or two occasions, called only to say they were glad my wife and child were dead. Eventually I left the house, remaining in touch by phone and fax with the lawyer who had been entrusted with the business of selling it.

I had found the community near Portland, Maine, when I was returning to Manhattan from Chicago after chasing up one more obscure non-lead, a suspected child-killer named Byron Able who was dead by the time I arrived, killed in the parking lot of a bar after he tangled with some local thugs. Maybe I was also looking for some peace in a place I knew, but I never got as far as the house in Scarborough, the house that my grandfather had left me in his will.

I was sick by that time. When the girl found me retching and crying in the doorway of a boarded-up electronics store and offered me a bed for the night I could only nod. When her comrades, huge men with muddied boots and shirts that smelt of sweat and pine needles, dragged me to their pick-up and dumped me in the back I half-hoped that they were going to kill me. They nearly did. By the time I left their community, out by Sebago Lake, six weeks later I had lost fourteen pounds and my stomach muscles stood out like the plates on an alligator's back. I worked on their small farm and attended group sessions where others like me tried to purge themselves of their demons. I still craved alcohol but fought back the desire as I had been taught. There were prayers in the evenings and every Sunday a pastor would give a sermon on abstinence, tolerance, the need for each man and woman to find a peace within himself or herself. The community funded itself through the produce it sold, some furniture it made and donations from those who had availed of its services, some of them now wealthy men and women.

But I was still sick, consumed by a desire to revenge myself upon those around me. I felt trapped in a limbo: the investigation had ground to a halt and would not resume again until a similar crime was committed and a pattern could be established.

Someone had taken my wife and child from me and escaped unpunished. Inside me, the hurt and anger and guilt ebbed and flowed like a red tide waiting to spill its banks. I felt it as a physical pain that tore at my head and gnawed at my stomach. It led me back to the city, where I tortured and killed the pimp Johnny Friday in the toilet of the bus station where he had been waiting to feast on the waifs and strays drifting into New York.

I think now that I had always set out to kill him but I had hidden the knowledge of what I intended to do in some corner of my mind. I draped it with self-serving justifications and excuses, the sort I had used for so long each time I watched a shot of whiskey poured in front of me, or heard the gassy snap of a beer cap. Frozen by my own inability and the inability of others to find the killer of Susan and Jennifer, I saw a chance to strike out and I took it. From the moment I packed my gun and gloves and set out for the bus station, Johnny Friday was a dead man.

Friday was a tall, thin black man who looked like a preacher in his trademark dark three-buttoned suits and his collarless shirts fastened to the neck. He would hand out small Bibles and religious pamplets to the new arrivals and offer them soup from a flask and, as the barbiturates it contained began to take effect, he would lead them from the station and into the back of a waiting van. Then they would disappear, as surely as if they had never arrived, until they turned up on the streets as beaten junkies, whoring for the fix that Johnny supplied at inflated prices while they pulled in the tricks that kept him rich.

His was a 'hands-on' operation and, even in a business not noted for its humanity, Johnny Friday was beyond any kind of redemption. He supplied children to paedophiles, delivering them to the doors of selected safe-houses where they were raped and sodomised before being returned to their owner. If they were rich and depraved enough, Johnny would give them access to 'The Basement' in an abandoned warehouse in the garment district. There, for a cash payment of $10,000, they could take one of Johnny's stable and, boy or girl, child or teen, they could torture, rape and, if they wished, kill, and Johnny would take care of the body. He was noted, in certain circles, for his discretion.

In my search for the killer of my wife and child, I had learned of Johnny Friday. I had not intended to kill him, or at least I did not admit that intention to myself. From a former snitch I learned that Johnny sometimes dealt in pictures and videos of sexual torture, that he was a leading source of this material and that anyone whose tastes ran in that direction would, at some point, come into contact with Johnny Friday or one of his agents.

And so I watched him for five hours from an Au Bon Pain in the station and when he went to the washroom I followed him. It was divided into sections, the first mirrored with sinks, the second lined with urinals along the end wall and two sets of stalls opposite, divided by a central aisle. An old man in a stained uniform sat in a small, glass-lined cubicle beside the sinks but he was engrossed in a magazine when I entered behind Johnny Friday. Two men were washing their hands at the sinks, two were standing at the urinals and three of the stalls were occupied, two in the section to the left, one in the section to the right. Piped music was playing, some unrecognisable tune.

Johnny Friday walked, hips swinging, to the urinal at the far right of the wall. I stood two urinals away from him as I waited for the other men to finish. As soon as they had finished I moved behind Johnny Friday, clasping my hand on his mouth and pressing the Smith & Wesson into the soft skin beneath his chin as I pushed him into the end stall, the furthest away from the other occupied stall on that side.

'Hey, don't, man, don't,' he whispered, his eyes wide.

I brought my knee up hard into his groin and he fell down heavily on his knees as I locked the door behind us. He tried weakly to rise and I hit him hard in the face. I brought the gun close to his head again. 'Don't say a word. Turn your back to me.'

'Please, man, don't.'

'Shut up. Turn.'

He inched slowly round on his knees. I pulled his jacket down over his arms and then cuffed him. From my other pocket I took a rag and a roll of duct tape. I stuffed the rag in his mouth and wrapped the tape around his head two or three times. Then I pulled him to his feet and pushed him down on to the toilet. His right foot came up and caught me hard on the shin and he tried to push himself up, but he was off balance and I hit him again. This time he stayed down. I held the gun on him and listened for a moment in case anyone came to see what the noise was. There was only the sound of a toilet flushing. No one came.

I told Johnny Friday what I wanted. His eyes narrowed as he realised who I was. Sweat poured from his forehead and he tried to blink it from his eyes. His nose was bleeding slightly and a thin trickle of red ran from beneath the duct tape and rolled down his chin. His nostrils flared as he breathed heavily through them.

'I want names, Johnny. Names of customers. You're going to give them to me.'

He snorted in disdain and blood bubbled from a nostril. His eyes were cold now. He looked like a long, black snake with his slicked-back hair and slitted, reptilian eyes. When I broke his nose they widened in shock and pain.

I hit him again, once, twice, hard blows to the stomach and head. Then I pulled the tape down hard and dragged the bloodied rag from his mouth.

'Give me names.'

He spat a tooth from his mouth. 'Fuck you,' he said. 'Fuck you and your dead bitches.'

What happened after is still not clear to me. I remember hitting him again and again, feeling bone crunch and ribs break and watching my gloves darken with his blood. There was a black cloud in my mind and streaks of red ran through it like strange lightning.

When I stopped, Johnny Friday's features seemed to have melted into a bloody blur of what they had once been. I held his jaw in my hands as blood bubbled from his lips.

'Tell me,' I hissed. His eyes rolled towards me and, like a

vision of some craggy entrance to Hell, his broken teeth showed behind his lips as he managed one last smile. His body arched and spasmed once, twice. Thick black blood rolled from his nose and mouth and ears and then he died.

I stood back, breathing heavily. I wiped my blood-spattered face as best I could and cleaned some of the blood from the front of my jacket, although it hardly showed against the black leather and my black jeans. I took the gloves from my hands, stuffed them in my pocket and then flushed the toilet before peering carefully out and pulling the door closed behind me as I left. Blood was already seeping out of the stall and pooling in the cracks between the tiles.

I realised that the noise of Johnny Friday's dying must have echoed around the washroom but I didn't care. As I left I passed only an elderly black man at the urinals and he, like a good citizen who knows when to mind his own business, didn't even glance at me. There were other men at the sinks who gave me a cursory look in the mirror. But I noticed that the old man was gone from his glass cubicle and I ducked into an empty departure gate as two cops came running towards the washroom from the upper level. I made my way to the street through the ranks of buses beneath the station.

Perhaps Johnny Friday deserved to die. Certainly, no one mourned his passing and the police made little more than a cursory effort to find his killer. But there were rumours, for Walter, I think, had heard them.

But I live with the death of Johnny Friday as I live with the deaths of Susan and Jennifer. If he did deserve to die, if what he got was no more than he deserved, yet it was not for me to act as his judge and executioner. 'In the next life we get justice', someone once wrote. 'In this one we have the law.' In Johnny Friday's last minutes there was no law and only a kind of vicious justice that was not for me to give.

I did not believe that my wife and child were the first to die at the hands of the Travelling Man, if that was who he was. I still believed that somewhere in a Louisiana swamp lay another, and in her identity was the clue that would open up the identity of this man who believed he was more than a man. She was part of a grim tradition in human history, a parade of victims stretching back to ancient times, back to the time of Christ and before that, back to a time when men sacrificed those around them to placate gods who knew no mercy and whose natures they both created and imitated in their actions.

The girl in Louisiana was part of a bloody succession, a modern-day Windeby Girl, a descendant of that anonymous woman found in the fifties in a shallow grave in a peat bog in Denmark where she had been led nearly two thousand years before, naked and blindfolded, to be drowned in twenty inches of water. A path could be traced through history leading from her death to the death of another girl at the hands of a man who believed he could appease the demons within himself by taking her life but who, once blood had been spilled and flesh torn, wanted more and took my wife and child.

We do not believe in evil any more, only evil acts, which can be explained away by the science of the mind. There is no evil and to believe in it is to fall prey to superstition, like checking beneath the bed at night or being afraid of the dark. But there are those for whom we have no easy answers, who do evil because that is their nature, because they are evil.

Men such as Johnny Friday and others like him prey on those who live on the periphery of society, on those who have lost their way. It is easy to stray in the darkness on the edge of modern life and, once lost and alone, there are things waiting for us there. Our ancestors were not wrong in their superstitions: there is reason to fear the dark.

And just as a trail could be followed from a bog in Denmark to a swamp in the South, so I came to believe that evil, too, could be traced throughout the life of our race. There was a tradition of evil, which ran beneath all human existence like the sewers beneath a city, which continued on even after one of its constituent parts was destroyed because it was simply one small part of a greater, darker whole.

Perhaps that was part of what made me want to find out the truth about Catherine Demeter; as I look back, I realise that evil had found its way to touch her life too and taint it beyond retrieval. If I could not fight evil as it came in the form of the Travelling Man, then I would find it in other forms. I believe what I say. I believe in evil because I have touched it, and it has touched me.

# Chapter Seventeen

When I telephoned Rachel Wolfe's private practice the following morning, the secretary told me that she was giving a
seminar at a conference in Columbia University. I took the
subway from the Village and arrived early at the main entrance
to the campus. I wandered for a time around the Barnard Book
Forum, students jostling me as I stood browsing in the literature section, before making my way to the main college
entrance.

I passed through the college's large quadrangle, with the
Butler library at one end, the administration building at the
other and, like a mediator between learning and bureaucracy,
the statue of Alma Mater in the grass centre. Like most city
residents, I rarely came to Columbia and the sense of tranquil-
lity and study only feet away from the busy streets outside was
always surprising to me.

Rachel Wolfe was just finishing her lecture as I arrived, so
I waited for her outside the theatre until the session ended.
She emerged talking to a young, earnest-looking man with
curly hair and round spectacles, who hung on her every
word like a devotee of a god. When she saw me she stopped
and smiled a goodbye at him. He looked unhappy and
seemed set to linger but then turned and walked away,
his head low.

'How can I help you, Mr Parker?' she asked, with a puzzled but not uninterested look.

'He's back.'

We walked over to the Hungarian Pastry Shop on Amsterdam Avenue, where intense young men and women sat reading textbooks and sipping coffee. Rachel Wolfe was wearing jeans and a chunky sweater with a heart-shaped design on the front.

Despite all that had happened the previous night, I was curious about her. I had not been attracted to a woman since Susan's death and my wife was the last woman with whom I had slept. Rachel Wolfe, her long, red hair brushed back over her ears, aroused a sense of longing in me that was more than sexual. I felt a deep loneliness within myself and an ache in my stomach. She looked at me curiously.

'I'm sorry,' I said. 'I was thinking of something.'

She nodded and picked at a poppy-seed roll before pulling off a huge chunk and stuffing it in her mouth, sighing with satisfaction. I must have looked slightly shocked, because she covered her mouth with her hand and giggled softly. 'Sorry, but I'm a sucker for these things. Daintiness and good table manners tend to go out the window when someone puts one in front of me.'

'I know the feeling. I used to be like that with Ben and Jerry's until I realised I was starting to look like one of the cartons.'

She smiled again and pushed at a piece of roll, which was trying to make a break for freedom from the side of her mouth. The conversation sagged for a time.

'I take it your parents were jazz fans,' she said eventually.

I was puzzled for a moment and she smiled in amusement as I tried to take in the question. I had been asked it many times before but I was grateful for the diversion, and I think she knew that.

'No, my father and mother didn't know the first thing about jazz,' I replied. 'My father just liked the name. The first time he heard about Bird Parker was at the baptismal font when the priest mentioned it to him. The priest was a big jazz fan, I was told. He couldn't have been happier if my father had announced that he was naming all of his children after the members of the Count Basie Orchestra.

'My father, by contrast, wasn't too happy at the idea of naming his first-born after a black jazz musician but by then it was too late to think of another name.'

'What did he call the rest of his children?'

I shrugged. 'He didn't get the chance. My mother couldn't have any more children after me.'

'Maybe she thought she couldn't do any better.' She smiled.

'I don't think so. I was nothing but trouble for her as a child. It used to drive my father crazy.'

I could see in her eyes that she was about to ask me about my father but something in my face stopped her. She pursed her lips, pushed away her empty plate and settled herself back in her chair.

'Can you tell me what happened?'

I went through the events of the night before, leaving nothing out. The words of the Travelling Man were burned into my mind.

'Why do you call him that?'

'A friend of mine led me to a woman who said that she was receiving, uh, messages from a dead girl. The girl had died in the same way as Susan and Jennifer.'

'Was the girl found?'

'No one looked. An old woman's psychic messages aren't enough to launch an investigation.'

'Even if she exists, are you sure it's the same guy?'

'I believe it is, yes.'

Wolfe looked like she wanted to ask more, but she let it go.

'Go back over what this caller, this "Travelling Man", said again, slowly this time.'

I did until she lifted her hand to stop me. 'That's a quote from Joyce: "mouth to mouth's kiss". It's the description of the "pale vampire" in *Ulysses*. This is an educated man we're dealing with. The stuff about "our kind" sounds Biblical, but I'm not sure of it. I'll have to check it. Give them to me again.' I spoke the words slowly as she took them down in a wire-bound notebook. 'I have a friend who teaches theology and Biblical studies. He might be able to identify a source for these.'

She closed the notebook. 'You know that I'm not supposed to get involved in this case?'

I told her that I hadn't known.

'Following our earlier discussions, someone got in touch with the Commissioner. He wasn't best pleased at the snub to his relative.'

'I need help with this. I need to know all I can.' Suddenly I felt nauseous and, when I swallowed, my throat hurt.

'I'm not sure that's wise. You should probably leave this to the police. I know that's not what you want to hear but, after all that's happened, you risk damaging yourself. Do you understand what I mean?'

I nodded slowly. She was right. Part of me wanted to draw back, to immerse myself once again in the ebb and flow of ordinary life. I wanted to unburden myself of what I felt, to restore myself to some semblance of a normal existence. I wanted to rebuild but I felt frozen, suspended, by what had happened. And now the Travelling Man had returned, snatching any possibility of that normality from me and, simultaneously, leaving me as powerless to act as I had been before.

I think Rachel Wolfe understood that. Maybe that was why I had come to her, in the hope that she might understand.

'Are you all right?' She reached over and touched my hand and I almost cried. I nodded again.

'You're in a terribly difficult situation. If he has decided to contact you, then he wants you to be involved and there may be a link that can be exploited. From an investigative point of view, you probably shouldn't deviate from your routine in case he contacts you again, but from the point of view of your own well-being . . .' She let the unstated hang in the air. 'You might even want to consider some professional help. I'm sorry for being so blunt about it, but it has to be said.'

'I know, and I appreciate the advice.' It was strange to find myself attracted to someone after all this time and then have her advise me to see a psychiatrist. It didn't hold out the promise of any relationship that wasn't conducted on an hourly basis. 'I think the investigators want me to stay.'

'I get the feeling you're not going to do it.'

'I'm trying to find someone. It's a different case, but I think this person may be in trouble. If I stay here, there's no one to help her if she is.'

'It may be a good idea to get away from this for a time but from what you're saying, well . . .'

'Go on.'

'It sounds like you're trying to save this person but you're not even sure if she needs saving.'

'Maybe I need to save her.'

'Maybe you do.'


I told Walter Cole later that morning that I would continue looking for Catherine Demeter and that I would be leaving the city to do so. We were sitting in the quietness of Chumley's, the Village's old speakeasy at Bedford. When Walter called, I had surprised myself by nominating it for our meeting, but as I sat sipping a coffee I realised why I had chosen it.

I enjoyed its sense of history, its place in the city's past, which could be traced back like an old scar or the wrinkle at the corner of an eye. Chumley's had survived the Prohibition era, when customers had escaped raids by leaving hastily through the back door, which led on to Barrow Street. It had survived world wars, stock-market crashes, civil disobedience and the gradual erosion of time, which was so much more insidious than all the rest. For a brief period, I wanted to be part of its stability.

'You have to stay,' said Walter. He still had the leather coat, now hanging loosely over the back of his chair. Someone had whistled at him when he entered wearing it.

'No.'

'What do you mean, "No"?' he said angrily. 'He's opened an avenue of communication. You stay, we wire up the phone and we try to trace him when he calls again.'

'I don't think he will call again, at least not for a while, and I don't believe we could trace him anyway. He doesn't want to be stopped, Walter.'

'All the more reason to stop him, then. My God, look at what he's done, what he's going to do again. Look at what you've done for his—'

I leaned forward and broke in on him, my voice low. 'What have I done? Say it, Walter. Say it!'

He stayed silent and I saw him swallow the words back. We had come close to the edge, but he had pulled back.

The Travelling Man wanted me to remain. He wanted me to wait in my apartment for a call that might never come. I could not let him do that to me. Yet both Cole and I knew that the contact he had established could well be the first link in a chain that would eventually lead us to him.

A friend of mine, Ross Oakes, had worked in the police department of Columbia, South Carolina, during the Bell killings. Larry Gene Bell abducted and smothered two girls, one aged seventeen and snatched close to a mail-box, the other aged nine and taken from her play area. When investigators eventually found the bodies they were too decomposed to determine if they had been sexually assaulted, although Bell later admitted to assaulting both.

Bell had been tracked through a series of phone calls he made to the family of the seventeen-year-old, conversing primarily with the victim's older sister. He also mailed them her last will and testament. In the phone calls he led the family to believe that the victim was still alive until her body was eventually found one week later. After the abduction of the younger girl he contacted the first victim's sister and described the abduction and killing of the girl. He told the first victim's sister that she would be next.

Bell was found through indented writing on the victim's letter, a semi-obliterated telephone number, which was eventually tracked to an address through a process of elimination. Larry Gene Bell was a thirty-six-year-old white male, formerly married and now living with his mother and father. He told Investigative Support Unit agents from the FBI that 'the bad Larry Gene Bell did it'.

I knew of dozens of similar cases where contact with the killer by the victim's family sometimes led to his capture, but I had also seen what this form of psychological torture had done to those who were left behind. The family of Bell's first victim were lucky because they only had to suffer Bell's sick wanderings for two weeks. A family in Tulsa, whose toddler daughter had been raped and dismembered by a male nurse, received phone calls from the killer for over two years.

Amid the anger and pain and grief that I had felt the night before, there was another feeling, which caused me to fear any further contact with the Travelling Man, at least for the present.

I felt relief.

For over seven months there had been nothing. The police investigation had ground to a halt, my own efforts had brought me no nearer to identifying the killer of my wife and child and I feared that he might have disappeared.

Now he had come back. He had reached out to me and, by doing so, opened the possibility that he might be found. He would kill again and, in the killing, a pattern would emerge that would bring us closer to him. All these thoughts raced through my head in the darkness of the night but, in the first light of dawn, I had realised the implications of what I felt.

The Travelling Man was drawing me into a cycle of dependency. He had tossed me a crumb in the form of a telephone call and the remains of my daughter and, in doing so, had caused me to wish, however briefly, for the deaths of others in the hope that their deaths might bring me closer to him. With that realisation came the decision that I would not form such a relationship with this man. It was a difficult decision to make but I knew that if he decided to contact me again, then he would find me. Meanwhile, I would leave New York and continue to hunt for Catherine Demeter.

Yet deep down, perhaps only half recognised by me and suspected by Rachel Wolfe, there was another reason for continuing the search for Catherine Demeter.

I did not believe in remorse without reparation. I had failed to protect my wife and child and they had died as a result. Maybe I was deluded, but I believed that if Catherine Demeter died because I stopped looking for her then I would have failed twice and I was not sure that I could live with that knowledge. In her, maybe wrongly, I saw a chance to atone.

Some of this I tried to explain to Walter – my need to avoid a dependent relationship upon this man, the necessity of continuing the search of Catherine Demeter for her sake, and my own – but most of it I kept to myself. We parted uneasily and on bad terms.

Tiredness had gradually taken hold of me throughout the morning and I slept fitfully for an hour before setting off for Virginia. I was bathed in sweat and almost delirious when I awoke, disturbed by dreams of endless conversations with a faceless killer and images of my daughter before her death.

Just as I awakened, I dreamed of Catherine Demeter surrounded by darkness and flames and the bones of dead children. And I knew then that some terrible blackness had descended on her and that I had to try to save her, to save us both, from the darkness.

# Part Two

Eadem mutata resurgo
Though changed, I shall arise the same.

*Epitaph on the tombstone of Jacob Bernoulli,*
*Swiss pioneer of fluid dynamics and*
*spiral mathematics.*

# Chapter Eighteen

I drove down to Virginia that afternoon. It was a long ride but I told myself that I wanted time to open out the engine of the car, to let it cut loose after its time off the road. As I drove, I tried to sort through what had happened in the last two days, but my thoughts kept coming back to the remains of my daughter's face resting in a jar of formaldehyde.

I spotted the tail after about an hour, a red Nissan four-wheel-drive with two occupants. They kept four or five vehicles behind but when I accelerated, so did they. When I fell back they kept me in view for as long as they could, then they began to fall back too. The plates were deliberately obscured with mud. A woman drove, her blonde hair pulled back behind her ears and sunglasses masking her eyes. A dark-haired male sat beside her. I put them both in their thirties but I didn't recognise them.

If they were feds, which was unlikely, then they were lame. If they were Sonny's hired killers, then it was just like Sonny to hire cheap labour. Only a clown would use a 4WD for a tail, or to try to take out another vehicle. A 4WD has a high centre of gravity and rolls easier than a drunk on a slope. Maybe I was just being paranoid, but I didn't think so.

They didn't make a move and I lost them in the back roads between Warrenton and Culpeper as I headed towards the Blue Ridge. If they came after me again, I'd know: their jeep stood out like blood in snow.

As I drove, fading sunlight speared the trees, causing the web-like cocoons of caterpillars to glisten. I knew that, beneath the strands, the white bodies of the larvae were twisting and writhing like victims of Tourette's syndrome as they reduced the leaves to brown lifelessness. The weather was beautiful for most of the journey and there was a kind of poetry to the names of the towns that skirted Shenandoah: Wolftown, Quinque, Lydia, Roseland, Sweet Briar, Lovingston, Brightwood. To that list could be added the town of Haven, but only if you decided not to spoil the effect by actually visiting it.

It was raining heavily by the time I reached Haven. The town lay in a valley south-east of the Blue Ridge, almost at the apex of a triangle formed with Washington and Richmond. A sign at the limits read 'A Welcome in the Valley' but there was little that was welcoming about Haven. It was a small town over which a pall of dust appeared to have settled and which even the driving rain seemed unable to dislodge. Rusting pick-ups sat outside some of the houses and, apart from a single fast-food joint and a convenience store attached to a garage, only the weak neon of the Welcome Inn bar and the lights of the late-nite diner opposite beckoned the casual visitor. It was the sort of place where, once a year, the local Veterans of Foreign Wars got together, hired a bus and went somewhere else to commemorate their dead.

I checked into the Haven View Motel at the outskirts of the town. I was the only guest and a smell of paint hung around the halls of what might once have been a considerable house but had now been converted into a functional, anonymous three-storey inn.

'Second floor's being redecorated,' said the clerk, who told me his name was Rudy Fry. 'Have to put you upstairs, top floor. Technically, we shouldn't be accepting guests at all but . . .' He smiled to indicate the big favour he was doing me by letting me stay. Rudy Fry was a small, overweight man in his forties. There were long-dried yellow sweat stains under his arms and he smelt vaguely of rubbing alcohol.

I looked around. The Haven View Motel didn't look like the sort of place that would attract visitors at the best of times.

'I know what you're thinkin',' said the clerk, his smile revealing sparkling dentures. 'You're thinkin': "Why would anyone bother throwin' good money away by decoratin' a motel in a shithole like this?"' He winked at me before leaning over the desk conspiratorially. 'Well, I'm tellin' you, sir, it ain't gonna be a shithole much longer. Them Japanese is comin', and when they do, this place is gonna be a goldmine. Where else they gonna stay round here?' He laughed. 'Shit, we gonna be wipin' our asses with dollar bills.' He handed me a key with a heavy wooden block chained to it. 'Room twenty-three, up the stairs. Elevator's busted.'

The room was dusty but clean. A connecting door led into the next room. It took me less than five seconds to break the lock with my pocket knife, then I showered, changed and drove back into town.

The recession of the seventies had hit Haven hard, putting paid to what little industry there was. The town might have recovered, might have found some other way to prosper had its history been other than it was, but the killings had tainted it and the town had fallen into decay. And so the rain fell and washed and sluiced its way over the stores and streets, over the people and the houses, over trees and pick-ups and cars and Tarmac, and when it ceased to fall there was no freshness about Haven, as if the rain itself had been sullied by the contact.

I called into the sheriff's office but neither the sheriff nor Alvin Martin was available. Instead, a deputy named Wallace sat scowling behind the desk and shovelling Doritos into his mouth. I decided to wait until the morning in the hope of finding someone more accommodating.

The diner was closing as I walked through the town, which

left only the bar or the burger joint. The interior of the bar was ill lit, as if it was expending too much power on the pink neon sign outside. *The Welcome Inn*: the sign glowed brightly, but the interior seemed to give the lie to the sign.

Some kind of bluegrass music was playing over a speaker and a TV above the bar was showing a basketball game with the volume turned down, but no one seemed to be listening or watching anyway. Maybe twenty people were scattered around the tables and the long, dark wood bar, including a mountainous couple who looked like they'd left the third bear with a babysitter. There was a low tide of conversation, which ebbed slightly when I entered, although it refused to cease entirely, and then resumed at its previous level.

Near the bar, a small knot of men lounged around a battered pool table, watching a huge, heavy-set man with a thick dark beard playing an older man who shot pool like a hustler. They eyed me as I walked by but continued playing. No conversation passed between them. Pool was obviously a serious business in the Welcome Inn. Drinking wasn't. The hard men around the pool table were all clutching bottles of Bud Light, the real drinker's equivalent of a lady's white umbrella.

I took an empty stool at the bar and asked for a coffee from a barman whose white shirt seemed dazzlingly clean for such a place. He studiously ignored me, his eyes seemingly intent on the basketball game, so I asked again. His glance moved lazily to me, as if I were a bug crawling on the bar and he had just had his fill of squashing bugs, but was wondering whether he couldn't squash one more for the road.

'We don't do coffee,' he said.

I glanced along the bar. Two stools down an elderly man in a lumber jacket and a battered Cat cap sipped at a mug of what smelt like strong black coffee.

'He bring his own?' I inquired, gesturing with a nod down the bar.

'Yep,' said the barman, still looking at the TV.

'A Coke'll do. Right behind your knees, second shelf down. Don't hurt yourself leaning over.'

For a long time it seemed he wasn't going to move, then he shifted slowly, leaned down without taking his eyes from the screen and found the opener on the edge of the counter by instinct. Then he placed the bottle in front of me and set an iceless glass beside it. In the mirror behind the bar, I saw the amused smiles of some of the other patrons and heard a woman's laugh, low and boozy with a promise of sex in it. In the mirror over the bar, I traced the laugh to a coarse-featured woman in the corner, her hair huge and dark. Beside her, a stout man whispered sour somethings in her ear like the cooings of a sick dove.

I poured the drink and took a long draught. It was warm and sticky and I felt it cleave to my palate, my tongue and my teeth. The barman spent a while idly polishing glasses with a bar-towel which looked like it had last been cleaned for Reagan's inauguration. When he got bored with redistributing the dirt on the glasses he wandered back towards me and put the bar-towel down in front of me.

'Passin' through?' he asked, although there was no curiosity in his voice. It sounded more like advice than a question.

'Nope,' I said.

He took it in and then waited for me to say more. I didn't. He gave in first.

'Whatcha doin' here, then?' He looked over my shoulder at the pool-players behind and I noticed that the sound of balls colliding had suddenly ceased. He smiled a big shit-eating grin. 'Maybe I can . . .' He stopped and the grin got wider, his tone changing to one of mock-formality. '. . . be of some *a*-ssis-tance.'

'You know anyone named Demeter?'

The shit-eating grin froze and there was a pause. 'No.'

'Then I don't believe you can be of any *a*-ssistance.' I stood up to leave, placing two dollar bills on the counter. 'For the welcome,' I said. 'Put it towards a new sign.'

I turned to find a small, rat-featured guy in a worn blue denim jacket standing in front of me. His nose was dotted with blackheads and his teeth were prominent and yellow-stained like walrus tusks. His black baseball cap was marked with the words 'Boyz 'N the Hood' but this wasn't any logo John Singleton would have liked. Instead of homies, the words were surrounded by the hooded heads of Klan figures.

Beneath his denim jacket, I could see the word Pulaski under a seal of some sort. Pulaski was the birthplace of the Ku Klux Klan and the site of an annual rally for Aryan crackers everywhere, although I bet the face of old Thom Robb, grand high ass-wipe of the Klan, must have just lit up at the sight of Rat Features and his pinched, sub-intelligent face arriving to take in the Pulaski air. After all, Robb was trying to make the Klan appeal to the educated élite, the lawyers and the schoolteachers. Most lawyers would have been reluctant to have Rat Features as a client, still less a brother in arms.

But there was probably still a place for Rat Features in the new Klan. Every organisation needs its foot-soldiers and this one had cannon fodder written all over him. When the time came for the Boyz to storm the steps of the Capitol and reclaim the Jewnited States for their own, Rat Features would be in the front line where he could be certain to lay down his life for the cause.

Behind him, the bearded pool-player loomed, his eyes small, piggy and dumb-looking. His arms were enormous but without definition and his gut bulged beneath a camouflage T-shirt. The T-shirt bore the legend 'Kill 'em all – Let God sort 'em out', but the big guy was no Marine. He looked as close to retarded as you can get without someone coming by twice a day to feed you and clean up your mess.

'How you doin'?' said the Rat. The bar was quiet now and the group of men at the pool table were no longer lounging but stood rigid in anticipation of what was to come. One of them smiled and poked his neighbour with an elbow. Obviously, the Rat and his buddy were the local double act.

'Great till now.'

He nodded as if I'd just said something deeply profound with which he had a natural empathy.

'You know,' I said, 'I once took a leak in Thom Robb's garden.'

Which was true.

'It'd be better if you just got back on the road and kept driving, I reckon,' said the Rat, after a pause to figure out who Thom Robb was. 'So why don't you just do that?'

'Thanks for the advice.' I moved to go past him but his pal put a hand like a shovel against my chest and pushed me back against the bar by flexing his wrist slightly.

'It wasn't advice,' said the Rat. He gestured back at the big guy with his thumb.

'This here's Six. You don't get back in your fuckin' car now and start raisin' dust on the highway, Six is gonna fuck you up bad.'

Six smiled dimly. The evolutionary curve obviously sloped pretty gently where Six came from.

'You know why he's called Six?'

'Let me guess,' I replied. 'There are another five assholes like him at home?'

It didn't look like I was going to find out how Six got his name, because he stopped smiling and lunged past the Rat, his hand clutching for my neck. He moved fast for a man his size, but not that fast. I brought my right foot up and released it heel-first on to Six's left knee. There was a satisfying crunching sound and Six faltered, his mouth wide with pain, and stumbled sideways and down.

His friends were already coming to his aid when there was a commotion from behind them and a small, tubby deputy in his late thirties pushed his way through, one hand on the butt of his pistol. It was Wallace, Deputy Dorito. He looked scared and edgy, the kind of guy who became a cop to give him some sort of advantage over the people who used to laugh at him in school, steal his lunch money and beat him up, except he found that now those people still laughed at him and didn't look as if they'd let the uniform stand in the way of another beating. Still, on this occasion he had a gun and maybe they figured he was scared enough to pull it on them.

'What's goin' on here, Clete?'

There was silence for a moment and then the Rat spoke up. 'Just some high spirits got out of hand, Wallace. Ain't nothin' to concern the law.'

'I wasn't talking to you, Gabe.'

Someone helped Six to his feet and brought him to a chair.

'Looks like more than high spirits to me. I reckon you boys better come on down to the station, cool off for a time.'

'Let it go, Wallace,' said a low voice. It came from a thin, wiry man with cold, dark eyes and a beard flecked with grey. He had an air of authority about him and an intelligence that went beyond the low cunning of his associates. He watched me carefully as he spoke, the way an undertaker might eye up a prospective client for his casket.

'Okay, Clete, but . . .' Deputy Dorito's words trailed off as he realised there was nothing he could say that would matter to any of the men before him. He nodded to the crowd, as if the decision not to pursue things any further had been his to make.

'You'd better leave, Mister,' he said, looking at me.

I stood up and walked slowly to the door. No one said anything as I left.

Back at the motel, I rang Walter Cole to find out if anything had developed in the Stephen Barton killing but he was out of the office and his machine was on at home. I left the number of the motel and tried to get some sleep.

# Chapter Nineteen

The sky was grey and dark the next morning, heavy with impending rain. My suit was wrinkled from the previous day's travel, so I abandoned it for chinos, a white shirt and a black jacket. I even dug out a black silk-knit tie, so I wouldn't look like a bum. I drove once through the town. There was no sign of a red jeep or the couple I had seen driving it.

I parked outside the Haven diner, bought a copy of the *Washington Post* in the gas station across the road and then went into the diner for breakfast. It was after nine but people still lounged around at the counter or at the tables, mumbling about the weather and, I guessed, about me, since some of them glanced knowingly in my direction, directing the attention of their neighbours towards me.

I sat at a table in the corner and scanned the paper. A mature woman in a white apron and blue uniform with 'Dorothy' embossed at her left breast walked over to me carrying a pad and took my order of white toast, bacon and coffee. She hovered over me after I finished ordering. 'You the fella whupped that Six boy in the bar last night?'

'That's me.'

She nodded in satisfaction. 'I'll give you your breakfast for free, then.' She smiled a hard smile, then added, 'But don't you go confusin' my generosity with an invitation to stay. You ain't that good-lookin'.' She strolled back behind the counter and pinned my order to a wire.

There wasn't much traffic on Haven's main street. Most of the cars and trucks seemed to be passing through on their way to someplace else. Haven didn't look much better in the daylight than it did at night. I could see a used-car dealership, the roof of a high school and, further down the street, some stores and the Inn. There was little human activity. Haven seemed to be permanently stuck in a grim Sunday afternoon.

I finished my food and left a tip on the table. Dorothy slouched forward over the counter, her breasts resting on its polished surface. ''Bye now,' she said, as I left. The other diners briefly looked over their shoulders at me before returning to their breakfast and coffee.

I drove to the Haven public library, a new single-storey building at the far side of the town. A pretty black woman in her early thirties stood behind the counter with an older white woman whose hair was like steel wool and who eyed me with obvious distaste as I entered.

'Morning,' I said. The younger woman smiled, slightly anxiously, while the older one tried to tidy the already immaculate area behind the counter. 'What's the local paper around here?'

'Used to be the *Haven Leader*,' answered the younger woman after a pause. 'It's gone now.'

'I was looking for something older, back issues.'

She glanced at the other woman, as if for guidance, but she continued to shift pieces of paper behind the counter.

'They're on microfiche, in the cabinets beside the viewer. How far back do you want to go?'

'Not far,' I said, and strolled over to the cabinets. The *Leader* files were arranged in date order in small square boxes in ten drawers but the three boxes of files for the years of the Haven killings were not in their place. I ran through them all, in case they had been misfiled, although I had a feeling that those files weren't available to the casual visitor.

I returned to the counter. The elderly woman was no longer in sight.

'The files I'm looking for don't appear to be there,' I said. The younger girl looked confused but I didn't get the impression that she was.

'What year were you looking for?'

'Years. Nineteen sixty-nine, 'seventy, maybe 'seventy-one.'

'I'm sorry, those files aren't . . .' She seemed to search for an excuse that might be plausible. '. . . available. They've been borrowed for research.'

'Oh,' I said. I smiled my best smile. 'Never mind, I'll manage with what's there.'

She seemed relieved and I returned to the viewer, idly flicking through the files for anything useful with no return other than boredom. It took thirty minutes before an opportunity presented itself. A party of schoolchildren entered the junior section of the library, separated from the adult lending by a half-wood, half-glass screen. The younger woman followed them and stood with her back to me, talking to the children and their teacher, a young blonde who didn't look long out of school herself.

There was no sign of the older woman, although a brown door was half open in the small lobby beyond the adult section. I slipped behind the counter, and began rifling through drawers and cupboards as quietly as I could. At one point I passed, crouching, by the entry door to the junior section but the librarian was still dealing with her young clients.

I found the missing files in a bottom drawer, beside a small coin-box. I slipped them into my jacket pockets and was just leaving the counter area when the office door outside slammed and I heard soft footsteps approaching. I darted beside a shelf as the senior librarian entered. She stopped short at the entrance to the counter and shot an unpleasant look in my direction and at the book in my hand. I smiled gamely and returned to the viewer. I wasn't sure how long it would be before the dragon behind the counter checked that drawer and decided to call for back-up.

I tried the 1969 files first. It took some time, even though the *Haven Leader* had only been a weekly newspaper in 1969. There was nothing about any disappearances in the paper. Even in 1969, it seemed that black folks didn't count for much. The paper contained a lot about church socials, history society lectures and local weddings. There was some minor crime stuff, mostly traffic offences and drunk and disorderlies, but nothing that might lead a casual reader to suppose that children were disappearing in the town of Haven.

Then, in a November issue, I came upon a reference to a man named Walt Tyler. There was a picture of Tyler beside the piece, a good-looking man being led away in handcuffs by a white deputy. 'Man held in Sheriff Attack', read the headline above the picture. The details contained in the piece below were sketchy but it seemed Tyler had come into the sheriff's office and started busting the place up before taking a swing at the sheriff himself. The only indication of a reason for the attack came in the last paragraph.

'Tyler was among a number of negroes questioned by the Haven County Sheriff's Office in connection with the disappearance of his daughter and two other children. He was released without charge.'

The 1970 files were more productive. On the night of 8 February 1970, Amy Demeter had disappeared after heading out to a friend's house to deliver a sample of her mother's jam. She never made it to the house and the jar was found broken on a sidewalk about five hundred yards from her home. A picture of her was printed beside the story, along with details of what she had been wearing and a potted history of the family: father

Earl an accountant, mother Dorothy a housewife and a school board member, younger sister Catherine a well-liked child with some artistic potential. The story ran for the next few weeks: 'Search Goes On for Haven Girl'; 'Five More Questioned in Demeter Mystery'; and, finally, 'Little Hope Left for Amy'.

I spent another half-hour going back and forth through the *Haven Leader* but there was nothing more on the killings or their resolution, if any. The only indication was a report of the death of Adelaide Modine in a fire four months later, with a reference to her brother's death buried in the piece. There was no indication of the circumstances of the death of either, but there was one hint, once again in the last paragraph. 'The Haven County Sheriff's Office had been anxious to talk to both Adelaide and William Modine in their ongoing investigation into the disappearance of Amy Demeter and a number of other children.'

It didn't take a genius to read between the lines and see that either Adelaide Modine or her brother William, or possibly both, had been the main suspects. Local newspapers don't necessarily print all the news: there are some things everyone knows already and sometimes the local press merely prints enough to throw outsiders off the scent. The old librarian was giving me the evil eye so I finished printing off copies of the relevant articles, then gathered them and left.

A Haven County Sheriff's Office cruiser, a brown and yellow Crown Victoria, was pulled up in front of my car and a deputy, wearing a clean, well-pressed uniform, was leaning against my driver's door, waiting. As I drew closer I could see the long muscles beneath his shirt. His eyes were dull and lifeless. He looked like an asshole. A fit asshole.

'This your car?' he asked, in a Virginia drawl, his thumbs tucked inside a gun-belt that glittered with the spotless tools of his trade. On his chest, the name Burns stood out on his perfectly straight identity badge.

'Sure is,' I said, mimicking his accent. It was a bad habit I had. His jaw tightened, if it was actually possible for it to tighten more than it was already.

'Hear you were looking up some old newspapers?'

'I'm a crossword fan. They were better in the old days.'

'You another writer?'

Judging from his tone I didn't think he read much, at least nothing that didn't have pictures or a message from God. 'No,' I said. 'You get a lot of writers around here?'

I don't think he believed I wasn't a writer. Maybe I looked bookish to him or maybe anyone with whom he wasn't personally acquainted was immediately suspected of covert literary leanings. The librarian had sold me out, believing me to be simply another hack trying to make a buck out of the ghosts of Haven's past.

'I'm escorting you to the town line,' he said. 'I've got your bag.' He moved to the patrol car and took my travelling bag from the front seat. I was starting to get very tired of Deputy Burns.

'I'm not planning on leaving just yet,' I said, 'so maybe you could put it back in my room. By the way, when you're unpacking, I like my socks on the left side of the drawer.'

He dropped the bag on the road and started towards me. 'Look', I began, 'I have ID.' I reached into the inside pocket of my jacket. 'I'm . . .'

It was a dumb thing to do but I was hot and tired and pissed at Deputy Burns and I wasn't thinking straight. He caught one flash of the butt of my gun and his own piece was in his hands. Burns was quick. He probably practised in front of the mirror. Within seconds I was up against his car, my gun was gone and Deputy Burns's shiny cuffs were biting into my wrists.

# Chapter Twenty

I was left cooling my heels in a cell for what I reckoned to be three or four hours, since the careful Deputy Burns had taken my watch along with my gun, my wallet and ID, my notes and my belt and laces, in case I decided to hang myself in a fit of remorse for annoying the librarians. These had been entrusted to the safe care of Deputy Wallace, who made some passing reference to Burns of my involvement in the previous night's incident in the bar.

Still, the cell was just about the cleanest one I had ever visited in my life – even the can looked like it could safely be used without needing a course of penicillin later. I passed the time by mulling over what I had learned from the library microfiche, trying to fit the pieces of the puzzle into some recognisable picture and refusing to let my mind drift to the Travelling Man and what he might be doing.

Eventually, there was a noise outside and the cell door opened. I looked up to see a tall black man in a uniform shirt watching me. He looked to be in his late thirties but something about the way he walked and the light of experience in his eyes told me he was older. I guessed he might have boxed at one time, probably middle to light-heavy, and he moved grace-fully on his feet. He looked smarter than Wallace and Burns put together, although no one was likely to hand out gold stars for that particular feat. This, I guessed, was Alvin Martin. I didn't rush to get up, in case he thought I didn't like his nice clean cell.

'You want to stay there another couple of hours or you waiting for someone to carry you out?' he asked. The voice wasn't Southern: Detroit, Chicago, maybe.

I stood and he moved aside to let me pass. Wallace waited at the end of the corridor, his thumbs tucked into his belt to take the weight off his shoulders.

'Give him back his things, Deputy.'

'Even his gun?' asked Wallace, not making a move to do as he was told. Wallace had that look about him, the look that told you he wasn't used to taking orders from a black guy and didn't like it when he had to. It struck me that he might have more in common with the Rat and his friends than was really wise for a conscientious lawman.

'Even his gun,' replied Martin calmly but wearily, giving Wallace the eye. Wallace shoved off from the wall like a particularly ugly ship setting out to sea and steamed behind the counter, surfacing eventually with a brown envelope and my gun. I signed and Martin nodded me towards the door.

'Get in the car, please, Mr Parker.' Outside, the light was starting to fade and there was a cool wind blowing from the hills. A pick-up rattled by on the road beyond, a covered gun rack on the back guarded by a mangy hound.

'Back or front?' I asked.

'Get in the front,' he replied. 'I trust you.'

He started the cruiser and we drove for a time in silence, the a/c blasting cool air into our faces and on to our feet. The town limits receded behind us and we entered woods thick with trees, the road twisting and winding as it followed the contours of the land. Then, in the distance, a light shone. We pulled up in the parking lot of a white diner, topped by a green neon sign blinking Green River Eaterie on to the road beyond.

We took a booth at the rear, far away from the handful of

other patrons, who cast a curious glance at us before returning to their food. Martin took off his hat, ordered coffee for both of us, then sat back and looked at me. 'It's usually considered good manners for an investigator packing a pistol to drop in to the local lawmen and state his business, at least before he goes around beating up pool-players and stealing library files,' he said.

'You weren't around when I called,' I said. 'Neither was the sheriff, and your friend Wallace wasn't too keen on offering me cookies and swapping race jokes.'

The coffee arrived. Martin added creamer and sugar to his. I stuck with milk.

'I made some calls about you,' said Martin, stirring his coffee. 'A guy called Cole vouched for you. That's why I'm not kicking your ass out of town, least not yet. That and the fact that you weren't afraid to whip some cracker ass last night. Shows you got a sense of civic pride. So maybe now you'd like to tell me why you're here.'

'I'm looking for a woman named Catherine Demeter. I think she might have come to Haven in the last week.'

Martin's brow furrowed.

'She anything to Amy Demeter?'

'Sister.'

'I figured. Why do you think she might be here?'

'One of the last calls she made from her apartment was to the home of Sheriff Earl Lee Granger. She made a number of calls to your office as well the same night. Since then, there's been no sign of her.'

'You hired to find her?'

'I'm just looking for her,' I replied neutrally.

Martin sighed. 'I came here from Detroit six months ago,' he said, after about a minute of silence. 'Brought my wife and boy. My wife's an assistant librarian. I think you may have met her.'

I nodded.

'The governor decided there weren't enough blacks in the police force here and that relations between the local minority population and the cops might not be the best. So, a post came up here and I applied, mainly to get my kid away from Detroit. My father came from Gretna, just a ways from here. I didn't know about the killings before I came here. I know more now.

'This town died along with those kids. No new people came to live here and anyone with an ounce of sense or ambition got the hell out. Now the gene pool here's so shallow you couldn't drown a rat in it.

'In the last month or two there's been signs that something might happen to change that. There's a Japanese firm interested in locating about half a mile out of town. They do research and development of computer software, I hear, and they like the idea of privacy and a quiet little backwater they can call Nippon. They'd bring a lot of money to this town, a lot of jobs for locals and maybe a chance to put the past to rest. Frankly, the people here don't much care for the idea of working for the Japanese but they know they're sucking shit as it is, so they'll work for anyone as long as he's not black.

'The last thing they want is someone sniffing around ancient history, digging up the past to come up with the bones of dead children. They may be dumb in a lot of cases. They may also be racists and shit-kickers and child-fuckers, but they're desperate for a second chance and they'll mess up anyone who gets in their way. If they don't do it, Earl Lee will.'

He raised a finger and waved it purposefully in my face. 'Do you understand what I'm saying here? Nobody wants questions asked about child-killings that took place thirty years ago. If Catherine Demeter came back here, and frankly I don't know why she would since she ain't got no one here to come back to, then she wouldn't be welcome either. But she ain't here, because if she had come back it would be all over this town like shit on a shoe.'

He took a sip of his coffee and gritted his teeth. 'Damn, it's cold.' He gestured to the waitress and called for a fresh mug.

'I don't want to stay here any longer than I have to,' I said. 'But I think Catherine Demeter may have come back here, or tried to come back here. She certainly wanted to talk to the sheriff and I want to talk to him too. So where is he?'

'He took a couple of days' leave to get out of town for a while,' said Martin, twisting the brim of his hat so that it spun on the vinyl seat. 'He's due back – well, he was due back today but he may leave it until tomorrow. We don't have too much crime here beyond drunks and wife-beaters and the usual shit that goes with a place like this. But he may not be too pleased to see you waiting for him when he returns. I'm not so pleased to see you myself, no offence meant.'

'None taken. I think I'll wait around for the sheriff anyway.' I was also going to have to find out more about the Modine killings, whether Martin liked it or not. If Catherine Demeter had reached into her past then I was going to have to reach into that past too, or I would understand nothing about the woman for whom I was searching.

'I'll also need to talk to someone about the killings. I need to know more.'

Martin closed his eyes and ran his hand over them in weariness. 'You're not listening to me—' he began.

'No, you're not listening. I'm looking for a woman who may be in trouble and who may have turned to someone here for help. Before I leave I'm going to find out whether or not that's the case, even if it means rattling every cage in this godforsaken dump and scaring your Japanese saviours back to Tokyo. But if you help me, then this can all be done quietly and I'll be out of your hair in a couple of days.'

We were both tensed now, leaning towards each other across the table. Some of the other diners were staring at us, their food ignored.

Martin looked around at them then turned back to me again. 'Okay,' he said. 'Most of the people who were around then and might know something useful have either left, or died, or won't talk about it for love or money. There are two who might, though. One is the son of the doc who was around at that time. His name's Connell Hyams and he has a law office in town. You'll have to approach him yourself.

'The other is Walt Tyler. His daughter was the first to die and he lives outside town. I'll talk to him first and maybe he'll see you.' He stood up to leave. 'When you've got your business done you'd better leave and I never want to see your face again, understand?'

I said nothing and followed him towards the door. He stopped and turned towards me, placing his hat on his head as he did so. 'One more thing,' he said. 'I've had a word with those boys from the bar but, remember, they ain't got no reason to like you. I'd watch my back if I was planning on poking my nose into this town's business.'

'I noticed one of them, I think his name was Gabe, had a Klan shirt on,' I said. 'You got much of that around here?'

Martin blew breath heavily from puffed cheeks. 'In a poor town, the dumb ones always look for someone to blame for being poor.'

'There was one guy – your deputy called him Clete – who didn't look so dumb.'

Martin eyed me from under his hat brim. 'No, Clete's not dumb. He sits on the council, says the only way anyone's gonna get him off the council is with a gun barrel. Whipping you could be good for another twenty, thirty votes. Shit, maybe he'll send you a campaign badge.

'But as for the Klan, this ain't Georgia or North Carolina, or even Delaware. Don't go reading too much into this. You can pay for the coffee.'

I left a couple of bucks at the till and walked out towards the car, but Martin was already pulling away. I noticed that he'd taken his hat off again inside the car. The man just didn't seem comfortable with that damn hat. I went back into the diner, called Haven's only cab operator and ordered another coffee.

# Chapter Twenty-One

It was after six when I got back to the town. Connell Hyams's office and home address were listed but when I drove by his office all the lights were out. I called Rudy Fry at the motel and got directions for Bale's Farm Road, where not only Hyams but also Sheriff Earl Lee Granger had homes.

I drove cautiously along the winding roads, looking for the concealed entrance Fry had mentioned and still glancing occasionally in my mirror for any sign of the red jeep. There was none. I passed the entrance to Bale's Farm Road once without seeing it and had to go back over my tracks again. The sign was semi-obscured by undergrowth and pointed towards a winding, rutted track, heavy with evergreens, which eventually opened out on to a small but well-kept row of houses with long yards and what looked like plenty of space out back. Hyams's home was near the end, a large, two-storey white wooden house. A lamp blazed by a wire frame, which opened on to a solid oak front door with a fan of frosted glass near the top. There was a light on in the hallway.

A grey-haired man, wearing a red wool cardigan over grey slacks and a striped, open-necked shirt, opened the inner door as I pulled up and watched me cautiously.

'Mr Hyams?' I said, as I approached the door.

'Yes?'

'I'm an investigator. My name's Parker. I wanted to talk to you about Catherine Demeter.'

He paused for a long time in silence with the wire screen between us.

'Catherine, or her sister?' he inquired eventually.

'Both, I guess.'

'May I ask why?'

'I'm trying to find Catherine. I think she may have come back here but I'm not sure why.'

Hyams opened the wire door and stood aside to let me enter. Inside, the house was furnished in dark wood, with large, expensive-looking mats on the floors. He led me into an office at the back, where papers were strewn over a desk on which a computer screen glowed.

'Can I offer you a drink?' he asked.

'No. Thank you.'

He took a brandy glass from his desk and gestured me towards a chair at the other side before seating himself. I could see him more clearly now. He was grave and patrician in appearance, his hands long and slim, the nails finely manicured. The room was warm and I could smell his cologne. It smelt expensive.

'That all took place a long time ago,' he began. 'Most people would rather not talk about it.'

'Are you "most people"?'

He shrugged and smiled. 'I have a place in this community and a role to play. I've lived here almost all my life, apart from the time I spent in college and in practice in Richmond. My father spent fifty years practising here and kept working until the day he died.'

'He was the doctor, I understand.'

'Doctor, medical examiner, counsellor, legal adviser, even dentist when the resident dentist wasn't around. He did everything. The killings hit him particularly hard. He performed the autopsies on the bodies. I don't think he ever forgot it, not even in his sleep.'

'And you? Were you around when they took place?'

'I was working in Richmond at the time, so I was back and forth between Haven and Richmond. I knew of what took place here, yes, but I'd really rather not talk about it. Four children died and theirs were terrible deaths. Best to let them rest now.'

'Do you remember Catherine Demeter?'

'I knew the family, yes, but Catherine would have been much younger than I. She left after graduating from high school, as I recall, and I don't think she ever came back, except to attend the funerals of her parents. The last time she returned was probably ten years ago at the very least and her family home has been sold since then. I supervised the sale. Why do you believe she might have come back now? There's nothing here for her – nothing good at any rate.'

'I'm not sure. She made some calls here earlier this week and hasn't been seen since.'

'It's not much to go on.'

'No,' I admitted. 'It's not.'

He twisted the glass in his hand, watching the amber liquid swirl. His lips were pursed in appraisal but his gaze went through the glass and rested on me.

'What can you tell me about Adelaide Modine and her brother?'

'I can tell you that, from my point of view, there was nothing about them that might have led one to suspect that they were child killers. Their father was a strange man, a philanthropist of sorts, I suppose. He left most of his money tied up in a trust when he died.'

'He died before the killings?'

'Five or six years before, yes. He left instructions that the interest on the trust fund should be divided among certain charities in perpetuity. Since then, the number of charities receiving donations has increased considerably. I should know, since it is my duty to administer the trust, with the assistance of a small committee.'

'And his daughter and son? Were they provided for?'

'Very adequately, I understand.'

'What happened to their money, their property, when they died?'

'The State brought an action to take over the property and assets. We contested it on behalf of the townspeople and eventually an agreement was reached. The land was sold and all assets absorbed into the trust, with a portion of the trust used to fund new developments in the town. That is why we have a good library, a modern sheriff's office, a fine school, a top-class medical centre. This town doesn't have much, but what it does have comes from the trust.'

'What it has, good or otherwise, comes from four dead children,' I replied. 'Can you tell me anything more about Adelaide and William Modine?'

Hyams's mouth twitched slightly. 'As I've said, it was a long time ago and I really would prefer not to go into it. I had very little to do with either of them: the Modines were a wealthy family, their children went to a private school. We didn't mix very much, I'm afraid.'

'Did your father know the family?'

'My father delivered both William and Adelaide. I do remember one curious thing, but it will hardly be of any great help to you. Adelaide was one of twins. The male twin died in the womb and their mother died from complications shortly after the birth. The mother's death was surprising. She was a strong, domineering woman. My father thought she would have outlived us all.' He took a long sip from his glass and his eyes grew sharp with a remembered perception. 'Do you know anything about hyenas, Mr Parker?'

'Very little,' I admitted.

'Spotted hyenas frequently have twins. The cubs are extremely well developed at birth: they have fur and sharp incisor teeth. One cub will almost invariably attack the other, sometimes while still in the amniotic sac and typically to the death. The victor is also usually female and, if she is the daughter of a dominant female, will in turn become the dominant female in the pack. It's a matriarchal culture. Female spotted-hyena foetuses have higher levels of testosterone than adult males and the females have masculine characteristics, even in the womb. In adulthood the sexes can still be difficult to differentiate.'

He put his glass down. 'My father was an avid amateur naturalist. The animal world always fascinated him and I think he liked to find points of comparison between the animal world and the human world.'

'And he found one in Adelaide Modine?'

'Perhaps, in some ways. He was not fond of her.'

'Were you here when the Modines died?'

'I returned home the evening before Adelaide Modine's body was found and I attended the autopsy. Call it gruesome curiosity. Now, I'm sorry, Mr Parker, but I have nothing more to say and a great deal of work to do.'

He led me to the door and pushed open the screen to let me out.

'You don't seem particularly anxious to help me find Catherine Demeter, Mr Hyams.'

He breathed in heavily. 'Who suggested that you talk to me, Mr Parker?'

'Alvin Martin mentioned your name.'

'Mr Martin is a good, conscientious deputy and an asset to this town, but he is still a comparatively recent arrival,' said Hyams. 'The reason why I am reluctant to talk is a matter of client confidentiality. Mr Parker, I am the only lawyer in this town. At some point, nearly everyone who lives here, regardless of colour, income, religious or political belief, has passed through the door of my office. That includes the parents of the children who died. I know a great deal about what happened here, Mr Parker, more than I might wish to know and certainly much more than I plan to share with you. I'm sorry, but that's the end of the matter.'

'I see. One more thing, Mr Hyams.'

'Yes?' he asked, wearily.

'Sheriff Granger lives on this road too, doesn't he?'

'Sheriff Granger lives next door, the house on the right here. This house has never been burgled, Mr Parker, a fact that is surely not unconnected. Goodnight.'

He stood at the screen door as I drove away. I cast a glance at the sheriff's house as I passed but there were no lights within and there was no car in the yard. As I drove back to Haven, raindrops began to strike the screen and by the time I reached the outskirts of the town it had turned into a harsh, ceaseless downpour. The lights of the motel appeared through the rain. I could see Rudy Fry standing at the door, staring out into the woods and the gathering darkness beyond.

By the time I had parked, Fry was back behind his desk.

'What do folks do around here for fun, apart from trying to run other folks out of town?' I asked.

Fry grimaced as he tried to separate the sarcasm from the substance of the question. 'There ain't much to do around here outside of drinking at the Inn,' he replied, after a while.

'I tried that. Didn't care for it.'

He thought for a little while longer. I waited for the smell of smoke but it didn't come.

'There's a restaurant in Dorien, 'bout twenty miles east of here. Milano's, it's called. It's Italian.' He pronounced it Eyetalian, in a tone that suggested Rudy Fry was not overfond of any Italian food that didn't come in a box with grease dripping from the vents. 'Never eaten there myself.' He sniffed, as if to confirm his suspicion of all things European.

I thanked him, then went to my room, showered and changed. I was getting tired of the unrelenting hostility of Haven. If Rudy Fry didn't like somewhere, then that was somewhere I probably wanted to be.

Dorien wasn't much bigger than Haven but it had a bookstore and a couple of restaurants, which made it a cultural oasis of sorts. I bought a typescript copy of *Viva* by e.e. cummings in the bookstore and wandered into Milano's to eat.

Milano's had red check tablecloths and candles set in miniatures of the Coliseum, but it was almost full and the food looked pretty good.

A slim maître d' in a red bow-tie bustled over and showed me to a table in the corner. I took out the copy of cummings and read 'somewhere i have never travelled' while I waited for a menu, enjoying the cadence and gentle eroticism of the poem.

Susan had never read cummings before we met and I sent her copies of his poems during the early days of our relationship. In a sense, I let cummings do my courting for me. I think I even incorporated a line of cummings into the first letter I sent her. When I look back on it, it was as much a prayer as a love-letter, a prayer that Time would be gentle with her, because she was very beautiful.

A waiter strolled over and I ordered bruschetta and a carbonara from the menu, with water. I cast a glance around the restaurant but no one seemed to be paying me much attention, which was fine with me. I had not forgotten the warning Angel and Louis had given to me, or the couple in the red jeep.

The food, when it arrived, was excellent. I was surprised at my appetite and, while I ate, I turned over in my mind what I had learned from Hyams and the microfiche, and I remembered the handsome face of Walt Tyler, surrounded by police.

And I wondered, too, about the Travelling Man, before forcing him from my mind along with the images that came with him. He was not to be so easily denied. After I finished the water and paid the bill, I left the restaurant and vomited in an alleyway until my throat ached. Then I got back in my car and returned to Haven.

# Chapter Twenty-Two

My grandfather used to say that the most terrifying sound in the world was the sound of a shell being loaded into a pump-action shotgun, a shell that was meant for you. It woke me from my sleep in the motel as they came up the stairs, the hands of my watch glowing the time at 3.30 a.m. They came through the door seconds later, the sound of the explosions deafeningly loud in the silence of the night as shot after shot was fired into my bed, sending feathers and shreds of cotton into the air like a cloud of white moths.

But by then I was already on my feet, my gun in my hand. The sound of the shots was blocked slightly by the closed connecting door, just as the sound of the door opening into the hall was blocked from them, even when the firing had stopped and their ears sang with the hard notes of the gun and their eyes widened as they realised I was not in the bed. The decision not to make myself an easy target by sleeping in my assigned room had paid off.

I came into the hall quickly, turned and aimed. The man from the red jeep stood in the hall, the barrel of the Ithaca 12-gauge pump close to his face. Even in the dim hall light I could see that there were no shell casings on the ground at his feet. It had been the woman who fired the shots.

Now he spun towards me as the woman swore from inside the room. The barrel of the shotgun came down as he turned in my direction. I fired one shot and a dark rose bloomed at his throat and blood fell like a shower of petals on his white shirt. The shotgun dropped to the carpet as his hands clutched for his neck. He folded to his knees and fell flat on the floor, his body thrashing and jerking like a fish out of water.

The barrel of a shotgun appeared from behind the door jamb and the woman fired indiscriminately into the hall, plaster leaping from the walls. I felt a tug at my right shoulder and then sharp white-hot pain through my arm. I tried to hold on to my gun but I lost it on the ground as the woman continued firing, deadly shot zinging through the air and exploding in the walls around me.

I ran down the hall and through the door leading to the fire stairs, tripping and tumbling down the steps as the shooting stopped. I knew she would come after me as soon as she had made certain that her partner was dead. If there had been any chance of him surviving, I think she might have tried to save him, and herself.

I made it to the second floor but I could hear her steps pounding on the stairs above me. The pain in my arm was intense and I felt certain she would reach me before I got to the ground level.

I slipped through the door into the hallway. Plastic sheeting lay upon the ground and two step-ladders stood like steeples at either wall. The air was heavy with the smell of paint and spirits.

Twenty feet from the door was a small alcove, almost invisible until you were upon it, which contained a fire hose and a heavy, old-style water-based extinguisher. There was an identical alcove near my own room. I slipped into it, leaning against the wall and trying to control my breathing. Lifting the extinguisher with my left hand I tried to hold it underneath with my right in a vain effort to use it as a weapon but my arm, bleeding heavily by now, was useless and the extinguisher was too awkward to be effective. I heard the woman's steps slowing and the door sighed softly as she moved into the hall. I listened to her steps on the plastic. There was a loud bang as she kicked open the door of the first room on the floor, then a second bang as she repeated the exercise at the next door. She was almost upon me now and, though she walked softly, the plastic betrayed her. I could feel blood pouring down my arm and dripping from the ends of my fingers as I unwound the hose and waited for her to come.

She was almost level with the alcove when I swung the hose forward like a whip. The heavy brass nozzle caught her in the middle of her face and I heard bone crunch. She staggered back, harmlessly loosing off a blast from the shotgun as she raised her left hand instinctively to her face. I swung the hose again, the rubber glancing against her outstretched hand while the nozzle connected with the side of her head. She moaned and I slipped from the alcove as quickly as I could, the brass nozzle of the hose now in my left hand, and wrapped the rubber around her neck like the coils of a snake.

She tried to move her hand on the shotgun, the stock against her thigh in an effort to pump a cartridge as blood from her battered face flowed between the fingers of her right hand. I kicked hard at the gun and it fell from her grasp as I pulled her tightly against my body, bracing myself against the wall, one leg entwined with hers so she could not pull away, the other holding the hose taut. And there we stood like lovers, the nozzle now warm with blood in my hand and the hose tight against my wrist, as she struggled and then went limp in my grip.

When she stopped moving I released her and she slumped to the ground. I unwound the hose from her neck and, taking her by the hand, I pulled her down the stairs to ground level. Her face was reddish-purple and I realised I had come close to killing her, but I still wanted her where I could see her.

Rudy Fry lay grey on the floor of his office, blood congealing on his face and around the dent in his fractured skull. I called the sheriff's office, and, minutes later, heard the sirens and saw the red and blue glow of the lights spinning and reflecting around the darkened lobby, the blood and the flashes reminding me once again of another night and other deaths. When Alvin Martin entered with his gun in his hand I was nauseous with shock and barely able to stand, the red light like fire in my eyes.

'You're a lucky man,' said the elderly doctor, her smile a mixture of surprise and concern. 'Another couple of inches and Alvin here would have been composing a eulogy.'

'I bet that would have been something to hear,' I replied.

I was sitting on a table in the Emergency room of Haven's small but well-equipped medical centre. The wound in my arm was minor but had bled heavily. Now it had been cleaned and strapped and my good hand clutched a bottle of pain-killers. I felt like I'd been sideswiped by a passing train.

Alvin Martin stood beside me. Wallace and another deputy I didn't recognise were down the hall, guarding the room in which the woman was being kept. She had not regained consciousness and, from what I had heard of the doctor's hurried conversation with Martin, I believed that she might have lapsed into a coma. Rudy Fry was also still unconscious, although he was expected to recover from his injuries.

'Anything on the shooters?' I asked Martin.

'Not yet. We've sent photos and prints to the feds. They're going to send someone from Richmond later today.' The clock on the wall read 6.45 a.m. Outside the rain continued to fall.

Martin turned to the doctor. 'Could you give us a minute or two in private, Elise?'

'Certainly. Don't strain him, though.' He smiled at her as she left but when he turned back to me the smile was gone. 'You came here with a price on your head?'

'I'd heard a rumour, that's all.'

'Fuck you and your rumour. Rudy Fry almost died in there and I've got an unidentified corpse in the morgue with a hole in his neck. You know who called out the hit?'

'I know who did it.'

'You gonna tell me?'

'No, not yet anyway. I'm not going to tell the feds, either. I need you to keep them off my back for a while.'

Martin almost laughed. 'Now why am I gonna do that?'

'I need to finish what I came down here to do. I need to find Catherine Demeter.'

'This shooting have anything to do with her?'

'I don't know. It could have but I don't see where she fits in. I need your help.'

Martin bit his lip. 'The town council's running wild. They reckon if the Japanese get wind of this they'll open up a plant in White Sands before they come here. Everyone wants you gone.'

A nurse entered the room and Martin stopped talking, preferring instead to seethe quietly as she spoke. 'There's a call for you, Mr Parker,' she said. 'A Detective Cole from New York.'

I winced at the pain in my arm as I rose and she seemed to take pity on me. I wasn't above accepting pity at that point.

'Stay where you are,' she said with a smile. 'I'll bring in an extension and we can patch the call through.'

She returned minutes later with the phone and plugged the jack into a box on the wall. Alvin Martin hovered uncertainly for a moment beside me and then stomped out, leaving me alone.

'Walter?'

'A deputy called. What happened?'

'Two of them tried to take me out in the motel. A man and a woman.'

'How badly are you hurt?'

'A nick on the arm. Nothing too serious.'

'The shooters get away?'

'Nope. The guy's dead. The woman's in a coma, I think. They're patching in the pics and the prints at the moment. Anything at your end? Anything on Jennifer?' I tried to block out the image of her face but it hung at the edge of my consciousness, like a figure glimpsed at the periphery of one's vision.

'The jar was spotless. It was a standard medical storage jar. We've tried checking the batch number with the manufacturers but they went out of business in nineteen ninety-two. We'll keep trying, see if we can access old records, but the chances are slim. The wrapping paper must be sold in every damn gift shop in the country. Again, no prints. The lab is looking at skin samples to see if we can pick up anything from them. Technical guys figure he bounced the call and there's probably no way we can trace it. I'll let you know if there's anything further.'

'And Stephen Barton?'

'Nothing there either. The amount I know, I'm starting to think that I may be in the wrong business. He was knocked unconscious by a blow to the head, like the ME said, and then strangled. Probably driven to the parking lot and tipped into the sewer.'

'The feds still looking for Sonny?'

'I haven't heard otherwise but I assume they're out of luck too.'

'There doesn't seem to be much luck around at the moment.'

'It'll break.'

'Does Kooper know what happened here?'

I could hear what sounded like a choked laugh at the other

end of the line. 'Not yet. Maybe I'll tell him later in the morning. Once the name of the Trust is kept out of it he should be okay, but I don't know how he feels about the hired help whacking people outside motel rooms. I don't imagine it's happened before. What's the situation at your end?'

'The natives aren't exactly greeting me with open arms and *leis*. No sign of her so far but something isn't sitting right here. I can't explain it, but everything feels wrong.'

He sighed. 'Keep in touch. Anything I can do here?'

'I guess there's no way you can keep Ross off my back?'

'None whatsoever. Ross couldn't dislike you more if he heard that you screwed his mother and wrote her name on the wall of the men's room. He's on his way.'

Walter hung up. Seconds later, there was a click on the line. I kind of guessed Deputy Martin might be the cautious sort. He came back in after allowing enough time to elapse so that it didn't look like he'd been listening. The expression on his face had changed, though. Maybe it hadn't been such a bad thing that Martin heard what he did.

'I need to find Catherine Demeter,' I said. 'That's why I'm here. When that's done, I'll be gone.'

He nodded.

'I had Burns call some of the motels in the area earlier,' he said. 'There's no Catherine Demeter checked in at any of them.'

'I tried that before I left the city. She could be using another name.'

'I thought of that. If you give me a description I'll send Burns around to check with the desk clerks.'

'Thanks.'

'Believe me, I ain't doing this out of the kindness of my heart. I just want to see you gone from here.'

'What about Walt Tyler?'

'If we get time, I'll drive out there with you later.' He went to check with the deputies guarding the shooter. The elderly doctor appeared again and checked the dressing on my arm.

'Are you sure you won't rest up here for a time?' she asked.

I thanked her for the offer but turned her down.

'I partly guessed as much,' she said. She nodded towards the phial of pain-killers. 'They may make you drowsy.'

I thanked her for the warning and slipped them in my pocket as she helped me to put on my jacket over my shirtless chest. I had no intention of taking the pain-killers. Her expression told me that she knew that as well.

Martin drove me to the sheriff's office. The motel had been sealed up and my clothes had been moved to his office. I showered, wrapping my bandaged arm with plastic first, and then slept fitfully in a cell until the rain stopped falling.

Two federal agents arrived shortly after midday and questioned me about what had taken place. The questioning was perfunctory, which surprised me until I remembered that Special Agent Ross was due to fly in later that evening. The woman had still not regained consciousness by 5.00 p.m., when Tyler came into the Haven diner.

'Did Burns turn up anything on Catherine Demeter?'

'Burns has been tied up with the feds since this afternoon. He said he'd check some of the motels before calling it a day. He'll let me know if there's any sign of her. You still want to see Walt Tyler, we'd better get going now.'

# Chapter Twenty-Three

Walt Tyler lived in a dilapidated but clean white clapboard house, against one side of which leaned a teetering pile of car tyres that were, according to a sign on the road, 'For Sale'. Other items of varying degrees of saleability, which rested on the gravel and the well-trimmed lawn, included two semi-restored lawn-mowers, various engines and parts of engines and some rusting gym equipment, including a full set of bars and weights.

Tyler himself was a tall, slightly stooped man with a full head of grey hair. He had been handsome once, as his picture had suggested, and he still held himself with a kind of loose-limbed grace, as if unwilling to admit that those looks were now largely gone, lost to cares and worries and the never-ending sorrow of a parent who has lost an only child.

He greeted Alvin warmly enough, although he shook my hand less cordially and seemed reluctant to invite us in. Instead he suggested that we sit on the porch, despite the prospect of further rain. Tyler sat in a comfortable-looking wicker chair and Martin and I on two ornate metal lawn chairs, the lost elements of a more complete set and also, according to the sign hung from the back of mine, 'For Sale'.

Without Tyler making any effort to ask for it, coffee was brought out in clean china cups by a woman younger than him by maybe ten years. She, too, had been more beautiful once, although in her the beauty of youth had matured into something perhaps more attractive yet, the calm elegance of a woman for whom old age held no fears and in whom lines and wrinkles would alter but not erase her looks. She cast a glance at Tyler and, for the first time since we arrived, he smiled slightly. She returned it and went back into the house. We didn't see her on the porch again.

The deputy began to speak but Tyler stopped him with a slight movement of his hand. 'I know why you're here, Deputy. There's only one reason why you'd bring a stranger to my home.' He looked hard at me, his eyes yellowing and rimmed with red but with an interested, almost amused, look in them.

'You the fella been shooting up folks in the motel?' he asked, and the smile flickered briefly. 'Excitin' life you lead. Your shoulder hurt?'

'A little.'

'I was shot once, in Korea. Shot in the thigh. Hurt more'n a little. Hurt like hell.' He winced exaggeratedly at the memory and then was quiet again. I heard thunder rumble above us, and the porch seemed to grow dark for a time, but I could still see Walt Tyler looking at me and now the smile was gone.

'Mr Parker's an investigator, Walt. He used to be a detective,' said Alvin.

'I'm looking for someone, Mr Tyler,' I began. 'A woman. You probably remember her. Her name is Catherine Demeter. She's Amy Demeter's younger sister.'

'I knew you weren't no writer. Alvin wouldn't bring one o' them . . .' he searched for the word '. . . *leeches* here.' He reached for his coffee and sipped long and quietly, as if to stop himself from saying more on the subject, and, I thought, to give him time to consider what I had said. 'I remember her, but she ain't been back since her pappy died and that's better'n ten years. She ain't got no reason to come back here.'

That statement was taking on the sensation of an echo. 'Still, I think she did, and I think it can only be connected with what happened before,' I replied. 'You're one of the only ones left, Mr Tyler, you and the sheriff and one or two others, the only ones involved with what took place here.'

I think it had been a long time since he had spoken of it aloud, yet I knew that no long period went by without him returning to it in his thoughts or without him being dimly or acutely aware of it, like an old ache that never fades but which is sometimes forgotten in the throes of another activity and then returns in the forgetting. And I thought that each return was etched with a line in his face, and so a once-handsome man could lose his looks like a fine marble statue slowly chipped away to a memory of its former self.

'I still hear her sometimes, y'know. Can hear her step on the porch at night, can hear her singing in the garden. At first, I used to run out when I heard her, not knowing but I was sleeping or waking. But I never saw her and after a time I stopped running, though I still waked to her. She don't come as often now.'

Perhaps he saw something in my face, even in the slow-darkening evening, which led him to understand. I do not know for certain and he gave no sign that he knew or that there was anything more between us than a need to know and a desire to tell, but he stopped for a moment in the telling and in that pause we all but touched, like two travellers who pass on a long, hard road and offer comfort to each other in the journey.

'She was my only child,' he continued. 'She disappeared on the way back from town on a fall day and I never saw her alive again. Next I saw her, she was bone and paper and I didn't know her. My wife – my late wife – she reported her missing to the police, but nobody came for a day or two and in that time we searched the fields and the houses and anywhere we could. We walked from door to door, knocking and asking, but nobody could tell us where she was or where she might have been. And then, three days after she went, a deputy came and arrested me and accused me of killing my child. They held me for two days, beat me, called me a rapist, an abuser of children, but I never said anything but what I knew to be true, and after a week they let me go. And my little girl never appeared.'

'What was her name, Mr Tyler?'

'Her name was Etta Mae Tyler and she was nine years old.'

I could hear the trees whispering in the wind and the boards of the house creaking and settling. In the yard, a child's swing moved back and forth as a gust caught it. It seemed that there was movement all around us as we spoke, as if our words had awoken something that had been asleep for a long time.

'Two other children disappeared three months later, black children both, one within a week of the other. Cold it was. Folks thought the first child, Dora Lee Parker, might have fallen through some ice while playing. She was the very devil for ice, that child. But all the rivers were searched, all the ponds dredged, and they didn't find her. The police, they came and questioned me again, and for a time even some of my own neighbours looked at me kinda funny. But then the police's interest all died away again. These were black children and they saw no reason to go connectin' the two vanishings.

'The third child didn't come from Haven, he came from Willisville, about forty miles away. 'Nother black child, little boy named . . .' He stopped and put the palm of his hand to his forehead, pressing lightly, his eyes closed tight. 'Bobby Joiner,' he finished quietly, nodding slightly. 'By then, people was getting scared and a deputation was sent to the sheriff and the mayor. People started keeping their children inside, 'specially after dark, and the police, they questioned every black man for miles around, and some white folks too, poor men they knew to be homosexuals, mostly.

'I think then there was a waiting period. Those people

waited for the black folks to breathe easy again, to get careless, but they did not. It went on and on, for months, till early in nineteen seventy. Then the little Demeter girl disappeared and everything changed. The police, they questioned people for miles around, took statements, organised searches. But nobody saw a thing. It was like the little girl had disappeared into thin air.

'Things got bad then for black folks. The police figured there might be a connection between the disappearances after all, and they called in the FBI. After that, black men walking around town after dark were liable to get arrested or beaten, or both. But those people . . .' He used the phrase again and there was a kind of mental shake of the head in his voice, a gesture of horror at the ways of men. 'Those people had a taste for what they were doing, and couldn't stop. The woman tried to snatch a little boy in Batesville but she was alone and the boy fought and kicked and scratched her face and ran away. She chased after him, too, but then she gave up. She knew what was coming.

'The boy was a sharp one. He remembered the make of the car, described the woman, even recalled some of the numbers on the license plate. But it wasn't till the next day that someone else recalled the car and they went looking for Adelaide Modine.'

'The police?'

'No, not the police. A mob of men, some from Haven, others from Batesville, two or three from Yancey Mill. The sheriff, he was out of town when it happened and the FBI men had gone. But Deputy Earl Lee Granger, as was, he was with them when they arrived at the Modine house, but she was gone. There was only the brother there and he shut himself in the basement, but they broke in.'

He was silent then and I heard him swallow in the gathering dark, and I knew that he had been with them. 'He said he didn't know where his sister was, didn't know nothing about no dead children. So they hanged him from a beam in the roof and called it suicide. Got Doc Hyams to certify it, though that basement was fourteen feet from floor to ceiling and there was no way that boy could have gotten up there to hang hisself 'less he could climb walls. Folks after used to joke that the Modine boy wanted to hang hisself real bad to get up without help.'

'But you said the woman was alone when she tried to snatch the last child,' I said. 'How did they know the Modine boy was involved?'

'They didn't, at least they weren't sure. But she needed someone to help her do what she did. A child is a hard thing to take sometimes. They struggle and kick and cry for help. That's why she failed the last time, because she had no one to help her. At least, that's what they figured.'

'And you?'

The porch was quiet again. 'I knew that boy and he wasn't no killer. He was weak and . . . soft. He was a homosexual – he'd been caught with some boy back in his private school and they asked him to leave. My sister heard that, when she was cleaning for white folks in the town. It was hushed up, though there were stories about him. I think maybe some people had suspected him for a time, just for that. When his sister tried to take the child, well, folks just decided he must have known. And he must have, I guess, or maybe suspected at least. I don't know but . . .'

He glanced at Deputy Martin and the deputy stared right back at him. 'Go on, Walt. There's some things I know myself. You won't say anything I haven't thought or guessed.'

Tyler still looked uneasy but nodded once, more to himself than to us, and went on. 'Deputy Earl Lee, he knew the boy wasn't involved. He was with him the night Bobby Joiner was taken. Other nights too.'

I looked at Alvin Martin, who stared at the floor nodding slowly. 'How did you know?' I asked.

'I saw 'em,' he said simply. 'Their cars were parked out of town, under some trees, on the night Bobby Joiner was taken. I used to walk the fields sometimes, to get away from here, though it was dangerous, given all that was happenin'. I saw the cars parked and crept up and saw them. The Modine boy was . . . down . . . on the sheriff and then they got in the back and the sheriff took him.'

'And you saw them together after that?'

'Same place, couple of times.'

'And the sheriff let them hang the boy?'

'He wasn't going to say nothin',' Tyler spat, 'case someone found out about him. And he watched them hang that boy.'

'And his sister? What about Adelaide Modine?'

'They searched for her too, searched the house and the fields, but she was gone. Then someone saw a fire in the shell of an old house on the East Road about ten miles from town and pretty soon the whole place was ablaze. Thomas Packer, he used to store old paint and inflammables there, away from the children. And when the fire was out, they found a body, badly burned, and they said it was Adelaide Modine.'

'How did they identify her?

Martin answered, 'There was a bag near the body, with the remains of a lot of money, some personal papers, bank account details mostly. Jewellery she was known to have was found on the body, a gold and diamond bracelet she always wore. It was her mother's, they said. Dental records matched too. Old Doc Hyams produced her chart – he shared a surgery with the dentist, but the dentist was out of town that week.

'Seems she had holed up, maybe waiting for her brother or someone else to come to her, and fell asleep with a cigarette in her hand. She'd been drinking, they said, maybe to try to keep warm. The whole place went up. Her car was found near by, with a bag of clothes in the trunk.'

'Do you remember anything about Adelaide Modine, Mr Tyler? Anything that might explain—'

'Explain what?' he interrupted. 'Explain why she did it? Explain why someone helped her to do what she did? I can't explain those things, not even to myself. She had somethin', sure enough, somethin' strong inside her, but it was a dark thing, a vicious thing. I'll tell you somethin', Mr Parker. Adelaide Modine was as close to pure evil as I've met on this earth, and I've seen brothers hanged from trees and burned while they were hangin'. Adelaide Modine was worse than the people who did the hangin' because, try as I might, I can't see any reason for the things she did. They're beyond explainin', 'less you believe in the Devil and Hell. That's the only way I can explain her. She was a thing out of Hell.'

I stayed silent for a time, trying to sort and balance what I had been told. Walt Tyler watched while these thoughts went through my head and I think he knew what I was thinking. I couldn't blame him for not telling what he knew of the sheriff and the Modine boy. An allegation like that could get a man killed and it didn't provide conclusive proof that the Modine boy wasn't directly involved in the killings, although if Tyler's character assessment was right then William Modine was an unlikely child-killer. But the knowledge that someone involved in the death of his child might have eluded capture must have tortured Tyler all these years.

One part of the story still remained.

'They found the children the next day, just as the search had begun,' concluded Tyler. 'A boy out hunting took shelter in an abandoned house on the Modine estate and his dog started scraping at the cellar door. It was built into the floor, like a trapdoor. The boy shot the lock off and the dog went down and he followed. Then he ran home and called the police.

'There were four bodies down there, my little girl and the three others. They—' He stopped and his face creased but he did not cry.

'You don't have to go on,' I said softly.

'No, you gotta know,' he said. Then louder, like the cry of a wounded animal: 'You gotta *know* what they did, what they did to those children, to my child. They raped them and they tortured them. My little girl, all her fingers were broken, crushed, and the bones pulled away from the sockets.' He was crying openly now, his large hands open before him like a supplicant before God. 'How could they do those things, to children? How?' And then he seemed to retreat into himself and I thought I saw the woman's face at the window, and her fingertips brushing the pane.

We sat with him for a time and then stood up to leave. 'Mr Tyler,' I said gently, 'just one more thing. Where is the house where the children were found?'

'About three, four miles up the road from here. The old Modine estate starts there. There's a stone cross at the start of the track leading up to it. The house is pretty much gone now. There's just a few walls, part of a roof. State wanted to knock it down but some of us protested. We wanted to remind them of what had happened here, so the Dane house still stands.'

We left him then, but as I was going down the porch steps I heard his voice behind me.

'Mr Parker.' The voice was strong again and there was no quaver in it, although there was the lingering sound of grief in its tones. I turned to look at him. 'Mr Parker, this is a dead town. The ghosts of dead children haunt it. You find the Demeter girl, you tell her to go back where she came from. There's only grief and misery for her here. You tell her that now. You tell her that when you find her, y' hear?'

At the margins of his cluttered garden the whispering grew in the trees and it seemed that just beyond the line of vision, where the darkness became almost too dark to penetrate, there was movement. Figures drifted back and forth, skipping just outside the light from the house, and there was childish laughter in the air.

And then there were only the limbs of evergreens fanning the darkness and the empty jangling of a chain in the wreckage of the yard.

# Chapter Twenty-Four

On the Casuarina Coast, at the delta area of Irian in Indonesian New Guinea, lives a tribe called the Asmat. They are twenty thousand strong and the terror of every other tribe near them. In their language Asmat means 'the people – the human beings', and if they define themselves as the only humans, then all others are relegated to the status of non-human, with all that that entails. The Asmat have a word for these others: they call them *manowe*. It means 'the edible ones'.

Hyams had no answers that would have indicated why Adelaide Modine behaved as she did and neither did Walt Tyler. Maybe she, and others like her, had something in common with the Asmat. Perhaps they, too, saw others as less than human so that their suffering ceased to matter, was below notice apart from the pleasure it gave.

I recalled a conversation with Woolrich, after the meeting with Tante Marie Aguillard. Back in New Orleans, we walked in silence down Royal Street, past Madame Lelaurie's old mansion where slaves were once chained and tortured in the attic until some firefighters found them and a mob ran Madame Lelaurie out of town. We ended up at Tee Eva's on Magazine, where Woolrich ordered sweet potato and a Jax beer. He ran his thumb down the side of the bottle, clearing a path through the moisture, and then rubbed his damp thumb along his upper lip.

'I read a Bureau report last week,' he began. 'I guess it was a "state of the nation" address on serial killers, on where we stand, where we're going.'

'And where are we going?'

'We're going to Hell is where we're going. These people are like a virus. They're like bacteria spreading and this country is just one big Petri dish to them. The Bureau estimates that we could be losing five thousand victims to serial killers each year. That's fourteen people every day. The folks watching Oprah and Jerry Springer, or subscribing to Jerry Falwell, they don't wanna know that. They read about them in the crime mags or see them on the TV, but that's only when we catch one of them. The rest of the time, they don't have the least idea what's going on around them.'

He drank a deep draught of Jax. 'There are at least two hundred of these killers operating at the present time. *At least* two hundred.' He was reeling off the numbers now, emphasising each statistic with a stab of the beer bottle. 'Nine out of ten are male, eight out of ten are white and one in five is never goin' to be found. Never.

'And you know what the strangest thing is? We've got more of them than anywhere else. The good old US of A is breeding these fuckers like fucking Elmo dolls. Three-quarters of them live and work in this country. We're the world's leading producer of serial killers. It's a sign of sickness, is what it is. We're sick and weak and these killers are like a cancer inside us: the faster we grow, the quicker they multiply.

'And you know, the more of us there are, the more distant from each other we become. We're practically livin' on top of each other but we're further away from each other spiritually, socially, morally, than we've ever been before. And then these guys come in, with their knives and their ropes, and they're even further removed than the rest of us. Some of them even have cop's instincts. They can sniff each other out. We found a guy in Angola in February who was communicating with a suspected child-killer in Seattle using Biblical codes. I don't know how these two freaks found each other, but they did.

'Strange thing is, most of them are even worse off than the rest of humanity. They're inadequate – sexually, emotionally, physically, whatever – and they're taking it out on those they see around them. They have no . . .' He shook his hands in the air, searching for the word. '. . . no vision. They have no larger vision of what they're doing. There's no purpose to it. It's just an expression of some kind of fatal flaw.

'And the people they're killing, they're so dumb that they can't understand what's happening around them. These killers should be a wake-up call, but nobody's listening, and that widens the gap even more. All they see is the distance and they reach across it and pick us off, one by one. All we can do is hope that, if they do it often enough, we'll spot the pattern and put together a link between us and them, a bridge across the distance.' He finished his beer and raised the bottle up, calling for another.

'It's the distance,' he said, his eyes on the street but his gaze beyond it, 'the distance between life and death, Heaven and Hell, us and them. They have to cross it to get close enough to us to take us, but it's all a matter of distance. They love the distance.'

And it seemed to me, as rain poured down on the window, that Adelaide Modine, the Travelling Man and the thousands of others like them who roamed the country were all united by this distance from the common crowd of humanity. They were like small boys who torture animals or take fish from tanks to watch them squirm and gasp in their death throes.

Yet Adelaide Modine seemed even worse than so many of

the others, for she was a woman and to do what she had done went not only against law and morality and whatever other titles we give to the common bonds that hold us together and prevent us from tearing each other apart, it went against nature, too. A woman who kills a child seems to bring out something in us that exceeds revulsion or horror. It brings a kind of despair, a lack of faith in the foundations upon which we have built our lives. Just as Lady Macbeth begged to be unsexed so as to kill the old king, so also a woman who killed a child appeared to be denatured, a being divorced from her sex. Adelaide Modine was like Milton's night-hag, 'lured with the smell of infant blood'.

I cannot countenance the death of children. The killing of a child seems to bring with it the death of hope, the death of the future. I recall how I used to listen to Jennifer breathe, how I used to watch the rise and fall of my infant daughter's chest, how I felt a sense of gratitude, of relief, with every inhalation and exhalation.

When she cried, I would lull her to sleep in my arms, waiting for the sobs to fade into the soft rhythms of rest. And when she was at last quiet, I would bend down slowly, carefully, my back aching from the strain of the position, and lay her in her cot. When she was taken from me it was like the death of a world, an infinite number of futures coming to an end.

I felt a weight of despair upon me as the motel drew closer. Hyams had said that he had seen nothing in the Modines that would have indicated the depths of evil that existed within them. Walt Tyler, if what he had said was true, saw that evil only in Adelaide Modine. She had lived among these people, had grown up with them, perhaps even played with them, had sat with them in church, had watched them marry, have children and then had preyed upon them, and no one had suspected her.

I think that I wanted a power I could not have: the power to perceive evil, the ability to look at the faces in a crowded room and see the signs of depravity and corruption. The thought sparked a memory of a killing in New York State some years before, in which a thirteen-year-old boy had killed a younger kid in the woods, beating him to death with rocks. It was the words of the killer's grandfather that had stayed with me. 'My God,' he said, 'I should have been able to see, somehow. There should have been something to see.'

'Are there any pictures of Adelaide Modine?' I asked eventually.

Martin's brow furrowed. 'There may be one in the files of the original investigation. The library may have some stuff too. There's a kind of town archive stored in its basement, y' know, yearbooks, photos from the paper. There may be something in there. Why d'you ask?'

'Curiosity. She was responsible for so much of what happened to this town but I find it hard to picture her. Maybe I want to see what her eyes looked like.'

Martin shot me a puzzled look. 'I can get Laurie to look in the library archives. I'll try to get Burns to look through our own files but it could take a while. They're all packed in boxes and the filing system is pretty obscure. Some of the files aren't even in date order. It's a lot of work to satisfy your idle curiosity.'

'I'd appreciate it anyway.'

Martin made a sound in his throat but didn't say anything else for a time. Then, as the motel appeared on our right, he pulled over to the side of the road. 'About Earl Lee,' he said.

'Go on.'

'The sheriff's a good man. He held this town together after the Modine killings, from what I hear, him and Doc Hyams and a couple of others. He's a fair man and I've no complaints about him.'

'If what Tyler said is true, maybe you should have.'

Martin nodded. 'That's as maybe. If he's right, then the sheriff's got to live with what he's done. He's a troubled man, Mr Parker, troubled by the past, by himself. I don't envy him anything but his strength.' He spread his hands wide and shrugged slightly. 'Part of me figures that you should stay here and talk to him when he comes back, but another part of me, the smart part, tells me that it would be better for all of us if you finished up your business as quickly as you can and then got out.'

'Have you heard from him?'

'No, I haven't. He had some leave coming to him and maybe he's a little overdue on returning, but I ain't gonna hold that against him. He's a lonely man. A man who likes the company of other men ain't gonna find much comfort here.'

'No,' I said, as the neon light of the Welcome Inn flickered beyond us. 'I guess not.'

The call came through almost as soon as Martin pulled away from the kerb. There had been a death at the medical centre: the unidentified woman who had tried to kill me the previous night.

When we arrived, two cruisers were blocking the entrance to the parking lot and I could see the two FBI men talking together at the door. Martin drove us through and as we got out of the car the two agents moved towards me in unison, their guns drawn.

'Easy! Easy!' shouted Martin. 'He was with me the whole time. Put them away, boys.'

'We're detaining him until Agent Ross arrives,' said one of the agents, whose name was Willox.

'You ain't detaining or arresting nobody, not until we find out what's going on here.'

'Deputy, I'm warning you, you're out of your league here.'

Wallace and Burns came out of the medical centre at that

point, alerted by the shouts. To their credit, they moved to Martin's side, their hands hanging close by their guns.

'Like I said, let it go,' said Martin quietly. The feds looked like they might push the issue but then they holstered their weapons and moved back.

'Agent Ross is going to hear of this,' hissed Willox to Martin, but the deputy just walked by.

Wallace and Burns walked with us to the room in which the woman had been kept.

'What happened?' asked Martin.

Wallace turned bright red and started blabbering. 'Shit, Alvin, there was a disturbance outside the centre and—'

'What kind of disturbance?'

'A fire in the engine of a car, belonged to one of the nurses. I couldn't figure it out. There weren't nobody in it and she hadn't used it since she got in this morning. I only left the door here for maybe five minutes. When I got back, she was like this . . .'

We arrived at the woman's room. Through the open door I could see the pale, waxy pallor of her skin and the blood on the pillow beside her left ear. Something metal, ending in a wooden handle, glinted in the ear. The window through which the killer had entered was still open and the glass had been shattered in order to unhook the latch. A small sheet of brown paper lay on the floor, with glass adhering to it. Whoever had killed the woman had taken the trouble to put syrup or glue on the paper before breaking the glass, in order to muffle the sound and to ensure that the glass didn't make any noise when it hit the floor.

'Who's been in here, apart from you?'

'The doctor, a nurse and the two feds,' said Wallace. The elderly doctor called Elise appeared behind us. She looked shaken and weary.

'What happened to her?' said Martin.

'A blade of some kind – I think it's an ice-pick – was thrust through her ear and into her brain. She was dead when we got to her.'

'Left the pick in her,' mused Martin.

'Clean and easy,' I said. 'Nothing to tie the killer to what happened if he – or she – gets picked up.'

Martin turned his back on me and began consulting the other deputies. I moved away as they talked and made my way towards the men's washroom. Wallace looked back at me and I made a gagging expression. He looked away with contempt in his eyes. I spent five seconds in the washroom and then slipped out of the centre through the rear exit.

Time was running out for me. I knew Martin would try to grill me on the source of the hit. Agent Ross wasn't far behind. At the very least, he'd hold me until he got the information he wanted and any hope I might have of finding Catherine Demeter would disappear. I made my way back to the motel, where my car was still parked, and drove out of Haven.

# Chapter Twenty-Five

The track to the ruin of the Dane house was heavy with mud and the car moved through it only with a great effort, as if nature itself was conspiring against my approach. It had started to rain heavily again, and the wind and rain combined to render the wipers almost useless. I strained my eyes for the stone cross and took the turning opposite. I missed the house the first time, only realising my mistake when the road turned into a mass of mud and fallen, rotting trees, forcing me to reverse slowly back the way I had come until I spotted two small ruined pillars to my left and, between them, the almost roofless walls of the Dane house briefly silhouetted against the darkening sky.

I pulled up outside the empty eyes of the windows and the gaping mouth of what was once the door, pieces of its lintel strewn on the ground like old teeth. I took the heavy Maglite from under my seat and climbed out, the rain painful on my head as I ran for what little shelter the interior of the ruin could offer.

Over half of the roof was gone and what remained still showed blackened and charred. There were three rooms: what had once been a kitchen and eating area, identifiable from the remains of an ancient stove in one corner; the main bedroom, now empty except for a stained mattress around which old prophylactics were scattered like the discarded skins of snakes; and a smaller room, which might have served as a children's bedroom once but was now a mass of old timber and rusting metal bars dotted with paint tins, left there by someone too lazy to haul them to the municipal dump. The rooms smelt of old wood, of long extinct fires and human excrement.

An old couch stood in one corner of the kitchen, its springs flowering through the rotting cushions. It formed a triangle with the corners of the wall, upon which the remains of some faded floral wallpaper hung tenaciously. I shone the flashlight over the back of the couch, my hand resting on the edge. It felt damp but not wet, for the remains of part of the roof still sheltered it from the worst of the elements.

Behind the couch and almost flush with the corners of the house was what appeared to be a trapdoor some three feet at each side. It was locked and its edges seemed filthy and choked with dirt. Its hinges were bloodied with rust and pieces of wood, and pieces of old metal covered most of its surface.

I pulled back the couch to take a closer look and started as I heard a rat scurry across the floor at my feet. It melted into the darkness in a far corner of the room and then was still. I squatted down to examine the lock and bolt, using my knife to scrape away some of the filth from around the keyhole. New steel shone through beneath the dirt. I ran the blade of the knife along the bolt, exposing a line of steel that shone like molten silver in the darkness. I tried the same experiment with the door but only flakes of rust greeted me.

I examined the bolt more closely. What had appeared at first sight to be rust now looked more like varnish, carefully applied so that it would blend in with the door. The bolt's battered look could easily have been achieved by tying it to the back axle of a car and pulling it over the rutted tracks of this part of the country. It wasn't a bad job, designed as it was to fool only necking teenagers seeking a thrill in a house of the dead, or children daring each other to tempt the ghosts of other children long gone.

I had a crowbar in the car but I was reluctant to brave the driving rain again. Shining the flashlight around the room, a steel bar some two feet long was caught in the beam. I picked it up, felt its weight, inserted it in the U of the lock and prised. For a moment it seemed the bar might bend or fracture under the strain but then there was a sharp crack as the lock broke. I pulled it free, released the bolt and raised the door on its complaining hinges.

A rich, heady stench of decay rose from the cellar, causing my stomach to churn. I covered my mouth and moved away, but seconds later I was vomiting by the couch, my nostrils filled with my own smell and the odour from the cellar below. When I had recovered and breathed in some fresh air outside the house, I ran to the car and took the window rag from the dashboard. I sprayed it with de-mister from the glove compartment and tied it around my mouth. The de-mister made my head reel but I stuck it in the pocket of my jacket in case I needed it again and re-entered the house.

Even breathing through my mouth and tasting the spray, the smell of putrefaction was overpowering. I descended the wooden stairs carefully, my strong left hand on the rail and the Maglite in my right with the beam shining at my feet. I didn't want to trip on a ruined step and plunge into the darkness below.

At the base of the steps the flashlight beam caught a glint of metal and blue-grey material. A heavy-set man in his sixties lay near the steps, his knees curled beneath him and his hands cuffed behind his back. His face was grey-white and there was a wound on his forehead, a ragged hole like a dark, exploding star. For a moment, as I shone the light upon it, I thought it was an exit wound but moving the light to the back of his head I saw the hole in his skull gape, saw the decaying matter within and the white totem of his spine.

The gun had probably been pressed right against his head. There was some gunpowder smudging around the forehead wound and the star-shaped rip had been caused by the gases shooting under the skin next to the bone, expanding and tearing open the forehead as they exploded. The bullet had exited messily, taking most of the back of his skull with it. The contact wound also explained the unusual position of the body: he had been shot while kneeling, looking up into the muzzle of the gun as it approached and falling sideways and back when the bullet entered. Inside his jacket was a wallet, with a driving license and police ID identifying him as Earl Lee Granger.

Catherine Demeter lay slumped against the far wall of the basement, nearly opposite the stairs. Granger had probably seen her as he walked or was pushed down. She was slouched like a doll at the wall, her legs spread out before her and her hands resting palms up on the floor. One leg was bent at an unnatural angle, broken below the knee, and I guessed that she had been thrown down the cellar stairs and dragged to the wall.

She had been shot once in the face at close range. Dried blood, brain tissue and bone fragments surrounded her head like a bloody halo on the wall. Both bodies had begun to decay rapidly in the cellar, which seemed to stretch the length and breadth of the house.

There were blisters on Catherine Demeter's skin and fluid leaked from her nose and eyes. Spiders and millipedes scuttled across her face and slipped through her hair, hunting the bugs and mites that were already feeding on the body. Flies buzzed. I guessed she had been dead for two or three days. I took a quick look around the cellar but it was empty apart from some bundles of rotting newspaper, some cardboard boxes filled with old clothes and a pile of warped timbers, the detritus of lives lived long before and now no more.

A scuffling noise on the floor above me, the sound of wood shifting despite careful footsteps, made me turn quickly and run for the stairs. Whoever was above me heard me, for the steps moved quicker with no regard for any noise that might be made. As my feet hit the first stairs the sound of the trapdoor hinges greeted me and I saw the patch of star-studded sky begin to shrink as the door came down. Two shots were fired randomly through the gap and I heard them impact on the wall behind.

The trapdoor was almost to the floor when I jammed the Maglite into the gap. There was a grunt from above and then I felt the flashlight being kicked repeatedly so that I had to grip it firmly to prevent it being wrenched from my hand. Still the bell-shaped end held firm but my injured right shoulder ached from the strain of pushing up and holding the torch.

Above me, the entire weight of my assailant was on the trapdoor as he continued to aim kicks at the flashlight. Below, I thought I heard the sound of rats scurrying in alarm but faced with the prospect of being trapped in that cellar it seemed like it might be something else. I felt that I might yet hear the sound of Catherine Demeter dragging her shattered leg across the floor and up the wooden steps, that her white fingers might grip my leg and pull me down to her.

I had failed her. I could not protect her from the violent end in this cellar where four young children before her had met muffled, terrified deaths. She had returned to the place where her sister had perished and, in a strange circularity, she had re-enacted a death that she had probably replayed many times in her mind before that day. In the moments before she died, she gained an insight into her sister's awful end. And so she would keep me company, console me for my weakness and my helplessness in the face of her passing, and lie beside me as I died.

As I breathed through gritted teeth, the stench of decay felt like a dead hand over my mouth and nostrils. I felt vomit rising once again and forced it down, for if I stopped pushing even for a moment I felt sure I would die in this cellar. Momentarily the pressure above me eased and I pushed upwards with all my remaining strength. It was an error that my opponent exploited to the full. The flashlight was kicked once, hard, and slipped through the enlarged gap. The trapdoor slammed shut like the door of my tomb, its echo mocking me from the walls of the cellar. I groaned in despair and began to press futilely against the door once again when there was an explosion from above and the pressure eased entirely, the trapdoor shooting upwards and coming to rest flat on the floor.

I flung myself out, my hand inside my jacket reaching for my gun and the Maglite casting wild shadows on the ceilings and walls as I landed awkwardly and painfully on the floor.

The beam caught the lawyer Connell Hyams leaning against the wall just beyond the rim of the door, his left hand to his wounded shoulder while his right hand tried to raise his gun. His suit was soaked and his clean white shirt clung to his body like a second skin. I held him in the beam, my gun outstretched in the other hand.

'Don't,' I said, but the gun was rising now and his mouth curled into a snarl of fear and pain as he brought it up to fire. Two shots sounded. Neither of them was from Hyams. He jerked as each bullet hit and his gaze moved from me to a place over my shoulder. As he fell I was already turning, the gun still following the beam of the flashlight. Through the glassless window I caught a glimpse of a thin besuited figure fading into the dark, its limbs like sheathed blades and a scar running across its narrow, cadaverous features.

Maybe I should have called Martin then and let the police and the FBI handle the rest. I was sick and weary inside and an almost overpowering sense of loss tore through me and threatened to unman me. The death of Catherine Demeter was like a physical pain, so that I lay for a moment on the ground, the body of Connell Hyams slumped opposite, and clutched my stomach in agony. I could hear the sound of a car as Bobby Sciorra drove away.

It was that sound that caused me to scramble to my feet. It had been Sciorra who had killed the assassin in the medical centre, probably under orders from the old man in case she implicated Sonny in the hit. Yet I couldn't understand why he had killed Hyams and why he had let me live. I staggered to my car, my shoulder aching, and started to drive towards Hyams's house.

# Chapter Twenty-Six

As I drove, I tried to piece together what had taken place. Catherine Demeter had returned to Haven in an effort to contact Granger, and Hyams had intervened. Maybe he had learned of Catherine's presence here by chance; the other possibility was that someone had informed him that she might be coming and had urged him to ensure that she never spoke to anyone when she got here.

Hyams had killed Catherine and Granger, that much seemed certain. At a guess, I reckoned that he had watched for the sheriff's return and followed him into his house. If Hyams had a key to the sheriff's house which, since he was a neighbour and a trusted citizen, was a likely possibility, Hyams could have listened to the messages on the sheriff's machine himself and, through that, could have learned of Catherine Demeter's location. Catherine Demeter was dead before the sheriff returned: Granger's body had not decayed to the same extent as Demeter's.

Hyams might even have erased the messages but he couldn't be certain that Granger had not picked them up by remote contact through a touch-tone phone. Either way, Hyams couldn't take any chances and acted, probably knocking the sheriff unconscious before cuffing him and then taking him to the Dane house, where he had already killed Catherine Demeter. The sheriff's car had probably been dumped or driven to another town and left somewhere it wouldn't attract undue attention, at least for the time being.

The use of the Dane house pointed to another part of the puzzle: Connell Hyams was almost certainly Adelaide Modine's accomplice in the killings, the man for whom William Modine had been hanged. That raised the question of why he had been forced to act now and I believed that I was close to an answer to that too, although it was a possibility that made me sick to my stomach.

Hyams's house was dark when I arrived. There was no other car parked near by but I kept my gun in my hand as I approached the door. The thought of facing Bobby Sciorra in the darkness made my skin crawl and my hands shook as I used the keys I had taken from Hyams's body to open the door.

Inside, the house was silent. I went from room to room, my heart pounding, my finger on the trigger of the gun. The house was empty. There was no sign of Bobby Sciorra.

I went through to Hyams's office, pulled the curtains and turned on the desk light. His computer was password-protected but a man like Hyams would have to keep hard copies of all his documents. I wasn't even sure what I was looking for, except that it was something that would connect Hyams to the Ferrera family. The connection seemed almost absurd and I was tempted to give up the search and return to Haven and explain it all to Martin and Agent Ross. The Ferreras were many things, but they were not the consorts of child-killers.

The key to Hyams's filing cabinets was also on the set I had taken from his body. I worked fast, ignoring local files and others that seemed irrelevant or unrelated. There were no files for the Trust, which seemed extraordinary until I remembered his office in town and my heart sank. If the Trust files were not kept in the house, there was a possibility that other files were not here either. If that was the case, the search could prove fruitless.

In the end, I almost passed over the link and only some half-remembered Italian phrases caused me to stop and consider it. It was a rental agreement for a warehouse property in Flushing, Queens, signed by Hyams on behalf of a company called Circe. The agreement was over five years old and had been made with a firm called Mancino Inc. Mancino, I remembered, meant 'left-handed' in Italian. It derived from another word meaning deceitful. It was Sonny Ferrera's idea of a joke: Sonny was left-handed and Mancino Inc. was one of a number of paper companies established by Sonny in the early part of the decade when he had not yet been reduced to the level of a sick, dangerous joke in the Ferrera operation.

I left the house and started driving. As I reached the town limits, I saw a pick-up by the side of the road. Two figures sat in the back, drinking beer from cans enclosed in brown paper bags, while a third stood leaning against the cab with his hands in his pockets. The headlights identified the standing man as Clete and one of the seated figures as Gabe. The third was a thin, bearded man whose face I didn't recognise. I caught Clete's eye as I passed and saw Gabe lean towards him and start talking, but Clete just raised a hand. As I drove away I could see him staring after me, caught in the headlights of the pick-up, a dark shadow against the light. I felt almost sorry for him: Haven's chances of becoming Little Tokyo had just taken a terminal beating.

I didn't call Martin until I reached Charlottesville.

'It's Parker,' I said. 'Anybody near you?'

'I'm in my office and you're in deep shit. Why'd you run out like that? Ross is here and wants all our asses, but yours especially. Man, when Earl Lee gets back there's gonna be hell to pay.'

'Listen to me. Granger's dead. So is Catherine Demeter. I think Hyams killed them.'

'*Hyams?*' Martin almost shrieked the name. 'The lawyer? You're out of your mind.'

'Hyams is dead too.' It was starting to sound like a sick joke, except I wasn't laughing. 'He tried to kill me out at the Dane house. The bodies of Granger and Catherine Demeter were dumped in the cellar there. I found them and Hyams tried to lock me in. There was some shooting and Hyams died. There's another player, the guy who took out the woman in the medical centre.' I didn't want to bring Sciorra's name into it, not yet.

Martin was silent for a moment. 'You gotta come in. Where are you?'

'It's not finished. You've got to hold them off for me.'

'I'm not holding anyone off. This town is turning into a morgue because of you and now you're a suspect in I don't know how many murders. Come in. You got enough trouble coming to you already.'

'I'm sorry, I can't do that. Listen to me. Hyams killed Demeter to prevent her contacting Granger. I think Hyams was Adelaide Modine's accomplice in the child-killings. If that's the case, if he escaped, then she could have escaped too. He could have rigged her death. He had access to her dental records through his father's surgery. He could have switched a set of records from another woman, maybe a migrant worker, maybe someone snatched from another town, I don't know. But something made Catherine Demeter run. Something sent her back here. I think she saw her. I think she saw Adelaide Modine because there's no other reason why she would have come back here, why she would have contacted Granger after all these years away.'

There was silence at the other end of the phone. 'Ross looks like a volcano in a linen suit. He's going to be on to you. He got your plates from your motel registration.'

'I need your help.'

'You say Hyams was involved?'

'Yes. Why?'

'I had Burns check our files. Didn't take as long as I thought it would. Earl Lee has . . . *had* the file relating to the killings. He used to check it out every so often. Hyams came looking for it, day before yesterday.'

'My guess is that, if you find it, any photos will be gone. I think Hyams probably searched the sheriff's house for it. He had to eliminate any traces of Adelaide Modine, anything that might link her to her new identity.'

It is hard to disappear. A trail of paper, of public and private records, follows us from birth. For most of us, they define what we are to the State, the Government, the law. But there are ways to disappear. Obtain a new birth certificate, maybe from a death index or by using someone else's birth name and DOB, and age the cert by carrying it around in your shoe for a week. Apply for a library card and, from that, obtain a voter's registration card. Head for the nearest DMV clerk, flash the birth certificate and the VRC, and you now have a driver's license. It's a domino effect, each step based on the validity of the documents obtained in the preceding step.

The easiest way of all is to take on another's identity, someone who won't be missed, someone from the margins. My guess was that, with Hyams's help, Adelaide Modine took on the identity of the girl who burned to death in a Virginia ruin. 'There's more,' said Martin. 'There was a separate file on the Modines. The photos from that are all gone as well.'

'Could Hyams have got access to those files?'

I could hear Martin sigh at the other end of the phone.

'Sure,' he said eventually. 'He was the town lawyer. He was trusted by everyone.'

'Check the motels again. I reckon you'll find Catherine Demeter's belongings in one of them. There might be something there.'

'Man, you gotta come back here, sort this out. There's a lot of bodies here and your name is connected with all of them. I can't do any more than I've done already.'

'Just do what you can. I'm not coming in.'

I hung up and dialled another number. 'Yeah,' answered a voice.

'Angel. It's Bird.'

'Where the fuck have you been? Things are going down here. Are you on the cellphone? Call me back on a land line.'

I rang him back seconds later from a call-box outside a convenience store.

'Some of the old man's goons have picked up Pili Pilar. They're holding him until Bobby Sciorra gets back from some trip. It's bad. He's being held in isolation at the Ferrera place – anyone talks to him and they get it in the head. Only Bobby gets access to him.'

'Did they get Sonny?'

'No, he's still out there, but he's alone now. He's gonna have to sort whatever it is out with his old man.'

'I'm in trouble, Angel.' I explained to him briefly what had taken place. 'I'm coming back but I need something from you and Louis.'

'Just ask, man.'

I gave him the address of the warehouse. 'Watch the place. I'll meet you there as soon as I can.'

I didn't know how long it would take them to start tracking

233

me. I drove as far as Richmond and parked the Mustang in a long-term parking bay. Then I made some calls. For $1500 I bought silence and a flight on a small plane from a private airfield back to the city.

# Chapter Twenty-Seven

'You sure you wanna be dropped here?' The cab driver was a huge man, his hair lank with sweat which dribbled down his cheeks and over the rolls of fat in his neck, eventually losing itself in the greasy collar of his shirt. He seemed to fill the whole front of the cab. The door looked too small for him to have entered through. He gave the impression that he had lived and eaten in the cab for so long that he had grown inside it, to the point where it was no longer possible for him to leave: the cab was his home, his castle, and his bulk gave the impression that it would be his tomb.

'I'm sure,' I replied.

'This is a tough area.'

'That's okay. I have tough friends.'

The Mancino wine warehouse was one of a number of similar premises that lined one side of a long, ill-lit street west of the Northern Boulevard in Flushing. It was a red-brick building, its name reduced to a white, flaking shadow below the edge of its roof. Wire panels covered the windows on both the ground and upper levels. There were no visible lights on the walls, leaving the area between the gate and the main building in almost total darkness.

On the other side of the street stood the entrance to a large yard filled with storage depots and railroad containers. The ground inside was pitted with ponds of filthy water and discarded pallets. I saw a mongrel dog, its ribs almost bursting through its fur, tearing at something in the dim light of the lot's filthy spotlights.

As I stepped from the cab, headlights flashed briefly from the alleyway by the warehouse. Seconds later, as the cab pulled away, Angel and Louis emerged from the black Chevy van, Angel carrying a heavy-looking training bag, Louis immaculate in a black leather coat, a black suit and a black polo-neck.

Angel screwed up his face as he drew nearer. It wasn't hard to see why. My suit was torn and covered with mud and dirt from the encounter with Hyams in the Dane house. My arm had begun to bleed again and the right cuff of my shirt was a deep red colour. I ached all over and I was tired of death.

'You look good,' said Angel. 'Where's the dance?'

I looked towards the Mancino warehouse. 'In there. Have I missed anything?'

'Not here. Louis just got back from Ferrera's place, though.'

'Bobby Sciorra arrived there about an hour ago by chopper,' said Louis. 'Reckon him and Pili are having a real heart-to-heart.'

I nodded. 'Let's go,' I said.

The warehouse was surrounded by a high brick wall topped with barbed wire and spiked fencing. The gate, inset slightly as the wall curved inwards at the entrance, was also wire-topped and solid except for a gap where a heavy lock and chain linked its two halves together. While Louis lounged semi-discreetly nearby, Angel removed a small, custom-built drill from his bag and inserted the bit into the lock. He pressed the trigger and a high-pitched grinding sound seemed to fill the night. Instantly, every dog in the vicinity started to bark.

'Shit, Angel, you got a fuckin' whistle built into that thing?' hissed Louis. Angel ignored him and moments later the lock fell open.

We entered and Angel gingerly removed the lock and placed

it inside the gate. He replaced the chain so that to a casual observer it would still appear secure if, oddly, locked from the inside.

The warehouse dated from the thirties but would have appeared functional even then. Old doors at the right and left sides had been sealed shut, leaving only one way in at the front. Even the fire exit at the back had been welded in place. The security lights, which might once have lit up the yard, now no longer functioned and the illumination from the street-lights did not penetrate the darkness here.

Angel went to work on the lock with a selection of skeleton keys, a flashlight in his mouth, and less than a minute later we were in, lighting our heavy Mags as we went. A small kiosk, which was probably once occupied by a security guard or watchman when the building was in use, stood directly inside the door. Empty shelves stretched along the walls of the room, paralleled by similar shelving through the centre creating two aisles. The shelves were separated into alcoves, each sufficient to hold a bottle of wine. The floor was stone. This had originally been the display area where visitors could examine the stock. Below, in the cellars, was where the cases were kept. At the far end of the room stood a raised office, reached by three stairs to the right.

Beside the small flight of stairs up to the office, a larger staircase descended down. There was also an old freight elevator, unlocked. Angel stepped in and pulled the lever, and the lift descended a foot or two. He brought it back to its original level, stepped out again and raised an eyebrow at me.

We started down the stairs. There were four flights, the equivalent of two storeys, but there were no other floors between the shop floor and the cellars. At the base was another locked door, this one wooden with a glass window through which the flashlight revealed the arches of the cellar. I left

Angel to the lock. It took him seconds to open the door. He looked ill-at-ease entering the cellars. The training bag appeared suddenly heavy in his hand.

'Want me to take that for a while?' asked Louis.

'When I'm that old you'll be feeding me through a straw,' replied Angel. Although the cellars were cool, he licked at sweat on his upper lip.

'Practically feeding you through a straw already,' muttered the voice from behind us.

In the basement, a series of curved, cave-like alcoves stretched away before us. Each had bars running vertically down from ceiling to floor, with a gate set in the middle. They were the old storage bins for the wine. They were obviously disused, strewn with litter and old packaging. The flashlight's beams caught the edge of the floor of one bin that differed from the others. It was the one nearest us on the right and had a coating of earth where the cement floor had been removed. Its gate stood ajar.

Our footsteps echoed around the stone walls as we approached. Inside, the floor was clean and the earth neatly raked. In one corner was a green metal table with two slits on either side through which ran leather restrainers. In another corner stood a large, industrial-sized roll of what appeared to be plastic sheeting.

Two layers of shelving ran around the walls. They were empty except for a bundle, tightly wrapped in plastic, which had been tucked in against the far wall. I walked towards it and the beam of the flashlight caught denim and a green check shirt; a pair of small shoes and a mop of hair; a discoloured face whose skin had cracked and burst and a pair of open eyes, the corneae milky and cloudy. The smell of decay was strong, but dulled somewhat by the plastic. I recognised the clothing. I had found Evan Baines, the child who had disappeared from the Barton estate.

'Sweet Jesus,' I heard Angel say. Louis was silent.

I drew closer to the body, checking the fingers and face. Apart from natural decay, the body was undamaged and the boy's clothing appeared undisturbed. Evan Baines had not been tortured before he died but there was some heavier discoloration at his temple and there was dried blood in his ear.

The fingers of his left hand were splayed against his chest but his small right hand had formed into a tightly closed fist.

'Angel. Come here. Bring the bag.'

He stood beside me and I saw the anger and despair in his eyes.

'It's Evan Baines,' I said. 'Did you bring the masks?'

He bent down and took out two dust masks and a bottle of Aramis aftershave. He sprinkled the aftershave on each mask, handed one to me and put the other one on himself. Then he handed me a pair of plastic gloves. Louis stood further back but didn't take a mask. Angel held the flashlight's beam on the body.

I took my penknife and sliced through the plastic by the child's right hand. Even through the mask the stench grew stronger and there was a hiss of escaping gas.

I took the blunt edge of the knife and prised at the boy's fist. The skin broke and a nail came loose.

'Hold the light steady, dammit,' I hissed. I could see something small and blue in the boy's grip. I prised again, heedless now of the damage I was causing. I had to know. I had to find the answer to what had happened here. Eventually, the object came loose and fell to the floor. I bent to pick it up and examined it by the light of my own flashlight. It was a shard of blue china.

Angel had begun scanning the far corners of the room with his flashlight as I examined the shard and then had left the room. As I clutched the piece of china, I heard the sound of his drill and then his voice calling us from above. We went back up the stairs and found him in a small room, little bigger than a closet, almost directly above the room where the boy lay. Three linked video-cassette recorders were stacked one above the other on some shelving and a thin cable snaked through a hole at the base of the wall and disappeared into the floor of the warehouse. On one of the VCRs the seconds ticked off inexorably until Angel stilled them.

'In the corner of that cellar there's a tiny hole, not much bigger than my fingernail but big enough to take a fish-eye and a motion sensor,' he said. 'An ordinary joe couldn't have found them unless he knew they were there and he knew where to look. I reckon the wire follows the ventilation system. Someone wanted to record what went on in that room any time it was entered.'

Someone, but not whoever went to work on the children in that room. A regular video camera set up in the room would give better quality pictures. There was no reason for concealment unless the viewer didn't want to be noticed.

There was no monitor in the room, so whoever was responsible either wanted to watch the tapes in the comfort of his or her own home or wanted to be sure that whoever picked them up couldn't sample what was on them before handing them over. I knew a lot of people who could put together a deal like that, and so did Angel, but I had one in particular in mind: Pili Pilar.

We went back down to the basement. I took the telescopic spade from Angel's bag and began to break the earth. I didn't take long to hit something soft. I dug wider and then began to scrape away the earth, Angel beside me using a small garden shovel to help. A film of plastic was revealed and through it, barely discernible, I could see brown, wrinkled skin. We scraped away the rest of the dirt until the child's body was visible, curled in a foetal position with its head hidden by its left arm. Even in decay, we could see the fingers had been broken, although I couldn't tell if it was a boy or a girl without moving it.

Angel looked slowly around the floor of the cellar and I knew what he was thinking. It was probably worse than that. This child had been buried barely six inches beneath the ground, which meant there were probably others below. This room had been in use for a long time.

Louis slipped into the room, his finger pressed to his lips. He glanced once at the child, then he pointed slowly above us with his right hand. We stayed still, hardly breathing, and I heard the sound of soft steps on the stairs. Angel retreated into the shadows beside the shelves, clicking off the flashlight as he went. Louis was already gone when I stood up. I moved to take up a position at the other side of the door and was reaching for my gun when a beam of light hit me in the face. The voice of Bobby Sciorra simply said, 'Don't,' and I withdrew my hand slowly.

He had moved quickly, surprisingly so. He emerged from the shadows, the sleek Five-seveN in his right hand and his flashlight focused on me as he neared the open gate. He stopped about ten feet away from me and I could see his teeth shining as he smiled.

'Dead man,' he said. 'Dead as the kids in the room behind you. I was gonna kill you back in that house but the old man wanted you left alive, 'less there was no other option. I just ran out of options.'

'Still doing Ferrera's dirty work,' I replied. 'Even you should have scruples about doing this.'

'We all have our weaknesses.' He shrugged. 'Sonny's is short-eyes. He likes looking, you know. Can't do nothing else with his limp dick. He's a sick fuck but his daddy loves him and now his daddy wants the mess cleaned up.'

And so it was Sonny Ferrera who had recorded the death agonies of these children, who had watched while Hyams and

Adelaide Modine tortured them to death, their screams echoing around the walls as the silent unblinking eye of the camera took it all in to spew out again into his living room. He must have known who the killers were, must have watched them kill again and again, yet he did nothing because he liked what he was seeing and didn't want it to end.

'How did the old man find out?' I asked, but I already knew the answer. I knew now what had been in the car with Pili when he crashed, or thought I knew. It turned out that I was as wrong in that as I had been in so much else.

There was a scuffle of movement in the corner of the alcove and Sciorra reacted with the swiftness of a cat. The light beam widened and he stepped back, the gun moving minutely from me to the corner.

The beam caught the bowed head of Angel. He glanced up into Bobby Sciorra's eyes and smiled. Sciorra looked puzzled for a moment and then his mouth opened in slow-dawning realisation. He was already turning to try to locate Louis when the darkness seemed to come alive around him and his eyes widened as he realised, too late, that death had come for him too.

Louis's skin gleamed in the a beam of the flashlight and his eyes were white as his left hand clamped tight over Sciorra's jaw. Sciorra seemed to tighten and spasm, his eyes huge with pain and fear. He rose up on his toes and his arms stretched wide at either side. He shook hard once, twice, then the air seemed to leave him and his arms and body sagged, yet his head remained rigid, his eyes wide and staring. Louis pulled the long, thin blade from the back of Sciorra's head and pushed him forward, and he fell to the ground at my feet, small shudders running through his body until they stopped entirely. I could smell the contents of his voided bladder and bowels.

Angel emerged from the darkness of the room behind me.

'I always hated that fucking spook,' he said, looking at the small hole at the base of Sciorra's skull.

'Yeah,' said Louis. 'I like him a whole lot better now.' He looked at me. 'What do I do with him?'

'Leave him. Give me his car keys.'

Louis frisked Sciorra's body and tossed me the keys.

'He's a made guy. Is that gonna be a problem?'

'I don't know. Let me handle it. Stay close to here. At some point, I'm going to call Cole. When you hear the sirens, disappear.'

Angel bent down and gingerly lifted the FN from the ground using the end of a screwdriver.

'We gonna leave this here?' he asked. 'That's some gun, what you say is true.'

'It stays,' I said. If I was right, Bobby Sciorra's gun was the link between Ollie Watts, Connell Hyams and the Ferrera family, the link between a set of child-killings that spanned thirty years and a Mob dynasty more than twice as old again.

I stepped over Sciorra's body and ran from the warehouse. His black Chevy was pulled into the yard, its trunk facing the warehouse, and the gates had been closed behind it. It looked a lot like the car that had taken out Fat Ollie Watts's killer. I reopened the gates and drove away from the Mancino warehouse and Queens itself. Queens, a mass of warehouses and cemeteries. And, sometimes, both together.

# Chapter Twenty-Eight

I was close now, close to an end, a termination of sorts. I was about to witness the cessation of something that had been happening for over three decades and that had claimed enough young lives to fill the catacombs of an abandoned warehouse. But no matter what the resolution might be, it was insufficient to explain what had taken place. There would be an ending. There would be a closure. But there would be no solution.

I wondered how many times each year Hyams had travelled up to the city in his neat lawyer's clothes, clutching an expensive yet understated overnight bag, in order to tear another child apart. As he boarded the train in front of the ticket collector, or smiled at the girl behind the airline check-in desk, or passed the woman at the toll booth in his Cadillac, the interior redolent with the scent of leather, had there been anything in his face which might have caused them to pause, to reconsider their assessment of this polite, reserved man with his trim grey hair and his conservative suit?

And I wondered also at the identity of the woman who had burned to death in Haven all those years ago, for it was not Adelaide Modine.

I remembered Hyams telling me that he had returned to Haven the day before the body was found. It was not difficult to put together a chain of events: the panicked call from Adelaide Modine; the selection of a suitable victim from the files of Doc Hyams; the alteration of the dental files to match the body; the planting of the jewellery and purse beside the corpse; and the flickering of the first flames, the smell like roasting pork, as the body began to burn.

And then she disappeared back into the darkness to hibernate, to find time to reinvent herself so the killing could continue. Adelaide Modine was like a dark spider squatting in the corner of a web, rushing out when a victim wandered into her sphere of influence and cocooning it in plastic. She had moved unhindered through thirty long years, presenting one face to the world and revealing another to the children. She was a figure glimpsed only by the young, a bogeyman, the creature waiting in the darkness when all the world was asleep.

I believed I could see her face now. I believed also that I understood why Sonny Ferrera had been hunted by his own father, why I had been tracked to Haven by Bobby Sciorra, why Fat Ollie Watts had fled in fear of his life and died in the roar of a gun in a street soaked in late summer sunlight.

The street-lights flashed by like pistol flares. There was dirt beneath my fingernails as I clutched the wheel and I had an almost irresistible desire to pull into a gas station and wash them clean, to take a wire brush and to scrub my skin until it bled, scraping away all the layers of filth and death that seemed to have adhered themselves to me in the past twenty-four hours. I could taste bile in my mouth and I swallowed back hard, focusing on the road ahead, on the lights of the car in front and, just once or twice, on the careless dusting of stars in the dark skies above.

When I arrived at the Ferrera house, the gates were open and there was no sign of the Feds who had watched the house earlier in the week. I drove Bobby Sciorra's car up the driveway and parked in the shadows beneath some trees. My shoulder ached badly now and bouts of nauseous sweating racked my body.

The front door of the house was ajar and I could see men moving inside. Beneath one of the front windows a dark-suited figure sat slouched with his head in his hands, his automatic lying discarded beside him. I was almost on top of him when he saw me.

'You ain't Bobby,' he said.

'Bobby's dead.'

He nodded to himself, as if this was no more than he expected. Then he stood up, frisked me and took my gun. Inside the house, armed men stood in corners talking in hushed tones. The place had a funereal air, a sense of barely suppressed shock. I followed my escort to the old man's study. He left me to open the door for myself, standing back to watch me as I did so.

There was blood and grey matter on the floor and a dark, black-red stain on the thick Persian carpet. There was blood also on the tan pants of the old man as he cradled his son's head in his lap. His left hand, its fingers red, toyed with Sonny's lank, thinning hair. A gun hung limply from the right, its barrel pointing at the floor. Sonny's eyes were open and in his dark pupils I could see the light of a lamp reflected.

I guessed that he had shot Sonny as he held his head in his lap, as his son knelt beside him pleading for . . . what? For help, for a reprieve, for forgiveness? Fat, depraved Sonny, with his thick, rubbery lips and his mad-dog eyes, dressed in a cheap cream suit and an open-necked shirt, gaudy with gold even in death. The old man's face was stern and unyielding but, when they turned to look at me, his eyes were weak with guilt and despair, the eyes of a man who has killed himself along with his son.

'Get out,' said the old man, softly but distinctly, but he wasn't looking at me now. A slight breeze blew in through the open French windows from the garden beyond, bringing with it some petals and leaves and the sure knowledge of the end of things. A figure had appeared, one of his own men, an older soldier whose face I recognised but whose name I did not know. The old man raised the gun and pointed it at him, his hand shaking now.

'*Get out!*' he roared, and this time the soldier moved, pulling the windows closed instinctively as he departed. The breeze simply blew them open again and the night air began to make the room its own. Ferrera kept the gun trained there for a few seconds longer and then it wavered and fell. His left hand, stilled by the arrival of his man, returned to its methodical stroking of his dead son's hair with the soothing, insane monotony of a caged animal stalking its pen.

'He's my son,' he said, not looking at me now but staring into a past that was and a future that might have been. 'He's my son but there's something wrong with him. He's sick. He's bad in the head, bad inside.'

There was nothing for me to say. I stayed silent.

'Why are you here?' he said. 'It's over now. My son is dead.'

'A lot of people are dead. The children . . .' For an instant the old man winced. '. . . Ollie Watts . . .'

He shook his head slowly, his eyes unblinking. 'Fucking Ollie Watts. He shouldn't have run. When he ran, we knew. Sonny knew.'

'What did you know?'

I think that if I had entered the room only minutes later the old man would have had me killed instantly, or would have killed me himself. Instead, he seemed to seek some sort of release through me. He would confess to me, unburden himself to me, and that would be the last time he would bring himself to speak it aloud.

'That he'd looked in the car. He shouldn't have looked. He shoulda just walked away.'

'What did he see? What did he find in the car? Videos? Pictures?'

The old man's eyes closed tightly, but he couldn't hide from what he had seen. Tears squeezed themselves from wrinkled corners and ran down the sides of his cheeks. His mouth formed silent words. No. No. More. Worse. When he opened his eyes again, he was dead inside. 'Tapes. And a child. There was a child in the trunk of the car. My boy, my Sonny, he killed a child.'

He turned to look at me again but this time his face was moving, twitching almost, as if his head could not contain the enormity of what he had seen. This man, who had killed and tortured and who had ordered others to kill and torture in his name, had found in his own son a darkness that was beyond naming, a dark, lightless place where slain children lay, the black heart of every dead thing.

Watching had no longer been enough for Sonny. He had seen the power these people had, the pleasure they took in tearing the life slowly from the children, and wanted to experience it too.

'I told Bobby to bring him to me but he ran, ran as soon as he heard about Pili.' His face hardened. 'Then I told Bobby to kill them all, all the rest, every one of them.' And then he seemed to be talking to Bobby Sciorra again, his face red with fury. 'Destroy the tapes. Find the kids, find where they are and then put them somewhere they'll never be found. Dump them at the bottom of the fucking ocean if you can. I want it like it never happened. It never happened.' Then he seemed to remember where he was and what he had done, at least for a time, and his hand returned to its stroking.

'And then you came along, trailing the girl, asking questions. How could the girl know? I let you go after her, to get you away from here, to get you away from Sonny.'

But Sonny had come after me through his hired killers and

they had failed. Their failure forced his father to act. If the woman lived and was forced to testify, Sonny would be cornered again. And so Sciorra had been dispatched, and the woman had died.

'But why did Sciorra kill Hyams?'

'What?'

'Sciorra killed a lawyer in Virginia, a man who was trying to kill me. Why?'

For a moment, Ferrera's eyes grew wary and the gun rose. 'You wearing a wire?' I shook my head wearily, and painfully ripped open the front of my shirt. The gun fell again.

'He recognised him from the tapes. That's how he found you. Bobby's driving through the town and suddenly he sees this guy driving in the opposite direction and it's the guy in the video, the guy who . . .' He stopped again and rolled his tongue in his mouth, as if to generate enough saliva to keep talking. 'All the traces had to be wiped out, all of them.'

'But not me?'

'Maybe he should've killed you too, when he had the chance, no matter what your cop friends would have done.'

'He should have,' I said. 'He's dead now.'

Ferrera blinked hard. 'Did you kill him?'

'Yes.'

'Bobby was a made guy. You know what that means?'

'You know what your son did?'

He was silent then, as the enormity of his son's crime swept over him once more, but when he spoke again there was a barely suppressed fury in his voice and I knew that my time with him was drawing to a close.

'Who are you to judge my son?' he began. 'You think because you lost a kid that you're the patron saint of dead children. Fuck. You. I've buried two of my sons, and now, now I've killed the last of them. You don't judge me. You don't judge my son.' The gun rose again and pointed at my head.

'It's all over,' he said.

'No. Who else was on the tapes?'

His eyes flickered. The mention of the tapes was like a hard slap to him.

'A woman. I told Bobby to find her and kill her too.'

'And did he?'

'He's dead.'

'Do you have the tapes?'

'They're gone, all burned.'

He stopped, as he remembered again where he was, as if the questions had briefly taken him away from the reality of what he had done and of the responsibility he bore for his son, for his crimes, for his death.

'Get out,' he said. 'If I ever see you again, you're a dead man.'

No one stood in my way as I left. My gun was on a small table by the front door and I still had the keys to Bobby Sciorra's car. As I drove away from the house it looked silent and peaceful in the rear-view, as if nothing had ever happened.

# Chapter Twenty-Nine

Each morning, after the deaths of Jennifer and Susan, I would wake from my strange, disordered dreams and, for an instant, it seemed that they might still be near me, my wife sleeping softly by my side, my child surrounded by her toys in a room near by. For a moment they still lived and I experienced their deaths as a fresh loss with each waking, so that I was unsure whether I was a man waking from a dream of death or a dreamer entering a world of loss, a man dreaming of unhappiness or a man waking to grief.

And amid all, there was the constant aching regret that I had never really known Susan until she was gone and that I loved a shadow in death as in life.

The woman and the child were dead, another woman and child in a cycle of violence and dissolution which seemed unbreakable. I was grieving for a young woman and a boy whom I had never encountered when they were alive, about whom I knew almost nothing, and through them I grieved for my own wife and child.

The gates of the Barton estate stood open; either someone had entered and planned to leave quickly or someone had already gone. There were no other cars in sight as I parked on the gravel drive and walked towards the house. Light was visible through the glass above the front door. I rang the bell twice but there was no answer, so I moved to a window and peered in.

The door into the hall was open and, in the gap, I could see a woman's legs, one foot bare, the other with a black shoe still clinging to its toes. The legs were bare to the tops of the thighs, where the end of a black dress still covered her buttocks. The rest of her body was obscured. I shattered the glass with the butt of my gun, half expecting to hear an alarm, but there was only the sound of the glass tinkling on the floor inside.

I reached in carefully to open the latch and climbed through the window. The room was illuminated by the hallway lights. I could feel my blood pounding through my veins, could hear it in my ears as I opened the door wider, sensed it tingling at the tips of my fingers as I stepped into the hall and looked at the body of the woman.

Blue veins marbled the skin on her legs and the flesh at the thighs was dimpled and slightly flabby. Her face had been pounded in and strands of grey hair adhered to the torn flesh. Her eyes were still open and her mouth was dark with blood. Only the stumps of teeth remained within, rendering her almost unrecognisable. There was only the gold, emerald-studded necklace, the deep red nail varnish and the simple yet expensive De La Renta dress to suggest the body was that of Isobel Barton. I touched the skin at her neck. There was no pulse – I hardly expected any – but she was still warm.

I stepped into the study where we had first met and compared the shard of china I had taken from Evan Baines's hand with the single blue dog on the mantelpiece. The pattern matched. I imagined Evan had died quickly when the damage was discovered, the victim of a fit of rage at the loss of one of Adelaide Modine's family heirlooms.

From the kitchen down the hall came a series of uneven clicking sounds and I could smell a faint odour of burning, like a pot left on a stove for too long. Above it, almost unnoticed until now, was the faint hint of gas. No light showed around the edge of the closed door as I approached, although the acrid smell grew more definite, more intense and the odour of gas was stronger now. I opened the door carefully and stepped back and to one side. My finger rested gently on the trigger but, even as I noticed the pressure, I was aware that the gun was useless if there was gas leaking.

There was no movement from within but the smell was very strong now. The strange, irregular clicking was loud, with a low drone above it. I took a deep breath and flung myself into the room, my useless gun attempting to draw a bead on anything that moved.

The kitchen was empty. The only illumination came from the windows, the hall and the three large, industrial microwave ovens side by side in front of me. Through their glass doors I could see blue light dance over a range of metal objects inside: pots, knives, forks, pans, all were alive with tiny flickers of silver-blue lightning. The stench of gas made my head swim as the tempo of the clicks increased. I ran. I had the front door open when there was a dull *whump* from the kitchen followed by a second louder bang and then I was flying through the air as the force of the explosion hurled me on to the gravel. There was the sound of glass breaking and the lawn was set aglow as the house burst into flames behind me. As I stumbled towards my car I could feel the heat and see the dancing fire reflected in the windows.

At the gate to the Barton estate, a pair of red brake lights glowed briefly and a car turned into the road. Adelaide Modine was covering her tracks before disappearing into the shadows once again. The house was ablaze, the flames escaping to scale the outside walls like ardent lovers, as I pulled into the road and followed the rapidly receding lights.

She drove fast down the winding Todt Hill road and in the silence of the night I could hear the shriek of her brakes as she negotiated the bends. I took her at Ocean Terrace, as she headed for the Staten Island Expressway. To the left, a steep slope dense with trees fell down to Sussex Avenue below. I gained on her, mounted the verge at Ocean and swung hard to the left, the weight of the Chevy forcing the BMW closer and closer to the verge, the tinted windows revealing nothing of the driver within. Ahead of me, I saw Todt Hill Road curve viciously to the right, and I pulled away to stay with the curve just as the BMW's front wheels left the road and the car plunged down the hill.

The BMW rolled on garbage and scree, striking two trees before coming to a stop half-way down the leaf-strewn slope, its progress arrested by the dark mass of a young beech. The roots of the tree were partially yanked from the ground and it arched backwards, its branches eventually coming to rest unsteadily against the trunk of another tree further down the slope.

I pulled the car on to the verge, its headlights still on, and ran down the slope, my feet slipping on the grass so that I was forced to steady myself with my good arm.

As I approached the BMW the driver's door opened and the woman who was Adelaide Modine staggered out. A huge gash had opened in her forehead and her face was streaked with blood so that amid the woods and the leaves, in the bleak reflected light of the heads, she seemed a strange, feral being, her clothes inappropriate trappings to be shed as she returned to her ferocious natural state. She was hunched over slightly, clutching her chest where she had slammed into the steering column, but she straightened painfully as I approached.

Despite her pain, Isobel Barton's eyes were alive with viciousness. Blood flowed from her mouth when she opened it and I saw her test something within with her tongue and then release a small bloodied tooth on to the ground. There was a cunning in her face, as if, even now, she was seeking a means of escape.

There was evil still in her, a foulness that went far beyond the limited viciousness of a cornered beast. I think concepts of justice, of right, of recompense, were beyond her. She lived in a world of pain and violence where the killing of children, their torture and mutilation, were like air and water to her. Without them, without the muffled cries and the futile, despairing twistings, existence had no meaning and would come to an end.

And she looked at me and seemed almost to smile. 'Cunt,' she said, spitting the word out.

I wondered how much Ms Christie had known or suspected before she died in that hallway. Not enough, obviously.

I was tempted to kill Adelaide Modine then. To kill her would be to stamp out one part of that terrible evil, which had taken my own child along with the lives of the children in the cellars, the same evil that had spawned the Travelling Man and Johnny Friday and a million other individuals like them. I believed in the Devil and pain. I believed in torture and rape and vicious, prolonged death. I believed in hurt and agony and the pleasure they gave to those who caused them, and to all these things I gave the name evil. And in Adelaide Modine I saw its red, sputtering spark exploded into bloody flame.

I cocked the pistol. She didn't blink.

Instead, she laughed once and then grimaced at the pain. She was now curled over again, almost foetal, near the ground. I could smell gasoline on the air as it flowed from the ruptured tank.

I wondered what Catherine Demeter had felt when she saw this woman in DeVries's department store. Had she glimpsed her in a mirror, in the glass of a display case? Had she turned in disbelief, her stomach tightening as if in the grip of a fist? And when their eyes met, when she knew that this was the woman who had killed her sister, did she feel hatred or anger, or simply fear, fear that this woman could turn on her as she had once turned on her sister? For a brief moment, had Catherine Demeter become a frightened child again?

Adelaide Modine might not have recognised her immediately but she must have seen the recognition in the eyes of the other woman. Maybe it was that slight overbite which gave it away, or perhaps she looked into the face of Catherine Demeter and was instantly back in that dark cellar in Haven, killing her sister.

And then, when Catherine could not be found, she had set about finding a resolution to the problem. She had hired me on a pretext and had killed her own stepson, not only so that he could not give the lie to her story but as the first step in a process which would lead to the eventual death of Ms Christie and the destruction of her home as she covered the traces of her existence.

Maybe Stephen Barton bore some blame for what happened, for only he could have provided a link between Sonny Ferrera, Connell Hyams and his stepmother, when Hyams was seeking somewhere to take the children, a property owned by someone who wouldn't ask too many questions. I doubt if Barton ever really knew what was taking place, and that lack of understanding killed him in the end.

And I wondered when Adelaide Modine had learned of the death of Hyams and realised that she was now alone, that the time had come to move on, leaving Ms Christie as a decoy just as she had left an unknown woman to burn in her place in Virginia.

But how would I prove all this? The videos were gone. Sonny Ferrera was dead, Pilar was certainly dead. Hyams, Sciorra, Granger, Catherine Demeter, all gone. Who would remember a child-killer from three decades ago? Who would recognise her in the woman before me? Would the word of Walt Tyler be enough? She had killed Christie, true, but even that might never be proved. Would there be enough forensic evidence in the wine cellars to prove her guilt?

Adelaide Modine, curled in a ball, unravelled like a spider that senses a shift in its web and sprang towards me, the nails of her right hand digging into my face, scratching for my eyes, while the left sought the gun. I struck her in the face with the heel of my hand, pushing her back simultaneously with my knee. She came at me again and I shot her, the bullet catching her above the right breast.

She stumbled back against the car, supporting herself on the open door, her hand clutching at the wound in her chest.

And she smiled.

'I know you,' she said, forcing the words out through the pain. 'I know who you are.'

Behind her, the tree shifted slightly as the weight of the car forced its roots up from the ground. The big BMW moved forward a little. Adelaide Modine swayed before me, blood pouring now from the wound in her chest. There was something bright in her eyes, something that made my stomach tighten.

'Who told you?'

'I know,' she said, and smiled again. 'I know who killed your wife and child.'

I moved towards her as she tried to speak again but her words were swallowed by the sound of grinding metal from the car as the tree finally gave way. The BMW shifted on the slope and then plummeted down the hill. As it rolled, impacting on trees and stones, the rending metal sparked and the car burst into flame. And as I watched, I realised that it was always meant to end this way.

Adelaide Modine's world exploded into yellow flame as the gasoline around her ignited; and then she was enveloped, her head back and her mouth wide for an instant before she fell, striking feebly at the flames as she toppled, burning, into the darkness. The car was blazing at the bottom of the slope, thick black smoke ascending in plumes into the air. I watched it from the road, the heat searing my face. Further down the hill, in the wooded dark, a smaller pyre burned.

# Chapter Thirty

I sat in the same police interview room with the same wooden table with the same wooden heart carved into its surface. My arm was freshly bandaged and I had showered and shaved for the first time in over two days. Despite Agent Ross's best effort, I was not in a jail cell. I had been interrogated comprehensively, first by Walter and another detective, then by Walter and the Chief of Detectives and, finally, by Ross and one of his agents, with Walter in attendance to make sure they didn't beat me to death out of frustration.

Once or twice I thought I caught glimpses of Philip Kooper striding around outside, like a corpse that had exhumed itself to sue the undertaker. I guessed that the Trust's public profile was about to take a serious hammering.

I told the cops nearly everything. I told them about Sciorra, about Hyams, about Adelaide Modine, about Sonny Ferrera. I did not tell them that I had become involved in the case at Walter Cole's instigation. The other gaps in my story I left them to fill in for themselves. I told them simply that I had taken some leaps of the imagination. Ross almost had to be forcibly restrained at that point.

Now there was only Walter and me and a pair of coffee cups.

'Have you been down there?' I asked eventually, breaking the silence.

Walter nodded. 'Briefly. I didn't stay.'

'How many?'

'Eight so far, but they're still digging.'

And they would continue digging, not just there but perhaps in scattered locations across the state and maybe even further afield. Adelaide Modine and Connell Hyams had been free to kill for thirty years. The Mancino warehouse had been rented for only a portion of that time, which meant that there were probably other warehouses, other deserted basements, old garages and disused lots that contained the remains of lost children.

'How long had you suspected?' I asked.

He seemed to think I was asking about something else, maybe a dead man in the toilet of a bus station, because he started and turned to me. 'Suspected what?'

'That someone in the Barton household was involved in the Baines disappearance.'

He almost relaxed. Almost. 'Whoever took him had to know the grounds, the house.'

'Assuming he was taken at the house and hadn't wandered.'

'Assuming that, yes.'

'And you sent me to find out.'

'I sent you.'

I felt culpable for Catherine Demeter's death, not only because of my failure to find her alive but because, unwittingly, I might have brought Modine and Hyams to her.

'I may have led them to Catherine Demeter,' I said to Walter after a while. 'I told Ms Christie I was going to Virginia to follow a lead. It might have been enough to give her away.'

Walter shook his head.

'She hired you as insurance. She must have alerted Hyams as soon as she was seen. He was probably on the look-out for her already. If she didn't turn up in Haven, then they were relying on you to find her. As soon as you did, I think you'd both have been killed.'

I had a vision of Catherine Demeter's body slumped in the basement of the Dane house, her head surrounded by a circle of blood. And I saw Evan Baines wrapped in plastic, and the decayed body of a child half covered in earth and the other corpses still to be discovered in the Mancino basement, and elsewhere.

And I saw my own wife, my own child, in all of them.

'You could have sent someone else,' I said.

'No, only you. If Evan Baines's killer was there, I knew you'd find out. I knew you'd find out because you're a killer yourself.'

The word hung in the air for a moment and then tore a rift between us, like a knife cutting through our past together. Walter turned away.

I stayed silent for a time and then, as if Walter had never spoken, I said: 'She told me that she knew who killed Jennifer and Susan.'

Walter seemed almost grateful for the break in the silence.

'She couldn't have known. She was a sick, evil woman and that was her way of trying to torture you after she died.'

'No, she knew. She knew who I was before she died, but I don't think she knew when she hired me. She would have suspected something. She wouldn't have taken the chance.'

'You're wrong,' he said. 'Let it go.'

I didn't say anything more, but I knew that, somehow, the dark worlds of Adelaide Modine and the Travelling Man had come together.

'I'm considering retirement,' said Walter. 'I don't want to look at death any more. I've been reading Sir Thomas Browne. You ever read Thomas Browne?'

'No.'

'*Christian Morals*: "Behold not Death's Heads til thou doest not see them, nor look upon mortifying objects til thou overlook'st them."' His back was to me but I could see his face reflected in the window and his eyes seemed far away. 'I've spent too long looking at death. I don't want to force myself to look any more.'

He sipped his coffee. 'You should go away from here, do something to put your ghosts behind you. You're no longer what you once were, but maybe you can still step back, before you lose yourself for ever.'

A film was forming on my untouched coffee. When I didn't respond, Walter sighed and spoke with a sadness in his voice which I had never heard before. 'I'd prefer it if I didn't have to see you again,' he said. 'I'll talk to some people, see if you can go.'

Something had changed within me, that much was true, but I was not sure that Walter could see it for what it was. Maybe only I could really understand what had happened, what Adelaide Modine's death had unlocked within me. The horror of what she had done through the years, the knowledge of the hurt and pain she had inflicted on the most innocent among us, could not be balanced in this world.

And yet it had been brought to an end. I had brought it to an end.

All things decay, all things must end, the evil as well as the good. What Adelaide Modine's death had done, in its brutal, flame-red way, was to show me that this was true. If I could find Adelaide Modine and could bring her to an end, then I could do the same with others. I could do the same with the Travelling Man.

And somewhere, in a dark place, a clock began to tick, counting off the hours, the minutes, the seconds, before it would toll the end for the Travelling Man.

All things decay. All things must end.

And as I thought of what Walter had said, of his doubts about me, I thought too of my father and of the legacy he left me. I have only fragmented memories of my father. I remember a large, red-faced man carrying a Christmas tree into the house, his breath rising into the air like the puffs of steam from an old train. I remember walking into the kitchen one evening to find him caressing my mother and her laughter at their shared embarrassment. I remember him reading to me at night, his huge fingers following the words as he spoke them to me so that they might be familiar to me when I returned to them again. And I remember his death.

His uniform was always freshly pressed and he kept his gun oiled and cleaned. He loved being a policeman, or so it seemed. I did not know then what it was that drove him to do what he did. Maybe Walter Cole gained some knowledge of it when he looked upon the bodies of those dead children. Maybe I too have knowledge of it. Maybe I have become like my father.

What is clear is that something inside him died and the world appeared to him in different, darker colours. He had looked upon death's heads for too long and became a reflection of what he saw.

The call had been a routine one: two kids fooling around in a car late at night on a patch of waste ground, flashing the lights and sounding the horn. My father had responded and found one of the local boys, a petty criminal well on the road to graduating into felonies, and his girlfriend, a middle-class girl who was flirting with danger and enjoying the sexual charge it brought.

My father couldn't recall what the boy said to him as he tried to impress his girl. Words were exchanged and I can imagine my father's voice deepening and hardening in warning. The boy made mocking movements towards the inside pocket of his jacket, enjoying the effect on my father's nerves and bathing in the ripples of laughter from the young woman beside him.

Then my father drew his gun and the laughter stopped. I can

see the boy raising his hands, shaking his head, explaining that there was no weapon there, that it was all just fun, that he was sorry. My father shot him in the face, blood streaking the interior of the car, the windows, the face of the girl in the passenger seat, his mouth wide in shock. I don't think she even screamed before my father shot her too. Then he walked away.

Internal Affairs came for him as he stripped in the locker room. They took him before his brother officers, to make an example of him. No one got in their way. By then, they all knew, or thought they knew.

He admitted everything instantly but could not explain it. He simply shrugged his shoulders when they asked. They took his gun and his badge – his back-up, the one I now keep, remained back in his bedroom – and then they drove him home, under the NYPD rule that prevented a policeman being questioned about a crime until forty-eight hours had elapsed. He looked dazed when he returned and wouldn't speak to my mother. The two Internal Affairs men sat outside in their car, smoking cigarettes, while I watched from my bedroom window. I think they knew what would happen next. When the gunshot sounded, they didn't leave their car until the echoes of the shot had faded into the cool night air.

I am my father's son, with all that entails.

The door of the interview room opened and Rachel Wolfe entered. She was dressed casually in blue jeans, hi-top sneakers and a black hooded cotton top by Calvin Klein. Her hair was loose, hanging over her ears and resting on her shoulders, and there was a sprinkling of freckles across her nose and at the base of her neck.

She took a seat across from me and gave me a look of concern and sympathy. 'I heard about the death of Catherine Demeter. I'm sorry.'

I nodded and thought of Catherine Demeter and how she

looked in the basement of the Dane house. They weren't good thoughts.

'How do you feel?' she asked. There was curiosity in her voice, but tenderness too.

'I don't know.'

'Do you regret killing Adelaide Modine?'

'She called it. There was nothing else I could do.' I felt numb about her death, about the killing of the lawyer, about the sight of Bobby Sciorra rising up on his toes as the blade entered the base of his skull. It was the numbness that scared me, the stillness inside me. I think that it might have scared me more, but for the fact that I felt something else too: a deep pain for the innocents who had been lost, and for those who had yet to be found.

'I didn't know you did house calls,' I said. 'Why did they call you in?'

'They didn't,' she said simply.

She touched my hand, a strange, faltering gesture in which I felt – I hoped? – that there was something more than professional understanding. I gripped her hand tightly in mine and closed my eyes. I think it was a kind of first step, a faltering attempt to re-establish my place in the world. After all that had taken place over the previous two days, I wanted to touch, however briefly, something positive, to try to awaken something good within myself.

'I couldn't save Catherine Demeter,' I said at last. 'I tried and maybe something came out of that attempt. I'm still going to find the man who killed Susan and Jennifer.'

She nodded slowly and held my gaze. 'I know you will.'

Rachel had been gone only a short time when the cellphone rang.

'Yes?'

'Mista Parker?' It was a woman's voice.

'This is Charlie Parker.'

'My name is Florence Aguillard, Mista Parker. My mother is Tante Marie Aguillard. You came to visit us.'

'I remember. What can I do for you, Florence?' I felt the tightening in my stomach but this time it was born of anticipation, born of the feeling that Tante Marie might have found something to identify the figure of the girl who was haunting us both.

In the background I could hear the music of a jazz piano and the laughter of men and women, thick and sensual as treacle.

'I been tryin' to get you all afternoon. My momma say to call you. She say you gotta come to her now.' I could hear something in her voice, something that conspired to trip her words as they tumbled from her mouth. It was fear and it hung like a distorting fog around what she had to say.

'Mista Parker, she say you gotta come now and you gotta tell no one you comin'. No one, Mista Parker.'

'I don't understand, Florence. What's happening?'

'*I don't know,*' she said. She was crying now, her voice wracked by sobs. 'But she say you gotta come, you gotta come *now*.' She regained control of herself and I could hear her draw a deep breath before she spoke again.

'Mista Parker, she say the Travellin' Man comin'.'

There are no coincidences, only patterns we do not see. The call was part of a pattern, linked to the death of Adelaide Modine, which I did not yet understand. I said nothing about the call to anyone. I left the interrogation room, collected my gun from the desk, then headed for the street and took a cab back to my apartment. I booked a first-class ticket to Moisant Field, the only ticket left on any flight leaving for Louisiana that evening, and checked in shortly before departure, declaring my gun at the desk, my bag swallowed up in the general confusion. The plane was full, half of the passengers tourists who didn't know better heading for the stifling August heat of New Orleans. The stewards served a ham roll with chips and a packet of dried raisins, all contained in the sort of carrier bag you got on school trips to the zoo.

There was darkness below us when the pressure began building in my nose. I was already reaching for a drinks napkin when the first drops came but then the pressure became pain, a ferocious, shooting pain that caused me to jerk back in my seat.

The passenger beside me, a businessman who had earlier been cautioned about using his laptop computer while the plane was still on the runway, stared at me in surprise and then shock as he saw the blood. I watched his finger pressing repeatedly to summon the steward and then my head was thrown back, as if by the force of a blow. Blood spurted violently from my nose, drenching the back of the seat in front of me, and my hands shook uncontrollably.

Then, just as it seemed that my head was going to explode from the pain and the pressure, I heard a voice, the voice of an old, black woman in the Louisiana swamps.

'Chile,' said the voice. 'Chile, he's here.'

And then she was gone and my world turned black.

# Part Three

The concavities of my body are like another hell for their capacity.

*Sir Thomas Urquhart*, 'Rabelais' "Gargantua"'

# Chapter Thirty-One

There was a loud thud as the insect hit the windscreen. It was a large dragonfly, a 'mosquito hawk'.

'Shit, that thing must have been as big as a bird,' said the driver, a young FBI agent named O'Neill Brouchard. Outside, it was probably in the nineties, but the Louisiana humidity made it seem much hotter. My shirt felt cold and uncomfortable where the air-conditioning had dried it against my body.

A smear of blood and wings lay across the glass and the wipers struggled to remove it. The blood matched the drops that still stained my shirt, an unnecessary reminder of what had happened on the plane since my head still ached and the bridge of my nose felt tender to the touch.

Beside Brouchard, Woolrich remained silent, intent upon loading a fresh clip into his SIG Sauer. The Assistant SAC was dressed in his usual garb of cheap tan suit and wrinkled tie. Beside me, a dark Windbreaker marked with the agency's letters lay crumpled on the seat.

I had called Woolrich from the satellite phone on the plane but couldn't get a connection. At Moisant Field, I left a number with his message service telling him to contact me immediately, then hired a car and set out towards Lafayette on I-10. Just outside Baton Rouge, the cellphone rang.

'Bird?' said Woolrich's voice. 'What the hell are you doing

down here?' There was concern in his voice. In the background, I could hear the sound of a car engine.

'You get my message?'

'I got it. Listen, we're already on our way. Someone spotted Florence out by her house, with blood on her dress and a gun in her hand. We're going to meet up with the local cops at Exit 121. Wait for us there.'

'Woolrich, it may be too late—'

'Just wait. No hotdogging on this one, Bird. I got a stake in this, too. I got Florence to think about.'

In front of us I could see the tail-lights of two other vehicles, patrol cars out of the St Martin Sheriff's Office. Behind us, its headlights illuminating the inside of the FBI Chevy and the blood on the windscreen, was an old Buick driven by two St Martin detectives. I knew one of them, John Charles Morphy, vaguely, having met him once before with Woolrich in Lafitte's Blacksmith Shop on Bourbon, as he swayed quietly to the sound of Miss Lily Hood's voice.

Morphy was a descendant of Paul Charles Morphy, the world chess champion from New Orleans who retired in 1859 at the grand old age of twenty-two. It was said that he could play three or four games simultaneously while blindfolded. By contrast, John Charles, with his hard body-builder's frame, never struck me as a man much given to chess. Dead-lift competitions, maybe, but not chess. He was a man with a past, according to Woolrich, a former New Orleans cop who had left the NOPD for the St Martin's Sheriff's Office in the shadow of an investigation by the Public Integrity Division over the killing of a young black man named Luther Bordelon in a goods yard off Chartres two years earlier.

I looked over my shoulder and saw Morphy staring back at me, his shaven head glowing in the Buick's interior light, his hands tight on the wheel as he negotiated the rutted track through the bayou. Beside him, his partner Touissant held the

Winchester Model 12 pump upright between his legs. The stock was pitted and scratched, the barrel worn, and I guessed that it wasn't regulation issue but Touissant's own. It had smelt of oil when I spoke to Morphy through the window of the car back where the Bayou Courtableau intersected with I-10.

The lights of the car caught the branches of palmetto, tupelo and overhanging willows, huge cypress heavy with Spanish moss, and, occasionally, the stumps of ancient trees in the swamps beyond. We turned into a road that was dark as a tunnel, the branches of the cypress trees above us like a roof against the starlight, and then we were rattling over the bridge that led to the house of Tante Marie Aguillard.

Before us, the two sheriff's office cars turned in opposing directions and parked diagonally, the lights of one shining out into the dark undergrowth, which led down to the swamp banks. The lights of the second hit the house, casting shadows over the tree trunks that raised it from the ground, the building's overlapping boards, the steps leading up to the screen door, which now stood open on the porch, allowing the night creatures easy access to the interior of the house.

Woolrich turned around as we pulled up. 'You ready for this?'

I nodded. I had my Smith & Wesson in my hand as we stepped from the car into the warm air. I could smell rotting vegetation and a faint trace of smoke. Something rustled through the undergrowth to my right and then splashed lightly into the water. Morphy and his partner came up beside us. I could hear the sound of a cartridge being jacked into the pump.

Two of the deputies stood uncertainly beside their car. The second pair advanced slowly across the neat garden, their guns drawn.

'What's the deal?' said Morphy. He was six feet tall with the V-shape of a lifter, his head hairless and a circle of moustache and beard around his mouth.

'No one enters before us,' said Woolrich. 'Send those two jokers around the back but tell them to stay out of the house. The other two stay at the front. You two back us up. Broussard, stay by the car and watch the bridge.'

We moved across the grass, stepping carefully around the discarded children's toys on the lawn. There were no lights on in the house, no sign of any occupants. I could hear the blood pumping in my head and the palms of my hands were slick with sweat. We were ten feet from the porch steps when I heard a pistol cock and the voice of the deputy to our right.

'Ah, sweet Jesus,' he said, 'sweet Jesus Lord, this can't be . . .'

A dead tree, little more than an extended trunk, stood about ten yards from the water's edge. Branches, some no more than twigs, others as thick as a man's arm, commenced some three feet up the trunk and continued to a height of eight or nine feet.

Against the tree trunk stood Tee Jean Aguillard, the old woman's youngest son, his naked body glistening in the torch-light. His left arm was hooked around a thick branch so that his forearm and empty hand hung vertically. His head rested in the crook of another branch, his ruined eyes like dark chasms against the exposed flesh and tendons of his flayed face.

Tee Jean's right arm was also wrapped around a branch but this time his hand was not empty. In his fingers he grasped a flap of his own skin, a flap that hung like an opened veil and revealed the interior of his body from his exposed ribs to the area above his penis. His stomach and most of the organs in his abdomen had been removed. They lay on a stone by his left foot, a pile of white, blue and red body parts in which coils of intestine curled like snakes.

Beside me, I heard one of the deputies begin to retch. I turned to see Woolrich grabbing him by the collar and hauling him to the water's edge some distance away. 'Not here,' he said. 'Not here.' He left the deputy on his knees by the water and turned towards the house.

'We've got to find Florence,' he said. His face looked sickly and pale. 'We gotta find her.'

Florence Aguillard had been seen standing at the bridge to her house by the owner of a local bait shop. She had been covered in blood and held a Colt Service revolver in her hand. When the bait-shop owner stopped, Florence raised the gun and fired a single shot through the driver's window, missing the bait-shop owner by a fraction of an inch. He had called the St Martin cops from a gas station and they, in turn, had called Woolrich, acting on his notice to the local police that any incident involving Tante Marie should be notified immediately to him.

Woolrich took the steps up the porch at a run and was almost at the door when I reached him. I put my hand on his shoulder and he spun towards me, his eyes wide.

'Easy,' I said. The wild look disappeared from his eyes and he nodded slowly. I turned back to Morphy and motioned him to follow us into the house. Morphy took the Winchester pump from Touissant and indicated that he should hang back with the deputy, now that his partner was indisposed.

A long central hallway led, shotgun style, to a large kitchen at the rear of the house. Six rooms radiated off the central artery, three on either side. I knew that Tante Marie's was the last door on the right and I was tempted to make straight for it. Instead we progressed carefully, taking a room at a time, the flashlights cutting a swathe through the darkness, dust motes and moths bobbing in the beams.

The first room on the right, a bedroom, was empty. There were two beds, one made and the second, a child's bed, unmade, the blanket lying half on the floor. The living room opposite was also empty. Morphy and Woolrich each took a room as we progressed to the second set of doors. Both were bedrooms. Both were empty.

'Where are all the children, the adults?' I said to Woolrich.

'Eighteenth birthday party at a house two miles away,' he replied. 'Only Tee Jean and the old lady supposed to be here. And Florence.'

The door opposite Tante Marie's room stood wide open and I could see a jumble of furniture, boxes of clothes and piles of toys. A window was open and the curtains stirred slightly in the night air. We turned to face the door of Tante Marie's bedroom. It was slightly ajar and I could see moonlight within, disturbed and distorted by the shadows of the trees. Behind me, Morphy had the shotgun raised and Woolrich had the SIG Sauer held double-handed close to his cheek. I put my finger on the trigger of the Smith & Wesson, flicked open the door with the side of my foot and dived low into the room.

A bloody handprint lay on the wall by the door and I could hear the sound of night creatures in the darkness beyond the window. The moonlight cast drifting shadows across a long sideboard, a huge closet filled with almost identically patterned dresses and a long, dark chest on the floor near the door. But the room was dominated by the giant bed that stood against the far wall, and by its occupant, Tante Marie Aguillard.

Tante Marie: the old woman who had reached out to a dying girl as the blade began to cut her face; the old woman who had called out to me in my wife's voice when I last stood in this room, offering me some kind of comfort in my sorrow; the old woman who had, in turn, reached out to me in her final torment.

She sat naked on the bed, a huge woman undiminished by death. Her head and upper body rested against a mountain of pillows, stained dark by her blood. Her face was a red and purple mass. Her jaw hung open, revealing long teeth stained yellow with tobacco. The flashlight caught her thighs, her thick arms and the hands that reached towards the centre of her body.

'God have mercy,' said Morphy.

Tante Marie had been split from sternum to groin and the skin pulled back to be held in place by her own hands. As with her son, most of her internal organs had been removed and her stomach was a hollow cavern, framed by ribs, through which a section of her spine gleamed dully in the torchlight. Woolrich's light moved lower, towards her groin. I stopped it with my hand.

'No,' I said. 'No more.'

Then a shout came from outside, startling in the silence, and we were running together towards the front of the house.

Florence Aguillard stood swaying on the grass in front of her brother's body. Her mouth was curled down at either side, the bottom lip turned in on itself in grief. She held the long-barrelled Colt in her right hand, the muzzle pointing at the ground. Her white dress was patterned with blue flowers, obscured in places by her mother's blood. She made no noise, although her body was racked by silent cries.

Woolrich and I came down the steps slowly. Morphy and a deputy stayed on the porch. The second pair of deputies had come from the back of the house and stood facing Florence, Touissant slightly to the right of them. To Florence's left, I could see the figure of Tee Jean hanging on the tree and, beside him, the fourth deputy and Broussard with his unholstered SIG.

'Florence,' said Woolrich softly, putting his gun back in his shoulder holster. 'Florence, put the gun down.'

Her body shook and her left hand wrapped itself tightly around her waist. She bent over slightly and shook her head slowly from side to side.

'Florence,' repeated Woolrich. 'It's me.'

She turned her head towards us. There was misery in her eyes, misery and hurt and guilt and rage all vying for supremacy in her troubled mind.

She raised the gun slowly and pointed it in our direction. I saw the deputies bring their weapons up quickly. Touissant had already assumed a sharp-shooter's stance, his arms in front of his body, his gun unwavering.

'*No!*' shouted Woolrich, his right hand raised. I saw the cops look towards him in doubt and then towards Morphy. He nodded and they relaxed slightly, still keeping their weapons trained on Florence.

The Colt moved from Woolrich to me and still Florence Aguillard shook her head slowly. I could hear her voice, soft in the night, repeating Woolrich's word like a mantra – 'no no no no no . . .' – and then she turned the gun towards her, placed the barrel in her mouth and pulled the trigger.

The explosion sounded like a cannon's roar in the night air. I could hear the sound of birds' wings flapping and small animals hurtling through the undergrowth as Florence's body crumpled to the ground, her ruined skull gaping. Woolrich stumbled to his knees beside her and reached out to touch her face with his left hand, his right reaching instinctively, futilely, for the pulse in her neck. Then he lifted her and buried her face in his sweat-stained shirt, his mouth wide in pain.

In the distance, red lights shone. Further away, I could hear the sound of a helicopter's blades scything at the darkness.

# Chapter Thirty-Two

The day dawned heavy and humid in New Orleans, the smell of the Mississippi strong in the morning air. I left my guest-house and skirted the Quarter, trying to clear the tiredness from my head and my bones. I eventually ended up on L'oyola, the traffic adding to the oppressive warmth. The sky overhead was grey and overcast with the threat of rain, and dark clouds hung over the city, seeming to lock in the heat. I bought a copy of the *Times-Picayune* from a vending machine and read it as I stood before City Hall. The newspaper was so heavy with corruption that it was a wonder the paper didn't rot: two policemen arrested on drug-trafficking charges, a federal investigation into the conduct of the last Senate elections, suspicions about a former governor. New Orleans itself, with its run-down build-ings, the grim shopping precinct of Poydras, the Woolworth's store with its 'Closing Down' notices, seemed to embody this corruption, so it was impossible to tell whether the city had infected the populace or if some of its people were dragging down the city with them.

Chep Morrison had built the imposing City Hall, shortly after he returned from the Second World War to dethrone the millionaire Mayor Maestri and drag New Orleans into the twentieth century. Some of Woolrich's old cronies still re-membered Morrison with fondness, albeit a fondness arising from the fact that police corruption had flourished under him, along with numbers rackets, prostitution and gambling. More than three decades later, the police department in New Orleans was still trying to deal with his legacy. For almost two decades, the Big Sleazy had been top of the league table of complaints about police misconduct, numbering over one thousand complaints per year.

The NOPD had been founded on the principle of the 'cut'; like the police forces in other southern cities – Savannah, Richmond, Charleston and Mobile – it had been formed in the eighteenth century to control and monitor the slave population, with the police receiving a portion of the reward for capturing runaways. In the nineteenth century, members of the force were accused of rapes and murders, lynchings and robberies, of taking graft to allow gambling and prostitution to continue. The fact that police were forced to stand for election annually meant that they were forced to sell their allegiance to the two main political parties. The force manipulated government elections, intimidated voters, even participated in the massacre of the moderates at the Mechanics Institute in 1866.

New Orleans's first black mayor, Dutch Morial, tried to clean up the department at the start of the eighties. If the independent Metropolitan Crime Commission, which had a quarter of a century's start on Morial, couldn't clean up the department, what hope did a black mayor have? The predominantly white police union went on strike and the Mardi Gras was cancelled. The National Guard had to be called in to maintain order. I didn't know if the situation had improved since then. I hoped that it had.

New Orleans is also homicide central, with about four hundred Code 30s – NOPD code for a homicide – each year. Maybe half get solved, leaving a lot of people walking the streets of New Orleans with blood on their hands. That's something the city fathers prefer not to tell the tourists, although maybe a lot of the tourists would still come anyway.

After all, when a city is so hot that it offers riverboat gambling, twenty-four-hour bars, strippers, prostitution and a ready supply of drugs, all within a few blocks of each other, there's got to be some kind of downside to it all.

I walked on, eventually stopping to sit on the edge of a potted tree outside the pink New Orleans Center, the tower of the Hyatt rising behind it, while I waited for Woolrich to show. In the midst of the previous night's confusion, we had arranged a meeting for breakfast. I had considered staying in Lafayette or Baton Rouge, but Woolrich indicated that the local cops might not like having me so close to the investigation and, as he pointed out, he himself was based in New Orleans.

I gave him twenty minutes and, when he didn't arrive, I began to walk down Poydras Street, its canyon of office buildings already thronged with business people and tourists heading for the Mississippi.

At Jackson Square, La Madelaine was packed with break-fasters. The smell of baking bread from its ovens seemed to draw people in like cartoon characters pulled along by a visible, snake-like scent. I ordered a pastry and coffee and finished reading the *Times-Picayune*. It's next to impossible to get *The New York Times* in New Orleans. I read somewhere that the New Orleans citizenry bought fewer copies of *The New York Times* than any other city in the US, although they made up for it by buying more formal wear than anywhere else. If you're going out to formal dinners every evening, you don't get much time to read *The New York Times*.

Amid the magnolia and banana trees of the square, tourists watched tap-dancers and mimes and a slim black man who maintained a steady, sensual rhythm by hitting his knees with a pair of plastic bottles. There was a light breeze blowing from the river, but it was fighting a losing battle with the morning heat and contented itself with tossing the hair of the artists hanging their paintings on the square's black iron fence and threatening the cards of the fortune-tellers outside the cathedral.

I felt strangely distant from what I had seen at Tante Marie's house. I had expected it to bring back memories of what I had seen in my own kitchen, the sight of my own wife and child reduced to flesh, sinew and bone. Instead, I felt only a heaviness, like a dark, wet blanket over my consciousness.

I flicked through the newspaper once again. The killings had made the bottom of the front page, but the details of the mutilations had been kept from the press. It was hard to tell how long that would last; rumours would probably begin to circulate at the funerals.

Inside, there were pictures of two bodies, those of Florence and Tee Jean, being taken across the bridge to waiting ambulances. The bridge had been weakened by the traffic and there were fears that it might collapse if the ambulances tried to cross. Mercifully, there were no pictures of Tante Marie being transported on a special gurney to her ambulance, her huge bulk seeming to mock mortality even as it lay shrouded in black.

I looked up to see Woolrich approaching the table. He had changed his tan suit for a light grey linen; the tan had been covered in Florence Aguillard's blood. He was unshaven and there were black bags beneath his eyes. I ordered him coffee and a plate of pastries and stayed quiet as he ate.

He had changed a great deal in the years I had known him, I thought. There was less fat on his face and, when the light caught him a certain way, his cheekbones were like blades beneath his skin. It struck me for the first time that he might be ill, but I didn't raise the topic. When Woolrich wanted to talk about it, he would.

While he ate, I recalled the first time that I had met him, over the body of Jenny Ohrbach. She had been pretty once, a thirty-year-old woman who had kept her figure through regular exercise and a careful diet and who had, it emerged, lived a life of considerable luxury without any obvious means of support.

I had stood over her in an Upper West Side apartment on a cold January night. Two large bay windows opened out on to a small balcony overlooking 79th Street and the river, two blocks from Zabar's Deli on Broadway. It wasn't our territory, but Walter Cole and I were there because the initial MO looked like it might have matched two aggravated burglaries we were investigating, one of which had led to the death of a young accounts executive, Deborah Moran.

All of the cops in the apartment wore coats, some with mufflers dangling around their necks. The apartment was warm and nobody was in any great hurry to head back out into the cold, least of all Cole and I, despite the fact that this seemed to be a deliberate homicide rather than an aggravated burglary. Nothing in the apartment appeared to have been touched and a purse containing three credit cards and over $700 in cash was found undisturbed in a drawer under the television set. Someone had brought coffee from Zabar's and we sipped from the containers, our hands cupped around them, enjoying the unaccustomed feeling of warmth on our fingers.

The ME had almost finished his work and an ambulance team was standing by to remove the body when an untidy figure shambled into the apartment. He wore a long brown overcoat, the colour of beef gravy, and the sole of one of his shoes had come adrift from the upper. Through the gap, a red sock and an exposed big toe revealed themselves. His tan pants were as wrinkled as a two-day-old newspaper and his white shirt had given up the struggle to keep its natural tones, settling instead for the unhealthy yellow pallor of a jaundice victim. A fedora was jammed on his head. I hadn't seen anyone wear a fedora at a crime scene since the last *film noir* revival at the Angelika.

But it was the eyes that attracted the most attention. They

were bright and amused and cynical, trailing lines like a jellyfish moving through water. Despite his ramshackle appearance, he was clean-shaven and his hands were spotless as he took a pair of plastic gloves from his pocket and pulled them on.

'Cold as a whore's heart out there,' he remarked, squatting down and placing a finger gently beneath Jenny Ohrbach's chin. 'Cold as death.'

I felt a figure brush my arm and turned to see Cole standing beside me.

'Who the hell are you?' he asked.

'I'm one of the good guys,' responded the figure. 'Well, I'm FBI, so whatever that makes me in your eyes.' He flicked his ID at us. 'Special Agent Woolrich.'

He rose, sighed, and pulled the gloves from his hands, then thrust both gloves and hands deep into the pockets of his coat.

'What brings you out on a night like this, Agent Woolrich?' I asked. 'Lose the keys to the Federal Building?'

'Oh, the witty NYPD,' said Woolrich, with a half-smile. 'Lucky there's an ambulance standing by in case my sides split.' He turned his head to one side as he took in the body again. 'You know who she is?' he asked.

'We know her name, but that's it,' said a detective I didn't recognise. I didn't even know her name at that point. I knew only that she had been pretty once and now she was pretty no longer. She had been beaten around the face and head with a piece of hollow-centred coaxial cable, which had been dumped beside her body. The cream carpet around her head was stained a deep, dark red, and blood had splashed on the walls and the expensive, and probably uncomfortable, white leather suite.

'She's Tommy Logan's woman,' said Woolrich.

'The garbage-collection guy,' I said.

'The very same.'

Tommy Logan's company had clinched a number of valuable garbage-collection contracts in the city over the previous two years. Tommy had also expanded into the window-cleaning business. Tommy's boys cleaned the windows in your building or you didn't have any windows left to clean, and possibly no building either. Anyone with those kinds of contacts had to be connected.

'Racketeering interested in Tommy?' It was Cole.

'Lots of people interested in Tommy. Lot more than usual, if his girlfriend is lying dead on the carpet.'

'You think maybe someone's sending him a message?' I asked.

Woolrich shrugged. 'Maybe. Maybe someone should have sent him a message telling him to hire a decorator whose eyesight didn't give out the year Elvis died. This place looks like the Osmonds decorated it.'

He was right. Jenny Ohrbach's apartment was so retro it should have been wearing flares and a goatee. Not that it mattered to Jenny Ohrbach any more.

No one ever found out who killed her. Tommy Logan seemed genuinely shocked when he was told that his girlfriend was dead, so shocked he even stopped worrying that his wife might find out about her. Maybe Tommy decided to be more generous to his business partners as a result of Jenny Ohrbach's death but, if he did, their arrangement still didn't last much longer. One year later, Tommy Logan was dead, his throat cut and his body dumped by the Borden Bridge in Queens.

But Woolrich I saw more of. Our paths crossed on occasion; we went for a drink once or twice before I returned home and he went back to his empty apartment in TriBeCa. He produced tickets to a Knicks game; he came to the house for dinner; he gave Jennifer an enormous stuffed elephant as a birthday present; he watched, but did not judge or interfere, as I drank myself away shot by shot.

I have a memory of him at Jenny's third birthday party, a

cardboard clown's hat jammed on his head and a bowl of Ben and Jerry's Cherry Garcia ice-cream in his hand. He looked embarrassed, sitting there in his crumpled suit surrounded by three- and four-year-olds and their adoring parents, but also strangely happy as he helped small children blow up balloons or drew quarters from behind their ears. He did farmyard impressions and taught them how to balance spoons on their nose. When he left, there was a sadness in his eyes. I think he was recalling other birthdays, when his child was the centre of attention, before he lost his way.

When Susan and Jennifer died, he followed me to the station and waited outside for four hours until they had finished questioning me. I couldn't go back to the house and, after that first night when I found myself crying in a hospital lobby, I couldn't stay with Cole, not only because of his involvement in the investigation but because I did not want to be surrounded by a family, not then. Instead, I went to Woolrich's small, neat apartment, the walls lined with books of poetry: Marvell, Vaughan, Richard Crashaw, Herbert, Jonson and Ralegh, whose 'Passionate Man's Pilgrimage' he sometimes quoted. He gave me his bed. On the day of the funeral, he had stood behind me in the rain and let the water wash over him, the drops falling from the brim of his hat like tears.

'How you doing?' I asked eventually.

He puffed his cheeks and breathed out, his head moving slightly from side to side like a nodding-dog figure on the back seat of a car. Grey was seeping through his hair from silver pools over his ears. There were lines like the cracks in fine china spreading from his eyes and the corners of his mouth.

'Not so good,' he said. 'I got three hours' sleep, if you can call waking up every twenty minutes to flashes of red "sleep". I keep thinking of Florence and the gun and the way it looked as it slid into her mouth.'

'Were you still seeing her?'

'Not so much. On and off. We got together a coupla times and I was out at the house a few days back to see if everything was okay. Jesus, what a mess.'

He pulled the newspaper towards him and scanned its coverage of the killings, his finger moving along the sides of each paragraph so that it became dark with print. When he had finished reading, he looked at his blackened fingertip, rubbed his thumb lightly across it then wiped them both on a paper napkin.

'We got a fingerprint, a partial print,' he said, as if the sight of his own lines and whorls had only just reminded him of it.

Outside, the tourists and the noise seemed to recede into the distance and there was only Woolrich and his dark eyes. He drained the last of his coffee then dabbed at his mouth with the napkin.

'That's why I was delayed. Confirmed it just an hour ago. We've compared it against Florence's prints, but it's not hers. There are traces of the old woman's blood in it.'

'Where did you find it?'

'Underside of the bed. He may have tried to steady himself as he cut, or maybe he slipped. Doesn't look like there was an attempt to erase it. We're comparing it against local files and our master fingerprint identification records. If he's in the system, we'll find him.' As well as criminals, the files covered federal employees, aliens, military personnel and those individuals who had requested that their prints be retained for identification purposes. Over the next twenty-four hours, the print found at the scene would be checked against about two hundred million others on record.

If it turned out to be the Travelling Man's print then it would be the first real break since the deaths of Susan and Jennifer, but I wasn't holding my breath. A man who took the time to clean my wife's fingernails after he killed her was unlikely to be so careless as to leave his own fingerprint at a crime scene. I looked at Woolrich and knew he thought the same thing. He raised his hand for more coffee as he looked out at the crowds on Jackson Square and listened to the snorting of the ponies hitched to the touring carriages pulled up on Decatur.

'Florence'd been shopping in Baton Rouge earlier in the day, then returned home to change for the birthday party, one of her second cousins. She called you from some juke joint in Breaux Bridge, then went back to the house. She stayed there until maybe eight thirty, then went to the cousin's birthday party at Breaux Bridge at about nine. According to witness statements taken by the local cops, she was distracted and didn't stay for long – seems that her momma insisted that she go, that Tee Jean could take care of her. She stayed one hour, maybe ninety minutes, then came back. Brennan, the bait-shop owner, spotted her maybe thirty minutes after that. So we're looking at a window of one to two hours, no more, for the killings.'

'Who's dealing with the case?'

'Morphy's bunch, in theory. In practice, a lot of it is likely to devolve mainly to us, since it matches the MO on Susan and Jennifer, and because I want it. Brillaud is going to hook up your phone, in case our man calls. It'll mean hanging around your hotel room for a while, but I don't see what else we can do.' He avoided my eyes.

'You're cutting me out.'

'You can't be too involved in this, Bird. You know that. I've told you before and I'm telling you again. We'll decide the extent of your involvement.'

'Limited.'

'Damn, yes, limited. Look, Bird, you're the link to this guy. He's called once, he *will* call again. We wait, we see.' He spread his hands wide.

'She was killed because of the girl. Are you going to look for the girl?'

Woolrich rolled his eyes in frustration. 'Look where, Bird? The whole fucking bayou? We don't even know that she existed. We have a print, we'll run with that and see where it takes us. Now pay the bill and let's get out of here. We've got things to do.'

I was staying in a restored Greek revival house, the Flaisance House, on Esplanade, a white mansion filled with dead men's furniture. I had opted for a room in the converted carriage house at the rear, partly for the seclusion but also because it contained a natural alarm in the form of two large dogs, who prowled the courtyard beneath and growled at anyone who wasn't a guest, according to the guy manning the night desk. In fact, the dogs just seemed to sleep a lot in the shade of an old fountain. My large room had a balcony, a brass ceiling fan, two heavy leather armchairs and a small refrigerator, which I filled with bottled water.

When we reached the Flaisance, Woolrich turned on an early-morning game show and we waited, unspeaking, for Brillaud to arrive. He knocked on the door about twenty minutes later, long enough for a woman from Tulsa to win a trip to Maui. Brillaud was a small, neatly dressed man with receding hair, through which he ran his fingers every few minutes as if to reassure himself that there was still some there. Behind him, two men in shirtsleeves awkwardly carried an array of monitoring equipment on a metal gurney, carefully negotiating the wooden external stairway, which led up to the four carriage-house rooms.

'Get cooking, Brillaud,' said Woolrich. 'I hope you brought something to read.' One of the men in shirtsleeves waved a sheaf of magazines and some battered paperbacks which he had removed from the base of the gurney.

'Where will you be if we need you?' asked Brillaud.

'The usual place,' said Woolrich. 'Around.' And then he was gone.

I had once visited, through Woolrich, an anonymous room in the FBI's New York office. This was the tech room, where the squads engaged in long-term investigations – organised crime, foreign counter-intelligence – monitored their wire taps. Six agents sat before a row of reel-to-reel voice-activated tape-recorders, logging the calls whenever the recorders kicked in, carefully noting the time, the date, the subject of the conversation. The room was almost silent, save for the click and whir of the machines and the sound of pens scratching on paper.

The Feds do love their wire taps. Back in 1928, when it was called the Bureau of Investigation, the Supreme Court allowed almost unrestricted access to wire taps of targets. In 1940, when the attorney general, Andrew Jackson, tried to end wire-tapping, Roosevelt twisted his arm and extended taps to cover 'subversive activities'. Under Hoover's interpretation, 'subversive activities' covered anything from running a Chinese laundry to screwing someone else's wife. Hoover was the god of wire taps.

Now the Feds no longer have to squat by junction boxes in the rain trying to protect their notebooks from the elements. Judicial approval, followed by a call to the telephone company in order to have the signal diverted, is usually enough. It's even easier when the subject is willing to co-operate. In my case, Brillaud and his men didn't even have to sit in a surveillance van, smelling each others' sweat.

I excused myself for five minutes while Brillaud worked to hook up both my own cellphone and the room phone, telling him that I was just heading for the kitchen of the main house. I left the Flaisance and strolled through the courtyard, attracting a bored glance from one of the dogs huddled in the shadows. I walked down to a telephone booth by a grocery store one block away. From there, I called Angel's number. The machine was on. I left a message telling them the situation and advising him not to call me on the cellphone.

Technically, the Feds are supposed to engage in minimisation on wire-tapping or surveillance duties. In theory, this means that the agents hit the pause button on the recorder and tune out of the conversation, apart from occasional checks, if it becomes apparent that it's a private call unconnected with the business in hand. In practice, only a moron would assume that his private business would remain private on a tapped line and it seemed unwise for me to have conversations with a burglar and an assassin while the FBI was listening. When I had left the message, I picked up four coffees in the grocery store, re-entered the Flaisance and went up to my room, where an anxious-looking Brillaud was waiting by the door.

'We can order coffee up, Mr Parker,' he said disapprovingly.

'It never tastes the same,' I replied.

'Get used to it,' he concluded, closing the door behind me.

The first call came at 4.00 p.m., after hours of watching bad TV and reading the problem pages in back issues of *Cosmo*. Brillaud rose quickly from the bed and clicked his fingers at the technicians, one of whom was already tugging at his head-phones. He counted down from three with his fingers and then signalled me to pick up the cellphone.

'Charlie Parker?' It was a woman's voice.

'Yes?'

'It's Rachel Wolfe.'

I looked up at the FBI men and shook my head. There was the sound of breath being released. I put my hand over the mouthpiece. 'Hey, minimisation, remember?' There was a click as the recorder was turned off. Brillaud went back to lying on my clean sheets, his fingers laced behind his head and his eyes closed.

Rachel seemed to sense that there was something happening at the other end of the line.

'Can you talk?'

'I have company. Can I call you back?'

She gave me her home number and told me she planned to be out until 7.30 p.m. I could call her then. I thanked her and hung up.

'Lady friend?' asked Brillaud.

'My doctor,' I replied. 'I have a low tolerance syndrome. She hopes that within a few years I'll be able to cope with idle curiosity.'

Brillaud sniffed noisily but his eyes stayed closed.

The second call came at six. The humidity and the sound of the tourists had forced us to close the balcony window and the air was sour with male scent. This time, there was no doubt about the caller.

'Welcome to New Orleans, Bird,' said the synthesised voice, in deep tones that seemed to shift and shimmer like mist.

I paused for a moment and nodded at the FBI men. Brillaud was already paging Woolrich. On a computer screen by the balcony, I could see maps shifting and I could hear the Travelling Man's voice coming thinly through the headphones of the FBI men.

'No point in welcoming your FBI friends,' said the voice, this time in the high, lilting cadences of a young girl's voice. 'Is Agent Woolrich with you?'

I paused again before responding, conscious of the seconds ticking by.

'Don't fuck with me, Bird!' Still the child's voice, but this time in the petulant tones of one who has been told that she can't go out and play with her friends, the swearing rendering the effect even more obscene than it already was.

'No, he's not here.'

'Thirty minutes.' Then the connection ended.

Brillaud shrugged. 'He knows. He won't stay on long enough to get a fix.' He lay back down on the bed to wait for Woolrich.

Woolrich looked exhausted. His eyes were red-rimmed from lack of sleep and his breath smelt foul. He shifted his feet constantly, as if they were too big for his shoes. Five minutes after he arrived, the phone rang again. Brillaud counted down and I picked up the phone.

'Yes.'

'Don't interrupt, just listen.' It sounded like a woman's voice, the voice of someone who was about to tell her lover one of her secret fantasies, but distorted, inhuman. 'I'm sorry about Agent Woolrich's lover, but only because I missed her. She was supposed to be there. I had something special planned for her, but I suppose she had ideas of her own.'

Woolrich blinked hard once, but gave no other indication that he was disturbed by what he heard.

'I hope you liked my presentation,' continued the voice. 'Maybe you're even beginning to understand. If you're not, don't worry. There's plenty more to come. Poor Bird. Poor Woolrich. United in grief. I'll try to find you some company.'

Then the voice changed again. This time it was deep and menacing.

'I won't be calling again. It's rude to listen in on private conversations. The next message you get from me will have blood on it.' The call ended.

'Fuck,' said Woolrich. 'Tell me you got something.'

'We got nothing,' said Brillaud, tossing his headphones on to the bed.

★　　★　　★

I left the FBI men to pack away their equipment in a white Ford van and walked down through the Quarter to the Napoleon House to call Rachel Wolfe. I didn't want to use the cellular. For some reason, it seemed soiled by its role as the means of contact with a killer. I also wanted the exercise, after being cooped up in my room for so long.

She picked up on the third ring.

'It's Charlie Parker.'

'Hi . . .' She seemed to struggle for a time as she tried to decide what to call me.

'You can call me Bird.'

'Well spotted.'

There was an awkward pause, then: 'Where are you? It sounds incredibly noisy.'

'It is. It's New Orleans.' And then I filled her in as best I could on what had taken place. She listened in silence and, once or twice, I heard a pen tapping rhythmically against the phone at the other end of the line.

'Any of those details mean anything to you?' I asked, when I had finished.

'I'm not sure. I seem to recall something from my time as a student but it's buried so far back that I'm not sure that I can find it. I think I may have something for you arising out of your previous conversation with this man. It's a little obscure, though.' She was silent for a moment. 'Where are you staying?'

I gave her the number of the Flaisance. She repeated the name and the number to herself as she wrote them down.

'Are you going to call me back?'

'No,' she said. 'I'm going to make a reservation. I'm coming down.'

I looked around the Napoleon after I hung up. It was packed with locals and vaguely Bohemian-looking visitors, some of them tourists staying in the rooms above the dimly-lit bar. A classical piece I couldn't identify was playing over the speakers and smoke hung thick in the air.

Something about the Travelling Man's calls bothered me, although I wasn't sure what. He knew I was in New Orleans when he made his calls. He knew where I was staying, too, since he was aware of the presence of the Feds, and that awareness meant that he was familiar with police procedures and was monitoring the investigation, which matched Rachel's profile.

He had to have been watching the crime scene as we arrived, or shortly after. His reluctance to stay on the line was understandable, given the Feds' surveillance, but that second call . . . I played it back in my mind, trying to discern the source of my unease, but it yielded nothing.

I was tempted to stay in the Napoleon House, to breathe in the sense of life and gaiety in the old bar, but instead I returned to the Flaisance. Despite the heat I walked to the large windows, opened them, and stepped out on to the balcony. I looked out at the faded buildings and wrought-iron balconies of the upper Quarter and breathed deeply of the smells of cooking coming from a restaurant near by, mingled with smoke and exhaust fumes. I listened to the strains of jazz music coming from a bar on Governor Nicholls, the shouts and laughter of those heading for the rip-off joints on Bourbon Street, the sing-song accents of the locals blending with the voices of the out-of-towners, the sound of human life passing beneath my window.

And I thought of Rachel Wolfe, and the way her hair rested on her shoulders and the sprinkling of freckles across her white neck.

# Chapter Thirty-Three

That night, I dreamed of an amphitheatre, with rising aisles filled with old men. Its walls were hung with damask and two high torches illuminated its central rectangular table, with its curved edges and legs carved like bones. Florence Aguillard lay on the table, the exterior of her womb exposed while a bearded man in dark robes tore at it with an ivory-handled scalpel. Around her neck and behind her ears was the mark of a rope-burn. Her head lay at an impossible angle on the table-top.

When the surgeon cut her, eels slithered from her uterus and tumbled to the floor and the dead woman opened her eyes and tried to cry out. The surgeon stifled her mouth with sacking, while the old men watched and skeletons jangled their bones in the darkness. He continued to cut, his body ankle-deep in black eels, until the light went from her eyes.

And in a corner of the amphitheatre, half in light, half in darkness, figures watched. They came to me from the shadows, my wife and child, but now they were joined by a third, one who stayed further back in the dimness, one who was barely a silhouette, one who was hardly there. She came from a cold, wet place and brought with her a dense, loamy smell, the smell of rotting vegetation, of dark, lily-green water, of flesh bloated and disfigured by gas and decay. The place where she lay was small and cramped, its sides unyielding, and sometimes the fish

bumped against it as she waited. I seemed to smell her in my
nostrils when I woke and could still hear her voice

*help me*

as the blood rushed in my ears

*i'm cold help me*

and I knew that I had to find her.


I was awakened by the sound of the telephone in my room.
Dim light lanced through the curtains and my watchface
glowed the time at 8.35 a.m. I picked up the phone.

'Parker? It's Morphy. Get your ass in gear. I'll see you at La
Marquise in an hour.'

I showered, dressed and walked down to Jackson Square,
following the early-morning worshippers into St Louis Cathedral. Outside the cathedral, a huckster tried to attract worshippers to his fire-eating act while a group of black nuns
crowded beneath a yellow and green parasol.

Susan and I had attended mass here once, beneath its ornately
decorated roof depicting Christ among the shepherds and,
above the small sanctuary, the figure of the Crusader King
Louis IX, Roi de France, announcing the Seventh Crusade.

The cathedral had effectively been rebuilt twice since the
original wooden structure, designed in 1724, burned down
during the Good Friday fire of 1788, when over eight hundred
buildings went up in flames. The present cathedral was less than
a hundred and fifty years old, its stained-glass windows overlooking the Place Jean Paul Deux, a gift from the Spanish
government.

It was strange that I should have remembered the details so
clearly after so many years. Yet I remembered them less for
their own intrinsic interest than for their connections to Susan. I
remembered them because she had been with me when I
learned them, her hand clasped in mine, her hair pulled back
and tied with an aquamarine bow.

For a brief moment it seemed that, by standing in the same place and remembering the same words spoken, I could reach back to that time and feel her close beside me, her hand in my hand, her taste still on my lips, her scent on my neck. If I closed my eyes, I could imagine her sauntering down the aisle, her arm against mine, breathing in the mingled smells of incense and flowers, passing beneath the windows, moving from darkness to light, light to darkness.

I knelt at the back of the cathedral, by the statue of a cherub with a font in its hands and its feet upon a vision of evil, and I prayed for my wife and child.

Morphy was already at La Marquise, a French-style patisserie on Chartres. He was sitting in the rear courtyard, his head freshly shaved. He wore a pair of grey sweatpants, Nike sneakers and a Timberland fleece top. A plate of croissants and two cups of coffee stood on the table before him. He was carefully applying grape jelly to one half of a croissant as I sat down across from him.

'I ordered coffee for you. Take a croissant.'

'Coffee's fine, thanks. Day off?'

'Nah, just avoided the dawn patrol.' He took the half-croissant and stuffed it into his mouth, using his finger to cram in the last part. He smiled, his cheeks bulging. 'My wife won't let me do this at home. Says it reminds her of a kid hogging food at a birthday party.'

He swallowed and set to work on the remaining half of the croissant. 'St Martin's been frozen out of the picture, 'part from running around looking under rocks for bloody clothes,' he said. 'Woolrich and his boys have pretty much taken over the running of the investigation. We don't have a helluva lot to do with it any more, legwork excepted.'

I knew what Woolrich would be doing. The killings of Tante Marie and Tee Jean now confirmed the existence of a serial killer. The details would be passed on to the FBI's investigative support unit, the hard-pressed section responsible for advising on interrogation techniques and hostage negotiation, as well as dealing with VICAP, ABIS – the arson and bombing programme – and, crucially for this case, criminal profiling. Of the thirty-six agents in the unit, only ten worked on profiling, buried in a warren of offices sixty feet below ground in what used to be the FBI director's fall-out shelter at Quantico.

And while the Feds sifted through the evidence, trying to build up their picture of the Travelling Man, the police on the ground continued to search for physical traces of the killer in the area around Tante Marie's house. I could picture them already, the lines of cops moving through the undergrowth, warm green light shedding down upon them from the trees above. Their feet would be catching in the mud, their uniforms snagging on briars, as they searched the ground before them. Others would be working through the brown waters of Atchafalaya, swatting at 'no-see-ums' and sweating heavily through their shirts.

There had been a lot of blood at the Aguillard house. The Travelling Man must have been awash with it by the time his work was done. He must have worn overalls, and it would have been too risky for him to hold on to them. They had either been dumped in the swamp, or buried, or destroyed. My guess was that he had destroyed them, but the search had to go on.

'I don't have a helluva lot to do with it any more, either,' I said.

'I hear that.' He ate some more croissant and finished off his coffee. 'You finished, we'll get going.' He left some money on the table and I followed him outside. The same battered Buick that had followed us to Tante Marie's was parked half a block away, a hand-lettered cop-on-duty sign taped to the dashboard with duct tape. A parking ticket flapped beneath the wiper.

'Shit,' said Morphy, tossing the ticket in a trash can. 'Nobody got respect for the law no more.'

We drove to the Desire projects, a harsh urban landscape where young blacks lounged by rubbish-strewn lots or shot hoops desultorily in wire-rimmed courts. The two-storey blocks were like barracks, lining streets with bad-joke names like Piety, Abundance and Humanity. We pulled in near a liquor store, which was barricaded like a fortress, causing young men to skip away from us at the smell of cop. Even here, Morphy's trademark bald head appeared to be instantly recognisable.

'You know much about New Orleans?' said Morphy, after a time.

'Nope,' I replied. Beneath his fleece top, I could see the trademark bulge of his gun. The palms of his hands were calloused from gripping dumb-bells and bar-bells and even his fingers were thickly muscled. When he moved his head, muscles and tendons stood out on his neck like snakes moving beneath his skin.

Unlike most body-builders, there was an air of suppressed danger about Morphy, a sense that the muscle wasn't just for show. I knew that he had killed a man once in a bar in Monroe, a pimp who had shot up one of his girls and the john she was with in a hotel room in Lafayette. The pimp, a 220-pound Creole who called himself Le Mort Rouge, had stabbed Morphy in the chest with a broken bottle and then tried to choke him on the ground. Morphy, after trying punches to the face and body, had eventually settled for a grip on Le Mort's neck and the two men had remained like that, locked in each other's grip, until something burst in Le Mort's head and he fell sideways against the bar. He was dead by the time the ambulance arrived.

It had been a fair fight but, sitting beside Morphy in the car, I wondered about Luther Bordelon. He had been a thug, that much was certain. He had a string of assaults stretching back to his years as a juvenile and he was suspected of the rape of a young Australian tourist. The girl had failed to identify Bordelon in a line-up and no physical evidence of the rapist had been left on the girl's body because her assailant had used a condom and then made her wash her pubic region with a bottle of mineral water, but the NOPD cops knew it was Bordelon. Sometimes, that's just the way things are.

On the night he died, Bordelon had been drinking in an Irish bar in the Quarter. He was wearing a white T-shirt and white Nike shorts, and three customers in the bar, with whom he had been playing pool, later swore statements that Bordelon had not been armed. Yet Morphy and his partner, Ray Garza, reported that Bordelon had fired on them when they attempted to routinely question him and that he had been killed in their return of fire. A gun, a Smith & Wesson Model 60 that was at least twenty years old, was found by his side with two shots fired. The serial number of the gun had been filed away from the frame under the cylinder crane, making the gun difficult to identify, and Ballistics reported that it was clean and had not been previously used in the commission of a crime in the city of New Orleans.

The gun looked like a throwdown and the NOPD's Police Integrity Division clearly felt that was the case, but Garza and Morphy stuck by their story. One year later Garza was dead, stabbed while trying to break up a brawl in the Irish Channel, and Morphy had transferred to St Martin, where he had bought a house. That was it. That was how it ended.

Morphy gestured towards a group of young blacks, the asses of their jeans around their knees and oversized sneakers slapping the sidewalk as they walked. They returned our gaze unflinchingly, as if daring us to make a move on them. From a beatbox they carried came the sound of the Wu-Tang Clan, music to kickstart the revolution. I felt a kind of perverse pleasure from recognising the music. Charlie Parker, honorary homeboy.

Morphy said, 'That is the worst goddamn racket I ever heard. Shit, these people invented the blues. Robert Johnson heard that crap, he'd know for sure that he'd sold his soul to the Devil and gone straight to Hell.' He turned on his car radio and flicked through the channels with an unhappy look. Resignedly, he pushed in a tape and the warm sound of Little Willie John filled the car.

'I grew up in Metairie, before the projects really took hold in this city,' he began. 'I can't say any of my best friends were black or nothing – most of the blacks went to public schools, I didn't – but we got along together.

'But when the projects went up, that was the end. Desire, Iberville, Lafitte, those were places you didn't want to end up, 'less you were armed to the teeth. Then fucking Reagan came along and the place got worse. You know, they say there's more syphilis now than there was fifty years ago. Most of these kids ain't even been immunised against measles. You have a house in the inner city, then it ain't worth shit. Might as well abandon it and let it rot.' He slapped the steering wheel.

'When you got that kind of poverty, a man can make a lot of money from it if he puts his mind to it. Lot of people fighting for a slice of the projects, fighting for a slice of other things too: land, property, booze, gambling.'

'Like who?'

'Like Joe Bonnano. His crew's been running things down here for the past decade or so, controlling the supply of crack, smack, whatever. They've been trying to expand into other areas too. There's talk that they want to open a big leisure centre between Lafayette and Baton Rouge, maybe build a hotel. Maybe they just want to dump some bricks and mortar there and write it off as a tax loss, launder money through it.'

He cast an appraising eye around the projects. 'And this is where Joe Bones grew up.' He said this with a sigh, as if he could not understand how a man would set out to undermine the place in which he had grown and matured. He started the car again and, as he drove, he told me about Joe Bones.

Salvatore Bonnano, Joe's father, had owned a bar in the Irish Channel, standing up against the local gangs who didn't believe that an Italian had any place in an area where people named their children after Irish saints and an 'oul sod' mentality still prevailed. There was nothing particularly honourable about Sal's stance; it was simply born out of pragmatism. There was a lot of money to be made in Chep Morrison's post-war New Orleans, if a man was prepared to take the knocks and grease the right palms.

Sal's bar was to be the first in a string of bars and clubs he acquired. He had loans to pay off, and the income from a single bar in the Irish Channel wasn't going to satisfy his creditors. He saved and bought a second bar, this time in Chartres, and from there his little empire grew. In some cases, only a simple financial transaction was required to obtain the premises he wanted. In others, some more forceful encouragement had to be used. When that didn't work, the Atchafalaya Basin had enough water to hide a multitude of sins. Gradually, he built up his own crew to take care of business, to make sure the city authorities, the police, the Mayor's office, were all kept happy, and to deal with the consequences when those lower down the food chain tried to better themselves at Sal's expense.

Sal Bonnano married Maria Cuffaro, a native of Gretna, east of New Orleans, whose brother was one of Sal's right-hand men. She bore him one daughter, who died of TB at the age of seven, and a son who died in Vietnam. She died herself in '58, of cancer of the breast.

But Sal's real weakness was a woman named Rochelle Hines. Rochelle was what they called a 'high yellow' woman, a negress whose skin was almost white following generations of interbreeding. She had, as Morphy put it, a complexion like butter oil, although her birth certificate bore the words 'black, illegitimate'. She was tall, with long dark hair framing almond eyes and lips that were soft and wide and welcoming. She had a figure that would stop a clock and there were rumours that she might once have been a prostitute, although, if that was the case, Sal Bonnano quickly put an end to those activities.

Bonnano bought her a place in the Garden District and began introducing her as his wife after Maria died. It probably wasn't a wise thing to do. In the Louisiana of the late 1950s, racial segregation was a day-to-day reality. Even Louis Armstrong, who grew up in the city, could not perform with white musicians in New Orleans because the state of Louisiana prohibited racially integrated bands from playing in the city.

And so, while white men could keep black mistresses and consort with black prostitutes, a man who introduced a black woman, no matter how pale her skin, as his 'wife' was just asking for trouble. When she gave birth to a son, Sal insisted that he bear his name and he took the child and his mother to band recitals in Jackson Square, pushing the huge white pram across the grass and gurgling at his son.

Maybe Sal thought that his money would protect him. Maybe he just didn't care. He ensured that Rochelle was always protected, that she didn't walk out alone, so that no one could come at her. But, in the end, they didn't come at Rochelle.

One hot July night in 1964, when his son was five years old, Sal Bonnano disappeared. He was found three days later, tied to a tree by the shore of Lake Cataoutche, his head almost severed from his body. It seems likely that someone decided to use his relationship with Rochelle Hines as an excuse to move in on his operation. Ownership of his clubs and bars was transferred to a business consortium with interests in Reno and Vegas.

As soon as her husband was found, Rochelle Hines vanished with her son and a small quantity of jewellery and cash before anyone could come after them. She resurfaced one year later in the area that would come to be called Desire, where her half-sister rented a property. The death of Sal had destroyed her: she was an alcoholic and had become addicted to morphine.

It was here, among the rising projects, that Joe Bones grew up, paler yet than his mother, and made his stand against both blacks and whites since neither group would accept him as its own. There was a rage inside Joe Bones and he turned it on the world around him. By 1990, ten years after his mother's death in a filthy cot in the projects, Joe Bones owned more bars than his father had thirty years before and, each month, planeloads of cocaine flew in from Mexico, bound for the streets of New Orleans and points north, east and west.

'Now Joe Bones calls himself a white man, and don't nobody differ with him,' said Morphy. 'Anyway, how's a man gonna talk with his balls in his mouth? Joe's got no time for the brothers now.' He laughed quietly. 'Ain't nothin' worse than a man who can't get on with his in-laws.'

We stopped at a gas station and Morphy filled the tank, then came back with two sodas. We sipped them by the pumps, watching the cars go by.

'Now there's another crew, the Fontenots, and they got their eyes on the projects too. Two brothers, David and Lionel. Family was out of Lafayette originally, I think – still got ties there – but came to New Orleans in the twenties. The Fontenots are ambitious, violent, and they think maybe Bonnano's time has come. All of this has been coming to a head for about a year now, and maybe the Fontenots have a piece of work planned for Joe Bones.'

The Fontenots were not young men – they were both in

their forties – but they had gradually established themselves in Louisiana and now operated out of a compound in Delacroix guarded by wire and dogs and armed men, including a hard-core of Cajuns from back in Acadiana. They were into gambling, prostitution, some drugs. They owned bars in Baton Rouge, one or two others in Lafayette. If they could take out Joe Bones, it was likely that they would muscle in on the drugs market in a big way.

'You know anything about the Cajuns?' asked Morphy.

'No, not beyond their music.'

'They're a persecuted minority in this state and in Texas. During the oil boom, they couldn't get any work because the Texans refused to employ coon-asses. Most of them did what we all do when times are tough: they knuckled down and made the best of things. There were clashes with the blacks, because the blacks and the Cajuns were competing for the same limited amount of work, and some bad things went down, but most people just did what they could to keep body and soul together without breaking too many laws.

'Roland Fontenot – that's the grandfather – he left all that behind when he came to New Orleans, following some other obscure branch of the family. But the boys, they never forgot their roots. When things were bad in the seventies, they gathered a pretty disaffected bunch around them: a lot of young Cajuns, some blacks, and somehow kept the mixture from blowing up in their faces.' Morphy drummed his fingers on the dashboard. 'Sometimes I think maybe we're all responsible for the Fontenots. They're a visitation on us, because of the way their people were treated. I think maybe Joe Bones is a visitation too, a reminder of what happens when you grind a section of the population into the dirt.'

Joe Bones had a vicious streak, said Morphy. He once killed a man by slowly burning him with acid over the space of an afternoon and was thought by some to be missing part of his brain, the part that controlled unreasonable actions in most men. The Fontenots were different. They killed, but they killed like businessmen closing down an unprofitable or unsatisfactory operation. They killed joylessly, but professionally. In Morphy's view, the Fontenots and Joe Bones were all as bad as each other. They just had different ways of expressing it.

I finished my soda and trashed the can. Morphy wasn't the type to tell a tale for its own sake. All of this was leading up to something.

'What's the point, Morphy?' I asked.

'The point is, the fingerprint that was found at Tante Marie's belongs to Tony Remarr. He's one of Joe Bones's men.' I thought about that as he started the car and moved into the traffic, tried to match the name to any incident that might have occurred back in New York, anything that might connect me to Remarr. I found nothing.

'You think he did it?' Morphy asked.

'Do you?'

'No, no way. At first I thought, yeah, maybe. You know, the old woman, she owned that land. Wouldn't have taken much drainage work to make something of it.'

'If a man was considering opening a big hotel and building a leisure centre.'

'Exactly, or if he wanted to convince someone he was serious enough about it to dump some bricks there. I mean, swamp's swamp. Assuming he could get permission to build, who wants to share the warm evening air with critters even God regrets making?

'Anyway, the old woman wouldn't sell. She was shrewd. Her people have been buried out there for generations. The original landowner, an old Southern type who traced his ancestry back to the Bourbons, died in sixty-nine. He stipulated in his will that the land should be offered for sale at a reasonable rate to the existing tenants.

'Now most of the tenants were Aguillards and they bought that land with all the money they had. The old woman, she made all the decisions for them. Their ancestors are there and they have a history with that land going back to the time when they wore chains around their ankles and dug channels through the dirt with their bare hands.'

'So Bonnano had been putting pressure on her to sell up, but she wouldn't, so he decides to take things a step further,' I said.

Morphy nodded. 'I figure maybe Remarr was sent out to put more than pressure on her – maybe he's going to threaten the girl or some of the children, maybe even kill one of them – but when he arrives she's already dead. And maybe Remarr gets careless from the shock, thinks he hasn't left any traces and heads off into the night.'

'Does Woolrich know all this?'

'Most of it, yeah.'

'You bringing Bonnano in?'

'Brought him in last night and let him go an hour later, accompanied by a fancy lawyer called Rufus Thibodeaux. He ain't movin', says he ain't seen Remarr for three or four days. Says he wants to find Remarr as much as anyone, something about money from some deal out in West Baton Rouge. It's bullshit, but he's sticking with the story. I think Woolrich is going to try to put some pressure on his operations through Anti-Racketeering and Narcotics, put the squeeze on him to see if he can change his mind.'

'That could take time.'

'You got a better idea?'

I shrugged. 'Maybe.'

Morphy's eyes narrowed. 'You don't be fuckin' with Joe Bones, now, y' hear? Joe ain't like your boys back in New York, sittin' in social clubs in Little Italy with their fingers curled around the handles of espresso cups, dreaming about the days when everyone respected them. Joe ain't got no time for that. Joe don't want folks to respect him, Joe wants folks to be scared to death of him.'

We turned on to Esplanade. Morphy signalled and pulled in about two blocks from the Flaisance. He stared out of the window, tapping the index finger of his right hand against the steering wheel to some internal rhythm in his head. I sensed he had something more to say. I decided to let him say it in his own time.

'You've spoken to this guy, the guy who took your wife and kid, right?'

I nodded.

'It's the same guy? The same guy who did Tee Jean and the old woman?'

'He called me yesterday. It's him.'

'He say anything?'

'The feds have it on tape. He says he's going to do more.'

Morphy rubbed the back of his neck with his hand and squeezed his eyes shut tightly. I knew he was seeing Tante Marie in his head again.

'You going to stay here?'

'For a time, yes.'

'Could be the feds ain't gonna like it.'

I smiled. 'I know.'

Morphy smiled back. He reached beneath his seat and handed me a long brown envelope. 'I'll be in touch,' he said. I slipped the envelope under my jacket and stepped from the car. He gave a small wave as he drove away through the midday crowd.

I opened the envelope in my hotel room. Inside were a set of crime-scene pictures and photocopied extracts of the police reports, all stapled together. Stapled separately was a copy of the ME's report. One section had been emphasised with a luminous yellow felt-tip.

The ME had found traces of ketamine hydrochloride in the bodies of Tante Marie and Tee Jean, equivalent to a dosage of one milligram per kilo of weight. According to the report, ketamine was an unusual drug, a special type of anaesthetic used for some minor surgical procedures. No one was too clear on its precise mode of action apart from the fact that it was a PCP analogue and worked on sites in the brain, affecting the central nervous system.

It was becoming the drug of choice in the clubs of New York and LA while I was still on the force, usually in capsules or tabs made by heating the liquid anaesthetic to evaporate the water, leaving ketamine crystals. Users described a ketamine trip as 'swimming in the K pool' since it distorted the perception of the body, creating a feeling that the user was floating in a soft yet supportive medium. Other side-effects included hallucinations, distortions in the perception of space and time, and out-of-body experiences.

What the ME did note was that ketamine could be used as a chemical restrainer on animals, since it induced paralysis and dulled pain while allowing the normal pharyngeal-laryngeal reflexes to continue. It was for this purpose, he surmised, that the killer had injected both Tante Marie and Tee Jean Aguillard with the drug.

When they were flayed and anatomised, the report concluded, Tante Marie and her son had been fully conscious.

# Chapter Thirty-Four

When I had finished reading the ME's report, I put on my sweats and running shoes and did about four miles on Riverfront Park, back and forth past the crowds queuing to take a trip on the Natchez paddle steamer, the sound of its wheezing calliope sending tunes like messengers across the Mississippi. I was thick with sweat when I was done, and my knees ached. Even three years ago, four miles wouldn't have troubled me to such a degree. I was getting old. Soon, I'd be looking at bathchairs and feeling impending rain in my joints.

Back at the Flaisance, Rachel Wolfe had left a message to say that she would be flying in later that evening. The flight number and the arrival time were listed at the bottom of the message slip. I thought about Joe Bones and decided then that Rachel Wolfe might like some company on the flight down to New Orleans.

I called Angel and Louis.

The Aguillard family collected the bodies of Tante Marie, Tee Jean and Florence later that day. A firm of Lafayette undertakers placed Tante Marie's coffin into a wide-back hearse. Tee Jean and Florence lay side by side in a second.

The Aguillards, led by the eldest son, Raymond, and accompanied by a small group of family friends, followed the hearses in a trio of pick-up trucks, dark-skinned men and women seated on pieces of sacking amid machine parts and farm tools. I stayed behind them as they slipped from the highway and made their way down the rutted track, past Tante Marie's where the police tape fluttered lightly in the breeze, and on to the house of Raymond Aguillard.

He was a tall, large-boned man in his late forties or early fifties, running to fat now but still an imposing figure. He wore a dark cotton suit, a white shirt and a slim black tie. His eyes were red-rimmed from crying. I had seen him briefly at Tante Marie's the night the bodies were found, a strong man trying to hold his family together in the face of violent loss.

He spotted me as the coffins were unloaded and carried towards the house, a small group of men struggling with Tante Marie. I stood out, since I was the only white face in the crowd. A woman, probably one of Tante Marie's daughters, shot me a cold look as she passed by, a pair of older women at each shoulder. When the bodies had been carried into the house, a raised, slatted-wood building not unlike the home of Tante Marie herself, Raymond kissed a small cross around his neck and walked slowly towards me.

'I know who you are,' he said, as I extended my hand. He paused for a moment before taking it in a short, firm grip.

'I'm sorry,' I said, 'sorry about it all.'

He nodded. 'I know that.' He walked on, past the white fence at the boundary of the property, and stood by the side of the road, staring out at the empty stretch of track. A pair of mallards flew overhead, their wing-beats slowing as they approached the water below. Raymond watched them with a kind of envy, the envy that a man deeply grieving feels for anything untouched by his sorrow.

'Some of my sisters, they think maybe you brought this man with you. They think you got no right to be here.'

'Is that what you think?'

He didn't answer. Then: 'She felt him comin'. Maybe that's

why she sent Florence to the party, to get her away from him. And that's why she sent for you. She felt him comin' and I think she knowed who he was. Deep down, I think she knowed.' His voice sounded thick in his throat.

He fingered the cross gently, rubbing his thumb back and forth along its length. I could see that it had originally been ornately carved – it was still possible to discern some details of spirals at its edges – but for the most part it had been rubbed smooth by the action of this man's hand over many years.

'I don't blame you for what happened to my momma and my brother and sister. My momma, she always done what she believed was right. She wanted to find that girl and to stop the man that killed her. And that Tee Jean . . .' He smiled sadly. 'The policeman said that he'd been hit three, maybe four times from behind, and there were still bruises on his knuckles where he tried to fight this man.'

Raymond coughed before he spoke again and then breathed deeply through his mouth, his head tipped back slightly like a man who has run a great distance in pain.

'He took your woman, your child?' he said. It was as much a statement as a question, but I answered it anyway.

'Yes, he took them. Like you said, Tante Marie believed that he took another girl too.'

He dug the thumb and forefinger of his right hand into the corners of his eyes and blinked out a tear.

'I know. I seen her.'

The world around me seemed to grow silent as I shut out the noise of the birds, the wind in the trees, the distant sound of water splashing on the banks. All I wanted to hear was Raymond Aguillard's voice.

'You saw the girl?'

'That's what I said. Down by a slough in Honey Island, three nights ago. Night before my momma died. Seen her other times too. My sister's husband, he got himself some traps down there.' He shrugged. Honey Island was a nature reserve. 'You a superstitious man, Mista Parker?'

'I'm getting there,' I replied. 'You think that's where she is, down in Honey Island?'

'Could be. My momma'd say she didn't know where she was, just *that* she was. She knew the girl was out there somewhere. I just don't know how, Mista Parker. I never did understand my momma's gift. But then I seen her, a figure out by a cypress grove and a kinda darkness over her face, like a hand was coverin' it, and I knowed it was her.'

He looked down and, with the toe of his shoe, began picking at a stone embedded in the dirt. When he eventually freed it, sending it skidding into the grass, tiny black ants scurried and crawled from the hole, the entrance to their nest now fully exposed.

'Other people seen her too, I hear, folks out fishin' or checkin' the hooch they got distillin' in a shack somewheres.' He watched as the ants swarmed around his foot, some of them climbing on to the rim of his sole. Gently, he lifted his foot, shook it, and moved it away.

There were seventy thousand acres of Honey Island, Raymond explained. It was the second-biggest swamp in Louisiana, forty miles long and eight miles wide. It was part of the flood plain of the Pearl river, which acts as a boundary line between Louisiana and Mississippi. Honey Island was better preserved than the Florida Everglades: there was no dredging allowed, no draining or timber-farming, no development and no dams, and parts of Honey Island weren't even navigable. Half of it was state-owned; some was the responsibility of the Nature Conservancy. If someone was trying to dump a body in a place where it was unlikely to be discovered, then, tourist boats apart, Honey Island sounded like a good place to do it.

Raymond gave me directions to the slough and drew a rough map on the back of an opened-out Marlboro pack.

'Mista Parker, I know you're a good man and that you're sorry for what happened, but I'd be grateful to you if you didn't come out here no more.' He spoke softly, but there was no mistaking the force in his voice. 'And maybe you'd be kind enough not to turn up at the burial. My family, it's gonna take us a long time to get over this.'

Then he lit the last cigarette from the pack, nodded a goodbye and walked back to his house trailing smoke behind him.

I watched him as he walked away. A woman with steel-grey hair came out on to the porch and placed her arm around his waist when she reached her. He put a big arm around her shoulders and held her to him as they walked into the house, the screen door closing gently behind them. And I thought of Honey Island, and the secrets that it held beneath its green waters, as I drove away from the Aguillard house, the dust rising behind me.

As I drove, the swamp was already preparing to reveal its secrets. Honey Island would yield a body within twenty-four hours, but it would not be the body of a girl.

# Chapter Thirty-Five

I arrived early at Moisant Field so I browsed around the bookstore for a while, taking care to avoid tripping over the piles of Anne Rice novels.

I had been sitting in the arrivals hall for about an hour when Rachel Wolfe walked through the gates. She was wearing dark blue jeans, white sneakers and a red and white Polo Sport top. Her red hair hung loose on her shoulders and her makeup had been so carefully applied that it was almost indiscernible.

The only luggage she carried herself was a brown leather shoulder bag. The rest of what I took to be her belongings were being toted by Angel and Louis, who walked slightly self-consciously at either side of her, Louis in a cream double-breasted suit with a snow-white dress shirt open at the neck, Angel in jeans, battered Reebok hi-tops and a green check shirt that had not felt an iron since it left the factory many years before.

'Well, well,' I said, as they stood before me. 'All human life is here.'

Angel raised his right hand, from which dangled three thick piles of books, tied together by string. The ends of his fingers were turning purple. 'We brought half the New York Public Library with us as well.' He groaned. 'Tied with string. I ain't seen books tied with string since *Little House on the Prairie* stopped reruns.'

Louis, I noticed, was carrying a lady's pink umbrella and a cosmetics case. He had the look of a man who is trying to pretend that a dog isn't screwing his leg. 'Don't say a word, man,' he warned. 'Not a word.'

Between them, the two men also carried two suitcases, two leather travelling bags and a suit-carrier. 'Car's parked outside,' I said, as I walked with Rachel to the exit. 'Might be just enough room for the bags.'

'They paged me at the airport,' whispered Rachel. 'They were very helpful.' She giggled and glanced over her shoulder. Behind us, I heard the unmistakable sound of Angel tripping on a bag and swearing loudly.

We ditched the luggage at the Flaisance, despite Louis's stated preference for the Fairmont at University Place. The Fairmont was where the Republicans usually stayed when they hit New Orleans, which was part of its appeal for Louis. He was the only gay, black, Republican criminal I knew.

'Gerald Ford stayed at the Fairmont,' he lamented, as he surveyed the small suite he was to share with Angel.

'So?' I countered. 'Paul McCartney stayed at the Richelieu and you don't hear me demanding to stay there.' I left the door open and headed back to my own room for a shower.

'Paul *who*?' said Louis.


We ate in the Grill Room of the Windsor Court on Gravier Street, in deference to Louis's wishes, its marbled floors and heavy Austrian drapes strangely uncomfortable for me after the informal setting of the smaller eateries in the Quarter. Rachel had changed into dark trousers and a black jacket over a red blouse. It looked fine but the hot night air had taken its toll on her and she was still pulling the damp cloth of her blouse away from her body as we waited for the main courses.

As we ate, I explained to them about Joe Bones and the Fontenots. They would be a matter for Angel, Louis and me.

Rachel remained silent for much of our conversation, interjecting occasionally to clarify things that had been said by Woolrich or Morphy. She scribbled notes in a small, wirebound notebook, her handwriting neat and even. At one point her hand brushed my bare arm lightly and she left it there for an instant, her skin warm against mine.

I watched Angel pulling at his lip as he considered what I had said. 'This Remarr must be pretty dumb, dumber than our guy at least,' he said eventually.

'Because of the print?' I said.

He nodded. 'Careless, very careless.' He wore the dissatisfied look of a respected theologian who has seen someone bring his calling into disrepute by identifying Jesus as an alien.

Rachel spotted the look. 'It seems to bother you a lot,' she commented. I glanced at her. She had an amused expression on her face, but her eyes were calculating and slightly distant. She was playing over in her mind what I had told her, even as she engaged Angel in a conversation that he would usually have avoided. I waited to see how he would respond.

He smiled at her and tilted his head. 'I have a certain professional interest in these things,' he admitted. He cleared a space in front of him and held up his hands before us.

'Anyone doing a B & E job – that's breaking and entering, for the benefit of our more respectable listener – needs to take certain precautions,' began Angel. 'The first and most obvious is to make sure that he – or she, B & E being an equal-opportunities profession – doesn't leave any fingerprints. So what do you do?'

'You wear gloves,' said Rachel. She leaned forward now, enjoying the lesson and putting aside any other thoughts.

'Right. Nobody, no matter how dumb, enters a place he shouldn't be without wearing gloves. Otherwise, you leave visuals, you leave latents, you pretty much sign your name and confess to the crime.'

Visuals are the visible marks left on surfaces by a dirty or bloody hand, latents the invisible marks left by natural secretions of the skin. Visuals can be photographed or lifted using adhesive tape, but latents need to be dusted, typically with a chemical reagent like iodine vapour or ninhydrin solution. Electrostatic and fluorescence techniques are also useful and, in the search for latents on human skin, specialised X-ray photography can be used.

But if what Angel had said was correct, Remarr was too much of a professional to risk a job without gloves and then to leave not merely a latent, but a visual. He must have been wearing gloves, but something had gone wrong.

'You working it through in your head, Bird?' smirked Angel.

'Go on, Sherlock, baffle us with your brilliance,' I responded.

His smirk widened to a grin, and he continued, 'It's possible to get a fingerprint from *inside* a glove, assuming you have the glove. Rubber or plastic gloves are best for obtaining prints: your hands get sweaty under them.

'But what most people don't know is that the exterior surface of a glove can act like a fingerprint as well. Say it's a leather glove, then you got wrinkles, you got holes, you got scars, you got tears and no two leather gloves are gonna be the same. Now, in the case of this guy Remarr, what we have is a print and no gloves. Unless Remarr can't tie his shoelaces without falling over, we know that he was probably wearing gloves, but he still manages to leave a print. It's a mystery.' He made a small, exploding gesture with his hands, like a magician making a rabbit disappear in a puff of smoke, then his face became serious.

'My guess is that Remarr was wearing only a single pair of gloves, probably latex. He imagined this was going to be an easy job: either he was gonna off the old lady and her son, or he was gonna put the frighteners on her, maybe leave a calling card in the house. Since the son, from what I hear, wasn't the kind of guy to let anyone frighten his momma, I'd say Remarr went in there thinking that he might have to kill someone.

'But when he arrives, they're either dead or they're in the process of being killed. Again, my guess is they were already dead. If Remarr stumbled in on the killer, Remarr would be dead as well.

'So Remarr is going in, his one pair of gloves on, and maybe he spots the kid and it throws him. He probably starts to sweat. He goes into the house and finds the old lady. Bam! Second shock, but he goes to take a closer look, steadying himself as he leans over her. He touches blood and maybe considers wiping it away, but he figures wiping it away will only attract more attention to it and, anyway, he's got his gloves.

'But the problem with latex gloves is that one pair isn't enough. You wear them for too long and your prints start coming through. You get thrown, you start to sweat, the prints are gonna come through faster. Could be Remarr has been eating before he came out, maybe some fruit or some kind of pasta with vinegar. That causes extra moisture on the skin, so now Remarr is in real trouble. He's left a print he doesn't even know about, and now the cops, the feds and difficult people like our good selves want to ask him about it. Ta-da!' He gave a small bow from the waist. Rachel gave him a round of applause.

'Fascinating,' said Rachel. 'You must read a lot of books.' Her tone was heavily ironic.

'He does, then Barnes and Noble gonna be grateful that their stolen stock being put to good use,' remarked Louis.

Angel ignored him. 'Maybe I dabbled in these things, in my younger days.'

'Did you learn anything else, in your "younger" days?' smiled Rachel.

'Lot of things, some of them hard lessons,' said Angel, with feeling. 'Best thing I ever learned: don't hold on to nothin'. If you don't have it, can't nobody prove you took it.

'And I *have* been tempted. There was this figure of a knight on a horse once. French, seventeenth century. Gold inlaid with diamonds and rubies. About this tall.' He held the palm of his hand flat about six inches above the table. 'It was the most beautiful thing I ever saw.' His eyes lit up at the memory. He looked like a child.

He sat back in his chair. 'But I let it go. In the end, you have to let things go. The things you regret are the things you hold on to.'

'So is nothing worth holding on to?' asked Rachel.

Angel looked at Louis for a time. 'Some things are, yeah, but they ain't made of gold.'

'That's so romantic,' I said. Louis made choking noises as he tried to swallow his water.

Before us, the remains of our coffee lay cold in the cups. 'Do you have anything to add?' I asked Rachel, when Angel had finished playing to the gallery.

She glanced back through her notes. Her brow furrowed slightly. She held a glass of red wine in one hand and the light caught it, reflecting a streak of red across her breast like a wound.

'You said you had pictures, crime-scene pictures?' she asked. I nodded.

'Then I'd like to hold off until I've had a chance to see them. I have an idea based on what you told me over the phone, but I'd prefer to keep it to myself until I've seen the pictures and done a little more research. I do have one thing, though.' She took a second notebook from her bag and flicked through the pages to where a yellow Post-it note stuck out. ' "I lusted for her, but that has always been a weakness of my kind," ' she read. ' "Our sin was not pride, but lust for humanity." '

She turned to me, but I already recognised the words. 'They were the words this "Travelling Man" said to you when he called,' she said. I was aware of Angel and Louis moving forward in their chairs. 'It took a theologian in the Archbishop's palace to track down the reference. It's pretty obscure, at least if you're not a theologian.' She paused, then asked, 'Why was the Devil banished from heaven?'

'Pride,' said Angel. 'I remember Sister Agnes telling us that.'

'It was pride,' said Louis. He glanced at Angel. 'I remember *Milton* telling us that.'

'*Anyway*,' said Rachel pointedly, 'you're right, or partially right. From Augustine onwards, the Devil's sin is pride. But before Augustine, there was a different viewpoint. Up until the fourth century, the Book of Enoch was considered to be part of the Biblical canon. Its origins are a matter of dispute – it may have been written in Hebrew or Aramaic, or a combination of both – but it does seem to have provided a basis for some concepts that are still found in the Bible today. The Last Judgement may have been based on the Similitudes of Enoch. The fiery hell ruled by Satan also appears for the first time in Enoch.

'What is interesting for us is that Enoch takes a different view of the Devil's sin.' She turned a page of her notebook and began to read again. ' "And it came to pass, when men began to multiply on the face of the earth, and daughters were born unto them, that the sons of God saw the daughters of men that they were fair; and they took them wives of all which they chose . . ." '

She looked up again. 'That's from Genesis, which derives from a similar source as Enoch. The "sons of God" were the angels, who gave in to sexual lust against the will of God. The leader of the sinning angels, the Devil, was cast into a dark hole in the desert and his accomplices were thrown into the fire for their punishment. Their offspring, "evil spirits upon the earth", went with them. The martyr Justin believed that the children of the union between angels and human women were responsible for all evil on the earth, including murder.

'In other words, lust was the sin of the Devil. Lust for humanity, the "weakness of our kind".' She closed the notebook and permitted herself a small smile of triumph.

'So this guy believes he's a demon,' said Angel eventually.

'Or the offspring of an angel,' added Louis. 'Depends on how you look at it.'

'Whatever he is, or thinks he is, the Book of Enoch is hardly likely to turn up on Oprah's book choice,' I said. 'Any idea what his source might have been?'

Rachel reopened the notebook. 'The most recent reference I could find is a nineteen eighty-three New York edition: *The Old Testament Pseudepigrapha: Enoch*, edited by a guy called Isaac, appropriately enough,' she said. 'There's also an older translation from Oxford, published in nineteen thirteen by R. H. Charles.'

I noted the names. 'Maybe Morphy or Woolrich can check with the University of New Orleans, see if anyone local has been expressing an interest in the obscure end of Biblical studies. Woolrich might be able to extend the search to the other universities. It's a start.'

We paid the bill and left. Angel and Louis headed off towards the lower Quarter to check out the gay nightlife while Rachel and I walked back to the Flaisance. We didn't speak for a time, both of us conscious that we were on the verge of some intimacy.

'I get the feeling that I shouldn't ask what those two currently do for a living,' said Rachel, as we paused at a crossing.

'Probably not. It's best to view them as independent operators and leave it at that.'

She smiled. 'They seem to have a certain loyalty to you. It's unusual. I'm not sure that I understand it.'

'I've done things for them in the past but, if there ever was a debt, it was paid a long time ago. I owe them a lot more now.'

'But they're still here. They still help when they're asked.'

'I don't think that's entirely because of me. They do what they do because they like it. It appeals to their sense of adventure, of danger. In their own separate ways, they're both dangerous men. I think that's why they came: they sensed danger and they wanted to be part of it.'

'Maybe they see something of that in you.'

'I don't know. Maybe they do.'

We walked through the courtyard of the Flaisance, stopping only to pat the dogs. Her room was three doors down from mine. Between our rooms were the room shared by Angel and Louis and one unoccupied single room. She opened the door and stood at the threshold. From inside, I could feel the coolness of the air conditioning and could hear it pumping at full power.

'I'm still not sure why you're here,' I said. My throat felt dry and part of me was not certain that it wanted to hear an answer.

'I'm still not sure either,' she said. She stood on her toes and kissed me gently, softly on the lips, and then she was gone.

I went to my room, took a book of Sir Walter Ralegh's writings from my bag and headed back out to the Napoleon House, where I took a seat by the portrait of the Little Corporal. I didn't want to lie on my bed, conscious of the presence of Rachel Wolfe so near to me. I was excited and troubled by her kiss, and by the thought of what might follow.

Almost until the very end, Susan and I had enjoyed an incredible intimacy together. When my drinking truly began to take its toll on us, that intimacy had disintegrated. When we made love it was no longer totally giving. Instead, we seemed to circle each other warily in our lovemaking, always holding something back, always expecting trouble to rear its head and cause us to spring back into the security of our own selves.

But I had loved her. I had loved her until the end and I still loved her now. When the Travelling Man had taken her he had severed the physical and emotional ties between us, but I could still feel the remains of those ties, raw and pulsing at the very extremity of my senses.

Maybe this is common to all those who lose someone whom they have loved deeply. Making contact with another potential partner, another lover, becomes an act of reconstruction, a building not only of a relationship but also of oneself.

But I felt myself haunted by my wife and child. I felt them, not only as an emptiness or a loss, but as an actual presence in my life. I seemed to catch glimpses of them at the edges of my existence, as I drifted from consciousness to sleep, from sleep to waking. Sometimes, I tried to convince myself that they were simply phantoms of my guilt, creations born of some psychological imbalance.

Yet I had heard Susan speak through Tante Marie and, once, like a memory from a delirium, I had awakened in the darkness to feel her hand on my face and I had caught a trace of her scent in the empty bed beside me. More than that, I saw traces of them in every young wife, in each female child. In a young woman's laughter, I heard the voice of my wife. In the footsteps of a little girl, I heard the echo of my daughter's feet falling.

I felt something for Rachel Wolfe, a mixture of attraction and gratitude and desire. I wanted to be with her but only, I thought, when my wife and child were at peace.

# Chapter Thirty-Six

David Fontenot died that night. His car, a vintage Jensen Interceptor, was found on 190, the road that skirts Honey Island and leads down to the shores of the Pearl. The front tyres of the car were flat and the doors were hanging open. The windscreen had been shattered and the interior was peppered with 9mm holes.

The two St Tammany cops followed a trail of broken branches and flattened scrub to an old trapper's shack made of bits of salvaged wood, its tin roof almost obscured by overhanging Spanish moss. It overlooked a bayou lined with gum trees, its waters thick with lime-green duckweed and ringing with the sound of mallards and wood ducks.

The shack had been abandoned for a long time. Few people now trapped in Honey Island. Most had moved further out into the bayous, hunting beaver, deer and, in some cases, alligators.

There were noises coming from the shack as the party approached, sounds of scuffling and thudding and heavy snorting drifting through the open door.

'Hog,' said one of the deputies.

Beside him, the local bank official who had called them in flicked the safety on his Ruger rifle.

'Shit, that sure won't be no good against no hog,' said the second deputy. The local, a thick-set, balding man in a Tulane

Green Wave T-shirt and an almost unused hunting jacket, reddened. He was carrying a 77V with a telescopic sight, what they used to call in Maine a 'varmint rifle'. It was good for small game and some police forces even used it as a sniper rifle, but it wouldn't stop a feral hog first time unless the shot was perfect.

They were only a few feet away from the shack when the hog sensed them. It erupted from the open door, its tiny, vicious eyes wild and blood dripping from its snout. The man with the Ruger dived into the bayou waters to avoid it as it came at him. The hog spun, cornered at the water's edge by the party of armed men, then lowered its head and charged again.

There was an explosion in the bayou, then a second, and the hog went down. Most of the top of its head was gone and it twitched briefly on the ground, pawing at the dirt, until eventually it ceased to move. The deputy blew smoke theatrically from the long barrel of a Colt Anaconda, ejected the spent .44 Magnum cartridges with the ejector rod, then reloaded.

'Jesus,' said the voice of his partner. He was standing in the open doorway of the shack, his gun by his side. 'Hog sure got at him but it's Dave Fontenot all right.'

The hog had ruined most of Fontenot's face and part of his right arm was gnawed away, but even the damage caused by the hog couldn't disguise the fact that someone had forced David Fontenot from his car, hunted him through the trees and then cornered him in the shack, where he was shot in the groin, the knees, the elbows and the head.

'Mon,' said the hog-killer, exhaling deeply. 'When Lionel hears about this, there's gonna be hell to pay.'

I learned most of what had taken place during a hurried telephone conversation with Morphy and a little more from

WDSU, the local NBC affiliate. Afterwards, Angel, Louis and I breakfasted at Mother's on Poydras Street. Rachel had barely worked up the energy to answer the phone when we called her room, and had decided to sleep on and eat later in the morning.

Louis, dressed in an ivory-coloured linen suit and a white T-shirt, shared my bacon and homemade biscuits, washed down with strong coffee. Angel opted for ham, eggs and grits.

'Old folks eat grits, Angel,' said Louis. 'Old folks and the insane.'

Angel wiped a white grit trail from his chin and gave Louis the finger.

'He's not so eloquent first thing in the morning,' said Louis. 'Rest of the day, he don't have no excuse.'

Angel gave Louis the finger again, scraped the last of the grits from the bowl and pushed it away. 'So, you figure Joe Bones took a pre-emptive strike against the Fontenots?' he said

'Looks that way,' I replied. 'Morphy figures he used Remarr to do the job – pulled him out of hiding then squirrelled him away again. He wouldn't entrust a job like that to anyone else. But I don't understand what David Fontenot was doing out by Honey Island without any back-up. He must have known that Joe Bones would take a crack at him if the opportunity arose.'

'Could be one of his own people set him up, hauled him out there on some dead-end pretext and let Joe Bones know he was coming?' said Angel.

It sounded plausible. If someone had drawn Fontenot out to Honey Island, then it must have been someone he trusted enough to make the trip. More to the point, that someone must have been offering something that Fontenot wanted, something to make him risk the drive to the reserve late at night.

I said nothing to Angel or Louis, but I was troubled that both

Raymond Aguillard and David Fontenot had, in their own different ways, drawn my attention to Honey Island in a period of less than one day. I thought that, after I had spoken to Joe Bones, I might have to disturb Lionel Fontenot in his time of grief.

My cellphone rang. It was the desk clerk from the Flaisance, informing us that a delivery addressed to a 'Mr Louis' had arrived and a courier was waiting for us to sign. We took a taxi back to the hotel. Outside, a black transit van was parked half on the kerb.

'Courier,' said Louis, but there were no markings on the van, nothing to identify it as a commercial vehicle.

In the lobby, the desk clerk sat nervously, watching a huge black man who was squeezed into an easy chair. He was shaven-headed and wearing a black T-shirt with 'Klan Killer' written in jagged white writing across the chest. His black combat trousers were tucked into nine-hole army boots. At his feet lay a long steel container, locked and bolted.

'Brother Louis,' he said, rising. Louis took out his wallet and handed over three hundred-dollar bills. The man tucked the money into the thigh pocket of his combats, removed a pair of Ray-Ban sunglasses from the same pocket and put them on before strolling out into the sunlight.

Louis motioned to the container. 'If you gentlemen would like to take that up to the room,' he said. Angel and I took an end each and followed him up to the suite. The case was heavy and something inside rattled as we walked.

'Those UPS couriers are sure getting bigger,' I said, as I waited for him to open the door.

'It's a specialised service,' said Louis. 'There are some things the airlines just wouldn't understand.'

When he had closed and locked the door behind us, he took a set of keys from the pocket of his suit and opened the case.

It was separated into three layers, which opened up like those in a tool kit. On the first layer were the constituent parts of a Mauser SP66, a three-round heavy-barrelled sniper rifle with a combined muzzle brake and flash hider. The parts were packed in a removable case. Beside it, a SIG P226 pistol and a belt holster lay in a fitted compartment.

In the second compartment sat two Calico M-960A mini-subs, made in the good old US of A, each hand-held sub fitted with a short barrel which extended less than an inch and a half beyond the fore-end. With the stock retracted, each gun measured a little over two feet in length and, empty, weighed just under five pounds. They were exceptionally lethal little guns, with a rate of fire of seven hundred and fifty rounds per minute. The third compartment contained an array of ammunition, including four one-hundred-round magazines of 9mm Parabellum for the subs.

'Christmas present?' I asked.

'Yup,' said Louis, loading a fifteen-round magazine into the butt of the SIG. 'I'm hoping to get a rail gun for my birthday.'

He handed Angel the case containing the Mauser, slipped on the belt holster and inserted the SIG. He then relocked the case and went into the bathroom. As we watched, he removed the panelling from beneath the sink with a screwdriver and shoved the case into the gap before replacing the panel. When he was satisfied that it was back in place, we left.

'You think Joe Bones will be pleased to see a bunch of strangers show up on his doorstep?' asked Angel, as we walked to my rental.

'We ain't strangers,' said Louis. 'We're just friends he ain't met yet.'

Joe Bones owned three properties in Louisiana, including a weekend house at Cypremort Point where his presence must have made the more respectable weekenders, with their expensive holiday houses bearing jokey names like Eaux-Asis and End of the Trail, distinctly uneasy.

His city residence lay across from Audubon Park, almost opposite the bus stop for the shuttle bus that took tourists to the New Orleans Zoo. I had taken a trip on the St Charles streetcar to inspect the house, a brilliantly white confection adorned with black wrought-iron balconies and a cupola topped with a gold weather-vane. Finding Joe Bones inside a place like that was like finding a cockroach in a wedding cake. In the carefully maintained garden, a flower I couldn't identify bloomed lushly. Its scent was sickly and heavy, its flower so large and red that it seemed more rotten than blooming, as if the flowers themselves would suddenly burst and send thick fluid down the branches of the plant, poisoning the aphids.

Joe Bones had deserted the house for the summer in favour of a restored plantation house out in West Feliciana Parish, over one hundred miles north of New Orleans. As impending hostilities with the Fontenots grew more and more likely, the decision to remain in West Feliciana allowed him to defend the country house with more force than he could in the city.

It was a white, eight-columned mansion set on about forty acres, bordered at two sides by an expanse of river flowing south towards the Mississippi. Four large windows looked out on to a wide gallery and the house was topped by two dormer windows set into its roof. An avenue of oaks led from a black iron gate through grounds set with camellias and azaleas until the trees stopped before a wide expanse of lawn. On the lawn, a small group of people stood around a barbecue or lounged on iron lawn furniture.

I spotted three security cameras within ten feet of the gate when we drew up, side-on. We had dropped Angel about half a mile back after cruising by the house once already, and I knew he was already making for the stand of cypress that stood opposite the gate. In the event of anything going down with Joe Bones, I decided that I had a better chance of dealing with it with Louis rather than Angel by my side.

A fourth camera overlooked the gate itself. There was no intercom and the gate remained resolutely closed, even when Louis and I leaned against the car and waved.

After two or three minutes a converted golf cart came from behind the house and hummed down the oak-lined avenue towards us. Three men in chinos and sports shirts stepped from it. They made no attempt to hide their Steyr machine pistols.

'Hi,' I said. 'We're here to see Joe Bones.'

'There ain't no Joe Bones here,' said one of the men. He was tanned and short, no more than five-six. His hair was braided tightly against his scalp, giving him a reptilian appearance.

'How about Mr Joseph Bonnano, is he there?'

'What are you, cops?'

'We're concerned citizens. We were hoping Mr Bones would make a donation to the David Fontenot funeral fund.'

'He already gave,' said the guy by the golf cart, a fatter version of the lizard man. His colleagues at the gate laughed fit to burst a gut.

I moved closer to the gate. Lizard Man's gun came up quickly.

'Tell Joe Bones that Charlie Parker is here, that I was in the Aguillard house on Sunday night and that I'm looking for Remarr. You think Funny Man back there can remember all that?'

He stepped back from the gate and, without taking his eyes off us, relayed what I had said to the guy by the golf cart. He took a walkie-talkie from the rear seat, spoke into it for a moment and then nodded at Lizard Man. 'He says let 'em through, Ricky.'

'Okay,' said Ricky, taking a remote signaller from his pocket, 'step back from the gate, turn around and put your hands against the car. You packing, then tell me now. I find anything you haven't told me about, I put a bullet in your head and feed you to the 'gators.'

We owned up to a Smith & Wesson and a SIG between us. Louis threw in an ankle knife for good measure. We left the car at the gate and walked behind the golf cart towards the house. One man sat in the back with his pistol pointing at us while Ricky walked behind us.

As we neared the lawn I could smell shrimp and chicken cooking on the barbecue. An iron table held an assortment of spirits and glasses. Abita and Heineken lay in a steel cooler packed with ice.

From the side of the house came a low growl, deep with viciousness and menace. At the end of a strong chain, which was anchored to a bolt set in concrete, was a huge animal. It had the thick coat of a wolf, flecked with the colouring of an Alsatian. Its eyes were bright and intelligent, which rendered its obvious savagery all the more threatening. It looked like it weighed at least one hundred and eighty pounds. Each time it tugged at its chain, it threatened to wrench the bolt from the ground.

I noticed that it seemed to be directing most of its attention at Louis. Its eyes focused on him intently and at one point it raised itself up on its hind legs in its efforts to strike at him. Louis looked at it with the detached interest of a scientist finding a curious new type of bacteria growing in his Petri dish.

Joe Bones speared a piece of spiced chicken with a fork and placed it on a china plate. He was only slightly taller than Ricky, with long dark hair swept back from his forehead. His nose had been broken at least once and a small scar twisted his upper lip on the left side. His white shirt was open to the waist and hung over a pair of Lycra running shorts. His stomach was hard and muscular, his chest and arms slightly overdeveloped for a man of his height. He looked mean and intelligent, like the animal on the chain, which probably explained how he had lasted for ten years at the top of the heap in New Orleans.

He placed some tomatoes, lettuce and cold rice mixed with peppers beside the chicken and handed the plate to a woman seated near by. She was older than Joe, I guessed, probably in her early or mid-forties. There was no darkness at her blonde roots and she wore little or no makeup, although her eyes were obscured by a pair of Wayfarers. She wore a short-sleeved silk robe over a white blouse and white shorts. Like Joe Bones, she was barefoot. To one side of them stood two more men in shirts and chinos, each armed with a machine pistol. I counted two more on the balcony and one sitting beside the main door to the house.

'You want something to eat?' asked Joe Bones. His voice was low, with only a faint trace of Louisiana in it. He looked at me until I responded.

'No, thanks,' I said. I noticed that he didn't offer any to Louis. I think Louis noticed, too.

Joe Bones helped himself to some shrimp and salad, then motioned to the two guards to help themselves to what was left. They took turns to do so, each eating a breast of chicken with his fingers.

'Those Aguillard murders. A terrible thing,' said Joe Bones. He waved me towards the only empty seat left after he sat down. I exchanged a look with Louis, shrugged and sat.

'Excuse me for presuming on an intimacy with you,' he continued, 'but I hear that the same man may have been responsible for the deaths of your family.' He smiled almost sympathetically. 'A terrible thing,' he repeated. 'A terrible thing.'

I held his gaze. 'You're well informed about my past.'

'When someone new comes to town and starts finding bodies in trees, I like to make it my business to find out about them. They might be good company.' He picked a piece of shrimp from his plate and examined it briefly before starting to eat.

'I understand you had an interest in purchasing the Aguillards' land,' I said.

Joe Bones sucked at a shrimp and placed the tail carefully to one side of his plate before responding. 'I have a lot of interests, and that wasn't Aguillard land. Just because some senile fuck decides to make up for a bad life by slipping land to the niggers doesn't make it nigger land.' He spat the word 'nigger' each time. His shell of courtesy had proved remarkably fragile and he seemed intent upon deliberately provoking Louis. It was an unwise course of action, even with guns around him.

'It seems that one of your men, Tony Remarr, may have been in the house the night that the Aguillards died. We'd be interested in talking to him.'

'Tony Remarr is no longer part of my operation,' said Joe Bones, returning to his formal mode of speech after the burst of profanity. 'We agreed a mutual parting of the ways and I haven't seen him in weeks. I had no idea he was in the Aguillard house until the police told me.'

He smiled at me. I smiled back.

'Did Remarr have anything to do with David Fontenot's death?'

Joe Bones's jaw tensed but he kept smiling. 'I have no idea. I heard about David Fontenot on the news this morning.'

'Another terrible thing?' I suggested.

'The loss of a young life is always terrible,' he responded. 'Look, I'm sorry about your wife and kid, I truly am, but I can't help you. And, frankly, now you're getting rude, so I'd like you to take your nigger and get the fuck off my property.'

The muscles in Louis's neck rippled, the only sign he gave that he had heard Joe Bones. Joe Bones leered at him, picked up a piece of chicken and tossed it towards the beast on the chain. It ignored the titbit until his owner snapped his fingers, when it fell on the chicken and devoured it in a single bite.

'You know what that is?' asked Joe Bones. He spoke to me, but his body language was directed at Louis. It expressed utter contempt. When I didn't respond, he continued.

'It's called a *boerbul*. A man named Peter Geertschen, a German, developed it for the army and anti-riot squads in South Africa by crossing a Russian wolf with an Alsatian. It's a white man's watchdog. It sniffs out niggers.' He turned his gaze on Louis and smiled.

'Careful,' I said. 'He might get confused and turn on you.' Joe Bones jerked in his chair as if he had been hit by a jolt of electricity. His eyes narrowed and searched my face for any indication that I was aware of a double meaning in what I had said. I stared right back at him.

'You better leave now,' said Joe Bones, with quiet, obvious menace. I shrugged and stood up, Louis moving close to me as I did so. We exchanged a look.

'Man got us on the run,' said Louis.

'Maybe, but if we leave like this he won't respect us.'

'Without respect, a man got nothing,' agreed Louis.

He picked a plate from the stack on the table and held it above his head. It exploded in a shower of china fragments as the .300 Winchester cartridge impacted and buried itself in the wood of the house behind. The woman in the chair dived to the grass, the two goons moved to cover Joe Bones and three men appeared running from the side of the house as the shot echoed in the air.

Ricky, the Lizard Man, was the first to reach us. He raised the pistol and his finger tightened on the trigger, but Joe Bones struck out at his gun arm, pushing it upwards.

'No! You dumb fuck, you want to get me killed?' He scanned the treeline beyond his property, then turned back to me. 'You come in here, you shoot at me, you scare my woman. The fuck do you think you're dealing with here?'

'You said the N-word,' said Louis quietly.

'He's right,' I agreed. 'You did say it.'

'I hear you got friends in New Orleans,' said Joe Bones, his voice threatening. 'I got enough troubles without the feds crawling on me, but I see you or your . . .' He paused, swallowing the word. '. . . friend anywhere near me again and I'll take my chances, you hear?'

'I hear you,' I said. 'I'm going to find Remarr, Joe. If it turns out that you've been holding out on us and this man gets away because of it, I'll come back.'

'You make us come back, Joe, and we gonna have to hurt your puppy,' said Louis, almost sorrowfully.

'You come back and I'll stake you out on the grass and let him feed on you,' snarled Joe Bones.

We backed away towards the oak-lined avenue, watching Joe Bones and his men carefully. The woman moved beside him to comfort him, her white clothes stained with grass. She kneaded gently at his trapezius with her carefully manicured hands, but he pushed her away with a hard shove to the chest. There was spittle on his chin.

Behind us, I heard the gate open as we retreated beneath the oaks.

'I didn't know Angel was such a good shot,' I said, as we reached the car. 'You been giving him lessons?'

'Uh-huh,' said Louis. He sounded genuinely shocked.

'Could he have hit Joe Bones?'

'Uh-uh. I'm surprised he didn't hit me.'

Behind us, I heard the door open as Angel slid into the back seat, the Mauser already back in its case.

'So, we gonna start hangin' out with Joe Bones, maybe shoot some pool, whistle at girls?'

'When did you ever whistle at girls?' asked Louis, bemused, as we pulled away from the gate and headed towards St Francisville.

'It's a guy thing,' said Angel. 'I can do guy things.'

# Chapter Thirty-Seven

It was late afternoon when we got back to the Flaisance, where there was a message waiting from Morphy. I called him at the sheriff's department and got passed on to a cellphone number.

'Where you been?' he asked.

'Visiting Joe Bones.'

'Shit, why'd you do a thing like that?'

'Making trouble, I guess.'

'I warned you, man. Don't be screwing with Joe Bones. You go alone?'

'I brought a friend. Joe didn't like him.'

'What'd your friend do?'

'He got born to black parents.'

Morphy laughed. 'I guess Joe is kind of sensitive about his heritage, but it's good to remind him of it now and then.'

'He threatened to feed my friend to his dog.'

'Yeah,' said Morphy, 'Joe sure does love that dog.'

'You got something?'

'Maybe. You like seafood?'

'No.'

'Good, then we'll head out to Bucktown. Great seafood there, best shrimp around. I'll pick you up in two hours.'

'Any other reason for seeing Bucktown other than seafood?'

'Remarr. One of his exes has a pad there. Might be worth a visit.'

Rachel wasn't in her room when I knocked. The desk clerk said she had gone out to the university campus earlier in the day. He also had a pile of faxes for her, he said. He looked queasily at the curled papers. I was tempted to flick through them but instead I went back to my room, showered and changed, and left a message for Rachel telling her that I'd call her later. I told Angel and Louis where I was going and asked them to watch out for her return. Louis was practising yoga exercises on the bedroom floor. Angel was watching *Welcome Back Kotter*.

Morphy was on time and we headed north on Canal Boulevard and then west on to Lakeshore Drive. The waters of Lake Pontchartrain sparkled in the early-evening light and, ahead of us, I could see the lights of cars heading towards Mandeville and Covington on the giant Lake Pontchartrain causeway. We passed the marina at West End Park and Morphy pointed out the tree-lined boulevard of the Southern Yacht Club. He had only once set foot in the club, the second oldest in the country, he said, when he was called to arrest a man who had set his business partner's yacht on fire after he learned that his partner was sleeping with his wife. The burning yacht had illuminated the bar where the firebug sat, nursing a glass of Chivas and waiting patiently for the police to arrest him.

Bucktown was pretty in a quaint sort of way, as long as you liked the smell of fish. I kept the window up to try to limit the damage but Morphy had his rolled right down and was taking deep, sinful breaths. All in all, Bucktown seemed an unlikely place for a man like Remarr to hole up, but that in itself was probably reason enough for him to choose it.

Carole Stern lived in a small camelback house, a single-storey at the front against a two-storey rear, set in a small garden a few blocks off Bucktown's main street. According to Morphy, Stern worked in a bar on St Charles but was currently serving time for possession of crack with intent to supply. Remarr was rumored to be keeping up the rental payments until she got out. We parked around the corner from the house and we clicked off the safeties of our guns in unison as we stepped from the car.

'You're a little out of your territory here, aren't you?' I asked Morphy.

'Hey, we just came out here for a bite to eat and decided to check on the off-chance,' he said, with an injured look. 'I ain't steppin' on no toes.'

He motioned me towards the front of the house while he took the back. I walked to the front door, which stood on a small raised porch, and peered carefully through the glass. It was caked with dirt, in keeping with the slightly run-down feel of the house itself. I counted five and then tried the door. It opened with a gentle creak and I stepped carefully into the hall. At the far end, I heard the tinkle of glass breaking and saw Morphy's hand reach in to open the rear door.

The smell was faint, but obvious, like meat that has been left in the sunlight on a warm day. The downstairs rooms were empty and consisted only of a kitchen, a small room with a sofa and an old TV, and a boxroom with a single bed and a closet. The closet contained women's clothes and shoes. The bed was covered only by a worn mattress.

Morphy took the stairs first. I stayed close behind, both of us with our guns pointing towards the second floor. The smell was stronger here now. We passed a bathroom with a dripping shower head, which had stained the ceramic bath brown. On a sink unit beneath a small mirror stood some shaving foam, blades and a bottle of Boss aftershave.

Three other doors stood partially open. On the right was a

woman's bedroom. It had white sheets, potted plants, which had begun to wither, and a series of Monet prints on the walls. There were cosmetics on a long dressing table and a white fitted closet ran the length of one wall. A window opposite looked out on to a small, overgrown garden.

There were more women's clothes in the closet, and more shoes. Carole Stern was obviously funding some kind of shopping addiction by selling drugs.

The second door provided the source of the smell. A large open pot sat on a camper stove by a window facing on to the street. It contained scummy water in which a stew of some kind was cooking on a low heat. From the stench, the meat had been allowed to simmer for some time, probably most of the day. It smelt foul, like offal. Two easy chairs stood in the room on a new red carpet. A portable TV with a coat-hanger aerial sat blankly on a small table.

The third room was also at the front of the house facing on to the street, but its door was almost closed. Morphy took one side of the door. I took the other. He counted three and then nudged the door open with his foot and went in fast to the right-hand wall. I moved in low to the left, my gun level with my chest, my finger resting on the trigger.

The setting sun cast a golden glow over the contents of the room: an unmade bed, a suitcase open on the floor, a dressing table, a poster on the wall advertising a concert by the Neville Brothers in Tipitina's, with the brothers' signatures scrawled loosely across their images. The carpeted floor felt damp beneath my feet.

Most of the plaster had been removed from the ceiling and the roof beams lay exposed. I guessed Carole Stern had been considering some sort of restoration before her prison sentence put her plans temporarily on hold. At the far end of the room, a series of what looked like climbing ropes had been strung over the beams and used to hold Tony Remarr in position.

His remains glowed with a strange fire in the dying sunlight. I could see the muscles and veins in his legs, the tendons in his neck, the yellow mounds of fatty deposits seeping at his waist, the muscles in his stomach, the shrivelled husk of his penis. Huge masonry nails had been driven into the far wall of the room and he hung partially on them, one beneath each arm, while the ropes took the main weight of his body.

As I moved to the right I could see a third nail in the wall behind his neck, holding his head in place. The head faced to the right, in profile, supported by another nail beneath his chin. In places, his skull gleamed whitely through the blood. His eye sockets were almost empty and his gritted teeth were white against his gums.

Remarr had been totally flayed, carefully posed and hung against the wall. His left hand stretched diagonally outwards and down from his body. A long-bladed knife, like a butcher's filleting tool but wider, heavier, hung from his hand. It looked like it had been glued in place.

But the viewer's gaze was drawn, like Tony Remarr's own blind stare, to the figure's right hand. It stood at a right angle to his body until it reached the elbow. From there, the forearm was raised vertically, pulled upwards by a rope around the wrist. In the fingers of his right hand and draped over his right arm, Tony Remarr held his own flayed skin. I could see the shape of the arms, the legs, the hair of his scalp, the nipples on his chest. Beneath the scalp, which hung almost at his knees, there were bloody edges where the face had been removed. The bed, the floor, the wall, all were shaded in red.

I looked to my left to see Morphy cross himself and softly say a prayer for the soul of Tony Remarr.

We sat against Morphy's car drinking coffee from paper cups as the feds and the New Orleans police milled around the Stern house. A crowd of people, some local, some on their way to eat in Bucktown's seafood joints, hung around the edges of the police cordon waiting to see the body being removed. They were likely to be disappointed: the crime scene was highly organised by the killer and both the police and the feds were anxious to document it fully before allowing the body to be taken away.

Woolrich, his tan suit now restored to its former tarnished glory, came over to us and offered us the remains of a bag of donuts from his suit pocket. Behind the cordon, I could see his own Chevy Nova, a red '96 model that shone like new.

'Here, you must be hungry.' Both Morphy and I declined the offer. I still had visions of Remarr in my head and Morphy looked pale and ill.

'You speak to the locals?' asked Woolrich.

We both nodded. We had given lengthy statements to a pair of homicide detectives from Orleans Parish, one of whom was Morphy's brother-in-law.

'Then I guess you can go,' said Woolrich. 'I'll want to talk to both of you again, though.' Morphy wandered around to the driver's side of his car. I moved to open the passenger door but Woolrich held my arm.

'You okay?' he asked.

'I think so.'

'It was a good hunch that Morphy followed, but he shouldn't have brought you along. Durand's gonna be on my back when he finds out that you were first on another crime scene.' Durand was the FBI's Special Agent in Charge in New Orleans. I had never met him but I knew what most SACs were like. They ruled their field offices like kingdoms, assigning agents to squads and giving the go-ahead to operations. The competition for SAC posts was intense. If nothing else, Durand was a tough customer.

'You're still at the Flaisance?'

'Still there.'

'I'll drop by. There's something I want to bounce off you.'

He turned and walked back towards the Stern house. On his way through the gate, he handed the bag of crushed donuts to a pair of patrolmen sitting in their car. They took the bag reluctantly, holding it like it was a bomb. When Woolrich had entered the house, one of them climbed out of the car and threw the donuts in a trash can.

Morphy dropped me at the Flaisance. Before he left, I gave him my cellphone number. He wrote it in a small black notebook, bound tightly with a rubber band. 'If you're free tomorrow, Angie's cooking dinner. It's worth the drive. You taste her cooking and you won't regret it.' The tone of his voice changed. 'Besides, there's some things I think we need to discuss.'

I told him it sounded okay, although part of me wanted never to see Morphy, Woolrich or another cop again. He was about to pull away from the kerb when I patted the roof of the car with my palm. Morphy leaned over and rolled down the window. 'Why are you doing this?' I asked. Morphy had gone to considerable lengths to involve me, to keep me posted on what was happening. I needed to know why. I think I also needed to know if I could trust him.

He shrugged. 'The Aguillards died on my beat. I want to get the guy who killed them. You know something about him. He's come at you, at your family. The feds are conducting their own investigation and are telling us as little as they can. You're all I got.'

'Is that it?' I could see something more in his face, something which was almost familiar.

'No. I got a wife. I'm starting a family. You know what I'm sayin'?'

I nodded and let it go, but there was something else in his

eyes, something that resonated inside me. I patted the roof of the car once again in farewell and watched as he drove away, wondering how badly Morphy wanted absolution for what he might have done.

# Chapter Thirty-Eight

As I returned to the Flaisance I felt an overpowering sense of decay which seemed to creep into my nostrils, almost stopping my breathing. It lodged itself beneath my nails and stained my skin. I felt it on the sweat on my back and saw it in the weeds breaking through the cracks in the pavement beneath my feet. It was as if the city was corroding around me. I went to my room and showered under a hot jet until my skin was red and raw, then changed into a sweater and chinos, called Angel and Louis in their room and arranged to meet them in Rachel's room in five minutes.

She answered the door with an ink-stained hand. She had a pencil tucked behind her ear and a pair of pencils held her red hair back in a bun. There were dark rims under her eyes, which were red from reading.

Her room had been transformed. A Macintosh PowerBook stood open on the room's only table, surrounded by a mass of paper, books and notes. On the wall above it were diagrams, yellow Post-it notes and a series of what appeared to be anatomy sketches. A pile of faxes lay on the floor by her chair, beside a tray of half-eaten sandwiches, a pot of coffee and a stained cup.

I heard a knock on the door behind me. I opened it to admit Angel and Louis. Angel looked at the wall in disbelief. 'Guy on the desk already thinks you're crazy, with all the shit that's been comin' in on his fax. He sees this, he's gonna call the cops.'

Rachel sat back in her chair and pulled the pencils from her bun, releasing her hair. She shook her tresses out with her left hand and then twisted her neck to ease her knotted muscles.

'So,' she said, 'who wants to start?'

I told them about Remarr and, instantly, the tiredness went from Rachel's face. She made me detail the position of the body twice and then spent a couple of minutes shuffling papers on her desk.

'There!' she said, handing me a sheet of paper with a flourish. 'Is that it?'

It was a black and white illustration, marked at the top of the page, in old lettering: 'TAB.PRIMERA DEL LIB. SEGVNDO'. At the bottom of the page, in Rachel's handwriting, was written 'Valverde 1556'.

The illustration depicted a flayed man, his left foot on a stone, his left hand holding a long knife with a hooked hilt, his right holding his own flayed skin. The outline of his face was visible on the skin and his eyes remained in his sockets but, with those exceptions, the illustration was profoundly similar to the position in which Remarr had been found. The various parts of the body were each marked with Greek letters.

'That's it,' I said quietly. 'That's what we found.'

I handed the illustration to Angel and Louis, who examined it in silence.

'The *Historia de la composición del cuerpo humano*,' said Rachel. 'It was written by the Spaniard Valverde in 1556 as a medical textbook. This drawing –' She reached out to take the page from Louis and held it up so we could all see it. '– is an illustration of the Marsyas myth. Marsyas was a satyr, a follower of the goddess Cybele. He was cursed when he picked up a bone flute discarded by Athene. The flute played itself, because it was still inspired by Athene, and its music was so beautiful that the peasants said it was greater even than that of Apollo himself.

'Apollo challenged Marsyas to a competition to be judged by the Muses and Marsyas lost because he couldn't play the flute upside down and sing at the same time. And so Apollo took his revenge on Marsyas. He flayed him alive and nailed his skin to a pine. According to the poet Ovid, at his moment of death Marsyas cried out, "*Quid me mihi detrahis?*" – "Who is it that tears me from myself?" The artist Titian painted a version of the myth. So did Raphael. My guess is that Remarr's body will reveal traces of ketamine. To fulfil the myth, the flaying would have to be carried out while the victim was still alive. After all, it's hard to create a work of art if the subject keeps moving.'

Louis interrupted, 'But in this picture he looks like he flayed himself. He's holding the knife *and* the skin. Why did the killer choose this depiction?'

'This is just a guess but maybe it's because, in a sense, Remarr did flay himself,' I said. 'He was at the Aguillard house when he shouldn't have been. I think the Travelling Man was concerned at what he might have seen. Remarr was somewhere he shouldn't have been, so he was responsible for what happened to him.'

Rachel nodded. 'It's an interesting point, but there may be something more to it, given what happened to Tee Jean Aguillard.' She handed me a pair of papers. The first was a photocopy of the crime-scene photo of Tee Jean. The second was another illustration, this time marked 'DE DISSECT. PARTIVM'. At the bottom of the page, the date '1545' had been handwritten by Rachel.

The illustration depicted a man crucified against a tree, with a stone wall behind it. His head was cradled by the branches of the tree, his arms spread by further branches. The skin below his chest had been flayed, revealing his lungs, kidneys and heart. Some unidentified organ, probably his stomach, lay on a raised platform beside him. His face was intact but, once again, the illustration matched the posture of Tee Jean Aguillard's body.

'Marsyas again,' said Rachel. 'Or at least an adaptation of the myth. That's from Estienne's *De dissectione partium corporis humani*, another early textbook.'

'Are you saying that this guy is killing according to a Greek myth?' asked Angel.

Rachel sighed. 'It's not that simple. I think the myth has resonances for him, for the simple reason that he's used it twice. But the Marsyas theory breaks down with Tante Marie, and Bird's wife and child. I found the Marsyas illustrations almost by accident, but I haven't found a match yet for the other deaths. I'm still looking. The likelihood is that they are also based on early medical textbooks. If that's the case, then I'll find them.'

'It raises the possibility that we're looking for someone with a medical background,' I said.

'Or a knowledge of obscure texts,' said Rachel. 'We already know that he has read the Book of Enoch, or some derivative of it. It wouldn't take a great deal of medical knowledge to carry out the kind of mutilation we've found on the bodies so far, but an assumption of some surgical skills, or even some mild familiarity with medical procedures, might not be totally amiss.'

'What about the blinding and the removal of the faces?' I asked. I pushed a flashing image of Susan and Jennifer to the back of my mind. 'Any idea where they fit in?'

Rachel shook her head. 'I'm still working on it. The face appears to be some form of token for him. Jennifer's was returned because she died before he could start working on her, I'd guess, but also because he wanted to shock you personally. The removal could also indicate the killer's disregard for them as individuals, a sign of his disregard for their own status as people. After all, when you remove a person's face, you take away the most immediate representation of their individuality, their main physical distinguisher.

'As for the eyes, there is a myth that the image of the killer stays on the retina of the victim. There were lots of myths like that attached to the body. Even at the start of the last century, some scientists were still examining the theory that a murder victim's body bled when it was in the same room as its killer. I need to do more work on it, then we'll see.'

She stood up and stretched. 'I don't mean to sound callous, but now I want to take a shower. Then I want to go out and get something decent to eat. After that, I want to sleep for twelve hours.'

Angel, Louis and I started to leave but she held up her hand to stop us. 'There's just one more thing. I don't want to give the impression that this is just some freak copying violent images. I don't know enough about this to make that kind of judgement and I want to consult some people who are more experienced in this area than I am. But I can't help feeling that there's some underlying philosophy behind what he's doing, some pattern that he's following. Until we find out what that is, I don't think we're going to catch him.'

I had my hand on the door handle when there was a knock at the door. I opened it slowly and blocked the view of the room with my body while Rachel cleared away her papers. Woolrich stood before me. In the light from the room, I noticed a thin growth of beard was forming on his face. 'Clerk told me you might be here if you weren't in your own room. Can I come in?'

I paused for a moment, then stepped aside. I noticed that Rachel was standing in front of the material on the wall, obscuring it from view, but Woolrich wasn't interested in her. His eyes had fixed on Louis.

'I know you,' he said.

'I don't think so,' said Louis. His eyes were cold.

Woolrich turned to me. 'You bringing your hired killers to my town, Bird?'

I didn't reply.

'Like I said, man, I think you're making a mistake,' said Louis. 'I'm a businessman.'

'Really? And what kind of business would you be in?'

'Pest control,' said Louis.

The air seemed to crackle with tension, until Woolrich turned around and walked from the room. He stopped in the hall and gestured to me. 'I need to talk to you. I'll wait for you in the Café du Monde.'

I watched him go, then looked at Louis. He raised an eyebrow. 'Guess I'm more famous than I thought.'

'Guess you are,' I said, and went after Woolrich.

I caught up with him on the street but he said nothing until we were seated and he had a *beignet* in front of him. He tore off a piece, sprinkling powdered sugar on his suit, then took a long draught of coffee, which half drained the cup and left a brown stain along its sides. 'C'mon, Bird,' he said. 'What are you trying to do here?' He sounded weary and disappointed. 'That guy, I know his face. I know what he is.' He chewed another piece of *beignet*.

I didn't reply. We stared at each other until Woolrich looked away. He dusted sugar from his fingers and ordered another coffee. I had hardly touched mine.

'Does the name Edward Byron mean anything to you?' he said eventually, when he realised that Louis was not going to be a topic of discussion.

'It doesn't ring any bells. Why?'

'He was a janitor in Park Rise. That's where Susan had Jennifer, right?'

'Right.' Park Rise was a private hospital in Long Island. Susan's father had insisted that we use it, arguing that its staff were among the best in the world. They were certainly among the best-paid. The doctor who delivered Jennifer earned more in a month than I made in a year.

'Where's this leading?' I asked.

'Byron was let go – quietly – following the mutilation of a corpse earlier this year. Someone performed an unauthorised autopsy on a female body. Her abdomen was opened and her ovaries and Fallopian tube removed.'

'No charges were pressed?'

'The hospital authorities considered it, then decided against it. Surgical gloves containing traces of the dead woman's blood and tissue were found in a bag in Byron's locker. He argued that someone was trying to frame him. The evidence wasn't conclusive – theoretically, someone could have planted that stuff in his locker – but the hospital let him go anyway. No court case, no police investigation, nothing. The only reason we have any record of it is because the local cops were investigating the theft of drugs from the hospital around the same time, and Byron's name was noted on the report. Byron was dismissed after the thefts began and they pretty much ceased, but he had an alibi each time there were found to be drugs missing.

'That was the last anyone heard of Byron. We have his social security number, but he hasn't claimed unemployment, paid tax, dealt with state government or visited a hospital since he was dismissed. His credit cards haven't been used since October nineteen ninety-six.'

'What brings his name up now?'

'Edward Byron is a native of Baton Rouge. His wife – his ex-wife – Stacey still lives there.'

'Have you spoken to her?'

'We interviewed her yesterday. She says she hasn't seen him since last April, that he owes her six months' alimony. The last cheque was drawn on a bank in East Texas but his old lady thinks he may be living in the Baton Rouge area, or somewhere near by. She says he always wanted to come back here, that he hated New York. We've also put out photos of him, taken from his employee record at Park Rise.'

He handed me a blown-up picture of Byron. He was a handsome man, his features marred only by a slightly receding chin. His mouth and nose were thin, his eyes narrow and dark. He had dark brown hair, swept from left to right. He looked younger than thirty-five, his age when the picture was taken.

'It's the best lead we've got,' said Woolrich. 'Maybe I'm telling you because I figure you have a right to know. But I'm telling you something else as well: you keep away from Mrs Byron. We've told her not to talk to anyone in case the press get wind of it. Secondly, stay away from Joe Bones. His guy Ricky was caught on one of our taps swearing blue hell about some stunt you pulled today, but you won't get away with it a second time.'

He laid some money on the table. 'Your little team back there got anything that might help us?'

'Not yet. I figured a medical background, maybe a sexual pathology. If I get anything more, I'll let you know. I've got a question for you, though. What drugs were taken from Park Rise?'

He tilted his head to one side and twisted his mouth slightly, as if debating with himself whether or not to tell me.

'Ketamine hydrochloride. It's related to PCP.' I gave no indication that I already knew about the drug. The feds would tear Morphy a new asshole if they knew he had been feeding me details like that, although they must have already had their suspicions. Woolrich paused for a moment and then went on. 'It was found in the bodies of Tante Marie Aguillard and her son. The killer used it as a form of anaesthetic.'

He spun his coffee cup on its saucer, waiting until it came to rest with the handle pointing in my direction.

'Are you scared of this guy, Bird?' he asked quietly. 'Because I sure am. You remember that conversation we had about serial killers, back when I brought you to meet Tante Marie?'

I nodded.

'Back then, I thought I'd seen it all. These killers were abusers and rapists and dysfunctionals who had crossed some line, but they were so pathetic that they were still recognisably human. But this one . . .'

He watched a family pass by in a carriage, the driver urging the horse on with the reins while he gave them his own history of Jackson Square. A child, a small, dark-haired boy, was seated at the edge of the family group. He watched us silently as they passed by, his chin resting on his bare forearm.

'We were always afraid that one would come who was different from the others, who was motivated by something more than a twisted, frustrated sexuality or wretched sadism. We live in a culture of pain and death, Bird, and most of us go through life without ever really understanding that. Maybe it was only a matter of time before we produced someone who understood that better than we did, someone who saw the world as just one big altar on which to sacrifice humanity, someone who believed he had to make an example of us all.'

'And do you believe that this is him?'

' "I am become Death, the destroyer of worlds." Isn't that what the Bhagavadgita says, Bird? "I am become Death." Maybe that's what he is: pure Death.'

He moved towards the street. I followed him, then remembered my slip of paper from the previous night. 'Woolrich, there is one more thing.' He looked testy as I gave him the references for the Book of Enoch.

'What the fuck is the Book of Enoch?'

'It's part of the Biblical Apocrypha. I think he may have some knowledge of it.'

Woolrich folded the paper and put it in the pocket of his

pants. 'Bird,' he said, and he almost smiled, 'sometimes I'm torn between keeping you in touch with what's happening and not telling you anything.' He grimaced, then sighed as if to indicate that this was something that just wasn't worth arguing about. 'Stay out of trouble, Bird, and tell your friends the same.' He walked away, to be swallowed up by the evening crowds.

I knocked on Rachel's door, but there was no reply. I knocked a second time, harder, and I heard some noises from inside the room. She answered the door with a towel wrapped around her body and her hair hidden by a second, smaller towel. Her face was red from the heat of the shower and her skin glowed.

'Sorry,' I said. 'I forgot that you'd be showering.'

She smiled and waved me in.

'Take a seat. I'll get dressed and let you buy me dinner.' She took a pair of grey pants and a white cotton shirt from the bed, picked some matching white underwear from her case and stepped back into the bathroom. She didn't close the door fully behind her so that we could talk while she dressed.

'Should I ask what that exchange was about?' she said.

I walked to her balcony window and looked out on to the street below.

'What Woolrich said about Louis is true. It's not as simple as that, maybe, but he has killed people in the past. Now, I'm not so sure. I don't ask, and I'm not in a position to pass judgement on him. But I trust both Angel and Louis. I asked them to come because I know what they're good at.'

She came out of the bathroom buttoning her shirt, her damp hair hanging. She dried her hair with a travel dryer, then applied a little makeup. I had seen Susan do the same things a thousand times, but there was a strange intimacy in watching Rachel perform them in front of me. I felt something stir inside me, a tiny yet significant shift in my feelings towards her. She sat on the edge of the bed and slipped her bare feet into a pair of black slingbacks, her finger moving inside each one to ease the progress of her heel. As she leaned foward, moisture glistened on the small of her back. She caught me looking at her and smiled cautiously, as if afraid of misinterpreting what she had seen. 'Shall we go?' she said.

I held the door open for her as we left, her shirt brushing my hand with a sound like water sizzling on hot metal.

We ate in Mr B's on Royal Street, the big mahogany room cool and dark. I had steak, tender and luscious, while Rachel ate blackened redfish, the spices causing her to gasp at the first bite. We talked of little things, of plays and films, of music and reading. It emerged that we had both attended the same performance of *The Magic Flute* at the Met in ninety-one, both of us alone. I watched her as she sipped her wine, the reflected light playing on her face and dancing in the darkness of her pupils like moonlight seen from a lakeshore.

'So, you often follow strange men to distant lands?'

She smiled. 'I bet you've been waiting to use that line all your life.'

'Maybe I use it all the time.'

'Oh, *puh*-lease. Next thing you'll be wielding a club and asking the waiter to step outside.'

'Okay, guilty as charged. It's been a while.'

I felt myself redden and caught something playful but uncertain in her glance – a kind of sadness, a fear of hurting and being hurt. Inside me, something twisted and stretched its claws, and I felt a little tear in my heart.

'I'm sorry. I know almost nothing about you,' I said quietly.

She reached out gently and brushed along the length of my left hand, from the wrist to the end of the little finger. She followed the curves of my fingers, delicately tracing the lines and whorls of my fingerprints, her touch soft as a leaf. At last, she let her hand rest on the table, the tips of her fingers resting on top of my own, and began to speak.

She was born in Chilson, near the foothills of the Adirondacks. Her father was a lawyer, her mother taught kindergarten. She liked basketball and running, and her prom date got the mumps two days before the prom, so her best friend's brother went with her instead and tried to feel her breast during 'Only the Lonely'. She had one brother of her own, Curtis, ten years her elder. For five of his twenty-eight years, Curtis had been a cop. He was two weeks short of his twenty-ninth birthday when he died. 'He was a detective with the county sheriff's office, newly promoted. He wasn't even on duty the day he was killed.' She spoke without hesitation, not too slowly, not too quickly, as if she had gone over the story a thousand times, examining it for flaws, tracing its beginning, its resolution, cutting all extraneous detail from it until she was left with the gleaming core of her brother's murder, the hollow heart of his absence.

'It was a quarter after two, a Tuesday afternoon. Curtis was visiting some girl in Moriah – he always had two or three girls trailing him at any one time. He just broke their hearts. He was carrying a bunch of flowers, pink lilies bought in a store five doors from the bank. He heard some shouting and saw two people come running out of the bank, both armed, both masked, a man and a woman. There was another man sitting in a car, waiting for them to come out.

'Curtis was drawing his gun when they saw him. They both had sawn-offs and they didn't hesitate. The man emptied both barrels into him and then, while he lay dying on the ground, the woman finished him off. She shot him in the face, and he was so handsome, so lovely.'

She stopped talking and I knew that this was a story she had told only in her mind, that it was something not to be shared, but to be safeguarded. Sometimes, we need our pain. We need it to call our own.

'When they caught them, they had three thousand dollars. That was all they got from the bank, all that my brother was worth to them. The woman had been released from an institution the week before. Someone decided that she no longer posed a threat to the community.'

She drained the last of her wine. I signalled for more and she remained silent as the waiter refilled her glass.

'And here I am,' she said at last. 'Now I try to understand, and sometimes I get close. And sometimes, if I'm lucky, I can stop things from happening to other people. Sometimes.'

I found that her hand was now gripped tightly in mine, and I could not recall how that had happened. Holding her hand, I spoke for the first time in many years about leaving New York and the move to Maine with my mother.

'Is she still alive?'

I shook my head. 'I got in trouble with a local big-shot named Daddy Helms,' I said. 'My grandfather and my mother agreed that I should go away to work for the summer, until things quietened down. A friend of his ran a store in Philly, so I worked there for a while, stacking shelves, cleaning up at night. I slept in a room above the store.

'My mother began taking physiotherapy for a trapped nerve in her shoulder, except it turned out that she had been mis-diagnosed. She had cancer. I think she knew, but she chose not to say anything. Maybe she thought that if she didn't admit it to herself, she could fool her system into giving her more time. Instead, one of her lungs collapsed as she left the therapist's office.

'I came back two days later on a Greyhound bus. I hadn't seen her in two months and when I tried to find her in the hospital ward, I couldn't. I had to check the names on the ends of the beds because she had changed so much. She lasted six weeks after that. Towards the end, she became lucid, even with the pain-killers. It happens a lot, I believe. It can fool you into thinking they're getting better. It's like the cancer's small joke. She was trying to draw a picture of the hospital the night before she died, so she would know where she was going when it was time to leave.'

I sipped some water. 'I'm sorry,' I said. 'I don't know why all those things should have come back to me.'

Rachel smiled and I felt her hand tighten again on mine.

'And your grandfather?'

'He died eight years ago. He left me his house in Maine, the one I'm trying to fix up.' I noticed that she didn't ask me about my father. I guessed that she knew all there was to know.

Later, we walked slowly back through the crowds, the music from the bars blending together into one blast of sound in which familiar tunes could sometimes be identified. When we came to the door of her room we held each other for a time, then kissed softly, her hand on my cheek, before we said goodnight.

Despite Remarr and Joe Bones and my exchanges with Woolrich, I slept peacefully that night, my hand still holding the spectre of her own.

# Chapter Thirty-Nine

It was a cool, clear morning and the sound of the St Charles streetcar carried on the air as I ran. A wedding limousine passed me on its way to the cathedral, white ribbons rippling on its hood. I jogged west along North Rampart as far as Perdido, then back through the Quarter along Chartres. The heat was intense, like running with my face in a warm, damp towel. My lungs struggled to pull in the air and my system rebelled, trying to reject it, but still I ran.

I was used to training three or four times each week, alternating circuits for a month or so with a split body-building workout. After a few days outside my training regimen I felt bloated and out of condition, as if my system was full of toxins. Given the choice between exercise and colon cleansers, I opted for exercise as the less uncomfortable option.

Back at the Flaisance I showered and changed the dressing on my wounded shoulder; it still ached a little, but the wounds were closing. Finally, I left a batch of clothes at the local laundry, since I hadn't figured on staying quite so long in New Orleans and my underwear selection was becoming pretty limited.

Stacey Byron's number was in the phone book – she hadn't reverted to her maiden name, at least not as far as the phone company was concerned – so Angel and Louis volunteered to hire a car and take a trip to Baton Rouge to see what they could find out from her, or about her. Woolrich wouldn't be pleased, but if he wanted her left in peace then he shouldn't have said anything at all.

Rachel e-mailed details of the kind of illustrations she was seeking to two of her research students in Columbia and to a retired professor in Boston named Father Eric Ward, a former lecturer at Loyola in New Orleans, who specialised in Renaissance culture. Instead of hanging around waiting for a response she decided to come with me to Metairie, where David Fontenot was due to be buried that morning.

We were silent as we drove. The subject of our growing intimacy and what it might imply had not come up between us, but it seemed that we were both acutely aware of it. I could see something of it in Rachel's eyes when she looked at me. I thought that she could probably see the same in mine.

'So what else do you want to know about me?' she asked.

'I guess I don't know too much about your personal life.'

'Apart from the fact that I'm beautiful and brilliant.'

'Apart from that,' I admitted.

'By personal, do you mean sexual?'

'It's a euphemism. I don't want to seem pushy. If it makes you happier you can start with your age, since you didn't tell me last night. The rest will seem easy by comparison.'

She gave me a twisted grin and the finger. I chose to ignore the finger.

'I'm thirty-three but I admit to thirty, if the lighting is right. I have a cat and a two-bedroom apartment on the Upper West Side, but no one to share it with currently. I do step aerobics three times each week and I like Chinese food, soul music and cream ale. My last relationship ended six months ago and I think my hymen may be growing back.'

I arched an eyebrow at her and she laughed. 'You do look shocked,' she said. 'You need to get out more.'

'Sounds like you do, too. Who was the guy?'

'A stockbroker. We'd been seeing each other for over a year and we agreed to live together on a test basis. He had a one-bed, I had a two-bed, so he moved in with me and we used the second bedroom as a shared study.'

'Sounds idyllic.'

'It was, for about a week. It turned out that he couldn't stand the cat, he hated sharing a bed with me because he said I kept him awake by turning over all the time and all my clothes started to smell of his cigarettes. That clinched it. Everything stank: the furniture, the bed, the walls, the food, the toilet paper, even the cat. Then he came home one evening, told me he was in love with his secretary and moved to Seattle with her three months later.'

'Seattle's nice, I hear.'

'Fuck Seattle. I hope it falls into the sea.'

'At least you're not bitter.'

'Very funny.' She looked out of her window for a while and I felt an urge to reach out and touch her, an urge enhanced by what she said next. 'I still feel reluctant to ask you too many questions,' she said, gently. 'After what happened.'

'I know.' Slowly, I extended my right hand and lightly touched her cheek. Her skin was smooth and slightly moist. She leaned her head towards me, increasing the pressure against my hand, and then we were pulling up outside the entrance to the cemetery and the moment was gone.

Branches of the Fontenots had lived in New Orleans since the late nineteenth century, long before the family of Lionel and David had moved to the city, and the Fontenots had a big vault in Metairie cemetery, the largest of the city's cemeteries at Metairie Road and Pontchartrain Boulevard. The cemetery covered one hundred and fifty acres and was built on the old Metairie racecourse. If you were a gambling man, it was an appropriate final resting place, even though it proved that, in the end, the odds are always stacked in favour of the house.

New Orleans cemeteries are strange places. While most cemeteries in big cities are carefully manicured and encourage discreet headstones, generations of the dead citizens of New Orleans rested in ornate tombs and spectacular mausoleums. They reminded me of Père Lachaise in Paris, or the Cities of the Dead in Cairo, where people still lived among the bodies. The resemblance was echoed by the Brunswig tomb, which was shaped like a pyramid and guarded by a sphinx.

It was not simply the funerary architecture of Spain and France that had caused the cemeteries to develop the way they did. Most of the city was below sea level and, until the development of modern drainage systems, graves dug in the ground had rapidly filled with water. Above-ground tombs were the natural solution.

The Fontenot funeral had already entered the cemetery when we arrived. I parked away from the main body of vehicles and we walked past the two police cruisers at the gate, their occupants' eyes masked by shades. We followed the stragglers past the four statues representing Faith, Hope, Charity and Memory at the base of the long Moriarity tomb, until we came to a Greek revival tomb marked with a pair of Doric columns. 'Fontenot' was inscribed on the lintel above the door.

It was impossible to tell how many Fontenots had come to rest in the family vault. The tradition in New Orleans was to leave the body for a year and a day, after which the vault was reopened, the remains moved to the back and the rotting casket removed to make way for the next occupant. A lot of the vaults in Metairie were pretty crowded by this point.

The wrought-iron gate, inlaid with the heads of angels, stood open and the small party of mourners had surrounded the vault in a semicircle. A man I guessed to be Lionel Fontenot towered above them. He was wearing a black, single-breasted suit and a thick black tie. His face had been weathered to a reddish-brown and deep lines etched his forehead and snaked out from the corners of his eyes. His hair was dark but streaked with grey at the temples. He was a big man, certainly six-three at least and weighing close on two hundred and forty pounds. His suit seemed to struggle to contain him.

Beyond the mourners, ranged at intervals around the vaults and tombs, or standing beneath trees scanning the cemetery, were four hard-faced men in dark jackets and pants. Their pistols caused the jackets to bulge slightly. A fifth man, a dark overcoat hanging loosely on his shoulders, turned at an old cypress and I caught a glimpse of the tell-tale sights of an M16-based submachine-gun concealed beneath its folds. Two others stood at either side of Lionel Fontenot. The big man wasn't taking any chances.

The mourners, both black and white – young white men in snappy black suits, old black women wearing black dresses gilded with lace at the neckline – grew silent as the priest began to read the rites of the dead from a tattered prayer book with gold-lined pages. There was no wind to carry away his words and they hung in the air around us, reverberating from the surrounding tombs like the voices of the dead themselves.

'*Our Father, who art in heaven . . .*'

The pall-bearers moved forward, struggling awkwardly to fit the casket through the narrow entrance to the vault. As it was placed inside, a pair of New Orleans policemen appeared between two round vaults about eighty feet west of the funeral party. Two more emerged from the east and a third pair moved slowly down past a tree to the north. Rachel followed my glance.

'An escort?'

'Maybe.'

'*Thy kingdom come, thy will be done on earth . . .*'

I felt uneasy. They could have been sent to ensure that Joe Bones wasn't tempted to disturb the mourners, but something was wrong. I didn't like the way they moved. They looked uncomfortable in the uniforms, as if their shirt collars were too tight and their shoes pinched.

'*Forgive us our trespasses . . .*'

Fontenot's men had spotted them, too, but they didn't look too concerned. The policemen's arms hung loosely by their sides and their guns remained in their holsters. They were about forty feet away from us when something warm splashed my face. An elderly moon-faced woman in a tight black dress, who had been sobbing quietly beside me, spun sideways and tumbled to the ground, a dark hole in her temple and a damp glistening in her hair. A chip of marble flew from the vault, the area around it stained a vivid red. The sound of the shot came almost simultaneously, a dull subdued noise like a fist hitting a punchbag.

'*But deliver us from evil . . .*'

It took the mourners a few seconds to realise what was happening. They looked dumbly at the fallen woman, a pool of blood already forming around her head as I pushed Rachel into the space between two vaults, shielding her with my body. Someone screamed and the crowd began to scatter as more bullets came, whining off the marble and stone. I could see Lionel Fontenot's bodyguards rush to protect him, pushing him to the ground as the bullets bounced from the tomb and rattled its iron gate.

Rachel covered her head with her arms and crouched to try to make herself a smaller target. Over my shoulder, I saw the two cops to the north separate and pick up machine pistols concealed in the bushes at either side of the avenue. They were Steyrs, fitted with sound suppressors: Joe Bones's men. I saw a woman try to run for the cover of the outspread wings of a stone angel, her dark coat whipping around her bare legs. The coat puffed twice at the shoulder and she sprawled face forward on the ground, her hands outstretched. She tried to drag herself forward but her coat puffed again and she was gone.

Now there were pistol shots and the rattle of a semi-automatic as Fontenot's men returned fire. I drew my own Smith & Wesson and joined Rachel as a uniformed figure appeared in the gap between the tombs, the Steyr held in a two-handed grip. I shot him in the face and he crumpled to the ground.

'But they're cops!' said Rachel, her voice almost drowned by the exchange of fire around us.

I reached out and pushed her down further. 'They're Joe Bones's men. They're here to take out Lionel Fontenot.' But it was more than that: Joe Bones wanted to sow chaos and to reap blood and fear and death from the consequences. He didn't simply want Lionel Fontenot dead. He also wanted others to die – women, children, Lionel's family, his associates – and for those left alive to remember what had taken place and to fear Joe Bones more because of it. He wanted to break the Fontenots and he would do it here, beside the vault where they had buried generations of their dead. This was the action of a man who had moved beyond reason and passed into a dark, flame-lit place, a place that blinded his vision with blood.

Behind me, there was a scuffling, tumbling sound and one of Fontenot's men, the overcoated man with the semi-automatic, fell to his knees beside Rachel. Blood bubbled from his mouth and I heard her scream as he fell forward, his head coming to rest by her feet. The M16 lay on the grass beside him. I reached for it but Rachel got to it first, a deep, unquenchable instinct for survival now guiding her actions. Her mouth and eyes were wide as she fired a burst over the prone frame of the body-guard.

I flung myself to the end of the tomb and aimed in the same direction, but Joe Bones's man was already down. He lay on his back, his left leg spasming and a bloody pattern etched across his chest. Rachel's eyes were wide, her hands shaking as the adrenaline coursed through her system. The M16 began to fall from her fingers. Its strap became entangled in her arm and she shook herself furiously to release it. Behind her, I could see mourners running low through the avenues of tombs. Two white women dragged a young black man by his arms over the grass. The belly of his white shirt was smeared with blood.

I figured that there must have been a fourth set of Joe Bones's men who approached from the south and fired the first shots. At least three were down: the two killed by Rachel and me and a third who lay sprawled by the old cypress. Fontenot's man had taken one of them out before he was hit himself.

I helped Rachel to her feet and moved her quickly to a grimy vault with a corroded gate. I struck at the lock with the butt of the M16 and it gave instantly. She slipped inside and I handed her my Smith & Wesson and told her to stay there until I came back for her. Then, gripping the M16, I ran east past the back of the Fontenot tomb, using the other vaults as cover. I didn't know how many shots were left in the M16. The selector switch was set for three-round bursts. Depending on the magazine capacity, I might have anything between ten and twenty rounds left.

I had almost reached a monument topped by the figure of a sleeping child when something hit me on the back of the head and I stumbled forward, the M16 slipping from my grasp. Someone kicked me hard in the kidneys, the pain lancing through my body as far as the shoulder. I was kicked again in the stomach, which forced me on to my back. I looked up to see Ricky standing above me, the reptilian coils of his hair and his small stature at odds with the NOPD uniform. He had lost his hat and the side of his face was cut slightly where he had been hit by splinters of stone. The muzzle of his Steyr pointed at my chest.

I tried to swallow but my throat seemed to have constricted. I was conscious of the feel of the grass beneath my hands and the glorious pain in my side, sensations of life and existence and survival. Ricky raised the Steyr to point it at my head.

'Joe Bones says hello,' he said. His finger tightened on the trigger in the same instant as his head jerked back, his stomach thrusting forward and his back arching. A burst of fire from the Steyr raked the grass beside my head as Ricky fell to his knees and then toppled sideways, his body lying prone across my left leg. There was a jagged red hole in the back of his shirt.

Behind him, Lionel Fontenot stood in a marksman's stance, the pistol in his hand slowly coming down. There was blood on his left hand and a bullet hole in the upper left arm of his suit. The two bodyguards who had stood beside him at the cemetery walked quickly from the direction of the Fontenot tomb. They glanced at me, then turned their attention back to Fontenot. I could hear the sound of sirens approaching from the west.

'One got away, Lionel,' said one. 'The rest are dead.'

'What about our people?'

'Three dead, at least. More injured.'

Beside me, Ricky stirred slightly and his hand moved feebly. I could feel his body move against my leg. Lionel Fontenot walked over and stood above him for a moment before shooting him once in the back of the head. He looked at me curiously once more, then picked up the M16 and tossed it to one of his men.

'Now go help the wounded,' he said. He cradled his injured left arm with his right hand and walked back towards the Fontenot tomb.

My ribs ached as I returned to where I had left Rachel, after kicking Ricky's corpse from my leg. I approached carefully, conscious of the Smith & Wesson I had left with her. When I reached the tomb, Rachel was gone.

I found her about fifty yards away, crouching beside the body of a young girl who was barely beyond her teens. As I approached, Rachel reached for the gun by her side and spun towards me.

'Hey, it's me. You okay?'

She nodded and returned the gun to its resting place. I noticed that she had kept her hand pressed on the young girl's stomach for the entire exchange.

'How is she?' I asked but, as I looked over her shoulder, I knew the answer. The blood oozing from the gunshot wound was almost black. Liver shot. The girl, shivering uncontrollably, her teeth gritted in agony, was not going to live. Around us, mourners were emerging from hiding, some sobbing, some trembling with shock. I saw two of Lionel Fontenot's men running towards us, both with pistols, and I took hold of Rachel's arm.

'We have to go. We can't afford to wait for the cops to arrive.'

'I'm staying. I'm not leaving her.'

'Rachel.' She looked at me. I held her gaze and we shared our knowledge of the girl's impending death. 'We can't stay.'

The two Fontenots were beside us now. One of them, younger than the other, dropped to his knee beside the girl and took her hand. She gripped it tightly and he whispered her name. 'Clara,' he said. 'Hold on, Clara, hold on.'

'Please, Rachel,' I repeated.

She took the younger man's hand and pressed it against Clara's stomach. Clara cried out as the pressure was reapplied.

'Keep your hand there,' hissed Rachel. 'Don't take it away until the medics get here.'

She picked up the gun and handed it to me. I took it from her, slipped the safety on and put it back in my holster. We made our way from the focus of the mayhem, until the shouting had diminished, then I stopped and she reached out and held me tightly. I cradled her in my arms and kissed the top of her head and breathed in the scent of her. She squeezed me and I gasped as the pain in my ribs increased dramatically.

Rachel pulled back quickly. 'Are you hurt?'

'I took a kick, nothing else.'

I held her face in my hands. 'You did all that you could for her.'

She nodded but her mouth trembled. The girl had an importance to her that went beyond the simple duty to save her life. 'I killed that man,' she said.

'He would have killed us both. You had no choice. If you hadn't done it, you'd be dead. Maybe I'd be dead too.' It was true, but it wasn't enough, not yet. I held her tightly as she cried, the pain in my side inconsequential beside her own suffering.

# Chapter Forty

I had not spoken of Daddy Helms in many years, not until I talked of him to Rachel, recalling the part he'd played in the lingering death of my mother.

Daddy Helms was the ugliest man I had ever seen. He ran most of Portland from the late sixties to the early eighties, building up a modest empire that had started with Daddy Helms boosting liquor warehouses and moved on to take in the sale of drugs over three states.

Daddy Helms weighed over three hundred pounds and suffered from a skin ailment that had left him with raised bumps all over his body, but most visible on his face and hands. They were a deep red colour and formed a kind of scaly skin over his features, blurring them so that the observer always seemed to be seeing Daddy Helms through a red mist. He wore three-piece suits and Panama hats and always smoked Winston Churchill cigars, so you smelt Daddy Helms before you saw him. If you were smart enough, this usually gave you just enough time to be somewhere else when he arrived.

Daddy Helms was mean, but he was also a freak. If he had been less intelligent, less bitter and less inclined towards violence, he would probably have ended up living in a little house in the woods of Maine and selling Christmas trees door-to-door to sympathetic citizens. Instead, his ugliness seemed to be an outward manifestation of some deeper spiritual and moral blight within himself, a corruption that made you think that Daddy Helms's skin might not be the worst thing about him. There was a rage inside him, a fury at the world and its ways.

My grandfather, who had known Daddy Helms since he was a young boy and was generally a man who empathised with those around him, even the criminals he was forced to arrest when he served as a sheriff's deputy, could see nothing but evil in Daddy Helms. 'I used to think maybe it was his ugliness that made him what he is,' he said once, 'that the way he behaves is because of the way he looks, that he's finding a way to strike back at the world he sees around him.' He was sitting on the porch of the house he shared with my grandmother, my mother and me, the house in which we had all lived since my father's death. My grandfather's basset hound Doc – named after the country singer Doc Watson for no reason other than that my grandfather liked his rendition of the song 'Alberta' – lay curled at his feet, his ribs expanding in deep sleep and small yelps occasionally erupting from his jowls as he enjoyed dog dreams.

My grandfather took a sip of coffee from a blue tin mug and laid it down by his feet. Doc stirred slightly, opened one bleary eye to make sure he wasn't missing anything interesting, and then went back to his dreams.

'But Daddy Helms isn't like that,' he continued. 'Daddy Helms just has something wrong with him, something I can't figure. Only thing I wonder is what he might have made of himself if he weren't so damn ugly. I reckon he could have been the President of the United States, if he'd wanted to be and if people could have beared to look at him, 'cept he would've been more like Joe Stalin than John Kennedy. You oughta have stayed outta his way, boy. You learned a hard lesson yesterday, a hard lesson at the hands of a hard man.'

I had come from New York with the idea that I was a tough guy, that I was smarter and faster and, if it came down to it, harder than those I would come up against in the Maine boondocks. I was wrong. Daddy Helms taught me that.

Clarence Johns, a kid who lived with his drunk father near what is now Maine Mall Road, learned that lesson too. Clarence was amiable but dumb, a natural sidekick. We had been hanging out together for about a year, firing off his air rifle on lazy summer afternoons, drinking beers stolen from his old man's stash. We were bored and we let everybody know it, even Daddy Helms.

He had bought an old, run-down bar on Congress Street and was slowly working to transform it into what he imagined would be a pretty high-class establishment. This was before the refurbishment of the port area, before the arrival of the T-shirt shops, the craft stores, the arthouse cinema and the bars that serve free nibbles to the tourist crowd between five and seven. Maybe Daddy Helms had a vision of what was to come, for he replaced all of the old windows in the bar, put a new roof on the place and bought up furnishings from some old Belfast church that had been deconsecrated.

One Sunday afternoon, when Clarence and I were feeling particularly at odds with the world, we sat on the wall at the back of Daddy Helms's half-finished bar and broke just about every goddamn window in the place, flinging stones with pinpoint accuracy at the new panes. Eventually, we found an old abandoned toilet cistern and, in a final act of vandalism, we hoisted it through the large arched window at the back of the premises, which Daddy Helms had intended would span the bar itself like a fan.

I didn't see Clarence for a few days after that and thought nothing of the consequences until one night, as we walked down St John with an illicitly bought six-pack of beer, three of Daddy Helms's men caught us and dragged us towards a black Cadillac Eldorado. They cuffed our hands and put duct tape over our mouths and tied dirty rags over our eyes, then dumped us in the trunk and closed it. Clarence Johns and I lay side by side as we were carried away and I was conscious of the sour, unwashed smell from him, until I realised that I probably smelt the same.

But there were other smells in that trunk beyond oil and rags and the sweat of two teenage boys. It smelt of human excrement and urine, of vomit and bile. It smelt of the fear of impending death and I knew, even then, that a lot of people had been brought for rides in that Cadillac.

Time seemed to fade away in the blackness of that car, so that I couldn't tell how far we had travelled until it ground to a halt. The trunk was opened and I saw the stars shining above me like the promise of heaven. I could hear waves crashing to my left and could taste the salt in the air. We were hauled from the trunk and dragged through bushes and over stones. I could feel sand beneath my feet and, beside me, I heard Clarence Johns start to whimper, or maybe it was my own whimperings I heard. Then we were thrown face down on the sand and there were hands at my clothes, my shoes. My shirt was ripped from me and I was stripped from the waist down, kicking frantically at the unseen figures around me until someone punched me hard with his knuckles in the small of the back and I stopped kicking. The rag was pulled away from my eyes and I looked up to see Daddy Helms standing above me. Behind him, I could see the silhouette of a large building: the Black Point Inn. We were on the Western Beach at Prouts Neck, beyond Scarborough itself. If I had been able to turn, I would have seen the lights of Old Orchard Beach, but I was not able to turn.

Daddy Helms held the butt of his cigar in his deformed hand and smiled at me. It was a smile like light flashing on a blade. He wore a white three-piece suit, a gold watch chain snaking across his vest and a red and white spotted bow-tie arranged neatly at the collar of his white cotton shirt. Beside me,

Clarence Johns's shoes scuffled in the sand as he tried to gain enough purchase to raise himself up, but one of Daddy Helms's men, a blond-haired savage called Tiger Martin, placed the sole of his foot on Clarence's chest and forced him back on to the sand. Clarence, I noticed, was not naked.

'You Bob Warren's grandson?' Daddy Helms observed after a time. I nodded. I thought I was going to choke. My nostrils were filled with sand and I couldn't seem to get enough air into my lungs.

'You know who I am?' asked Daddy Helms, still looking at me.

I nodded again.

'But you can't know who I am, boy. You knew me, you wouldn't'ta done what you did to my place. 'Less you're a fool, that is, and that's worse than not knowin'.'

He turned his attention briefly to Clarence, but he didn't say anything to him. I thought I caught a flash of pity in his eyes as he looked at Clarence. Clarence was dumb, there was no doubt about that. For a brief instant, I seemed to be looking at Clarence with new eyes, as if he alone was not part of Daddy Helms's gang and all five of us were about to do something terrible to him. But I was not with Daddy Helms and the thought of what was about to happen brought me back again. I felt the sand beneath my skin and I watched as Tiger Martin came forward, carrying a heavy-looking black refuse sack in his arms. He looked to Daddy Helms, Daddy Helms nodded and then the bag was tipped upside down and the contents poured over my body.

It was earth, but something else too: I sensed thousands of small legs moving on me, crawling through the hairs on my legs and groin, exploring the crevasses of my body like tiny lovers. I felt them on my tightly closed eyes and shook my head to clear them away. Then the biting started, tiny pinpoints of pain on my arms, my eyelids, my legs, even my penis, as the fire ants began to attack. I felt them crawling into my nostrils, and then the biting started there as well. I twisted and writhed, rubbing myself on the sand in an effort to kill as many of them as I could but it was like trying to remove the sand itself, grain by grain. I kicked and spun and felt tears running down my cheeks and then, just as it seemed that I couldn't take any more, I felt a gloved hand on my ankle and I was dragged through the sand towards the surf. My wrists were freed and I plunged into the water, ripping the tape from my mouth, ignoring the pain as the adhesive tore my lips in my desire to rub and scratch myself. I submerged my head as the waves crashed above me, and still it seemed that I felt thread-like legs moving on me and felt the final bites of the insects before they drowned. I was shouting in pain and panic and then I was crying too, crying in shame and hurt and anger and fear.

For days afterwards, I found the remains of ants in my hair. Some of them were longer than the nail on my middle finger, with barbed pincers that curved forward to embrace the skin. My body was covered in raised bumps, almost an imitation of those of Daddy Helms himself, and the inside of my nose felt tender and swollen.

I pulled myself from the water and staggered on to the sand. Daddy Helms's men had gone back to the car, leaving only Clarence and me on the beach with Daddy Helms himself. Clarence was untouched. Daddy Helms saw the realisation in my face and he smiled as he puffed on his cigar.

'We found your friend last night,' he said. He placed a thick, melted-wax hand on Clarence's shoulders. Clarence flinched, but he didn't move. 'He told us everything. We didn't even have to hurt him.'

The pain of betrayal superseded the bites and the itching, the lingering sensation of movement on my skin. I looked at Clarence Johns with new eyes, adult eyes. He stood on the sand, his arms wrapped around his body, shivering. His eyes were filled with a pain that sang out from the depths of his being. I wanted to hate him for what he had done, and Daddy Helms wanted me to hate him, but instead I felt only a deep emptiness and a kind of pity.

And I felt a kind of pity, too, for Daddy Helms, with his ravaged skin and his mounds and folds of heavy flesh, forced to visit this punishment on two young men because of some broken glass, punishing them not only physically but by severing the bonds of their friendship.

'You learned two lessons here tonight, boy. You learned not to fuck with me, ever, and you learned something about friendship. In the end, the only friend you got is yourself, 'cos all the others, they'll let you down in the end. We all stand alone, in the end.' Then he turned and waddled, through the marram and dunes, back to his car.

They left us to walk back, my clothes torn and soaked through from the seawater. We said nothing to each other, not even when we parted at the gate to my grandfather's property and Clarence headed off into the night, his cheap plastic shoes slapping on the road. We didn't hang out together after that and I largely forgot Clarence until he died in a failed robbery attempt at a computer warehouse on the outskirts of Austin fifteen years later. Clarence was working as a security guard. He was shot by the raiders as he tried to defend a consignment of PCs.

When I entered my grandfather's house I took some antiseptic from the medicine cabinet, then stripped and stood in the bath, rubbing the liquid into the bites. It stung. When I had finished, I sat in the empty bath and wept, and that was where my grandfather found me. He said nothing for a time, then disappeared and came back with a red bowl containing a paste made from baking soda and water. He rubbed it painstakingly across my shoulders and chest, my legs and arms, then poured a little into my hand so I could rub it into my groin. He wrapped me in a white cotton sheet and sat me down in a chair in the kitchen, before pouring each of us a large glass of brandy. It was Remy Martin, I remember, XO, the good stuff. It took me some time to finish it, but neither of us spoke a word. As I had stood to go to bed, he'd patted me lightly on the head.

'A hard man,' repeated my grandfather, draining the last of his coffee. He stood and the dog rose with him.

'You want to walk the dog with me?'

I declined. He shrugged his shoulders and I watched him as he walked down the porch steps, the dog already running ahead of him, barking and sniffing and looking back to make sure the old man was following, then running on further again.

Daddy Helms died ten years later of stomach cancer. When he died, it was estimated that he had been involved, directly or indirectly, with over forty killings, some of them as far south as Florida. There was no more than a handful of people at his funeral.

I thought of Daddy Helms again as Rachel and I made our way from the killings in Metairie. I don't know why. Maybe I felt there was something of his rage in Joe Bonnano, a hatred of the world that stemmed from something rotten inside him. I remembered my grandfather, I remembered Daddy Helms and I recalled the lessons they had tried to teach me, lessons that I still had not yet fully learned.

# Chapter Forty-One

Outside the main cemetery gate, the New Orleans police were corralling witnesses and clearing the way for the injured to be carried to waiting ambulances. TV crews from WWDL and WDSU were trying to talk with survivors. I stayed close to one of Lionel Fontenot's men, the one who had been entrusted with the care of the M16, as we approached the gates at an angle. We followed him until he arrived at a portion of ruptured fencing by the highway, then made his way through it to a waiting Lincoln. As he drove away, Rachel and I climbed over the fence and walked back to our car, unspeaking, approaching it from the west. It was parked away from the main centre of activity and we were able to slip off without attracting any attention.

'How did that happen?' asked Rachel, in a quiet voice, as we drove back into the city. 'There should have been police. There should have been someone to stop them . . .' Her voice trailed away and she remained silent as we drove back to the Quarter, her hands clasped across her upper body. I didn't disturb her.

One of a number of things had happened. Someone in charge could have screwed up by assigning insufficient police to Metairie, believing that Joe Bones would never try to take out Lionel Fontenot at his brother's funeral in front of witnesses. The guns had been stashed either late the previous night, or early that morning, and the cemetery had not been searched.

It could also have been the case that Lionel warned off the cops, just as he had warned off the media, anxious not to turn his brother's funeral into a circus. The other possibility was that Joe Bones had paid off or threatened some or all of the cops at Metairie and they had turned their backs while his men went about their business.

When we reached the hotel, I took her to my room – I didn't want her surrounded by the images she had pinned to the walls of her own room. She went straight to the bathroom and closed the door behind her. I could hear the sound of the shower starting up. She stayed there for a long time.

When she eventually emerged, she had a big white bath towel draped around her from her breasts to her knees and was drying her hair with a smaller towel. Her eyes were red as she looked at me, then her chin trembled and she began to cry again. I held her, kissing the top of her head, then her forehead, her cheeks, her lips. Her mouth was warm as she responded to the kiss, her tongue darting around my teeth and entwining with my own tongue. I felt myself become aroused and pressed hard against her, pulling the towel from her as I did. Her fingers fumbled at my belt and my zipper, then reached inside and held me tightly. Her other hand worked at the buttons on my shirt as she kissed my neck and ran her tongue across my chest and around my nipples.

I kicked off my shoes and leaned over awkwardly to try to take off my socks. Damn socks. She smiled a little as I almost fell over while removing the left one and then I was on top of her as she pushed down my pants and shorts.

Her breasts were small, her hips slightly wide, the small triangle of hair at their centre a deep, fiery red. She tasted sweet. When she came, her back arched high and her legs wrapped around my thighs, I felt like I had never been held so tightly, or loved so hard.

Afterwards, she slept. I slipped from the bed, put on a T-shirt and jeans and took the key to her room from her bag. I walked barefoot down the gallery to the room, closed the door behind me and stood for a time before the pictures on the wall. Rachel had bought a large draughtsman's pad on which to work out patterns and ideas. I took two sheets from it, taped them together and added them to the images on the wall. Then, surrounded by pictures of the anatomised Marsyas and photocopies of the crime-scene photos of Tante Marie and Tee Jean, I took a felt-tip and began to write.

In one corner I wrote the names of Jennifer and Susan, a kind of pang of regret and guilt hitting me as I wrote Susan's name. I tried to put it from my mind and continued writing. In another corner I put the names of Tante Marie, Tee Jean and, slightly to one side, Florence. In the third corner I wrote Remarr's name and in the fourth I placed a question mark and the word 'girl' beside it. In the centre I wrote 'Trav Man' and then, like a child drawing a star, I added a series of lines emanating from the centre and tried to write down all that I knew, or thought I knew, about the killer.

When I had finished, the list included: a voice synthesis program or unit; the Book of Enoch; a knowledge of Greek myths/early medical texts; a knowledge of police procedures and activities, based on what Rachel had said following the deaths of Jennifer and Susan, the fact that he had known that the feds were monitoring my cellphone, and the killing of Remarr. Initially I thought that if he had seen Remarr at the Aguillard house, then Remarr would have died there and then, but I reconsidered on the basis that the Travelling Man would have been reluctant to remain at the scene or to engage an alerted Remarr, and had decided to wait for another chance. The other option was that the killer had found out about the fingerprint and, somehow, the killer had also later found Remarr.

I added other elements based on standard assumptions: white

male killer, probably somewhere between his twenties and forties; a Louisiana base from which to strike at Remarr and the Aguillards; a change of clothing, or overalls worn over his own clothes, to protect him from the blood; and access to and knowledge of ketamine.

I drew another line from Trav Man to the Aguillards, since the killer knew that Tante Marie had been talking, and a second line connecting him to Remarr. I added a dotted line to Jennifer and Susan, and wrote Edward Byron's name with a question mark beside it. Then, on impulse, I added a third dotted line and wrote David Fontenot's name between those of the Aguillards and Remarr, based only on the Honey Island connection and the possibility that, if the Travelling Man had lured him to Honey Island and tipped off Joe Bones that David Fontenot would be there, then the killer was someone known to the Fontenot family. Finally, I wrote Edward Byron's name on a separate sheet and pinned it beside the main diagram.

I sat on the edge of Rachel's bed and smelt the scent of her in the room as I looked at what I had written, shifting the pieces around in my head to see if they would match up anywhere. They didn't, but I made one more addition before I returned to my own room to wait for Angel and Louis to return from Baton Rouge: I drew a light line between David Fontenot's name and the question mark representing the girl in the swamp. I didn't know it then, but by drawing that line I had made the first significant leap into the world of the Travelling Man.

I returned to my own room and sat by the balcony, watching Rachel in her uneasy sleep. Her eyelids moved rapidly, and once or twice she let out small groans and made pushing movements with her hands, her feet scrabbling beneath the blankets. I heard Angel and Louis before I saw them, Angel's voice raised in what seemed to be anger, Louis responding in measured tones with a hint of mockery beneath them.

Before they could knock, I opened the door and indicated that we should talk in their room. They hadn't heard about the shootings at Metairie since, according to Angel, they hadn't been listening to the radio in the rental car. His face was red as he spoke and his lips were pale. I don't think that I had ever seen him so angry.

In their room, the bickering started again. Stacey Byron, a bottle-blonde in her early forties who had kept her figure remarkably well for a woman of her age, had apparently come on to Louis in the course of their interrogation of her. Louis had, in a manner, responded.

'I was pumping her for information,' he explained, his mouth twitching in amusement as he looked sideways at Angel. Angel was unimpressed.

'You wanted to pump her, all right, but the only information you were after was her bra size and the dimensions of her ass,' he spat. Louis rolled his eyes in exaggerated bafflement and I thought, for a moment, that Angel was going to strike him. His fists bunched and he moved forward slightly before he managed to restrain himself.

I felt sorry for Angel. While I didn't believe there was anything in Louis's courting of Edward Byron's wife, beyond the natural response of any individual to the favourable attentions of another and Louis's belief that, by leading her on, she might give away something about her ex-husband, I knew how much Louis mattered to Angel. Angel's history was murky, Louis's more so, but I remembered things about Angel, things that I sometimes felt Louis forgot.

When Angel was sent down to Rikers Island, he attracted the attentions of a man named William Vance. Vance had killed a Korean shopkeeper in the course of a botched robbery in Brooklyn and that was how he ended up in Rikers, but there were other things suspected of him: that he had raped and killed an elderly woman in Utica, mutilating her before she died; that he may have been linked to a similar killing in Delaware. There was no proof, other than rumour and conjecture, but when the opportunity came to put Vance away for the killing of the Korean, the DA, to his credit, seized it.

And for some reason, Vance decided that he wanted Angel dead. I heard that Angel had dissed him when Vance had tried it on with him, that he had knocked out one of Vance's teeth in the showers. But there was no telling with a man like Vance: the workings of his mind were obscure and confused by hatred and strange, bitter longing. Now Vance didn't just want to rape Angel: he wanted to kill him, and kill him slowly. Angel had pulled three to five. After one week in Rikers, the odds of him surviving his first month had plummeted.

Angel had no friends on the inside and fewer still outside, so he called me. I knew that it pained him to do so. He was proud and I think that, under ordinary circumstances, he would have tried to work out his problems for himself. But William Vance, with his tattoos of bloodied knives on his arms and a spider's web over his chest, was far from ordinary.

I did what I could. I pulled Vance's files and copied the transcripts of his interrogation over the Utica killing and a number of similar incidents. I copied details of the evidence assembled against him and the account of an eyewitness who later retracted after Vance made a call and threatened to fuck her and her children to death if she gave evidence against him. Then I took a trip to Rikers.

I spoke to Vance through a transparent screen. He had added an Indian ink tattoo of a tear below his left eye, bringing the total number of tattooed tears to three, each one representing a life taken. A spider's silhouette was visible at the nape of his neck. I spoke to him softly for about ten minutes. I warned him that if anything happened to Angel, anything at all, I would make sure that every con in the place knew that he was only a hair's breadth away from sexual homicide charges involving old, defenceless women. Vance had five years left to serve before he became eligible for parole. If his fellow inmates found out what he was suspected of doing, he would have to spend those five years in solitary or in a special unit to avoid death. Even then, he would have to check his food every day for powdered glass, would have to pray that a guard's attention didn't wander for an instant while he was being escorted to the yard for his hour's recreation, or while he was being brought to the prison doctor when the stress began to take its toll on his health.

Vance knew all this and yet, two days after we spoke, he tried to castrate Angel with a shank. Only the force of Angel's heel connecting with Vance's knee saved him, although Angel still needed twenty stitches across his stomach and thigh after Vance slashed wildly at him as he fell to the ground.

Vance was taken in the shower the next morning. Persons unknown held him down, used a wrench to hold his mouth open and then pumped water mixed with detergent into his body. The poison destroyed his insides, tearing apart his stomach and almost costing him his life. For the remainder of his life he was a shell of a man, racked by pains in his gut that made him howl in the night. It had taken one telephone call. I live with that, too.

After he was released, Angel hooked up with Louis. I'm not even sure how these two solitary creatures met, exactly, but they had now been together for six years. Angel needed Louis and, in his way, Louis needed Angel too, but I sometimes thought that the balance of the relationship hinged on Angel. Men and men, men and women, whatever the permutation, in the end one partner always feels more than the other and that partner usually suffers for it.

It emerged that they hadn't learned much from Stacey

Byron. The feds, or maybe the local cops, had been watching the house from the front but Louis and Angel, dressed in the only suit he owned, had come in from the back. Louis had flashed his fitness-club membership and his smile as he told Mrs Byron that they were just conducting a routine search of her garden and they spent the next hour talking to her about her ex-husband, about how often Louis worked out and, in the end, whether or not he'd ever had a white woman. It was at that point that Angel had really started to get annoyed.

'She says she hasn't seen him in four months,' said Louis. 'Says that last time she saw him, he didn't say much, just asked after her and the kids and took some old clothes from the attic. Seems he had a carrier-bag from some drugstore in Opelousas and the feds are concentrating their search there.'

'Does she know why the feds are looking for him?'

'Nope. They told her that he might be able to assist them with information on some unsolved crimes. She ain't dumb, though, and I fed her a little more to see if she'd bite. She said that he always had an interest in medical affairs – seems he might have had ambitions to be a doctor at one time, although he didn't have the education to be a tree surgeon.'

'Did you ask her if she thought he could kill?'

'I didn't have to. Seems he threatened to kill her once, while they were arguing over the terms of the divorce.'

'Did she remember what he said?'

Louis nodded deeply, once.

'Uh-huh. He said he'd tear her fucking face off.'

Angel and Louis parted on bad terms, with Angel retiring to Rachel's room while Louis sat on the balcony of their room and took in the sounds and smells of New Orleans, not all of them pleasant.

'I was thinking of getting a bite to eat,' he said. 'You interested?'

I was surprised. I guessed that he wanted to talk but I had never spent time with Louis without Angel being present as well.

I checked on Rachel. The bed was empty and I could hear the shower running. I knocked gently on the door.

'It's open,' she said.

When I entered, she had the shower curtain wrapped around her. 'Suits you,' I said. 'Clear plastic is in this season.'

The sleep hadn't done her any good. There were dark rings under her eyes and she looked ill and drawn. She made a half-hearted effort to smile, but it was more like a grimace of pain than anything else.

'You want to go out and eat?'

'I'm not hungry. I'm going to do some work, then take two sleeping pills and try to sleep without dreaming.'

I told her that Louis and I were heading out, then went to tell Angel. I found him flicking through the notes Rachel had made. He motioned to my chart on the bedroom wall. 'Lot of blank spaces on that.'

'I still have one or two details to work out.'

'Like who did it and why.' He gave me a twisted grin.

'Yeah, but I'm trying not to get too hung up on minor problems. You okay?'

He nodded. 'I think this whole thing is gettin' to me, all this . . .' He waved an arm at the illustrations on the wall.

'Louis and I are heading out to eat. You wanna come?'

'Nah, I'd only be the lemon. You can have him.'

'Thanks. I'll break the bad news of my sexual awakening to the *Swimsuit Illustrated* models tomorrow. They'll be heart-broken. Look after Rachel, will you? This hasn't been one of her better days.'

'I'll be right across the hall.'

\*     \*     \*

Louis and I sat in Felix's Restaurant and Oyster Bar on the corner of Bourbon and Iberville. There weren't too many tourists there; they tended to gravitate towards the Acme Oyster House across the street, where they served red beans and savoury rice in a hollowed-out boat of French bread, or a classier French Quarter joint like Nola. Felix's was plainer. Tourists don't care much for plain. After all, they can get plain at home.

Louis ordered an oyster po'boy and doused it in hot sauce, sipping an Abita beer between bites. I had fries and a chicken po'boy, washed down with mineral water.

'Waiter thinks you're a sissy,' commented Louis, as I sipped my water. 'The ballet was in town, he'd hit on you for tickets.'

'Shows what he knows,' I replied. 'You're confusing things by not conforming to the stereotype. Maybe you should mince more.'

His mouth twitched and he raised his hand for another Abita. It came quickly. The waiter performed the neat trick of making sure we weren't left waiting for anything while trying to spend as little time as possible in the vicinity of our table. Other diners chose to take the scenic route to their tables rather than pass too close to us and those forced to sit near us seemed to eat at a slightly faster pace than the rest. Louis had that effect on people. It was as if there was a shell of potential violence around him, and something more: the sense that, if that violence erupted, it would not be the first time that it had done so.

'Your friend Woolrich,' he said, as he drained the Abita half-way with one mouthful. 'You trust him?'

'I don't know. He has his own agenda.'

'He's a fed. They only got their own agendas.' He eyed me over the top of the bottle. 'I think, if you were climbing a rock with your friend and you slipped, found yourself dangling on the end of the rope with him at the other end, he'd cut the rope.'

'You're a cynic.'

His mouth twitched again. 'If the dead could speak, they'd call all cynics realists.'

'If the dead could speak, they'd tell us to have more sex while we can.' I picked at my fries. 'The feds have anything on you?'

'Suspicions, maybe, nothing more. That's not really what I'm getting at.'

His eyes were unblinking and there was no warmth in them now. I think that, if he believed Woolrich was close to him, he would kill him and it would not cost him another thought afterwards.

'Why is Woolrich helping us?' he asked, eventually.

'I've thought about that too,' I said. 'I'm not sure. Part of it could be that he empathises with the need to stay in touch with what's going on. If he feeds me information, then he can control the extent of my involvement.'

But I knew that wasn't all. Louis was right. Woolrich had his own agenda. He had depths to him that I only occasionally glimpsed, as when the different shifting colours on the surface of the sea hint at the sharp declivities and deep spaces that lie beneath. He was a hard man to be with in some ways: he conducted his friendship with me on his own terms and, in the time I had known him, months had gone by without any contact from him. He made up for this with a strange loyalty, a sense that, even when he was absent from their lives, he never forgot those closest to him.

But as a fed, Woolrich played hardball. He had progressed to Assistant SAC by making collars, by attaching his name to high-profile operations, and by fixing other agents' wagons when they got in his way. He was intensely ambitious and maybe he saw the Travelling Man as a way of reaching greater heights: SAC, assistant director, a deputy directorship, maybe even eventually to becoming the first agent to be appointed directly to the post of director. He had already ensured that the cops were effectively locked out of the Travelling Man investigation and he had done his best to limit my direct involvement while feeding me enough information to keep me keen. The pressure on him was intense, but if Woolrich were to be responsible for bringing an end to the Travelling Man, he would be assured a bright, powerful future within the Bureau.

I had a part to play in this, and Woolrich knew it and felt it strongly enough that he would use whatever friendship existed between us to bring about an end to what was taking place. 'I think he's using me as bait,' I added. 'And he's holding the line.'

'How much you think he's holding back?' Louis finished his beer and smacked his lips appreciatively.

'He's like an iceberg. We're only seeing the ten per cent above the surface. Whatever the feds know, they're not sharing it with the local cops and Woolrich sure isn't sharing it with us. There's something more going on here, and only Woolrich and maybe a handful of feds are privy to it. You play chess?'

'In my way,' he replied drily. Somehow, I couldn't see that way including a standard board.

'This whole thing is like a chess game,' I continued. 'Except we only get to see the other player's move when one of our pieces is taken. The rest of the time, it's like playing in the dark.'

Louis raised a finger for the check. The waiter looked relieved.

'And our Mr Byron?'

I shrugged. I felt strangely distant from what was happening. Part of it was because we were players on the periphery of the investigation, but part of it was also because I needed that distance. I needed the distance to think. In one way, what had taken place with Rachel that afternoon, and what it meant to my feelings of grief and loss about Susan, had given me some of that distance.

'I don't know.' We were only beginning to construct a picture of Byron, like a figure at the centre of a jigsaw puzzle around which other pieces might interlock. 'We'll work our way towards him. First, I want to find out what Remarr saw the night Tante Marie and Tee Jean were killed. And I want to know why David Fontenot was out at Honey Island alone.'

It was clear now that Lionel Fontenot would move against Joe Bones. Joe Bones knew that too, which was why he had risked an assault at Metairie. Once Lionel was back in his compound, he would be out of the reach of Joe Bones's men. The next move was Lionel's.

The check arrived. I paid and Louis left a twenty-dollar tip, more than the meal itself cost. The waiter looked at the bill like Andrew Jackson was going to bite his finger when he tried to lift it.

'I think we're going to have to talk to Lionel Fontenot,' I said, as we left. 'And Joe Bones.'

Louis actually smiled. 'Joe ain't gonna be too keen on talking to you, seeing as how his boy tried to put you in the ground.'

'I kinda figured that,' I replied. 'Could be that Lionel Fontenot might help us out there. Anyway, if Joe Bones doesn't want to see me again, you can be damn sure that the sight of you waltzing across his lawn is not going to set his world alight. You might get to use those mini-subs yet.'

We walked back to the Flaisance. The streets of New Orleans aren't the safest in the world but I didn't think that anyone would bother us.

I was right.

# Chapter Forty-Two

I slept late the next morning. Rachel had returned to her own room to sleep. When I knocked, her voice sounded harsh with tiredness. She told me she wanted to stay in bed for a time and, when she felt better, she would go out to Loyola again. I asked Angel and Louis to watch out for her, then drove from the Flaisance.

The incident at Metairie had left me shaken, and the prospect of facing Joe Bones again was unappealing. I also felt a crushing sense of guilt for what had happened to Rachel, for what I had drawn her into and for what I had forced her to do. I needed to get out of New Orleans, at least for a short time. I wanted to clear my head, to try to see things from a different angle. I ate a bowl of chicken gumbo in the Gumbo Shop on St Peter and then headed out of the city.

Morphy lived about four miles from Cecilia, a few miles north-west of Lafayette. He had bought and was refurbishing a raised plantation home by a small river, a budget version of the classic old Louisiana houses, which had been built at the end of the nineteenth century in a blend of French Colonial, West Indian and European architectural influences.

The house presented a strange spectacle. Its main living quarters were on top of an above-ground basement area, which had once been used for storage and as protection from flooding. This section of the house was brick and Morphy had reworked the arched openings with what looked like hand-carved frames. The living quarters above, which would usually have been weatherboard- or plaster-covered, had been replaced with timber slats. A double-pitched roof, which had been partially reslated, extended over the gallery.

I had called ahead and told Angie I was on my way. Morphy had just got home when I arrived. I found him in the yard at the rear of the house, benching two hundred in the evening air.

'What do you think of the house?' he asked, as I approached, not even pausing in his reps as he spoke.

'It's great. Looks like you still have some way to go before it's finished.'

He grunted with the effort of the final rep and I slotted the bar back on to its rest. He stood up and stretched, then looked at the back of his house with barely concealed admiration.

'It was built by a Frenchman in eighteen eighty-eight,' he said. 'He knew what he was doing. It's built on an east–west axis, with principal exposure to the south.' He pointed out the lines of the building as he spoke. 'He designed it the way the Europeans designed their houses, so that the low angle of the sun in winter would heat the building. Then, in the summer, the sun would only shine on it in the morning and evening. Most American houses aren't built that way, they just put 'em up whatever way suits 'em, throw a stick in the air and see where it lands. We were spoiled by cheap energy. Then the Arabs came along and hiked up their prices and people had to start thinking again about the layout of their houses.' He smiled. 'Don't know how much good an east–west house does around here, though. Sun shines all the goddamn time any-way.'

When he had showered, we sat at a table in the kitchen with Angie and talked as she cooked. Angie was almost a foot smaller than her husband, a slim, dark-skinned woman with auburn hair that flowed down her back. She was a junior-school teacher, but she did some painting in her spare time. Her canvases, dark, impressionistic pieces set around water and sky, adorned the walls of the house.

Morphy drank a bottle of Breaux Bridge and I had a soda. Angie sipped a glass of white wine as she cooked. She cut four chicken breasts into about sixteen pieces and set them to one side as she set about preparing the roux.

Cajun gumbo is made with roux, a glutinous thickener, as a base. Angie poured peanut oil into an iron-based pan over a hot flame, added in an equal amount of flour, and beat it with a whisk continuously so it wouldn't burn, gradually turning the roux from blond to beige and through mahogany until it reached a dark chocolate colour. Then she took it off the heat and allowed it to cool, still stirring.

While Morphy looked on, I helped her chop the trinity of onion, green pepper and celery and watched as she sweated them in oil. She added a seasoning of thyme and oregano, paprika and cayenne peppers, onion and garlic salt, then dropped in thick pieces of chorizo sausage. She added the chicken and more spices, until their scent filled the room. After about half an hour, she spooned white rice on to plates and poured the thick rich gumbo over it. After that, we ate in silence, savouring the flavours in our mouths.

When we had washed and dried the dishes, Angie left us and went to bed. Morphy and I sat in the kitchen and I told him about Raymond Aguillard and his belief that he had seen the figure of a girl at Honey Island. I told him of Tante Marie's dreams and my feeling that, somehow, David Fontenot's death at Honey Island could be linked to the girl.

Morphy didn't say anything for a long time. He didn't sneer at visions of ghosts, or at an old woman's belief that the voices she heard were real. Instead, all he said was: 'You sure you know where this place is?'

I nodded.

'Then we'll give it a try. I'm free tomorrow, so you better stay here tonight. We got a spare room you can use.' I called Rachel at the Flaisance and told her what I intended to do the next day and where in Honey Island we were likely to be. She said that she would tell Angel and Louis, and that she felt a little better for her sleep. It would take her a long time to get over the death of Joe Bones's man.

It was early morning, barely ten before seven, when we prepared to leave. Morphy wore heavy steel-toed Caterpillar workboots, old jeans and a sleeveless sweatshirt over a long-sleeved T-shirt. The sweat was dappled with paint and there were patches of tar on the jeans. His head was freshly shaved and smelt of liniment.

While we drank coffee and ate toast on the gallery, Angie came out in a white robe and rubbed her husband's clean scalp, smirking at him as she took a seat beside him. Morphy acted like it annoyed the hell out of him, but he doted on her every touch. When we rose to go, he kissed her deeply with the fingers of his right hand entwined in her hair. Her body instinctively rose from the chair to meet him, but he pulled away, laughing, and she reddened. It was only then that I noticed the swelling at her belly: she was no more than five months gone, I guessed. As we walked across the grass at the front of the house, she stood on the gallery, her weight on one hip and a light breeze tugging at her robe, and watched her husband prepare to leave.

'Been married long?' I asked, as we walked towards a cypress glade that obscured the view of the house from the road.

'Two years in January. I'm a contented man. Never thought I would be, but that girl changed my life.' There was no embarrassment as he spoke and he acknowledged it with a smile.

'When is the baby due?'

He smiled again. 'Late December. Guys held a party for me when they found out, to celebrate the fact that I was shooting live ones.'

A breakdown truck was parked in the glade, with a trailer attached, on which a wide, flat-bottomed aluminium boat lay covered in tarpaulin, its engine tilted forward so that it rested on the bed. 'Touissant's brother dropped it over late last night,' he explained. 'Does some hauling on the side.'

'Where's Touissant?'

'In bed with food poisoning. He ate some bad shrimp, least that's how he tells it. Personally, I think he's just too damn lazy to give up his morning in bed.'

In the back of the truck, beneath some more tarpaulin, were an axe, a chainsaw, two lengths of chain, some strong nylon rope and an icebox. There was also a dry suit and mask, a pair of waterproof flashlights and two oxygen tanks. Morphy added a flask of coffee, some water, two sticks of French bread and four chicken breasts coated in K-Paul's Cajun spices, all contained in a waterproof bag, then climbed into the driver's seat of the truck and started her up. She belched smoke and rattled a bit, but the engine sounded good and strong. I climbed in beside him and we drove towards Honey Island, a Clifton Chenier tape on the truck's battered stereo.

We entered the reserve at Slidell, a collection of shopping malls, fast-food joints and Chinese buffets on the north shore of Lake Pontchartrain named for the Democratic senator John Slidell. In the 1844 federal election, Slidell arranged for two steamboats to carry a bunch of Irish and German voters from New Orleans to Plaquemines Parish to vote. There was nothing illegal about that; what was illegal was letting them vote at all the other polling stations along the route.

A mist still hung over the water and the trees as we unloaded the boat at the Pearl River ranger station, beside a collection of run-down fishing shacks that floated near the bank. We loaded the chains, rope, chainsaw, the diving gear and the food. In a tree beside us, the early-morning sun caught the threads of a huge, intricate web, at the centre of which lay, unmoving, a Golden Orb spider. Then, with the sound of the motor blending with the noise of insects and birds, we moved on to the Pearl.

The banks of the river were lined with high tupelo gum, water birch, willows and some tall cypress with trumpet creeper vines, their red flowers in bloom, winding up their trunks. Here and there, trees were marked with plastic bottles, signs that catfish lines had been sunk. We passed a village of riverside homes, most of them down-at-heel, with flat-bottomed pirogues tied up outside them. A blue heron watched us calmly from the branches of a cypress; on a log beneath him, a yellow-bellied turtle lay soaking up the sun.

I still had Raymond Aguillard's map but it took us two attempts to find the trevasse, the trappers' channel that he had marked. There was a stand of gum trees at its entrance, their swollen buttresses like the bulbs of flowers, with a sole green ash leaning almost across the gap. Further in, branches, weighed down with Spanish moss, hung almost to the surface of the water and the air was redolent with the mingled scents of growth and decay. Misshapen tree trunks surrounded by duckweed stood like monuments in the early-morning sun. East, I could see the grey dome of a beaver lodge and, as we watched, a snake slithered into the water not five feet from us.

'Diamondback,' said Morphy.

Around us, water dripped from cypress and tupelo, and birdsong echoed in the trees.

'Any chance of 'gators here?' I asked.

He shrugged. 'Maybe. Don't bother people much, though, unless people bother them. There's easier pickings in the swamps, and they've been known to take dogs that wander too close to the bank. If you see any while I'm down there, fire a shot to let me know what's happening.'

The bayou started to narrow until it was barely wide enough to allow the boat passage. I felt the bottom scrape on a tree trunk resting below the surface. Morphy killed the engine and we used our hands and a pair of wooden paddles to pull ourselves through.

It seemed then that we might somehow have made a mistake in our map-reading, because we were faced with a wall of wild rice, the tall, green stalks like blades in the water. There was only one narrow gap visible, big enough for a child to pass through. Morphy shrugged and restarted the engine, aiming us for the gap. I used the paddle to beat back the rice stalks as we moved forward. Something splashed close by us and a dark shape, like a large rat, sliced through the water.

'Nutria,' said Morphy. I could see the big rodent's nose and whiskers now as it stopped beside a tree trunk and sniffed the air inquisitively. 'Taste worse than 'gators. I hear we're trying to sell their meat to the Chinese since no one else wants to eat it.'

The rice blended into sharp-edged grass, which cut at my hands as I worked the paddle, and then the boat was free and we were in a kind of lagoon formed by a gradual accumulation of silt, its banks surrounded mainly by gum and willows that dragged the fingers of their branches in the water. There was some almost firm ground at the eastern edge, near an accumulation of arrowroot lilies, with wild pig tracks in the dirt, the animals attracted by the promise of the arrowroot at the lilies' base. Further in, I could see the rotting remains of a T-cutter, probably one of the craft that had originally cut the channel. Its big V8 engine was gone, and there were holes in its hull.

We tied the boat up at a sole red swamp maple, which was almost covered with resurrection fern waiting for the rains to bring it back to life. Morphy stripped down to a pair of Nike cycling shorts, rubbed himself down with grease and put the dry suit on. He added the flippers, then strapped on the tank and tested it. 'Most of the waters around here are no more than ten, maybe fifteen feet deep, but this place is different,' he said. 'You can see it in the way the light reflects on the water. It's deeper, twenty feet or more.' Leaves, sticks and logs floated on the water and insects flitted above the surface. The water looked dark and green.

He washed the mask in the swamp water then turned to me. 'Never thought I'd be looking for swamp ghosts on my day off,' he said.

'Raymond Aguillard says he saw the girl here,' I replied. 'David Fontenot died up the river. There's something here. You know what you're looking for?'

He nodded. 'Probably a container of some sort, heavy, sealed.'

Morphy flicked on the flashlight, slipped on his mask and began sucking oxygen. I tied one end of the climbing rope to his belt and another to the trunk of the maple, yanked it firm then patted him on the back. He raised a thumb and waded into the water. Two or three yards out, he began to dive and I started to feed the rope out through my hands.

I had had little experience of diving, beyond a few basic lessons taken during a holiday with Susan on the Florida Keys. I didn't envy Morphy, swimming around in that swamp. During my teens, we went swimming in the Stroudwater river, beyond what are now the Portland city limits, during the summer. Long, lean gars dwelt in those waters, vicious things that brought a hint of the primeval with them. When they brushed your bare legs, it made you think of stories you had heard about them biting small children or dragging swimming dogs down to the bottom of the river.

The waters of Honey Island swamp were like another world compared to the Stroudwater. With its glittering snakes and its cowens, the name the Cajuns give to the swamp's snapping turtles, Honey Island seemed so much more feral than the backwaters of Maine. But there were alligator gar here too, and scaled shortnoses, as well as perch and bass and bowfins. And 'gators.

I thought of these things as Morphy disappeared below the surface of the bayou, but I also thought of the young girl who might have been dumped in these waters, where creatures she couldn't name bumped and clicked against the side of her tomb while others searched for rust holes through which to get at the rotting meat inside.

Morphy surfaced after five minutes, indicated the short, north-eastern bank, and shook his head. Then he submerged again and the line on the ground snaked south as he swam. After another five minutes the rope began to pull out quickly. Morphy broke the surface again, but this time some distance from where the rope entered the water. He swam back to the bank, removed the mask and mouthpiece and breathed in short gasps as he gestured back towards the southern end of the bayou.

'We got a couple of metal boxes, maybe four feet long, two feet wide and eighteen inches deep, dumped down there,' he said. 'One's empty, the other's locked and bolted. Couple of hundred yards away there's a bunch of oil barrels marked with red fleurs-de-lys. They belong to the old Brevis Chemical Company, used to operate out of West Baton Rouge until a big fire in 'eighty-nine put it out of business. That's it. Nothing else down there.'

I looked out towards the edge of the bayou, where thick roots lay obscured beneath the water.

'Could we pull in the box using the rope?' I asked.

'Could do, but that box is heavy and if we bust it open while hauling it in we'll destroy whatever's inside. We'll have to bring the boat out and try to pull it up.'

It was getting very warm now, although the trees on the bank provided some shade from the sun. Morphy took two bottles of still mineral water from the icebox and we drank them sitting on the bank. Then Morphy and I got into the boat and took it out to his marker.

Twice the box caught on some obstacle on the bottom as I tried to pull it up, and I had to wait for Morphy to signal before I could start hauling it in again. Eventually, the grey metal box broke the surface of the water, Morphy pushing up from beneath before he went back down to tie the marker rope to one of the oil barrels in case we had to search them.

I brought the boat back to the landing and dragged the box up on to the shore. The chain and lock securing it were old and rusted, probably too old to yield anything of any use to us. I took the axe and struck at the rusty lock that held the chain in place. It broke as Morphy walked on to the bank. He knelt beside me, the oxygen tank still on his back and the mask pushed up on to his forehead as I pulled at the lid of the box. It was stuck fast. I took the blunt head of the axe and struck upward along the edges until the lid lifted.

Inside was a consignment of breech-loading Springfield .50 calibre rifles and the bones of what seemed to be a small dog. The butts of the rifles had almost rotted but I could still see the letters 'LNG' on the metal butt plates.

'Stolen rifles,' said Morphy, pulling one free and examining it. 'Maybe eighteen seventy or 'eighty. The authorities probably issued a stolen arms proclamation after these were taken and the thief dumped them or left them there with the intention of coming back.'

He prodded at the dog's skull with his fingers. 'The bones are an indicator of some kind. Pity nobody been seein' the Hound of the Baskervilles out here, else we'd have the whole mystery cleared up.' He looked at the rifles, then back out towards the oil drums. He sighed, then began to swim out towards the marker.

Hauling in the drums was a laborious process. The chain slipped off three times as we tried to haul in the first. Morphy came back for a second chain and wrapped it, parcel style, around the drum. The boat almost overturned when I tried to open the barrel while I was still on the water, so we were forced to bring it back to dry land. When we eventually got it on to the bank, brown and rusting, it contained only stale sump. The drums had a hole for loading and pouring the oil, but the entire lid could also be prised off. When we opened the second drum it didn't even contain sump, just some stones which had been used to weigh it down.

By now, Morphy was exhausted. We stopped for a time to eat some of the chicken and bread, and drink some of the coffee. It was now past midday and the heat in the swamp was heavy and draining. After we had rested, I offered to do some of the diving. Morphy didn't refuse, so I handed him my shoulder holster then suited up and strapped on the spare tank.

The water was surprisingly cool as I slipped into it. As it reached my chest, it almost took my breath away. The chains were heavy across my shoulder as I guided myself along the marker rope with one hand. When I reached the spot where the rope entered the water, I slipped the flashlight from my belt and dived.

The water was deeper than I expected and very dark, the duckweed above me blacking out the sunlight in patches. At the periphery of my vision, fish twisted and spun. The barrels, of which five remained, all piled in a heap, were gathered around the submerged trunk of an ancient tree, its roots buried deep in the bottom of the swamp. Any boat that might have been using the swamp bank to land on would have avoided the tree, which meant that the barrels were in no danger of being disturbed. The water at the base of the tree was darker than the rest, so that without the meagre light the barrels would have been invisible.

I wrapped the top barrel in chains and yanked once to test its weight. It tumbled from the top of the pile, yanking the rope from my grasp as it headed for the bottom. The water muddied and dirt and vegetation obscured my vision, and then everything went black as oil began to leak from the drum. I was kicking back to get into clearer water when I heard the dull, echoing sound of a gunshot from above me. For a moment, I thought that Morphy might be in trouble until I remembered what the gunshot was supposed to signal and realised that it was I, not Morphy, who was in trouble.

I was breaking for the surface when I saw the 'gator. It was small, maybe only six feet long, but the glare caught the wicked-looking teeth jutting out along its jaws and its light-coloured underbelly. It was as disorientated by the oil and dirt as I was, but it seemed to be angling towards the beam of my flashlight. I turned it off and instantly lost sight of the 'gator as I made a final kick for the surface.

When I broke the water the marker rope was fifteen feet in front of me, Morphy beside it.

'Come on!' he shouted. 'There's no other landing around you.'

I splashed hard as I swam towards him, all the time aware of the reptile cruising beneath me. As I splashed, I spotted it on the surface to my left, about twenty feet away from me. I could see the scales on its back, its hungry eyes and the line of its jaw pointed in my direction. I turned on my back so I could keep the 'gator in my sight and kicked out, sometimes using the rope to pull myself along, at other times using my hands.

I was still five feet from the boat when the 'gator moved, working its way swiftly through the water in my direction. I spat the mouthpiece out.

'Shoot it, goddammit,' I shouted. I heard the boom of a gun and a spume of water kicked up in front of the 'gator, then a second. The creature stopped short and then a sprinkling of pink and white fell to my right and it turned in that direction. It reached the objects just as a second shower fell, further away to the right, and I felt the boat against my back and Morphy's hands helping me to haul myself up. We turned for the bank as Morphy sent a third handful of marshmallows into the air. When I looked at him, he was grinning as he popped a last marshmallow into his mouth. Out on the bayou, the 'gator was snapping at the remains of the candy.

'Scared you, huh?' smiled Morphy, as I shrugged off the oxygen tank and lay flat on the bottom of the boat.

I nodded and kicked off a flipper.

'I think you're going to have to get your dry suit cleaned,' I said.

We sat on a log and watched the 'gator for a time. It cruised the waters looking for more marshmallows, eventually settling for a wait-and-see policy, which consisted of it lying partially submerged near the marker rope. We sipped coffee from tin cups and finished off the last of the chicken.

'You should have shot it,' I said.

'This *is* a nature reserve and there are laws about killing 'gators,' responded Morphy testily. 'Not much point in having a nature reserve if people can come in when they please and shoot the wildlife.'

We sipped the coffee some more, until I heard the sound of a boat coming towards us through the rice and grass.

'Shit,' said a familiar Brooklyn drawl, as the prow of the boat broke the grass, 'it's the Donner Party.'

Angel emerged first, then Louis behind him, controlling the rudder. They moved steadily towards us and tied up at the maple. Angel splashed into the water, then followed our gaze out towards the 'gator. He caught one sight of the partially submerged reptile and ran awkwardly on to the bank, his knees high and his elbows pumping.

'Man, what is this? Jurassic Park?' he said. He turned to Louis, who jumped from his boat to ours and then on to the bank. 'Hey, didn't you tell your sister not to be swimmin' in no strange ponds?'

Angel was dressed in his usual jeans and battered sneakers, with a denim jacket over a Doonesbury T-shirt, which depicted Duke and the motto 'Death Before Unconsciousness'. Louis was wearing crocodile-skin boots, black Levi's and a white collarless Liz Claiborne shirt.

'We dropped by to see how you were,' said Angel, casting anxious glances at the 'gator after I had introduced him to Morphy. He held a bag of donuts in his hand.

'Our friend's gonna be real upset if he sees you wearing one of his relatives, Louis,' I said.

Louis sniffed and approached the water's edge. 'Is there a problem?' he asked at last.

'We were diving and then Wally Gator appeared and we weren't diving any more,' I explained.

Louis sniffed again. 'Hmm,' he said. Then he drew his SIG and blew the tip of the 'gator's tail off. The reptile thrashed in pain and the water around it turned bright red, then it spun and headed off into the bayou, trailing blood behind it. 'You should have shot it,' he said.

'Let's not get into it,' I responded. 'Roll up your sleeves, gentlemen, we're going to need some help.'

I still had the dry suit on so I offered to keep diving.

'Trying to prove to me that you ain't chicken?' grinned Morphy.

'Nope,' I said, as we untied the boat. 'Trying to prove it to myself.'

We rowed out to the marker rope and then I dived down with the hook and chains, leaving Angel topside with Morphy and his gun in case the 'gator showed up again. Louis joined us in the second boat. A thick black film of oil had formed on the surface of the water and hung in the depths below. The barrels had scattered when the topmost drum fell. I checked the ruptured barrel with the flashlight but it appeared to contain nothing except the oil that remained.

It was laborious work, tying the barrel and hauling it up each time, but with two boats it meant that we could transport two barrels at a time to the bank. There was probably an easier way to do it, but we hadn't figured it out.

The sun was growing low and the waters were bathed in gold when we found her.

# Chapter Forty-Three

It seems to me now that when I touched the barrel for the first time to attach the chains, something coursed through my system and tightened in my stomach like a fist. I felt a jolt. A blade flashed before my eyes and the depths were coloured by a fountain of blood, or maybe it was simply the dying sunset on the water above reflected on my mask. I closed my eyes for a moment and felt movement around me, not just the water of the swamp or the fish in its depths but another swimmer who twisted around my body and legs. I thought I felt her hair brush my cheek but when I reached out I caught only swamp weed in my hand.

This barrel was heavier than the others, weighed down, it emerged, with masonry bricks that had been split neatly in half. It would need the combined efforts of Morphy and Angel to pull it up.

'It's her,' I said to Morphy. 'We've found her.' And then I swam down to the barrel and manoeuvred it slowly over the rocks and tree trunks at the bottom as we brought it up. We all seemed to handle this barrel more gently than the rest, as if the girl inside was merely sleeping and we didn't want to disturb her, as if she was not long decayed but had been laid within it only yesterday. On the bank, Angel took the crowbar and carefully applied it to the rim of the lid, but it refused to move. He examined it more closely.

'It's been sealed,' he said. He scraped the crowbar over the surface of the barrel and checked the mark left. 'The barrel's been treated with something as well. That's why it's in better condition than the others.'

It was true. The barrel had hardly rusted and the fleur-de-lys on its side was as clear and bright as if it had been painted only days before.

I thought for a moment. We could use the chainsaw to cut it but, if I was right and the girl was inside, I didn't want to damage the remains. We could also have called for assistance from the cops, or even the feds. I suggested it, more out of duty than desire, but even Morphy declined. He might have been concerned at the embarrassment that would be caused if the barrel was empty, but when I looked in his eyes I could see that wasn't the case. He wanted us to take it as far as we could.

In the end, we tested the barrel by gently tapping along its length with the axe. From the difference in sound, we judged as best we could where we could safely cut. Morphy carefully made an incision near the sealed end of the barrel and, using a combination of chainsaw and crowbar, we cut an area that was roughly half the circumference, then pushed it up with the crowbar and shone a light inside.

The body was little more than bones and shreds of material, the skin and flesh entirely rotted away. She had been dumped in head first and her legs had been broken to fit her into the barrel. When I shone the flashlight to the far end, I glimpsed bared teeth and strands of hair. We stood silently beside her, surrounded by the lapping water and the sounds of the swamp.

It was late that night when I got back to the Flaisance. While we waited for the Slidell police and the rangers, Angel and Louis departed, with Morphy's agreement. I stayed on to give my statement and back up Morphy's version of what had taken place. On Morphy's advice, the locals called the FBI. I didn't wait around. If Woolrich wanted to talk, he knew where to find me.

The light was still on in Rachel's room as I passed, so I stopped and knocked. She opened the door wearing a pink Calvin Klein nightshirt, which stopped at mid-thigh level.

'Angel told me what happened,' she said, opening the door wider to let me enter. 'That poor girl.' She hugged me and then ran the shower in the bathroom. I stayed in there for a long time, my hands against the tiles, letting the water roll over my head and back.

After I had dried myself, I wrapped the towel around my waist and found Rachel sitting on the bed, leafing through her papers. She cocked an eyebrow at me.

'Such modesty,' she said, with a little smile.

I sat on the edge of the bed and she wrapped her arms around me from behind. I felt her cheek and her warm breath against my back. 'How are you feeling?' I asked.

Her grip tightened a little. 'Okay, I think.'

She turned me around so that I was facing her. She knelt on the bed before me, her hands clasped between her legs and bit her lip. Then she reached out and gently, almost tentatively, ran her hand through my hair.

'I thought you psychology types were supposed to be good at all this,' I said.

She shrugged. 'I get just as confused as everybody else, except I know all the terminology for my confusion.' She sighed. 'Listen, what happened yesterday . . . I don't want to put pressure on you. I know how hard all this is for you, because of Susan and . . .'

I held my hand against her cheek and rubbed her lips gently with my thumb. Then I kissed her and felt her mouth open beneath mine. I wanted to hold her, to love her, to drive away the vision of the dead girl.

'Thanks,' I said, my mouth still against her, 'but I know what I'm doing.'

'Well,' she said, as she eased back slowly on to the bed, 'at least one of us does.'

The following morning, the remains of the girl lay on a metal table, curled foetally by the constriction of the barrel as if to protect herself for eternity, On the instructions of the FBI, she had been brought to New Orleans, weighed and measured, X-rayed and fingerprinted. The body bag in which she had been removed from Honey Island had been examined for debris that might have fallen from her while she was being transported.

The white tiles, the shining metal tables, the glinting medical instruments, the white lights hanging above them, all seemed too harsh, too relentless in their mission to expose, to examine, to reveal. It seemed a final indignity, after the terrors of her final moments, to display her here in the sterility of this room, with these men looking upon her. A part of me wanted to cover her with a shroud and carry her carefully, gently, to a dark hole beside flowing water, where green trees would shade the ground under which she lay and where no one would disturb her again.

But another part of me, the rational part, knew that she deserved a name, that she needed an identity to put an end to the anonymity of her sufferings and, perhaps, to close in on the man who had reduced her to this. And so we stood back as the gowned ME and his assistants moved in with their tapes and their blades and their white-gloved hands.

The pelvis is the most easily recognisable distinguishing feature between the male and female skeletons. The greater sciatic notch, situated behind the inominate bone – which itself consists of the hip, the ischium, the ilium and the pubis – is wider in the female, with a sub-pubic angle roughly the size of that between the thumb and forefinger. The pelvic outlet is also larger in the female but the thigh sockets are smaller, the sacrum wider.

Even the female skull is different from that of the male, a reflection in miniature of the physical differences between the two sexes. The female skull is as smooth and rounded as the female breast, yet smaller than the male skull; the forehead is higher and also more rounded; the eye sockets, too, are higher and the edges less sharply defined: the female jaw, palate and teeth are smaller.

The skeletal remains before us conformed to the general pelvic and skull rules governing the female body. In estimating the age of the body at the time of death, the ossification centres or areas of bone formation were examined, as were the teeth. The femur of the girl's body was almost completely fused at the head, although there was only partial joining of the collarbone to the top of the breastbone. Combined with an examination of the sutures on her skull, the ME estimated her age at twenty-one or twenty-two. There were marks on her forehead, the base of her jaw and on her left cheekbone, where the killer had cut through to the bone as he removed her face.

Her dental features were recorded, a process known as forensic odontology, to be checked against missing-persons files, while samples of bone marrow and hair were removed for possible use in DNA profiling. Then Woolrich, Morphy and I watched as the remains were wheeled away, covered in a plastic wrap. We exchanged a few words before we each went our separate ways but, to be honest, I don't recall what they were. All I could see was the girl. All I could hear was the sound of water in my ears.

If the DNA profiling and the dental records failed to reveal her identity, Woolrich had decided that facial reconstruction might prove valuable, using a laser reflected from the skull to establish the contours, which could then be compared against a known skull of similar dimensions. He decided to contact

Quantico to make the initial arrangements as soon as he had had time to wash and grab a cup of coffee.

But facial reconstruction proved unnecessary. It took less than two hours to identify the body of the young woman in the swamp. Although she had lain in the dark waters for almost six months, she had been reported missing only three months before.

Her name was Lutice Fontenot. She was Lionel Fontenot's half-sister.

# Chapter Forty-Four

The Fontenot compound lay five miles east of Delacroix. It was approached via a raised private road, newly built, which wound through swamps and decaying trees until it reached an area that had been cleared of all vegetation and was now only dark earth. High fencing, topped with razor wire, enclosed two or three acres, at the centre of which lay a low single-storey, horseshoe-shaped concrete building. A Corniche convertible and three black Explorers were parked in a line in the concrete lot created by the arms of the building. To the rear was an older house, a standard single-storey wooden dwelling with a porch and what looked like a series of parallel linked rooms. No one seemed to be around as I pulled up the rented Taurus at the compound gate, Louis in the passenger seat beside me. Rachel had taken the other rental with her on a final visit to Loyola University.

'Maybe we should have called ahead,' I said, as I looked towards the silent compound.

Beside me, Louis raised his hands slowly above his head and gestured in front of him with his chin. Two men, dressed in jeans and faded shirts, stood before us pointing Heckler & Koch HK53s with retracted stocks. I caught two more in the rear-view mirror and a fifth, wearing an axe in his belt, opposite the passenger window. They were hard, weathered-looking men, some of them with beards already tinged with grey. Their boots were muddy and their hands were the hands of manual labourers, scarred in places, the fingers thick and muscled.

I watched as a man of medium height, dressed in a blue denim shirt, jeans and workboots, walked towards the gate from the main compound building. When he reached the gate he didn't open it but stood watching us through the fencing. He had been burned at some point: the skin on the right of his face was heavily scarred, the right eye useless, and the hair hadn't grown back on that side of his scalp. A fold of skin hung over his dead eye and, when he spoke, he did so out of the left side of his mouth.

'What you want here?' The voice was heavily accented: Cajun stock.

'My name's Charlie Parker,' I replied, through the open window. 'I'm here to see Lionel Fontenot.'

'Who this?' He motioned at Louis with a finger.

'Count Basie,' I said. 'The rest of the band couldn't make it.'

Pretty Boy didn't crack a smile, or even a half-smile. 'Lionel don't see no one. Get yo' ass outta here 'fo you get hurt.' He turned and walked back towards the compound.

'Hey,' I said. 'You accounted for all of Joe Bones's goons at Metairie yet?'

He stopped and turned back towards us.

'What you say?' He looked like I'd just insulted his sister.

'I figure you have two bodies at Metairie that no one can account for. If there's a prize, I'd like to claim it.'

He seemed to consider this for a moment, then: 'You a joker? You are, I don't think you funny.'

'You don't think I'm funny?' I said. There was an edge to my voice now. His left eyelid flickered and a H&K ended up two inches from my nose. It smelt like it had been used recently. 'Try this for funny: I'm the guy who hauled Lutice Fontenot from the bottom of Honey Island. You want to tell Lionel that, see if he laughs?'

He didn't reply, but pointed an infra-red signaller at the compound gate. It opened almost noiselessly.

'Get outta the car,' he said. Two of the men kept our hands in view and their guns trained on us as we opened the car doors, then two others came forward and frisked us against the car, looking for wires and weapons. They handed Louis's SIG and knife and my S&W to the scarred guy, then checked the interior of the car for concealed weapons. They opened the hood and trunk and checked under the car.

'Man, you like the Peace Corps,' whispered Louis. 'Make friends wherever you go.'

'Thanks,' I replied. 'It's a gift.'

When they were satisfied that it was clean, we were allowed to drive slowly up to the compound with one of Fontenot's men, the axeman, in the back. Two men walked alongside the car. We parked beside the Corniche and were escorted up to the older house.

On the porch, waiting for us with a china cup of coffee in his hand, was Lionel Fontenot. The burn victim went up to him and spoke a few words in his ear, but Lionel stopped him with a raised hand and turned a hard stare on us. I felt a raindrop fall on my head and within seconds we were standing in a downpour. Lionel left us in the rain. I was wearing my blue linen Liz Claiborne suit and a white shirt with a blue silk-knit tie. I wondered if the dye would run. The rain was heavy and the dirt around the house was already turning to mud when Lionel ordered his men to leave, took a seat on the porch and indicated with a nod of his head that we should come up. We sat on a pair of wooden chairs with woven seats while Lionel took a wooden recliner. The burn victim stood behind us. Louis and I moved our chairs slightly as we sat so that we could keep him in view.

An elderly black maid, with a face that I recognised from the Metairie funeral party, emerged from the house with a silver coffee pot and sugar and cream in a matching set, all on an ornate silver tray. There were three china cups and saucers on the tray. Multi-coloured birds chased each other's tails around the rim of the cups and a heavy silver spoon with a sailing ship at the end lay neatly positioned beneath the handle of each one. The maid placed the tray on a small wicker table and then left us.

Lionel Fontenot was wearing a pair of black cotton pants and a white shirt with an open collar. A matching black jacket lay over the back of his chair and his brogues were newly polished. He leaned over the table and poured three cups of coffee, added two sugars to one and handed it wordlessly to the burn victim.

'Cream and sugar?' he asked, looking to Louis and me in turn.

'Black's fine,' I said.

'Likewise,' said Louis.

Lionel handed us each a cup. It was all very polite. Above us, the rain hammered on the porch roof.

'You want to tell me how you came to be looking for my sister?' Lionel said at last. He looked like someone who finds a strange guy cleaning the windscreen of his car and can't decide whether to tip him a buck or hit him with a tyre iron. He held his cup with his little finger cocked while he sipped his coffee. I noticed that the burn victim did the same.

I told Lionel some of what I knew then. I told him about Tante Marie's visions and her death and about the stories of the ghost of a girl at a Honey Island slough. 'I think the man who killed your sister killed Tante Marie Aguillard and her son. He also killed my wife and my little girl,' I said. 'That's how I came to be looking for your sister.'

I didn't say that I was sorry for his pain. He probably knew that anyway. If he didn't, then it wasn't worth saying.

'You take out two men at Metairie?'

'One,' I answered. 'Someone else killed the other.'

Lionel turned to Louis. 'You?'

Louis didn't reply.

'Someone else,' I repeated.

Lionel put his cup down and spread his hands. 'So why are you here now? You want my gratitude? I'm going to New Orleans now to take away my sister's body. I don't know that I want to thank you for that.' He turned his face away. There was pain in his eyes, but no tears. Lionel Fontenot didn't look like a man with well-developed tear ducts.

'That's not why I'm here,' I said quietly. 'I want to know why Lutice was only reported missing in the last three months. I want to know what your brother was doing out at Honey Island on the night he was killed.'

'My brother,' he said. Love and frustration and guilt chased each other in his voice like the birds on his pretty cups. Then he seemed to catch himself. I think he was about to tell me to go to Hell, to keep out of his family's business if I wanted to stay alive, but I held his gaze and for a time he said nothing.

'I got no reason to trust you,' he said.

'I can find the man who did this,' I said. My voice was low and even. Lionel nodded, more to himself than to me, and appeared to make his decision.

'My sister left at the end of January, start of February,' he began. 'She didn't like . . .' He waved his left hand gently at the compound. '. . . all this. There was trouble with Joe Bones, some people got hurt.' He paused and chose his next words carefully. 'One day she closed her bank account, packed a bag and left a note. She didn't tell us to our faces. David wouldn't have let her leave, anyways.

'We tried to trace her. We looked up friends in the city, even people she knew in Seattle and Florida. There was nothing, not a trace. David was real cut up about her. She was our half-sister. When my momma died, my father married again. Lutice came out of that marriage. When my father and her momma died –

that was in nineteen eighty-three, in an automobile accident – we took care of her, David especially. They were real close.

'Few months back, David started having dreams about Lutice. He didn't say nothing at first, but he got thinner and paler and his nerves started to play at him. When he told me, I thought he was going crazy and told him so, but the dreams just kept comin'. He dreamed of her under water, he said, heard her banging against metal in the night. He was sure that something had happened to her.

'But what could we do? We had searched half of Louisiana. I'd even made approaches to some of Joe Bones's men, to see if there was something that maybe needed to be sorted out. There was nothing. She was gone.

'Next thing I knew, he reported her missing and we had the cops crawling over the compound. Mon, I nearly killed him that day, but he insisted. He said something had happened to Lutice. He was beyond reason by then, and I had to take care of things on my own, with Joe Bones hangin' over me like a sword 'bout to fall.'

He looked to the burn victim.

'Leon here was with him when the call came. He wouldn't say nothin' about where he was goin', just took off in his damned yellow car. When Leon tried to stop him, he pulled a gun on him.' I glanced at Leon. If he felt any guilt about what had happened to David Fontenot, he kept it well hidden.

'Any idea who made the call?' I asked.

Lionel shook his head.

I put my cup on the tray. The coffee was cold and untasted.

'When are you going to hit Joe Bones?' I asked. Lionel blinked like he had just been slapped and, out of the corner of my eye, I saw Leon step forward.

'The hell you talkin' about?' said Lionel.

'You've got a second funeral coming up, at least as soon as the police release your sister's body. Either you won't have too many mourners or the funeral will be overrun with police and media. Whatever happens, I figure you'll try to take out Joe Bones before then, probably at his place in West Feliciana. You owe him for David, and, anyway, Joe won't rest easy until you're dead. One of you will try to finish it.'

Lionel looked at Leon. 'They clean?' Leon nodded.

Lionel leaned forward. There was menace in his voice. 'The fuck does any of this have to do with you?'

I wasn't fazed by him. The threat of violence was in his face, but I needed Lionel Fontenot.

'You heard about Tony Remarr's death?'

Lionel nodded.

'Remarr was killed because he was out at the Aguillard place after Tante Marie and her son were murdered,' I explained. 'His fingerprints were found in Tante Marie's blood, Joe Bones heard about it and told Remarr to lie low. But the killer found out – I don't know how, yet – and I think he used your brother to lure Remarr into making the hit so he could take him out. I want to know what Remarr told Joe Bones.'

Lionel considered what I had said. 'And you can't get to Joe Bones without me.'

Beside me, Louis's mouth twitched. Lionel caught the movement.

'That's not entirely true,' I said. 'But if you're going to be calling on him anyway, we might tag along.'

'I go calling on Joe Bones, his fucking place is gonna be real fucking quiet by the time I leave,' said Lionel softly.

'You do what you have to do,' I replied. 'But I need Joe Bones alive. For a while.'

Lionel stood and tied the top button on his shirt. He took a wide black silk tie from the inside pocket of his jacket and began to put it on, using his reflection in the window to check the knot.

'Where you staying?' he asked. I told him, and gave Leon the number of my phone. 'We'll be in touch,' said Lionel. 'Maybe. Don't come out here again.'

Our discussions appeared to be at an end. Louis and I were almost at the car when Lionel spoke again. He pulled on his jacket and adjusted the collar, then smoothed down the lapels.

'One thing,' he said. 'I know Morphy out of St Martin was there when Lutice was found. You got cop friends?'

'Yeah. I got federal friends too. That a problem?'

He turned away. 'Not as long as you don't make it one. If you do, the crabs gonna be feeding on you and your buddy.'

Louis fooled around with the radio until he found a station that seemed to be playing back-to-back Dr John. 'This is music, right?' he said.

The music segued uneasily from 'Makin' Whoopee' to 'Gris Gris Gumbo Ya-Ya' and John's throaty rumble filled the car. Louis flicked the pre-sets again, until he found a country station playing three-in-a-row from Garth Brooks.

'This be the Devil's music,' mumbled Louis. He turned the radio off and tapped his fingers on the dash.

'You know,' I said, 'you don't have to hang around if you don't want to. Things could get difficult, or Woolrich and the feds could decide to make them difficult for you.' I knew that Louis was what Angel diplomatically referred to as 'semi-retired'. Money, it appeared, was no longer an issue. The 'semi' indicated that it might have been replaced by something else, although I wasn't sure yet what that was.

He looked out the window, not at me. 'You know why we're here?'

'Not entirely. I asked, but I wasn't sure that you'd come.'

'We came because we owe you, because you'd look out for us if we needed it and because someone has to look out for you after what happened to your woman and your little girl. More than that, Angel thinks that you're a good man. Maybe I think so too and maybe I think that what you brought to an end with the Modine bitch, what you're trying to bring to an end here, they're things that should be brought to an end. You understand me?'

It was strange to hear him talk this way, strange and affecting. 'I think I understand,' I replied quietly. 'Thank you.'

'You are going to end this thing here?' he said.

'I think so, but we're missing something, a detail, a pattern, something.' I kept catching glimpses of it, like a rat passing under streetlights. I needed to find out more about Edward Byron. I needed to talk to Woolrich.

Rachel met us in the hall of the main Flaisance house. I guessed that she had been watching for the car. Angel lounged beside her, eating a Lucky Dog, which looked like the business end of a baseball bat topped with onion, chilli and mustard.

'The FBI came,' said Rachel. 'Your friend Woolrich was with them. They had a warrant. They took everything – my notes, the illustrations, everything they could find.' She led the way to her room. The walls had been stripped of their notes. Even the diagram I had drawn was gone.

'They searched our room too,' remarked Angel to Louis. 'And Bird's.' My head jerked up as I thought of the case of guns. Angel spotted the move. 'We ditched them soon as your FBI friend put the stare on Louis. They're in a storage depot on Bayonne. We both have keys.'

I noticed that Rachel seemed more irritated than upset as we followed her to her room. 'Am I missing something here?'

She smiled. 'I said they took everything they could *find*. Angel saw them coming. I hid some of the notes in the waistband of my jeans, under my shirt. Angel took care of some of the rest.'

She took a small pile of papers from under her bed and

waved them with a small flourish. She kept one separate in her hand. It was folded over once.

'I think you might want to see this,' she said, handing the paper to me. I unfolded it and felt a pain in my chest.

It was an illustration of a woman seated naked on a chair. She had been split from neck to groin and the skin on each side had been pulled back so that it hung over her arms like the folds of a gown. Across her lap lay a young man, similarly opened but with a space where his stomach and other internal organs had been removed. Apart from the detail of the anatomisation and the alteration in the sex of one of the victims, it resembled in its detail what had been done to Jennifer and Susan.

'It's Estienne's *Pietà*,' said Rachel. 'It's very obscure, which is why it took so long to track down. Even in its day, it was regarded as excessively explicit and, more to the point, blasphemous. It bore too much of a resemblance to the figure of the dead Christ and Mary for the liking of the Church authorities. Estienne nearly burned for it.'

She took the illustration from me and looked at it sadly, then placed it on her bed with the other papers. 'I know what he's doing,' she said. 'He's creating *memento mori*, death's heads.' She sat on the edge of the bed and put her hands together beneath her chin, as if in prayer. 'He's giving us lessons in mortality.'

# Part Four

He had a mind to be acquainted with your inside, Crispin.

*Edward Ravenscroft*, 'The Anatomist'

# Chapter Forty-Five

In the medical school of the Complutense University of Madrid there is an anatomical museum. Founded by King Carlos III, much of its collection derives from the efforts of Doctor Julian de Velasco in the early to mid-nineteenth century. Dr Velasco was a man who took his work seriously. He was reputed to have mummified the corpse of his own daughter, just as William Harvey was assisted in his discovery of circulation by his decision to autopsy the bodies of his own father and sister.

The long rectangular hall is arrayed with glass cases of exhibits: two giant skeletons, the wax model of a foetal head and, at one point, two figures labeled '*despellejados*'. They are the 'flayed men', who stand in dramatic poses, displaying the movement of the muscles and the tendons without the white veil of the skin to hide it from the eye of the beholder. Vesalius, Valverde, Estienne, their forebears, their peers, their successors, worked in the knowledge of this tradition. Artists such as Michelangelo and Leonardo da Vinci created their own *écorchés*, as they termed their drawings of flayed figures, basing their work on their own participation in dissections.

And the figures they created were more than merely anatomical specimens: they served, in their way, as reminders of the flawed nature of our humanity, a reminder of the body's capacity for pain and, eventually, mortality. They warned of the futility of the pursuits of the flesh, the reality of disease and pain and death in this life and the promise of something better in the next.

In eighteenth-century Florence, the practice of anatomical modelling reached its peak. Under the patronage of the Abbot Felice Fontana, anatomists and artists worked side by side to create natural sculptures from beeswax. Anatomists exposed the cadavers, the artists poured the liquid plaster, and moulds were created. Layers of wax were poured into them, with pig fat used to alter the temperature of the wax where necessary, allowing a process of layering that reproduced the transparency of human tissue.

Then, using threads and brushes and fine point, the lineaments and striations of the body were reproduced. Eyebrows and eyelashes were added, one by one. In the case of the Bolognese artist Lelli, real skeletons were used as frames for his wax creations. The Emperor of Austria, Joseph II, was so impressed by the collection that he ordered 1192 models to promote medical teaching in his own country. By contrast, Frederik Ruysch, Professor of Anatomy at the Atheneum Illustre in Amsterdam, used chemical fixatives and dyes to preserve his specimens. His house contained an exhibition of the skeletons of infants and children in various poses, reminders of the transience of life.

Yet nothing could compare to the reality of the actual human body exposed to view. Public demonstrations of anatomisation and dissection attracted huge crowds, some of them in carnival disguise. Ostensibly, they were there to learn. In reality, the dissection was little more than an extension of the public execution. In England, the Murder Act of 1752 provided a direct link between the two events by permitting the bodies of murderers to be anatomically dissected and post-mortem penal dissection became a form of further punishment for the criminal, who would now be denied a proper burial. In 1832, the Anatomy Act extended the deprivation of the poor into the next life by allowing the confiscation of the bodies of dead paupers for dissection.

So death and dissection walked hand-in-hand with the extension of scientific knowledge. But what of pain? What of the Renaissance disgust with the workings of the female body, which led to a particularly morbid fascination with the uterus? In the acts of flaying and anatomisation, the realities of suffering, sex and death were not far away.

The interior of the body, when revealed, speaks to us of mortality. But how many of us can ever bear witness to our own interiors? We see our own mortality only through the prism of the mortality of others. Even then, it is only in exceptional circumstances, in cases of war, or violent accidental death or murder, when the viewer is a witness to the act itself or its immediate consequences, that mortality in all its deep red reality is made clear to us.

In his violent, pain-filled way, Rachel believed, the Travelling Man was trying to break down these barriers. In killing his victims in this way, he was making them aware of their own mortality, exposing to them their own interiors, introducing them to the meaning of true pain; but they also served as a reminder to others of their own mortality and the final, dreadful pain that would some day find them.

The Travelling Man crisscrossed the boundaries between torture and execution, between intellectual and physical curiosity and sadism. He was part of the secret history of mankind, the history recorded in the thirteenth-century *Anatomia Magistri Nicolai Physici*, which observed that the ancients practised dissection upon both the living and the dead, binding condemned criminals hand and foot and gradually dissecting them, beginning with their legs and arms and moving on to their internal organs. Celsus and Augustine made similar allegations about live dissections, still contested by medical historians.

And now the Travelling Man had come to write his own history, to offer his own blending of science and art, to make his own notes on mortality, to create a Hell within the human heart.

All this Rachel explained as we sat in her room. Outside, it had grown dark and the strains of music floated on the air.

'I think the blinding may be related to ignorance, a physical representation of a failure to understand the reality of pain and death,' she said. 'But it indicates just how far the killer himself is removed from ordinary humanity. We all suffer, we all experience death in various ways before we die ourselves. He believes that only he can teach us this . . .'

'That, or he believes we've lost sight of it and need to be reminded, that it's his role to tell us just how inconsequential we are,' I added. Rachel nodded her assent.

'If what you say is true, then why was Lutice Fontenot dumped in a barrel?' It was Angel. He sat by the balcony, staring out on to the street below.

''Prentice work,' said Rachel. Louis cocked an eyebrow but stayed silent.

'This Travelling Man believes he's creating works of art: the care he takes in displaying the bodies, their relation to old medical texts, the links with mythology and artistic representations of the body all point in that direction. But even artists have to start somewhere. Poets, painters, sculptors all serve an apprenticeship of sorts, formal or otherwise. The work they create during their apprenticeships may go on to influence their later work, but it's usually not for public display. It's a chance to make mistakes without criticism, to see what you can and cannot achieve. Maybe that's what Lutice Fontenot was to him: 'prentice work.'

'But she died after Susan and Jennifer,' I added softly.

'He took Susan and Jennifer because he wanted to, but the results were unsatisfactory. I think he used Lutice to practise again before he returned to the public arena,' she answered, not looking at me. 'He took Tante Marie and her son for a combination of reasons, out of both desire and necessity, and this time he had the time he needed to achieve the effect for which he was searching. He then had to kill Remarr, either because of what he actually saw or the mere possibility that he might have seen something, but again he created a *memento mori* out of him. He's practical, in his way: he's not afraid to make a virtue out of necessity.'

Angel looked unhappy with the thrust of Rachel's words. 'But what about the way most of us react to death?' he began. 'It makes us want to live. It even makes us want to *screw*.'

Rachel glanced at me, then returned to her notes.

'I mean,' continued Angel, 'what does this guy want us to do? Stop eating, stop loving, because he's got a thing about death and he thinks the next world is going to be something better?'

I picked up the illustration of the *Pietà* again and examined the detail of the bodies, the carefully labelled interiors, and the placid expressions on the faces of the woman and the man. The faces of the Travelling Man's victims had looked nothing like this. They were contorted in their final agonies.

'He doesn't give a damn about the next world,' I said. 'He's only concerned with the damage he can do in this one.'

I stood and joined Angel at the window. Beneath us, the dogs scampered and sniffed in the courtyard. I could smell cooking and beer and imagined that, beneath it all, I could smell the mass of humanity itself, passing us by.

'Why hasn't he come after us? Or you?' It was Angel. His words were directed at me, but it was Rachel who answered.

'Because he wants us to understand,' she said. 'Everything he's done is an attempt to lead us to something. All of this is an effort to communicate, and we're the audience. He doesn't want to kill us.'

'Yet,' said Louis.

Rachel nodded once, her eyes locked on mine. 'Yet,' she repeated softly.

I arranged to meet Rachel and the others later in Vaughan's. Back in my room, I called Woolrich and left a message on his machine. He returned the call within five minutes and told me he'd meet me at the Napoleon House within the hour.

He was as good as his word. Shortly before ten he appeared, dressed in off-white chinos and carrying a matching jacket over his arm, which he put on as soon as he entered the bar.

'Is it chilly in here, or is it just the reception?' There was sleep caked at the corners of his eyes and he smelled sour and unwashed. He was no longer the assured figure I recalled from Jenny Ohrbach's apartment, wresting control of the room from a group of vaguely hostile cops. Instead he looked older, more uncertain. Taking Rachel's papers in the way he did was out of character for him; the old Woolrich would have taken them anyway, but he would have asked for them first. He ordered an Abita for himself and another mineral water for me.

'You want to tell me why you seized materials from the hotel?'

'Don't look on it as a seizure, Bird. Consider it borrowing.' He sipped at his beer and looked at himself in the mirror. He didn't seem to like what he saw.

'You could just have asked,' I said.

'Would you have given it to me?'

'No, but I'd have discussed why I wouldn't.'

'I don't think that Durand would have been too impressed with that. Frankly, I wouldn't have been too impressed either.'

'Durand called it? Why? You have your own profilers, your own agents on it. Why were you so sure that we could add something?'

He spun around on his stool and leaned close to me, close

enough that I could smell his breath. 'Bird, I know you want this guy. I know you want him for what he did to Susan and Jennifer, to the old woman and her son, to Florence, to Lutice Fontenot, maybe even to that fuck Remarr. I've tried to keep you in touch with what's been going down and you've walked all over this case like a fucking child in new boots. You've got an assassin staying in the room next door, God alone knows what his pal does, and your lady friend is collecting graphic medical imagery like box tops. You ain't given me shit, so I did what I had to do. You think I'm holding back on you? With the shit you're pulling, you're lucky I don't put you back on a plane to Noo Yawk.'

'I need to know what you know,' I said. 'What are you holding back about this guy?'

We were almost head to head now. Then Woolrich leaned back.

'Holding back? Jesus, Bird, you're unbelievable. Here's something: Byron's wife? You want to know what she majored in when she was at college? Art. Her thesis was on Renaissance art and depictions of the body. You think that might have included medical representations, that maybe that was where her ex got some of his ideas?'

He took a deep breath and a long draught of beer. 'You're bait, Bird. You know it, and I know it. And I know something else too.' His voice was cold and hard. 'I know you were at Metairie. There's a guy in the morgue with a bullet hole in his head and the cops have the remains of a 10-millimetre Smith & Wesson bullet, which was dug out of the marble behind him. You want to tell me about that, Bird? You want to tell me if you were alone in Metairie when the killing started?'

I didn't reply.

Then: 'You screwing her, Bird?'

I looked at him. There was no mirth in his eyes and he wasn't smiling. Instead, there was hostility and distrust. Whatever I needed to know about Edward Byron and his ex-wife, I would have to find out myself. If I had hit him then, we would have hurt each other badly. I didn't waste any more words on him and I didn't look back as I left the bar.

I took a cab to Bywater and stopped off right outside Vaughan's Lounge on the corner of Dauphine and Lesseps. I paid the five-dollar cover at the door. Inside, Kermit Ruffins and the Barbecue Swingers were lost in a rhapsody of New Orleans brass and there were plates of red beans scattered on the tables. Rachel and Angel were dancing around chairs and tables while Louis looked on with a long-suffering expression. As I approached, the tempo of the music slowed a little and Rachel made a grab for me. I moved with her for a while as she stroked my face, and I closed my eyes and let her. Then I sipped a soda and thought my own thoughts until Louis moved from his seat and sat beside me.

'You didn't have much to say back in Rachel's room,' I said.

He nodded. 'It's bullshit. All this stuff, the religion, the medical drawings, they're all just trappings. And maybe he believes them and maybe he don't. It's nothing to do with mortality, it's to do with the beauty of the colour of meat.'

He took a sip of beer.

'And this guy just likes red.'

Back at the Flaisance, I lay beside Rachel and listened to her breathing in the dark.

'I've been thinking,' she said. 'About our killer.'

'And?'

'I think the killer may not be male.'

I raised myself up on my elbows and looked at her. I could see the whites of her eyes, wide and bright.

'Why?'

'I'm not sure, exactly. There just seems to be something

almost feminine about the sensibility of whoever is committing these crimes, a . . . *sensitivity* to the interconnectedness of things, to their potential for symbolism. I don't know. I guess I'm thinking out loud, but it's not a sensibility typical of a modern male. Maybe "female" is wrong – I mean, the hall-marks, the cruelty, the capacity to overpower, all point to a male – but it's as close as I can get, at least for now.'

She was silent again.

'Are we becoming a couple?' she asked at last.

'I don't know. Are we?'

'You're avoiding the question.'

'No, not really. It's not one that I'm used to answering, or that I ever thought that I'd have to answer again. If you're asking if I want us to stay together, then the answer is yes, I do. It worries me a little, and I'm bringing in more baggage than the handlers at JFK, but I want to be with you.'

She kissed me softly.

'Why did you stop drinking?' she asked, adding, 'Since we're having this heart-to-heart.'

I started at the question. 'Because if I took one drink now, I'd wake up in Singapore with a beard a week later,' I replied.

'It doesn't answer the question.'

'I hated myself and that made me hate others, even the people closest to me. I was drinking the night Susan and Jennifer were killed. I'd been drinking a lot, not just that night but other nights too. I drank because of a lot of things, because of the pressure of the job, because of my failings as a husband, as a father, and maybe other things as well, things from way back. If I hadn't been a drunk, Susan and Jennifer might not have died. So I stopped. Too late, but I stopped.'

She didn't say anything else. She didn't say, 'It wasn't your fault,' or 'You can't blame yourself.' She knew better than that.

I think I wanted to say more, to try to explain to her what it was like without alcohol, about how I was afraid that, without it, each day would now leave me with nothing to which to look forward. Each day would simply be another day without a drink. Sometimes, when I was at my lowest ebb, I wondered if my search for the Travelling Man was just a way to fill my days, a way to keep me from going off the rails.

Later, as she slept, I lay on the bed, on top of the sheets, and thought about Lutice Fontenot and bodies turned into art, before I, too, faded into sleep.

# Chapter Forty-Six

I slept badly that night, wound up by my conversation with Woolrich and troubled by dreams of dark water. The next morning, I had breakfast alone after tracking down what seemed to be the only copy of *The New York Times* in Orleans Parish over at Riverside News, by the Jax Brewery. Later, I met Rachel at Café du Monde and we walked through the French Market, wandering between the stalls of T-shirts and CDs and cheap wallets, and on to the fresh produce at the Farmers' Market. There were pecans like dark eyes, pale, shrunken heads of garlic, melons with dark red flesh that held the gaze like a wound. White-eyed fish lay packed in ice beside crawfish tails; headless shrimp rested by racks of ''gator-on-a-stick' and murky tanks in which baby alligators lay on display. There were stalls loaded with eggplants and militones, sweet onions and elephant-toe garlic, fresh Roma tomatoes and ripe avocados.

Over a century before, this had been a two-block stretch of Gallatin Street on the riverfront docks between Barracks and Ursuline. Outside of maybe Shanghai and the Bowery, it was one of the toughest places in the world, a strip of brothels and low-life gin mills where hard-faced men mixed with harder women and anyone without a weapon had taken a wrong turning somewhere that he was bound to regret.

Gallatin is gone now, erased from the map, and instead

tourists mix with Cajun fishermen from Lafayette and beyond, come to sell their wares surrounded by the thick, heady smell of the Mississippi. The city was like that, it seemed: streets disappeared; bars opened and, a century later, were gone; buildings were torn down or burned to the ground and others rose to take their place. There was change, but the spirit of the city remained the same. On this muggy morning, it seemed to brood beneath the clouds, feeling the people as a passing infection which it would cleanse from itself with rain.

The door of my room was slightly ajar when we returned through the courtyard. I motioned Rachel against the wall and drew my Smith & Wesson, keeping to the sides of the wooden stairway so that the steps wouldn't creak. The noise of Ricky's Steyr sending bullets raking past my ear had stayed with me. '*Joe Bones says hello.*' I figured that if Joe Bones tried to say hello again, I could spare enough powder to blow him back to Hell.

I listened at the door but no sounds came from inside. If it had been the maid in my room, she'd have been whistling and bumping, maybe listening to a blues station on her tinny portable radio. If there was a maid in my room now, she was either asleep or levitating.

I hit the door hard with my shoulder and entered fast, my gun at arm's length, scanning the room with the sight. It came to rest on the figure of Leon sitting in a chair by the balcony, flicking through a copy of *GQ* that Louis had passed on to me. Leon didn't look like the kind of guy who bought much on *GQ*'s recommendation, unless the Q had made a big play for the JC Penney contract. Leon glanced at me with even less interest than he gave to *GQ*. His damaged eye glistened beneath its fold of skin like a crab peering out of a shell.

'When you're finished, there are hairs in the shower and the closet door sticks,' I said.

'Room falls down around your ears, I could give a fuck,' he replied. That Leon, what a kidder.

He threw the magazine on the floor and looked past me to Rachel, who had followed me into the room. His eyes didn't register any interest there either. Maybe Leon was dead and no one had worked up the guts to tell him.

'She's with me,' I said. Leon looked like he could have keeled over from apathy.

'Ten tonight, at the 966 junction at Starhill. You *et ton ami noir*. Anyone else, Lionel cornhole ·you both with a shotgun.'

He stood to leave. As I moved aside to let him pass, I made a pistol of my finger and thumb and fired it at him. There was a flash of steel in each of his hands and two barb-edged knives appeared inches from each of my eyes. I could see ·the tops of the spring loaders in his sleeves. That explained why Leon didn't seem to feel the need to carry a gun.

'Impressive,' I said, 'but it's only funny until someone loses an eye.' Leon's dead right eye seemed to gaze into my soul, as if to rot it and turn it to dust, then he left. I couldn't hear his footsteps as he walked down the gallery.

'A friend of yours?' asked Rachel.

I walked out of the room and looked down at the already empty courtyard. 'If he is, I'm lonelier than I thought.'

When Louis and Angel returned from a late breakfast, I went to their door and knocked. A couple of seconds went by before there was a response.

'Yeah?' shouted Angel.

'It's Bird. You two decent?'

'Jeez, I hope not. C'mon in.'

Louis sat upright in bed, reading the *Times-Picayune*. Angel sat beside him outside the sheets, naked but for a towel across his lap.

'The towel for my benefit?'

'I'm afraid you might become confused about your sexuality.'

'Might take away what little I have.'

'Very witty for a man screwing a psychologist. Why don't you just pay your eighty bucks an hour like everyone else?'

Louis gave us both bored looks over the top of his newspaper. Maybe Leon and Louis were related way back.

'Lionel Fontenot's boy just paid me a visit,' I said.

'The beauty queen?'

'None other.'

'We on?'

'Tonight at ten. Better get your stuff out of hock.'

'I'll send my boy.' He kicked Angel in the leg from beneath the sheets.

'The ugly queen?'

'None other,' said Louis.

Angel continued to watch his game show. 'It's beneath my dignity to comment.'

Louis returned to his paper. 'You got a lot of dignity for a guy with a towel on his dick.'

'It's a big towel,' sniffed Angel.

'Waste of a lot of good towel space, you ask me.'

I left them to it. Back in my room, Rachel was standing by the wall, her arms folded and a fierce expression on her face.

'What happens now?' she asked.

'We go back to Joe Bones,' I said.

'And Lionel Fontenot kills him,' she spat. 'He's no better than Joe Bones. You're only siding with him out of expediency. What will happen when Fontenot kills him? Will things be any better?'

I didn't answer. I knew what would happen. There would be

a brief disturbance in the drugs trade, as Fontenot renegotiated existing deals or ended them entirely. Prices would go up and there would be some killing, as those who felt strong enough to challenge him for Joe Bones's turf made their play. Lionel Fontenot would kill them, of that I had no doubt.

Rachel was right. It was only expediency that made me side with Lionel. Joe Bones knew something about what had happened the night Tante Marie died, something that could bring me a step closer to the man who had killed my wife and child. If it took Lionel Fontenot's guns to find out what that was, then I would side with the Fontenots.

'And Louis will stand beside you,' said Rachel quietly. 'My God, what have you become?'

Later, I drove to Baton Rouge, Rachel accompanying me at my insistence. We were uneasy together, and no words were exchanged. Rachel contented herself with looking out of the window, her elbow resting against the door, her right hand supporting her cheek. The silence between us remained unbroken until we reached Exit 166, heading for LSU and the home of Stacey Byron. Then I spoke, anxious that we should at least try to clear the air between us.

'Rachel, I'll do what I have to do to find whoever killed Susan and Jennifer,' I said. 'I need this, else I'm dead inside.'

She did not reply immediately. For a time, I thought she was not going to reply at all.

'You're already dying inside,' she said at last, still staring out of the window. I could see her eyes, reflected in the glass, following the landscape. 'The fact that you're prepared to do these things is an indication of that.'

She looked at me for the first time. 'I'm not your moral arbiter, Bird, and I'm not the voice of your conscience. But I am someone who cares about you, and I'm not sure how to deal with these feelings right now. Part of me wants to walk away and never look back, but another part of me wants, needs, to stay with you. I want to stop this thing, all of it. I want it all to end, for everybody's sake.' Then she turned away again and left me to deal with what she had said.

Stacey Byron lived in a small white clapboard house with a red door and peeling paint, close to a small mall with a big supermarket, a photo shop and a twenty-four-hour pizzeria. This area by the LSU campus was populated mainly by students and some of the houses now had stores on their first floor, selling used CDs and books or long hippie dresses and over-wide straw hats. As we drove by Stacey Byron's house and pulled into a parking space in front of the photo shop, I spotted a blue Probe parked close by. The two guys sitting in the front seats looked bored beyond belief. The driver had a newspaper folded in four resting on the wheel and was sucking a pencil as he tried to do the crossword. His partner tapped a rhythm on the dashboard as he watched the front door of Stacey Byron's house.

'Feds?' asked Rachel.

'Maybe. Could be locals. This is donkey work.'

We watched them for a while. Rachel turned on the radio and we listened to an AOR station: Rush, Styx, Richard Marx. Suddenly the middle of the road seemed to be running straight through the car, musically speaking.

'Are you going in?' asked Rachel.

'May not have to,' I replied, nodding towards the house.

Stacey Byron, her blonde hair tied back in a ponytail and her body encased in a short white cotton dress, emerged from the house and walked straight towards us, a straw shopping basket over her left arm. She nodded at the two guys in the car. They tossed a coin and the one in the passenger seat, a medium-sized man with a small belly protruding through his jacket, got out of the car, stretched his legs and followed her towards the mall.

She was a good-looking woman, although the short dress was a little too tight at the thighs and dug slightly into the fat below her buttocks. Her arms were strong and lean, her skin tanned. There was a grace to her as she walked: when an elderly man almost collided with her as she entered the supermarket, she spun lightly on her right foot to avoid him.

I felt something soft on my cheek and turned to find Rachel blowing on it.

'Hey,' she said, and for the first time since we left New Orleans there was a tiny smile on her lips. 'It's rude to lech when you're with another woman.'

'It's not leching,' I said, as we climbed from the car, 'it's surveillance.'

I wasn't sure why I had come here, but Woolrich's remarks about Stacey Byron and her interest in art made me want to see her for myself, and I wanted Rachel to see her as well. I didn't know how we might get to talk to her but I figured that these things had a habit of working themselves out.

Stacey took her time browsing on the aisles. There was an aimlessness about her shopping as she picked up items, glanced at the labels and then discarded them. The cop followed about ten feet behind her, then fifteen, before his attention was distracted by some magazines. He moved to the checkout and took up a position where he could see down two aisles at once, limiting his care of Stacey Byron to the occasional glance in her direction.

I watched a young black man in a white coat and a white hat with a green band stacking pre-packaged meat. When he had emptied the tray and marked off its contents on a clipboard, he left the shop floor through a door marked 'Staff Only'. I left Rachel to watch Byron and followed him. I almost hit him with the door as I went through, since he was squatting to pick up another plastic tray of meat. He looked at me curiously.

'Hey, man,' he said, 'you can't come in here.'

'How much do you earn an hour?' I asked.

'Five twenty-five. What's it to you?'

'I'll give you fifty bucks if you lend me your coat and that clipboard for ten minutes.'

He thought it over for a few seconds, then said, 'Sixty, and anyone asks I'll say you stole it.'

'Done,' I said, and counted out three twenties as he took off the coat. It fitted a bit tightly across the shoulders, but no one would notice as long as I left it unbuttoned. I was stepping back into the store when the young guy called me.

'Hey, man, 'nother twenty, you can have the hat.'

'For twenty bucks, I could go into the hat business myself,' I replied. 'Go hide in the men's room.'

I found Stacey Byron by the toiletries, Rachel close by.

'Excuse me, ma'am,' I said, as I approached, 'can I ask you some questions?'

Up close, she looked older. There was a network of broken veins beneath her cheekbones and a fine tracery of lines surrounded her eyes. There were tight lines, too, around her mouth, and her cheeks were sunken and stretched. She looked tired and something else: she looked threatened, maybe even scared.

'I don't think so,' she said, with a false smile, and started to step around me.

'It's about your ex-husband.'

She stopped then and turned back, her eyes searching for her police escort.

'Who are you?'

'An investigator. What do you know about Renaissance art, Mrs Byron?'

'What? What do you mean?'

'You studied it in college, didn't you? Does the name Valverde mean anything to you? Did your husband ever use it? Did you?'

'I don't know what you're talking about. Please, leave me alone.'

She backed away, knocking some cans of deodorant to the floor.

'Mrs Byron, have you ever heard of the Travelling Man?'

Something flashed in her eyes and behind me I heard a low whistle. I turned to see the fat cop moving down the aisle in my direction. He passed Rachel without noticing her and she began moving towards the door and the safety of the car, but by then I was already heading back to the staff area. I dumped the coat and walked straight through and on to the back lot, which was crowded with trucks making deliveries, before slipping around the side of the mall where Rachel already had the car started. I stayed low as we drove off, turning right instead of passing Stacey Byron's house again. In the side mirror, I could see the fat cop looking around and talking into his radio, Byron beside him.

'And what did we achieve there?' asked Rachel.

'Did you see her eyes when I mentioned the Travelling Man? She knew the name.'

'She knows something,' agreed Rachel. 'But she could have heard it from the cops. She looked scared, Bird.'

'Maybe,' I said. 'But scared of what?'

That evening, Angel removed the door panels of the Taurus and we strapped the Calicos and the magazines into the space behind them, then replaced the panels. I cleaned and loaded my Smith & Wesson in the hotel room while Rachel watched.

I put the gun in my shoulder holster and put on a black Alpha Industries bomber jacket over my black T-shirt and black jeans. With my black Timberlands, I looked like the doorman at a nightclub.

'Joe Bones is living on borrowed time. I couldn't save him if

445

I wanted to,' I told her. 'He was dead from the moment the Metairie hit went wrong.'

Rachel spoke. 'I've decided. I'm leaving in a day or two. I don't think I can be part of this any longer, the things you're doing, the things I've done.' She wouldn't look at me and there was nothing that I could say. She was right, but she wasn't simply preaching. I could see her own pain in her eyes. I could feel it every time we made love.

Louis was waiting by the car, dressed in a black sweat top and black denim jacket over dark jeans and Ecco boots. Angel checked the door panels one last time to make sure they slipped off without any trouble, then stood beside Louis.

'You don't hear anything from us by three a.m, you take Rachel and clear out of the hotel. Book into the Pontchartrain and get the first plane out in the morning,' I said. 'I don't want Joe Bones trying to even up scores if this turns bad. Handle the cops whatever way you think is best.'

He nodded, exchanged a look with Louis, and went back into the Flaisance. Louis put an Isaac Hayes tape into the stereo and we rolled out of New Orleans to the strains of 'Walk On By'.

'Dramatic,' I said.

He nodded. 'We the men.'

Leon lounged by a gnarled oak, its trunk knotted and worn, as we reached the Starhill intersection. Louis's left hand was hanging loosely by his side, the butt of the SIG jutting from beneath the passenger seat. I had slipped the Smith & Wesson into the map compartment on the driver's door as we approached the meeting place. Seeing Leon alone against the tree didn't make me feel any better.

We slowed and turned on to a small side-road which ran past the oak tree. Leon didn't seem to register our presence. I killed the engine and we sat in the car, waiting for him to make a move. Louis had his hand on the SIG now and drew it up so that it lay along his thigh.

We looked at each other. I shrugged and got out of the car, leaning against the open door with the Smith & Wesson within reach. Louis climbed from the passenger side, stretched slightly to show Leon that his hands were empty and then rested against the side of the car, the SIG now on the seat beside him.

Leon hauled himself from the tree and walked towards us. Other figures emerged from the trees around us. Five men, H&Ks hanging from their shoulders, long-bladed hunting knives at their belts, surrounded the car.

'Up against the car,' said Leon. I didn't move. From around us came the sound of safeties clicking.

'Don't move, you die now,' he said. I held his gaze, then turned and put my hands on the roof of the car. Louis did the same. As he stood behind me, Leon must have seen the SIG on the passenger seat but he didn't seem concerned. He patted my chest, beneath my arms and checked my ankles and thighs. When he was satisfied that I wasn't wearing a wire, he did a similar check on Louis then stepped back.

'Leave the car,' he instructed. Headlights shone as engines started up around us. A brown Dodge sedan and a green Nissan Patrol burst through from behind the tree line, followed by a flat-bed pick-up with three pirogues lashed down on the bed. If the Fontenot compound was under surveillance, then whoever was responsible needed his eyesight tested.

'We got some stuff in the car,' I said to Leon. 'We're gonna take it out.' He nodded and watched as I removed the mini-subs from behind the door panels. Louis took two magazines and handed one to me. The long cylinder stretched over the rear end of the receiver as I checked the safety at the front edge of the trigger guard. Louis placed a second magazine inside his jacket and tossed me a spare.

As we climbed into the back of the Dodge, two men drove our car out of sight and then jumped into the Nissan. Leon sat in the passenger seat of the Dodge beside the driver, a man in his fifties with long grey hair tied back in a ponytail, and indicated to him to move off. The other vehicles followed at a distance, so that we wouldn't look like a convoy to any passing cops.

We drove along the border of East and West Feliciana, Thompson Creek to our right, until we came to a turn-off that led down to the riverbank. Two more cars, an ancient Plymouth and what looked like an even older Volkswagen Beetle, were pulled up at the riverbank and two more pirogues lay beside them. Lionel Fontenot, dressed in blue jeans and a blue workshirt, stood by the Plymouth. He cast an eye over the Calicos but didn't say anything.

There were fourteen of us in all, most armed with H&Ks, two carrying M16 rifles, and we split three to a pirogue, with Lionel and the driver of the Dodge taking the lead in a smaller boat. Louis and I were separated and each handed a paddle, then we moved off up-river.

We rowed for twenty minutes, staying close to the western bank, before a darker shape appeared against the night sky. I could see lights flickering in windows and then, through a stand of trees, a small jetty against which a motorboat lay moored. The grounds of Joe Bones's house were dark.

There was a low whistle from in front of us and hands were raised in the pirogues to indicate that we should stop rowing. Sheltered by the trees, which hung out over the water, we waited in silence. A light flashed on the jetty and, briefly, the face of a guard was illuminated as he lit a cigarette. I heard a low splash somewhere in front of me and, high on the bank, an owl hooted. I could see the guard moving against the moon-haunted water, could hear the sound of his boots scuffing against the wooden jetty. Then a dark shape rose up beside him

448

and the pattern of the moonlight on the water was disturbed. A knife flashed and the red ember of the cigarette tumbled through the night air like a signal of distress as the guard crumpled to the ground. He made hardly a sound as he was lowered into the water.

The ponytailed man stood waiting at the jetty as we paddled by, moving as close as we could to the grass bank beyond before we climbed from the pirogues and dragged them on to dry land. The bank rose up to join an expanse of green lawn, undisturbed by flowers or trees. It rolled uphill to the back of the house, where steps led up to a patio over-looked by two french windows at ground level and a gallery on the second floor, which mirrored the one on the front of the house. I caught a movement on the gallery and heard voices from the patio. Three guards at least, probably more at the front.

Lionel raised two fingers and singled out two men to my left. They moved forward cautiously, keeping low against the ground as they moved towards the house. They were about twenty yards in front of us when the house and grounds were suddenly illuminated with bright white light. The two men were caught like rabbits in headlights as shouts came from the house and automatic fire burst from the gallery. One of them spun like an ice-skater who has missed his jump, blood bursting forth from his shirt like fresh blooms. He fell to the ground, his legs twisting, as his partner dived for the cover of a metal table, part of a lawn set which stood, semi-obscured, by the river-bank.

The french windows opened and dark figures spilled out on to the patio. On the gallery, the guard was joined by two or three others, who raked the grass in front of us with heavy fire. From the sides of the house, muzzles flashed as more of Joe Bones's men inched their way around.

Close to where I lay, Lionel Fontenot swore. We were partly

protected by the slope of the lawn as it curved down to meet the river, but the guards on the gallery were angling for clear shots at us. Some of Fontenot's men returned fire, but each time they did so, they exposed themselves to the guards at the house. One, a sharp-faced man in his forties with a mouth like a paper cut, grunted as a bullet hit him in the shoulder. He kept firing, even as the blood turned his shirt red.

'It's fifty yards from here to the house,' I said. 'There are guards moving in from the sides to cut us off. We don't move now, we're dead.' A spray of earth kicked up by Fontenot's left hand. One of Joe Bones's men had progressed almost to the riverbank by approaching from the front of the house. Two bursts of M16 fire came from behind the metal lawn table and he tumbled sideways, rolling along the grass into the river.

'Tell your men to get ready,' I hissed. 'We'll cover you.' The message was passed down the line.

'Louis!' I shouted. 'You ready to try these things out?' A figure two men down from me responded with a wave and then the Calicos burst into life. One of the guards on the gallery bucked and danced as the 9-mm bullets from Louis's gun tore into him. I pushed the selector on the trigger guard fully forward and sent a burst of automatic fire across the patio. The french windows exploded in a shower of glass and a guard tumbled down the steps and lay unmoving on the lawn. Lionel Fontenot's men sprang from their cover and raced across the lawn, firing as they did so. I switched to single-shot and concentrated on the eastern side of the house, sending wood splinters shooting into the air as I forced the men there to take cover.

Fontenot's men were almost at the patio when two fell, hit by fire from behind the ruined windows. Louis sent a burst into the room beyond and Fontenot's men moved on to the patio and entered the house. Exchanges of fire were coming from within as Louis and I rose and ran across the lawn.

To my left, the guy behind the lawn table abandoned his cover to join us. As he did so, something huge and dark appeared out of the shadows and launched itself from the grass with a deep, ferocious growl. The *boerbul* struck him on the chest, knocking him to the ground with its enormous weight. He shouted once, his hands pounding at the creature's head, and then the huge jaws closed on his neck and the *boerbul*'s head shook as he tore the man's throat apart.

The animal lifted its head and its eyes gleamed in the darkness as it found Louis. He was turning the Calico in its direction when it bounded from the dead body and sprang into the air. Its speed was astonishing. As it moved towards us, its dark form blotted out the stars in the sky above. It was at the apex of its jump when Louis's Calico sang and bullets ripped into it, causing it to spasm in mid-air and land with a crunch on the grass not two feet from us. Its paws scrambled for purchase and its mouth worked in biting motions, even as blood and froth spilled from between its teeth. Louis pumped more rounds into it until it lay still.

My eye caught movement at the western corner of the house as we neared the steps. A muzzle flashed and Louis yelled in pain. The Calico dropped to the ground as he leaped for the steps, cradling his injured hand. I fired three shots and the guard dropped. Behind me, one of Fontenot's men fired single shots from his M16 as he advanced towards the house, then let the gun hang from its shoulder strap as he reached the corner. I saw moonlight catch the blade of his knife as he stood waiting. The short muzzle of a Steyr appeared, followed by the face of one of Joe Bones's men. I recognised him as the one who had driven the golf cart to the plantation gates on our first visit here, but the flash of recognition became one with the flash of the knife as it struck across his neck. A crimson jet flew into the air from his severed arteries, but even as he fell Fontenot's man raised the M16 once again and fired past him as he moved in the direction of the front of the house.

Louis was examining his right hand as I reached him. The bullet had torn across the back of the hand, leaving a bad gash and damaging the knuckle of his forefinger. I tore a strip from the shirt of a dead guard who lay sprawled across the patio and wrapped it around Louis's hand. I handed him the Calico and he worked the strap over his head, then fitted his middle finger into the trigger guard. With his left hand he freed his SIG, then nodded to me as he rose. 'We better find Joe Bones.'

Through the patio doors lay a formal dining room. The dining table, which could seat at least eighteen people comfortably, was splintered and pitted by shots. On the wall, a portrait of a Southern gentleman standing by his horse had sustained a large hole through the horse's belly and a selection of antique china plates lay shattered in the remains of their glass-fronted display cabinet. There were two bodies in the room. One of them was the ponytailed man who had driven the Dodge.

The dining room led out into a large carpeted hallway and a white chandeliered reception area, from which a staircase wound up to the next floor. The other doors at ground level stood open, but there were no sounds coming from inside. There was sustained firing on the upper levels as we made our way to the stairs. At their base, one of Joe Bones's men lay in a pair of striped pyjama bottoms, blood pooling from an ugly head wound.

From the top of the stairs, a series of doors stretched left and right. Fontenot's men seemed to have cleared most of the rooms, but they had been pinned down in the alcoves and doorways by gunfire from the rooms at the western end of the house, one on the river side to the right, its panels already pockmarked by bullets, and the other facing out to the front of the house. As we watched, a man in blue overalls carrying a short-handled axe in one hand and a captured Steyr in the other moved quickly from his hiding place to within one doorway of the front-facing room. Shots came through the door on the right and he fell to the ground, clutching his leg.

I leaned into an alcove in which the remains of long-stemmed roses lay in a pool of water and shattered pottery and fired a sustained burst at the door on the front-facing side. Two of Fontenot's men moved forward at the same time, keeping low on the ground as they did so. Across from me, Louis fired shots at the semi-closed river-side door. I stopped firing as Fontenot's men reached the room and rushed the occupant. There were two more shots, then one of them emerged wiping his knife on his trousers. It was Lionel Fontenot. Behind him was Leon.

The two men took up positions at either side of the last room. Six more of his men moved forward to join him.

'Joe, it's over now,' said Lionel. 'We gon' finish this thing.'

Two shots burst through the door. Leon raised his H&K and appeared to be about to fire, but Lionel lifted his hand, looking past Leon to where I stood. I advanced forward and waited behind Leon's back as Lionel pushed open the door with his foot, then pressed himself flat against the wall as two more shots rang out followed by the click of a hammer on an empty chamber, a sound as final as the closing of a tomb.

Leon entered the room first, the H&K now replaced by his knives. I followed him, with Lionel behind me. The walls of Joe Bones's bedroom were pitted with holes and the night air entered through the shattered window and sent the white curtains swirling in the air like angry ghosts. The blonde who had lunched with Joe on his lawn earlier in the week lay dead against the far wall, a red stain on the left breast of her white nightgown.

Joe Bones stood before the window in a red silk dressing gown. The Colt in his hand hung uselessly at his side but his eyes glowed with anger and the scar on his lip seemed painfully pinched and white against his skin. He dropped the gun.

'Do it, you fuck,' he hissed at Lionel. 'Kill me, you got the fucking guts.'

Lionel closed the bedroom door behind us as Joe Bones turned to look at the woman.

'Ask him,' said Lionel.

Joe Bones didn't seem to hear. His face appeared consumed with a look of terrible grief as his eyes traced the contours of the dead woman's face.

'Eight years,' he said softly. 'Eight years she was with me.'

'Ask him,' repeated Lionel Fontenot.

I stepped forward and Joe Bones sneered as he turned, that look of sadness now gone. 'The fucking grieving widower. You bring your trained nigger with you?'

I slapped him hard and he took a step back.

'I can't save you, Joe, but if you help me maybe I can make it quicker for you. Tell me what Remarr saw the night the Aguillards died.'

He wiped blood from the corner of his mouth, smearing it across his cheek. 'You have no idea what you're dealing with, no fucking idea in the world. You're so out of your fucking depth, the fucking pressure should be making your nose bleed.'

'He kills women and children, Joe. He's going to kill again.'

Joe Bones twisted his mouth into the semblance of a grin, the scar distorting his full lips like a crack in a mirror. 'You killed my woman and now you're gonna kill me, no matter what I say. You got nothing to bargain with,' he said.

I glanced at Lionel Fontenot. He shook his head almost imperceptibly, but Joe Bones caught it. 'See, nothing. All you can offer is a little less pain, and pain don't hold no surprises for me.'

'He killed one of your own men. He killed Tony Remarr.'

'Tony left a print at the nigger's house. He was careless and he paid the price. Your guy, he saved me the trouble of killing the old bitch and her brood myself. I meet him, I'll shake his hand.'

Joe Bones smiled a broad smile like a flash of sunshine through dark, acrid smoke. Haunted by visions of tainted blood flowing through his veins, he had moved beyond ordinary notions of humanity and empathy, love and grief. In his shimmering red robe, he looked like a wound in the fabric of space and time.

'You'll meet him in Hell,' I said.

'I see your bitch there, I'll fuck her for you.' His eyes were bland and cold now. The smell of death hung around him like old cigar fumes. Behind me, Lionel Fontenot opened the door and the rest of his men walked quietly into the room. It was only now, seeing them all together in the ruined bedroom, that the resemblance between them became clear. Lionel held the door open for me.

'It's a family thing,' he said as I left. Behind me, the door closed with a soft click like the knocking of bones.

After Joe Bones died, we gathered the bodies of the Fontenot dead on the lawn in front of the house. The five men lay side by side, crumpled and torn as only the dead can be. The gates to the plantation were opened and the Dodge, the VW and the pick-up sped in. The bodies were loaded gently but quickly into the trunks of the cars, the injured helped into the rear seats. The pirogues were doused in gasoline, set on fire and left to float down the river.

We drove from the plantation and kept driving until we reached the rendezvous point at Starhill. The three black Explorers I had seen at the Delacroix compound stood waiting, their motors idling, their lights dimmed. As Leon sprayed gasoline into the cars and the pick-up, the bodies of the dead were removed, wrapped in tarpaulin and placed in the backs of two of the Jeeps. Louis and I watched it all in silence.

As the Jeeps roared into life and Leon threw lighted rags into the discarded vehicles, Lionel Fontenot walked over to us and stood with us as they burned. He took a small green notebook from his pocket, scribbled a number on a sheet and tore it out.

'This guy will look after your friend's hand. He's discreet.'

'He knew who killed Lutice, Lionel,' I said.

He nodded. 'He wouldn't tell, not even at the end.' He rubbed his index finger along a raw cut on the palm of his right hand, picking dirt from the wound. 'I hear the feds are looking for someone around Baton Rouge, used to work in a hospital in New York.'

I stayed silent and he smiled. 'We know his name. Man could hide out in the bayou for a long time, he knew his way around. Feds might not find him, but we will.' He gestured with his hand, like a king displaying his finest troops to his worried subjects. 'We're looking. We find him, it'll end there.'

Then he turned and climbed into the driver's seat of the lead Jeep, Leon beside him, and they disappeared into the night, the red tail-lights like falling cigarettes in the darkness, like burning boats floating on black water.

I called Angel as we drove back to New Orleans. At an all-nite drugstore I picked up antiseptic and a first-aid kit so we could work on Louis's hand. There was a sheen of sweat on his face as I drove and the white rags binding his fingers were stained a deep red. When we arrived back at the Flaisance, Angel cleansed the wound with the antiseptic and tried to stitch it with some surgical thread. The knuckle looked bad and Louis's mouth was stretched tight with pain. Despite his protests, I called the number we had been given. The bleary voice that answered the phone on the fourth ring shook the sleep from its tones when I mentioned Lionel's name.

Angel drove Louis to the doctor's surgery. When they had gone, I stood outside Rachel's door and debated whether or not to knock. I knew she wasn't asleep: Angel had spoken to her after I called, and I could sense her wakefulness. Still, I didn't knock, but as I walked back towards my own room her door opened. She stood in the gap, a white T-shirt reaching almost to her knees, and waited for me. She stood carefully aside to let me enter.

'You're still in one piece, I see,' she said. She didn't sound particularly pleased.

I felt tired and sick from the sight of blood. I wanted to plunge my face into a sink of ice-cold water. I wanted a drink so badly my tongue felt swollen inside my mouth and only a bottle of Abita, ice frosting on its rim, and a shot of Redbreast whiskey could restore it to its normal size. My voice sounded like the croak of an old man on his deathbed when I spoke.

'I'm in one piece,' I said. 'A lot of others aren't. Louis took a bullet across the hand and too many people died out at the house. Joe Bones, most of his crew, his woman.'

Rachel turned her back and walked to the balcony window. Only the bedside lamp lit the room, casting shadows over the illustrations she had kept from Woolrich and which were now restored to their places on the walls. Flayed arms and the face of a woman and a young man emerged from the semi-darkness.

'What did you find out, for all that killing?'

It was a good question. As usual with good questions, the answer didn't live up to it.

'Nothing, except that Joe Bones was happier to die painfully than to tell us what he knew.'

'What are you going to do now?'

I was getting tired of questions, especially questions as difficult as these. I knew Rachel was right and I felt disgusted at myself. It felt as if she had become tainted through her contact with me. Maybe I should have told her all of those things then, but I was too tired and too sick and I could smell blood in my nostrils; and, anyway, I think she already knew most of it.

'I'm going to bed,' I said. 'After that, I'm winging it.' Then I left her.

# Chapter Forty-Seven

The next morning I awoke with an ache in my arms from toting the Calico, exacerbated by the lingering pain of the gunshot wound inflicted in Haven. I could smell powder on my fingers, in my hair and on my discarded clothes. The room stank like the scene of a gunfight, so I opened the window and let the hot New Orleans air slip heavily into the room like a clumsy burglar.

I checked on Louis and Angel. Louis's hand had been expertly bound after the doctor picked the shards of bone from the wound and padded the knuckle. Louis barely opened his eyes as I exchanged a few quiet words with Angel at the door. I felt guilty for what had happened, although I knew that neither of them blamed me.

I sensed, too, that Angel was anxious now to return to New York. Joe Bones was dead, and the police and the feds were probably closing in on Edward Byron, despite Lionel Fontenot's doubts. Besides, I didn't believe that it would take long for Woolrich to connect us to what had happened to Joe Bones, especially if Louis was walking around with a bullet crease on his hand. I told Angel all of this and he agreed that they would leave as soon as I returned, so that Rachel would not be left alone. The whole case seemed to have ground to a kind of halt for me. Elsewhere, the feds and the Fontenots were hunting Edward Byron, a man who still seemed as distant from me as the last emperor of China.

I left a message for Morphy. I wanted to see what his people had on Byron; I wanted to add flesh to the figure. As things stood, he was as shorn of identity as the faceless figures of the slain which the feds believed he had left behind. The feds might well have been right. With the local police, they could conduct a better search than a bunch of visitors from New York with delusions of adequacy. I had hoped to work my way towards him from a different direction, but with the death of Joe Bones that path seemed to have come to an end in a tangle of dark undergrowth.

I took my phone and my book of Ralegh's writings and headed for Mother's on Poydras Street, where I drank too many cups of coffee and picked at some bacon and brown toast. When you reach one of life's dead ends, Ralegh is good company. 'Go, soul . . . since I needs must die/And give the world the lie.' Ralegh knew enough to take a stoical attitude to adversity, although he didn't know enough to avoid getting his head cut off.

Beside me, a man ate ham and eggs with the concentrated effort of a bad lover, yellow egg yolk tinging his chin like sunlight reflected from a buttercup. Someone whistled a snatch of 'What's New?', then lost his thread in the complicated chord changes of the song. The air was filled with the buzz of late-morning conversation, a radio station easing into neutral with a bland rock song and the low, aggravated hum of distant, slow-moving traffic. Outside, it was another humid New Orleans day, the kind of day that leads lovers to fight and makes children sullen and grim.

An hour passed. I rang the detective squad in St Martin and was told that Morphy had taken a day's leave to work on his house. I had nothing better to do now, so I paid my bill, put some gas in the car and started out once again towards Baton

Rouge. I found a Lafayette station playing some scratchy Cheese Read, followed by Buckwheat Zydeco and Clifton Chenier, an hour of classic Cajun and Zydeco, as the DJ put it. I let it play until the city fell away and the sound and the landscape became one.

A sheet of plastic slapped drily in the early-afternoon wind rolling from the river as I pulled up outside Morphy's place. He was replacing part of the exterior wall on the west side of the house, and the lines holding the plastic in place over the exposed joints sang as a breeze tried to yank them from their moorings. It tugged at one of the windows, which had not been fastened properly, and made the screen door knock at its frame like a tired visitor.

I called his name but there was no reply. I walked to the rear of the house, where the back door stood open, held in place by a piece of brick. I called again but my voice seemed to echo emptily through the central hallway. The rooms on the ground level were all unoccupied and no sounds came from upstairs. I drew my gun and climbed the stairs, newly planed in preparation for treating. The bedrooms were empty and the bathroom door stood wide open, toiletries neatly arranged by the sink. I checked the gallery and then went back downstairs. As I turned back towards the rear door cold metal touched the base of my neck.

'Drop it,' said a voice.

I let the gun slip from my fingers.

'Turn around. Slowly.'

The pressure was removed from my neck and I turned to find Morphy standing before me, a nail gun held inches from my face. He let out a deep breath of relief and lowered the gun.

'Shit, you scared the hell out of me,' he said.

I could feel my heart thumping wildly in my chest. 'Thanks,' I said. 'I really needed that kind of adrenaline rush on top of five cups of coffee.' I sat down heavily on the bottom step.

'You look terrible, mon. You up late last night?'

I looked up to see if there was an edge to what he had said, but he had turned his back.

'Kind of.'

'You hear the news? Joe Bones and his crew were taken out last night. Someone cut Joe up pretty bad before he died, too. Locals weren't even sure it was him until they checked the prints.' He walked down to the kitchen and came back with a beer for himself and a soda for me. I noticed it was caffeine-free cola. Under his arm he held a copy of the *Times-Picayune*.

'You see this today?'

I took the paper from him. It was folded into quarter-size, the bottom of the front page facing up. The headline read: POLICE HUNT SERIAL KILLER IN RITUAL MURDERS. The story below contained details of the deaths of Tante Marie Aguillard and Tee Jean that could only have come from the investigation team itself: the display of the bodies, the manner of their discovery, the nature of some of the wounds. It went on to speculate on a possible link between the discovery of Lutice Fontenot's body and the death of a man in Bucktown, known to have links with a leading crime figure. Worst of all, it said that police were also investigating a connection to a similar pair of murders in New York late the previous year. Susan and Jennifer were not named, but it was clear that the writer – anonymous beneath a '*Times-Picayune* Journalists' byline – knew enough about the murders to be able to put a name on the victims.

I put the paper down wearily. 'Did the leak come from your guys?' I asked.

'Could have done, but I don't think so. The feds are blaming us. They're all over us, accusing us of sabotaging the investigation.' He sipped his beer before saying what was on his mind. 'One or two people maybe felt that it could have been you who leaked the stuff.' He was obviously uncomfortable saying it, but he didn't look away.

'I didn't do it. If they've got as far as Jennifer and Susan, it won't be too long before they connect me to what's happening. The last thing I need is the press crawling all over me.'

He considered what I said, then nodded. 'I guess you're right.'

'You speak to the editor?'

'He was contacted at home when the first edition came out. We got freedom of the press and the protection of sources coming out our ass. We can't force him to tell but . . .' He rubbed at the tendons on the back of his neck. '. . . it's unusual for something like this to happen. The papers are real careful about jeopardising investigations. I think it had to come from someone close to all this.'

I thought about it. 'If they felt okay about using this stuff, then it must be cast-iron and the source impeccable,' I said. 'It could be that the feds are playing their own game on this.' It seemed to reaffirm our belief that Woolrich and his team were holding back, not only from me but probably from the police investigating team as well.

'It wouldn't be anything new,' said Morphy. 'Feds wouldn't tell us what day it is, they thought they could get away with it. You think they might have planted the story?'

'Somebody did.'

Morphy finished his beer and crushed the can beneath his foot. A small stain of beer spread itself on the bare wood. He picked up a tool belt from where it hung on a hatstand near the door and strapped it on.

'You need any help?'

He looked at me. 'Can you carry planks without falling over?'

'No.'

'Then you're perfect for the job. There's a spare pair of workgloves in the kitchen.'

For the rest of the afternoon I worked with my hands,

hoisting and carrying, hammering and sawing. We replaced most of the wood on the west side, a gentle breeze spraying sawdust and shavings around us as we worked. Later, Angie returned from a shopping trip to Baton Rouge, carrying groceries and boutique bags. While Morphy and I cleaned up, she grilled steaks with sweet potatoes, carrots and Creole rice, and we ate them in the kitchen as the evening drew in and the wind wrapped the house in its arms.

Morphy walked me out to my car. As I put the key in the ignition, he leaned in the window and said softly, 'Someone tried to get to Stacey Byron yesterday. Know anything about it?'

'Maybe.'

'You were there, weren't you? You were there when they took Joe Bones?'

'You don't want to know the answer to that,' I replied. 'Just like I don't want to know about Luther Bordelon.'

As I drove away, I could see him standing before his uncompleted house. Then he turned away and returned to his wife.

When I arrived back at the Flaisance, Angel and Louis were packed and ready to go. They wished me luck and told me that Rachel had gone to bed early. She had booked a flight for the next day. I decided not to disturb her and went to my own room. I don't even remember falling asleep.

The luminous dial on my watch read 8.30 a.m. when the pounding came at my door. I had been in deep sleep and I pulled myself slowly into wakefulness like a diver struggling for the surface. I had got as far as the edge of the bed when the door exploded inwards and there were lights shining in my face and strong arms hauled me to my feet and pushed me hard against the wall. A gun was held to my head as the main light came on in the room. I could see NOPD uniforms, a couple of plainclothes men and, directly to my right, Morphy's partner Touissant. Around me, men were tearing the room apart.

And I knew then that something had gone terribly, terribly wrong.

They allowed me to pull on a tracksuit and a pair of sneakers before cuffing me. I was marched through the hotel, past guests peering anxiously from their rooms, to a waiting police car. In a second car, her face pale and her hair matted from sleep, sat Rachel. I shrugged helplessly at her before we were driven in convoy from the Quarter.

I was questioned for three hours, then given a cup of coffee and grilled again for another hour. The room was small and brightly lit. It smelt of cigarette smoke and stale sweat. In one corner, where the plaster was pitted and worn, I could see what looked like a bloodstain. Two detectives, Dale and Klein, did most of the questioning, Dale assuming the role of aggressive interrogator, threatening to dump me in the swamp with a bullet in the head for killing a Louisiana cop, Klein taking the part of the reasonable, sensitive man trying to protect me while ensuring that the truth was told. Even with other cops as the object of their attentions, the 'good cop, bad cop' thing never went out of fashion.

I told them all I could, again and again and again. I told them of my visit to Morphy, the work on the house, the dinner, the departure, all of the reasons why my prints were all over the place. No Morphy hadn't given me the police files found in my room. No, I couldn't say who did. No, only the night porter saw me re-enter the hotel, I didn't speak to anyone else. No, I didn't leave my room again that night. No, there was no one to confirm that fact. No. No. No. No. No.

Then Woolrich arrived and the merry-go-round started all over again. More questions, this time with the feds in atten-dance. And still, no one told me why I was there or what had happened to Morphy and his wife. In the end, Klein returned and told me I could go. Behind a slatted rail divider, which separated the detective squad-room from the main corridor, Rachel sat with a mug of tea while the detectives around her studiously ignored her. In a cage ten feet behind her, a skinny white man with tattooed arms whispered obscenely to her.

Touissant appeared. He was an overweight, balding man in his early fifties, with straggly white curls around his pate like the top of a hill erupting from out of a mist. He looked red-eyed and nauseous and was as out of place here as I was.

A patrolman motioned to Rachel. 'We'll take you back to your hotel now, ma'am.' She stood. Behind her, the guy in the cage made sucking noises and grabbed his crotch in his hand.

'You okay?' I asked, as she passed by.

She nodded dumbly, then: 'Are you coming with me?'

Touissant was at my left hand. 'He'll follow later,' he said. Rachel looked over her shoulder at me as the patrolman led her away. I gave her a smile and tried to make it look reassuring, but my heart wasn't in it.

'Come on, I'll drive you back and buy you a coffee on the way,' said Touissant, and I followed him from the building.

We ended up in Mother's, where less than twenty-four hours before I had sat waiting for Morphy's call and where Touissant would tell me how John Charles Morphy and his wife Angela had died.

Morphy had been due to work a special early shift that morning and Touissant had dropped by to pick him up. They alternated pickup duties as it suited. That day, it happened to be Touissant's turn.

The screen door was closed, but the front door behind stood open. Touissant called Morphy's name, just as I had the afternoon before. He followed in my footsteps through the central hallway, checking the kitchen and the rooms to the right and left. He thought Morphy might have slept in, although he had never been late before, so he called up the stairs to the bedroom. There was no reply. He recalled that his stomach was already tightening as he worked his way up the stairs, calling Morphy's name, then Angie's, as he advanced. The door of their bedroom was partially open, but the angle obscured their bed.

He knocked once, then slowly opened the door. For a moment, the merest flashing splinter of a second, he thought he had disturbed their lovemaking, until the blood registered and he knew that this was a parody of all that love stood for, of all that it meant, and he wept then for his friend and his wife.

Even now, I seem to recall only snatches of what he said, but I can picture the bodies in my head. They were naked, facing each other on what had once been white sheets, their bodies locked together at the hips, their legs intertwined. From the waist, they leaned backwards at arm's length from each other. Both had been cut from neck to stomach. Their rib-cages had been split and pulled back and each had a hand buried in the breast of the other. As he neared, Touissant saw that each was holding the other's heart in the palm of a hand. Their heads hung back so that their hair almost touched their backs. Their eyes were gone, their faces removed, their mouths open in their final agony, their moment of death like an ecstasy. In them, love was reduced to an example to other lovers of the futility of love itself.

As Touissant spoke, a wave of guilt swept over me and broke across my heart. I had brought this thing to their house. By helping me, Morphy and his wife had been marked for a terrible death, just as the Aguillards too seemed to have been tainted by their contact with me. I stank of mortality.

And, in the midst of it all, some lines of verse seemed to float into my head and I could not recall how I had resurrected them, or who had given them to me in the first place. And it seemed to me that their source was important, although I could not tell why, except that in the lines there seemed to be echoes of what Touissant had seen. But as I tried to remember a voice speaking them to me, it slipped away and, try as I might, I could not bring it back. Only the lines remained. Some metaphysical poet, I thought. Donne, perhaps. Yes, almost certainly Donne.

> If th'unborne
> Must learne, by my being cut up, and torne:
> Kill, and dissect me, Love; for this
> Torture against thine owne end is,
> Rack't carcasses make ill Anatomies.

A *remedia amoris*, wasn't that the term? The torture and death of lovers as a remedy for love.

'He helped me,' I said. 'I involved him in this.'

'He involved himself,' Touissant said. 'He wanted to do it. He wanted to bring this guy to an end.'

I held his gaze.

'For Luther Bordelon?'

Touissant looked away. 'What does it matter now?'

But I couldn't explain that in Morphy I saw something of myself, that I had felt for his pain, that I wanted to believe he was better than me. I wanted to know.

'Garza called it,' said Touissant at last. 'Garza killed him and then Morphy supplied the throwdown. That's what he said. Morphy was young. Garza shouldn't have put him in that situation, but he did and Morphy's been paying for it ever since.' And then he caught himself using the present tense and went silent.

Outside, people were living another day: working, touring, eating, flirting still continued despite all that had taken place, all that was happening. It seemed, somehow, that it should all have come to a halt, that the clocks should have been stopped and the mirrors covered, the doorbells silenced and the voices reduced to a respectful, hushed volume. Maybe if they had seen the pictures of Susan and Jennifer, of Tante Marie and Tee Jean, of Morphy and Angie, then they would have stopped and reconsidered. And that was what the Travelling Man wanted: to provide, in the deaths of others, a reminder of the deaths of us all and the worthlessness of love and loyalty, of parenthood and friendship, of sex and need and joy, in the face of the emptiness to come.

As I stood to leave, something else came to me, something awful which I had almost forgotten, and I felt a deep, violent ache in my gut, which spread through my body until I was forced to lean against the wall, my hand scrabbling for purchase.

'Ah, God, she was pregnant.'

I looked at Touissant and his eyes briefly fluttered closed.

'He knew, didn't he?'

Touissant said nothing, but there was despair in his eyes. I didn't ask what the Travelling Man had done to the unborn child but, in that instant, I saw a terrible progression over the last months of my life. It seemed that I had moved from the death of my own child, my Jennifer, to the deaths of many children, the victims of Adelaide Modine and her accomplice Hyams, and now, finally, to the deaths of all children. Everything this Travelling Man did signified something beyond itself: in the death of Morphy's unborn child, I saw all hope for the future reduced to tattered flesh.

'I'm supposed to bring you back to your hotel,' said Touissant, at last. 'The New Orleans PD will make sure you get on the evening flight back to New York.'

But I hardly heard him. All I could think was that the Travelling Man had been watching us all along and that his game was still going on around us. We were all participants, whether we wanted to be or not.

And I recalled something that a con-man named Saul Mann had once told me back in Portland, something that seemed important to me, yet I couldn't recall why.

You can't bluff someone who isn't paying attention.

# Chapter Forty-Eight

Touissant dropped me at the Flaisance. Rachel's door was half open when I reached the carriage house. I knocked gently and entered. Her clothes had been thrown across the bedroom floor and the sheets from her bed were tossed in an untidy pile in the corner. All of her papers were gone. Her suitcase sat open on the bare mattress. I heard movement from the bathroom and she emerged carrying her cosmetics case. It was stained with powder and foundation and I guessed that the cops had broken some of its contents during their search.

She was wearing a faded blue Knicks sweat top, which hung down over her dark blue denims. She had washed and showered and her damp hair clung to her face. Her feet were bare. I had not noticed before how small they were.

'I'm sorry,' I said.

'I know.' She didn't look at me. Instead, she started to pick up her clothes and fold them as neatly as she could into her suitcase. I bent down to pick up a pair of socks, which lay in a ball by my feet.

'Leave it,' she said. 'I can do it.'

There was another knock at the door and a patrolman appeared. He was polite, but he made it clear that we were to stay in the hotel until someone arrived to take us to the airport.

I went back to my room and showered. A maid came and

made up the room and I sat on my clean sheets and listened to the sounds from the street. I thought about how badly I had screwed up, and how many people had been killed because of it. I felt like the Angel of Death; if I stood on a lawn, the grass would die.

I must have dozed for a while, because the light in the room had changed when I awoke. It seemed that it was dusk, yet that could not have been the case. There was a smell in the room, an odour of rotting vegetation and water filled with algae and dead fish. When I tried to take a breath, the air felt warm and humid in my mouth. I was conscious of movement around me, shapes shifting in the shadows at the corners of the room. I heard whispered voices and a sound like silk brushing against wood and, faintly, a child's footsteps running through leaves. Trees rustled and there came a flapping of wings from above me, beating unevenly as if the bird was in distress or pain.

The room grew darker, turning the wall facing me to black. The light through the window frame was tinged with blue and green and shimmered as seen through a heat haze.

Or through water.

They came from out of the dark wall, black shapes against green light. They brought with them the coppery scent of blood, so strong that I could taste it on my tongue. I opened my mouth to call out something – even now, I am not sure what I could have called, or who would have heard – but the dank, humid air stilled my tongue like a sponge soaked in warm, filthy water. It seemed that a weight was on my chest, preventing me from rising, and I had trouble taking air into my lungs. My hands clasped and unclasped until they, too, were still and I knew then how it felt to have ketamine coursing through one's veins, stilling the body in preparation for the anatomist's knife.

The figures stopped at the edge of the darkness, just beyond the reach of the window's dim light. They were indistinct, their edges forming and re-forming like figures seen through frosted glass or a projection losing and then regaining its focus.

And then the voices came,

*birdman*

soft and insistent,

*birdman*

fading and then strong again,

*birdman*

voices that I had never heard and others that had called out to me in passion,

*bird*

in anger, in fear, in love.

*daddy*

She was the smallest of them all, linked hand in hand with another who stood beside her. Around them, the others fanned out. I counted eight in all and, behind them, other figures, more indistinct, women, men, young girls. As the pressure built on my chest and I struggled to draw the shallowest of breaths, it came to me that the figure which had haunted Tante Marie Aguillard, which Raymond believed he had seen at Honey Island, the girl who seemed to call out to me through dark waters, might not have been Lutice Fontenot.

*chile*

Each breath felt like my last, none getting further than the back of my throat before it was choked in a gasp.

*chile*

The voice was old and dark as the ebony keys on an ancient piano singing out from a distant room.

*wake up, chile, his world is unravelling*

And then my last breath sounded in my ears and all was stillness and quiet.


I woke to the sound of a tapping on my door. Outside, daylight had passed its height and was ebbing towards evening. When I opened the door, Touissant stood before me. Behind him, I could see Rachel waiting. 'It's time to go,' he said.

'I thought the New Orleans cops were taking care of that.'

'I volunteered,' he replied. He followed me into the room as I threw my shaving gear loosely into my suit carrier, folded it over and attached the clasps. It was London Fog, a present from Susan.

Touissant nodded to the NOPD patrolman.

'You sure this is okay?' said the cop. He looked distracted and uncertain.

'Look, New Orleans cops got better things to be doing than babysitting,' replied Touissant. 'I'll get these people to their plane, you go out and catch some bad guys, okay?'

We drove in silence to Moisant Field. I sat in the passenger seat, Rachel sat in the back. I waited for Touissant to take the turn to the airport but he continued straight on 10.

'You missed your turn,' I said.

'No,' said Touissant. 'No, I didn't.'


When things start to unravel, they unravel fast. We got lucky that day. Everybody gets lucky some time.

On a junction of the Upper Grand River, south-east of 10 on the road to Lafayette, a dredging operation to remove silt and junk from the bottom of the river got some of its machinery caught up on a batch of discarded barbed wiring that was rusting away on the riverbed. They eventually freed it and tried to haul it up, but there were other things caught in the wire as well: an old iron bedstead; a set of slave irons, more than a century and a half old; and, holding the wire to the bottom, an oil drum marked with a fleur-de-lys.

It was almost a joke to the dredging crew as they worked to free the drum. The report of the discovery of a girl's body in a fleur-de-lys drum had been all over the news bulletins and it had taken up ninety lines below the fold on the *Times-Picayune* on the day of its discovery.

Maybe the crew joshed each other morbidly as they worked the barrel out of the water in order to get at the wire. Perhaps they went a little quieter, barring the odd nervous laugh, as one of them worked at the lid. The drum had rusted in places and the lid had not been welded shut. When it came off, dirty water, dead fish and weeds flowed out.

The legs of the girl, partially decayed but surrounded by a strange, waxy membrane, emerged from the open lid as well, although her body remained jammed, half in, half out of the drum. The river life had fed on her but when one man shone his flashlight to the end of the drum he could see the tattered remains of skin at the forehead and her teeth seemed to be smiling at him in the darkness.

Only two cars were at the scene when we arrived. The body had been out of the water for less than three hours. Two uniformed cops stood by with the dredging crew. Around the body stood three men in plain clothes, one of them wearing a slightly more expensive suit than the rest, his silver hair cut short and neat. I recognised him from the aftermath of Morphy's death: Sheriff James Dupree of St Martin Parish, Touissant's superior.

Dupree motioned us forward as we stepped from the car. Rachel hung back slightly but still moved towards the body in the drum. It was the quietest crime scene at which I had ever been present. Even when the ME appeared later, it remained restrained.

Dupree pulled a pair of plastic gloves from his hands, making sure that he didn't touch their exterior with his exposed fingers. His nails were very short and very clean, I noticed, although not manicured.

'You want to take a closer look?' he asked.

'No,' I said. 'I've pretty much seen all I want to see.'

There was a rotten, pungent odour coming from the mud and silt dredged up by the crew, stronger even than the smell from the girl's body. Birds hovered over the detritus, trying to target dead or dying fish. One of the crew lodged his cigarette in his mouth, bent to pick up a stone and hurled it at a huge grey rat that scuttled in the dirt. The stone hit the mud with a wet, thudding sound like a piece of meat dropped on a butcher's slab. The rat scurried away. Around it, other grey objects burst into activity. The whole area was alive with rodents, disturbed from their nests by the actions of the dredging crew. They bumped and snapped at each other, their tails leaving snaking lines in the mud. The rest of the crew now joined in, casting stones in a skimming motion close to the ground. Most of them had better aim than their friend.

Dupree lit a cigarette with a gold Ronson lighter. He smoked Gitanes, the only cop I had ever seen do so. The smoke was acrid and strong and the breeze blew it directly into my face. Dupree apologised and turned so that his body partially shielded me from the smoke. It was a peculiarly sensitive gesture and it made me wonder, once again, why I was not sitting at Moisant Field.

'They tell me you tracked down that child-killer in New York, the Modine woman,' said Dupree eventually. 'After thirty years, that's no mean feat.'

'She made a mistake,' I said. 'In the end, they all do. It's just a matter of being in the right place at the right time to take advantage of the situation.'

He tilted his head slightly to one side, as if he didn't entirely agree with what I had said but was prepared to give it a little thought in case he'd missed something. He took another long drag on his cigarette. It was an upmarket brand, but he smoked it the way I had seen longshoremen on the New York docks smoke, the butt held between the thumb and the first two fingers of the hand, the ember shielded by the palm. It was the sort of hold you learned as a kid, when smoking was still a furtive pleasure and being caught with a cigarette was enough to earn you a smack across the back of the head from your old man.

'I guess we all get lucky sometimes,' said Dupree. He looked at me closely. 'I'm wondering if maybe we've got lucky here.'

I waited for him to continue. There seemed to be something fortuitous in the discovery of the girl's body, or perhaps I was still remembering a dream in which shapes came out of my bedroom wall and told me that a thread in the tapestry being woven by the Travelling Man had suddenly come loose.

'When Morphy and his wife died, my first instinct was to take you outside and beat you to within an inch of your life,' he said. 'He was a good man, a good detective, despite everything. He was also my friend.

'But he trusted you, and Touissant here seems to trust you too. He thinks maybe you provide a linking factor in all this. If that's true, then putting you on a plane back to New York isn't going to achieve anything. Your FBI friend Woolrich seemed to feel the same way, but there were louder voices than his shouting for you to be sent home.'

He took another drag on his cigarette. 'I reckon you're like gum caught in someone's hair,' he continued. 'The more they try to prise you out, the more you get stuck in, and maybe we can use that. I'm risking a storm of shit by keeping you here, but Morphy told me what you felt about this guy, how you believed he was observing us, manipulating us. You want to tell me what you make of this, or do you want to spend the night at Moisant sleeping on a chair?'

I looked at the bare feet and exposed legs of the girl in the drum, the strange yellow accretion like a chrysalis, lying in a pool of filth and water on a rat-infested stretch of a river in western Louisiana. The ME and his men had arrived with a body bag and a stretcher. They positioned a length of plastic on the ground and carefully manoeuvred the drum on to it, one of them supporting the girl's legs with a gloved hand. Then slowly, gently, the ME's hands working inside the drum, they began to free her.

'Everything we've done so far has been dogged and predicted by this man,' I began. 'The Aguillards learned something, and they died. Remarr saw something, and he was killed. Morphy tried to help me, and now he's dead as well. He's closing off the options, forcing us to follow a pattern that he's already set. Now someone's been leaking details of the investigation to the press. Maybe that person has been leaking things to this man as well, possibly unintentionally, possibly not.'

Dupree and Touissant exchanged a look. 'We'd been considering that possibility as well,' said Dupree. 'There are too many damn people crawling over this for anything to stay quiet for long.'

'On top of all that,' I continued, 'the feds are keeping something back. You think Woolrich has told you everything he knows?'

Dupree almost laughed. 'I know as much about this guy Byron as I know about the poet, and that's sweet FA.'

From inside the drum came a scraping sound, the sound of bone rubbing on metal. Gloved hands supported the girl's naked, discoloured body as it was freed from the confines of the drum.

'How long can we keep the details quiet?' I asked Dupree.

'Not long. The feds will have to be informed, the press will find out . . .' He spread his hands in a gesture of helplessness. 'If you're suggesting that I don't tell the feds . . .' But I could see in his face that he was already moving in that direction, that the reason why the ME was examining the body so soon after its discovery, the reason why there were so few police at the scene, was to keep the details limited to the minimum number of people.

I decided to push him. 'I'm suggesting you don't tell *anyone* about this. If you do, the man who did this will be alerted and he'll cut us off again. If you're put in a position where you have to say something, then fudge it. Don't mention the barrel, obscure the location, say you don't believe the discovery is connected to any other investigation. Say nothing until the girl is identified.'

'Assuming that we can identify her,' said Touissant mournfully.

'Hey, you want to rain someplace else?' snapped Dupree.

'Sorry,' said Touissant.

'He's right,' I said. 'We may not be able to identify her, That's a chance we'll have to take.'

'Once we exhaust our own records, we'll have to use the feds',' said Dupree.

'We'll burn that bridge when we come to it,' I responded. 'Can we do this?'

Dupree shuffled his feet and finished his cigarette. He leaned through the open window of his car and put the butt into the ashtray.

'Twenty-four hours max,' he said. 'After that, we'll be accused of incompetence or deliberately impeding the progress of an investigation. I'm not even sure how far we'll get in that time, although . . .' He looked at Touissant, then back to me. '. . . it may not come to that.'

'You want to tell me,' I said, 'or do I have to guess?'

It was Touissant who answered.

'The feds think they've found Byron. They're going to move on him by morning.'

'In which case, this is just a back-up,' said Dupree. 'The joker in our pack.'

But I was no longer listening. They were moving on Byron,

479

but I would not be there. If I tried to participate, then a sizeable portion of the Louisiana law-enforcement community would be used to put me on a plane to New York or to lock me in a cell.

The crew were likely to be the weakest link. They were taken aside and given cups of coffee, then Dupree and I were as honest with them as we felt we could be. We told them that if they didn't keep quiet about what they had seen for at least one day, then the man who had killed the girl would probably get away and that he would kill again. It was at least partly true; cut off from the hunt for Byron, we were continuing the investigation as best we could.

The crew was made up of hard-working local men, most of them married with children of their own. They agreed to say nothing until we contacted them and told them that it was okay to do so. They meant what they said, but I knew that some of them would tell their wives and their girlfriends as soon as they got home and word of what had happened would spread from there. A man who says he tells his wife everything is either a liar or a fool, my first sergeant used to say. Unfortunately, he was divorced.

Dupree had been in his office when the call came through and had picked pairs of deputies and detectives whom he trusted implicitly. With the addition of Touissant, Rachel and me, along with the ME's team and the dredging crew, maybe twenty people knew of the discovery of the body. It was nineteen people too many to keep a secret for long, but that couldn't be helped.

After the initial examination and photography, it was decided to bring the body to a private clinic outside Lafayette, where the ME sometimes consulted, and he agreed to commence his work almost immediately. Dupree prepared a statement detailing the discovery of a woman of unspecified age, cause of death unknown, some five miles from the actual location of the discovery. He dated it, timed it, then left it under a sheaf of files on his desk.

By the time we both arrived at the autopsy room, the remains had been X-rayed and measured. The gurney that had brought the body in had been pushed into a corner, away from the autopsy table on its cylindrical tank, which delivered water to the table and collected the fluids that drained through the holes on the table itself. A scale for the weighing of organs hung from a metal frame and, beside it, a small-parts dissection table on its own base stood ready for use.

Only three people, apart from the ME and his assistant, attended the autopsy. Dupree and Touissant were two. I was the third. The smell was strong and only partly masked by the antiseptic. Dark hair hung from her skull and the skin that was left was shrunken and torn. The girl's remains were almost completely covered by the yellow-white substance.

It was Dupree who asked the question. 'Doc, what is that stuff on the body?'

The examiner's name was Dr Emile Huckstetter, a tall, stocky man in his early fifties with a ruddy complexion. He ran a gloved finger over the substance before he responded.

'It's a condition called adipocere,' he said. 'It's rare – I've seen maybe two or three cases at most, but the combination of silt and water in that canal seems to have resulted in its development here.'

His eyes narrowed as he leaned towards the body. 'Her body fats broke down in the water and they've hardened to create this substance, the adipocere. She's been in the water for a while. This stuff takes at least six months to form on the trunk, less on the face. I'm taking a stab here, but I figure she's been in the water for less than seven months, certainly no more than that.'

Huckstetter detailed the examination into a small microphone attached to his green surgical scrubs. The girl was seventeen or eighteen, he said. She had not been tied or bound. There was evidence of a blade's slash at her neck, indicating a deep cut across her carotid artery as the probable cause of death. There were marks on her skull where her face had been removed and similar marks in her eye sockets.

As the examination drew to a close, Dupree was paged and, minutes later, he arrived back with Rachel. She had checked into a Lafayette motel, storing both her own baggage and mine, then returned. She recoiled initially at the sight of the body, then stood beside me and, without speaking, took my hand.

When the ME was done, he removed his gloves and commenced scrubbing. Dupree took the X-rays from the case envelope and held them up to the light, each in turn. 'What's this?' he said, after a time.

Huckstetter took the X-ray from his hand and examined it himself. 'Compound fracture, right tibia,' he said, pointing with his finger. 'Probably two years old. It's in the report, or it will be as soon as I can compile it.'

I felt a falling sensation and an ache spreading across my stomach. I reached out to steady myself and the scales jangled as I glanced against their frame. Then my hand was on the autopsy table and my fingers were touching the girl's remains. I pulled my hand back quickly.

'Parker?' said Dupree. He reached out and gripped my arm to steady me. I could still feel the girl on my fingers.

'My God,' I said. 'I think I know who she is.'

In the early-morning light, near the northern tip of Bayou Courtableau, south of Krotz Springs and maybe twenty miles from Lafayette, a team of Federal agents, backed up by St Landry Parish sheriff's deputies, closed in on a shotgun house, which stood with its back to the bayou, its front sheltered by overgrown bushes and trees. Some of the agents wore dark raingear with FBI in large yellow letters on the back, others helmets and body armour. They advanced slowly and quietly, their safeties off. When they spoke, they did so quickly and with the fewest possible words. Radio contact was kept to a minimum. They knew what they were doing. Around them, deputies armed with pistols and shotguns listened to the sound of their breathing and the pumping of their hearts as they prepared to move on the house of Edward Byron, the man they believed to be directly responsible for the deaths of their colleague, John Charles Morphy, his young wife and at least five other people.

The house was run-down, the slates on the roof damaged and cracked in places, the roof beams already rotting. Two of the windows at the front of the house were broken and had been covered with cardboard held in place by duct tape. The wood on the gallery was warped and, in places, missing altogether. On a metal hook to the right of the house hung the carcass of a wild pig, newly skinned. Blood dripped from its snout and pooled on the ground below.

On a signal from Woolrich, shortly after 6.00 a.m., agents in Kevlar body armour approached the house from the front and the rear. They checked the windows at either side of the front door and adjoining the rear entrance. Then, simultaneously, they hit the doors, moving into the central hallway with maximum noise, their flashlights burning through the darkness of the interior.

The two teams had almost reached each other when a shotgun roared from the back of the house and blood erupted in the dim light. An agent named Thomas Seltz plunged forward as the shot ripped through the unprotected area of his armpit, the vulnerable point in upper-body armour, his finger tightening in a last reflex on the trigger of his machine pistol as he died. Bullets raked across the wall, ceiling and floor as he fell, sending dust and splinters through the air and injuring two agents, one in the leg and one in the mouth.

The firing masked the sound of another shell being pumped into the shotgun. The second shot blasted wood from the frame of an interior door as agents hit the ground and began firing through the now empty rear door. A third shot took out an agent moving fast around the side of the house. A mass of logs and old furniture, destined for firewood, lay scattered on the ground, dispersed when the shooter broke from his hiding place beneath it. The sound of small-arms fire directed into the bayou reached the agents as they knelt to tend to their injured colleagues or ran to join the chase.

A figure in worn blue jeans and a white and red check shirt had disappeared into the bayou. The agents followed warily, their legs sinking almost to the knee at times in the muddy swamp water, dead tree trunks forcing them to deviate from a straight advance, before they reached firm ground. Using the trees as cover, they moved slowly, their guns at their shoulders, sighting as they went.

There was the roar of a shotgun from ahead. Birds scattered from the trees and splinters shot out at head height from a huge cypress. An agent screamed in pain and stumbled into view, impaled in the cheek by the shards of wood. A second blast rang out and shattered the femur in his left leg. He collapsed on to the dirt and leaves, his back arched in agony.

Automatic fire raked the trees, shattering branches and blasting foliage. After four or five seconds of concentrated firing, the order went out to cease fire and the swamp was quiet once again. The agents and police advanced once more, moving quickly from tree to tree. A shout went up as blood was found by a willow, its broken branches white as bone.

From behind came the sounds of dogs barking as the tracker, who had been kept in reserve three miles away, was brought in to assist. The dogs were allowed to sniff around Byron's clothing and the area of the woodpile. Their handler, a thin, bearded man with his jeans tucked into muddy boots, let them sniff at the blood by the willow as soon as he caught up with the main party. Then, the dogs straining at their leashes, they moved on cautiously.

But no more shots came at them from Edward Byron, because the lawmen were not the only ones hunting him in the swamp.

While the hunt continued for Byron, Touissant, two young deputies and I were in the sheriff's office at St Martinville, where we continued our trawl through Miami's dentists, using emergency numbers from answering-machines where necessary.

Rachel provided the only interruption, when she arrived with coffee and hot Danishes. She stood behind me and gently laid a hand on the back of my neck. I reached around and clasped her fingers, then pulled them forward and lightly kissed their tips.

'I didn't expect you to stay,' I said. I couldn't see her face.

'It's almost at an end, isn't it?' she asked quietly.

'I think so. I feel it coming.'

'Then I want to see it out. I want to be there at the end.'

She stayed for a little longer, until her exhaustion became almost contagious. Then she returned to the motel to sleep.

It took thirty-eight calls before the dental assistant at Erwin Holdman's dental surgery at Brickell Avenue found the name of Lisa Stott on her records, but she declined even to confirm if Lisa Stott had attended during the last six months. Holdman was on the golf course and didn't like being disturbed, the assistant said. Touissant told her that he didn't give a good goddamn what Holdman liked or didn't like and she gave him a cellphone number.

She was right. Holdman didn't like being disturbed on the

golf course, especially when he was about to make a birdie on the fifteenth. After some shouting, Touissant requested Lisa Stott's dental records. The dentist wanted to seek the permission of her mother and stepfather. Touissant handed the phone to Dupree, and Dupree told him that, for the present, that wasn't possible, that they only wanted the records in order to eliminate the girl from their inquiries and it would be unwise to disturb the parents unnecessarily. When Holdman continued to refuse to cooperate, Dupree warned him that he would ensure that all his records were seized and his tax affairs subjected to microscopic examination.

Holdman co-operated. The records were kept on computer, he said, along with copies of X-rays and dental charts that had been scanned in. He would send them on as soon as he returned to his office. His dental assistant was new, he explained and wouldn't be able to send on the records electronically without his password. He would just finish his round . . .

There was some more shouting and Holdman decided to suspend his golfing activities for that day. It would take him one hour, traffic permitting, to get back to his office. We sat back to wait.

Byron had made it about a mile into the swamp. The cops were closing and his arm was bleeding badly. The bullet had shattered the elbow of his left arm and a steady current of pain was coursing through his body. He paused in a small clearing and reloaded the shotgun by tensing the stock against the ground and pumping awkwardly with his good hand. The barking was closer now. He would take the dogs as soon as they came in sight. Once they were gone, he would lose the lawmen in the swamp.

It was probably only when he rose that he first became aware of the movement in front of him. The pack couldn't have got around him already, he reasoned. The waters were deeper to the west. Without boats, they would not have been able to make it into the swamp from the road. Even if they had, he would have heard them coming. His senses had become attuned to the sounds of the swamp. Only the hallucinations threatened to undo him, but they came and went.

Byron crooked the shotgun awkwardly beneath his right arm and moved forward, his eyes moving constantly. He advanced slowly toward the tree line, but the movement seemed to have stopped. Maybe he shook his head then to clear his sight, fearing the onset of the visions, but they didn't come. Instead, death came for Edward Byron as the woods came alive around him and he was surrounded by dark figures. He loosed off one shot before the gun was wrenched from his grip and he felt a pain shoot across his chest as the blade opened his skin from shoulder to shoulder.

The figures surrounded him – hard-faced men, one with an M16 slung over his shoulder, the others armed with knives and axes, all led by a huge man with reddish-brown skin and dark hair streaked with grey. Byron fell to his knees as blows rained down on his back and arms and shoulders. Dazed with pain and exhaustion, he looked up in time to see the big man's axe scything through the air above him.

Then all was darkness.


We were using Dupree's office, where a new PC sat ready to receive the dental records Holdman was sending. I sat in a red vinyl chair, which had been repaired so often with tape that it was like sitting on cracking ice. The chair squeaked as I shifted in it, my feet on the window-sill. Across from me was the couch on which I had earlier caught three hours of uncomfortable sleep.

Touissant had gone off to get coffee thirty minutes before. He still hadn't come back. I was starting to get restless when I heard the sound of voices raised from the squad-room beyond. I passed through the open door of Dupree's office and into the squad-room, with its rows of grey metal desks, its swivel chairs and hatstands, its bulletin boards and coffee cups, its half-eaten bagels and donuts.

Touissant appeared, talking excitedly to a black detective in a petrol-blue suit and open-collar shirt. Behind him, Dupree was talking to a uniformed deputy. Touissant saw me, patted the black detective on the shoulder, and walked toward me.

'Byron's dead,' he said. 'It was messy. The feds lost two men, couple more injured. Byron broke for the swamp. When they found him, someone had cut him up and split his skull with an axe. They've got the axe and a lot of boot prints.' He fingered his chin. 'They think maybe Lionel Fontenot decided to finish things his way.'

Dupree ushered us into his office, but didn't close the door. He stood close to me and touched my arm gently.

'It's him. Things are still confused, but they've got sample jars matching the one in which your daughter's . . .' He paused, then rephrased it. '. . . the jar which you received. They've got a laptop computer, the remains of some kind of home-made speaker attachment and scalpels with tissue remains, most of it found in a shed at the back of the property. I talked to Woolrich, briefly. He mentioned something about old medical texts. Said to tell you that you were right. They're still searching for the faces of the victims, but that could take some time. They're going to start digging around the house later today.'

I wasn't sure what I felt. There was relief, a sense of a weight being lifted and taken away, a sense that it had all come to a close. But there was also something more: I felt disappointment that I had not been there at the end. After all that I had done, after all the people who had died, both at my hands and the hands of others, the Travelling Man had evaded me right until the end.

Dupree left and I sat down heavily in the chair, the sunlight filtering through the shades on the window. Touissant sat on the edge of Dupree's desk and watched me. I thought of Susan and Jennifer and of days spent in the park together. And I remembered the voice of Tante Marie Aguillard, and I hoped that she was now at peace.

A low, two-note signal beeped from Dupree's PC at regular intervals. Touissant hauled himself from the desk and walked around to where he could see the screen of the PC. He tapped some keys and read what was on-screen.

'It's Holdman's stuff coming through,' he said.

I joined him at the screen and watched as Lisa Stott's dental records appeared, detailed in words, then as a kind of two-dimensional map of her mouth with fillings and extractions marked, and then in the form of a mouth X-ray.

Touissant called up the ME's X-ray from a separate file and set the two images side-by-side.

'They look the same,' he said.

I nodded. I didn't want to think of the implications if they were.

Touissant called up Huckstetter, told him what we had and asked him to come over. Thirty minutes later, Dr Emile Huckstetter was running through Holdman's file, comparing it with his own notes and the X-ray images he had taken from the dead girl. At last, he pushed his glasses up on his forehead and pinched the corners of his eyes.

'It's her,' he said.

Touissant let out a long, jagged breath and shook his head in sorrow. It was the Travelling Man's last jest, it seemed, the old jest. The dead girl was Lisa Stott or, as she once was known, Lisa Woolrich, a young girl who had become an emotional casualty of her parents' bitter divorce, who had been abandoned by a mother anxious to start a new life without the complication of an angry, hurt teenage daughter, and whose father was unable to provide her with the stability and support she needed.

She was Woolrich's daughter.

# Chapter Forty-Nine

The voice on the telephone was heavy with tiredness and tension. I spoke as I drove; a St Martin's deputy had retrieved the rental car from the Flaisance.

'Woolrich, it's Bird.'

'Hey.' There was no life to the word. 'What have you heard?'

'That Byron's dead, some of your men too. I'm sorry.'

'Yeah, it was a mess. They call you in New York?'

'No.' I debated whether or not to tell him the truth and decided not to. 'I missed the flight. I'm heading towards Lafayette.'

'*Lafayette*? Shit, what you doin' in Lafayette?'

'Hanging around.' With Touissant and Dupree, it had been agreed that I should talk to Woolrich, that I should be the one to tell him that his daughter had been found. 'Can you meet me?'

'Shit, Bird, I'm on my last legs here.' Then, resignedly: 'Sure, I'll meet you. We can talk about what happened today. Give me an hour. I'll meet you in the Jazzy Cajun, off the highway. Anyone will tell you where it is.' I could hear him coughing at the other end of the phone.

'Your lady friend go home?'

'No, she's still here.'

'That's good,' he said. 'It's good to have someone with you at times like this.' Then he hung up.

★    ★    ★

The Jazzy Cajun was a small dark bar annexed to a motel, with pool tables and a country-music juke-box. Behind the bar, a woman restocked the beer cabinet while Willie Nelson played over the speakers.

Woolrich arrived shortly after I began drinking my second coffee. He was carrying a canary-yellow jacket and the armpits of his shirt were stained with sweat. The shirt itself was marked with dirt on the back and sleeves and one elbow was torn. His tan trousers were heavy with mud at the cuffs and hung over mud-encrusted, ankle-high boots. He ordered a bourbon and a coffee, then took a seat beside me near the door. We didn't say anything for a time, until Woolrich drained half of his bourbon and began sipping at his coffee.

'Listen, Bird,' he began. 'I'm sorry for what went down between us this last week or so. We were both trying to bring this to an end our own way. Now that it's done, well . . .' He shrugged and tipped his glass at me before draining it and signalling for another. There were black stains beneath his eyes and I could see the beginnings of a painful boil at the base of his neck. His lips were dry and cracked and he winced as the bourbon hit the inside of his mouth. He noticed my look. 'Canker sores,' he explained. 'They're a bitch.' He took another sip of coffee. 'I guess you want to hear what happened.'

I wanted to put off the moment, but not like that.

'What are you going to do now?' I asked.

'Sleep,' he said. 'Then maybe take some time off, go down to Mexico and see if I can't rescue Lisa from these goddamn religious freaks.'

I felt a pain in my heart and stood suddenly. I wanted a drink as badly as I had ever wanted anything before in my life. Woolrich didn't seem to notice my lack of composure, or even register that I was walking towards the mensroom. I could feel sweat on my forehead and my skin felt hypersensitive, as if I was about to come down with a fever.

'She's been asking after you, Birdman,' I heard him say, and I stopped dead.

'What did you say?' I didn't turn around.

'She asks after you,' he repeated.

I turned then. 'When did you hear from her last?'

He waved the glass. 'Couple of months back, I suppose. Two or three.'

'You sure?'

He stopped and stared at me. I hung by a thread over a dark place and watched as something small and bright separated from the whole and disappeared into the blackness, never to be found again. The surroundings of the bar fell away and there was only Woolrich and me, alone, with nothing to distract one from the other's words. There was no ground beneath my feet, no air above me. I heard a howling in my head as images and memories coursed through my mind.

Woolrich standing on a porch, his finger on the cheek of Florence Aguillard, a gentle, trusting girl with a scarred face. In her final moments, I think she knew what he had done, what he had led her to do.

'*I call this my metaphysical tie, my George Herbert tie.*'

A couplet from Ralegh, from the 'Passionate Man's Pilgrim-age', the poem from which Woolrich so loved to quote:

'*Blood must be my bodies balmer/No other balme will there be given*'

The second phone call I had received in the Flaisance, the one during which the Travelling Man had allowed no questions, the one during which Woolrich was in attendance.

'*They have no vision. They have no larger view of what they're doing. There's no purpose to it.*'

Woolrich and his men seizing Rachel's notes.

'*I'm torn between keeping you in touch and telling you nothing.*'

Cops throwing a bag of donuts he had touched into a trash can.

'*Are you fucking her, Bird?*'

You can't bluff someone who isn't paying attention.

And a figure in a New York bar, fingering a Penguin volume of metaphysical verse and quoting lines from Donne.

*Rack't carcasses make ill Anatomies.*

A metaphysical sensibility: that was what the Travelling Man had, what Rachel had tried to pinpoint only days before, what united the poets whose works had lined the shelves of Woolrich's East Village apartment on the night he took me back there to sleep, on the night after he killed my wife and child.

'Bird, you okay?' His pupils were tiny, like little black holes sucking the light from the room.

I turned away. 'Yeah, just a moment of weakness, that's all. I'll be back.'

'Where are you going, Birdman?' There was doubt in his voice, and something else, a note of warning, of violence, and I wondered if my wife had heard it as she tried to escape, as he came after her down the hall of our home, as he broke her nose against the wall.

'I have to go to the john,' I said.

Bile was rising in my throat, threatening to make me gag and vomit on the floor. A fierce, burning pain dug at my stomach and clawed at my heart. It was as if a veil had been pulled aside at the moment of my death, revealing only a cold, black emptiness beyond. I wanted to turn away. I wanted to turn away from it all and, when I returned, everything would be normal again. I would have a wife and a daughter who looked like her mother. I would have a small, peaceful home and a patch of lawn to tend and someone who would stand by me, even to the end.

The toilet was dark and smelt of stale urine from the unflushed bowl but the tap worked. I splashed cold water on my face then reached into my jacket pocket for my phone.

It wasn't there. I had left it on the table with Woolrich. I wrenched the door open and moved around the bar, my right hand drawing my gun, but Woolrich was gone.

I called Touissant but he had already left. Dupree had gone home. I convinced the switchboard operator to ring Dupree's home number and to ask him to call me back. Five minutes later he did. His voice was bleary.

'This had better be good,' he said.

'Byron isn't the killer,' I said.

'What?' He was wide awake now.

'He didn't kill them,' I repeated. I was outside the bar, gun in hand, but there was no sign of Woolrich. I stopped two black women passing with a child between them, but they backed off as soon as they saw the gun. 'Byron wasn't the Travelling Man. Woolrich was. He's running. I caught him out with a lie about his daughter. He said he had spoken to her two or three months back. You and I both know that's not possible.'

'You could have made a mistake.'

'Dupree, listen to me. Woolrich set Byron up. He killed my wife and daughter. He killed Morphy and his wife, Tante Marie, Tee Jean, Lutice Fontenot, Tony Remarr and he killed his own daughter too. He's running, do you hear me? He's running.'

'I hear you,' said Dupree. His voice was dry with the realisation of how wrong we had been.

One hour later, they hit Woolrich's apartment in Algiers, on the south bank of the Mississippi. It lay on the upper floor of a restored house on Opelousas Avenue above an old grocery store, approached by a flight of cast-iron stairs girded with gardenias that led on to a gallery. Woolrich's apartment was the only one in the building, with two arched windows and a solid oak door. The New Orleans police were backed up by six

FBI men. The cops led, the feds taking up positions at either side of the door. There was no movement visible in the apartment through the windows. They had not expected any.

Two cops swung an iron battering ram with 'Hi, y'all' painted in white on its flat head. It took one swing to knock the door open. The FBI men poured into the house, the police securing the street and the surrounding yards. They checked the tiny kitchen, the unmade bed, the lounge with the new television, the empty pizza cartons and beer cans, the Penguin poetry editions which sat in a milk crate, the picture of Woolrich and his daughter smiling from on top of a nest of tables.

In the bedroom was a closet, open and containing an array of wrinkled clothes and two pairs of tan shoes, and a metal cabinet sealed with a large steel lock.

'Break it,' instructed the agent in charge of the operation, Assistant SAC Cameron Tate. O'Neill Brouchard, the young FBI man who had driven me to Tante Marie's house centuries before, struck at the lock with the butt of his machine pistol. It broke on the third attempt and he pulled the doors open.

The explosion blew O'Neill Brouchard backwards through the window, almost tearing his head off in the process, and sent a hailstorm of glass shards into the narrow confines of the bedroom. Tate was blinded instantly, glass embedding itself in his face, neck and his Kevlar vest. Two other FBI men sustained serious injuries to the face and hands as part of Woolrich's store of empty glass jars, his laptop computer, a modified H3000 voice synthesiser and a flesh-coloured mask, designed to obscure his mouth and nose, were blown to pieces. And amid the flames and the smoke and the shards of glass, burning pages fluttered to the ground like black moths, a mass of Biblical apocrypha disintegrating into ash.

★ ★ ★

As O'Neill Brouchard was dying, I sat in the detective squad-room in St Martinville as men were pulled in from holidays and days off to assist in the search. Woolrich had switched off his cellphone but the phone company had been alerted. If he used it, they would try to pinpoint a location.

Someone handed me a cup of coffee in an alligator cup and, while I drank it, I tried Rachel's room at the motel again. On the tenth ring the desk clerk interrupted. 'Are you . . . Do they call you the Birdman?' he said. He sounded young and un-certain.

'Yes, some people do.'

'I'm sorry, sir. Did you call before?'

I told him that this was my third call. I was aware of an edge in my voice.

'I was buying lunch. I have a message for you, from the FBI.'

He said the three letters with a sort of wonder in his voice. Nausea bubbled in my throat.

'It's from Agent Woolrich, Mr Birdman. He said to tell you that he and Ms Wolfe were taking a trip, and that you'd know where to find them. He said he wanted you to keep it to just the three of you. He doesn't want anyone else to spoil the occasion. He told me to tell you that specifically, sir.'

I closed my eyes and his voice grew further away.

'That's the message, sir. Did I do okay?'


Touissant, Dupree and I laid the map across Dupree's desk. Dupree took out a red felt-tip and drew a circle around the Crowley-Ramah area, with the two towns acting as the diameters of the circle and Lafayette as its centre.

'I figure he's got a place in there somewhere,' said Dupree. 'If you're right and he needed to be close to Byron, if not to the Aguillards as well, then we're looking at an area as far as Krotz Springs to the north and, damn, maybe as far as Bayou Sorrel to the south. If he took your friend, that probably delayed him a little: he needed time to check motel reservations – not much, but enough if he was unlucky with the places he called – and he needed time to get her out. He won't want to stay on the roads, so he'll hole up, maybe in a motel or, if it's close enough, his own place.'

He tapped the pen in the centre of the circle. 'We've alerted the locals and the state police. That leaves us – and you.'

I had been thinking of what Woolrich had said, that I would know where to find them, but so far nothing had come to me. 'I can't pin anything down. The obvious ones, like the Aguillard house and his own place in Algiers, are already being checked, but I don't think he's going to be at either of those places.'

I put my head in my hands. My fears for Rachel were obscuring my reasoning. I needed to pull back. I took my jacket and walked to the door, almost bumping into a deputy in the process. He handed me two sheets of paper.

It was a fax message from Agent Ross in New York, a copy of a series of surveillance details on Stephen Barton and, briefly, his stepmother. Most of the names appeared repeatedly over a period of weeks. One, ringed in felt-tip, appeared just twice: Woolrich. At the bottom of the page, Ross had written just two words: 'I'm sorry.'

*they can sniff each other out*

'I need space to think,' I said. 'I'll stay in touch.'

Dupree seemed about to object, but he said nothing. Outside, my car was parked in a police space. I sat in it, rolled down the windows and took my Louisiana map from the glove compartment. I ran my fingers over the names: Arnaudville, Grand Coteau, Carencro, Broussard, Milton, Catahoula, Coteau Holmes, St Martinville itself. I started to drive out of town.

The last name seemed familiar from somewhere, but by that point all the towns seemed to resonate with some form of

meaning, which left them all meaningless. It was like repeating
your name over and over and over again in your head, until the
name itself lost its familiarity and you began to doubt your
own identity.

Still, St Martinville came back to me again. Something
about New Iberia and a hospital. A nurse. Nurse Judy Neubolt.
Judy the Nut. As I drove the car, I recalled the conversation
that I had had with Woolrich when I arrived in New Orleans
for the first time after the deaths of Susan and Jennifer. Judy the
Nut. '*She said I murdered her in a past life.*' Was the story true, or
did it mean something else? Had Woolrich been toying with
me, even then?

The more I thought about it, the more certain I became. He
told me that Judy Neubolt had moved to La Jolla on a one-year
contract after their relationship broke up. I doubted that Judy
had ever got as far as La Jolla.

Judy Neubolt wasn't in the current directory. I found her in
an old directory in a gas station – her phone had since been
disconnected – and I figured I could get directions in St
Martinville. Then I called Huckstetter at home, gave him
Judy's address and asked him to call Dupree in an hour if he
hadn't heard from me. He agreed, reluctantly.

As I drove, I thought of David Fontenot and the call from
Woolrich that had almost certainly brought him to Honey
Island, a promise of an end to the search for his sister. He
couldn't have known how close he was to her resting place
when he died.

I thought of the deaths I had brought on Morphy and Angie;
the echo of Tante Marie's voice in my head as he came for
her; and Remarr, gilded in fading sunlight. I think I realised,
too, why the details had appeared in the newspaper: it was
Woolrich's way of bringing his work to a larger audience, a
modern-day equivalent of the public anatomisation.

And I thought of Lisa: a small, heavy, dark-eyed girl, who

had reacted badly to her parents' separation, who had sought refuge in a strange Christianity in Mexico and who had returned at last to her father. What had she seen to force him to kill her? Her father washing blood from his hands in a sink? The remains of Lutice Fontenot or some other unfortunate floating in a jar?

Or had he simply killed her because he could, because the pleasure he took in disposing of her, in mutilating his own flesh and blood, was as close as he could come to turning the knife on his own body, to enduring his own anatomisation and finding at last the deep, red darkness within himself?

# Chapter Fifty

Neat lawns mixed with thick growths of cypress as I drove along the blacktop of 96 back to St Martinville, past a 'God is Pro-Life' sign and the warehouse-like structure of Podnuh's nightclub. At Thibodeaux's Café, on the neat town square, I asked for directions to Judy Neubolt's address. They knew the place, even knew that the nurse had moved to La Jolla for a year, maybe longer, and that her boyfriend was maintaining the house.

Perkins Street started almost opposite the entrance to Evangeline State Park. At the end of the street was a T-junction, which disappeared on the right into a rural setting, with houses scattered at distant intervals. Judy Neubolt's house was on this stretch, a small, two-storey dwelling, strangely low despite the two floors, with two windows on either side of a screen door and three smaller windows on the upper level. At the eastern side, the roof sloped down, reducing it to a single storey. The wood of the house had been newly painted a pristine white and damaged slates on the roof had been replaced, but the yard was overgrown with weeds and the woods beyond had begun to make inroads on the boundaries of the property.

I parked some way from the house and approached it through the woods, stopping at their verge. The sun was already falling from its apex and it cast a red glow across the roof and walls. The rear door was bolted and locked. There seemed to be no option but to enter from the front.

As I moved forward, my senses jangled with a tension I had not felt before. Sounds, smells and colours were too sharp, too overpowering. I felt as if I could pick out the component parts of every noise which came to me from the surrounding trees. My gun moved jerkily, my hand responding too rapidly to the signals from my brain. I was conscious of the firmness of the trigger against the ball of my finger and every crevasse and rise of the grip against the palm of my hand. The sound of the blood pumping in my ears was like an immense hand banging on a heavy oak door, my feet on the leaves and twigs like the crackling of some huge fire.

The drapes were pulled on the windows, top and bottom, and across the inner door. Through a gap in the drapes on the door I could see black material, hung to prevent anyone from peering through the cracks. The screen door opened with a squeak of rusty hinges as I eased it ajar with my right foot, my body shielded by the wall of the house. I could see a thick spider's web at the upper part of the door frame, the brown, drained husks of trapped insects shivering in the vibrations from the opening door.

I reached in and turned the handle on the main door. It opened easily. I let it swing to its fullest extent, revealing the dimly lit interior of the house. I could see the edge of a sofa, one half of a window at the other side of the house and, to my right, the beginning of a hallway. I took a deep breath, which echoed in my head like the low, pained gasp of a sick animal, then moved quickly to my right, the screen door closing behind me.

I now had a full, uninterrupted view of the main room of the house. The exterior had been deceptive. Judy Neubolt, or whoever had decided on the design of the house's interior, had removed one floor entirely so that the room reached right to the roof, where two skylights, now encrusted with filth and partly obscured by black drapes stretched beneath them, allowed thin shafts of sunlight to penetrate to the bare boards below. The only real illumination came from a pair of dim floor lamps, one at each end of the room.

The room was furnished with a long sofa, decorated with a red and orange zigzag pattern, which stood facing the front of the house. At either side of it were matching chairs, with a low coffee table in the centre and a TV cabinet beneath one of the windows facing the seating area. Behind the sofa was a dining table and six chairs, with a fireplace to their rear. The walls were decorated with samples of Indian art and one or two vaguely mystical paintings of women with flowing white dresses standing on a mountain or beside the sea. It was hard to make out details in the dim light.

At the eastern end was a raised wooden gallery, reached by a flight of steps to my left, which led up to a sleeping area with a pine bed and a matching closet.

Rachel hung upside down from the gallery, a rope attached from her ankles to the rail above. She was naked and her hair stretched to within two feet of the floor. Her arms were free and her hands hung beyond the ends of her hair. Her eyes and mouth were wide open, but she gave no indication that she saw me. A small, clear Band Aid was attached to her left arm. A needle emerged from beneath it, attached to the plastic tube of a drip. The drip bag hung from a metal frame, allowing the ketamine to seep slowly and continuously into her system. On the floor beneath her was stretched an expanse of clear plastic sheeting.

Beneath the gallery was a dark kitchen area, with pine cupboards, a tall refrigerator and a microwave oven beside the sink. Three stools stood empty by a breakfast nook. To my right, on the wall facing the gallery, hung an embroidered tapestry with a pattern similar to the sofa and chairs. A thin patina of dust lay over everything.

I checked the hallway behind me. It led into a second bedroom, this one empty but for a bare mattress on which lay a military-green sleeping bag. A green kit-bag lay open beside the bed and I could see some jeans, a pair of cream trousers and some men's shirts inside. The room, with its low, sloping roof, took up about half the width of the house, which meant that there was a room of similar size on the other side of the wall.

I moved back towards the main room, all the time keeping Rachel in sight. There was no sign of Woolrich, although he could have been standing hidden in the hallway at the other side of the house. Rachel could give me no indication of where he might be. I began moving slowly along the tapestried wall towards the far wall of the house.

I was about half-way across when a movement behind Rachel caught my eye and I spun, my gun raised to shoulder level as I instinctively assumed a marksman's stance.

'Put it down, Birdman, or she dies now.' He had been waiting in the darkness behind her, shielded by her body. He stood close to her now, most of his body still hidden by her own. I could see the edge of his tan pants, the sleeve of his white shirt and a sliver of his head, nothing more. If I tried to shoot, I would almost certainly hit Rachel.

'I have a gun pointing at the small of her back, Bird. I don't want to ruin such a beautiful body with a bullet hole, so *put the gun down.*'

I bent down and placed the gun gently on the ground.

'Now kick it away from you.'

I kicked it with the side of my foot and watched it slide across the floor and spin to rest by the foot of the nearest chair.

He emerged from the shadows then, but he was no longer the man that I had known. It was as if, with the revelation of his true nature, a metamorphosis had occurred. His face was more gaunt than ever and the dark shadows beneath his eyes gave

him a skeletal look. But those eyes: they shone in the semi-
darkness like black jewels. As my eyes grew more accustomed
to the light, I saw that his irises had almost disappeared. His
pupils were large and dark and fed greedily on the light in the
room.

'Why did it have to be you?' I said, as much to myself as to
him. 'You were my friend.'

He smiled then, a bleak, empty smile that drifted across his
face like snow.

'How did you find her, Bird?' he asked, his voice low. 'How
did you find Lisa? I gave you Lutice Fontenot, but how did you
find Lisa?'

'Maybe she found me,' I replied.

'It doesn't matter,' he said softly. 'I don't have time for those
things now. I got a whole new song to sing.'

He was fully in view now. In one hand he held what looked
like a modified, wide-barrelled air pistol, in the other a scalpel.
A SIG was tucked into the waistband of his pants. I noticed that
they still had mud on the cuffs.

'Why did you kill her?'

Woolrich twisted the scalpel in his hand. 'Because I could.'

Around us, the light in the room changed, darkening as a
cloud obscured the sunlight filtering through the skylights
above us. I moved slightly, shifting my weight, my eye on
my gun where it lay on the floor. My movement seemed
exaggerated, as if, faced with the potential of the ketamine,
everything shifted too quickly by comparison. Woolrich's gun
came up in a single fluid moment.

'Don't, Bird. You won't have long to wait. Don't rush the
end.'

The room brightened again, but only marginally. The sun
was setting fast. Soon, there would only be darkness.

'It was always going to end this way, Bird, you and me in a
room like this. I planned it, right from the start. You were

always going to die this way. Maybe here, or maybe later, in some other place.' He smiled again. 'After all, they were going to promote me. It would have been time to move on again. But, in the end, it was always going to come down to this.'

He moved forward, one step, the gun never wavering.

'You're a little man, Bird. Do you have any idea how many little people I've killed? Trailer-park trash in penny-ass towns from here to Detroit. Cracker bitches who spent their lives watching Oprah and fucking like dogs. Addicts. Drunks. Haven't you ever hated those people, Bird, the ones you know are worthless, the ones who will never amount to anything, will never do anything, will never contribute anything? Have you ever thought that you might be one of them? I showed them how worthless they were, Bird. I showed them how little they mattered. I showed your wife and your daughter how little they mattered.'

'And Byron?' I asked. 'Was he one of the little people, or did you turn him into one of them?' I wanted to keep him talking, maybe work my way towards my gun. As soon as he stopped, he would try to kill both Rachel and me. But more than that, I wanted to know why, as if there could ever be a why that would explain all of this.

'Byron,' said Woolrich. He smiled slightly. 'I needed to buy myself some time. When I cut up the girl, everyone believed the worst of him and he fled, back to Baton Rouge. I visited him, Bird. I tested the ketamine on him and then I just kept giving it to him. He tried to run once, but I found him.

'In the end, I find them all.'

'You warned him that the Feds were coming, didn't you? You sacrificed your own men to ensure that he would lash out at them, to ensure that he died before he could start raving to them. Did you warn Adelaide Modine too, after you sniffed her out? Did you tell her I was coming after her? Did you make her run?'

Woolrich didn't answer. Instead, he ran the blunt edge of the scalpel down Rachel's arm. 'Have you ever wondered how skin so thin . . . can hold so much blood in?' He turned the scalpel and ran the blade across her scapula, from the right shoulder to the space between her breasts. Rachel did not move. Her eyes remained wide, but something glittered and a tear trickled from the corner of her left eye and lost itself in the roots of her hair. Blood flowed from the wound, running along the nape of her neck and pooling at her chin before it fell on to her face, drawing red lines along her features.

'Look, Bird,' he said. 'I think the blood is going to her head.'

His head tilted. 'And then I drew you in. There's a circularity to this which you should appreciate, Bird. After you die, everybody is going to know about me. Then I'll be gone – they won't find me, Bird, I know every trick in the book – and I'll start again.'

He smiled slightly.

'You don't look very appreciative,' he said. 'After all, Bird, I gave you a gift when I killed your family. If they had lived, they'd have left you and you would have become just another drunk. In a sense, I kept the family together. I chose them because of you, Bird. You befriended me in New York, you paraded them in front of me, and I took them.'

'Marsyas,' I said quietly.

Woolrich glanced at Rachel. 'She's a smart lady, Bird. Just your type. Just like Susan. And soon she'll be just another of your dead lovers, except this time you won't have long to grieve over her.'

His hand flicked the scalpel back and forth, tearing fine lines across Rachel's arm. I don't think he even realised what he was doing, or the manner in which he was anticipating the acts to come.

'I don't believe in the next world, Bird. It's just a void. This is Hell, Bird, and we are in it. All the pain, all the hurt, all the misery you could ever imagine, you can find it here. It's a culture of death, the only religion worth following. The world is my altar, Bird.

'But, I don't think you'll ever understand. In the end, the only time a man really understands the reality of death, of the final pain, is at the moment of his own. It's the flaw in my work but, somehow, it makes it more human. Look upon it as my conceit.' He turned the scalpel in his hand, dying sunlight and blood mingling on the blade. 'She was right all along, Bird. Now it's time for you to learn. You're about to receive, and become, a lesson in mortality.

'I'm going to re-create the *Pietà* again, Bird, but this time with you and your ladyfriend. Can't you see it? The most famous representation of grief and death in the history of the world, a potent symbol of self-sacrifice for the greater good of humanity, of hope, of resurrection, and you're going to be a part of it. Except this is the Anti-resurrection we're creating, darkness made flesh.'

He moved forward, his eyes terrifyingly bright.

'You're not going to come back from the dead, Bird, and the only sins you're dying for are your own.'

I was already moving to the right when the gun fired. I felt a sharp, stinging pain in my left side as the aluminium-bodied syringe struck and the sound of Woolrich's footsteps approaching across the wooden floor. I lashed out at it with my left hand, dislodging the needle painfully from my flesh. It was a huge dose. I could already feel it taking effect as I reached for my gun. I gripped the butt hard and tried to draw a bead on Woolrich.

He killed the lights. Caught in the centre of the floor, away from Rachel's body, he moved to the right. I found a shape moving past the window and I loosed off two shots. There was a grunt of pain and the sound of glass breaking. A finger of sunlight lanced into the room.

I worked my way backwards until I reached the second hallway. I tried to catch a glimpse of Woolrich but he seemed to have disappeared into the shadows. A second syringe whacked into the wall beside me and I was forced to dive to my left. My limbs were heavy now, my arms and legs propelling me with difficulty. I felt as if there was a pressure on my chest and I knew I would not be able to support my own weight if I tried to rise.

I kept moving backwards, every movement a huge effort, but I felt certain that, if I stopped, I would never be able to move again. The creaking of boards came from the main room and I heard Woolrich breathing harshly. He barked out a short laugh and I could hear the pain in it.

'Fuck you, Bird,' he said. '*Shit*, that hurts.' He laughed again. 'I'm going to make you pay for that, Bird, you and the woman. I'm going to tear your fucking souls apart.'

His voice came to me as if through a heavy fog, which distorted the sound and made it difficult to tell distances or direction. The walls of the hallway rippled and fragmented and black gore oozed from the cracks. A hand reached out to me, a slim, female hand with a narrow gold loop on its wedding finger. I saw myself reach out to touch it, although I could still feel my hands on the floor beneath me. A second female hand appeared, flailing blindly.

*bird*

I backed away, shaking my head to try to clear the vision. Then two smaller hands emerged from the darkness, delicate and childlike, and I closed my eyes tightly and gritted my teeth.

*daddy*

'*No*,' I hissed. I dug my nails into the floor until I heard one crack and pain coursed through the index finger of my left hand. I needed the pain. I needed it to fight off the effects of the ketamine. I pressed down hard on the injured finger and the pain made me gasp. There were still shadows moving along the wall, but the figures of my wife and child had gone.

I was conscious now of a reddish glow bathing the hallway. My back struck something cold and heavy, which moved slowly as I pressed against it. I was leaning against a partially open reinforced steel door, with three bolts on its left side. The central bolt was a monster, easily an inch in diameter with a huge open brass lock hanging from it. A dim reddish light seeped out from the crack in the door.

'Birdman, it's almost over,' said Woolrich. His voice sounded very close now, although I still could not see him. I guessed he was standing at the very edge of the corner, waiting for me finally to stop moving. 'The drug is going to stop you soon. Throw the gun away, Bird, and we can get started. The sooner we start, the sooner we finish.'

I leaned back harder on the door and felt it give fully. I pushed back with my heels once, twice, a third time, until I came to rest against a set of shelving that reached from ceiling to floor. The room was lit by a single red bulb, which hung unshaded from the centre of the ceiling. The windows had been bricked up, the brickwork left uncovered. There was no natural light to illuminate the contents of the room.

Opposite me, to the left of the door, was a row of metal shelving, perforated bars holding the shelves in place with screws. On each shelf sat a number of glass jars and, in each jar, glowing in the dim red light, lay the remains of a human face. Most were beyond recognition. Lying in the formaldehyde, they had sunken in on themselves. Eyelashes were still visible on some, lips bleached almost white on others, the skin at their edges tattered and torn. On the lowest shelf, two dark faces lay almost upright against the glass and, even violated in this way, I recognised the faces of Tante Marie Aguillard and her son. I counted maybe fifteen bottles in front of me. Behind me, the shelving moved slightly and I heard the sound of glass knocking against glass and the slick movement of liquid.

I raised my head. Row upon row of bottles reached up to the ceiling, each bearing its faint, white human remains. Beside my left eye, a face leaned against the front of a jar, its empty eyes gaping, as if trying to peer into eternity.

And I knew that somewhere among these faces, Susan lay preserved.

'What do you think of my collection, Bird?' The dark bulk of Woolrich moved slowly down the hallway. In one hand, I could see the outline of the pistol. In the other, he rubbed his thumb along the clean line of the scalpel.

'Wondering where your wife is? She's on the middle shelf, third from the left. Shit, Bird, you're probably sitting beside her right now.'

I didn't move. I didn't blink. My body lay slumped against the shelves, surrounded by the faces of the dead. My face would be there soon, I thought, my face and Rachel's and Susan's, side by side for ever.

Woolrich moved forward until he stood in the doorway. He raised the air pistol.

'No one ever lasted this long before, Bird. Even Tee Jean, and he was a strong kid.' His eyes glowed redly. 'I gotta tell you, Bird: in the end, this is going to hurt.'

He tightened his finger on the pistol and I heard the crack as the syringe shot from the barrel. I was already raising my gun as the sharp pain struck my chest, my arm achingly heavy, my vision blurred by the shadows moving across my eyes. I tightened my finger on the trigger, willing it to increase the pressure. Woolrich moved forward, alive to the danger, the scalpel raised to slash at my arm.

The trigger moved back slowly, infinitesimally slowly, and the world slowed down with it. Woolrich seemed to hang in space, the blade curving down in his hand as if through water, his mouth wide and a sound like a wind howling in a tunnel coming from his throat. The trigger moved back another tiny measure and my finger froze as the gun boomed loudly in the enclosed space. Woolrich, barely three feet from me now, bucked as the first shot took him in the chest. Then the automatic fire kicked in under the sustained pressure and the next eight shots seemed to come together, the sound of their firing joined together seamlessly as the bullets tore into him, ripping through cloth and flesh before the gun locked empty. Glass shattered as the bullets exited and the floor became awash with formaldehyde. Woolrich fell backwards and lay on the floor, his body shaking and spasming. He rose once, his shoulders and head lifting from the ground, the light already dying in his eyes. Then he lay back and moved no more.

My arm gave in under the weight of the gun and it fell to the floor. I could hear liquid dripping, could feel the presence of the dead as they crowded around me. From a distance, there came the sound of approaching sirens and I knew that, whatever happened to me, Rachel at least would be safe. Something brushed my cheek with a touch light as gossamer, like the last caress of a lover before the time to sleep, and a kind of peace came over me. With a last act of will, I closed my eyes and waited for the stillness to come.

# Epilogue

*I turn left at the Scarborough intersection, down the steep hill, past the big Catholic church and the old cemetery, the fire department on my right, the late-evening sun shining bleakly on the expanse of marsh-land to the east and west of the road. Soon it will be dark and lights will appear in the houses of the locals, but the summer houses on Prouts Neck Road will not be lit.*

*The sea rolls in gently at Prouts Neck, washing slowly over sand and stone. The season is over now and behind me the bulk of the Black Point Inn looms darkly, its dining room deserted, its bar quiet, the screen doors of the staff dormitories locked. In the summer, the old and wealthy from Boston and upstate New York will come to stay, eating buffet lunches by the pool and dressing for dinner, the candlelight reflecting on their heavy jewellery and dancing around the table like golden moths.*

*Across the water, I can see the lights of Old Orchard Beach. A chill wind is coming in over the sea, tossing and buffeting the last of the gulls. I pull my coat tightly around me and stand on the sand, watching the grains swirl and twist before me. They make a sound like a mother hushing her child as the wind raises them from the dunes and lifts them like the shapes of old ghosts before laying them to rest again.*

*I am standing near the spot where Clarence Johns stood all those years ago, as he watched Daddy Helms's man pour dirt and ants over my body. It was a hard lesson to learn, harder still to learn it twice. I recall the look on his face as he stood shivering before me, the desolation, the realisation of what he had done, of what he had lost.*

*And I want to put my arm around the shoulders of Clarence Johns and tell him that it's all right, that I understand, that I bear him no malice for what he did. I want to hear the soles of his cheap shoes slapping on the road. I want to watch him skim a stone over the water and know that he is still my friend. I want to walk the long walk home beside him and hear him whistling the only three bars he knows of some tune that he can't get out of his head, a tune that returns again and again to haunt him as he makes his way along the road.*

*But instead I will climb back in my car and return to Portland in the waning autumn light. I have a room at the Inn on St John, with big bay windows and clean white sheets and a separate bathroom two doors down the hall. I will lie on my bed as the traffic passes beneath my window, as the Greyhound buses arrive and depart from the terminal across the street, as the street people push their shopping carts filled with bottles and cans down the sidewalk to the depot on Congress.*

*And in the gathering darkness I will call Rachel's number in Manhattan. The phone will ring – once, twice – and then her machine will kick in: 'Hi, no one can come to the phone right now, but . . .' I have heard the same message again and again since she left the hospital. Her receptionist says that she cannot tell me where Rachel is. She has cancelled her college lectures. And, from my hotel room, I will talk to the machine.*

*I could find her, if I chose. I found the others, but they were dead when I found them. I do not want to chase her down.*

*It is not supposed to end this way. She should be beside me now, her skin perfect and white, not scarred by Woolrich's knife; her eyes bright and inviting, not wary and haunted by the visions that torment her in the night; her hands reaching for me in the darkness, not raised to ward me off, as if even my touch might cause her pain. We will both reach an accommodation with the past, with all that has taken place, but for now we will each do so alone.*

In the morning, Edgar will have the radio playing and there will be orange juice and coffee on the table in the lobby, and muffins wrapped in plastic. From there, I will drive out to my grandfather's house and start working. A local man has agreed to help me fix my roof and mend my walls, so that the house can be made habitable for the winter.

And I will sit on my porch as the wind takes the evergreens in hand, pressing and moulding their branches into new shapes, creating a song from their leaves. And I will listen for the sound of a dog barking, its paws scraping on the worn boards, its tail moving lazily in the cool evening air; or the tap-tap-tap on the rail as my grandfather prepares to tamp the tobacco into his pipe, a glass of whiskey beside him warm and tender as a familiar kiss; or the rustle of my mother's dress against the kitchen table as she lays out plates for the evening meal, blue on white, older than she is, old as the house.

Or the sound of plastic-soled shoes fading into the distance, disappearing into the darkness, embracing the peace that comes at last to every dead thing.

# Acknowledgements

A number of books proved particularly valuable in the course of researching this novel. Chief among them was *The Body Emblazoned* (Routledge, 1995), Jonathan Sawday's brilliant study of dissection and the human body in Renaissance culture. Other works to which I returned included F. Gonzalez-Crussi's *Suspended Animation* (Harcourt Brace & Co., 1995); Denis C. Rousey's *Policing the Southern City* (Louisiana State University Press, 1996); Luther Link's *The Devil* (Reaktion Books, 1995); Lyall Watson's *Dark Nature* (Hodder & Stoughton, 1995); and the *Crime Classification Manual* (Simon & Schuster, 1993) by Ressler, Douglas, Burgess and Burgess.

On a more personal note, I wish to thank my agent, Darley Anderson, without whom *Every Dead Thing* would not have seen the light of day. I also wish to acknowledge the faith, advice and encouragement of my editor at Hodder & Stoughton, Sue Fletcher, and Bob Mecoy, my editor at Simon & Schuster in New York. Finally, thanks to my family and Ruth, for everything.

# Dark Hollow

## John Connolly

For my Father

# Part One

Alone, alone, about a dreadful wood
Of conscious evil runs a lost mankind,
Dreading to find its Father.

W.H. Auden, *For the Time Being*

# Prologue

The Dodge Intrepid stood beneath a stand of firs, its windshield facing out to sea, the lights off, the key in the ignition to keep the heater running. No snow had fallen this far south, not yet, but there was frost on the ground. From nearby came the sound of the waves breaking on Ferry Beach, the only sound to disturb the stillness of this Maine winter night. A floating jetty bobbed close to the shore, lobster pots piled high upon it. Four boats lay shrouded in tarpaulin behind the red wooden boathouse, and a catamaran was tied down close to the public access boat ramp. Otherwise, the parking lot was empty.

The passenger door opened and Chester Nash climbed quickly into the car, his teeth chattering and his long brown coat drawn tightly around him. Chester was small and wiry, with long dark hair and a sliver of a moustache on his upper lip that stretched down beyond the corners of his mouth. He thought the moustache made him look dashing. Everyone else thought it made him look mournful, ergo Cheerful Chester. If there was one thing guaranteed to make Chester Nash mad, it was people calling him Cheerful Chester. He had once stuck his gun in Paulie Block's mouth for calling him Cheerful Chester. Paulie Block had almost ripped his arm off for doing it, although, as he explained to Cheerful Chester while he slapped him repeatedly across the head with hands as big as shovels, he understood the reason why Chester had done it. Reasons just didn't excuse everything, that was all.

'I hope you washed your hands,' said Paulie Block, who sat in the driver's seat of the Dodge, maybe wondering why Chester couldn't have taken a leak earlier like any normal individual instead of insisting on pissing against a tree in the woods by the shore and letting all of the heat out of the car while he did it.

'Man, it's cold,' said Chester. 'This is the coldest goddamn place I have ever been in my whole goddamn life. My meat nearly froze out there. Any colder, I'da pissed ice cubes.'

Paulie Block took a long drag on his cigarette and watched as the tip flared briefly red before returning to grey ash. Paulie Block was aptly named. He was six-three, weighed two-eighty and had a face that looked like it had been used to shunt trains. He made the interior of the car look cramped just by being there. All things considered, Paulie Block could have made Giants Stadium look cramped just by being there.

Chester glanced at the digital clock on the dash, the green numerals seeming to hang suspended in the dark.

'They're late,' he said.

'They'll be here,' said Paulie. 'They'll be here.'

He returned to his cigarette and stared out to sea. He probably didn't look too hard. There was nothing to be seen, just blackness and the lights of Old Orchard Beach beyond. Beside him, Chester Nash began playing with a Game Boy.

Outside, the wind blew and the waves washed rhythmically on the beach, and the sound of their voices carried over the cold ground to where others were watching, and listening.

'. . . Subject Two is back in vehicle. Man, it's cold,' said FBI Special Agent Dale Nutley, unconsciously repeating the words that he had just heard Chester Nash speak. A parabolic microphone stood beside him, positioned close to a small gap in the wall of the boathouse. Next to it, a voice-activated Nagra tape recorder whirred softly and a Badger Mk II low-light camera kept a vigil on the Dodge.

Nutley wore two pairs of socks, long johns, denims, a T-shirt, a cotton shirt, a wool sweater, a Lowe ski jacket, thermal gloves and a grey alpaca hat with two little flaps that hung down over the headphones and kept his ears warm. Special Agent Rob Briscoe, who sat beside him on a tall stool, thought the alpaca hat made Nutley look like a llama herder, or the lead singer with the Spin Doctors. Either way, Nutley looked like a clown in his alpaca hat, with its damn flaps to keep his ears warm. Agent Briscoe, whose ears were very cold, wanted that alpaca hat. If it got any colder, he figured he might just have to kill Dale Nutley and take the hat from his dead head.

The boathouse stood to the right of the Ferry Beach parking lot, giving its occupants a clear view of the Dodge. Behind it, a private road followed the shore, leading to one of the summer houses on the Neck. From the lot, Ferry Road snaked back to Black Point Road, leading ultimately to Oak Hill and Portland to the north and Black Point itself to the south. The boathouse windows had received a reflective coating barely two hours before, in order to prevent anyone from seeing the agents inside. There had been a brief moment of apprehension when Chester Nash had peered in the window and tested the locks on the doors before running quickly back to the Dodge.

Unfortunately, the boathouse had no heating, at least none that worked, and the FBI had not seen fit to provide the two special agents with a heater. As a result, Nutley and Briscoe were about as cold as they had ever been. The bare boards of the boathouse were icy to the touch.

'How long we been here?' asked Nutley.

'Two hours,' replied Briscoe.

'You cold?'

'What sort of a stupid question is that? I'm covered in frost. Of course I'm fucking cold.'

'Why didn't you bring a hat?' asked Nutley. 'You know, you lose most of your body heat through the top of your head? You should have brought a hat. That's why you're cold. You should have brought a hat.'

'You know, Nutley?' said Briscoe.

'What?' said Nutley.

'I hate you.'

Behind them, the voice-activated recorder whirred softly, taking in the conversation of the two agents through the microphones attached to their jackets. Everything was to be recorded, that was the rule on this operation: everything. And if that included Briscoe's hatred of Nutley because of his alpaca hat, then so be it.

The security guard, Oliver Judd, heard her before he saw her. Her feet made a heavy, shuffling noise on the carpeted floor and she was speaking softly to herself as she walked. Regretfully, he stood up in his booth and walked away from his TV and the heater that had been blasting warm air onto his toes. Outside, there was a kind of stillness that presaged further snow. There was no wind, though, which was something. It would soon get worse – December always did – but, this far north, it got worse sooner than it did anywhere else. Sometimes, living in northern Maine could be a bitch.

He walked swiftly towards her. 'Hey, lady, lady! What are you doing out of bed? You're gonna catch your death.'

The old woman started at the last word and looked at Judd for the first time. She was small and thin but carried herself straight, which gave her an imposing air among the other occupants of St Martha's Home for the Elderly. Judd didn't think she was as old as some of the other folks in the home, who were so old that they'd bummed cigarettes from people who died in World War I. This one, though, was maybe sixty at most. Judd figured that if she wasn't old then she was probably infirm which meant, in layman's terms, that she was mad, plumb loco. Her hair was silver grey and hung loose over her shoulders and almost to her waist. Her eyes were bright blue and looked straight through Judd and off into the distance. She wore a pair of brown, lace-up boots, a nightgown, a red muffler and a long blue overcoat, which she was buttoning as she walked.

'I'm leaving,' she replied. She spoke quietly but with absolute determination, as if it was nothing out of the ordinary that a sixty-year-old woman should try to leave a home for the elderly in northern Maine wearing only a nightdress and a cheap coat on a night when the forecast promised more snow to add to the six inches that already lay frozen on the ground. Judd couldn't figure out how she had slipped past the nurses' station, still less almost to the main door of the home. Some of these old folks were cunning as foxes, Judd reckoned. Turn your back on them and they'd be gone, heading for the hills or their old house or off to wed a lover who had died thirty years before.

'Now you know you can't leave,' said Judd. 'Come on, you got to go back to bed. I'm going to call for a nurse now, so you stay where you are and we'll have someone down to take care of you before you know it.'

The old woman stopped buttoning her coat and looked again at Oliver Judd. It was then that Judd realised for the first time that she was scared: truly, mortally afraid for her life. He couldn't tell how he knew, except that maybe some kind of primitive sense had kicked in when she came near him. Her eyes were huge and pleading and her hands shook now that they were no longer occupied with her buttons. She was so scared that Judd began to feel a little nervous himself. Then the old woman spoke.

'He's coming,' she said.

'Who's coming?' asked Judd.

'Caleb. Caleb Kyle is coming.'

The old woman's stare was almost hypnotic, her voice trembling with terror. Judd shook his head and took her by the arm.

'Come on,' he said, leading her to a vinyl seat beside his booth. 'You sit down here while I call the nurse.' Who in hell was Caleb Kyle? The name was almost familiar, but he couldn't quite place it.

He was dialing the number for the nurses' station when he heard a noise from behind. He turned to see the old woman almost on top of him, her eyes now narrow with concentration, her mouth set firmly. Her hands were raised above her head and he lifted his eyes to see what she was holding, his face rising just in time to see the heavy glass vase falling towards him.

Then all was darkness.

'I can't see a fucking thing,' said Cheerful Chester Nash. The windows of the car had steamed up, giving Chester an uncomfortably claustrophobic feeling that the huge bulk of Paulie Block did nothing to ease, as he had just told his companion in no uncertain terms.

Paulie wiped the side window with his sleeve. In the distance, headlights raked the sky.

'Quiet,' he said. 'They're coming.'

Nutley and Briscoe had also seen the headlights, minutes after Briscoe's radio had crackled into life to inform the agents that a car was on its way down Old County Road, heading in the direction of Ferry Beach.

'You think it's them?' asked Nutley.

'Maybe,' replied Briscoe, brushing icy condensation from his jacket as the Ford Taurus emerged from Ferry Road and pulled up alongside the Dodge. Through their 'phones, the agents heard Paulie Block ask Cheerful Chester if he was ready to rumble. They heard only a click in response. Briscoe couldn't be certain, but he thought it was the sound of a safety clicking off.

In St Martha's Home for the Elderly, a nurse placed a cold compress on the back of Oliver Judd's head. Ressler, the sergeant out of Dark Hollow, stood by with a reserve patrolman, the patrolman still laughing quietly to himself. There was the faintest trace of a fading smile on Ressler's lips. In another corner stood Dave Martel, the chief of police in Greenville, five miles south of Dark

Hollow, and beside him one of the Fisheries and Wildlife wardens from the town.

St Martha's was technically in the jurisdiction of Dark Hollow, the last town before the big industrial forests began their sweep towards Canada. Still, Martel had heard about the old woman and had come to offer his help in the search if it was needed. He didn't like Ressler, but liking had nothing to do with whatever action needed to be taken.

Martel, who was sharp, quiet and only Greenville's third chief since the foundation of the town's small department, didn't see anything particularly funny about what had just happened. If they didn't find her soon, she would die. It didn't require too much cold to kill an old woman, and there was plenty to spare that night.

Oliver Judd, who had always wanted to be a cop but was too short, too overweight and too dumb to make the grade, knew the Dark Hollow cops were laughing at him. He figured that they probably had a right to laugh. After all, what kind of security guard gets cold-cocked by an old lady? An old lady, what's more, who now had Oliver Judd's new Smith & Wesson 625 somewhere on her person.

The search team prepared to move off, headed by Dr Martin Ryley, the director of the home. Ryley was wrapped up tightly in a hooded parka, gloves and insulated boots. In one hand he carried an emergency medical kit, in the other a big Maglite flashlight. At his feet lay a backpack containing warm clothing, blankets and a thermos filled with soup.

'We didn't pass her on the way in here, so she's moving across country,' Judd heard someone say. It sounded like Will Patterson, the warden, whose wife ran a drugstore in

Guilford and who had an ass like a peach waiting to be bitten.

'It's all hard going,' said Ryley. 'South is Beaver Cove, but Chief Martel didn't see her on his way up here. West is the lake. Looks like she may be just wandering aimlessly through the woods.'

Patterson's radio buzzed and he moved away to talk. Almost immediately, he turned back. 'Plane's spotted her. She's about two miles north east of here, moving farther into the forest.'

The two Dark Hollow cops and the warden, accompanied by Ryley and a nurse, moved off, one of the cops shouldering the backpack of clothing and blankets. Chief Martel looked at Judd and shrugged. Ressler didn't want his help, and Martel wasn't about to stick his nose in where it wasn't wanted, but he had a bad feeling about what was happening, a very bad feeling. As he watched the group of five heading into the trees, the first small flurries of snow began to fall.

'Ho Chi Minh,' said Cheerful Chester. 'Pol Pot. Lychee.'

The four Cambodians looked at him coldly. They wore matching blue wool overcoats, blue suits with sombre ties, and black leather gloves on their hands. Three were young, probably no more than twenty-five or twenty-six, Paulie reckoned. The fourth was older, with strands of grey seeping through his slicked-back dark hair. He wore glasses and smoked an unfiltered cigarette. In his left hand, he held a black leather briefcase.

'Tet. Chairman Mao. Nagasaki,' continued Cheerful Chester.

'Will you shut up?' said Paulie Block.

'I'm trying to make them feel at home.'

The older guy took a last drag on his cigarette and flicked it toward the beach.

'When your friend is finished making a fool of himself, perhaps we can begin?' he said.

'See,' said Paulie Block to Cheerful Chester. 'That's how wars start.'

'That Chester sure is an asshole,' said Nutley. The conversation between the six men carried clearly to them in the chill night air. Briscoe nodded in agreement. Beside him, Nutley adjusted the camera to zoom in on the case in the Cambodian's hand, clicked off a frame, then pulled back a little to take in Paulie Block, the Cambodian and the case. Their brief was to watch, listen and record. No interference. The interference part would come later, as soon as all of this – whatever 'this' was, since all they had was the meeting point – could be traced back to Tony Celli in Boston. A car containing two other agents was waiting to pick up the Dodge at Oak Hill, while a second car would follow the Cambodians.

Briscoe picked up a Night Hawk scope and trained it on Cheerful Chester Nash.

'You see anything unusual about Chester's coat?' he said.

Nutley moved the camera a little to the left.

'No,' he said. 'Wait. It looks like it's fifty years old. He doesn't have his hands in his pockets. He's got them in those slits below the breast. Pretty awkward way to keep warm, don't you think?'

'Yeah,' said Briscoe. 'Real awkward.'

'Where is she?' said the older Cambodian to Paulie Block.

Paulie gestured to the trunk of the car. The Cambodian

nodded and handed the briefcase to one of his associates. The case was flicked open and the Cambodian held it, facing forward, so that Paulie and Chester could see what was inside.

Chester whistled. 'Shit,' he said.

'Shit,' said Nutley. 'There's a lot of cash in that case.'

Briscoe trained the scope on the notes. 'Ouch. We're talking maybe three mil.'

'Enough to buy Tony Celli out of whatever jam he's in,' said Nutley.

'And some.'

'But who's in the trunk?' asked Nutley.

'Well, son, that's what we're here to find out.'

The group of five moved carefully over the hard ground, their breath puffing white as they went. Around them, the tips of evergreens scraped the sky and welcomed the flakes with their spread branches. The ground here was rocky, and the new snow had made it slick and dangerous. Ryley had already stumbled once, painfully scraping his shin. In the sky above them, they could hear the sound of the Cessna's engine, one of Currier's planes from Moosehead Lake, and could see its spotlight picking out something on the ground ahead of them.

'If this snow keeps up, the plane's going to have to turn back,' said Patterson.

'Nearly there,' said Ryley. 'Another ten minutes and we'll have her.'

A gunshot exploded in the darkness ahead of them, then a second. The light on the plane tilted and started to rise. Patterson's radio burst out with an angry blast of speech.

'Hell,' said Patterson, with a look of disbelief on his face. 'She's shooting at them.'

The Cambodian stayed close to Paulie Block as he moved to the rear of the car. Behind them, the younger men pulled back their coats to reveal Uzis hanging from straps on their shoulders. Each kept a hand on the grip, one finger just outside the trigger guard.

'Open it,' said the older man.

'You're the boss,' said Paulie, as he inserted the key in the lock and prepared to lift the trunk. 'Paulie's just here to open the trunk.' If the Cambodian had been listening more intently, he would have noticed that Paulie Block said the words very loudly and very distinctly.

'Gun slits,' said Briscoe suddenly. 'Fucking gun slits, that's what they are.'

'Gun slits,' repeated Nutley. 'Oh, Jesus.'

Paulie Block opened the trunk and stepped back. A blast of heat greeted the Cambodian as he moved forward. In the trunk was a blanket, and beneath it was a recognisably human form. The Cambodian leaned in and pulled the blanket back.

Beneath it was a man: a man with a sawn-off shotgun.

'What is this?' said the Cambodian.

'This is goodbye,' said Paulie Block, as the barrels roared and the Cambodian jerked with the impact of the shots.

'Fuck,' said Briscoe. 'Move! Move!' He drew his SIG and ran for the back door, flipping a switch on his handset and calling for the Scarborough backup to move in as he flipped the lock and headed into the night in the direction of the two cars.

'What about non-interference?' said Nutley as he followed the older man. This wasn't the way it was supposed to happen. It wasn't supposed to go down like this at all.

Cheerful Chester's coat flew open, revealing the twin short barrels of a pair of Walther MPK submachine guns. Two of the Cambodians were already raising their Uzis when he pulled the triggers.

'Sayonara,' said Chester, his mouth exploding into a grin.

The 9mm parabellums ripped into the three men, tearing through the leather of the briefcase, the expensive wool of their coats, the pristine whiteness of their shirts, the thin shell of their skin. They shattered glass, pierced the metal of the car, pockmarked the vinyl of the seats. It took less than four seconds to empty sixty-four rounds into the three men, leaving them wrinkled and slumped, their warm blood melting the thin layer of frost on the ground. The briefcase had landed face down, some of the tightly packed wads scattering as it fell.

Chester and Paulie saw what they had done, and it was good.

'Well, what are you waiting for?' said Paulie. 'Let's get the money and get the fuck out of here.'

Behind him, the man with the shotgun, whose name was Jimmy Fribb, climbed from the cramped trunk and stretched his legs, his joints creaking. Chester loaded a fresh clip into one of the MPKs and dumped the other in the trunk of the Dodge. He was just leaning down to pick up the fallen money when the two shouts came almost together.

'Federal Agents,' said the first voice. 'Let me see your hands *now*.'

The other voice was less succinct, and less polite, but probably strangely familiar to Paulie Block.

'Get the fuck away from the money,' it said, 'or I'll blow your fucking heads off.'

The old woman stood in a patch of clear ground, watching the sky. Snow fell on her hair, on her shoulders and on her outstretched arms, the gun clasped in her right hand, her left hand open and empty. Her mouth was gaping and her chest heaved as her aging body tried to cope with its exertions. She seemed not to notice Ryley and the others until they were only thirty feet from her. The nurse hung back behind the others. Ryley, despite Patterson's objections, took the lead.

'Miss Emily,' he said softly. 'Miss Emily, it's me, Dr Ryley. We're here to take you home.'

The old woman looked at him and Ryley suspected, for the first time since they had set out, that the old woman was not mad. Her eyes were calm as she watched him, and she almost grinned as he approached.

'I'm not going back,' she said.

'Miss Emily, it's cold. You're going to die out here if you don't come with us. We've brought you blankets and warm clothes and I have a thermos of chicken soup. We'll get you warm and comfortable, then we'll bring you safely back.'

The old woman actually smiled then, a broad smile with no humour to it, and no trust.

'You can't keep me safe,' she said softly. 'Not from him.'

Ryley frowned. He recalled something about the old

woman now, an incident with a visitor and a report the night before from one of the nurses after Miss Emily claimed that someone had tried to climb in her window. They'd dismissed it, of course, although Judd had taken to wearing his gun on duty as a result. These old folks were nervous, fearful of illness, of strangers, of friends and relatives sometimes, fearful of the cold, of the possibility of falling, fearful for their meagre possessions, for their photos, for their fading memories.

Fearful of death.

'Please, Miss Emily, put the gun down and come back with us. We can keep you safe from harm. No one's going to hurt you.'

She shook her head slowly. Above them, the plane circled, casting a strange white light over the old woman, turning her long grey hair to silver fire.

'I'm not going back. I'll face him out here. This is his place, these woods. This is where he'll be.'

Her face changed then. Behind Ryley, Patterson thought he had never seen an expression of such abject terror. Her mouth curled down at the edges, her chin and lips trembled and then the rest of her body began to shake, a strange, violent quivering that was almost like an ecstasy. Tears flowed down her cheeks as she began to speak.

'I'm sorry,' she said. 'I'm sorry, I'm sorry, I'm sorry, I'm sorry . . .'

'Please, Miss Emily,' said Ryley, as he moved toward her. 'Put the gun down. We have to take you back.'

'I'm not going back,' she repeated.

'Please, Miss Emily, you must.'

'Then you'll have to kill me,' she said simply, as she

pointed the Smith & Wesson at Ryley and pulled the trigger.

Chester and Paulie looked first to their left and then to their right. To their left, in the parking lot, stood a tall man in a black jacket with a handset in one hand and a SIG held before him in the other. Behind him stood another, younger man, also holding a SIG, this time in a two-handed grip, with a grey alpaca hat on his head and flaps hanging down over his ears.

To their right, beside a small wooden hut used to collect parking fees during the summer, stood a figure dressed entirely in black, from the tips of his boots to the ski-mask covering his head. He held a Ruger pump-action in his hands and he breathed heavily through the round slit in the mask.

'Cover him,' said Briscoe to Nutley. Nutley's SIG shifted from Paulie Block to the black-garbed figure near the edge of the woods.

'Drop it, asshole,' said Nutley.

The Ruger wavered slightly.

'I said *Drop it*,' repeated Nutley, his voice rising to a shout.

Briscoe's eyes moved briefly to take in the figure with the shotgun. It was all Chester Nash needed. He spun and opened fire with the MPK, hitting Briscoe in the arm and Nutley in the chest and head. Nutley died instantly, his alpaca hat turning red as he fell.

Briscoe opened fire from where he lay on the road, hitting Chester Nash in the right leg and the groin, the MPK tumbling from his hands as he fell. From the woods came the sound of the Ruger opening up and Paulie Block, his gun in his right hand, bucked as he was hit, the window behind him shattering as the shots exited. He slumped to his knees and then fell face down on the ground. Chester Nash tried to reach for the MPK with his right hand, his left hand clasping his injured groin, when Briscoe fired two more shots into him and he ceased moving. Jimmy Fribb dropped his shotgun and raised his hands, just in time to stop Briscoe from killing him.

Briscoe was about to rise when, from in front of him, he heard the sound of a shotgun shell being jacked.

'Stay down,' said the voice.

He did as he was told, placing the SIG on the ground beside him. A black-booted foot kicked the gun away, sending it spinning into the undergrowth.

'Put your hands on your head.'

Briscoe lifted his hands, his left arm aching as he did so, and watched as the masked figure moved towards him, the Ruger still pointing down. Nutley lay on his side close by, his open eyes staring out at the sea. Christ, thought Briscoe, what a mess. Beyond the trees, he could see headlights and hear the sound of approaching cars. The man with the shotgun heard them too, his head twisting slightly as he placed the last of the cash in the briefcase and closed it. Jimmy Fribb used the distraction to make a lunge for the discarded SIG but the gunman killed him before he could reach it, firing a shot into his back. Briscoe tightened his grip on his head, his injured arm aching, and started to pray.

'Stay flat on the ground and don't look up,' he was told.

Briscoe did as he was told, but kept his eyes open. Blood flowed on the ground beneath him and he moved his head slightly to avoid it. When he looked up again, there were headlights in his eyes and the figure in black was gone.

Dr Martin Ryley was forty-eight, and was anxious to see forty-nine. He had two children, a boy and a girl, and a wife called Joanie who cooked him pot roast on Sundays. He wasn't a very good doctor, which was why he ran an old folks' home. When Miss Emily Watts fired at him, he hit the ground, covered his head with his hands and began alternately praying and blaspheming. The first shot went somewhere to his left. The second sprayed wet dirt and snow on his face. Behind him, he heard the sound of safety catches clicking off and he shouted: 'No, leave her, please. Don't shoot.'

Once again the woods were silent, with only the high buzzing of the Cessna as a distraction. Ryley risked a glance up at Miss Emily. She was crying openly now. Carefully, Ryley rose to his feet.

'It's all right, Miss Emily.'

The old woman shook her head. 'No,' she replied. 'It will never be all right.' And she put the mouth of the Smith & Wesson to her left breast and fired. The impact spun her backwards and to her left, her feet tangling beneath her as she fell and the fabric of her coat igniting briefly from the muzzle flare. She bucked once then lay still upon the ground, her blood staining the earth around her, the snow falling on her open eyes, her body lit by the light from above.

And around her, the woods watched silently, their branches shifting occasionally to allow the passage of the snow.

This is how it began for me, and for another generation: two violent occurrences, taking place almost simultaneously one winter's night, bound together by a single dark thread that lost itself in tangled memories of distant, brutal acts. Others, some of them close to me, had lived with it for a long, long time, and had died with it. This was an old evil, and old evil has a way of permeating bloodlines and tainting those who played no part in its genesis: the young, the innocent, the vulnerable, the defenceless. It turns life to death and glass to mirrors, creating an image of itself in everything that it touches.

All of this I learned later, after the other deaths, after it became clear that something terrible was happening, that something old and foul had emerged from the wilderness. And in all that would come to pass, I was a participant. Perhaps, looking back into the past, I had always been a participant without ever really understanding how, or why. But that winter, a whole set of circumstances occurred, each incident separate yet ultimately connected. It opened a channel between what had been and what should never have been again, and worlds ended in the collision.

I look back over the years and see myself as I used to be, frozen in former times like a figure in a series of vignettes. I see myself as a young boy waiting for the first sight of my father as he returns from his day's exertions in the city, his policeman's uniform now put away, a black gym bag in his left hand, his once muscular form now running a little to fat, his hair greyer than it used to be, his eyes a little more tired. I run to him and he sweeps me up into the crook of his right arm, his fingers closing gently on my thigh, and I am amazed at his strength, at the muscles bunched below his shoulder, his biceps tight and hard. I want to be him, to emulate his achievements and to sculpt my body in his likeness. And when he begins to come apart, when his body is revealed only as the flawed shield for a fragile mind, then I, too, start to fall to pieces.

I see myself as an older boy, standing by my father's grave, only a handful of policemen straight and tall beside me, so that I too have to be straight and tall. These are his closest friends, the ones who are not ashamed to come. This is not a place where many wish to be seen: there is bad feeling in the city at what has taken place, and only a loyal few are willing to have their reputations frozen in the flare of a newsman's flashbulb.

I see my mother to my right, coiled in grief. Her husband – the man she has loved for so long – is gone, and with him the reality of him as a kind man, a family man, a father who could sweep his boy into the air like a leaf on the wind. Instead, he will forever be remembered as a murderer, a suicide. He has killed a young man and a young woman, both unarmed, for reasons that no one will ever properly explain, reasons that lay in the depths of those tired eyes. They had taunted him, this thug making the transition from juvenile to adult courts and his middle-class girlfriend with his dirt under her manicured nails, and he had killed them, seeing in them something beyond what they were, beyond even what they might become. Then he had put his gun in his mouth and pulled the trigger.

I see myself as a young man, standing at another grave, watching as they lower my mother down. Beside me now is the old man, my grandfather. We have travelled down from Scarborough, Maine – the place to which we fled after the death of my father, the place in which my mother was born – for the funeral, so that my mother can be buried beside my father, as she has always wished, for she has never stopped loving him. Around us, old men and women have gathered. I am the youngest person present.

I see snowfalls in winter. I see the old man grow older. I leave Scarborough. I become a policeman, like my father, like my grandfather. There is a legacy to be acknowledged, and I will not be found wanting. When my grandfather dies, I return to Scarborough and fill in the grave myself, spadefuls of earth carefully falling on the pine casket. The morning sun shines down on the cemetery and I can smell the salt on the air, carried from the marshes to the east and the west. Nearby, a golden-crowned kinglet chases cluster flies, filthy grey vermin that parasitise earthworms by laying their eggs in them and seek shelter from the winter in the chinks and cracks of houses. Above, the first of the Canada geese fly south for the winter, a pair of ravens flanking them like black fighters escorting a flight of bombers.

And as the last patch of wood disappears, I hear the sound of children's voices coming from the Lil Folks Farm nursery school which borders on the cemetery, the noise of their games high and joyful, and I cannot help but smile, for the old man would have smiled as well.

And then there is one more grave, one more set of prayers read from a tattered book, and this one tears my world apart. Two bodies are lowered down to rest side by side, just as I used to find them resting close to each other when I returned at night to our Brooklyn home, my three-year-old daughter sleeping quietly in the curled quarter-moon of her mother's form. In one instant, I ceased to be a husband. I ceased to be a father. I had failed to protect them, and they had been punished for my failings.

All of these images, all of these memories, like the

forged links of a chain, stretch back into the darkness. They should be put away, but the past is not so easily denied. Things left unfinished, things left unsaid, they all, in the end, come back to haunt us.

For this is the world, and the echo of worlds.

# Chapter One

Billy Purdue's knife bit deeper into my cheek, sending a trickle of blood down my face. His body was pressed hard against mine, his elbows pinning my arms to the wall, his legs tensed against my legs so that I couldn't go for his groin. His fingers tightened on my neck and I thought:

Billy Purdue. I should have known better . . .

Billy Purdue was poor, poor and dangerous with some bitterness and frustration added to spice up the pot. The threat of violence was always imminent with him. It hung around him like a cloud, obscuring his judgment and influencing the actions of others, so that when he stepped into a bar and took a drink, or picked up a pool cue for a game, then sooner or later, trouble would start. Billy Purdue didn't have to pick fights. Fights picked him.

It acted like a contagion, so that even if Billy himself managed to avoid conflict – he generally didn't seek it, but when he found it he rarely walked away – five would get you ten that he would have raised the testosterone level in the bar sufficiently to cause someone else to consider starting something. Billy Purdue could have provoked a fight at a conclave of cardinals just by looking

25

into the room. Whichever way you considered it, he was bad news.

So far, he hadn't killed anybody and nobody had managed to kill him. The longer a situation like that goes on, the more the odds are stacked in favour of a bad end, and Billy Purdue was a bad beginning looking for a worse end. I'd heard people describe him as an accident waiting to happen, but he was more than that. He was a constantly evolving disaster, like the long, slow death of a star. His was an ongoing descent into the maelstrom.

I didn't know a whole lot about Billy Purdue's past, not then. I knew that he'd always been in trouble with the law. He had a rap sheet that read like a catalogue entry for minor crimes, from disrupting school and petty larceny to DWD, receiving stolen goods, assault, trespassing, disorderly conduct, non-payment of child support . . . The list went on and on. He was an adopted child and had been through a succession of foster homes in his youth, each one keeping him for only as long as it took the foster parents to realise that Billy was more trouble than the money from social services was worth. That's the way some foster parents are: they treat the kids like a cash crop, like livestock or chickens, until they realise that if a chicken acts up you can cut its head off and eat it for Sunday dinner, but the options are more limited in the case of a delinquent child. There was evidence of neglect by many of Billy Purdue's foster parents, and suspicion of serious physical abuse in at least two cases.

Billy had found some kind of home with an old guy and his wife up in the north of the state, a couple who specialised in tough love. The guy had been through about twenty foster kids by the time Billy arrived and, when he got to know Billy a little, maybe he figured that this was one too many. But he'd tried to straighten Billy out and, for a time, Billy was happy, or as happy as he could ever be. Then he started to drift a little. He moved to Boston and fell in with Tony Celli's crew, until he stepped on the wrong toes and got parcelled back to Maine, where he met Rita Ferris, seven years his junior, and they married. They had a son together, but Billy was always the real child in the relationship.

He was now thirty-two and built like a bull, the muscles on his arms like huge hams, his hands thick and broad, the fingers almost swollen in their muscularity. He had small pig eyes and uneven teeth, and his breath smelt of malt liquor and sourdough bread. There was dirt under his nails and a raised rash on his neck, the heads white, where he had shaved himself with an old, worn blade.

I was given the opportunity to observe Billy Purdue from close quarters after I failed to put an arm-lock on him and he pushed me hard against the wall of his silver Airstream trailer, a run-down thirty-footer out by Scarborough Downs that stank of unwashed clothes, rotting food and stale seed. One of his hands was clasped hard around my neck as he forced me upwards, my toes barely touching the floor. The other held the short-bladed knife that had pierced my skin an inch beneath my left eye. I could feel the blood dripping from my chin.

The arm-lock probably hadn't been a good idea. In fact, on the scale of good ideas, it ranked somewhere between voting for Ross Perot and invading Russia in the winter. I would have had a better chance of successfully arm-locking the trailer itself; even with all of my strength pulling on it, Billy Purdue's arm had stayed as rigid and immobile as the statue of the poet in Longfellow Square.

While my mind was registering just how bad an idea it had been to go for the lock, Billy had pulled me forward and slapped me hard across the head, open palmed, with his enormous right hand, then pushed me up against the side wall of the trailer, his huge forearms holding my arms in place. My head was still ringing from the blow and my ear ached. I thought my eardrum had burst but then the pressure on my neck started to increase and I realised that I might not have to worry about my eardrum for much longer.

The knife twisted in his hand and I felt a fresh burst of pain. The blood was running freely now, spilling from my chin onto the collar of my white shirt. Billy's face was almost purple with rage and he was breathing heavily through clenched teeth, spittle erupting as he wheezed out.

He was completely focused on squeezing the life from me as I moved my right hand inside my jacket and felt the cool grip of the Smith & Wesson. I thought I was about to black out when I managed to wrench it free and move my arm enough to stick the muzzle into the soft flesh beneath Billy's jaw. The red light in his eyes flared briefly and then began to fade. The pressure on my neck eased, the knife slid out of the wound and I slumped to the floor. My throat ached as I pulled shallow, rattling breaths into my starved lungs. I kept the gun on Billy but he had turned away. Now that his tide of rage had begun to ebb he seemed unconcerned about the gun, and about me. He took a cigarette from a pack of Marlboros and lit up. He offered the pack to me. I shook my head and the pain in my ear started raging again. I decided to stop shaking my head.

'Why'd you put the lock on me?' asked Billy in an

aggrieved tone. He looked at me and there was genuine hurt in his eyes. 'You shouldn't have put the lock on me.'

The guy was certainly a character. I drew some more breaths, deeper now, and spoke. My voice sounded hoarse and my throat felt as if someone had rubbed grit into it. If Billy had been less of a child, I might have used the butt of the gun on him.

'You said you were going to get a baseball bat and beat the living shit out of me, as I recall,' I said.

'Hey, you were being rude,' he said and the red light seemed to glow again for a brief moment. I still had the gun pointed at him and he still didn't seem concerned. I wondered if he knew something about the gun that I didn't. Maybe the stench in the trailer was rotting the bullets as we spoke.

Rude. I was about to shake my head again when I remembered my ear and decided that it might be better, all things considered, to keep my head steady. I had come to visit Billy Purdue as a favour to Rita, now his ex-wife, who lived in a small apartment over on Locust Street in Portland with her two-year-old son, Donald. Rita had been granted her divorce six months before and since then Billy hadn't paid over a nickel of child support. I knew Rita's family when I was growing up in Scarborough. Her father had died in a botched bank raid in Bangor in '83 and her mother had struggled and failed to keep her family together. One brother was in jail, another was on the run from drug charges and Rita's elder sister was living in New York and had cut off all contact with her siblings.

Rita was slim and pretty and blonde but already the raw deal life had dealt her was taking its toll on her looks. Billy Purdue had never hit her or physically abused her but he was prone to black rages and had destroyed the two apartments in which they had lived during their marriage, setting fire to one after a three-day binge in South Portland. Rita had woken up just in time to get her then one-year-old son out, before hauling Billy's unconscious body from the apartment and setting off the alarm to evacuate the rest of the building. She filed for divorce the next day.

Now Billy marked time in his bullet-shaped trailer and lived a life that was on nodding terms with poverty. During the winter he did some lumber work, cutting Christmas trees or heading farther north to the timber company forests. The rest of the time he did what he could, which wasn't a lot. His trailer stood on a patch of land owned by Ronald Straydeer, a Penobscot Indian from Old Town who had settled in Scarborough after returning from Vietnam. Ronald was part of the K-9 corps during the war, leading army patrols down jungle trails with his German shepherd dog Elsa by his side. The dog could smell Vietcong on the wind, Ronald told me, even found freshwater once when a platoon ran dangerously low. When the Americans pulled out, Elsa was left behind as 'surplus equipment' for the South Vietnamese army. Ronald had a picture of her in his wallet, tongue lolling, a pair of dog tags hanging from her collar. He figured the Vietnamese ate her as soon as the Americans left, and he never got himself another dog. Eventually, he got Billy Purdue instead.

Billy knew his ex-wife wanted to move to the West Coast and start a new life and that she needed the money Billy owed her to do that. Billy didn't want her to go. He still believed that he could salvage their relationship, and a divorce and an order preventing him from going within one hundred feet of his ex-wife hadn't altered this belief.

I had agreed to approach him as a favour to Rita, after she called me and I met her back at her apartment. It was about the time that I told Billy Purdue that she wasn't coming back to him and that he had a legal obligation to pay her the money she was owed that Billy had gone for the baseball bat and things had fallen apart.

'I love her,' he said, puffing on his cigarette and sending twin columns of smoke shooting from his nostrils like the exhalations of a particularly mean-tempered bull. 'Who's gonna look out for her in San Francisco?'

I struggled to my feet and wiped some of the blood from my cheek. The sleeve of my jacket came back damp and stained. It was lucky my jacket was black, although the fact that I considered that lucky said a lot about the kind of day I was having.

'Billy, how can she and Donald survive if you don't pay her the money the judge told you to pay?' I replied. 'How's she going to get by without that? If you do care about her, then you have to pay her the money.'

He looked at me and then looked at his feet. His toe shifted on the filthy linoleum.

'Sorry I hurt you, man, but . . .' He reached behind his neck and scratched at his dark, unruly hair. 'You gonna go to the cops?'

If I was going to the cops, I wouldn't tell Billy Purdue. Billy's regret was about as genuine as Exxon's when the *Exxon Valdez* went down. Plus, if I went to the cops, Billy would be banged up and Rita still wouldn't get her money. But there was something in his tone when he asked about the cops, something that I should have picked up on but didn't. His black T-shirt was soaked with sweat, and there was mud caked at the cuffs of his pants. He had so much adrenaline coursing through his system, he made ants look calm. It should have told me that Billy wasn't concerned about the cops because of some assault beef, or unpaid child support. Hindsight: it's a wonderful thing.

'If you pay the cash, I'll let it go,' I said.

He shrugged. 'I ain't got much. Ain't got a thousand dollars.'

'Billy, you owe nearly two thousand dollars. I think you're missing the point here.'

Or maybe he wasn't. The trailer was a dump, he drove a Toyota with holes in the floor and he made one hundred, maybe one-fifty, each week hauling junk and lumber. If he had two thousand dollars, he'd be some-place else. He'd also be somebody else, because Billy Purdue was never going to have two thousand dollars to his name.

'I got five hundred,' he said eventually, but there was something new in his eyes as he said it, a kind of low cunning.

'Give it to me,' I replied.

Billy didn't move.

'Billy, if you don't pay me, the cops are going to come and lock you up until you do pay. If you're locked up, you can't make any cash to pay anyone and that looks like a vicious circle to me.'

He considered that for a time, then reached beneath the filthy sofa at the end of the trailer and produced a crumpled envelope. He turned his back to me and counted out five hundred-dollar bills, then replaced the envelope. He handed over the cash with a flourish, like a magician producing someone's wristwatch after a particularly impressive conjuring trick. The bills were brand new, consecutively numbered. From the look of the envelope, they had left a lot of friends behind.

'You go to the cash machine over at Fleet Bank, Billy?' I asked. It seemed unlikely. The only way Billy Purdue would get money from a cash machine was by breaking it out of the wall with a bulldozer.

'You tell her something from me,' he said. 'You tell her that maybe there's more where this came from, understand? You tell her that maybe I ain't such a loser no more. You hear me?' He smiled a knowing smile, the kind of smile someone really dumb shoots at you when he thinks he knows something that you don't. I figured that if Billy Purdue knew it, then it wasn't anything I'd want to share. I was wrong.

'I hear you, Billy. Tell me you're not still doing work for Tony Celli. Tell me that.'

His eyes retained that gleam of dim cunning, but the smile faltered a little. 'I don't know no Tony Celli.'

'Let me refresh your memory. Tall wiseguy out of Boston, calls himself Tony Clean. Started off running whores, now he wants to run the world. He's into drugs, porn, shylocking, anything there's a statute against, so his hopes of a good citizen award are currently so low they're off the scale.' I paused. 'You used to work for him, Billy. I'm asking if you still do.'

He twitched his head as if trying to dislodge water from his ear, then looked away. 'Y'know, I did stuff, maybe, sometimes, y'know, for Tony. Sure, sure I did. It beat hauling junk. But I ain't seen Tony in a long time. *Long* time.'

'You'd better be telling the truth, Billy, or else a lot of people are going to have some harsh words to say to you.'

He didn't respond and I didn't push it. As I took the bills from his hand he moved closer to me and I brought the gun up again. His face was an inch from mine, the muzzle of the gun against his chest.

'Why are you doing this?' he asked, and I could smell his breath and see the embers of that red glare flickering into life again. The smile was gone now. 'She can't afford no private dick.'

'It's a favour,' I said. 'I knew her family.'

I don't think he even heard me.

'How's she gonna pay you?' His head turned to one side as he considered his own question. Then: 'You fucking her?'

I held his gaze. 'No. Now back off.'

He stayed where he was, then scowled and moved slowly away. 'You better not be,' he said as I backed out of the trailer and into the dark December night.

The money should have alerted me, of course. There was no way Billy Purdue could have come by it honestly, and maybe I should have pushed him on it, but I was sore and just glad to be getting away from him.

My grandfather, who was himself once a policeman, until he found the tree with the strange fruit far to the north, used to tell a joke that was more than a joke.

A guy tells his buddy that he's heading off to a card game.

'But it's crooked,' protests his buddy.

'I know,' says the guy. 'But it's the only game in town.'

That joke, a dead man's joke, would come back to me in the days that followed, as things began to fall apart. Other things that my grandfather had told me came back to me as well, things that were far from jokes for him, although many had laughed at them. Within seventy-two hours of the deaths of Emily Watts and the men at Prouts Neck, Billy Purdue would be the only game in town, and an old man's fancies would flame into violent being.

I stopped off at the bank at Oak Hill and withdrew two hundred dollars from my account through the automatic teller. The cut beneath my eye had stopped bleeding, but I figured if I tried to clean away the encrusted blood it would start bleeding all over again. I called into Ron Archer's office on Forest Avenue, where he saw patients two nights a week, and he put in three stitches.

'What were you doing?' he asked, as he prepared to give me a shot of anaesthetic. I was going to ask him not to bother, but I figured he'd just think I was playing up to him. Dr Archer was sixty, a handsome, distinguished-looking man with fine silver hair and the kind of bedside manner which made lonely women want him to climb into bed beside them and conduct intimate and unnecessary medical examinations.

'Trying to get an eyelash out,' I said.

'Use eyedrops, you'll find they don't hurt as much and you'll still have an eye afterwards.'

He cleaned the wound with a swab, then leaned over me with the needle. I winced a little as he delivered the shot.

'That's the big, brave boy,' he muttered. 'If you don't cry, I'll give you an M & M when it's all over.'

'I'll bet you were the talk of med school with your doctor-patient wit.'

'Seriously, what happened?' he asked, as he began to stitch. 'Looks like someone stuck a sharp blade into this and you've got some bruising coming up on your neck.'

'I tried to put an arm-lock on Billy Purdue. It wasn't a big success.'

'Purdue? The crazy sonofabitch who nearly burned his wife and child to death?' Archer's eyebrows shot to the top of his forehead like a pair of startled crows. 'You must be even more postal than he is.' He began stitching. 'You know, as your doctor, I should advise you that if you keep doing dumb things like that you're likely to need more specialised treatment than I can offer.' He slipped the needle through once more then cut the thread. 'Although I imagine you'll find the transition to senility pretty smooth.'

He stepped back and examined his handiwork proudly. 'Wonderful,' he said with a sigh. 'A lovely piece of embroidery.'

'If I look in the mirror and find you've stitched a little heart on my face, I'll have to burn your surgery down.'

He wrapped the used needles carefully and dumped them in a protective container. 'Those stitches will dissolve in a few days,' he said. 'And don't play with them. I know what you kids are like.'

I left him laughing to himself and drove to Rita Ferris's apartment, close by the Cathedral of the Immaculate Conception and the Eastern Cemetery, where the two young fools Burrows and Blythe were buried. They died in an unneccessary naval combat between the American brig *Enterprise* and the British *Boxer*, of which they were the respective captains, off Monhegan Island during the War of 1812. They were interred in the Eastern Cemetery after a huge double funeral which paraded through the streets of Portland. Close by them is a marble memorial to Lieutenant Kervin Waters, who was injured in the same battle and took two agonising years to die. He was just sixteen when he was injured, and eighteen when he died. I don't know why I thought of them as I approached

Rita Ferris's apartment. Maybe, after meeting Billy Purdue, I was acutely conscious of young, wasted lives.

I turned into Locust, passing St Paul's Anglican on my right and the St Vincent de Paul thrift shop on my left. Rita Ferris's building was at the end of the street, across from the Kavanagh School. It was a run-down, white three-storey, with stone steps leading up to a door lined on one side with buzzers and apartment numbers and on the other with a row of unlocked mailboxes.

A black woman with a small girl, probably her daughter, opened the door of the building as I approached and looked at me with suspicion. There are comparatively few black people in Maine: in the early nineties, the state was still ninety-nine per cent white. It takes a long time to catch up on that kind of lead, so maybe she was right to be cautious.

I tried to give the woman my best smile to reassure her. 'I'm here to see Rita Ferris. She's expecting me.'

If anything, her features hardened even more. Her profile seemed to have been carved from ebony. 'She's expecting you, then ring the buzzer,' she said, as she closed the door in my face. I sighed and rang the buzzer. Rita Ferris answered, the door clicked and I headed up the stairs to the apartment.

Through the closed door of Rita's second floor apartment I could hear the sound of *Seinfeld* on the TV and an infant's soft cough. I knocked twice and the door opened. Rita stood aside to let me in, Donald, dressed in blue rompers, resting on her right hip. Her hair was tied back in a bun and she wore a shapeless blue sweatshirt over blue jeans with black sandals. The sweatshirt was stained with food and child spit. The apartment, small and neat despite the worn furniture, smelt of the child as well.

A woman stood a couple of feet behind Rita. As I watched, she placed a cardboard box filled with diapers, canned food and some fresh produce on the small couch. A plastic bag filled with second-hand clothes and one or two used children's toys lay on the floor, and I noticed that Rita was holding some bills in her hand. When she saw me, she blushed bright red, crumpled the cash and shoved it into the pocket of her denims.

The woman with her looked at me curiously and, I thought, hostilely. She was probably in her late sixties, with permed silver hair and large brown eyes. She wore a long wool coat, which looked expensive, with a silk sweater and tailored cotton pants beneath it. Gold twinkled discreetly at her ears, her wrists and around her neck.

Rita closed the door behind me and turned to the older woman.

'This is Mr Parker,' she said. 'He's been talking to Billy for me.' She slipped her hands into the back pockets of her denims and nodded her head shyly to the older woman. 'Mr Parker, this is Cheryl Lansing. She's a friend.'

I stretched out a hand in greeting. 'Pleased to meet you,' I said. After a moment's hesitation, Cheryl Lansing took my hand. Her grip was surprisingly strong.

'Likewise,' she said.

Rita sighed, and decided to elaborate a little on her introduction. 'Cheryl helps us out,' she explained. 'With food and clothes and stuff. We couldn't get by without her.'

Now it was the older woman's turn to look uncomfortable. She raised a hand in dismissal and said 'Hush, child' once or twice. Then she pulled her coat tightly around her, and kissed Rita lightly on the cheek before turning her attention to Donald. She ruffled his hair, and the infant smiled.

'I'll drop in on you again in a week or two,' she said to Rita.

Rita looked a little pained, as if she felt that she was somehow being rude to her guest. 'You sure you won't stay?' she asked.

Cheryl Lansing glanced at me, and smiled. 'No, thank you. I have quite a ways to go tonight, and I'm sure you and Mr Parker have a lot to talk about.'

With that, she nodded a goodbye to me, and left. I watched her as she walked down the stairs: social services, I guessed, maybe even someone from St Vincent de Paul. After all, they were only across the street. Rita seemed to guess what I was thinking.

'She's a friend, that's all,' she said softly. 'She knew Billy. She knew what he was like, what he's still like. Now, she tries to make sure that we're okay.'

She closed and locked the door, then took a look at my eye. 'Did Billy do that?'

'We had a misunderstanding.'

'I'm sorry. I really didn't think he'd try to hurt you.' There was genuine concern on her face and it made her seem pretty, despite the dark patches beneath her eyes and the frown lines that were working their way across her features like cracks through old plaster.

She sat down and balanced Donald on her knee. He was a large child, with huge blue eyes and a permanent expression of mild curiosity on his face. He smiled at me, raised a finger, then dropped it again and looked at his mother. She smiled down at him and he laughed, then hiccuped.

'Can I get you some coffee?' she asked. 'I don't have any beer, otherwise I'd offer you a drink.'

'Thanks, I don't drink. I just came by to give you this.'

I handed her the seven hundred dollars. She looked a little shocked, until Donald tried to take a fifty-dollar bill and stick it in his mouth.

'Uh-uh,' she said, moving the money beyond his reach. 'You're expensive enough to keep as it is.' She peeled away two fifties and offered them to me.

'Please, take it,' she said. 'For what happened. Please.'

I folded her hand over the money and pushed it gently back towards her.

'I don't want it,' I told her. 'Like I told you, it's a favour. I've had a talk with Billy. I think he has a little cash right now and maybe he might start coming around to his obligations. If he doesn't, it may be a matter for the cops.'

She nodded. 'He's not a bad person, Mr Parker. He's just confused, and he hurts a lot inside, but he loves Donnie more than anything in the world. I think he'd do just about anything to keep me from taking him away.'

That was what worried me. That red flame in Billy's eyes flared up a little too easily, and he had enough rage and resentment inside him to keep it burning for a long, long time.

I stood up to leave. On the floor beside my feet I saw one of Donald's toys, a red plastic truck with a yellow hood that squeaked when I picked it up and placed it on a chair. The noise briefly distracted Donald, but then his attention returned to me.

'I'll drop by next week, see how you are.' I reached out a finger to Donald and he gripped it in his little fist. I was suddenly seized by an image of my own daughter doing the same thing to me and a terrible sadness welled up inside me. Jennifer was dead now. She had died with my wife at the hands of a killer who believed that they were worthless enough to tear apart and display as a warning to others. He was dead as well, hunted to death in Louisiana, but it didn't make me feel any better. The books don't balance that way.

I gently removed my finger from Donald's grip and patted his head. Rita followed me to the door, Donald once again at her hip.

'Mr Parker . . .' she began.

'Bird,' I said, opening the door. 'That's what my friends call me.'

'Bird. Please stay.' With her free hand, she reached out and touched my cheek. 'Please. I'm putting Donald to bed now. I got no other way to thank you.'

I carefully removed her hand and kissed her palm. It smelt of hand cream and Donald.

'I'm sorry, I can't,' I said.

She looked a little disappointed. 'Why not? You don't think I'm pretty enough?'

I reached out and ran my fingers through her hair, and she leaned her head into my hand.

'It's not that,' I said. 'It's not that at all.'

She smiled then, a small smile but a smile nonetheless.

'Thank you,' she said and kissed me softly on the cheek. Our reverie was disturbed by Donald, whose face had darkened when I touched his mother and who now began to strike at me with his little hand.

'Hey!' said his mother. 'Stop that.' But still he struck, until I took my hand away from her.

'He's very protective of me,' she said. 'I think he thought you were trying to hurt me.' Donald buried his head in her breast, his thumb in his mouth, and looked out at me with suspicious eyes. Rita stood in the dark hallway as I went down the stairs, framed by the light of the apartment. She lifted Donald's hand to make him wave goodbye, and I waved back.

It was the last time I saw either of them alive.

# Chapter Two

I rose early the day after Rita Ferris spoke to me for the last time. The darkness outside was still and oppressive as I drove to the airport to catch the first commuter flight to New York. There were early reports on the news bulletin of a shooting incident at Scarborough, but the details were still sketchy.

From JFK, I caught a cab, the Van Wyck and Queens Boulevard dense with traffic, to Queens Boulevard and 51st. There was already a small crowd gathered at the New Calvary Cemetery: groups of police in uniform smoking and talking quietly at the gates; women in funeral black, their hair carefully arranged, their makeup delicately applied, nodding solemnly to one another; younger men, some barely out of their teens, uncomfortable in too-tight collars, with cheap, borrowed black ties knotted untidily at their necks, the knots too small, too thin. Some of the cops glanced at me and nodded, and I nodded back. I knew many of them by their last names, but not their first.

The hearse approached from Woodside, three black limousines following, and entered the cemetery. The waiting crowd moved behind in twos and threes as, slowly, we made our way towards the grave. I saw a mound of earth, green matting thrown across it, wreaths and other floral tributes ranged against it. There was a larger crowd here: more police in uniform, others in plain clothes, more women, a sprinkling of children. I spotted some deputy chiefs, an assistant chief, half a dozen captains and lieutenants, all come to pay their last respects to George Grunfeld, the old sergeant in the 30th Precinct, who had finally succumbed to his cancer two years before he was due to retire.

I knew him as a good man, a decent cop in the old mould who had the misfortune to work a precinct which had been plagued for years by rumours of shakedowns and corruption. The rumours eventually became complaints: guns and drugs, mainly cocaine, were routinely confiscated from dealers and resold; homes were raided illegally; threats were made. The precinct, over at 151st Street and Amsterdam Avenue, was investigated. In the end, thirty-three officers, who had been involved in two thousand prosecutions, were convicted, many for perjury. On top of the Dowd incident in the 75th – more arms and cocaine dealing, more payoffs – it made for bad coverage for the NYPD. I guessed that there was more to come: there were whispers that Midtown South was under the gun, the result of an ongoing deal with local prostitutes involving recreational sex for officers on duty.

Maybe that was why so many people had turned out for Grunfeld's funeral. He represented something good and fundamentally decent, and his passing was something to mourn. I was there for very personal reasons. My wife and child were taken from me in December 1996, while I was still a homicide detective in Brooklyn. The ferocity and brutality of the manner in which they were torn from this world, and the inability of the police to find their killer, caused a rift to develop between me and my fellow officers. The murders of Susan and Jennifer tainted me in their eyes, exposing the vulnerability of even a policeman and his family. They wanted to believe that I was the exception, that somehow, as a drunk, I had brought it on myself, so that they would not have to consider the alternative. In a way, they were right: I did bring it on myself, and on my family, but I had never forgiven them for forcing me to confront this alone.

I resigned from the NYPD barely one month after the deaths. Few people had tried to argue me out of my decision, but one of them was George Grunfeld. He met me one bright Sunday morning at John's on Second Avenue, close by the UN building. We ate pink grapefruit and English muffins while sitting in a booth by the window, Second Avenue quiet with little traffic and few pedestrians. Slowly, patiently, he listened to my reasons for leaving: my growing ostracisation, the pain of living in a city where everywhere reminded me of what I had lost; and my belief that maybe, just maybe, I could find the man who had taken everything I valued from me.

'Charlie,' he said (he never called me Bird), thick grey hair topping a full-moon face, eyes dark like craters, 'those are all good reasons, but if you quit then you're alone and there's a limit to the help anyone can give you. With the force, you still have family, so stay. You're a good cop. It's in your blood.'

'I can't, I'm sorry.'

'You leave, and maybe a lot of people will think you're running away. Some of them will probably be glad that you are, but they'll hate you for caving in.'

'Let them. Those ones aren't worth worrying about anyway.'

He sighed, sipped his coffee. 'You were never the easiest man to get along with, Charlie. You were too smart, too likely to go off the handle. We all have our demons, but you wore yours on your sleeve. I think you made people nervous, and if there's one thing a cop doesn't like, it's being made to feel nervous. It goes against the grain.'

'But I don't make you nervous?'

Grunfeld twisted his mug on the table with his little finger. I could tell that he was debating whether or not to tell me something. What he said when he spoke made me feel a little ashamed, and increased my admiration for him tenfold, if such a thing were possible with a man like this.

'I have cancer,' he said quietly. 'Lymphosarcoma. They tell me I'm going to get real sick in the next year, and I've got maybe another year after that.'

'I'm sorry,' I said, the words so small that they were quickly lost in the enormity of what he was facing.

Grunfeld raised a hand and gave a little shrug. 'I'd like to have more time. I got grandchildren. I'd like to watch them grow. But I've watched my own kids grow, and I feel for you because that's been taken away from you. Maybe it's the wrong thing to say, but I hope that you get a second chance at that. In the end, it's the best thing you get in this world.

'As for you making me nervous, the answer's no. I got death coming for me, Charlie, and that puts things in perspective. Every day I wake up and thank God that I'm still here and that the pain isn't too bad. And I go into the 30th, and I take my seat at the muster desk and watch people piss their lives away for nothing, and I envy them every minute they waste. Don't you go doing that, Charlie, because when you're angry and grieving and you're looking for someone to blame, the worst thing you can do is turn on yourself. And the next worst thing is to turn on someone else. That's where the structure, the routine can help. That's why I'm still at that desk, because otherwise I'd tear myself and my family to pieces.'

He finished his coffee and pushed the mug away. 'In the end, you'll do what you have to do, and nothing I can say will change that. You still drinking?'

I didn't resent the bluntness of the question, because it contained no deeper implication. 'I'm trying to quit,' I said.

'That's something, I guess.' He raised his hand for the check, then scribbled a number on a napkin. 'My home number. You need to talk, you give me a call.' He paid the check, shook my hand, and walked out into the sunlight. I never saw him again.

At the graveside, a figure raised its head and I felt its attention focus on me. Walter Cole gave a small nod in my direction, then returned his attention to the priest as he read from a leather-bound prayer-book. Somewhere, a woman cried softly and, in the dark skies above, a hidden jet roared its way through the clouds. And then there were only the low, muted tones of the priest, the soft rustle as the flag was folded, and the final, muffled echo as the first handfuls of earth hit the casket.

I stood by a willow as the mourners began to move away. And I watched, with bitterness, sorrow and regret, as Walter Cole walked away with them without saying a word to me. We had been close once: partners for a time, then friends and, of all those whose friendship I had lost, it was Walter that I missed the most. He was an educated man. He liked books, and movies that didn't star Steven Seagal or Jean-Claude Van Damme, and good food. He had been best man at my wedding, the box holding the rings clutched so hard in his hand that it had left deep ridges in his palm. I had played with his children. Susan and I had enjoyed dinners, the theatre and walks in the park, with Walter and his wife Lee. And I had sat with him for hours and hours, in cars and bars, in courtrooms and back rooms, and felt the deep, steady pulse of life throbbing beneath our feet.

I remembered one case in Brooklyn, when we were trailing a painter and decorator whom we believed had killed his wife and had somehow disposed of her remains. We were in a bad neighbourhood, just north east of Atlantic Avenue, and Walter smelt so much of cop they could have named a scent after him, but the guy didn't seem to suspect we were there. Maybe nobody told him. We weren't bothering the junkies or the pushers or the whores, and we were so obvious that we couldn't be undercover, so the local colour decided that the best thing to do would be to let us be and not to interfere in whatever we were planning.

Each morning, the guy would fill his van with paint cans and brushes and head off to work and we would follow him. Then, from a distance, we watched as he painted first a house and, a day or two later, the storefront on which he was working, before he dumped the empty cans and headed home.

It took a few days to figure out what he was doing. It was Walter who took a screwdriver and flipped open the lid, as the can lay with its fellows in a Dumpster. It took him two tries, because the paint had dried along the edge. That was what had alerted us, of course: the fact that the paint on the can was dry, not wet.

Inside the can was a hand, a woman's hand. There was

still a wedding ring on one of the fingers, and the stump had adhered to the paint at the bottom of the can, so the hand seemed to be emerging from the base. Two hours later we had our warrant and, when we kicked in the door of the painter's place, there were paint cans stacked almost to the ceiling in one corner of the bedroom, each containing a section of his wife's body. Some of them were packed tight with flesh. We found her head in a two-gallon can of white gloss.

That night, Walter had taken Lee out for dinner, and when they went home he held her the whole night through. He didn't make love to her, he said, he just held her, and she understood. I couldn't even remember what I did that night. That was the difference between us; at least, it *was*. I knew better now.

I had done things since then. I had killed in an effort to find, and avenge myself upon the killer of my family, the Travelling Man. Walter knew this, had even used it for his own ends, recognising that I would tear apart who-ever stood in my way. I think that, in some ways, it was a test, a test to see if I would realise his worst fears about me.

And I did.

I caught up with him near the cemetery gate, with the roar of the traffic in our ears, the city's version of the sound of the sea. Walter was talking with some captain who used to be with the 83rd: Emerson, who was now with Internal Affairs, which maybe explained the look he gave me as I approached. The murder of the paedophile pimp Johnny Friday was now a cold case, and I didn't think they'd ever get the guy who killed him. I knew, because I was the guy. I had killed him in a burst of black rage in the months following the deaths of Jennifer and Susan. By the end, I didn't care what Johnny Friday knew or didn't know. I just wanted to kill him for what he had helped to do to a hundred Susans, a thousand Jennifers. I regretted the manner of his death, like I regretted so much else, but regrets weren't going to bring him back. There had been rumours since then, but nothing would ever be proved. Still, Emerson had heard the rumours.

'Parker,' he nodded. 'Didn't think we'd see you back here.'

'Captain Emerson,' I replied. 'How are things in Infernal Affairs? Being kept busy, I imagine.'

'Always time for one more, Parker,' he said, but he didn't smile. He raised a hand to Walter and walked towards the gates, his back straight, his spine held together by the cords of righteousness.

Walter looked at his feet, his hands in his pockets, then raised his eyes to me. Retirement didn't seem to be doing him much good. He looked uncomfortable and pale, and there were burn marks and cuts where he had shaved that morning. I guessed that he was missing the force, and occasions like this just made him miss it more.

'Like the man said,' Walter muttered at last, 'I didn't think we'd see you back here.'

'I wanted to pay my respects to Grunfeld. He was a good man. How's Lee?'

'She's good.'

'And the kids.'

'They're good.' Walter and Emerson were proving to be tough crowds to play one after the other. 'Where are you now?' he asked, although his tone said he was only inquiring out of awkwardness.

'I'm back in Maine. It's peaceful. I haven't killed anyone in weeks.'

Walter's eyes remained cold. 'You should stay up

there. You get itchy, you can shoot a squirrel. I've got to go now.'

I nodded. 'Sure. Thanks for your time.'

He didn't reply and, as I watched him walk away, I felt a deep, humiliating grief, and I thought: they were right. I should not have come back, not even for a day.

I took the subway to Queensboro Plaza, where I changed onto the N train for Manhattan. As I sat opposite a man reading a Bible tract, the sound of the subway and the smell in the train set off a chain of memories, and I recalled something that had happened seven months before, in early May, just as the heat of the summer was beginning to tell. They had been dead for almost five months.

It was late, very late one Tuesday night. I was taking the subway from Café Con Leche at 81st and Amsterdam back to my apartment in the East Village. I must have dozed off for a time, because when I awoke the car was empty, and the light in the next car down was flickering on and off, black to yellow to black again.

There was a woman sitting in the next car, looking down at her hands, her hair obscuring her face. She wore dark pants and a red blouse. Her arms were spread, her palms raised upward, as if she were reading a newspaper, except that her hands were empty.

Her feet were bare and there was blood on the floor beneath them.

I stood and moved down the car until I came to the connecting door. I had no idea where we were, or what the next stop might be. I opened the door, felt the rush of heat from the tunnel, the taste of filth and smog in my mouth as I stepped across the gap and into the darkness of the next car.

The lights flickered on again, but the woman was gone, and there was no blood on the floor where she had been sitting only moments before. There were three other people in the car: an elderly black woman clutching four oversized plastic bags; a slim, neatly dressed white male wearing glasses, a briefcase on his knees; and a drunk with a ragged beard who lay across four seats, snoring. I was about to turn to the businessman when, ahead of me, I saw a shape in black and red briefly illuminated. It was the same woman, sitting in the same position – arms spread, palms up – as she had been when I first saw her. She was even occupying more or less the same seat, except one car farther down.

And I noticed that the flickering light seemed to have moved down with her, so that once again she was a figure briefly frozen by the faulty lighting. Beside me, the old woman looked up and smiled; and the executive with the briefcase gazed at me unblinking; and the drunk shifted on his seat and awoke, and his eyes were bright and knowing as he watched me.

I moved down the car, closer and closer to the door. Something about the woman was familiar, something in the way she held herself, something in the style of her hair. She did not move, did not look up, and I felt my gut tighten. Around her, the lights flickered, and then were gone. I stepped into the car, the last car before the driver, and I could smell the blood on the floor. I took one step, then another, and another, until my feet slid on something wet and I knew then who she was.

'Susan?' I whispered, but the darkness was silent, a silence broken only by the rushing of the wind in the subway, the rattle of the wheels on the tracks. As the tunnel lights flashed by, I saw her silhouetted against the far door, head down, her arms raised. The light flickered for a second, and I realised that she was not wearing a red blouse. She was not wearing anything. There was only blood: thick, dark blood. The light shone dimly through the skin that had been pulled back from her breasts and arrayed like a cloak over her outstretched arms. She lifted her head, and I saw a deep-red blur where her face had been, and the sockets of her eyes were empty and ruined.

And the brakes shrieked and the car rocked as the train approached the station. All light left the world and there was only a void until we burst into Houston Street, unnatural illumination flooding the car. The smell of blood and perfume lingered in the air, but she was gone.

That was the first time.

The waitress brought us dessert menus. I smiled at her. She smiled back. What's seldom is wonderful.

'She's got a fat ass,' remarked Angel, as she walked away. He was dressed in the traditional Angel garb of faded denims and wrinkled check shirt over a black T, and sneakers that were now a filthy mockery of their original white. A black leather jacket hung on the back of his chair.

'I wasn't looking at her ass,' I replied. 'She has a pretty face.'

'Then she's the acceptable face of fat-assed women.'

'Yeah,' chipped in Louis. 'She like the spokeswoman for the lard-asses, the one they wheel out when they want to look good on TV. Folks look at her and say, "Hey, maybe them lard-asses ain't so bad after all."'

As always, Louis looked as if he had been constructed as a deliberate riposte to his lover. He wore a black, single-breasted Armani suit and a snow-white dress shirt with the collar unbuttoned, the virgin white of the shirt in stark contrast to his own dark features and his shaven, ebony head.

We were sitting in J. G. Melon's at the corner of Third and 74th. I had not seen them in over two months, but these men, this diminutive, white ex-burglar and his enigmatic, soft-spoken boyfriend, were now the closest things to friends I had left. They had stood by me when Jennifer and Susan died and they had been with me in those last, terrible days in Louisiana as we drew nearer to a final confrontation with the Travelling Man. They were outsiders – perhaps that was one of the reasons for our closeness – and Louis in particular was a dangerous man, a hired killer now enjoying a murky, indefinite form of semi-retirement, but they were on the side of the angels, even if the angels were not entirely sure that this was a positive development.

Angel laughed loudly – 'Spokeswoman for the lard-asses,' he repeated to himself – and scanned the menu. I tossed a discarded French fry at him.

'Hey, Slim,' I said. 'Looks like you could skip a couple of sundaes every now and again. You tried to burgle somewhere now, you'd get stuck in the door. The only places you could break into would be ones with big windows.'

'Yeah, Angel,' said Louis, stone-faced. 'Maybe you could specialise in cathedrals, or the Met.'

'I can afford to fill out,' replied Angel, throwing him a glare.

'Man, you fill out any more, you be twins.'

'Funny, Louis,' shrugged Angel. 'She's still two tokens on the subway, if you see what I mean.'

'What does it matter to you anyway?' I said. 'You

don't have any right to pass comments about the opposite sex. You're gay. You don't *have* an opposite sex.'

'That's just prejudice, Bird.'

'Angel, it's not prejudice when someone points out that you're gay. It's just a statement of fact. It's prejudice when you start baiting the wider members of society.'

'Hey,' he said. 'Doesn't change the fact that if you're looking for company, maybe we can help.'

I stared at him, and raised an eyebrow. 'I think that's unlikely. I get that desperate, I'll blow my head off.'

He smiled. 'Well, you know, you got that look. I hear that website, "Womenbehindbars.com", is worth a visit.'

'Excuse me?' I replied. His smile widened so much you could have slotted toasting bread into it.

'Lot of women out there looking for a guy like you.' He turned his right hand into a little gun and fired his index finger at me with a movement of his thumb. It made him look like the cabaret act from gay hell.

'What exactly is "Womenbehindbars.com"?' I asked. I knew I was being baited, but I sensed something more from both Angel and Louis. You're up there alone, Bird, they seemed to say. You don't have too many people you can fall back on, and we can't look out for you from New York City. Sometimes, maybe even before you think you're really ready to do so, you have to reach out and find something that you can rely on. You have to try to find a foothold, otherwise you're going to fall and you're going to keep falling until it all goes dark.

Angel shrugged. 'Y'know, it's one of those internet dating services. Some places have more lonely women than others: San Francisco, New York, state prisons . . .'

'You're telling me there's a dating service for women in jail?'

He raised his hands wide. 'Sure there is. You know, cons have needs too. You just log on, take a look at the pictures, and pick your woman.'

'They're in jail, Angel,' I reminded him. 'It's not as if I can invite them out for dinner and a movie without committing a felony. Plus, I might have *put* them in jail. I'm not going to try to date anyone I jailed. It'd be too weird.'

'So date out of state,' said Angel. 'You declare anywhere from Yonkers to Lake Champlain a no-go zone, and the rest of the Union's your oyster.' He toasted me with his glass, then he and Louis exchanged a look, and I envied them that intimacy.

'Anyway, what are these women in for?' I asked, resigned by now to playing the role of straight man.

'The site don't say,' replied Angel. 'All it says is their ages, what they're looking for in a guy, and then it gives you a picture. One without numbers underneath it,' he added. 'Oh, and it tells you whether or not they're willing to relocate, although the answer's pretty obvious. I mean, they *are* in jail. Relocation's probably top of their list of priorities.'

'So what does it matter why they're in there?' asked Louis. I noticed that his eyes were watering. I was glad I was providing amusement for him. 'The ladies do the crime, do the time, then their debt to society is paid. Long as they ain't cut off a guy's dick and tied it to a helium balloon, you're home free.'

'Yeah,' said Angel. 'You just set some ground rules, and then dip your toes in the pool. Suppose she was a thief. Would you date a thief?'

'She'd steal from me.'

'A hooker?'

'Couldn't trust her.'

'That's a terrible thing to say.'

'Sorry. Maybe you could start a campaign.'

Angel shook his head in mock sorrow, then brightened. 'How about an assault case? Broken bottle, maybe a kitchen knife. Nothing too serious.'

'A kitchen knife and it's nothing too serious? What planet do you live on, Angel? Plastic cutlery world?'

'Okay then, a murderer.'

'Depends who she killed.'

'Her old man.'

'Why?'

'The fuck do I know why? You think I was wearing a wire? Do you date her or not?'

'No.'

'Shit, Bird, if you're going to be fussy you're never going to meet anyone.'

The waitress returned. 'Would you gentlemen like to order dessert?'

We all declined, Angel adding: 'Nah, I'm sweet enough as it is.'

'Cheesy enough, too,' said the waitress, and flashed me another grin. Angel reddened and Louis's mouth twitched in an approximation of a smile.

'Three coffees,' I said, and grinned back at her. 'You just earned yourself a substantial tip.'

After the meal, we took a walk in Central Park, stopping to rest by the statue of Alice on the mushroom by the model boat pond. There were no kids sailing their boats on the pond, although one or two couples sat huddled together by the bank, watched impassively by Louis. Angel hoisted himself up onto the mushroom, his legs dangling beside me, Alice in turn watching over him.

'How old are you?' I said.

'Young enough to appreciate this,' he replied. 'So how you doin'?'

'I'm surviving. I have good days and bad days.'

'How do you tell them apart?'

'On the good days, it doesn't rain.'

He smiled sympathetically. 'Thanksgiving must have been a blast.'

'I gave thanks that it didn't rain.'

'The house coming along?' I was completing the renovations on my grandfather's old house in Scarborough. I had already moved in, although there were some repairs still needed.

'Nearly finished. Roof just needs fixing, that's all.'

He stayed quiet for a time. 'We were only yanking your chain back in the restaurant,' he said at last. 'We know this is maybe not such a good time for you. It'll be the first anniversary soon, won't it?'

'Yeah, December twelfth.'

'You okay with that?'

'I'll visit the grave, have a mass said. I don't know how difficult it will be.' In truth, I was dreading the day. For some reason, it was important to me that the house be finished by then, that I be firmly established there. I wanted its stability, its links to a past that I remembered with happiness. I wanted a place that I could call home, and in which I could try to rebuild my life.

'Let us know the details. We'll come up.'

'I'd appreciate it.'

He nodded. 'Until then, you need to look out for yourself, you know what I mean? You spend too much time alone, you're likely to go crazy. You hear from Rachel?'

'No.' Rachel Wolfe and I had been lovers, for a time. She had come down to Louisiana to assist in the hunt for the Travelling Man, bringing with her a background in psychology and a love for me that I did not understand and that I was unable to fully return, not then. She had been hurt that summer, physically and emotionally. We had not spoken since the hospital, but I knew she was in Boston. I had even watched her cross the campus one day, her red hair glowing in the late morning light, but I could not bring myself to intrude upon her solitude, or her pain.

Angel stretched and changed the subject. 'Meet anyone interesting at the funeral?'

'Emerson.'

'The Internal Affairs schmuck? That must have been a joy.'

'Always a pleasure meeting Emerson. Guy just stopped short of measuring me up for a set of manacles and a suit with arrows on it. Walter Cole was there too.'

'He have anything to say to you?'

'Nothing good.'

'He's a righteous man, and they're the worst kind. Speaking of Emerson, you hear two-forty-seven Mulberry is coming up for sale? Louis and I are thinking of buying it, opening up a museum of law enforcement.'

Two-forty-seven Mulberry was the former site of the Ravenite Social Club, headquarters of John Gotti Sr before Sammy the Bull's testimony ensured that Gotti's business was transferred to a prison cell. His son John Junior had taken over the Gambino crime family, in the process earning himself an arrest and a reputation as the most inept godfather in mob history.

'John Junior, man,' said Angel, shaking his head. 'Just goes to show, the father's genes don't automatically pass intact to the eldest son.'

'I guess not,' I said. I glanced at my watch. 'I've got to go. I have a flight to catch.'

Louis turned and strolled back to us, the muscles on his slim, six-six frame obvious even beneath the suit and overcoat. 'Angel,' he said, 'I found you on a mushroom, I'd burn the crop. You makin' Alice look ill.'

'Uh-huh. Alice saw you coming for her, she'd figure she was going to be mugged. The White Rabbit you ain't.' I watched as Angel eased himself down, using his hands to arrest his slide. Then he raised them, the palms now lightly coated with grime, and approached Louis's immaculate form.

'Angel, you touch me, man, you be wavin' goodbye with a stump. I'm warnin' you . . .'

I walked past them and looked out over the park and the stillness of the pond. I had a growing feeling of unease for which I could find no cause, a sense that, while I was in New York, there were events happening elsewhere that somehow affected me.

And in the water of the pond, dark clouds gathered, forming and reforming, and birds flew through the shallows as if to drown. In the dimness of this reflected world, the bare trees sent searching branches down into the depths, like fingers digging deeper and deeper into a half-remembered past.

# Chapter Three

For me, the first sign that winter is coming has always been the change in the coloration of the paper birches. Their trunks, usually white or grey, turn yellow-green in the fall, blending into the riot of chimney red, burning gold and dying amber as the trees turn. I look at the birches and know that winter is on its way.

In November, the first heavy frosts arrive and the roads become treacherous, the blades of grass fragile as crystal, so that when you walk the ghosts of your footsteps trail behind like the ranks of lost souls. In the skeletal branches above, tree sparrows huddle together; cedar waxwings trapeze from tree to tree; and, at night, the hawk owls come, hunting for prey in the darkness. In Portland harbour, which never entirely freezes, there are mallards, and harlequin ducks, and eiders.

Even in the coldest weather, the harbour, the fields, the woods, all are alive. Blue jays fly, and brown winter wrens call; finches feed on birch seed. Tiny, unseen things crawl, hunt, live, die. Lacewings hibernate under the loose bark on the trees. Caddisfly larvae carry houses made from plant debris on their backs, and aphids huddle on the alders. Wood frogs sleep frozen beneath piles of leaf-mould, while beetles and back swimmers, newts and spotted salamanders, their tails thick with stored fat, all flicker in the icy waters above. There are carpenter ants, and snow fleas, and spiders, and black mourning cloak butterflies which flit across the snow like burnt paper. White-footed mice and woodland voles and pygmy shrews scurry through the slash, ever-wary of the foxes and weasels and the vicious, porcupine-hunting fishers that share the habitat. The snowshoe hare changes its coat to white in response to the diminishing daylight hours, the better to hide itself from its predators.

Because the predators never go away.

It is dark by four when winter comes, and lives are compressed to meet the new restrictions set by nature. People return to a lifestyle that would have been familiar in ways to their ancestors, to the earliest settlers who travelled along the great river valleys into the interior in search of timber and farmland. They move about less, remaining in the warmth of their homes. They complete their daily tasks before the darkness sets in. They think of seeding, of the welfare of animals, of children, of their old. When they do leave their houses they wrap up warm and keep their heads down, so that the wind does not blow the sand from the road into their eyes.

On the coldest nights, the branches of the trees crack in the darkness, the sky is lit by the passing angels of the aurora borealis, and young calves die.

There will be false thaws in January, more in February and March, but the trees will still be bare. The ground turns to mud in the warmth after the dawn, then freezes again at night; tracks become impassable by day, and dangerous by dark.

And still the people will gather in the warmth, and wait for the ice to crack in April.

At Old Orchard Beach, south of Portland, the amusement parks stand silent and empty. Most of the motels are closed, the AC vents covered with black plastic bags. The waves break grey and cold, and the wheels of the cars make a deep thudding sound as they cross the old railroad tracks on the main street. It has been this way for as long as I can remember, ever since I was a boy.

When the trees began to turn, before the paper birches changed from bone white to the colours of a beautiful decay, the grifter Saul Mann would pack his bags and prepare to leave Old Orchard for Florida.

'Winter is for rubes,' he would say, as he laid his clothes – his huckster's ties, his bright JCPenney jackets, his two-tone shoes – into a tan suitcase. Saul was a small, dapper man, with hair that was jet black for as long as I knew him and a small belly that strained only slightly the buttons of his vest. His features were relentlessly average, strangely unmemorable, as if he had expressly ordered them for that purpose. His manner was friendly and unthreatening, and he wasn't greedy, so he rarely, if ever, overstepped his own limits. He took people for tens and twenties, sometimes a fifty, occasionally, if he thought the mark could take the loss, for a couple of hundred. He generally worked alone although, if the con required it, he would hire a steerer to draw in the pigeons. Sometimes, if things were not going well, he would find work with the carnies and fleece folk with rigged games.

Saul had never married. 'A married man's a mark for his wife,' Saul would say. 'Never marry, unless she's richer than you, dumber than you, and prettier than you. Anything less than that, you're a pigeon.'

He was wrong, of course. I married a woman who took walks in the park with me, who made love to me and gave me a child, and whom I never really knew until she was gone. Saul Mann never had that joy: he was so worried about becoming a mark that life swindled him without him even noticing.

Beside Saul as he packed, in a second, smaller, black patent-leather bag, were the tools of the bunco, the armoury of the short-con artist. There was the wallet stuffed with twenty dollar bills which, on closer examination, revealed themselves to be one twenty dollar bill plus half of the *Maine Sunday Telegram* carefully cut up to resemble twenty dollar bills. The con artist 'finds' the wallet, asks the mark's advice on what to do with it, agrees to entrust it to his safekeeping until the legal obligation to hand it over is negated by the passage of time, encourages him to give over a one-hundred dollar deposit as a gesture of goodwill, just to be sure that he's not going to swindle anyone out of a share of the cash and, hey, the con man is up eighty bucks on the deal, minus the cost of a new wallet and another copy of the *Maine Sunday Telegram* for the next mish roll.

There were fake diamond rings, all glass and paste and metal so cheap it took a week to get the green stain from your finger, and bottle caps for the three-shell game. There were cards with more marks than Omaha Beach on D-Day. And there were other, more elaborate cons too: papers, heavy with official-looking seals, which promised the bearer the sun, the moon and the stars; lotteries guaranteeing the winner precisely zero percent of nothing; cheque-books for ten or twenty different accounts, each with barely enough in them to keep them active but still sufficiently open to enable cheques to be successfully written on them on a Friday night, giving them a whole two days of fiscal respectability before they bounced.

During the summer months, Saul Mann would trawl the resorts of the Maine coast looking for pigeons. He would arrive at Old Orchard Beach religiously on the third day of July, hire himself the cheapest room he could find, and work the beach for a week, maybe two at most, until his face started to become familiar. Then he would head up towards Bar Harbor and do the same, always moving, never staying too long, picking his marks carefully. And when he had amassed sufficient funds and the crowds began to peter away after Labor Day, when the trees slowly began to turn, Saul Mann would pack his bags and move to Florida to scam the winter tourists.

My grandfather didn't like him or, at least, he didn't trust him, and trust and like were the same thing in my grandfather's book. 'He asks you to lend him a dollar, don't do it,' he warned me, time and time again. 'You'll get back ten cents if you get back anything at all.'

But Saul never asked me for a thing. I met him first when I was doing summer work in the arcades at Old Orchard, taking money from little kids in exchange for soft toys whose eyes were held in place by half-inch-long pins and whose limbs were connected to their torso by the will of God. Saul Mann told me about the carny, about the joint scams: the basketball shoot with the over-inflated ball and the too-small ring; the balloon darts with the soft balloons; the shooting gallery with the skewed sights. I watched him work the crowds, and I learned as I watched. He targeted the elderly, the greedy, the desperate, the ones who were so uncertain of themselves that they would trust another man's judgment above their own. He sometimes went for the dumb ones, but he knew that the dumb ones could turn mean, or that maybe they wouldn't have enough cash to make the scam worthwhile, or that they sometimes possessed a low cunning which made them naturally distrustful.

Better still were the ones who thought they were smart, the ones who had good jobs in medium-sized towns, who believed that they could never be taken in by a grifter. They were the prime targets, and Saul relished them when they came. He died in 1994, in a retirement home in Florida, among the people he used to take as his marks, and he probably swindled them at canasta until the last breath left his body, until God reached down and showed him that, in the end, everybody is a mark.

Here is what Saul Mann told me.

Never give the suckers a break: they'll run if you do. Never have pity: pity is the mother of charity, and charity is giving money away, and a grifter never gives money away. And never force them to do anything, because the best scams of all are the ones where they come to you.

Lay the bait, wait, and they will always come to you.

The snows came early that December to Greenville and Beaver Cove and Dark Hollow and the other towns on the very rim of the great northern wilderness. The first flurries fell and people looked to the skies before hurrying on, a new quickness in their steps, spurred on by the cold they could already feel in their bones. Fires were lit, and children were wrapped up warm in bright red scarves and mittens coloured like rainbows, and warnings were given about staying out late, about hurrying home before darkness fell, and stories were told in school yards about little children who strayed from the path and were found cold and dead when the thaws came.

And in the woods, among the maples and birches and oaks, through the spruce and hemlock and white pine, something moved. It walked slowly and deliberately. It knew these woods, had known them for a long, long time. Every footfall was surely placed, every fallen tree anticipated, every ancient stone wall, long overtaken by the renewed forests and lost amid the undergrowth, was a place to rest, to draw breath, before moving on.

In the winter blackness, it moved with a new purpose. Something that had been lost had now been found again. Something unknown had been revealed, like a veil drawn back by the hand of God. It passed by the derelict remains of an old farmhouse, its roof long collapsed, its walls now no more than a shelter for mice. It reached the crest of a hill and moved along its edge, the moon bright above it, the trees whispering in the darkness.

And it devoured the stars as it went.

# Chapter Four

I had been back in Scarborough for almost three months, back in the house where I had spent my teenage years after my father died and that my grandfather had left to me in his will. In the East Village, where I lived for some time after my wife and child died, the old lady who owned my rent-controlled apartment had ushered me out with a smile on her face as she calculated the potential increase she could apply to the next tenant. She was a seventy-two-year-old Italian-American who had lost her husband in Korea, and she was usually about as friendly as a hungry rat. Angel suggested that her husband had probably handed himself over to the enemy to avoid being sent home to her again.

The Scarborough house was where my mother had been born and where my grandparents still lived at the time of my father's death. After three hundred years, Scarborough was already changing when I arrived at the end of the seventies. Economic prosperity meant that it was becoming a satellite town for Portland and, although some of the older residents still held on to their land, land which had been in some families for generations, the developers were paying premium prices and more and more people were selling up. But Scarborough was still the kind of community where you knew your mailman and who his family was and he, in turn, knew the same about you.

From my grandfather's house on Spring Street, I could cycle north into Portland or south to Higgins Beach, Ferry Beach, Western Beach or Scarborough Beach itself, or down to the head at Prouts Neck to look out on Bluff Island and Stratton Island and the Atlantic Ocean.

Prouts Neck is a small point of land that protrudes into Saco Bay about twelve miles south of Portland itself. It was where the artist Winslow Homer set up house near the end of the nineteenth century. His family bought up most of the land on the Neck and Winslow vetted his prospective neighbours carefully since, by and large, he wanted to be left to his own devices. The folks out on the Neck are still that way. There has been a fancy yacht club there since 1926 and a private beach club with membership limited to those who live or rent summer homes in the area and who belong to the Prouts Neck Association. Scarborough Beach remains public and free and there's public access to Ferry Beach, close by the Black Point Inn on the Neck. Since it was beside Ferry Beach that Chester Nash, Paulie Block and six other men had lost their lives, the Neckers were going to have a lot to talk about when they returned in the summer.

In the old house, the past hung in the air like motes of dust waiting to be illuminated by the sharp rays of memory. It was there, surrounded by remembrances of a happier youth, that I hoped to set about putting old ghosts to rest: the ghosts of my wife and child, who had haunted me for so long but had maybe now achieved a kind of peace, a peace not yet mirrored in my own soul; of my father; of my mother, who had taken me away from the city in an effort to find peace for both of us; of Rachel, who now seemed lost to me; and of my grandfather, who had taught me about duty and humanity and the importance of making enemies of whom a man could be proud.

I had moved out of the Inn on St John at Congress Street in Portland as soon as most of the house had been made habitable. At night, the wind made the plastic on the roof slap like the beating of dark, leathery wings. The final job left to do was the slating, which was why I was sitting on my porch with a cup of coffee and the *New York Times* at 9 a.m. the next morning, waiting for Roger Simms. Roger was fifty, a straight-backed man with long, thin muscles and a face the colour of rosewood. He could do just about anything that involved a hammer, a saw and a natural craftsman's ability to bring order out of the chaos of nature and neglect.

He arrived right on time, his aged Nissan belching blue fumes which tainted the air behind like nicotine on a lung. He stepped out of the car wearing paint-splattered, old man's jeans, a denim shirt and a blue sweater that was little more than an assortment of holes held together by yarn. A pair of brown cowhide work gloves hung from one of the ass pockets of his jeans and a black watch cap was pulled down over his ears. From beneath it, strands of dark hair hung like the legs of a hermit crab. A cigarette dangled between his lips, a gravity-defying pillar of ash forming at the tip.

I gave him a mug of coffee and he drank it quickly while examining the roof critically, as if seeing it for the first time. He had been up there about three times already, checking the rafters and the roof supports and measuring the angles, so I didn't think it was likely to hold any surprises for him. He thanked me for the coffee and handed back the mug. 'Thanks' was the first word he had said to me since he arrived; Roger was a great worker but the amount of air he wasted on unnecessary small talk wouldn't have saved a gnat's life.

It seemed to me that, by putting the roof on the old house, I was at last confirming my place in it. Stripped of its old broken slates and left with only the plastic to shield it from the elements, it had been reduced to a lifeless shell, the memories of the past lives it held within its walls reduced to dormancy as if to protect them from the ravages of the natural world. With its roof restored, the house would be warm and enclosed once again and I could become one with its past by guaranteeing its future and my presence in it.

We had already laid down straps in preparation for the shingles, using pieces of two-by-four cut lengthwise in half and oiled with wood preservative. Now, with the air crisp and cold and no promise of rain in the sky, we began the process of shingling. There was something in the placing of shingles, its rhythms and routines, that made it an almost meditative exercise. Travelling methodically across the face of the roof, I reached for a shingle, placed it on the one below, adjusted its exposure using a notch on the handle of my hammer, flipped the hammer, nailed down the shingle, reached for another and began the process again. I found a kind of peace in it and the morning passed quickly. I decided not to share my meditative speculations with Roger. Somehow, those who do jobs like roofing for a living tend to resent the musings of amateurs on the nature of the task. Roger would probably have thrown his hammer at me.

We worked for four hours, each of us resting when the

mood took him, until I climbed carefully down and told Roger that I was heading up to the Seng Thai on Congress to get us some food. He grunted something that I took as assent and I started up the Mustang and drove towards South Portland. As usual, there were plenty of cars on Maine Mall Road, people nosing about in Filene's or heading for the movies, eating in the Old Country Buffet or sizing up the motels on the strip. I drove past the airport, along Johnson and, finally, onto Congress. I parked in the lot behind the Inn on St John between a Pinto and a Fiat, then headed down a block, bought the food and dumped it on the backseat of the car.

Edgar still had a crate of my stuff behind the reception desk at the inn and I figured I might as well pick it up while I was in the area. I opened the door and entered the ornate, old-style lobby, with its ancient radio and its neat piles of tourist brochures. Edgar wasn't there but some other guy I didn't recognise hauled the crate out, gave me a smile and then went back to counting receipts. I left him to it.

When I stepped back into the lot, I saw that someone had boxed me in. A huge black Cadillac Coupe de Ville, forty years old and virtually an antique, was parked behind the Mustang, leaving me with no way to get out. The car had whitewall tyres and restored tan upholstery, and the distinctive pontoon bumpers at the front were shiny and intact. A map of Maine lay on the backseat and it had Massachusetts plates but, apart from that, there was nothing about the car to identify its owner. It could have come straight from a museum exhibit.

I placed the crate in the trunk of the Mustang and headed back into the inn, but the guy on the desk said

he'd never seen the Cadillac before. He offered to have it
towed but I decided to try to track down the owner first. I
asked in Pizza Villa across the street but they didn't know
anything about it either. I even tried the Dunkin' Donuts
and the Sportsman's Bar until, still unsuccessful, I re-
crossed the street and slapped the roof of the Cadillac in
frustration.

'Nice car,' said a voice, as the echo of the slap faded.
The voice was high, almost girlish, the words drawn out
with what sounded more like malice than admiration, the
sibilance in the first word almost menacing.

At the entrance to the inn's back lot, a man was leaning
against the wall. He was short and squat, probably no
more than five-five and maybe two hundred and thirty
pounds. He wore a tan raincoat, belted at the front, with
brown pants and a pair of brown brogues.

He had a face from a horror movie.

His head was completely bald, with a rounded crown
that ran into wrinkles of fat at the back. The head seemed
to grow wider instead of narrower from the temples to
the mouth, before it lost itself in his shoulders. He had no
neck, or at least nothing that was worthy of the name. His
face was deathly pale, apart from his long, thick, red lips,
which were stretched into a rictus of a grin. He had wide
dark nostrils, set in a flattened snout of a nose, and his eyes
were so grey as to be almost colourless, the pupils like
black pinpoints at their centre, tiny dark worlds in a cold,
hostile universe.

He pulled himself from the wall and advanced
slowly and steadily, and as he did so I caught the
smell. It was indistinct and masked by some cheap
cologne, but it caused me to hold my breath and take a
step back from him nonetheless. It was the smell of

earth and blood, the stench of rotting meat and stale animal fear that hangs in a slaughterhouse at the end of a long day's butchering.

'Nice car,' he repeated, and a fat white hand emerged from one of his pockets, the fingers like thick, pale slugs that had spent too long in dark places. He caressed the roof of the Mustang appreciatively, and it seemed as if the paint would corrode spontaneously beneath his fingers. It was the touch a child molester would give a kid in a playground when its mother's back was turned. For some reason, I felt the urge to push him away but I was stopped by a stronger instinct that told me not to touch him. I couldn't have explained why, but something foul appeared to emanate from him that discouraged any contact. To touch him, it seemed, would be to blight oneself, to risk contamination or contagion.

But it was more than that. He exuded a sense of extreme lethality, a capacity for inflicting hurt and pain that was so profound as to be almost sexual. It seeped from his pores and flowed viscously over his skin, seeming almost to drip visibly from the tips of his fingers and the end of his ugly, brutish nose. Despite the cold, tiny beads of perspiration glittered on his forehead and upper lip, spangling his soft features with moisture. Touch him, I sensed, and your fingers would sink into his flesh, the skin yielding clammily to the pressure as it sucked you in.

And then he would kill you, because that was what he did. I was certain of it.

'Your car?' he asked. Those grey eyes glittered coldly and the tip of a pink tongue appeared between his lips, like a snake testing the air.

'Yes, it's my car,' I replied. 'That your Cadillac?'

He didn't seem to notice the question, or decided not to

notice it. Instead, he passed another long caressing movement along the roof of the Mustang.

'Good car, the Mustang,' he said, nodding to himself, and again there was that intense sibilance on the S sound, like water dropped on a hot stove. 'Me and the Mustang, we got a lot in common.'

He moved closer to me, as if to share some deep, darkly funny secret. I could smell his breath on me, sweet and overripe as late-summer fruit.

'We both went to hell after nineteen seventy.'

And then he laughed, a low hissing sound like gas escaping from a corpse. 'Better take care of that car, make sure nothing happens to it,' he said. 'A man's got to look out for what's his. He should take care of his own business, and keep his nose out of other people's.' He walked around the back of the car before entering the Cadillac, so I had to turn to watch him.

'Be seeing you again, Mr Parker,' he said. Then the Caddy started with a low, confident rumble and the car made an illegal left onto Congress and headed in the direction of downtown Portland.

# Chapter Five

Roger didn't look too happy about being kept waiting for his food, because the permanent frown lines on his forehead had dipped by about half an inch by the time I got back.

'You were a coon's age,' he muttered as he took the food. It was one of the longest sentences I had ever heard him speak.

I picked at my chicken and rice, but my appetite was gone. I was bothered by the appearance of the fat, bald man on Congress, although I couldn't tell why, exactly, apart from the fact that he knew my name and made my skin crawl.

Roger and I returned to the roof, a chill wind now forcing the pace a little so that we had finished by mid afternoon just as the light was starting to fade. I paid Roger and he nodded his thanks, then headed back to town. My fingers were numb from working on the roof but the job had to be done before the heavy snows came, or else I'd be living in an ice castle. I took a hot shower to remove the grit from my hair and fingers, and was just making a pot of coffee when I heard a car pull up outside.

For a moment, I didn't recognise her as she stepped from the Honda Civic. She had grown since I last saw her, and her hair was lighter, tinted with some kind of colouring. She had a woman's body, large-breasted and generous at the hips. I felt a little embarrassed noticing the changes in her. After all, Ellen Cole was barely into her twenties, and Walter Cole's daughter to boot.

'Ellen?' I stepped from the porch and opened my arms to her as she hugged me.

'It's good to see you, Bird,' she said softly, and I hugged her tightly in response. Ellen Cole: I had watched her grow up. I could remember dancing with her at my wedding, the shy grin she threw back at her younger sister Lauren, her tongue stuck out teasingly between her lips at Susan in her bridal gown. I remembered, too, sitting on the steps of Walter's porch with a beer, and Ellen beside me, her hands clasped around her knees, as I tried to explain why boys sometimes behaved like assholes to even the most beautiful of girls. I liked to think that was one area in which my expertise was beyond doubt.

She had been a friend to Susan, and Jennifer had loved her. My daughter never cried out when Susan and I left her for an evening, as long as Ellen was there to baby-sit her. The child would sit in the older girl's arms, toying with her fingers, eventually falling asleep with her head on her lap. Ellen had about her a kind of strength that found its roots in an immense store of kindness and compassion, a strength that inspired trust in those smaller and weaker than she.

Two days after Susan and Jennifer had died, I discovered her waiting for me alone at the funeral home as I arrived to make arrangements for the bodies. Others had offered to accompany me, but I didn't want them there. I think I was already retreating into my own, strange world of loss at that point. I didn't know how long she had been waiting for me there, her car parked in the lot, but she came to me, and she held me for a long, long time, and then she stood beside me as I looked at pictures of caskets and limousines, never letting go of my hand. In her eyes, I saw the depths of my own pain reflected and I knew that, like me, she felt the loss of Jennifer as an absence in her arms, and the loss of Susan as a silence in her heart.

And when we left, the strangest thing happened. I sat with her in her car and, for the first time in days, I cried. That deep, still, placid thing inside Ellen drew the pain and hurt and grief from me, like the lancing of a wound. She held me again and, for a time, the clouds cleared, and I was able to go on.

Behind Ellen, a young man stepped from the passenger side of the car. He had dark skin and long black hair that hung lankly to his shoulders. His dress code was slacker chic, apart from his Zamberlain hiking boots: jeans, T-shirt loose over the top of his jeans, denim shirt hanging open over everything else. He shivered a little as he watched me with suspicious eyes.

'This is Ricky,' said Ellen. '*Riccardo*,' she added, with a vaguely Spanish inflection on the word. 'Ricky, come meet Bird.'

He shook hands firmly, then put one arm protectively around Ellen's shoulders. It seemed to me that Ricky was territorial and insecure, a bad combination. I kept an eye on him as we went into the house, just in case he decided to make his mark by pissing against my door.

We sat in my kitchen and drank coffee from big blue mugs. Ricky didn't say a whole lot, not even 'Thanks'. I wondered if he'd ever met Roger. Put the two of them together and you'd have the world's shortest conversation.

'What are you doing here?' I asked Ellen.

She shrugged. 'We're heading north. I've never been far north before. We're going to make for Moosehead Lake, see Mount Katahdin, whatever. Maybe we'll rent some ski-doos.'

Ricky stood up and asked where the john was. I directed him and he sloped off, slouching from side to side as he walked, like a man with his feet in parallel ditches.

'Where did you find the Latin lover?' I asked.

'He's a psychology major,' she replied.

'Really?' I tried to keep the cynicism out of my voice. Maybe Ricky was trying to kill two birds with one stone by taking psychology so he could analyse himself.

'He's really nice, Bird. He's just a little shy with strangers.'

'You make him sound like a dog.'

She stuck her tongue out at me in response.

'School finished?'

She dodged the question. 'I have some study time coming.'

'Hmm. What are you planning on studying? Biology?'

'Ha ha.' She didn't smile. I guessed that Ricky had pushed thoughts of semester exams from her mind.

'How's your mom?'

'Good.'

She stayed silent for a moment.

'She worries about you and Dad. He told her you were at the funeral in Queens yesterday, but that you didn't have much to say to each other. I think she feels that you should sort out whatever happened between you.'

'It's not that easy.'

She nodded. 'I've heard them talking,' she said softly. 'Is what he says about you true?'

'Some of it, yes.'

She bit down on her lip, then seemed to reach a decision. 'You should talk to him. You were his friend, and he doesn't have many of those.'

'Most of us don't,' I replied. 'And I've tried talking to him, Ellen, but he's judged me and found me wanting. Your father's a good man, but not everything good fits his definition.'

Ricky came back into the room and the conversation sort of died. I offered them my bed for the night but was kind of glad when Ellen declined. I'd probably never be able to sleep there again if I had visions of Ricky humping in it. They decided to spend the night in Portland instead of Augusta, with the intention of heading straight for the Great North Woods the next morning. I suggested the Inn on St John, and told them to say that I had sent them. Apart from that, I left them to it, although I was pretty sure I didn't want to know what 'it' was. Somehow, I didn't imagine Walter Cole would want to know either.

After they had gone, I got in the car and drove back into Portland to work out in the Bay Club at One City Center. Slating the roof had been exercise in itself, but I was trying to work off the little handles of fat that were clinging to my sides like determined children. I spent forty-five minutes doing peripheral hard-flow circuits, constantly alternating leg and upper-body exercises until my heart was pounding and my shirt was soaked with sweat. When I had finished, I showered and looked at the little fat deposits in the mirror to see if they were getting any smaller. I was almost thirty-five, I had grey hairs invading the blackness of my hair, and I was one hundred and eighty pounds of insecurity in a five-eleven frame. I needed to get a life – that, or liposuction.

The white Christmas lights glowed in the trees of the Old Port as I left the Bay Club, so that, from a distance, they seemed to be burning. I walked to Exchange to pick up some books in Allen Scott's, then continued down to Java Joe's to nurse a large one and read the newspapers. I rustled through the *Village Voice* to find out Dan Savage's latest views on sex with eggs or urinary games. This week, Dan was dealing with a guy who said he wasn't homosexual, he just liked having sex with men. Dan Savage didn't seem to see the difference. Frankly, neither did I. I tried to imagine what Angel would have said to the guy and then figured even the *Voice* wouldn't print what Angel would have said to him.

It had started to rain and wet streaks marked the windows like cuts on crystal and fell on the kids heading for the bars in the Old Port. I watched the rain for a time, then returned to the *Voice*. As I did so, I was conscious of a figure moving towards me and a rank smell in my nostrils. My skin prickled with unease.

'Can I ask you a question?' said a distinctive voice. I looked up and started. The same coldly amused eyes watched me from the doughlike face, rain glistening on the bald head. The mingled scents of blood and cologne were stronger now, and I drew back a little from the table.

'Do you want to find God?' he continued, with the kind of concerned look that doctors give smokers when they start patting their pockets for cigarettes in the waiting room. In his pale hand, he held a crumpled Bible pamphlet, a crude pen drawing of a child and its mother visible on one side.

I looked at him in puzzlement, then my face cleared. I thought for a moment that he might be some kind of Jesus freak, although if he was then Jesus was scraping the bottom of the barrel for recruits. 'When God wants me, he'll know where to find me,' I replied and went back to reading the *Voice*, my eyes on the page but my attention riveted to the man before me.

'How do you know that this isn't God looking for you now?' he said, as he sat down across from me.

I realised that I should have kept my mouth shut. If he was a religious nut, then talking to him would only encourage him. These types act like monks who've just been given a weekend off from their vows of silence. Except this guy didn't seem like the religious kind, and I got the feeling that there was a subtext to his questions which I hadn't quite grasped.

'I'd always hoped He'd be taller,' I told him.

'There's a change coming,' said the bald man. His eyes had a kind of intense look to them now. 'There'll be no place for sinners, for divorcees, for fornicators, for sodomites, for women who don't respect their husbands.'

'I think you've just covered some of my hobbies, and all of my friends,' I said, folding the paper and taking a last, regretful sip of my coffee. It just wasn't my day. 'Wherever they end up sounds good to me too.'

He watched me carefully, like a snake preparing to strike if it saw an opening. 'No place for a man who comes between another man and his wife, or his little boy.' There was audible menace in his words now. He smiled and I could see his teeth, small and yellow like the fangs of a rodent. 'I'm looking for someone, Mr Parker. I think you may be able to help me find him.' His obscenely soft red lips stretched so far that I thought they might burst and shower me with blood.

'Who are you?' I asked.

'It doesn't matter who I am.'

I looked around the coffee house. The kid behind the counter was distracted by a girl at the window table and there was no one else sitting down here at the rear of the premises.

'I'm looking for Billy Purdue,' he continued. 'I was hoping you might know where he is.'

'What do you want with him?'

'He has something that belongs to me. I want to claim it.'

'I'm sorry, I don't know any Billy Purdue.'

'I think you're telling lies, Mr Parker.' The tone and volume of his voice didn't change, but the threat of danger it contained rose a notch.

I flipped back my jacket to reveal the butt of my gun.

'Mister, I think you have the wrong person,' I said. 'Now I'm going to leave and if you get up before I've gone, I'll use this gun on your head. You understand me?'

The smile didn't flicker, but his eyes were now dead. 'I understand,' he said, and again there was that terrible sibilance in his voice. 'I don't think you can be of help to me after all.'

'Don't let me see you again,' I said.

He nodded to himself. 'Oh, you won't see me,' he replied, and this time the threat was explicit. I kept him in sight until I reached the door and watched as he took the pamphlet and set it alight with a brass Zippo. All the time, his eyes never left my face.

★   ★   ★

I retrieved my car from the parking garage at Temple and took a ride by Rita Ferris's place, but the lights were out and there was no reply when I tried the buzzer. Then I drove from Portland to Scarborough Downs until I came to Ronald Straydeer's place close by the junction of Payne Road and Two Rod Road. I pulled in beside Billy Purdue's silver trailer and knocked on the door, but the trailer was quiet and no lights burned inside. I peered in the window, cupping my fingers at the glass, but the place still looked a mess. Billy's car stood to the right of the trailer. The hood was cold.

I heard a noise from behind me and turned, half expecting to see that strange head erupting like a white sore from its tan raincoat. Instead, there was only Ronald Straydeer, dressed in black denims, sandals and a Sea Dogs T-shirt, his short dark hair hidden by a white baseball cap decorated with a red lobster. He held an AK-47 in his hands.

'I thought you were someone else,' he said, looking at the gun with embarrassment.

'Like who? The Vietcong?' I knew that Ronald swore by his AK. A lot of men who had served in Vietnam did likewise. Ronald once told me that their standard-issue rifle, the MI, used to jam in the rains of Southeast Asia, and they would routinely replace them with AK-47s stolen from the bodies of Vietcong. Ronald's gun looked old enough to be a war souvenir, which it probably was.

Ronald shrugged. 'T'ain't loaded anyhow.'

'I'm looking for Billy. Have you seen him?'

He shook his head. 'Not since yesterday. He hasn't been around.' He looked unhappy, as if he wanted to say more.

'Has anyone else been looking for him?'

'I don't know. Maybe. I thought I saw someone last night looking in the trailer, but I could be mistaken. I didn't have my glasses on.'

'You're getting old,' I said.

'Yuh, he could have been old,' replied Ronald, seemingly mishearing me.

'What did you say?'

But he had already lost interest. 'I ever tell you about my dog?' he began, and I figured that Ronald had told me just about everything I might find useful.

'Yeah, Ronald,' I said, as I walked back to the car. 'Maybe we'll talk about him again, another time.'

'You don't mean that, Charlie Parker,' he said, but he smiled as he spoke.

'You're right,' I smiled back, 'I don't.'


That night, cold rain fell like nails on my newly-shingled roof. It didn't leak, not even from the parts that I had done. I felt a deep satisfaction as I drifted off to sleep, the wind rattling the windows and causing the boards of the house to creak and settle. I had spent many years falling asleep to the sounds of those boards, to the gentle murmur of my mother's voice in the living room beyond, to the rhythmic tapping of my grandfather's pipe on the porch rail. There was still a mark on the rail, an ochre stain of tobacco and worn wood. I had not painted over it, a sentimental gesture that surprised me.

I can't recall why I awoke, but some deep sense of disquiet had penetrated through my REM sleep and drawn me back into the darkness of night. The rain had stopped and the house seemed peaceful, but the hairs on the back of my neck were almost rigid and my perceptions were immediately razor-sharp, the mugginess of sleep dispelled by the instinctive knowledge that some danger was near.

I slipped silently from my bed and pulled on a pair of jeans. My Smith & Wesson lay in its holster by my bed. I removed the gun and thumbed the safety. The bedroom door was open, the way I had left it. I pulled it a little farther, the well-oiled hinges moving silently, and carefully placed a foot on the bare boards of the hallway.

My foot hit something soft and wet and I drew it back immediately. The moonlight shone through the windows beside the front door, bathing the hallway in a silvery light. It illuminated an old coatrack, and some paint cans and a ladder that lay to my right. It also shone on a set of muddy footprints that ran from the back door, through the kitchen, up to my bedroom door and then into the living room. The mark of my bare foot lay in the print nearest the bedroom door.

I checked the living room and the bathroom before making my way to the kitchen. I could feel my heart thumping in my chest and my breath was white in the cold night air. I counted to three in my head then came in fast through the kitchen door, the gun panning around the room.

It was empty, but the back door was open slightly. Someone had jimmied the lock then made his way – I assumed it was male by the size of the boot prints – through the house, and watched me while I slept. I recalled the bald-headed grotesque I had encountered the day before and the thought of him observing me from the shadows made me sick to my stomach. I opened the back door fully and scanned the yard. Leaving the kitchen and porch light off, I slipped on a pair of work boots that I kept in the kitchen beside the door, then stepped outside and walked once around the house. There were more prints on the porch and in the mud below. At my bedroom window they turned slightly, where the visitor had stood watching from outside.

I went back into the house, dug out my Maglite and threw on a sweater, then traced the tracks through the mud and out onto the road. There had been little traffic and it was still possible to see where the boot marks petered out on the tarmac. I stood on the empty road, looking left and right, then returned to the house.

It was only when I turned on the kitchen light that I noticed what lay on the table in the corner of the room. I picked it up using a piece of paper towel and turned it over in my hand.

It was a small wooden clown, its body made up of a series of brightly painted rings which could be removed by twisting the clown's smiling head off. I sat looking at it for a time, then placed it carefully in a plastic bag and left it by the sink. I locked the back door, checked all the windows and returned to bed.

I must have drifted off into an uneasy sleep at some point, because I dreamed. I dreamed that I saw a shape moving through the night, black against the stars. I saw a tree standing alone in a clearing and shapes moving beneath it. I smelt blood and sickly-sweet perfume. Squat, white fingers moved across my bare chest.

And I saw a light die, and I heard a child crying in the darkness.

# Chapter Six

The first grey light of dawn had appeared at the window and the ground had frozen again when I rose and returned to the kitchen. I looked at the shape of the clown in the bag, its contours masked, its long red nose jutting through the white plastic, its colours dimly visible like a faded ghost of itself.

I slipped on my running gear and started for US 1. Before I left, I made sure all the doors and windows were locked, something that I didn't ordinarily do. I turned onto Spring Street and headed south to the Mussey Road intersection, the red brick exterior and the white wood steeple of the Scarborough First Baptist Church to my left and the 8 Corners store straight ahead. I continued down Spring onto 114 and kept going, the road quiet, the pine trees whispering above me. I passed Scarborough High School on my right, where I had attended school after moving to Maine, even getting a few games with the Redskins one spring when half the team went down with flu. To my left, the parking lot of the Shop n Save was silent, but there was already traffic ahead on the untidy strip of US 1. It had always been untidy: by the time zoning began in the 1980s, it was too late to save it. Then again, maybe it's in the nature of US 1 to be this way, because it looks the same in just about every place I've been.

When I first arrived in Scarborough there was only one mall in the town, the Orion Center. It had the Mammoth Mart department store, which was kind of like Woolworths, and Martin's grocery store, and a Laundromat and a liquor store, the kind my grandfather used to refer to as a 'Dr Green's' from the days when they were all painted uniformly green in compliance with the regulations of the state liquor commission.

At Dr Green's we bought Old Swilwaukee and Pabst Blue Ribbon – the legal drinking age was still eighteen then, not that it mattered – to drink on Higgins Beach, down at the quiet end beside the bird sanctuary, where the piping plover marks its territory with a song like small bells tolling.

I remember, in the summer of eighty-two, trying to convince Becky Berube to lie down on the sand there with me. I was unsuccessful, but it was that kind of summer, the kind that makes you think you're going to die a virgin. Becky Berube has five kids now, so I guess she learned to lie down pretty quickly after that. We drove sixties' automobiles – Pontiac convertibles, MGs, Thunderbirds, Chevy Impalas and Camaros with big V-8 engines; even, in one case, a Plymouth Barracuda convertible. We took summer jobs at the ClamBake at Pine Point, or as waiters and busboys at the Black Point Inn.

I recall a fight at the Orion Center, one hot summer night when a group of us clashed with some kids from Old Orchard Beach who had journeyed north up US 1 seeking just such a turn of events. Words had been exchanged, then threats, then blows. I had not been able to handle myself, not then, and had taken a fierce shot to the nose from a guy whose name I never learned, some-one we had never seen before and would never see again, somebody's cousin from Chicago. He had mean, dumb eyes, I recalled, and wore bleach-stained denims and an Aerosmith T-shirt beneath a black leather biker jacket.

His fist headed for the bridge of my nose as surely and certainly as a wrecking ball cleaving the air before it strikes a condemned building, the cartilage buckling beneath the onslaught when the punch landed. It was a bad break and I fell to the ground, my blood warm on my face. Around me the scuffling continued, and someone ended up curled into a ball on the ground taking kicks to the belly and head, but the events came to me dully through a mist of pain and fear and nausea. The fight broke up as the final blows, the last threats and promises, were exchanged, but I stayed kneeling on the ground, my hands cupped around my busted nose, tears mingling with blood.

Anthony Hutchence, 'Tony Hutch', who had wrestled before he came to Scarborough High and would wrestle again when he went on to study in the University of New England, who would have competed in the Olympics had it not been for a back injury, carefully moved my hands from my face and cupped my cheeks in his palms, examining my face with a detached professionalism born out of his own experience both on and off the mat. Then he called two pairs of arms to him, and they held my hands and my head as he reset my nose using his thumbs.

The pain was shocking, almost profound. Lightning shot through my head and my vision turned white, then bright, hard red. I screamed, but I do not even recall what I screamed, only that the sound was like no other I had ever heard before. And then the needle-sharp pain receded into a dull, hard ache, and Tony Hutch stepped back, and there was blood on his thumbs and I knew that the lines and whorls of them were clear on the skin of my face.

But, after that, the fear of my nose breaking would never be the same again. I knew the pain, and had no desire to court it, but the way I felt about it had changed: I had coped, and I would cope again, if the need arose. But there would never be the same shock, the same powerlessness, the same hurt. All of that was behind me, and I was stronger for it. When Jennifer and Susan died, something similar occurred, but this time it killed something inside me; instead of strengthening me, I think it cut off part of me forever.

I crossed US 1 at Amato's Italian restaurant and continued down Old County Road, through the salt marshes that flooded once a month with the phases of the moon, and past the Maximilian Kolbe Catholic Church until I reached the cemetery. My grandfather was buried on Fifth Avenue, a joke he liked to share with my grandmother after they bought the plot. They lay there together now, and while I rested I cleared some of the weeds away and said a small prayer for them.

When I got back to the house I put on a pot of coffee, ate some grapefruit and thought again about what had happened the night before. It was almost nine by the clock on the wall when Ellis Howard arrived at my door.

Ellis looked like lard poured into a flexible, vaguely human-shaped mould and left to set. Wrapped in a brown sheepskin coat, the deputy chief in charge of the Portland Police Department's Bureau of Investigations climbed, with some difficulty, from his car. The detective division of the Portland PD was divided into sections dealing with Narcotics and Vice, Crimes Against Persons, Crimes Against Property, and Admin., with Ellis pretty much in charge, assisted by a detective lieutenant and four sergeants, each with responsibility for a section. In total, there were twenty-two officers involved, and four evidence technicians. It was a small, efficient division.

Ellis rolled up to the porch, like a bowling ball that someone had wrapped in fur to keep the frost out. He didn't look like he could move at even half the pace of a bowling ball, didn't look like he could run to save his life or anyone else's. But then Ellis's job wasn't to run around and, anyway, looks could be deceptive. Ellis watched and thought and asked questions and watched and thought some more. Little got past Ellis. He was the kind of man who could eat soup with a fork and not spill a drop.

His wife was a fearsome woman named Doreen, who wore her makeup so thick that you could have carved your initials into her face without drawing blood. When she smiled, which wasn't too often, it was as if someone had just stripped a section of peel from an orange. Ellis seemed to tolerate her the way saints tolerated the rack although I guessed that, deep down, really deep down, he still didn't like her very much.

Instead, Ellis found his solace in work and baseball statistics. Without blinking, Ellis could tell you the only game in Major League history in which two men threw no-hit balls against each other for nine innings or more – May second, 1917, when Fred Toney of the Reds and Hippo Vaughn of the Cubs went through nine innings until Larry Kopf hit a clean single in the tenth and came home on a Jim Thorpe roller – or the details of Lou Gehrig's performance in the Yanks' four-game sweep of the 1932 World Series: three homers, eight RBIs, a .529 batting average and a 1.118 slugging mark. Babe Ruth may have got the press, but it was Lou Gehrig whom Ellis remembered. Lou had his beloved Eleanor, Ellis had Doreen. That seemed just about to sum things up for Ellis.

I stood aside to let him enter the house. I didn't have a whole lot of choice. 'Looking good, Ellis,' I said. 'The doughnut diet is really paying dividends.'

'I see you got someone to fix your roof,' he replied. 'Know you were from the city, only man in the durned state doing roofing in the winter. Do any of it yourself?'

'As a matter of fact, yes.'

'Jesus, maybe we'd be safer talking outside.'

'Funny guy,' I said, as he sat down heavily in a kitchen chair. 'Maybe you should be more concerned about the floor collapsing under you.'

I poured him some coffee. He sipped it and I noticed that his face had grown serious, almost sad.

'Something wrong?'

He nodded. 'Very. You know Billy Purdue?'

I guessed that he knew the answer to that question already. I fingered the scar on my cheek. I could feel the edges of the stitches beneath my finger.

'Yeah, I know him.'

'Heard you had a run-in with him a few days back. He say anything to you about his ex-wife?'

'Why?' I wasn't about to get Billy into trouble unnecessarily, but I already had a sinking feeling in the pit of my stomach.

'Because Rita and her child turned up dead this morning in her apartment. No sign of forced entry and no one heard a thing.'

I breathed out deeply and felt a sharp pang of sorrow as I recalled Donald's hand on my finger, as I remembered the touch of his mother's hand on my cheek. A burning anger at Billy Purdue coursed through my system as I briefly, instinctively, assumed his guilt. The feeling didn't last long but the intensity of it remained with me. I thought: why couldn't he have stood by them? Why couldn't he have been there for them? Maybe I didn't have the right to ask those questions; or maybe, given all that had happened in the last year, nobody else had a greater right.

'What happened to them?'

Ellis leaned forward and rubbed his hands together with a soft, rustling sound.

'From what I hear, the woman was strangled. The boy, I don't know. No obvious signs of sexual assault on either.'

'You haven't been at the apartment?'

'No. This was supposed to be my day off, but I'm on my way now. ME's already on the scene. Unlucky for him, he was in Portland for a wedding.'

I stood up and walked to the window. Outside, the wind brushed the evergreens and a pair of black-capped chickadees flew high into the sky.

'You think Billy Purdue killed his own child and his ex-wife?' I said.

'Maybe. He wouldn't be the first to do something like it. She called us three nights ago, said he was hanging around outside, shouting, roaring drunk, demanding to be let in to see her. We sent a car and took him in, let him cool off for a time, then told him to keep away from her or we'd lock him up. Could be he decided that he wasn't going to let her leave him, whatever it took.'

I shook my head. 'Billy wouldn't do that.' But I had some doubts, even as I said it. I recalled that red glare in his eyes, and the way that he had almost choked the life from me in his trailer, and Rita's belief that he would do anything to stop her from taking his son away from him.

Ellis was keeping pace with my thoughts. 'Maybe, maybe not,' he said. 'That's a nice scar you got on your cheek. You want to tell me how you came by it?'

'I went to his trailer to try to get some child-support money. He threatened to take a baseball bat to me, I tried to stop him and things got a little out of hand.'

'Did she hire you to get her money?'

'I did it as a favour.'

Ellis turned his mouth down at the corners. 'A favour,' he repeated, nodding to himself. 'And when you were doing this . . . *favour*, did he say anything to you about his ex-wife?' There was an edge to Ellis's voice now.

'He said he wanted to look out for her, for them both. Then he asked me if I was sleeping with her.'

'What did you tell him?'

'I told him no.'

'Probably the right answer, under the circumstances. Were you sleeping with her?'

'No,' I said, and looked hard at him. 'No, I wasn't. You pick up Billy yet?'

'He's gone. No sign of him at the trailer and Ronald Straydeer hasn't seen him since day before yesterday.'

'I know. I was out there last night.'

Ellis arched an eyebrow. 'Want to tell me why?'

I told him about my encounter with the white-faced freak at the inn and later at Java Joe's. Ellis took out his notebook and wrote down the number of the Coupe de

Ville. 'We'll run it through the system, see what comes up. Anything else I should know?'

I went to the sink unit and handed him the plastic bag with the clown toy in it. 'Someone came into the house last night when I was sleeping. He took a look around, watched me for a time, then left this.'

I opened the bag and placed it on the table in front of Ellis. He took an evidence glove from his pocket, then reached in and touched the toy clown gently.

'I think you'll find that it's Donald Purdue's.'

Ellis looked at me. 'And where were you last night?'

'Jesus, Ellis, don't ask me that.' I could feel a huge surge of anger welling up inside me. 'Don't even imply that.'

'Take it easy, Bird. Don't cry before you're hurt. You know I have to ask. May as well get it done now as have to go through it later.'

He waited.

'I was here during the afternoon,' I said through gritted teeth. 'I went into Portland yesterday evening, worked out, bought some books, had a coffee, dropped by Rita's apartment . . .'

'What time?'

I thought for a moment. 'Eight. Eight-thirty at the latest. There was no reply.'

'And then?'

'I headed out to Ronald Straydeer's place, came back here, read, went to bed.'

'When did you find the toy?'

'Maybe three a.m. You might want to get someone down here to take moulds of the boot prints outside my house. The frost will have held the marks in the mud.'

He nodded. 'We'll do that.' He stood to leave, then stopped. 'I had to ask. You know that.'

'I know.'

'And here's something else: the presence of this – ' he raised the bag containing the clown ' – means someone has marked you out. Someone's drawn a line between you and Rita Ferris, and it seems to me that there's only one likely candidate.'

Billy Purdue. Still, it just didn't sit right, unless Billy had decided that I was to blame for the events leading up to the death of his son; that, by my actions in helping Rita, I had forced him to act as he did.

'Look, let me go with you, see if there's anything about it that strikes a chord,' I said, at last.

Ellis leaned against the door frame. 'Hear you applied to Augusta for a PI licence.'

That was true. I still had some cash left from Susan's insurance policy and the sale of our home, and from some work I had undertaken in New York, but I figured that sooner or later I'd have to make a living somehow. I'd already been offered some work in 'corporate competitive intelligence', a euphemism which covered tackling industrial espionage. It sounded more interesting than it was: a sales rep suspected of selling a competitor's goods in violation of a non-competition agreement; sabotage of a production line in a software factory in South Portland; and the leaking of information on bids for a new public housing development in Augusta. I was still debating whether or not to take on any of them.

'Yeah, the licence came through last week.'

'You're better than that. We all know what you did, the people you've hunted down. We could do with someone like that.'

'What are you saying?'

'I'm saying there's a badge waiting, if you want it. There's something coming up in CAP pretty soon.'

'Property or Persons?'

'Don't be a jerk.'

'A minute ago you were implying that I might be a suspect in a double homicide. You sure are a changeable man, Ellis.'

He smiled. 'So how about it?'

I nodded. 'I'll think about it.'

'You do that,' he said. 'You do that.'


Rita Ferris lay facedown on the floor of her apartment, close to the TV. The coiled ends of a rope hung at her neck, and the tip of one ear, visible through the twisted strands of her hair, was blue. Her skirt was pushed up almost to her waist but her panty-hose and panties were in place and undamaged. I felt a rush of pity for her, and something more: a kind of love born out of a brief feeling of intense loss. It made my stomach tighten and my eyes burn and, on my face, I could feel, once again, her last, brief touch, as if I had been branded by her hand.

And in that small room, clean and neat but for the toys and clothes, the diapers and pins, the everyday beauty of her child's slow-forming life, I made myself feel her last moments. I felt –

*I see – the blur of movement as the ligature is flipped over her head, the sudden instinctive shifting of her own hands to her throat in an effort to slip her fingers beneath the rope, the brief burn at her fingertips as she fails and the rope tightens around her.*

*It is a long death, this slow choking of life from her body. It is a bitter, terrible struggle against the gradual, remorseless crushing of her throat, the progressive destruction of the cricoid cartilage and the eventual soft death knell as the fragile hyoid bone snaps.*

*She panics as her pulse rate increases; her blood pressure soars as she struggles and gasps for breath. She tries to kick back at the body behind her, but the action is anticipated and the rope is pulled tighter. Her face becomes congested, her skin gradually turning blue as cyanosis develops. Her eyes bulge and her mouth froths and she feels as though her head must explode under the pressure.*

*Then her body convulses and she can taste the blood in her mouth, can feel it flowing from her nose and over her lips. Now she knows that she is going to die and she makes a final desperate effort to release herself, to save her child, but her body is already failing, her mind darkening, and she can smell herself as the light fades, as she loses control of her bodily functions and she thinks to herself:*

*but I have always been so clean . . .*

'You finished?' said a voice. It was the medical examiner, Dr Henry Vaughan, speaking to the police photographer. Vaughan was grey haired and erudite, a philosopher as much as a doctor, and had been the ME for over twenty years. The post of ME was an appointed job with a seven-year term, which meant that Democrat governors, Republican governors and independent governors had all appointed, or reappointed, Vaughan down the years. He was due to retire soon, I knew, and was set to leave his storage room in Augusta lined with old peanut, mayonnaise and sauce bottles, each now containing some small part of someone's remains. He wasn't too unhappy about it: according to Ellis, he wanted 'more time to think'.

The photographer took one final photograph of the

knot, then nodded his assent. The preliminary sketches had already been made, the measurements taken. The evidence technician with responsibility for this room had finished his work around the bodies and had moved on to the periphery of the crime scene. A pair of medics waited in one corner with a stretcher, but they prepared to move forward as Vaughan spoke.

'We're going to flip her,' said Vaughan. Two detectives, both wearing plastic gloves, took up positions beside the body, one at her legs, one at her torso, their feet at the edge of the taped outline surrounding her, while Vaughan held her head.

'Ready?' he said, then: 'Here we go.'

They flipped the body, gently but expertly, and I heard one of the cops, a muscular, balding man in his forties, softly whisper: 'Ah, Jesus.'

Her eyes were wide open and filled with blood where the tiny capillaries had burst under the pressure of the rope, the pupils like dark suns in a red sky. Her fingertips were blue and her nostrils and mouth were covered in blood and dried white froth.

And her lips, the lips that had kissed me softly barely three nights before, that once were red and welcoming and now were cold and blue,

*say bye-bye*

her lips had been sewn together with thick black thread, the stitches crisscrossing from top to bottom in ragged 'v' shapes, a tangled knot of thread at one corner so that it would not work itself through the hole while the stitches were still being put in place.

I moved closer and it was only then that I saw the child. His body had been obscured by the couch but, as I walked, his small, covered feet became visible, and then the rest of his body, dressed in purple Barney the dinosaur rompers. There was blood around his head, blood caked in his fine blonde hair and blood on the corner of the windowsill where his head had impacted.

Ellis was beside me. 'There's bruising to his face. We figure whoever did this hit him, maybe while he was crying, maybe because he got in the way. The force of the blow knocked him into the windowsill and broke his skull.'

I shook my head and remembered how the little boy had flailed at me as I touched his mother the night before.

'No,' I said, and I squeezed my eyes shut hard as the burning became too much. And I thought of my own child, lost to me now, and the others, their bodies wrapped in plastic, bodies buried beneath the earth of a damp cellar in Queens, tiny faces in jars, a small host of the lost stretching into the darkness, walking hand in hand to oblivion.

'No, he didn't just cry,' I said. 'He was trying to save her.'

While the bodies were placed in white body bags to be taken to Augusta for autopsy, I walked through the apartment. There was only one bedroom, although it was wide and long and held a double bed and a smaller bed with retractable side bars for Donald. There was a pine chest of drawers and a matching pine wardrobe, and a box piled high with toys beside a small bookshelf stacked with picture books. In one corner, beside an open drawer, an evidence technician dusted for fingerprints.

And the sight of the clothes stacked neatly on the shelves, and the toys packed away in their box, brought back a memory that speared me through the heart. Less than one year before, I had stood in our small house on Hobart Street in Brooklyn and, in the space of one night, had gone through the possessions of my dead wife and child, sorting, discarding, smelling the last traces of them that clung to their clothing like the ghosts of themselves. My Susan and my Jennifer: their blood was still on the kitchen walls and there were chalk marks on the floor where the chairs had stood, the chairs to which they had been tied and in which they had been mutilated while the husband and father who should have protected them was propping up a bar.

And I thought, as I stood in Rita's bedroom: who will take their clothes and sort them now? Who will feel the cotton of her blouse between his fingers, caressing it until the material holds the stains of his prints like a seal? Who will take her underwear, her pink bras without the support wiring (for her breasts were so very small), and hold them carefully, recalling, before he puts them away forever, how he used to undo the clasps with just one hand, the weight of her forcing the straps apart, the cups gently falling?

Who will take her lipstick and run his finger along the edge, knowing that this, too, was a place she touched, that no lips but hers had ever touched it before, or would ever touch it again? Who will see the small traces of a fingertip in her blusher, or carefully unwind each strand of hair from her brush, as if by doing so he might begin to remake her again, piece by piece, atom by atom?

And who will take the child's toys? Who will spin the wheels on a bright, plastic truck? Who will test a button nose, the glass eyes of a bear, the upraised trunk of a white elephant? And who will pack away those small clothes, those little shoes with laces that young fingers had not yet learned to master?

Who will do all of these things, these small services for the dead, these acts of remembrance more powerful in their way than the most ornate memorial? In parting with what was once theirs they became, in that moment, intimately, intensely present, for the ghost of a child is still, for all that, a child, and the memory of a love is still, even decades later, love.

I stood outside the apartment in the cold winter sunlight and watched as the bodies were removed. They had been dead for no more than ten hours, according to Vaughan, possibly less; the precise time of death would take longer to establish, for a number of reasons, including the cold in the drafty old apartment and the nature of Rita Ferris's death. Rigor mortis had set into the small muscles at the eyelids, the lower jaw and the neck, gradually spreading to the other muscles of their bodies, although in Rita Ferris the process of rigor mortis was hastened by her death struggles.

Rigor mortis is caused by the disappearance of the energy source for muscle contraction, called adenosine triphosphate, or ATP. ATP usually dissipates entirely four hours after death, leaving the muscles rigid until decomposition starts to occur. But if the victim struggles before death, then the ATP energy source becomes depleted during the struggle and rigor mortis sets in more quickly. That would have to be taken into account in the case of Rita, so Vaughan reckoned that Donald Ferris would provide a more accurate estimate of the time of death.

There was fixed lividity on the underside of both bodies, where gravity had drawn the blood down, which normally occurs six to eight hours after death, and pressure applied to the area of lividity did not cause 'blanching' or whitening, since the blood had already clotted, meaning that they had been dead for at least five hours. Thus the window for a time of death was certainly greater than five hours but probably not in excess of eight hours to ten hours. There was no fixed lividity on the backs of either body, which meant that they had not been moved after death. They had not been dead when I had tried to find Rita the night before. Maybe she had gone shopping, or visiting friends. If I had found her, could I have warned her? Could I have saved her, saved them both?

Ellis walked over to me, where I stood away from the throng of curious onlookers.

'Anything strike you about it?' he asked.

'No,' I said. 'Not yet.'

'You think of anything, you let us know, y'hear?'

But my attention had already been distracted. Two men in plain-clothes flashed ID at the cop keeping the crowds back and made their way into the building. I didn't need to see what was in their wallets to know what they were.

'Feds,' I said.

Behind them, a taller figure with jet black hair and wearing a conservative blue suit followed.

'Special Agents Samson and Doyle,' said Ellis. 'And the Canadian cop, Eldritch. They were here earlier. Guess they don't trust us.'

I turned to him. 'What do I not know here?'

He reached into his pocket and removed a clear plastic evidence bag. It contained four hundred-dollar bills, still crisp and new except a single fold on each.

'Let's barter,' said Ellis. 'Know anything about these?'

There was no way to avoid the issue. 'They look like the bills Billy Purdue gave me for Rita as part of the child-support payments.'

'Thanks,' he said, and started to walk away. I could see that he was angry at me, although I wasn't sure why.

I reached out and gripped him by the upper arm. He didn't look happy about it but I didn't care. My gesture attracted the attention of two uniformed cops, but Ellis waved them away.

'Don't be presuming on my good humor, Bird,' he warned, looking at my hand on his arm. 'Why didn't you tell me that he gave you this money?'

I didn't release my grip. 'You owe me something,' I said. 'I couldn't have known then the money was important.'

He frowned, then replied: 'Just testing, I guess. You want to let go of my arm now? My fingers are going numb.'

I took away my hand and he rubbed his arm gently.

'Still working out, I see.' He glanced back towards the apartment building, but the feds and the Canadian cop were still inside.

'That business out at Prouts Neck a couple of nights back?' he began.

'Yeah, I watch the news. A dead Irish-American fed, three dead Italians and four dead Cambodians: an equal-opportunity slaughter. What about it?'

'There was another player. Took out Paulie Block and Jimmy Fribb with a pump-action, and that's not all he took.'

'Go on.'

'There was an exchange going on at the Neck: cash for something else. The feds were tipped off to it when Paulie

Block and Chester Nash turned up in Portland. They figure a ransom, for someone who was already dead. Norfolk County Sheriff's Office down in Massachusetts dug up a body out by the Larz Anderson Park yesterday, a Canadian national named Thani Pho. A dog sniffed her out.'

'Let me guess,' I interrupted. 'Thani Pho was of Cambodian extraction.'

Ellis nodded. 'Seems she was a freshman student at Harvard; her bag was found with her. Autopsy indicated that she'd been raped, then buried alive. They found earth in her throat. The way the feds and this guy Eldritch figure it, Tony Celli's crew kidnapped the girl, pulled a double-cross on the Cambodians and then blew them away under the noses of the feds. The main focus of the investigation is Boston. Despite the sideshow at the Neck, the feds are concentrating their attention on Tony Celli. Those two agents are just clearing up loose ends.'

'Who paid the ransom?'

He shrugged. 'The FBI Free Information Store closed for business at that point, but they believe that the exchange and the murder of Thani Pho are connected, and maybe there's a Canadian angle if this guy Eldritch is involved. These bills came from a bank in Toronto, and so did the bills that fell from the ransom stash out at the Neck. Trouble is, the rest of the cash is gone, and that's where the other player comes in.'

'How much?'

'I heard two mil.'

I pushed my hands through my hair and kneaded the muscles on the back of my neck. Billy Purdue: the guy was like some kind of infernal ricocheting bullet, bouncing off people and destroying lives until he ran out of energy or something stopped him. If what Ellis said was true, then Billy had somehow heard of Tony Celli's deal at the Neck, may even have been involved somewhere lower down the scale, and decided to make a big score, maybe in the hope of getting his ex-wife and son back and carving out a new life somewhere else, somewhere he could leave the past behind.

'You still think Billy killed Rita and his own son?' I asked quietly.

'Possibly,' shrugged Ellis. 'I don't see anyone else on the horizon.'

'And sewed her mouth shut with black thread?'

'I don't know. If he's crazy enough to cross Tony Celli, he's crazy enough to sew up his old lady.'

But I knew that he didn't believe what he was saying. The money changed everything. There were people who would cause a lot of pain to get their hands on that kind of cash, and Tony Celli was one of them, especially since he probably felt that it was his money to begin with. Still, the damage to Rita's mouth didn't fit in. Neither did the fact that she hadn't been tortured. Whoever killed her didn't do it in the course of trying to find out something from her. She was killed because someone wanted her dead, and her mouth was sewn up because that same someone wanted to send a message to whoever found her.

Two million dollars: that money was going to bring a storm of trouble down on everybody's head – from Tony Celli, maybe from the guys he tried to double-cross. Jesus, what a mess. I didn't know it then, but the money had attracted others too, individuals who were anxious to secure it for their own ends and didn't care who they killed to get it.

But Billy Purdue, by his actions, had also drawn

someone else, someone who didn't care about money, or the Boston crew, or a dead child, or a young woman who was trying to make a better life for herself. He had come back to claim something as his own, and to avenge himself on all those who had kept him from it, and God help anyone who got in his way.

Winter had come howling down from the north, and he had come with it.

# Chapter Seven

When Ellis had left I stood for a time, considering whether or not to leave the police to their work. Instead of simply driving away, I re-entered the apartment building and walked up to the third floor. The door to apartment five had been freshly painted a bright, cheerful yellow, small paint flecks still freckling the brass numeral. I knocked gently and the door opened on a chain. In the gap, a small dark face appeared about four feet from the ground, its features framed by black curls, its eyes wide and wondering.

'Come away from there, child,' said a voice and then a taller, darker figure filled the gap. I could see the resemblance in the two faces almost instantly.

'Mrs Mims?' I asked.

'*Ms* Mims,' she corrected. 'And I just finished talking to a police officer not twenty minutes ago.'

'I'm not with the police, ma'am.' I showed her my ID. She examined it carefully without touching it, her daughter straining up on her toes to do the same, then glanced back at my face. 'I remember you,' she said. 'You called here, couple of nights back.'

'That's right. I knew Rita. Can I come in for a moment?'

She bit down gently on her lower lip, then nodded and closed the door. I could hear the chain being removed and then the door swung open, revealing a bright, large-ceilinged room. The couch inside was blue and decorated with yellow throws, its legs set on a bare varnished floor. Two tall bookshelves crammed with paperbacks stood at either side of an old, stained, marble fireplace, and there was a portable stereo on a stand by the window close to a combination TV and VCR. The room smelt of flowers and opened to the right onto a short hallway, presumably leading to the bedroom and bathroom, and on the left into a small, clean kitchen. The walls had been newly painted a soft yellow, so that the room seemed to be bathed in sunlight.

'You have a nice place. You do all this yourself?'

She nodded, proud despite herself.

'I helped her,' piped the girl. She was maybe eight or nine, and it was possible to see in her the seeds of a beauty that would eventually grow to outshine her mother's.

'You'll have to start hiring yourself out,' I said. 'I know people who'd pay a lot of money for a job as good as this. Including me.'

The girl giggled shyly and her mother reached out and gave her a little hug around the shoulders. 'Go on now, child. Go and play while I talk with Mr Parker here.'

She did as she was told, casting a small, anxious look over her shoulder as she entered the hallway. I smiled to reassure her, and she gave a little smile back.

'She's a beautiful girl,' I said.

'Takes after her father,' she replied, her voice thick with sarcasm.

'I don't think so. He around?'

'No. He was a worthless sonofabitch, so I kicked him

out. Last I heard, he was a drain on the economy of New Jersey.'

'Best place for him.'

'Amen to that. You want coffee? Tea maybe?'

'Coffee would be fine.' I didn't really want it, but I figured it might take the strain out of the situation a little. Ms Mims seemed like a pretty tough woman. If she decided to be unhelpful, a steel hull wouldn't be enough to break the ice.

After a few minutes, she emerged from the kitchen with two mugs, placed them carefully on coasters on a low pine table, then went back to the kitchen for milk and sugar. When she returned we sat. Her hand was shaking, as she held her coffee. She caught my look, and raised her left hand to try to still the mug.

'It's not easy,' I said softly. 'When something of this kind happens, it's like a stone dropped in a pool. It ripples out, and everything gets tossed in its wake.'

She nodded. 'Ruth's been asking me about it. I haven't told her that they're dead. I haven't figured out how to tell her yet.'

'Did you know Rita well?'

'I knew her a little. I knew more by reputation. I knew about her husband, knew he almost killed them in a fire.' She paused. 'You think he did this?'

'I don't know. I hear he was around lately.'

'I've seen him, once or twice, watching the place. I told Rita, but she only called the police that last time he got roaring drunk. The rest of the time, she seemed content to let him be. I think she felt sorry for him.'

'Were you here last night?'

She nodded, then paused. 'I went to bed early – women's troubles, you know? I took two Tylenol, drank a shot of whiskey and didn't wake up until this morning. I went downstairs, saw Rita's door was open, and went in. That's when I found them. I can't help thinking that if I hadn't taken the pills, hadn't had a drink . . .' She swallowed loudly and tried not to cry. I looked away for a moment, and when I turned back she seemed to have composed herself.

'Was there anything else bothering her, anyone else?' I continued.

Again, there was a pause, but this one spoke volumes. I waited, but she didn't speak. 'Ms Mims . . .' I began.

'Lucy,' she said.

'Lucy,' I said gently. 'You can't say anything to hurt her now. But if you do know something that might help to find whoever did this then, please, tell me.'

She sipped her coffee. 'She was short of money. I knew, because she told me. There was a woman helped her out, but it still wasn't enough. I offered her some, but she wouldn't take it. Said she had found a way to make a little on the side.'

'Did she say how?'

'No, but I looked after Donnie while she was gone. Three times, each at short notice. The third time, she came back and I could see she'd been crying. She looked scared, but wouldn't tell me what had happened, just said that she wouldn't need me to watch Donnie no more, that the job hadn't worked out.'

'Did you tell the police this?'

She shook her head. 'I don't know why I didn't. It was just that . . . she was a good person, you know? I think she was just doing what she had to do to make ends meet. But if I told the police, it would have become something else, something low.'

'Do you know who she was working for?'

She rose and went into the hallway, and I could hear her footsteps on the bare floor as she walked. When she appeared again, there was a piece of paper in her hands.

'She told me that if there was any trouble with Donnie or Billy, or if she didn't come back on time, I was to call this number and talk to this man.' She handed me the piece of paper. On it, written in Rita Ferris's tight, neat script, was a telephone number and the name Lester Biggs.

'When did the crying incident happen, Lucy?'

'Five days ago,' she said, which meant that Rita had called me the day after looking for help and money to get out of Portland.

I held up the piece of paper. 'Can I keep this?'

She nodded and I placed it in my wallet. 'Do you know who he is?' she asked.

'He runs an escort service out of South Portland,' I replied. There was no point in sugaring it. Lucy Mims had already guessed the truth.

For the first time, tears glistened in her eyes. A drop hung from her eyelash, then slowly trickled down her cheek. At the hallway, her daughter appeared and ran to her mother to hug her tight. She looked at me, but there was no blame in her eyes. She knew that, whatever had happened, it was not my fault that her mother was crying.

I took my card from my wallet and handed it to Lucy. 'Call me if you think of anything else, or if you just want to talk. Or if you need help.'

'I don't need help, Mr Parker,' she said. In her voice, I could hear the echo of someone being kicked all the way to New Jersey.

'I guess not,' I said, and opened the door. 'And most people call me Bird.'

She walked across the room to close the door behind me, her daughter's arms still clutched tightly around her.

'You will find the man who did this, won't you?' she asked.

Passing clouds dappled the winter sunshine, creating movement on the walls behind her. And, for a moment, it seemed to assume a human shape, the shape of a young woman passing through the room, and I had to shake my head slightly to make it disappear. It lingered for a second, then the clouds cleared and it was gone.

I nodded. 'Yes, I'll find him.'

Lester Biggs operated out of an office on Broadway, above a hairdressing salon. I rang the intercom on the door and waited about thirty seconds before a male voice answered.

'I'm here to see Lester Biggs,' I said into the speaker.

'What's your business with Mr Biggs?' came the reply.

'Rita Ferris. My name's Charlie Parker. I'm a private investigator.'

Nothing happened. I was about to ring again when the door buzzed and I pushed it open to reveal a narrow staircase carpeted in faded green, with a small, grimy window on the landing. I went up two flights of stairs to where a door stood open on to an office overlooking the street. There was the same green carpet on the floor, a desk with a telephone, two wooden chairs without cushions and a pile of skin magazines on the floor, twin stacks of videocassettes beside them. Three sets of filing cabinets stood along the wall. Opposite them, beneath and alongside the two big windows that looked out onto

Broadway, stood a selection of electrical items in boxes: microwave ovens, hairdryers, cookware, stereos, even some computers, although they were made by no company that I knew. The writing on the box appeared to be Cyrillic: trust Lester Biggs to buy and sell Russian computers.

Behind the desk, in a leather seat, sat Lester himself, and to his right, on one of the chairs, sat a bearded man with a huge pot belly and biceps the size of melons. His buttocks hung over the edges of the chair, like balloons filled with water.

Lester Biggs was slim and kind of well-groomed, if your definition of well-groomed was a disc jockey at his sister-in-law's wedding. He looked about forty and was dressed in a cheap three-button pinstripe suit, a white shirt and a slim pink tie. He wore his hair in a mullet-cut, the top short, the back long and permed. His face was tanning salon-brown, his eyes slightly hooded, like a man caught between sleeping and waking. In his right hand he held a pen, which he tapped lightly on the desk as I entered, causing the gold bracelet on his arm to jangle.

Biggs wasn't a bad man by the standards of his profession, according to some. He had started out running a used electronics store, had progressed rapidly into buying and selling stolen goods, then branched out into a number of other areas. The escort service was a recent one, maybe six or seven months old. From what I heard, he took the calls, contacted the girl, provided a car to take her to the address and a guy, sometimes the big man Jim who sat beside him, to make sure everything went smoothly. For that, he took fifty per cent. He wasn't morally bankrupt, just overdrawn.

'The local celebrity sleuth,' he said. 'Welcome. Take a

seat.' He gestured with the pen to the remaining un-occupied wooden chair. I sat. The back creaked a little and started to give way, so I leaned forwards to take the pressure off.

'Business is booming, I see.'

Biggs shrugged. 'I do pretty good. It doesn't pay to maintain a high profile in my line of work.'

'And that would be . . . ?'

'I buy and sell things.'

'Like people?'

'I provide a service. I don't force anybody to do what they do. Nobody, apart from Jim here, works for me. They work for themselves. I just act as the facilitator.'

'Tell me how you facilitated Rita Ferris.'

Biggs didn't reply, just twisted in his seat to look out the window. 'I heard about it. I'm sorry. She was a nice woman.'

'That's right, she was. I'm trying to find out if her death was connected in any way to what she was doing for you.'

He flinched a little. 'Why should it matter to you?'

'It just does. It should matter to you too.'

He exchanged a look with Jim, who shrugged. 'How'd you find me?' he said.

'I followed the trail of cheap porn.'

Biggs smiled. 'Some men need a little something extra to get them going. There are a lot of screwed-up people out there, and every day I thank God for them.'

'Did Rita Ferris meet one of those screwed-up people?'

Biggs kicked back from his desk until his chair came to rest against the wall. He didn't say anything, just sat sizing me up.

'Tell me, or tell the cops,' I said. 'I'm sure Narcotics

and Vice would be happy to discuss the nature of facil-
itation with you.'

'What do you want to know?'

'Tell me about last Monday night.'

Again, he exchanged a look with Jim, then seemed to
resign himself to talking. 'It was a freak call, that's all.
Guy rang from the Radisson over on High Street, wanted
a girl. I asked him if he had any preferences and he gave
me short, blonde, small tits, neat ass. Said that was what
he liked. Well, that was Rita. I gave her a call, offered her
the job, and she said yes. It was only her third time, but
she was keen to make some cash. Cash for gash.' He
smiled emptily. 'Anyway, Jim picked her up, dropped
her off, parked the car and waited in the lobby while she
went up to the room.'

'What room?'

'Nine-twenty-seven. Ten minutes later Rita comes
down, runs into the lobby and straight over to Jim,
demands to be taken home. Jim hauls her into a corner
and tries to calm her down, find out what happened.
Seems she got to the room and an old guy opened the
door and let her in. She said he was dressed kind of funny
– ' He looked to Jim for confirmation.

'Old,' said Jim. 'He was dressed old-fashioned, like his
suit was thirty, forty years out of date. It smelt of
mothballs, she said.'

For the first time, Biggs looked uneasy. 'It was strange,
she said. There were no clothes in the room, no cases or
bags, nothing but the old guy in his old suit. And she got
scared. She couldn't say why, but the old guy frightened
her.'

'He smelt bad,' said Jim. 'That's what she told me. Not
bad like rotten fish or eggs, but bad like there was

something rotten inside him. Bad like . . . like if evil had a smell, it would have smelt like him.' He looked embarrassed by his own words, and started examining his fingers.

'So he puts his hand on her shoulder,' continued Lester, 'and, immediately, she just wants to run. She pushes out at him and he falls back on the bed, and while he's down there she makes for the door, but he's locked it and she loses some time trying to get it open. By the time she gets it unlocked, he's behind her so she starts to scream. He's pulling at her dress, trying to cover her mouth, and she strikes out at him again, catches him on the head. Before he can recover, she has the door open and she's running down the corridor. She can hear him behind her, too, pounding after her, and he's gaining. Then she turns a corner and there's a group of people getting in the elevator. She reaches them just before the doors close, jamming her foot in the opening. The door opens and she gets in. There's no sign of the old guy, but she can still smell him, she says, and knows that he's close. She was lucky, I guess. The Radisson only has one functioning elevator in that bank. If she'd missed that, he'd have gotten her, no question. Then the elevator brings her down to the lobby, and to Jim.'

Jim was still looking down at his hands. They were big and heavily veined, with scars on the knuckles. Maybe he was wondering if Rita Ferris might still have been alive if he'd had a chance to use them on the old man. 'I told her to wait for me in the lobby, by the reception desk,' he said, as he took up the story. 'I went up to the room, but the door was open and the room was empty. Like she said, there were no bags, nothing. So I went back down to the desk, told them that I was supposed to meet a friend of mine who was staying in the hotel. Room nine-twenty-seven.'

He pursed his lips, and tugged at one of his scars with a long fingernail. 'There was no guest in room nine-twenty-seven,' he said at last. 'The room was unoccupied. The old guy must have bullshitted one of the staff so he could get in. I took Rita to the bar, got her a brandy and waited until she had calmed down before taking her home. That's all there is.'

'You find any way to tell the cops about this guy?'

Biggs shook his head. 'How could I?'

'You have a telephone.'

'I have a business,' he replied.

Not for long, I thought. Biggs, for all his posturing, was no better than a cluster fly, insinuating himself into young women's lives and then draining them from the inside. 'He could try again,' I said. 'Maybe he did try, and Rita Ferris ended up dead because of it.'

Biggs shook his head. 'Nah, these things happen. The freak probably went home and jerked off instead.' His eyes told me that he didn't believe his own lies. Beside him, Jim still hadn't lifted his face. Guilt rolled off him like a fog.

'She give you a description?'

'Like we told you: old, tall, grey hair, smelt bad. That's it.'

I rose. 'Thanks, you've been a big help.'

'Anytime,' he said. 'You ever want to party, you give me a call.'

'Yeah, you'll be the first to know.'

When I stepped outside, a car drew up: Ellis Howard's car. He didn't look overly happy to see me.

'What are you doing here?' he asked.

'Same thing you are, I guess.'

'We got an anonymous tip-off.'

'Lucky you.' I guessed that Lucy Mims's conscience had got the better of her in the end.

Ellis rubbed his hand across his face, dragging his skin down so I could see the red beneath his eyes. 'You still haven't answered the question,' he said. 'How did you know she was working as a prostitute?'

'Maybe the same way you did. It doesn't matter.'

'But you weren't going to tell us?'

'I would have, eventually. I didn't want her labelled as a hooker, that's all, not with the press around and not before I had a chance to find out more.'

'I didn't know you were so sentimental,' said Ellis. He wasn't smiling.

'I have hidden shallows,' I replied, as I turned and walked to my car. 'See you around, Ellis.'

# Chapter Eight

After I left Lester Biggs's office, I headed down to the Green Mountain Coffee Roasters at Temple Street, where I ate a muffin, drank some French roast and watched the cars go by on Federal Street. A handful of people queued to see cheap movies in the Nickelodeon movie theatre next door, or took the air around Monument Square. Nearby, Congress Street was bustling. It had suffered when the suburban malls drew the retail businesses out of the city, but now had restaurants, and the Keystone theatre café, and was reinventing itself as Portland's cultural district.

This was a survivor's city: it had burned twice at the hands of the Indians in 1676 and 1690, burned again under the guns of the Englishman Henry Mowatt in 1775 following a dispute over masts, and burned once more in 1866 when someone threw a firecracker into a boat-builder's yard on Commercial Street and turned the eastern half of the city to ash. And still the city remained, and still it grew.

I felt about the city as I felt about the house in Scarborough: it was a place where the past was alive in the present, where a man could find a place for himself as long as he understood the fact that he was a link in the chain, for a man cut off from his past is a man adrift in the present. Maybe that was part of Billy Purdue's problem. There had been little stability in his life. His past was a series of unconnected episodes, united only by the unhappiness provoked by the memory of them. A man like Billy could not make a marriage work because, by and large, when one unhappy person enters a marriage it frequently ends up as two unhappy people, maybe even two unhappy people getting a divorce.

In the end, I figured that Billy Purdue was probably none of my business. Whatever he had done to Tony Celli, for whatever reason, was between him and Tony. Billy was a big boy now and his actions at Ferry Beach meant that he was playing by big boys' rules. So if Billy Purdue was none of my business, why did I feel that I should try to save him?

If I stretched the point then Rita and Donald were none of my business either, but it didn't feel that way. In their apartment, as the two bodies lay on the floor, frozen briefly by the flashbulbs of the camera, I felt something ripple through me, something I recognised from before, something that had come to me as a gift from another. In the crowded coffee shop, as people sheltered from the cold, talked about their children, gossiped about their neighbours, touched the hands of girlfriends, boyfriends, lovers, I moved the fingers of my left hand gently over the palm of my right and recalled a touch more intense than that of any lover, and I smelt again the rich heady odour of the Louisiana swamps.

Almost eight months before, I had sat in the bedroom of an old, blind woman named Tante Marie Aguillard, a huge ebony form with dead, sightless eyes whose consciousness moved through the darkness of her own life, and the lives of others. I wasn't sure what I was looking for from her, except that she said she could hear the voice of a dead girl calling her from the swamps. I believed then that the man who killed the girl might also have been responsible for the deaths of my own wife and child – assuming the old woman wasn't crazy, or vindictive, or just plain lonely and seeking attention.

But when she touched my hand in that darkening room, something shot through me like a jolt of electricity and I knew that she was not lying, that somehow she heard that girl crying amid the rotting vegetation and the deep green waters, and that Tante Marie had tried to comfort her as she died.

And through Tante Marie, I heard the voices also of Susan and Jennifer, faint but distinct, and I took those voices away with me, and on a subway train a week later my wife appeared to me for the first time. That was Tante Marie's gift to me: I saw and heard my dead wife and child, and I saw and heard others too. Eventually, Tante Marie was among them. That was her gift, passed in the touch of a hand, and yet I could not explain it.

I think that it may be a kind of empathy, a capacity to experience the suffering of those who have been taken painfully, brutally, without mercy. Or perhaps what I experience is a form of madness, a product of grief and guilt; maybe I am disturbed, and in my disturbance I have imagined alternative worlds where the dead seek reparation from the living. I do not know for certain. All I can say is that those who are absent, by its means become present.

But some gifts are worse than curses, and the dark side of the gift is that they know. The lost, the stragglers, those who should not have been taken but were, the innocents, the struggling, tormented shades, the gathering ranks of the dead, they know.

And they come.

Despite my misgivings, I spent that afternoon moving from bar to bar, talking to those who had known Billy Purdue, who might have some idea of where he had gone. In some cases, the Portland PD had been there before me, which usually meant that my welcome was pretty frosty. No one could, or would, tell me anything, and I had almost given up hope when I found James Hamill.

I guessed that there weren't too many forks in Hamill's family tree. He was a scrawny piece of lowlife, one hundred and twenty pounds of bitterness, repressed anger and redneck mentality, the kind of guy who wouldn't willingly do someone a good turn if he could do a bad one instead. Hamill's position was pretty low down on the food chain: where he existed, they ate it raw.

He was playing alone in Old Port Billiards down on Fore Street when I came upon him, his baseball cap turned backwards on his head as he lined up a shot, his scrawny moustache curled in concentration. He missed the shot and swore loudly. If the ball had been iron and the pocket magnetised, he still would have missed the shot. Hamill was just that kind of guy.

Someone in Gritty McDuff's had told me that Hamill hung out with Billy Purdue on occasion. I couldn't imagine why. Maybe Billy just wanted to be with someone who could make him look good.

'James Hamill?' I asked.

He scratched his ass and offered me his hand. His smile was a dentist's nightmare.

'Pleased to meet you, whoever you are. Now go fuck yourself.'

He went back to his game.

'I'm looking for Billy Purdue.'

'Get in line.'

'Someone else been asking after him?'

'Just about anyone with a uniform and a badge, from what I hear. You a cop?'

'Nope.'

'Private?' He drew back his cue slowly, aiming to put a stripe in the centre pocket.

'I guess.'

'You the one he hired?'

I lifted the stripe and the cue ball went straight into the pocket.

'Hey!' said Hamill. 'Gimme back my ball.' He sounded like a small, spoiled child, although I figured you'd have a hard time getting any mother to claim Hamill as her own.

'Billy Purdue hired a private investigator?' I said.

My tone betrayed me, for the look of profound unhappiness disappeared from Hamill's face to be replaced by a greedy leer.

'What's it to you?'

'I'm interested in talking to anyone who can help me to trace Billy. Who's the PI?' If Hamill didn't tell me, I could probably find out by calling around, assuming that whomever he had hired would admit to working for him.

'I wouldn't want to get my amigo into trouble,' said Hamill, rubbing his chin with a rough approximation of a thoughtful expression. 'What's your angle?'

'I worked for his ex-wife.'

'She's dead. Hope you got paid up front.'

I hefted the pool ball in my hand and thought about letting fly at Hamill's head. Hamill saw the intent in my face.

'Look, I need some cash,' he said, his manner softening. 'Let me have something, I'll give you his name.'

I took out my wallet and put a twenty on the table.

'Shit, twenty bucks,' spat Hamill. 'You're a regular Jack Benny without the laughs. It'll cost more than that.'

'I'll give you more. I want the name.'

Hamill considered for a moment. 'I don't know his first name, but he's called Wildon or Wifford or something.'

'Willeford?'

'Yeah, yeah, that's it. Willeford.'

I nodded my thanks and moved off.

'Hey! Hey!' shouted Hamill, and I could hear his sneakered feet shuffling across the floor behind me. 'What about my extra?'

I turned back. 'Sorry, I almost forgot.'

I put a dime on top of the twenty and gave him a wink as I returned the ball to the table.

'That's for the crack about his ex-wife. Enjoy it in good health.'

I walked away and headed for the stairs.

'Hey, Mr Trump,' shouted Hamill at my retreating back. 'You hurry back now, y'hear?'

Marvin Willeford wasn't in his office, a one-desk job above an Italian restaurant across from the blue Casco Bay ferry terminal, but a handwritten sign on the door said he had gone to lunch – a long lunch, obviously. I asked in the restaurant where Willeford usually hung out and the waiter gave me the name of a waterfront bar, the Sail Loft Tavern at Commercial and Silver.

During the eighteenth and nineteenth centuries, Portland harbour was a thriving centre for fishing and shipping. In those days, the wharves would be piled high with lumber bound for Boston and the West Indies. There would be lumber on them again soon, but now that wood was bound for China and the Middle East. Meanwhile, the redevelopment of the harbour, the building of new condos and stores to attract the tourists and the young professionals, was still the subject of controversy. It's hard to have a proper working harbour when folks in tie-dyes and sandals are hanging around taking pictures of one another and eating snow-cones. The Sail Loft looked like a throwback to the old days, the kind of place some people liked to call home.

I knew Willeford to see but I had never spoken to him and knew almost nothing about his past. He looked older than I remembered when I found him at the dark bar, watching the rerun of a basketball game on TV surrounded by sea horses and starfish on the walls. I figured he must be in his early sixties by now, jowly and bald, with a few strands of white hair flicked across his skull like seaweed on a rock. His skin was pale, almost translucent, with a fine tracery of veins at his cheeks and a bulbous red nose pitted with craters, like a relief map of Mars. His features seemed misty and inexact, as if they were slowly dissolving into the alcohol that coursed through his system, gradually becoming blurred versions of their original form.

He held a beer in one hand, an empty shot glass beside it, and the remains of a sandwich and potato chips lay on a plate before him as he watched the screen. He didn't slouch at the bar, though; he sat tall and straight, leaning slightly into the rest at the back of the chair.

'Hi,' I said as I took a seat beside him. 'Marvin Wille-ford?'

'He owe you money?' asked Willeford, without re-moving his gaze from the screen.

'Not yet,' I replied.

'Good. You owe him money?'

'Not yet,' I repeated.

'Pity. Still, I'd keep it that way if I were you.' He turned himself towards me. 'What can I do for you, son?'

It felt odd to have someone call me 'son' at thirty-four. I almost felt compelled to show some ID. 'My name's Charlie Parker.'

He nodded in recognition. 'I knew your grandaddy, Bob Warren. He was a good man. Hear you may be moving in on my patch, Charlie Parker.'

I shrugged. 'Maybe. Hope there'll be enough work for both of us. Buy you a beer?'

He drained his glass and called for a refill. I ordered coffee.

' "The old order changeth, yielding place to new," ' said Willeford sadly.

'Tennyson,' I said.

He smiled approvingly. 'Nice to see there are still some romantics left.' There was more to Willeford than long lunches in a dark bar. With his kind, there usually is.

He smiled and saluted with his new beer. 'Well at least you're not a total philistine, son. Y'know, I've been coming to this place for too many years. I look around and wonder how long more it'll be here, now that they're building fancy apartments and cute little stores on the port. Sometimes I think I ought to chain myself to some railings in protest, 'cept I got a bad hip and the cold makes me want to pee.' He shook his head sadly. 'So, what brings you to my office, son?'

'I was hoping you could tell me about Billy Purdue.'

He pursed his lips as he swallowed his beer. 'This professional, or personal? 'Cause if it's personal, then we're just talking, right? But if it's professional, then you got your ethics, you got your client confidentiality, you got your poaching, although – and here I'm speaking personally, you understand – you want to take Billy Purdue as a client, then be my guest. He lacked some of the basic qualities I look for in a client, like money, though from what I hear he needs a lawyer more'n a PI.'

'Let's call it personal, then.'

'Personal it is. He hired me to find his birth parents.'

'When?'

'Month or so back. He paid me two-fifty up front – in ones and fives, straight out of the cookie jar – but then couldn't pay anything more, so I dropped him. He wasn't real pleased about it, but business is business. Anyway, that boy was more trouble than arthritis.'

'How far did you get?'

'Well, I took the usual steps. I applied to the state for non-identifying information – you know, ages of the parents, professions, birth states, ethnicity. Got zilch, nada. The kid was found under a cabbage leaf.'

'No birth records at all?'

He held up his hands in mock amazement, then took another huge mouthful of beer. I reckoned it took him three mouthfuls to a glass. I was right.

'Well, I headed up to Dark Hollow. You know where that is, up north past Greenville?' I nodded. 'I had some other business up by Moosehead, figured I'd do Purdue a favour and carry on some of his work on my other client's time. The last guy who fostered him lives up thataways, though he's an old man now, older than me. His name's

Payne, Meade Payne. He told me that, far as he knew, Billy Purdue's was originally a private adoption arranged through some woman in Bangor and the sisters at St Martha's.'

St Martha's rang a bell, but I couldn't remember why. Willeford seemed to sense my struggle. 'St Martha's,' he repeated. 'Where that old lady killed herself few days back, the one who ran away. St Martha's used to be a convent and the nuns took in women who had, you know, fallen by the wayside. Except now all the nuns are dead, or Alzheimered out, and St Martha's is a private nursing home, strictly low end. Place smells of pee and boiled vegetables.'

'So no records?'

'Nothing. I looked through whatever files remained, which wasn't a whole lot. They kept a record of the births and retained copies of the relevant documents, but there was nothing that matched Billy Purdue. It didn't go through the books or, if it did, then somebody made sure to hide the traces. No one seemed to know why.'

'You talk to this woman, the one who arranged the adoption?'

'Lansing. Cheryl Lansing. Yeah, I spoke to her. She's old too. Jeez, even her kids were getting old. All I seem to meet is old people – old people and clients. I think I need to make some young friends.'

'People will talk,' I said. 'You'll get a reputation.'

He laughed to himself. 'Can you be a sugar daddy without having any cash?'

'I don't know. You could try, but I don't think you'd get very far.'

He nodded and finished his beer. 'Story of my life. Dead folks get more action than I ever did.'

So Cheryl Lansing was the woman who had arranged Billy Purdue's adoption. She obviously had more than a professional interest in him, if she was still trying to help out his ex-wife and his son three decades later. I pictured the bag of clothes, and the box of food, and the small wad of bills in Rita Ferris's hand. Cheryl Lansing had seemed like a nice woman. The news of the two deaths would hit her hard, I thought.

I called for another beer and Willeford thanked me. He was pretty stewed by now. I felt like a great guy, getting him so drunk that he wouldn't be able to work for the rest of the day just so I could satisfy my crusading urge.

'What about Cheryl Lansing?' I pressed.

'Well, she didn't want to talk about Purdue. I kept at her but it was no use. All she would say was that the woman was from up north, that she arranged the adoption as a favour to the sisters, that she didn't even know the woman's name. Apparently, she made some money brokering adoptions for the nuns and passed on a portion of the proceeds to them, except this one was *pro bono*. She had a copy of a birth certificate, though, but the parents were John and Jane Doe. I figured there had to be a record of the birth somewhere.'

'What did you do?'

'Well, through what Payne could tell me and by checking the records, I found that most of the people who fostered Billy Purdue also came from up north. Farthest south he got was Bangor, until he left for Boston when he was old enough. So I asked questions, put up notices with approximate dates of birth, even took out an advertisement in some of the local papers, then sat around and waited. Anyway, the money had run out by then and

I didn't see as how Purdue would be able to come up with any more.

'Then I got a call, saying I should talk to a woman in the old folks' home up in Dark Hollow, which brought the focus back to St Martha's.' He paused and took a long slug of beer. 'Well, I told Billy that I might have something and asked him if he wanted me to continue. He told me he had no more money, so I told him that, regretfully, I would have to cease our business relationship. Then he chewed me out some, threatened to smash up my office if I didn't help him out. I showed him this –' He pushed back his jacket to reveal a Colt Python with a long, eight-inch barrel. It made him look like an aging gunfighter. 'And he went on his way.'

'Did you give him the name of the woman?'

'I would have given him the coat off my back to get rid of him. I figured it was time to beat a strategic retreat. If I'd retreated any faster, I'd have been going forward again.'

My coffee was cold in the mug before me. I leaned over the bar and poured it into a sink.

'Any idea where Billy might be now?'

Willeford shook his head. 'There is one more thing,' he said.

I waited.

'The woman in St Martha's? Her name was Miss Emily Watts or, least, that's what she called herself. That name ring a bell with you?'

I thought for a while but came up with nothing. 'I don't think so. Should it?'

'She's the old lady who died in the snow. Strange stuff, don't you think?'

I remembered the full story now. The deaths of the

men at Prouts Neck had forced it from the forefront of my memory.

'You think Billy Purdue went to see her?'

'I don't know, but something spooked her enough to make her run off into the woods and kill herself when they tried to take her back.'

I stood and thanked him, then shrugged on my over-coat.

'It was my pleasure, son. You know, you look something like your grandaddy. You act like him too and you'll give no one cause to regret meeting you.'

I felt another pang of guilt. 'Thanks. You want me to give you a ride anywhere?'

He shook his glass to order another beer, and called for a whiskey chaser as well. I put down ten bucks on the bar to cover it, and he raised the empty glass in salute.

'Son,' he said, 'I ain't goin' nowhere.'

It was already growing dark when I left the bar and I pulled my coat tightly round me to protect myself from the cold. From off the harbour a wind came, running icy hands through my hair and rubbing my skin with chill fingers. I had parked the Mustang in the lot at One India, a corner of Portland with a dark history. One India was the original site of Fort Loyal, erected by the colonists in 1680. It only survived for ten years, before the French and their native allies captured it and butchered the one hundred and ninety settlers who had surrendered. Eventually, the India Street Terminal was built on the same spot, marking milepost 0.0 for the Atlantic and St Lawrence Railroad, the Grand Trunk Railway of Canada and the Canadian National Railways, when Portland was still an important rail centre. At One India, now occupied by an insurance company, it was still possible to see the sign for the Grand Trunk and Steamship Offices over the door.

The railroads had been gone for almost three decades now, although there was talk of rebuilding Union Station on St John and reopening the passenger railway from Boston. It was strange how things from the past, once thought lost and gone forever, should now be resurrected and made vivid once again in the present.

The windows of the Mustang were already beginning to frost over as I approached it, and a mist which sharpened every sound hung over the warehouses and the boats on the water. I was almost at the car when I heard the footsteps behind me. I began to turn, my coat now open, my right hand making a leisurely movement towards my gun, but something jammed into the small of my back and a voice said:

'Let it go. Keep them wide.'

I kept my hands horizontally away from my sides. A second figure limped from my right, his left foot curved slightly inwards, distorting his walk, and took my gun from its holster. He was small, maybe five-four, and probably in his late forties. His hair was thick and black over brown eyes and his shoulders were wide beneath his overcoat, his stomach hard. He might even have been handsome, but for a harelip that slashed his soft cupid's bow like a knife wound.

The second man was taller and bulkier, with long dark hair that hung over the collar of a clean white shirt. He had hard eyes and an unsmiling mouth that contrasted with the bright Winnie the Pooh tie neatly knotted at his neck. His head was almost square, set on wide, rectangular shoulders, with a thick muscular neck intervening.

He moved the way a kid moves an action figure, loping from side to side without bending his knees. Together, the two made quite a pair.

'Jeez, fellas, I think you may be a little late for trick or treat.' I leaned conspiratorially towards the shorter guy. 'And you know,' I whispered, 'if the wind changes direction, you'll be left that way.' They were cheap shots, but I didn't like people sneaking around in the mist poking guns in my back. As Billy Purdue might have said, it was kind of rude.

The shorter guy turned my gun over in his hand, examining the third generation Smith & Wesson with an expert's appreciation.

'Nice piece,' he said.

'Give it back and I'll show you how it works.'

He smiled a strange, jagged smile.

'You gotta come with us.' He waved me in the direction of India Street, where a pair of headlights had just flashed on in the darkness.

I looked back at the Mustang.

'Shit,' said Harelip, with a look of mock concern on his face. 'You worried about your car?'

He flicked the safety on my gun and fired at the Mustang, blowing out the front and rear tyres on the driver's side. From somewhere close by, a car alarm began to sound.

'There,' he said. 'Nobody's gonna steal it now.'

'I'll remember you did that,' I replied.

'Uh-huh. You want me to spell my name for you, you let me know.'

The taller guy gave me a shove in the direction of the car, a silver Seven Series BMW, which moved over to us and swung to the right, the rear door popping open.

Inside sat another handsome devil with short brown hair and a gun resting on his thigh. The driver, younger than the rest, popped bubble gum and listened to an AOR station on the car stereo. Bryan Adams came on as I climbed into the car, singing the theme song from *Don Juan de Marco*.

'Any possibility we could change the station?' I asked, as we drove off.

Beside me, Harelip prodded me hard with his gun.

'I like this song,' he said, humming along. 'You got no soul.'

I looked at him. I think he was serious.

We drove to the Regency Hotel on Milk Street, the nicest hotel in Portland, which occupied the former site of an old red brick armory in the Old Port. The driver parked in back and we walked to the side entrance near the hotel gym, where another young guy in a neat black suit opened the door for us before speaking into a mike on his lapel to advise that we were on our way up. We took an elevator to the top floor, where Harelip knocked respectfully at the end door on the right. When it opened, I was led in and brought to meet Tony Celli.

Tony sat in a big armchair with his shoeless feet on a matching footstool. His black stockings were silk and his grey trousers were immaculately pressed. He wore a blue-striped shirt with a white collar and a dark red tie marked with an intricate pattern of black spirals. Gold gleamed at his white cuffs. He was clean shaven and his black hair was neatly combed and parted to one side. His eyes were brown beneath thin, plucked eyebrows. His nose was long and unbroken, his mouth a little soft, his chin a little fat. There were no rings on his fingers, which lay clasped in his lap. In front of him, the TV was tuned to the nightly financial report. On a table beside him lay a pair of headphones and a bug detector, indicating that the room had already been searched for listening devices.

I knew Tony Celli by reputation. He had worked his way up through the ranks, running porn shops and whores in Boston's Combat Zone, paying his dues, gradually building up a power base. He took cash from the people below him and paid a lot of it to the people above him. He met his obligations and was now regarded as a hot tip for the future. I knew that he already had a certain amount of responsibility in money matters, based on a perception that he was gifted with financial acumen, a perception he now reinforced with his striped shirt and the attention he was paying to the stock prices that flashed past at the bottom of the screen.

I guessed that he was forty by now, certainly no more than that. He looked good. In fact, he looked like the sort of guy you could bring home to meet your mother, if you didn't think that he'd probably torture her, fuck her, then dump her remains in Boston harbour.

The nickname Tony Clean had stuck for a number of reasons: his appearance was part of it, but mainly it was because Tony never got his hands dirty. People had washed a lot of blood off their hands for Tony's sake, watching it spiral down into cracked porcelain bathtubs or stainless steel sinks, but Tony never got so much as a speck of it on his shirt.

I heard a story about him once, back in 1990 when he was still slashing up pimps who forgot how territorial Tony could be. A guy called Stan Goodman, a Boston real estate developer, owned a weekend house in Rockport, a big old gabled place with vast green lawns and an oak tree which was about two centuries old out by the boundary wall. Rockport's a pretty nice place, a fishing village north of Boston at Cape Ann where you can still park for a penny and the Salt Water trolley will haul you around town for four dollars a day.

Goodman had a wife and two teenage children, a boy and a girl, and they loved that house as well. Tony offered Stan Goodman a lot of money for the house, but he refused. It had belonged to his father, he said, and his father had bought it from the original owner back in the forties. He offered to find Tony Clean a similar property nearby, because Stan Goodman figured that if he kept on the good side of Tony Clean then everything would turn out okay. Except Tony Clean didn't have a good side.

One night in June, someone entered the Goodman house, shot their dog, bound and gagged the four members of the family and took them out to the old granite quarries at Halibut Point. My guess is that Stan Goodman died last, after they had killed his wife, his daughter and his son by placing their heads on a flat rock and cracking them open with a sledgehammer. There was a lot of blood on the ground when they were found the next morning, and I reckon it took the men who killed them a long time to wash it from their clothes. Tony Celli bought the house the following month. There were no other bidders.

The mere fact that Tony was here after what had taken place at Prouts Neck indicated that he wasn't screwing around. Tony wanted that money, and he wanted it bad, and he was willing to risk bringing down heat on himself to find it.

'You watch the news?' he said at last. He didn't look

away from the screen, but I knew that the question was directed at me.

'Nope.'

He looked at me for the first time.

'You don't watch any news?'

'Nope.'

'Why not?'

'It depresses me.'

'You must depress easy.'

'I have a sensitive nature.'

He stayed quiet for a moment, returning his attention to the screen as the report detailed the collapse of some bank in Tokyo.

'You don't watch the news?' he repeated, like I'd just told him I didn't like sex or Chinese food. 'Ever?'

'Like you say, I depress easy. Even the weather forecast depresses me.'

'That's because you live here. Try living in California, then the forecast won't depress you so much.'

'I hear it's sunny all year round.'

'Yeah, it's always sunny.'

'Then I'd get depressed by the monotony.'

'Doesn't sound like you're ever going to be truly happy.'

'You may be right, but I try to stay cheerful.'

'You're so cheerful, I'm starting not to like you.'

'That's a real shame. I thought we could hang out together, maybe take in a movie.'

The financial report ended. He clicked off the TV using a manicured finger on the remote, then turned his full attention to me.

'You know who I am?' he said.

'Yeah, I know who you are.'

'Good. Then, being an intelligent man, you probably know why I'm here.'

'Christmas shopping? Looking to buy a house?'

He smiled coldly. 'I know all about you, Parker. You're the one that took down the Ferreras.' The Ferreras were a New York crime family, 'were' being the operative word. I had become mixed up in their business, and it had ended badly for them.

'They took themselves down. I just watched.'

'That's not what I heard. A lot of people in New York would be happier if you were dead. They think you lack respect.'

'I'm sure.'

'So why aren't you dead?'

'I brighten up a dull world?'

'They want to brighten up their world, they can turn on a light. Try again.'

'Because they know I'll kill whoever comes after me, then I'll kill whoever sent them.'

'I could kill you now. Unless you can come back from the dead, your threats aren't going to disturb my sleep.'

'I have friends. I'd give you a week, maybe ten days. Then you'd die too.'

He pulled a face, and a couple of the men around him snickered. 'You play cards?' he asked, when they had finished laughing.

'Only solitaire. I like playing with someone I can trust.'

'You know what "fucking the deck" means?'

'Yeah, I know.' Fucking the deck was something neophyte gamblers did: they screwed up the cards by making dumb calls. That was why some experienced gamblers didn't play with amateurs, no matter how much money they had. There was always the chance that they'd fuck the deck so badly that the risk of losing increased to the extent that it wasn't worth gambling.

'Billy Purdue fucked my deck, and now I think you might be about to fuck my deck too. That's no good. I want you to stop. First I want you to tell me what you know about Purdue. Then I'll pay you to walk away.'

'I don't need money.'

'Everybody needs money. I can pay whatever debts you owe, maybe make some others disappear.'

'I don't owe anybody.'

'Everybody owes somebody.'

'Not me. I'm free and clean.'

'Or maybe you figure you got debts that money can't pay.'

'That's very perceptive. What does it mean?'

'It means I am running out of reasonable ways to alter your current course of action, Bird-*man*.' He made a little quotation marks sign with his fingers as he spoke the last syllable, then his voice lowered and he stood up. Even in his stocking feet, he was taller than I was.

'Now you listen to me,' he said, when he was only inches from me. 'Don't make me tear your wings off. I hear you did some work for Billy Purdue's ex-wife. I hear also that he gave you money, my money, to give to her. That makes you a very interesting individual, Birdman, because I figure you were one of the last people to talk to both of them before they went their separate ways. Now, do you want to tell me what you know so that you can go back to your little birdhouse and curl up for the night?'

I held his gaze. 'If I knew anything useful and told you, my conscience wouldn't let me sleep,' I said. 'As it happens, I don't know anything, useful or otherwise.'

'You know that Purdue has my money?'

'Has he?'

He shook his head, almost in sorrow. 'You're going to make me hurt you.'

'Did you kill Rita Ferris and her son?'

Tony took a step back then punched me hard in the stomach. I saw it coming and braced myself for the blow but the force was strong enough to send me to my knees. As I gasped for breath I heard a gun cock behind me and felt cold steel against my skull.

'I don't kill women and children,' said Tony.

'Since when?' I replied. 'New Year's?'

A clump of my hair was gripped in someone's hand and I was dragged to my feet, the gun still behind my ear.

'How stupid are you?' said Tony, rubbing the knuckles of his right hand. 'You want to die?'

'I don't know anything,' I repeated. 'I did some work for his ex-wife as a favour, crossed swords with Billy Purdue and walked away. That's all.'

Tony Clean nodded. 'What were you talking to the rummy in the bar about?'

'Something else.'

Tony drew his fist back again.

'It was something else,' I said again, louder this time. 'He was a friend of my grandfather's. I just wanted to look him up, that's all. You're right, he's just a rummy. Leave him be.'

Tony stepped back, still rubbing his knuckles.

'I find out you're lying to me, you'll die badly, you understand? And if you're a smart guy, and not just a guy with a smart mouth, you'll stay out of my affairs.'

The tone of his voice grew gentler, but his face hardened as he spoke again: 'I'm sorry we have to do this to you, but I need to be sure that you understand what we've discussed. If at any point you feel you have something to add to what you've told me, just moan louder.'

He nodded at whoever was behind me and I was forced down to my knees again. A rag was stuffed in my mouth, and my arms were pulled back and then secured with cuffs. I looked up to see Harelip limping towards me. In his hand, he held a black metal rod. Crackling blue lightning danced along its length.

The first two shots from the cattle prod knocked me backwards and sent me spasming to the ground, my teeth gritted in pain against the rag. After the third or fourth contact I lost control of myself and blue flashes moved through the blackness of my mind until, at last, the clouds took me and all went quiet.

When I came to, I was lying behind my Mustang, hidden from anyone walking on the street. The tips of my fingers were raw and my coat glittered with crystals of frost. My head ached badly, my body still trembled and there was dried blood and vomit on the side of my face and the front of my coat. I smelt bad. I got unsteadily to my feet and checked my coat pockets. My gun was in one, its clip gone, and my cell phone was in the other. I called a cab and, while I waited for it to arrive, made a call to a mechanic over by the Veteran's Memorial Bridge and asked him to take care of the car.

When I got back to Scarborough, the right side of my face had swollen badly and there were small burn marks where the prod had touched my skin. There were also two or three gashes on my head, one of them deep. I reckoned that Harelip had kicked me a couple of times for good measure. I put ice on my head and spray on the burns, then swallowed some painkillers, pulled on a pair of sweatpants and a T-shirt to guard against the cold, and tried to sleep.

I don't recall why I awoke, but when I opened my eyes the room seemed to hang between darkness and brightness, as if the universe had paused to draw a breath when the morning sun first sent shafts of light through the dark winter clouds.

And from somewhere in the house came a sound like the scuffling of feet, as if small delicate steps were padding over the floorboards. I drew my gun and rose. The floor was cold and the windows rattled gently. I opened the door slowly and stepped into the hallway.

To my right, a figure moved. I caught the motion out of the corner of my eye, so that I was not sure that I even saw a figure as such or merely a shifting of shadows in the kitchen. I turned and walked slowly to the back of the house, the boards creaking slightly beneath my feet.

Then I heard it: a soft burst of childlike laughter, a giggle of amusement, and the padding of feet again, moving to my left. I reached the entrance to the kitchen, the gun half raised, and turned in time to see another flash of movement by the door frame connecting the kitchen to the living room, to hear another cry of childish delight at the game we were playing. And I felt certain that what I had seen was a child's foot, its sole protected by the enclosures of purple rompers. And I knew too that I had seen that tiny foot before and the remembrance of it made my throat go dry.

I entered the dining room. Something small waited for me beyond the far door. I could see its form in the shadows and the light in its eyes, but no more than that.

As I moved in its direction, the form shifted and I heard the front door creak open on its hinges and impact against the wall, the wind now rushing through the house, pulling at the drapes, setting frames rattling and raising spirals of dust in the hallway.

I walked faster now. As I reached the door, I caught another glimpse of the little figure, something dressed in purple that flitted between the trees, moving farther and farther into the darkness beyond. I stepped from the porch and into the yard, felt the grass beneath my feet, the small stones digging into the soles, and tensed as something tiny and multilegged scuttled across my toes. I stood at the verge of the woods, and I was afraid.

She was waiting for me there. She stood unmoving, masked by bushes and trees that hid her body from me, her face now obscured by the shadows of branches, now clear again. Her eyes were full of blood and the thick black thread wove back and forth across her face like the crudely constructed mouth of an old cloth doll. She stood there unspeaking, watching me from the woods, and behind her the smaller figure danced and skipped in the undergrowth.

I closed my eyes and concentrated, trying to wake myself, but the cold in my feet was real, and the throbbing pain in my head, and the sound of the child's laughter carrying on the wind.

I felt movement behind me and something touched me on the shoulder. I almost turned, but the pressure on my shoulder increased and I knew that I must not turn, that I was not meant to see what stood at my back. I looked to my left, to the point of pressure, and I could not restrain the shudder that ran through my body. I closed my eyes instantly but what I had seen was imprinted on my mind like an image seen against bright sunlight.

The hand was soft and white and delicate, with long, tapering fingers. A wedding band gleamed in the strange, predawn light.

*bird*

How many times had I heard that voice whisper to me in the darkness, a prelude to the soft caress of a warm hand, the feel of her breath against my cheek, my lips, her small breasts hard against my body, her legs like ivy curling around me? I had heard it in times of love and passion when we were happy together, in moments of anger and rage and sadness as our marriage fell apart. And I had heard it since in the rustling of leaves on the grass and the sound of branches rubbing against one another in the autumn breezes, a voice that carried from far away and called to me from the shadows.

Susan, my Susan.

*bird*

The voice was close now, almost beside my ear, but I could feel no breath on my skin.

*help her*

In the woods beyond, the woman watched me, her red eyes wide and unblinking.

How?

*find him*

Find who? Billy?

The fingers tightened their grip.

*yes*

He's not my responsibility.

*they are all your responsibility*

And in the patches of moonlight beneath the trees, shapes twisted and turned, suspended above the earth, their feet not touching the ground, and their ruined stomachs shone dark and wet. All of them, my responsibility.

Then the pressure on my shoulder eased and I sensed her moving away. Ahead of me came a sound from the undergrowth and the woman who had been Rita Ferris receded into the trees. I caught a final glimpse of purple moving swiftly beyond the line of trees, laughter like music carrying back to me.

And I saw something else.

I saw a small girl with long blonde hair who looked back at me with something like love before she followed her playmate into the darkness.

# Chapter Nine

I woke to a bright room, winter sunlight spearing through a gap in the drapes. My head ached and my jaw felt stiff and sore where I had gritted my teeth as the shocks hit my body. It was only when I sat up and the pain in my head increased that I remembered my dream from the night before, if a dream were what it was.

My bed was full of leaves and twigs, and there was mud on my feet.

I had some homeopathic remedies which Louis had recommended to me, so I took them with a glass of water while I waited for the shower to heat up. I downed a combination of phosphorus, to combat nausea, and gelsemium, which Louis claimed countered feelings of shakiness. I also took some hypericum, which was supposed to act as a natural painkiller. Frankly, I felt like a flake taking the stuff but there was no one around to see me do it, so that made it all right.

I started a pot of coffee, filled a mug and watched it grow cold on the kitchen table. I felt pretty low and was considering taking up a different profession – gardening, maybe, or lobster fishing. After the coffee had developed a nice film, I called Ellis Howard. I figured that, since he had turned up at Lester Biggs's place, Ellis was taking a hands-on approach to the case. It took a while for him to come to the phone. He was probably still sore over the Biggs affair.

'You're awake early,' were his first words when he got to the phone. I could hear him sigh as he eased his bulk into a chair. I could even hear the chair squeaking in protest. If Ellis had sat on me, I'd have squeaked too.

'I could say the same about you,' I said. 'I trust you've had your coffee and doughnuts?'

'Mine, and someone else's. You aware that Tony Celli turned up in town yesterday?'

'Yeah. Bad news travels fast.' Particularly when it's being passed into your jaw in the form of an electric current.

'He blew out again this morning. Looks like he's gone to ground.'

'It's a shame. I thought he was going to move here and open a florist's.'

At the other end of the phone there was the sound of the receiver being covered, a muffled exchange and then the rustling of papers. Then: 'So what do you want, Bird?'

'I wanted to know if there was any movement on Rita Ferris, or Billy Purdue, or on that Coupe de Ville.'

Ellis laughed dully. 'Ixnay on the first two, but the third one is interesting. Turns out the Coupe de Ville is a company car, registered to one Leo Voss, a lawyer in Boston.' There was a pause on the other end of the line. I waited until I realised that, once again, I was supposed to be playing the role of straight man in a conversation.

'But . . . ?' I said at last.

'*But,*' said Ellis, 'Leo Voss is no longer with us. He's dead, died six days ago.'

'Damn, a dead lawyer. Only another million to go.'

'We live in hope,' said Ellis.

'Did he fall, or was he pushed?'

'That's the interesting part. His secretary found him and called the cops. He was sitting behind his desk still dressed in his running outfit – sneakers, socks, T-shirt, sweatpants – with an opened bottle of mineral water in front of him. Their first impression was that he'd had a heart attack. According to the secretary, he'd been feeling ill for a day or too. He thought it might be flu.

'But when he was autopsied, there was evidence of inflammation of the nerves in the hands and feet. He'd also lost some hair, probably only in the previous day or two. Tests on a hair sample turned up traces of thallium. You know what thallium is?'

'Yeah, I know.' My grandfather had used it as ratbait, until its sale was restricted. It was a metallic element, similar to lead or mercury, but far more poisonous. Its salts were soluble in water, almost tasteless and produced symptoms similar to influenza, meningitis or encephalitis. A lethal dose of thallium sulphate, maybe eight hundred milligrams or more, could kill in anything from twenty-four to forty hours.

'So what sort of work did this Leo Voss do?' I asked.

'Fairly straightforward stuff, mainly corporate, although what he did must have been pretty lucrative. He had a house in Beacon Hill, a summer place in the Vineyard, and still had some money in the bank, probably because he was single and there was no one putting fur coats on *his* credit card.'

Doreen, I thought. If Ellis could have afforded it, he'd have pasted pictures of her outside churches as a warning to others.

'They're still going through his files, but he seems to have been squeaky clean,' concluded Ellis.

'Which probably means that he wasn't.'

Ellis tut-tutted. 'Such cynicism in one so young. Now I've got something for you: I hear you were talking to Willeford.'

'That's right. Is that a problem?'

'Could be. He's gone, and I'm starting to resent arriving in places to find that you've already been there. It's making me feel inadequate, and I get enough of that at home.'

I felt my grip tighten on the phone. 'Last I saw of him, he was sitting in the Sail Loft nursing a drink.'

'Willeford never nursed a drink in his life. They don't survive in the glass long enough to be nursed. He give any indication that he might be planning to go away somewhere?'

'No, nothing.' I recalled Tony's Celli's interest in Willeford and felt my mouth go dry.

'What did you two talk about?'

I paused before I spoke. 'He did some work for Billy Purdue: tracing of birth parents.'

'That it?'

'That's it.'

'He have any luck?'

'I don't think so.'

Ellis went quiet, then said distinctly: 'Don't hold back on me, Bird. I don't like it.'

'I'm not.' It wasn't quite a lie, but I'm not sure that it qualified as the truth either. I waited for Ellis to say something more, but he didn't push the issue.

'Stay out of trouble, Bird,' was all he said, before he hung up.

★　　★　　★

I had just finished cleaning off the table and was in my bedroom slipping on my boots when I heard the sound of a car pulling up outside. Through the gap in the drapes I could see the rear of a gold Mercury Sable parked near the side of the house. I took my Smith & Wesson, wrapped it in a towel and walked onto the porch. And as I stepped into the cold morning sunlight, I heard a voice that I knew say:

'Why would anybody plant so many trees? I mean, who has that kind of time? I can't even find time to get my laundry done.'

Angel stood with his back to me, staring out at the trees at the edge of my property. He wore a Timberland fleece top, a pair of brown corduroy pants and tan work boots. At his feet was a hard plastic suitcase that was so pitted and battered it looked like it had been dropped from an airplane. A piece of blue climbing rope and the whim of fortune held it closed.

Angel breathed in deeply then bent over as his body was racked by a fit of coughing. He spat something large and unpleasant onto the ground before him.

'That's the clean air getting the shit out of your lungs,' said a deep, drawling voice. From behind the raised trunk door of the car Louis appeared holding a matching Delsey case and suit carrier. He wore a black Boss overcoat beneath which a grey double-breasted suit shimmered. A black shirt was buttoned to the neck and his shaved head gleamed. In the open trunk, I could see a long, metal storage case. Louis never went anywhere without his toys.

'I think that *was* my lung,' said Angel, using the tip of his boot to poke with interest at whatever piece of matter had expelled itself from his body. As I looked at them both, my spirits lifted. I wasn't sure why they were here instead of back in New York but, whatever the reason, I was glad. Louis glanced at me and nodded, which was usually as close as Louis ever came to looking pleased about anything.

'You know, Angel,' I said, 'you make nature look untidy just by standing there.'

Angel turned and raised an arm in a sweeping gesture.

'Trees,' he said, shaking his head in bafflement and smiling. 'So many trees. I ain't seen this many trees since I got thrown out of the Indian Scouts.'

'You know, I don't think I even want to know why,' I said.

Angel picked up his case. 'Bastards. And I was just about to get my explorer's badge too.'

'Didn't think they had badges for the shit you was exploring,' said Louis, from behind. 'Badge like that could get a man thrown in jail in Georgia.'

'Funny,' barked Angel. 'It's just a myth that you can't be gay and do macho things.'

'Uh-huh. Just like it's a myth that all homosexuals wear nice clothes and take care of their skin.'

'That better not be aimed at me.'

It was nice to see that some things hadn't changed.

'How you doin' today?' said Angel, as he pushed past me. 'And lose the gun. We're staying, like it or not. You look like shit, by the way.'

'Nice suit,' I remarked to Louis, as he followed Angel.

'Thanks,' he replied. 'Never forget: no such thing as a brother with no taste, just a brother with no money.'

I stood on the porch for a moment, feeling a little stupid holding the towel-wrapped gun. Then, figuring that the matter had obviously been decided long before they got to Maine, I followed them into the house.

I showed them to the spare bedroom, where the furniture consisted only of a mattress on the floor and an old closet.

'Jesus,' said Angel. 'It's the Hanoi Hilton. If we knock on the pipes, someone better answer.'

'You gonna supply sheets, or we have to roll some drunks and steal their coats?' asked Louis.

'I can't sleep here,' said Angel, with an air of finality. 'If the rats want to feed on me, fuckers should at least have to go to the trouble of climbing up a bedframe.'

He brushed past me again and, seconds later, I heard his voice call:

'Hey, this one's much nicer. We'll take this.'

There came the unmistakable sound of someone bouncing up and down on my bed. Louis looked at me.

'Might need that gun after all,' he said. Then he shrugged and followed the sound of the springs.

When I eventually got them out of my bedroom and had arranged to have some extra furniture, including a bed, taken out of the Kraft Mini-Storage on Gorham Road and delivered to the house, we sat around the kitchen table and I waited for them to tell me why they were here. It had begun to rain: hard, cold drops that spoke of the coming of snow.

'We're your fairy godparents,' said Angel.

'I'm not sure that was meant to be taken quite so literally,' I replied.

'Maybe we just heard that this is the place to be,' continued Angel. 'Anybody who's anybody is here right now. You got your Tony Celli, you got your feds, you got your local shit-kickers, you got your dead Asians. Shit, this place is like the UN with guns.'

'What do you know?' I asked.

'We know that you've been pissing people off already,' he replied. 'What happened to your face?'

'Guy with a harelip tried to educate me with a cattle-prod, then rearranged my hair-line with his shoe.'

Angel grimaced in sympathy. 'Guys with harelips, they just want to share their physical defects with everybody.'

'That's Mifflin,' said Louis. 'He have another guy with him, looked like someone dropped a safe on his head and the safe lost?'

'Yeah,' I said. 'He didn't kick me, though.'

'That's 'cause the message probably got halfway from his brain to his foot then forgot where it was going. His name's Berendt. He's so dumb he makes dirt look smart. Tony Clean was with them?' While he spoke, he balanced one of my carving knives on the tip of his index finger and amused himself by tossing it in the air and catching it by the handle. It was a pretty neat trick. If the circus came to town, he was a shoo-in.

'They were staying at the Regency,' I said. 'I got to visit Tony's room.'

'Was it nice?' said Angel, pointedly running a hand along the underside of the table and examining the accumulated dust on the tips of his fingers.

'Yeah, pretty nice, apart from the kicks in the head and the electric shocks.'

'Fuck him. We should make him stay here. A bit of squalor would put him back in touch with his roots.'

'You criticize my house again, you can sleep in the yard.'

'Probably be cleaner,' he muttered. 'And warmer.'

Louis tapped a long, slim finger gently on the tabletop. 'Hear there's a lot of money got misdirected around these parts. A *lot* of money.'

'Yeah, so I gather.'

'Any idea where it is?'

'Maybe. I think it's with a guy called Billy Purdue.'

'That's what I hear too.'

'From Tony Celli's end?'

'Disaffected employees. They figure this Billy Purdue's so dead, someone should name a cemetery after him.'

I told them about the deaths of Rita and Donald. I noticed Angel and Louis exchange a glance and I knew that there was more to come.

'Billy Purdue take out Tony's men?' asked Angel.

'Two of them, at least. Assuming he's the one who took the money, and that's what Tony Celli and the law have assumed.'

Louis stood and carefully washed his mug. 'Tony's in trouble,' he said at last. 'Got involved in some deal on Wall Street that fell through.' I had heard stories that the Italians had moved into Wall Street, establishing paper companies and getting crooked brokers to float them and rip off investors. There was a lot of money to be made if it was done right.

'Tony screwed up,' continued Louis, 'and now you got a guy whose days are numbered in single figures.'

'How bad is it?'

Louis placed the mug upside down to drain, then leaned against the sink. 'You know what PERLS is?'

'PERLS *are*,' I corrected him, incorrectly as it turned out. 'Things found in oysters?'

'Not unless an oyster can take you for one-point-five mil. Easy to know you never had no money to invest.'

'I live an ascetic existence, like Father Damien without the lepers.'

'PERLS,' said Louis, 'stands for Principal Exchange Rate Linked Security. It's a structured note, a kind of bond sold by investment banks. It's packaged to look safe, except it's risky as sex with a shark. Basically, the buyer bets a certain amount of money and the return is based on the changes in the exchange rate of a number of different currencies. It's a formula, and if things go right, you can make a killing.'

I always found it fascinating that Louis could drop the monosyllabic black gunman shtick if the subject required it, but I didn't point it out to him.

'So Tony Celli thinks he's a financial wizard, and some people in Boston believe him,' he went on. 'He takes care of laundering, passes a lot of money through offshore banks and paper companies, until it finds its way back into the right accounts. He deals with the accountants, but he's also the first point of contact for any cash. He's like the thinnest part of an hourglass: everything has to go through him to get to somewhere else. And sometimes, Tony makes a few investments on the side using other people's money, or makes a little on currency exchanges, and keeps what he makes. No one cares, long as he doesn't get too greedy.'

'Let me guess,' I interrupted. 'Tony got too greedy.'

Louis nodded. 'Tony's tired of being an Indian and now he wants to be a chief. He figures he needs money to do that, more than he's got. So he gets talking to some derivatives salesman who doesn't have a fucking clue who Tony is beyond the fact that he's a wop in a striped shirt with money to spend, because Tony is trying to keep his dealings as low-key as possible. He convinces Tony to

buy a variation on these PERLS, linked to the difference
between the value of some south-east Asian currencies
and a basket of other currencies – dollars, Swiss francs,
German marks, I heard – and pockets the commission.
The thing is so dangerous it should be ticking, but Tony
buys in for one and a half million dollars, most of which
isn't his own money, because there are midwestern insurance companies and pension funds in on the deal too
and Tony figures wrongly that they're too conservative
to bet on a risky hand. It's purely a short-term investment, and Tony figures he'll have his money made before
anybody notices he's holding onto the cash for longer
than usual.'

'So what happened?'

'You read the papers. The yen plummets, banks fail,
the whole economy of south-east Asia starts to come
unstuck. The value of Tony's bonds falls by ninety-five
per cent in forty-eight hours, and his life expectancy falls
by roughly the same amount. Tony sends some people to
look for the salesman and they find him in Zip City down
on 18th Street, laughing about how he ripped some guy's
face off, 'cause that's what these salesmen call it when they
sell someone an exploding bond.'

And with those words, according to Louis, the salesman had signed his own death warrant. He was taken
when he went to the bathroom, brought to a basement in
Queens and tied to a chair. Then Tony came in, stuck his
fingers in the soft flesh beneath the guy's chin, and started
to pull. It took him less than two minutes to tear the guy's
face apart, then they put him in a car and beat him to
death in some woods upstate.

Louis picked up the knife again, gave it a couple of
extra spins for good luck, then put it back in its wooden

block. There was no blood on his fingertip, despite the pressure of the knifepoint. 'So Tony's in the hole for the cash, and some people higher up start getting concerned about the length of time it's taking for their money to reach them. Then Tony gets lucky: some mook in Toronto, who owes Tony big time, tells him about this old Cambodian guy living the quiet life in Hamilton, south of the city. It seems the old man was Khmer Rouge, used to be a deputy director in the Tuol Seng camp in Phnom Peng.'

I had heard of Tuol Seng. It had once been a school in the Cambodian capital, but was converted into a place of torture and execution by the Khmer Rouge when they took over the country. Tuol Seng had been run by the big-eared camp director known as Comrade Deuch, who had used whips, chains, poisonous reptiles and water to torture and kill maybe sixteen thousand people, including westerners who strayed too close to the Cambodian coast.

'Seems like this old man had friends in Thailand, and made a lot of money on the side by acting as a conduit for heroin smuggling,' said Louis. 'When the Vietnamese invaded, he disappeared and reinvented himself as a restaurateur in Toronto. His daughter had just started school in Boston, so Tony targeted her, took her and sent her old man a ransom demand to cover his debts, and then some. The old man couldn't go to the cops because of his past, and Tony gave him seventy-two hours to comply, though his daughter was already dead by then. The old man comes up with the money, sends his men down to Maine for the drop and – bam! – it all goes haywire.'

That explained the presence of the Toronto cop, Eldritch. I mentioned him to Louis and he raised a slim finger. 'One more thing: at the same time that the killings were going down here, the old man's house in Hamilton burned to the ground, with him, the rest of his family and his personal guards still in it. Seven people, all told. Tony wanted it to be clean, because he's a clean kind of guy.'

'So Tony's got a price on his head and then Billy Purdue takes his get-out-of-jail-free card,' I remarked. 'Now, you want to tell me what that look that passed between you and Angel was about?' When Louis had finished talking, Angel had once again glanced at him in a way that told me that there was something more to hear, and it wasn't good.

Louis watched as the rain speckled the window.

'You got more problems than Tony and the law,' he said quietly. His face was serious, his expression mirrored by the usually ebullient Angel.

'How bad?'

'Don't think it gets any worse. You ever hear of Abel and Stritch?'

'No. What do they do, make soap?'

'They kill people.'

'With all due respect, that hardly makes them unique in the present company.'

'They enjoy it.'

And for the next half hour, Louis traced the path of the two men known only as Abel and Stritch, a trail marked by torture, burnings, gassings, casual sexual homicide, the rape and violent abuse of women and children, paid and unpaid assassinations. They broke bones and spilled blood; they electrocuted and asphyxiated. Their trail wound its way around the world like a coil of barbed wire, stretching from Asia and South Africa to South and Central America, through every trouble spot where people might pay to have their enemies terrorised and killed, whether those enemies were guerillas, agents of the government, peasants, priests, nuns or children.

Louis told me of an incident in Chile, when a family suspected of harbouring Mapuche Indians was targeted by agents of Pinochet's National Intelligence Directorate. The family's three sons, aged seventeen, eighteen and twenty, were taken to the basement of an abandoned office building, gagged and tied to the concrete supports of the building. Their mother and sisters were led in and forced at gunpoint to sit facing the men. Nobody spoke.

Then a figure had appeared from the darkness at the back of the room, a squat, pale man with a bald head and dead eyes. Another man remained in the shadows, but they could see his cigarette flare occasionally and could smell the smoke he exhaled.

In his right hand, the pale man held a large, five-hundred watt soldering iron, adapted so that its glowing tip was almost half an inch long and burned at two or three hundred degrees. He walked to the youngest son, pulled back the boy's shirt and applied the tip to his breast, just below the sternum. The iron hissed as it entered the flesh, and the smell of burning pork filled the room. The boy struggled as the iron went deeper and deeper, and muffled noises of panic and pain came from his mouth. His tormentor's eyes had changed now, had become bright and alive, and his breathing came in short, excited gasps. With his free hand, he fumbled at the zipper of the boy's pants, and he reached in and held him as the iron moved upward towards the boy's heart. As it pierced the wall of muscle, the pale man's grip tightened and he smiled as the boy shook and died.

The women told them what they knew, which was little, and the other boys died quickly, as much because the pale man had spent himself as because of what had been revealed.

Now these men had come north, north as far as Maine.

'Why are they here?' I said at last.

'They want the money,' said Louis. 'Men like them, they make enemies. If they're good at what they do, most of those enemies don't live long enough to do them any harm. But the longer they keep working, the more the chances of someone slipping through the net increase. These two have been killing for decades. The clock is ticking on them now. That money would help to provide a pretty cool retirement fund. I got a feeling they may be calling on you, which is why we're here.'

'What do they look like?' I asked, but I already had my suspicions.

'That's the problem. Nothing on Abel, 'cept he's tall with silver, almost white, hair. But Stritch, the torturer . . . The guy is a fucking freak-show: small, with a wide, bald head, a mouth like an open wound. Looks like Uncle Fester but without the good nature.'

I thought of the strange, goblinlike man outside the inn, the same man who had later turned up at Java Joe's ostensibly proselytising for the Lord, with his crudely-drawn picture of a mother and child and his soft, implicit threats.

'I've seen him,' I said.

Louis wiped his hand across his mouth. I had never before found him so concerned about the threat posed by anyone. In my mind, I still had an image of the darkness coming alive in an old warehouse back in Queens and one of the city's most feared killers rising up on his toes, his mouth wide, as Louis's blade entered the base of his skull. Louis didn't frighten easily. I told him about the car and the encounter in the coffee shop, and the lawyer named Leo Voss.

'My guess is that Voss was their point of contact, the guy people came to if they wanted to hire Abel and Stritch,' said Louis. 'If he's dead, then they killed him. They're closing down the operation, and they don't want no loose ends. If Stritch is here, then so is Abel. They don't work separately. He make any other move?'

'No. I got the feeling he just wanted to make his presence felt.'

'Takes a special guy to drive around in a dead man's Caddy,' said Angel. 'Kind of guy who wants to draw attention to himself.'

'Or away from someone else,' I said.

'He's watching,' said Louis. 'So is his partner, somewhere. They're waiting to see if you can lead them to Billy Purdue.' He thought for a moment. 'The woman and the boy, were they tortured?'

I shook my head. 'The woman was strangled. No sign of other injuries or sexual assault. The boy died because he got in the way.' I recalled the sight of Rita Ferris's mouth as the cops turned her over. 'There was one thing: the killer sewed the woman's mouth shut with black thread after she died.'

Angel screwed up his face. 'Makes no sense.'

'Makes no sense if it's Abel and Stritch,' agreed Louis. 'They'd have ripped her fingers off and hurt the boy to find out what she knew about the money. Doesn't sound like their work.'

'Or Tony Celli's,' added Angel.

'The cops think Billy may have killed them,' I said. 'It's possible, but there's still no reason for him to mutilate the mouth.'

We were silent then as we balanced and weighed what we knew. I think we all moved towards the same conclusion, but it was left to Louis to voice it:

'There's someone else.'

Outside, the rain fell hard, hammering on the tiles and raking at the windowpanes. I felt a coldness at my shoulder, or perhaps it was just the memory of a touch, and the voice of the rain seemed to whisper to me in a language that I could not comprehend.

A couple of hours later, a truck arrived with some of my furniture and we set up a bed in the spare room, added some throw rugs and generally made the place look like a home away from home, as long as the original home was nothing too fancy. Then, when we had all freshened up, we drove into Portland, past the blue-and-white lights of the Christmas tree at Congress Square and the second, larger tree at Monument Square. We parked the car, then strolled down to the Stone Coast Brewing Company on York Street, where Angel and Louis drank microbrew beer while we decided where to eat.

'You got a sushi bar around here?' asked Louis.

'I don't eat seafood,' I said.

'You don't eat seafood?' Louis's voice rose an octave. 'The fuck you mean, you don't eat seafood? You live in Maine. Lobsters practically hand you a knife and fork and invite you to chew on their ass.'

'You *know* I don't eat seafood,' I replied patiently. 'It's just a thing.'

'It's not just a thing, man, it's a *phobia*.'

Beside me, Angel smiled. It was good to be out like this, to be acting in this way, after what we had spoken of earlier.

'Sorry,' I continued, 'but I draw the line at anything with more than four legs, or no legs at all. I bet you even eat the lungs out of crabs.'

'Lungs, the crab juice . . .'

'That's not juice, Louis, it's the contents of their digestive system. Why do you think it's yellow?'

He waved a hand dismissively. 'Ain't no crab shit in sushi anyways.'

Angel drained the last of his beer. 'Well I'm with Bird on this one,' he said. 'Last time I was in LA I ate in a sushi bar. Pretty much ate them out of anything that had gills. Went outside, took one last look in the window, and the place had a "C" grading from the health department. A fucking "C"! I might eat in a burger joint with a "C" grade, worst you could expect would be a dose of Ronald McDonald's Revenge, but C-graded sushi . . . Man, that stuff'll kill you. Damn fish was so bad, it almost pulled a gun and tried to steal my wallet.'

Louis put his head in his hands and prayed to whomever it was that people like Louis prayed to – Smith & Wesson, probably.

We ate in Tony's Thai Taste on Wharf Street, down in the Old Port. As it happened, sitting three tables away from us were Samson and Doyle, the two feds I had seen at Rita Ferris's apartment, and the Toronto policeman, Eldritch. They gave us interested but unfriendly looks, then went back to their red curries.

'Friends of yours?' said Angel.

'The federal boys, plus their cousin from north of the border.'

'Feds got no reason to like you, Bird. Not that they need a reason not to like anyone.'

Our own food came: one Paradise Chicken for Louis

and two chef's favourites for Angel and me, made up of beef with peppers, pineapple and green peas, spiced with lemon grass and a garlic and chili sauce. Louis caught the smell of the garlic and wrinkled his nose. I figured no one would be kissing either of us good night tonight.

We ate in silence. The feds and Eldritch left in the course of our meal. I got the feeling that I'd be hearing from them again. When they were gone, Louis dabbed his lips carefully with a napkin and drained the last of his Tsing-Tsao beer. 'You got a plan of campaign on the Billy Purdue thing?'

I shrugged. 'I've asked around, but he's gone to earth. Part of me says that he's here, but another part tells me that he may be heading north. If he's in trouble, my guess is that he may look for someone who's been sympathetic to him in the past, and those people are precious few. There's a guy up by Moosehead Lake in a place called Dark Hollow, acted as Billy Purdue's foster parent for a time. It may be that he knows something, or has heard from him.'

I told them about my conversation in the bar with Willeford and his subsequent disappearance. 'I'm also going to pay a call on Cheryl Lansing, see if she can add anything to what she told Willeford.'

'Sounds like your curiosity's been sparked,' remarked Angel.

'Maybe, but . . .'

'But?'

I didn't want to tell him about my experience the night before, no matter how much I trusted him. That was the stuff of madness. 'But I owe something to Rita and her son. And, anyhow, it seems like other people have decided to involve me whether I like it or not.'

'Ain't that always the way?'

'Yeah.' I reached into my wallet, took out the bill from the furniture removal firm and waved it pointedly at Angel. 'Ain't that always the way?' I echoed.

He smiled. 'Take that attitude and we might never leave.'

'Don't even go there, Angel,' I warned. 'And pick up the check. It's the least you can do.'

# Chapter Ten

I woke late and refreshed for the trip to Bangor. Angel and Louis were still in bed, so I drove to Oak Hill, intending to stop off at the bank to withdraw some cash for the trip north. But when I had finished, I headed on down Old County Road, then onto Black Point Road and past the White Caps Sandwich Shop until I reached Ferry Road. To my left was the golf course, to my right the summer homes, and ahead of me was the parking lot where the men had died. The rain had washed away the evidence, but lengths of tattered crime scene tape still fluttered on one of the barriers as the wind howled in off the sea.

As I stood, taking in the scene, a car pulled up behind me, a cruiser driven by one of the Neck cops.

'You okay, sir?' he asked, as he stepped from the car.

'Yeah, just looking,' I replied. 'I live up on Spring Street.'

He sized me up, then nodded. 'I recognise you now. Sorry, sir, but after what happened here, we have to be careful.'

I waved a hand at him, but he seemed to be in the mood for conversation. He was young, certainly younger than I was, with straw-coloured hair and soft, serious eyes. 'Strange business,' he said. 'It's usually pretty quiet and peaceful here.'

'You from around these parts?' I asked.

He shook his head. 'No sir. Flint, Michigan. Moved east after GM screwed us over, and started again here. Best move I ever made.'

'Yeah, well, this place hasn't always been so peaceful.' My grandfather could trace his family's roots back to the mid seventeenth century, maybe two decades after Scarborough was first settled in 1632 or 1633. Back then, the whole area was called Black Point and the settlement was abandoned twice because of attacks by the natives. In 1677, the Wabanaki had attacked the English fort at Black Point on two occasions, killing over forty English soldiers and a dozen of their Indian allies from the Protestant mission village at Natick, near Boston. Maybe ten minutes by car from where we were standing was Massacre Pond, where Richard Hunnewell and nineteen others had died in an Indian attack in 1713.

Now, with its summer homes and its yacht club, its bird sanctuary and its tennis courts, it was easy to forget that this was once a violent, troubled place. There was blood beneath the ground here, layer upon layer of it like the marks left in rock faces by seas that had ceased to exist hundreds of millions of years before. I sometimes felt that places retained memories – houses, lands, towns, mountains, all holding within themselves the ghosts of past experiences – and that history had a way of repeating itself that might lead a man to believe that sometimes these places acted just like magnets, attracting bad luck and violence to them like iron filings. In that way of thinking, once a lot of blood was spilled somewhere then there was a pretty good chance that it would be spilled there again.

If that was true, then it wasn't strange that eight men should have ended their lives so bloodily here. It wasn't strange at all.

When I returned to the house I toasted some English muffins, made some coffee to go with them and had a quiet breakfast in the kitchen while Louis and Angel showered and dressed.

We had decided the night before that Louis would stay at the house, maybe take a look round Portland and see if he could find any signs of Abel and Stritch. Also, in the event that anything developed while we were away, he could call me on the cell phone and let me know.

Portland to Bangor is one hundred and twenty five miles north on I-95. As we drove, Angel flipped through my cassette tape collection impatiently, listening to something for one or two songs then discarding it on the back seat. The Go-Betweens, The Triffids, The Gourds out of Austin, Jim White, Doc Watson, they all ended up in the pile, so that the car started to look like an A&R man's nightmare. I put on a Lambchop cassette, and the gentle, sad chords of *I Will Drive Slowly* filled the car.

'What'd you say this is?' asked Angel.

'Alternative country,' I replied.

'That's when your truck starts, your wife comes back and your dog gets resurrected,' he snickered.

'Willie Nelson heard you talking like that, he'd whip your ass.'

'This the same Willie Nelson whose wife once tied him up in a bedsheet and beat him unconscious with a broom handle? That pothead comes after me, I reckon I can handle myself.'

Eventually, we settled for a discussion of local news on

PBS. There was some talk of a timber company surveyor who might have gone missing up north, but I didn't pay a whole lot of attention to it.

At Waterville, we took the off ramp and stopped for soup and coffee. Angel toyed with saltine crumbs as we waited for the check. He had something on his mind, and it didn't take long for it to emerge.

'Remember when I asked you about Rachel, back in New York?' he said at last.

'I remember,' I replied.

'You weren't too keen on talking about it.'

'I'm still not.'

'Maybe you should.'

There was a pause. I wondered when Louis and Angel had discussed Rachel and me, and guessed that it might have come up between them more than once. I relented a little.

'She doesn't want to see me,' I said.

He pursed his lips. 'And how do you feel about that?'

'You going to charge me by the hour for this?'

He flicked a crumb at me. 'Just answer the question.'

'Not so good but, frankly, I've got other things on my mind.'

Angel's eyes flicked up at me, then back down again. 'Y'know, she called once, to ask how you were.'

'She called *you*? How'd she get your number?'

'We're in the book.'

'No, you're not.'

'Well, then, we must have given it to her.'

'You're so helpful.' I sighed, and ran my hands over my face. 'I don't know, Angel. The whole thing is screwed up. I don't know if I'm ready yet and, anyway,

I frighten her. She's the one who pushed me away, remember?'

'You didn't need a whole lot of pushing.'

The check came, and I put down a ten and some ones on top of it. 'Yeah, well . . . I had my reasons. Just like she did.'

I stood, and Angel stood with me.

'Maybe,' he said. 'Pity neither of you could come up with one good reason between you.'

As we drove back onto I-95, Angel stretched contentedly beside me and, as he did so, the sleeve of his oversized shirt fell down to his elbow. On his arm, a scar, white and ragged, ran from the hollow curve on his elbow to within an inch or two of his wrist. It was maybe six inches long in total and I couldn't imagine why I hadn't noticed it before but, as I thought about it, I realised it was a combination of factors: the fact that Angel rarely wore only a T-shirt or, if he did so, it was one with long sleeves; my own self-absorption while we were in Louisiana hunting the Travelling Man; and Angel's basic lack of inclination to discuss anything about past pains.

He caught me looking at the scar and reddened, but he did not try to hide it immediately. Instead, he looked at it himself and went quiet, as if recalling its making.

'You want to know?' he asked.

'You want to tell?'

'Not particularly.'

'Then don't.'

He didn't respond for a time, then: 'It kind of concerns you, so maybe you got a right to know.'

'If you tell me you've always been in love with me, I'm stopping the car and you can walk to Bangor.'

Angel laughed. 'You're in denial.'

'You have no idea how deep.'

'Anyway, you ain't that good lookin'.' He touched the scar gently with the index finger of his right hand. 'You been in Rikers, right?'

I nodded. I'd been at Rikers Island in the course of investigations. I had also been there while Angel was a prisoner, when another inmate named William Vance had threatened to take Angel's life and I had intervened. Vance was dead now. He had died, at last, in October from injuries received after persons unknown poured detergent down his throat, after they learned that he was a suspected sex killer who would never stand trial for his crimes because of a lack of evidence. I had provided the information on which his attackers had acted. I had done it to save Angel, and Vance was no loss to the world, but it still weighed on my conscience.

'First time Vance came at me, I knocked out one of his teeth,' Angel said quietly. 'He'd been threatening it for days, saying how he was gonna fuck me up bad. Fucking guy just had it in for me, you know that. The blow wasn't bad or nothing, but a corrections officer found him bleeding and me standing over him and I got twenty days in the bing.'

The 'bing' was solitary confinement: twenty-three-hour lockdown, with one hour's exercise permitted in the yard. The yard was basically a cage, not much bigger than a cell, and prisoners were kept handcuffed while they walked. The yard had basketball hoops but no basketballs, even assuming anyone could play basketball with cuffs on. The only thing the prisoners could do was fight, which is what they usually did when they were let out.

'Most of the time, I didn't leave my cell,' said Angel.

'Vance had been given ten days, just for getting his mouth cut, and I knew he was waiting for me out there.' He went quiet, his teeth working at his bottom lip. 'You think it's going to be easy – you know, peace and quiet, sleep, safe most of the time – but it isn't. You can't bring nothing in with you. They take your clothes and give you three jumpsuits instead. You can't smoke, but I boofed the best part of a pack of tobacco in three condoms, rolled it in toilet paper to smoke it.' 'Boofing' meant taking contraband and inserting it in the anus in order to transport it.

'The tobacco was gone in five days, and I never smoked again. After those five days in that cell, I couldn't take it any more: the noise, the screams. It's psychological torture. I went out into the yard for the first time and Vance came at me straight off, caught me on the side of the head with his balled fists, then started kicking me on the ground. He got five, maybe six good ones in before they hauled him off, but I knew then that I couldn't take any more time in that place. There was no way I could do it.

'I was taken to the infirmary after the beating. They looked me over, decided nothing was broken, then sent me back to the bing. I brought a screw back with me, maybe three inches long, that I'd worked out of the base of a medicine cabinet. And when they put me in the cell, and the lights went out, I tried to cut myself.'

He shook his head and, for the first time since he started the story, he smiled. 'You ever try to cut yourself with a screw?'

'Can't say that I have.'

'Well, it's kinda hard to do. Screws just weren't designed with that particular purpose in mind. After a lot of effort, I managed to get some serious blood flowing, but if I was hoping to bleed to death I'd probably have finished my twenty days before it happened. Anyway, they found me hacking away at my arm and hauled me off to the infirmary again. That's when I called you.

'After some talk, and a psychological profile, and whatever you told them, they put me back in the general population. They figured I wasn't going to harm no one, except maybe myself, and they needed the bing space for someone more deserving.'

I had spoken to Vance shortly afterwards, before he was due to be released from solitary, and told him what I knew about him, and what I would tell the others if he made a move on Angel. It didn't do any good, and Vance's first act on release was to try to kill Angel in the showers. After that, he was a dead man.

'If they'd put me back in the bing, I'd have found a way to kill myself,' concluded Angel. 'Maybe I'd have let Vance do it, just to get done with it. There are some debts that will never be paid, Bird, and that's no bad thing sometimes. Louis knows, and I know. The fact that you do what you do because it's right makes it easier to take your side, but you decide you want to take out Congress and Louis will find a way to light the fuse. And I'll hold his coat while he does it.'

Cheryl Lansing lived in a clean, white, two-storey house at the western edge of Bangor itself, surrounded by neat lawns and twenty-year-old pine trees. It was a quiet neighbourhood with prosperous-looking homes and new cars in the drives. Angel stayed in the Mustang while I tried the bell. No one answered. I cupped my hands and peered in through the glass, but the house was quiet.

I walked around the side and into a long garden with a swimming pool at the end nearest the house. Angel joined me.

'Baby-brokering business must pay good,' he remarked. Smiling, he waved a black wallet, about six inches by two inches: the tools of his trade. 'Just in case,' he said.

'Great. The local cops drop by and I'll tell them I was making a citizen's arrest.'

The back of the house had a glass-walled extension that allowed Cheryl Lansing to look out on her green lawn in the summer and watch the snow fall on it in the winter. The pool hadn't been cleaned in a while, and there was no cover over it. It didn't look too deep, sloping from maybe three feet at one end to six or seven feet at the other, but it was full of leaves and dirt.

'Bird.'

I walked over to where Angel was looking into the house. There was a kitchen area to one side and a large oak table opposite surrounded by five chairs, with a doorway behind it leading into a living room. On the table stood cups, saucers, a coffee pot and an assortment of muffins and breads. A bowl of fruit stood in the centre. Even from here, I could see the mould on the food.

Angel pulled a pair of double-thick gloves from his pocket and tried the sliding door. It opened to his touch.

'You want to take a look around?'

'I guess.'

Inside, I could smell sour milk and the lingering stench of food gone bad. We moved through the kitchen and into the living room, which was furnished with thick couches and armchairs with a pink floral motif. I searched downstairs while Angel went through the upper rooms. When he called me, I was already on the stairs to follow him up.

He stood in what was obviously a small office, with a dark wood desk, a computer and a pair of filing cabinets. On the shelves along the wall sat a series of expanding files, each marked with a year. The files for 1965 and '66 had been removed from the shelves and their contents lay scattered on the floor.

'Billy Purdue was born early in sixty-six,' I said quietly.

'You figure he came calling?'

'Someone did.'

How badly did Billy Purdue want to trace his roots, I wondered? Bad enough to come here and ransack an old woman's office to find out what she knew?

'Check the cabinets,' I said to Angel. 'Then see if there's anything relating to Billy Purdue that we can salvage from those files. I'm going to have another run through the house, see if I can find anything that might have been discarded.'

He nodded and I went through the house again, searching bedrooms, the bathroom and eventually ending up once again in the downstairs rooms. In the kitchen, the rotting fruit on the table was surrounded by the compass points of four settings, two with coffee cups, two with glasses of rancid milk.

I went back out into the yard. At the far eastern side stood a toolshed, an open lock hanging below the bolt. I walked down, took a handkerchief from my pocket and slipped the bolt. Inside, there was only a gas-powered mower, flowerpots, seeding trays and an assortment of short-handled garden tools. Old paint cans sat on the shelves beside jars filled with old brushes and nails. An empty birdcage hung from a hook on the roof. I closed the shed and started back towards the house.

As I walked, a breeze arose and pulled at the branches of the trees and the blades of the grass beneath my feet. It lifted the leaves in the unfilled pool, sending them tumbling softly over one another with a crisp, rustling sound. Amid the greens and browns and soft yellows at the deep end, something bright red showed.

I squatted by the edge of the pool and looked at the shape. It was a doll's head, topped by a tuft of red hair. I could make out a glass eye and the edge of a set of ruby lips. The pool was wide and I thought for a moment of going back to the shed and trying to find a tool long enough to grip the doll, but I couldn't remember seeing anything there that might serve my purpose. Of course, the doll might mean nothing. Kids lost things in the oddest places all of the time. But dolls . . . They tended to look after their dolls. Jennifer had one called Molly, with thick dark hair and a movie-star pout, that would sit beside her at the dinner table and stare emptily at the food. Molly and Jenny, friends forever.

I moved to the end of the pool nearest the house, where a set of steps led into the shallow end, the bottom step obscured by leaves. I walked down and stepped carefully into the pool itself, anxious not to lose my footing on the slope. As I progressed, the depth of the leaves began to increase, covering first the toes of my shoes, then the cuffs of my pants, then rising almost to my knees. By the time I came close to the doll, they were halfway up my thighs and I was conscious of a sense of dampness from the rotting vegetation and the feel of water seeping into my shoes. I was walking with caution now, the tiles slick beneath my feet and the slope more pronounced.

The glass eye looked to the heavens, a spread of brown leaves and dirt masking the other side of the doll's face. I reached down carefully, dug into the leaves and lifted the doll's head free from below. As it came away, the leaves fell and the doll's right eye, which had been held closed by the pressure, clicked open gently. Its blouse, slowly revealed, was blue and its skirt green. Its chubby knees were filthy with mud and decaying vegetation.

The entire body of the doll came away from the leaves with a soft sucking sound, and something else came with it. The hand clutching the doll's legs was small, but decay had swollen it and mottled it with winter colours. Two nails had begun to come loose and there were tears in the skin exposing long striations of muscle. At the elbow, above a large gas blister, I could see the end of a rotting sleeve, its pretty pink colour now almost black with leaf mould, dirt and dried blood.

I stepped back instinctively, my hand still clutching the doll, and, with a flash of shock and fear, I felt my feet slide from beneath me on the tiles at the bottom of the pool. I fell backwards into the leaves, my feet shooting out ahead of me and impacting on something soft and wet and yielding. There were leaves in my mouth and the odour of decay was in my nostrils as the child rose, forced upwards by my struggling legs and my sustained grip on the doll. I saw damp hair and grey skin and eyes like milk as I slid down, my feet still struggling to find purchase. In my fear I released my grip on the doll and instinctively pushed the child's body away, my hand heavy with the smell of her as she slid back into the mould. And then my slide was stopped by a heavier form, there were dead fingers against my calf and I knew that they were all there beneath the rotting leaves, decay on decay, and that, if I sank farther beneath those leaves, I would see them and I might never rise again.

A hand gripped my own right hand and I heard Angel shout: 'Bird, easy. Easy!' I looked up and found that I was almost at the right-hand side of the pool. With Angel's help, I got a grip on the rim and pulled myself up. I crawled away from the pool edge and lay on the cold, damp grass as I rubbed my hands on the blades, again and again and again, in a vain and terrible effort to remove the smell of that poor, lost girl from my fingers.

'They're down there,' I said. 'They're all down there.'

Angel called Louis, then I called the Bangor police. Angel left before they arrived; with his record, his presence would only complicate matters. I told him to take a cab, check into the Days Inn by the huge Bangor Mall out of town and wait for me there. And then I stood by the side of the pool, the young girl's hair and blouse now clearly visible amid the wind-danced leaves, and waited for the police to come.

I met Angel back in the Days Inn four hours later. I had told the cops everything, including the fact that I had made a search of the house. They were none too pleased but Ellis Howard reluctantly vouched for me from back in Portland, then asked for me to be put on the line.

'So you weren't holding anything back?' The receiver almost vibrated with the depth of the anger in his voice. 'I should have let them lock you up for interfering with a crime scene.'

There was no point in apologising, so I didn't. 'Willeford told me about her. She arranged Billy Purdue's adoption. She was with Rita Ferris a couple of nights before Rita and Donald were killed.'

'First his wife and child, now this adoption woman. Looks like Billy Purdue has a grudge against the world.'

'You don't believe that, Ellis.'

'Fuck do you know what I believe? You want to be a bleeding heart, go bleed somewhere else. We're all full up here.' He was so annoyed it took him three noisy tries to hang up. I gave the Bangor cops my cell phone number and told them I'd help in any way I could.

There were four bodies in the pool. Cheryl Lansing was at the bottom of the deep end, beneath the body of her daughter-in-law Louise. Her two granddaughters, Sophie and Sarah, were farther away, both of them in their nightgowns. The leaves had been heaped on them from all around the yard, and topped off with a pile of mulch from behind the toolshed.

The throats of all four had been cut, left to right. Cheryl Lansing's jaw had also been broken by a blow to the left side of her face and her mouth gaped strangely as her head was revealed by the medics working in the empty pool. And as she lay beneath the body of her daughter-in-law, mouth wide, it became clear that her killer had visited one final indignity on her body.

Before she died, Cheryl Lansing's tongue had been ripped out.

If Cheryl Lansing was dead, then someone – Billy Purdue, Abel and his partner Stritch, or an individual as yet unrevealed – was tracing a path through Billy's life, a path that appeared now to be related to the abortive investigation into his roots carried out by Willeford. I decided then to continue north. Angel offered to come with me but I told him instead to catch a commuter flight back to Portland the next morning, while I used the Mustang to move on.

'Bird?' he asked, as I started the car. 'You've told me about Billy Purdue, about his wife and his kid. What I don't get is: how did she end up with a guy like that?'

I shrugged. She came from a dysfunctional family, I guessed, and she seemed to be repeating the cycle by starting her own dysfunctional family with Billy Purdue. But there was more to it than that: Rita Ferris had something good inside her, something that had remained untouched and uncorrupted despite all that had happened to her. Maybe, just maybe, she believed that she saw something similar in Billy and thought that if she could find the place where it was, and touch him there, she could save him, that she could make him need her as much as she needed him, because she thought that love and need were the same. A host of abused wives and beaten lovers, bruised women and unhappy children, could have told her that she was wrong, that there is a wilful blindness in believing that one person can somehow redeem another. People have to redeem themselves, but some of them just don't want redemption, or don't recognise it when it shines its light upon them.

'She loved him,' I said, at last. 'In the end, it was all she had to give, and she needed to give it.'

'It's not much of an answer.'

'I don't have the answers, Angel, just different ways of phrasing the questions.' Then I pulled out of the parking lot and headed north to the junction of I-95 and 15, towards Dover-Foxcroft, and Greenville, and Dark Hollow. Looking back, it was the first step on a journey that would force me to confront not only my own past, but also my grandfather's; that would disturb old ghosts long believed to have been laid to rest; and that would lead me at last to face what had waited for so long in the darkness of the Great North Woods.

# Chapter Eleven

For much of its history, Maine was little more than a series of fishing settlements clinging to the Atlantic coastline. Beneath the sea off that coast lay the remains of another world, a world that had ceased to exist when the waters rose. Maine has a drowned coastline: its islands were once mountains, and forgotten fields lie on the bed of the ocean. Its past lies submerged, fathoms deep, beyond the reach of the sunlight.

And so the present came into existence at the very precipice of the past, and the people clung to the coast of the region. Few ventured into the wilderness at its heart, apart from French missionaries seeking to bring Christianity to the tribes – which never numbered much more than three thousand to begin with, and most of them also lived along the coast – or trappers trying to make a living from the fur trade. The soil that covered the bedrock of the coast was good and fertile and the Indians farmed it using rotting fish as fertilizer, the smell of it mixing with the scents of wild roses and sea lavender. Later came the saltwater farms, the digging for clams in the flats, and the huge icehouses where Maine ice was stored before being exported to the farthest reaches of the globe.

But as the possibilities offered by the forests came to be

realised, settlers pushed deeper and deeper north and west. On the king's orders, they harvested those white pines which measured over twenty-four inches in diameter one foot from the ground for use as masts on his ships. The masts of Admiral Nelson's ship HMS *Victory*, which fought Napoleon's forces at the Battle of Trafalgar, were grown in Maine.

But it was not until the early nineteenth century, when the financial opportunities represented by Maine's forests were recognised, that the interior was fully explored and surveyed, leading the way into the Great North Woods. Mills were built in the wilderness to produce paper, pulp and two-by-fours. Schooners sailed up the Penobscot to load pine and spruce timber that had been brought downstream from the farthest reaches of the north. Saw-mills lined the river's banks and those of the Merrimack, the Kennebec, the Saint Croix, the Machias. Lives were ended in the struggle to break jams or hold a million board feet of logs together, until the era of the industrial river drives came to an end in 1978. The land was remodelled to meet the demands of the timber barons: the paths of rivers were altered, lakes raised, dams built. Fires ravaged the dry slash left behind by the loggers and entire streams were denuded of life by the discarded sawdust waste. The first growth of pine has been gone for two centuries; the hardwood second growth of birch, maple and oak followed.

Now, much of the north country is industrial forest owned by the timber companies and lumber trucks make their way along the roads carrying stacks of freshly-cut trees. The companies cut swaths through acres of forest in the winter, removing every tree in their path and piling them during March and April. Wood is the state's wealth.

and even my grandfather, like many on the coast, used to grow spruce and fir for sale as Christmas trees, harvesting and selling them from early November to mid-December.

But there are still a few places where the mature forest remains untouched, with animal trails and moose droppings leading to secluded watering holes fed by waterfalls that tumble over rocks and stones and fallen trees. This was one of the last regions to have wolves and mountain lions and caribou. There are still ten million uninhabited acres in Maine and the state is greener now than it was one hundred years ago, when the exhaustion of the thin soil caused agriculture to decline and the forest reclaimed the land, as is its way, and walls that had once sheltered families now guarded only hemlock and pine.

A man could lose himself in that wilderness, if he chose.

Dark Hollow lay about five miles north of Greenville, close by the eastern shore of Moosehead Lake and the two hundred thousand acres of protected wilderness in Baxter State Park, where Mount Katahdin dominates the skyline at the northern end of the Appalachian Trail. I had half considered stopping off in Greenville – the road was dark and the evening cold – but I knew that finding Meade Payne was more important. People who had been close to Billy Purdue – his wife, his child, the woman who had organised his adoption – were dying, and dying badly. Payne had to be warned.

Greenville was the gateway to the north woods, and wood had long been the wealth of this town and the surrounding area. There had even been a lumber mill in the town providing jobs for the people of Greenville and its surrounds, until it closed in the mid-seventies, when the economic situation made it unprofitable to operate. A lot of people left the area then and those who remained tried to make new lives in tourism, fishing and hunting, but Greenville and the smaller towns scattered farther north – Beaver Cove, Kokadjo, and Dark Hollow, where the power lines ended and the wilderness truly began – were still poor. When the golf club at Greenville had raised its fees from ten dollars to twelve dollars per round, there had been uproar.

I drove up Lily Bay Road, for many years the winter road used for hauling heavy supplies to the logging camps, snow piled high on each side, the woods stretching beyond, until I came to Dark Hollow. It was a small town, barely more than two blocks at its centre, with a police department at the farthest limit of the northern end. Dark Hollow got some of the tourism and hunting overflow from Greenville, but not much. There was no view of the lake from its streets, only the mountains and the trees. There was one motel, the Tamara Motor Inn, which looked like a relic from the fifties, with a high arched frontage across which its name glowed in red and green neon. There were one or two handicraft shops selling scented candles and the kind of furniture that left pieces of bark on your pants if you sat on it. A bookstore-cum-coffee shop, a diner and a drugstore made up a considerable part of the town's commercial area, where piles of icy snow still lay in the gutters and in the shadows of the buildings.

Only the diner was still open. It had been painted in cute psychedelic colours outside, making it look like the kind of place the Scooby Doo crew might have opened when the Mystery Machine eventually broke down, like those air-cooled Volkswagens that burned out in Santa Fe when their hippie owners tried to drive them cross-country during the sixties.

Inside, there were reproductions of old concert posters and landscapes by what I took to be local artists. In one corner there was a framed photo of a kid in an army uniform beside an older man, some faded red, white and blue ribbon around the picture, but I didn't look too closely. A couple of old folks sat in a booth drinking coffee and shooting the breeze and four young guys tried to look cool and vaguely menacing without bursting their pimples when they sneered.

I ordered a club sandwich and a mug of coffee. It was good and almost made me forget, for a moment, what had happened back in Bangor. I asked the waitress, whose name was Annie, for directions to the Payne place and she gave them to me with a smile, although she told me that there was frost and maybe more snow expected and that the road was poor at the best of times.

'You a friend of Meade's?' she asked. Annie seemed keen to talk, more keen than I was. She had red hair and red lipstick, and dark blue makeup around her eyes. Combined with her naturally pale features, the total effect was of an unfinished drawing, like something abandoned by a distracted child.

'No,' I replied. 'I just want to talk to him about something.'

Her smile faltered a little. 'It's nothing bad, is it? Because that old man has had his share of bad times.'

'No,' I lied. 'It's nothing bad. I'm sorry to hear that things haven't been going well for Meade.'

She shrugged, and the smile regained some of its vigour. 'He lost his wife a couple of years back, then his nephew died in the Gulf during Desert Storm. He's kept himself pretty much to himself since then. We don't see him around too often these days.'

Annie leaned over, her breasts brushing my arm as she took away the remains of my sandwich. 'You want anything else?' she asked brightly, bringing an end to the Meade Payne conversation. I wasn't sure if there was a subtext to the question. I decided that there wasn't. Life tended to be simpler that way.

'No, thanks.'

She tore the check from her pad with a flourish. 'Then I'll just leave you with this.' She flashed me another smile as she slipped the check beneath the bowl of creamers. 'You take care now, sugar,' she said, as she sashayed away.

'I will,' I replied. I felt kind of relieved when she was gone.

Meade Payne didn't have a phone, or at least his name wasn't in the book. Reluctantly, I decided not to talk to him until the morning. I got a room at the Tamara for twenty-eight dollars and slept in an old bed with a high, thick mattress and a carved wood bedstead. I woke once during the night, when the smell of rotting leaves and the sound of heavy decaying things moving beneath them became unbearable.

The waitress had been right: a heavy frost covered the ground when I left the Tamara the next morning and the blades of grass on the motel's narrow strip of lawn were like carved crystal as I walked. In the bright morning sunlight, cars passed slowly down the main street and folks in coats and gloves puffed their way along like steam engines. I left the car at the Tamara and made my way on foot to the diner. From outside, I could see that most of the booths were already full and there was a welcoming air of community, of belonging, among those seated inside. Waitresses – Annie didn't seem to be among them – flitted from table to table like butterflies and a fat, bearded man in an apron chatted with patrons beside the register. I was almost at the door when a voice behind me said – gently, softly, familiarly – 'Charlie?' and I turned around and the past and the present collided in the memory of a kiss.

Lorna Jennings was six years older than I was and lived a mile from my grandfather's house. She was small and lithe, no taller than five-two and certainly no more than one hundred and ten pounds, with short, dark hair cut in a bob and a mouth that always seemed to be entering into, or emerging from, a kiss. Her eyes were blue-green and her skin was porcelain white.

Her husband's name was Randall, but his friends called him Rand. He was tall and had been a hockey hopeful once. Rand was a cop, still in uniform but angling for a transfer to the detective bureau. He had never hit his wife, never hurt her physically and she believed that their marriage was sound until he told her about his first and, he said, his only affair. That was before I knew her, before we became lovers.

It was my first summer out of the University of Maine, where I had majored – barely – in English. I was twenty-three. I had worked some after I finished high school, lousy jobs mainly, then taken some time out to travel to the West Coast before taking up a place at college. Now I had returned to Scarborough for what would be my final summer there. I had already applied to the NYPD, using what few contacts remained with those who had some fond memories of my father. Maybe I had some idealistic notion that I could remove the stain from his name by my presence there. Instead, I think I just stirred up old memories for some people, like mud disturbed from the bottom of a pond.

My grandfather got me a job in an insurance firm, where I worked as an office boy, a runner. I made the coffee and swept the floors and answered the phones and polished the desks and learned enough about the insurance business to know that anybody who believed what they were told by an insurance salesman was either naive or desperate.

Lorna Jennings was the personal assistant to the office manager. She was never less than polite to me but we spoke little in the beginning, although once or twice I found her looking at me in a kind of amused way before she went back to studying her papers or typing her letters. I spoke to her properly for the first time during a retirement party for one of the secretaries, a tall woman with blue-rinsed hair who was committed a year later after she killed one of her dogs with an axe. Laura strolled up to me as I sat at the bar, drinking a beer and trying to pretend that the insurance business and I were not even remotely acquainted.

'Hi,' she said. 'You look kind of lonesome. You trying to keep your distance from us?'

'Hi,' I replied, twisting the glass. 'No, not really.'

She arched an eyebrow, and I confessed.

'Well, maybe just a little. Although not from you.'

The eyebrow moved up another notch. I wondered if it was possible to burst a blood vessel from embarrassment.

'I saw you reading something today,' she said, taking the stool across from me. She was wearing a long, dark wool dress that hugged her body like a sheath and she smelt of flowers: body lotion, I later learned. She rarely wore perfume. 'What was it?'

I was still a little embarrassed, I guess. I had been reading Ford Madox Ford's *The Good Soldier*. I'd picked it up thinking it was something other than what it was: an examination of a series of characters who were unfaithful to one another in their various ways. In the end, as our relationship developed, it came to seem more like a textbook than a novel.

'It's Ford Madox Ford. Have you read him?'

'No, I just know the name. Should I?'

'I guess.' This didn't seem like a particularly hearty recommendation and, as literary criticism, it left a lot to be desired, so I pressed on. 'If you want to read about weak men and bad marriages.'

She winced a little at that and, although I knew almost nothing about her, not then, a little piece of my world fell off and bounced across the floor amid the cigarette butts and the peanut shells. I figured if I dug a hole halfway to China and pulled the earth down on top of me, then I might be far enough underground to hide my discomfort. I had hurt her in some way, but I wasn't sure how.

'Really?' she said at last. 'Maybe you might let me borrow it sometime.'

We talked a little more, about the office, about my grandfather, before she stood to leave. As she did so, she moved her hand across the material of her dress, above the knee, rubbing at a tiny piece of white lint that had caught in the fabric. It made the material stretch and tighten further against her thighs, revealing the shape of her almost to her knees. And then she looked at me curiously, her head to one side, and there was a light in her eyes that I had never seen until then. No one had ever looked at me that way before. No one, I thought, would ever look at me that way again. She touched my arm gently, and the touch burned.

'Don't forget that book,' she said.

Then she left.

That was how it began, I suppose. I gave her the book to read and, somehow, it gave me a strange pleasure to know that her hands were touching my book, her fingers caressing the pages gently. I left the job a week later. More accurately, I was fired after an argument with the office manager in the course of which he called me a lazy sonofabitch and I told him he was a cocksucker, which he was. My grandfather was kind of angry at first that I had lost the job, although he was secretly pleased that I had called the office manager a cocksucker. My grandfather thought he was a cocksucker too.

It was another week before I worked up the courage to call Lorna. We met for coffee in a little place near the Veterans Memorial Bridge. She said she had loved *The Good Soldier*, although it had made her sad. She had brought the book back to give to me but I told her to keep it. I think I wanted to believe that she might be thinking of me as she looked at it. That's what infatuation does to a person, I suppose, although the infatuation soon became something more.

We left the coffee shop and I offered her a ride home in the MG my grandfather had bought for me as a graduation present, one of the American-built models made before British Leyland bought the company and screwed it up. It was kind of a chick car, but I liked the way it moved. She declined.

'I have to meet Rand,' she said. I think the hurt must

have shown in my face, because she leaned forward and kissed me softly on the cheek.

'Don't leave it so long the next time,' she said. I didn't.

We met often after that day but it was a warm July night when we kissed properly for the first time. We had been to see some lousy movie and we were walking to our separate cars. Rand didn't like the movies, lousy or not. She didn't tell Rand that she was going to a movie with me and she asked me if I thought that was okay. I said that I guessed it was, although it probably wasn't. Certainly Rand didn't see it that way, when things started to come apart at the end.

'You know, I don't want to stop you from meeting some nice girl,' she said. She didn't look at me when she said it.

'I won't,' I lied.

'Because I don't let us come between me and Rand,' she lied back.

'That's fine then,' I lied again.

We were at the cars by that point and she stood with her keys in her hand, staring ahead, her eyes on the sky. Then, still holding her keys, she put her hands in her pockets and bowed her head.

'Come here,' I said. 'Just for a moment.'

And she did.

The first time we made love was in my bedroom, one Friday afternoon when Rand had gone to Boston to attend a funeral. My grandfather was in town with some of his old cop buddies, remembering old times and catching up on the obituaries. The house was quiet.

She walked from her home. Even though we had agreed that she would come, I was still surprised when I saw her standing there, dressed in jeans and a denim shirt with a white T-shirt underneath. She didn't say anything as I led her to my room. We kissed awkwardly at first, her shirt still buttoned, then harder. My stomach danced with nerves. I was acutely conscious of her presence, of her scent, of the feel of her breasts beneath her shirt, of my own inexperience, of my desire for her, of, even then, I think, my love for her. She stepped back and unbuttoned her shirt, then pulled off her T-shirt. She wasn't wearing a bra and her breasts rose slightly with the movement. Then I was beside her, fumbling at her jeans as she pulled at my shirt, my tongue slipping and coiling around her own, my hips hard against her.

And in the dappled sunlight of a July afternoon, I lost myself in the warmth of her kiss and the soft yielding of her flesh as I entered her.

I think we had four months together before Rand found out about us. I would meet her when she could get away. I was working by then as a waiter, which meant my afternoons were pretty much free, and two or three nights as well if I decided I didn't want to work flat out. We made love where we could and when we could, and communicated mostly by letter and snatched phone conversations. We made love on Higgins Beach once, which kind of made up for my lack of success with the Berube girl, and we made love when my letter of acceptance came through from New York, although I could feel her regret even as we moved together.

My time with Lorna was different from any of the previous relationships I had had. They were short, abortive things blighted by the small-town environment of Scarborough where guys would come up to you and tell you how many ways they had screwed your girl when she was with them, and how good she was with her mouth. Lorna seemed beyond those things, although she had been touched by them in another way, evident in the gradual, insidious corrosion of a marriage between high-school sweethearts.

It ended when some friend of Rand's spotted us in a coffee shop, holding hands across a table covered with doughnut sugar and creamer stains. It was that mundane. They fought and Rand offered to give her the child she had wanted for so long. In the end, she decided not to throw away seven years of marriage on a boy. She was probably right, although the pain she caused me tore through me for two years after and stayed as a lingering ache for longer than that. I didn't call or see her again. She was not among the mourners at my grandfather's funeral, although she had been his neighbour for almost a decade. It turned out that she and Rand had left Scarborough, but I didn't bother trying to find out where they might have gone.

There is a kind of postscript to this. About one month after our relationship ended I was drinking in a bar off Fore Street, catching up with a few people who had stayed on in Portland while the rest moved on to college, or out-of-state jobs, or marriage. I went to the men's room and was washing my hands when the door opened behind me. I looked in the mirror to see Rand Jennings standing there, out of uniform, and behind him a fat, burly guy who leaned back against the door to hold it closed.

I nodded at him in the mirror; after all, there wasn't a whole lot else I could do. I dried my hands on the towel, turned and took his fist in the pit of my stomach. It was a hard blow, with the full force of his body behind it, and it expelled every breath of air from my lungs. I fell to my knees, clutching at my midriff, and he kicked me hard in the ribs. And then, as I lay there on the filth and piss of the floor, he kicked me again and again and again: on my thighs, my buttocks, my arms, my back. He stayed away from my head until the end, when he lifted it up by the hair and slapped me hard across the face. Throughout the whole beating he never said a word, and he left me there, bleeding on the floor, for my friends to find. I was lucky, I suppose, although I didn't believe it then. Worse things happened to people who messed with a cop's wife.

And now, in this small town on the edge of the wilderness, the years tumbled away and she was before me again. Her eyes were a little older, the lines streaking away from them more pronounced. There were tiny striations around her mouth too, as if she had spent too long with her lips pinched closed. Yet, when she smiled cautiously, there was that same look in her eyes and I knew that she was still beautiful and that a man could fall in love with her all over again, if he wasn't careful.

'It is you, isn't it?' she said, and I nodded in reply. 'What in the Lord's name are you doing in the Hollow?'

'Looking for someone,' I replied, and I could see in her eyes that, for one brief moment, she thought it might be her. 'You want to get a cup of coffee?'

She appeared doubtful for a moment, looked around as if to make sure that Rand wasn't watching from somewhere, then smiled again. 'Sure, I'd like that.'

Inside, we found an empty booth away from the window and ordered mugs of steaming coffee. I had some toast and bacon, which she nibbled at in spite of herself. For those few seconds, ten years fell away and we were back in a coffee shop in South Portland, talking about a future that would never be and stealing touches across the table.

'How've you been?' I asked.

'Okay, I guess. It's a nice place to live; a little isolated, maybe, but a nice place.'

'When did you come here?'

'In eighty-eight. Things weren't going so well for us in Portland. Rand couldn't get his detective's badge, so he took a post up here. He's chief now.'

Heading up to the edge of nowhere to save your marriage seemed like a dumb thing to do, but I kept my mouth closed. They'd stayed together this long, so I figured that they knew what they were doing.

I figured wrong, of course.

'So you two are still together?'

For the first time, something flickered across her face: regret or anger, maybe, or a recognition that this was true yet with no idea why it should be so. Or it may simply have been my own memories of that time transferred on to her, like recollecting an ancient injury and wincing at the recall.

'Yeah, we're together.'

'Kids?'

'No.' She looked flustered, and pain flashed across her face. I recalled Rand's promise to her when he was trying to win her back, but I said nothing. She took a sip of her coffee, and when she spoke again the pain was hidden, put back in whatever box she used to hide it away. 'I'm sorry. I heard about what happened to your own family, back in New York.'

'Thanks.'

'Someone paid for it, didn't they?'

It was a curious way of putting it. 'A lot of people paid.'

She nodded, then looked at me with her head to one side for a time. 'You've changed. You look . . . older, *harder* somehow. It's strange seeing you this way.'

I shrugged. 'It's been a long time. A lot of things have happened since I saw you last.'

We moved on to talk of other things: about life in Dark Hollow, about her job teaching part-time in Dover-Foxcroft, about my return to Scarborough. To anyone passing by, we must have looked like old friends relaxing together, catching up, but there was a tension between us that was only partly to do with our past together. Maybe I was wrong, but I sensed a need within Lorna, something unsettled and unfocused looking for somewhere to alight.

She drained the last of her coffee in a single mouthful. When she put the mug down, her hand was shaking a little. 'You know,' she said, 'after it ended between us, I still thought about you. I'd listen for snatches of information about you, about what you were doing. I spoke to your gramps about you. Did he tell you that?'

'No, he never said.'

'I asked him not to. I was afraid, I guess, afraid that you might take it the wrong way.'

'And what way would that be?'

I meant it lightly, but she didn't take it that way. Instead, her lips tightened and she held my gaze with a look half of pain, half of anger. 'You know, I used to stand at the edge of the cliffs out at the Neck and pray that a wave would come, one of the big twenty-footers, and wash me away. There were times when I'd think of you and Rand and the whole sad fucking business and dream about losing myself beneath the ocean. Do you know what that kind of pain is like?'

'Yes,' I said. 'Yes, I do.'

She stood then, and buttoned her coat, and gave me a little half smile before she left. 'Yes,' she said. 'I guess you do. It was good seeing you, Charlie.'

'And you.'

The door closed behind her with a single, soft slap. I watched her through the windows, looking left and right, running a little as she crossed the street, her hands deep in her pockets, her head low.

And I thought of her standing at the edge of the black cliffs at Prouts Neck, the wind blowing her hair, the taste of salt on her lips: a woman dark against the evening sky, waiting for the sea to call her name.

Meade Payne lived in a red, wooden house overlooking Ragged Lake. A long, poorly-kept driveway wound up to the yard, where a Dodge pickup was parked, old and partially eaten by rust. The house was quiet and no dog barked as I drew the Mustang up alongside the truck, icy snow crunching beneath the tyres.

I knocked on the door, but no one answered. I was about to go to the back of the house when the door opened and a man peered out. He was in his late twenties or early thirties, I guessed, with dark hair and sallow, windblown skin. There was a hardness about him, and his hands were tough and pitted with scars across the backs of the fingers. He wore no rings, no watch and his clothes looked like they didn't fit him quite as well as they should. His shirt was a little too tight on his shoulders and chest, his jeans a little too short, revealing heavy wool socks above black, steel-toed shoes.

'Help you?' he said, in a tone of voice that indicated that, even if he could, he'd prefer not to.

'I'm looking for Meade Payne.'

'Why?'

'I want to talk to him about a boy he fostered once. Is Mr Payne around?'

'I don't know you,' he said. For no reason, his tone was becoming belligerent.

I kept my temper. 'I'm not from around these parts. I've come from Portland. It's important that I talk to him.'

The young man considered what I had said, then left me to wait in the snow as he closed the door behind him. A few minutes later, an elderly man appeared from the side of the house. He was slightly bent over and walked slowly, shuffling a little as if the joints in his knees hurt him, but I guessed that he might once have been close to my own height, maybe even six feet. He wore a pair of dungarees over a red check shirt and dirty white sneakers. A Chicago Bears cap was pulled down low on his head and wisps of grey hair tried to escape from beneath the rim. His eyes were bright blue and very clear. He kept his hands in his pockets and looked me over, his head slightly to one side, as if trying to place me from somewhere.

'I'm Meade Payne. What can I do for you?'

'My name's Charlie Parker. I'm a private investigator out of Portland. It's about a boy you fostered some years back: Billy Purdue.'

His eyes widened a little as I said the name and he waved me in the direction of a pair of old rocking chairs at the end of the porch. Before I sat down, he took a rag from his pocket and carefully cleaned the seat. 'Sorry, but I don't get many visitors. Always tried to discourage them, mostly for the sake of the boys.'

'I'm not sure I understand.'

He indicated the house with a movement of his chin.

His skin was still quite taut, its colour a reddish brown. 'Some of the boys I fostered down the years, they were troublesome types. They needed a firm hand to guide them and they needed to be kept away from temptations. Out here' – He waved a hand towards the lake and the trees – 'only temptations are hunting rabbits and jacking off. I don't know how kindly the Lord takes to either, but I don't reckon they count for much in the great scheme of things.'

'When did you stop fostering?'

'Back a ways,' he said, but added nothing more. Instead, he reached out a hand and rapped a long finger on the arm of my chair. 'Now, Mr. Parker, you tell me: is Billy in some kind of trouble?'

I told him as much as I felt I could: that his wife and child had been killed; that he was a suspect in the killings but that I didn't believe he was responsible; that certain people outside the law believed that he might have stolen some money belonging to them and they would hurt him to get it back. The old man listened silently to all that I said. The hostile young man leaned on the frame of the open door, watching us.

'Do you know where Billy might be now?' he asked.

'I was hoping you might have some idea.'

'I ain't seen him, if that's what you're asking,' he said. 'And if he comes to me, I can't say as I'll hand him over to anyone, 'less I'm sure he'll get a fair hearing.'

Out on the lake, a motor boat was moving through the waters. Birds flew from its path, but they were too far away to identify.

'There may be something more to this,' I said, weighing carefully what I was going to say next. 'You remember Cheryl Lansing?'

'I recall her.'

'She's dead. She was murdered along with three members of her family. I'm not sure how long ago; certainly only a few days. If there's a connection to Billy Purdue, then you could be in danger.'

The old man shook his head gently. He pinched his lips with his fingers and said nothing for a time. Then: 'I appreciate you taking the time to come up here, Mr Parker, but, like I said, I ain't heard from Billy and, if I do, I'll have to think long and hard about what to do next. As for being in danger, I can handle a gun and I've got the boy with me.'

'Your son?'

'Caspar. Cas, to them what knows him. We can look out for each other and I don't fear no man, Mr Parker.'

There didn't seem to be anything more I could say. I gave Meade Payne the number of my cell phone and he stuffed it into one of the pockets of his dungarees. He shook my hand and walked slowly, stiffly, back to the door, humming softly to himself. It was an old song, I thought. I seemed to recall it from somewhere but couldn't place it, something about tender ladies and a handsome gambler and memories haunting the mind. I found myself whistling a little of it as, through the rearview, I saw Caspar help the old man into the house. Neither of them looked back as I drove away.

# Chapter Twelve

Back in Dark Hollow, I stopped off at the diner and went through the phone book. I got Rand Jennings's address and the chef gave me directions to his house. Rand and Lorna lived about two miles out of town, in a two-storey house painted yellow and black with a neat garden and a black fence at its boundary. Smoke rose from the chimney. Behind the house, a river ran from the lakes to the west of town. I slowed as I drove by, but didn't stop. I wasn't even sure why I was there: old memories stirred up, I supposed. I still felt something for her, I knew, although it wasn't love. I think, and I had no reason to feel it, that it was a kind of sorrow for her. Then I turned back to head south for Greenville.

I found the Greenville Police Department at the town's Municipal Building on Minden Street, where it occupied an unattractive tan-sided office with green shutters and Christmas wreaths on the windows in an effort to make it look prettier. There was a fire department office close by, and a police car and a green Department of Conservation forest ranger truck in the lot.

Inside, I gave my name to a pair of cheerful secretaries, then took a seat on a bench across from the door. After twenty minutes, a stocky man with dark hair and a moustache and brown, watchful eyes came out of an office down the hall, his blue uniform neatly pressed, and extended his hand in greeting.

'Sorry for keeping you waiting,' he said. 'We have a contract for policing Beaver Cove. I've been out there most of the day. My name's Dave Martel. I'm chief of police.'

At Martel's instigation, we left the police building and walked past the Union Evangelical Church to the Hard Drive Café at Sanders Store. There were a couple of cars in the parking lot across the street, the white hull of the steamboat *Katahdin* looming behind them. A mist hung over the lake and created a white wall at the end of the street through which cars occasionally burst. Inside the café, we ordered French vanilla coffee and took a seat close by one of the computer terminals that folks used to pick up their e-mail.

'I knew your granddaddy,' said Martel, as we waited for the coffee to arrive. Sometimes it was easy to forget how tightly knit the ties still were in parts of the state. 'Knew Bob Warren from back in Portland, when I was a boy. He was a good man.'

'You been here long?'

'Ten years now.'

'Like it?'

'Sure. This is an unusual place. You got a lot of people in this part of the country who don't care much for the law, who've come up here because they don't like being regulated. Funny thing is, here they've got me, they've got the game wardens, they've got the county sheriff and the Highway Patrol all keeping an eye on 'em. Mostly we get along just fine, but we got crime here so it's not like I'm not kept busy.'

'Anything serious?'

Martel smiled. 'Serious is shooting a moose out of season, if you talk to the wardens.'

I winced. Grouse, pheasant, rabbit, maybe even squirrel I could understand – at least squirrels moved fast enough to constitute a challenge – but not moose. The moose population in the state had risen from about three thousand in the thirties to its present level of thirty thousand, and moose hunting was now allowed for one week in October. It brought a lot of revenue to places like Greenville at a time when there weren't too many tourists around, but it also brought in its share of assholes. That year, about one hundred thousand people had applied for maybe two thousand permits, every one of them trying to put a moose head above the fireplace.

It's not difficult to kill a moose. In fact, the only thing easier to hit than a moose is a dead moose. Their sight is poor, although their sense of smell and hearing are good, and they don't move unless they have to. Most hunters get their moose on their first or second day out, and boast about it to all the other assholes. Then, after all the hunters have gone with their fat bikes and their orange caps, you can head out and look at the animals that have survived, the glory of them as they come down to lick salt from the rocks by the side of the road, put there to melt the snow and instead used by the moose to supplement their diet.

'Still,' continued Martel, 'if you're asking what's current, there's a timber company man, a freelance surveyor name of Gary Chute, who hasn't delivered his report yet.'

I recalled the PBS news programme, although I hadn't noticed any sense of urgency in its discussion of the situation. 'I heard them talking about it on the radio,' I said. 'How bad is it?'

'Hard to say. Seems his wife hasn't seen him in a while, although that's not unusual. He had a couple of projects to work on, and was set to spend some time away from home. Plus rumour has it he keeps some sweet stuff stashed over in Troy, Vermont. Add to that his fondness for the bottle, and you got a guy who maybe isn't the most reliable. He doesn't turn up in the next twenty-four hours, there may have to be a search organised. It'll probably be down to the wardens and the Piscataquis sheriff, but could be we'll all have to lend a hand. Talking of serious, I hear you want to know about Emily Watts?'

I nodded. I figured that it would be easier to talk to Martel first and then try to deal with Rand Jennings than to try to find out what I wanted to know by talking to Jennings alone. I thought I might slip it past Martel without him noticing, but he was too good for that.

'Can I ask why you're not talking to Rand Jennings up in Dark Hollow about this?' There was a smile on his face, but his eyes were still and watchful.

'Rand and I have some history,' I replied. 'You get on with him?' Something in the way that Martel asked the question told me that I wasn't the only one with a little history behind him.

'Have to try,' said Martel diplomatically. 'He's not the most sympathetic of men, but he's conscientious in his way. His sergeant, Ressler, now he's another matter. Ressler's so full of shit his eyeballs are brown. Haven't seen too much of him lately, which is fine by me. They've been kept busy, what with the trouble over Emily Watts dying and all.'

Outside, a car crawled sluggishly up the street, heading north, but there didn't appear to be anybody walking around. Beyond, I could see the shapes of pine-covered islands out on the lake, but they were little more than dark patches in the mist.

The coffee arrived and Martel told me about what took place the night Emily Watts died, the same night that Billy Purdue took some two million dollars for which a lot more people had died. It was a strange death, out there in the woods. She would have died anyway from the cold, if they hadn't tracked her down, but to kill herself out in the woods at the age of sixty . . .

'It was a mess,' said Martel. 'But these things, they happen sometimes and there's no way to call them before they go down. Maybe if the security guard hadn't been packing, and the nurse on the old woman's floor had been watching less TV, and the doors had been locked more securely, and a dozen other things hadn't been out-of-sync that night, then things might have been different. You want to tell me what your interest is in all this?'

'Billy Purdue.'

'Billy Purdue. Now there's a name to warm your heart on a winter's night.'

'You know him?'

'Sure I know him. His ass was rousted not so long ago. Ten days, maybe. He was out at St Martha's, kicking and screaming with an ass pocket of whiskey. Said he wanted to speak to his momma, but no one knew him from Cain himself. He was hauled in, allowed to cool off in one of Jennings's cells, then packed off home. They told him that, if he came back, he'd be charged with trespassing and disturbing the peace. He even made the local papers. From what I hear, the last few days haven't made him a reformed character.'

It looked like Billy Purdue had followed up on the information supplied by Willeford. 'You know his wife and child were killed?' I asked.

'Yeah, I know. Never figured him for a killer, though.' He gave me a thoughtful look. 'My guess is, you don't either.'

'I don't know. You think he could have been looking for the woman who shot herself?'

'Why would you think that?'

'I'm not overfond of coincidences. They're God's way of telling you that you're not seeing the big picture.' Plus, I knew that Willeford, for good or bad, had given Emily Watts's name to Billy.

'Well, you see that picture, you let me know, because I sure as hell don't know why that old woman did what she did. Could be it was her nightmares that drove her to it.'

'Nightmares?'

'Yeah, she told the nurses that she saw the figure of a man watching her window and that someone tried to break into her room.'

'Any sign of an attempt at forced entry?'

'Nothing. Shit, the woman was on the fourth floor. Anyone trying to get in would have had to climb up the drainpipe. There might have been someone in the grounds earlier in the week, but that happens sometimes. Could have been a drunk taking a leak, or kids fooling around. In the end, I think the old lady was just starting to lose it, because there's no other way to explain it, or the name she called when she died.'

I leaned forward. 'What name did she call?'

'She called the bogeyman,' said Martel with a smile. 'She called the guy that mothers use to scare their children into bed, the hobgoblin.'

'What was the name?' I repeated, and something like fear crept into my voice.

Martel's smile gave way to a look of puzzlement as he said it.

'Caleb,' he said. 'She called on Caleb Kyle.'

# Part Two

For the thing which
I greatly feared is come upon me,
and that which I was afraid of
Is come unto me.

Job

# Part Two

# Chapter Thirteen

The years tumble by like leaves driven before the breeze, intricate and veined, fading from the green of recent memory to the gold autumnal shades of the distant past. I see myself as a child, as a young man, as a lover, a husband, a father, a mourner. I see old men around me in their old men pants and their old men shirts; old men dancing, their feet moving delicately, following a pattern lost to those younger than them; old men telling tales, their liver-spotted hands moving before the fire, their skin like crumpled paper, their voices soft as the rustle of empty corn husks.

An old man walks through the lush August grass with wood in his arms, brushing away loose bark with a gloved hand; an old man, tall and unbowed, with a halo of white hair like an ancient angel, a dog stepping slowly beside him, older, in its way, than the man himself, its grey-beard muzzle flecked with foam, its tongue lolling, its tail swinging gently through the warm evening air. The first patches of red are showing in the trees, and the clamour of the insects has begun to subside. The ash trees, the last to unfurl their leaves in spring, are now the first to let them fall to the ground. Pine needles decay on the forest floor and the blackberries are ripe and dense as the old man passes by, at one with the rhythms of the world around him.

These are the things he does, open-coated, firm footsteps leaving the clear imprint of his passing as he goes: the woodcutting, savouring the weight of the axe in his hands, the perfection of the swing, the fresh crack as the blade splits the sugar maple log, the sweep of the head to clear the two halves, the careful positioning of the next log, the heft of the axe, the feel of his old man muscles moving, stretching, beneath his old man shirt. Then the piling, wood on wood, fitting one to the other, shifting, turning, forming the pile so that it remains steady, so that none will fall, so that not even one will be lost. Finally, he stretches the sheeting, a brick at each corner to hold it in place – always the same bricks for he is, and has ever been, a methodical man. And when the time comes in winter to set the fire, he will return to his pile and bend down, the buckle of the belt on his old man pants digging into the softness of his belly, and he will remember that it was firm once, when he was a young man, when the belt held a gun and a nightstick and cuffs, and his badge shone like a silver sun.

I will be old too, and I will be this man, if I am spared. I will find a kind of happiness in repeating his motions, in the aptness of the action as I feel the circle closing, as I become him, as he made her, who made me. And in doing what he once did, in front of that same house, with the same trees moving in the wind, the same axe in my hand cleaving the wood beneath its blade, I will create an act of remembrance more powerful than a thousand prayers. And my grandfather will live in me, and the ghost of a dog will taste the air with its tongue, and bark at the joy of it.

Now it is his hands that I see moving before the fire, his voice that tells the tale, about Caleb Kyle and the tree with the strange fruit at the edge of the wilderness. He has never told me the tale before and he will never tell me how it ends, because it has no end, not for him. It will be I who will finish the tale for him, and I who will complete the arc.

Judy Giffen was the first to disappear, in Bangor in 1965. She was a slim girl, nineteen, with a mane of dark hair and soft red lips with which she tasted men, savouring them like berries. She worked in a hat shop and went missing on a warm April evening redolent with the promise of summer. They searched and they searched, but they didn't find her. Her face looked out from ten thousand newspapers, frozen in her years as surely as if she had been trapped in amber.

Ruth Dickinson from Corinna, another thin beauty, with long blonde hair that hung to her waist, was next to go, in late May when she was just short of her twenty-first birthday. To their names would be added Louise Moore from East Corinth, Laurel Trulock from Skowhegan and Sarah Raines from Portland, all disappearing within a period of not more than a few days in September. Sarah Raines was a schoolteacher and, at twenty-two, the eldest of the women to disappear. Her father, Samuel Raines, had been to school with Bob Warren, my grandfather, and Sarah was Bob's goddaughter. The last to go missing was an eighteen-year-old student named Judith Mundy, who disappeared after a party in Monson in the first week of October. Unlike the others, she was a chubby, plain girl, but by then people had figured out that there was something very wrong and the break in the pattern didn't seem so important. A search was organised for the Mundy girl to the north and a lot of folks helped out, some, like my grandfather, from as far south as Portland. He drove up on a Saturday morning but, by then, all hope was pretty much gone. My grandfather joined a small party out by Sebec Lake, a few miles east of Monson. There were only three men, then two, then just my grandfather.

That evening, he got himself a room in Sebec and had dinner in a bar outside town. It was bustling, what with all the people who had been out looking for Judith Mundy, and the newspapermen and the police. He sat drinking a beer at the counter when a voice beside him said:

'You know what all this fuss is about?'

He turned and saw a tall, dark-haired man with a knife slash for a mouth and hard, unloving eyes. There was a trace of the south in his voice, he thought. He wore tan corduroy pants and a dark sweater pitted with holes, through which patches of a dirty yellow shirt were visible. A brown slicker hung to his calves, and the toes of heavy black boots peered from under the too-long cuffs of his pants.

'They're looking for the girl who's gone missing,' replied my grandfather. The man made him uneasy. There was something in his voice, he recalled, something sour-sweet, like syrup laced with arsenic. He smelt of earth and sap and something else, something he couldn't quite place.

'You think they're gonna find her?' A light flickered in the man's eyes, and my grandfather thought that it might have been amusement.

'Maybe.'

'They ain't found the others.'

He was watching my grandfather now, his face solemn but the strange glimmer still in his eyes.

'No, they haven't.'

'You a cop?'

My grandfather nodded. There was no point in denying it. Some people just knew.

'You're not from around here, though?'

'No. I'm from Portland.'

'Portland?' said the man. He seemed impressed. 'And where you been searching?'

'Out by Sebec Lake, the south shore.'

'Sebec Lake's nice. Me, I prefer the Little Wilson Stream, up there by the Elliotsville Road. It's pretty, worth a look if a man had the time. Lot of coverage on the banks.' He gestured for a whiskey, tossed some coins on the bar, then drained the glass in a single mouthful. 'You going back out there again tomorrow?'

'I guess.'

He nodded, wiping the back of his right hand across his mouth. My grandfather saw scarring on the palm, and dirt beneath the fingernails. 'Well, maybe you'll have better luck than them other fellas, seeing as how you're from Portland and all. Sometimes it takes new eyes to see an old trick.' Then he left.

That Sunday, the day when my grandfather found the tree with the strange fruit, dawned crisp and bright, with birds in the trees and blossoms by the shining waters of Sebec Lake. He left his car by the lake at Packard's Camps, showed his badge and joined a small party, made up of two brothers and a cousin from the same family, which was heading for the northern shore. The four men searched together for three hours, not talking much, until the family returned home for Sunday lunch. They asked my grandfather if he wanted to join them, but he had wrapped sourdough bread in a napkin with some fried chicken, and he had a thermos of coffee in his backpack, so he turned down their offer. He returned to Packard's Camps and ate seated on a stone by the bank, the water lapping behind him, and watched rabbits skipping through the grass.

When the other men didn't return, he got in his car and began to drive. He took the road north till he came to a steel bridge that crossed the waters of the Little Wilson. Its roadway was a series of grilles through which could be seen the brown rushing torrent of the stream. Across the bridge the road sloped upwards before splitting in two, heading for Ontwa and Borestone Mountain along the Elliotsville Road to the west and Leighton to the east. On each side of the river, the trees grew thickly. A hermit thrush shot from a birch and looped across the water. Somewhere, a warbler called.

My grandfather did not cross the bridge, but parked his car by the side of the road and followed a rough trail of stones and dirt down to the riverbank. The water was fast moving, and there were rocky outcrops and fallen branches to negotiate as he began to walk, so that he had to step into the flow at times to bypass them. Soon, there were no more houses on the slopes above him. The bank grew increasingly wild, and he was forced more and more often to take to the water in order to continue upriver.

He had been walking for almost thirty minutes when he heard the flies.

Ahead of him, a huge slab of rock rose up from the

bank, its end almost tapering to a point. He climbed it, using its ridges and alcoves for footholds and handholds, until he reached the plateau. To his right was the river, to his left a space in the trees through which the buzzing sounded louder. He walked through the gap, over which the trees hung in an arch like the entry into a cathedral, until he reached a small clearing. The sight that met him made him stop short and caused his food to erupt from his gut in a rush.

The girls hung from an oak, an old, mature tree with a thick, gnarled trunk and heavy extended branches like splayed fingers. They turned slowly, black against the sun, their bare feet pointing at the ground, their hands loose by their sides, heads lolling to one side. A fury of flies surrounded them, excited by the stench of decay. As he moved towards them, he could make out the colour of their hair, the twigs and leaves caught in the strands, the yellowing of their teeth, the eruptions on their skin, their mutilated bellies. Some were naked, while tattered dresses still clung to the others. They pirouetted in mid air, like the ghosts of five dancers no longer restricted by the pull of gravity. A heavy, rough rope around the neck of each anchored the girls to the branches above.

There were only five. When the bodies were taken down and identified, Judith Mundy's was not among them. And when she didn't appear, when no trace was ever found of her, it was decided that whoever was responsible for the deaths of the five others had probably had nothing to do with the disappearance of the Mundy girl. It would be more than thirty years before that piece of reasoning was proved wrong.

My grandfather told the police about the man in the bar and what he had said. The details were taken down and it was found that a man roughly fitting that description had been seen in Monson about the time of Judith Mundy's disappearance. There were similar descriptions of a fellow in Skowhegan, although folks differed about his height, or the colour of his eyes, or the cut of his hair. This anonymous man was a suspect, for a time, until something broke in the case.

Ruth Dickinson's clothes, soiled with blood and grime, were found in a shed in Corinna owned by the family of Quintin Fletcher. Fletcher was twenty-eight and somewhat retarded: he made a little money by selling handicrafts he created from wood picked up in the forest, travelling around the state by Greyhound bus with his case of wooden dolls, toy trucks and candlesticks. Ruth Dickinson had complained to his family and, later, to the police, that Fletcher had followed her on occasion, leering and making lewd suggestions. After he tried to touch her breast at a county fair the police told his family that they would have him put away if he approached the Dickinson girl again. Fletcher's name came up in the course of the investigation into the girls' deaths. He was questioned, the house searched, and the discovery made. Fletcher started crying, claiming that he didn't know where the clothing came from, that he hadn't hurt anybody. He was remanded for trial and placed in a secure unit in Maine State Prison, for fear that someone might try to get to him if he was kept locally. He might still have been there now, making toys and nautical gifts for the store out on US 1 in York that sells prisoners' crafts, but for the fact that a trusty, who was related distantly to Judy Giffen, attacked Fletcher when he was undergoing a checkup in the prison hospital and stabbed him three times in the neck and chest with a scalpel. Fletcher died twenty-four hours later, two days before his case was due to go to trial.

And there it lay, for most people at least: the killings ended with Fletcher's capture and subsequent death. But my grandfather couldn't forget the man in the bar, and the glimmer in his eyes, and the reference to the Elliotsville Road. For months afterwards, he countered hostility and the desire to mourn and forget with quiet persistence and sensitivity. And what he got was a name, which folks had heard but couldn't quite remember how, and sightings of the man from the bar in each town where a girl had been lost. He mounted a campaign of sorts, speaking to any newspaper or radio show that would listen, putting across his view that the man who had killed the five girls and used them to decorate a tree was still at large. He even convinced some people, for a time, until the family of Quintin Fletcher weighed in behind him and folks took a turn against the whole affair, even his old friend Sam Raines.

In the end, the hostility and indifference proved too much even for him. Under some pressure, my grandfather left the force and took up construction and then woodworking to support his family, carving lamps and chairs and tables and selling them through the HOME service for cottage industries run by the Franciscan nuns in Orland. He carved each piece of work with the same care and sensitivity he had used to question the families of the girls who died. He only spoke of the affair once thereafter, that night in front of the fire with the smell of the wood on him and the dog sleeping at his feet. The discovery he had made on that warm day had blighted his life. It haunted him in his sleep, the possibility that the man who had killed those girls had somehow escaped justice.

After he told me the tale, I knew that on those occasions when I found him sitting on the porch, his pipe cold between his lips, his eyes fixed somewhere beyond the sunset, he was thinking about what had taken place decades before. When he pushed away food almost untouched, after reading in the papers about some young girl who had strayed from home and not yet been found, he was back on the Elliotsville Road, his feet wet in his boots and the ghosts of dead girls whispering in his ear.

And the name that he found all those years before had, by then, become a kind of talisman in towns in the north, although no one could figure out how that might have happened. It was used to scare bad children who wouldn't do what they were told, who wouldn't go to sleep quietly or who headed off into the woods with their friends without telling anyone where they were going. It was a name spoken at night, before the light was switched off and the hair tousled by a familiar hand, the soft scent of a mother's perfume lingering after a final good night kiss: 'Be good now and go to sleep. And no more trips into the forest, else Caleb will get you.'

I can see my grandfather poking at the logs in the fire, letting them settle before he adds another, the sparks flying up the chimney like sprites, the melting snow sizzling in the flames.

'Caleb Kyle, Caleb Kyle,' he intones, repeating the words of the children's rhyme, the fire casting shadows on his face. 'If you see him, run a mile.'

And the snow hisses, and the wood cracks, and the dog whimpers softly in its sleep.

# Chapter Fourteen

St Martha's stood on its own grounds, surrounded by a stone wall fifteen feet in height and guarded by wrought-iron gates from which black paint bubbled and flaked in preparation for a slow, fluttering fall to the earth and snow below. The ornamental pond was filled with leaves and trash, the lawn was overgrown and the trees had not been pruned for so long that the branches of some intertwined with those of their neighbours, creating a woven canopy beneath which the grass had probably died. The building itself was grimly institutional: four floors of grey stone with a gabled roof beneath which a carved cross betrayed its religious origins.

I drove to the main entrance and parked in a space reserved for staff, then walked up the granite steps and into the home itself. To one side stood the security guard's booth where the old woman had cold-cocked Judd before racing off to her death. Straight ahead was a reception desk where a female attendant in a white coat was busy rearranging some papers. Behind her, a door opened into an office lined with books and files. The attendant was a plain-faced woman with white, doughy cheeks and dark eye shadow that made her look like a Mardi Gras skeleton. She had no name tag on her lapel;

close up, her coat was stained at the breast and white threads hung like cobwebs from the fraying collar. Willeford had been right: the place smelled of overboiled vegetables and human waste, unsuccessfully masked by disinfectant. All things considered, Emily Watts might have done the smart thing by making a break for the woods.

'Can I help you?' said the woman. Her face was neutral but her voice had the same tone as Meade Payne's boy. It made 'help' sound like a dirty word. The way she said 'you' wasn't much better.

I gave her my name and told her that Chief Martel had called ahead to arrange for me to talk to someone about the death of Emily Watts.

'I'm sorry, but Dr Ryley, the director, is at a meeting in Augusta until tomorrow.' She sounded superficially pleasant, but her face told me that anyone asking about Emily Watts was about as welcome as Louis Farrakhan at a Klan dinner. 'I told the chief, but you'd already left.' Now her face matched her tone, with the addition of a look of malicious amusement at the trip I'd been forced to make unnecessarily.

'Let me guess,' I said. 'You can't let me talk to anyone without the director's permission, the director isn't here and you have no way of contacting him.'

'Exactly.'

'Happy to save you the trouble of saying it.'

She bristled and gripped her pen tightly, as if in preparation for ramming it into my eye. From out of the security booth stepped a pudgy guy in a cheap, badly fitting uniform. He pulled on his hat as he walked towards me, but not quickly enough to hide the scars at the side of his head.

'Everything all right here, Glad?' he asked the woman behind the desk. Glad: some people were just like a big finger raised to the universe.

'Now I *am* scared,' I said. 'Big security man and no old lady to protect me.'

He blushed a deep red and sucked in his stomach a little.

'I think you'd better leave. Like the lady said, there's nobody here who can help you.'

I nodded and pointed to his belt. 'I see you got a new gun. Maybe you should get a lock and chain for it. A passing child might try to steal it.'

I left them in the reception area and walked back into the grounds. I felt a little petty for picking on Judd but I was tired and antsy and the mention of the name Caleb Kyle after all those years had thrown me. I stood on the grass and looked up at the stained, unlovely façade of the home. Emily Watts's room was at the western corner, top floor, according to Martel. The drapes were drawn and there were bird droppings on the window ledge. In the room beside it, a figure moved at the window and an elderly woman, her hair pulled back in a bun, watched me. I smiled at her but she didn't respond. When I drove away, I could see her in the rear-view, still standing at the window, still watching.

I had planned to stay another day in Dark Hollow, since I hadn't yet spoken to Rand Jennings. The sight of his wife had stirred up feelings in me that had been submerged for a long time: anger, regret, the embers of some old desire. I remembered the humiliation of lying on the toilet floor as Jennings's blows rained down on me, his fat friend snickering as he held the door closed. It surprised me, but part of me still wanted a confrontation with him after all that time.

On my way back to the motel, I tried to call Angel using the cell phone but I seemed to be out of range. I called him instead from a gas station, listening to the newly installed telephone in the Scarborough house ring five times before he eventually picked up.

'Yeah?'

'It's Bird. What's happening?'

'Lots, none of it good. While you've been doing your Perry Mason thing up north, Billy Purdue was spotted in a convenience store down here. He got away before the cops could pick him up but he's still in the city, somewhere.'

'He won't be for long, now that he's been seen. What about Tony Celli?'

'Nothing, but the cops found the Coupe de Ville in an old barn out by Westbrook. Louis picked it up on the police band. Looks like the freak show ditched his wheels for something less showy.'

I was about to tell him what little I had learned when he interrupted.

'There's something else. You got a visitor here, arrived this morning.'

'Who is it?'

'Lee Cole.'

I was surprised, given the deterioration of my friendship with her husband. Maybe she had hopes of rebuilding bridges between Walter and me.

'Did she say what she wanted?'

There was a hesitation in Angel's voice, and I immediately felt my stomach turn. 'Kinda. Bird, her daughter Ellen is missing.'

\*　　\*　　\*

I drove back immediately, doing a steady eighty as soon as I hit I-95. I was almost on the outskirts of Portland when the cell phone rang. I picked it up, half expecting it to be Angel again. It wasn't.

'Parker?' I recognised the voice almost immediately.

'Billy? Where are you?'

Billy Purdue's voice was panicky and scared. 'I'm in trouble, man. My wife, she trusted you, and now I'm trusting you too. I didn't kill them, Parker. I wouldn't do that. I couldn't kill her. I couldn't kill my little boy.'

'I know, Billy, I know.' As we spoke, I kept repeating his name in an effort to calm him and develop whatever tentative trust he might have towards me. I tried to put Ellen Cole out of my mind, at least for the present. I would deal with that as soon as I could.

'The cops are after me. They think I killed 'em. I loved 'em. I'd never have hurt 'em. I just wanted to keep 'em.' His voice bubbled on the edge of hysteria.

'Calm down, Billy,' I said. 'Look, tell me where you are and I'll come and get you. We'll take you somewhere safe and we can talk this thing through.'

'There was an old guy at their place, Parker. I saw him watching it, that night the cops picked me up. I was trying to look out for them, but I couldn't.' I wasn't even sure that he had heard my offer of help, but I let him talk as I drove past the Falmouth exit about three miles from the city.

'Did you recognise him, Billy?'

'No, I never seen him before, but I'd know him if I saw him again.'

'Good, Billy. Now tell me where you are and I'll come and get you.'

'I'm at a phone box on Commercial, but I can't stay

here. There's people, cars. I've been hiding out in the Portland Company complex at Fore Street, down by the locomotive museum. There's a vacant building just inside the main entrance. You know it?'

'Yeah, I know it. Go back inside. I'll be there as soon as I can.'

I called Angel again and told him to meet me, with Louis, at the corner of India and Commercial. Lee Cole was to be left at Java Joe's. I didn't want her at the house in case Tony Celli, or anyone else, decided to pay a visit.

There was no one else around when I arrived at the corner of India and Commercial. I pulled into the parking lot of the old India Street Terminal, the car nestling in the shadow of the old three-storey building. As I stepped from the car, the first drops of rain began to fall, a heavy, skin-soaking rain that exploded dramatically on the hood of the car and left splashes the size of quarters on the windshield. I walked round the terminal, past a picnic table and a single-storey office building, painted red, until I was on the harbour side, looking out over the dark waters. Thunder rumbled and, on Casco Bay, a ship was frozen in a flash of lightning. Ahead of me, on a restored stretch of line used to give tourists a taste of a narrow gauge railway, stood a flat-bed car with a storage tank on top, marking the start of the line. A row of locked cargo containers was ranged behind the car. To my right was the Casco Bay ferry terminal, the dinosaur body of a blue eighteen-ton crane standing above it on four spindly legs like a mutilated bug.

I was about to turn back to my car when, from behind me, I heard a noise on the gravel and a familiar voice said:

'Bad weather for birds. You should be curled up in your coop.' The voice was accompanied by the cocking of a hammer on a pistol.

I slowly raised my hands from my coat and turned to see Mifflin, Tony Celli's harelipped enforcer, smiling crookedly at me. He held a Ruger Speed Six in his hand, the rounded butt gripped hard in his stubby fist.

'It's like déjà vu all over again,' I said. 'I'll have to park someplace else in future.'

'I think your parking problem is about to be solved. Permanently. How's your head feel?' The smile was still fixed in place.

'A little tender. Hope I didn't hurt your foot too badly.'

'I get the soles specially made to absorb impact. I didn't feel a thing.' He was close to me, maybe only six or seven feet away. I didn't know where he had come from; maybe he had been waiting in the shadows behind One India all along, or had followed me to the meeting place, although I couldn't figure out how he might have known about it. Behind me, the rain made cracking noises as it hit the water.

Mifflin nodded in the direction of the lot. 'See you got your Mustang fixed.'

'Accidents will happen. That's why I have insurance.'

'You should have saved your money, spent it on dames. You ain't gonna need a car no more, unless they have demolition derbies in hell.'

He raised the gun and his finger tightened on the trigger. 'Bet your insurance doesn't cover you for this.'

'Bet it does,' I said, as Louis appeared from behind the red office building, his dark hand gripping Mifflin's gun arm tightly as I moved quickly to my left. Louis's right hand pressed the barrel of a SIG into the soft jowl of the would-be assassin.

'Gently,' said Louis. 'Wouldn't want that thing to go off and scare somebody, make them loose off a shot into someone else's fat jaw.'

Mifflin carefully removed his finger from within the guard and slowly eased the hammer down. Angel joined Louis and took the Ruger from the gunman's hand.

'Hi, gorgeous,' he said, pointing it at Mifflin's head. 'That's a big gun for a little guy.'

Mifflin said nothing as Louis eased the SIG away from his mouth and slipped it into the side pocket of his dark overcoat, his hand still gripping the gunman's arm. Louis made a sudden, swift movement and there was a hard, sharp crack as he broke Mifflin's right arm at the elbow, then struck the smaller man's head twice against the side of the building. The gunman folded to the ground. Angel disappeared and returned a minute later driving the Mercury. He flipped the trunk and Louis dumped Mifflin's prone form inside. Then we followed the car as Angel drove to the end of the Island parking lot, close by a gap in the fencing that led to the edge of the dock. When we had stopped, Louis took Mifflin's body from the trunk, dragged him to the edge, and threw him into the sea. There was a loud splash as he hit the water, the noise quickly drowned by the steady sound of the rain.

Louis would have regarded me as weak, I think, if I had said it, but I regretted the death of Mifflin. Certainly, the fact that he had been about to kill me indicated that Tony Celli felt my limited usefulness was now at an end. If we had let him live, he would have come back and tried again, probably with more guns to back him up. But the finality of that soft splash made me weary.

'His car's parked a block away,' said Angel. 'We found this on the floor.' In his hand was a mobile VHF three-channel receiver, maybe five inches wide and an inch and a half in width, designed to draw power from the car battery. If there was a receiver, then there had to be a transmitter.

'They bugged the house,' I said. 'Probably while I was in Celli's room. I should have known, when they didn't kill me.'

Angel shrugged, and tossed the receiver into the sea. 'If he was here, then his friends are already on their way to the complex,' he said. To my left, Fore Street wound north, parallel to the harbour, and I could see the silhouettes of the Portland Company buildings in the distance.

'We'll follow the railway line, come in from the harbour side,' I said. I drew my gun and clicked off the safety, but Louis tapped me on the shoulder as I did so and withdrew a Colt Government Model .380 from his right coat pocket. From his inside pocket, he produced and fitted a suppressor. 'You use your Smith & Wesson and anything goes down, they can trace it back to you,' he said. 'Use this, and we can dump it later. Plus, it'll be a whole lot quieter.' Not surprisingly, Louis knew his guns: semi-automatics chambered for subsonic ammunition are about the only pistols that function effectively with a suppressor. If the Hertz people knew the kind of luggage Louis was keeping in their car, they'd have suffered a collective seizure.

Louis handed his SIG to Angel, took a matching .380 from his left pocket and once again fitted a suppressor. His actions should have alerted me to what would happen later – not even Louis just 'happened' to be carrying a pair of silenced weapons – but I was too concerned about Billy Purdue to give it much thought.

Louis and I walked down the line, Angel behind us. Rust-red railroad tracks lay in forgotten piles, beside ties that were pitted and knotted, the wood almost black in places. Beyond the storage yards, where old wrecking balls lay side by side and concrete supports bled rust from their innards, wooden pilings moved in the tide like the remains of a primeval forest.

The Portland Company complex stood across from the marina, its entrance marked by the Sandy River Railroad car used to carry the tourists, its red guard's car and green carriages now standing silent. The complex had served the railroads once, when the Portland Company had built engines and steam locomotives, but it closed in the seventies and the buildings had now been redeveloped as a business park. Inside the yard, an old black steel tractor with a restored chimney stood at the entrance to the Narrow Gauge Railroad Museum. The building, like all those in the complex, was red brick, and three stories at its highest point, with a machine tool company housed in a similar, though larger, structure behind it, the two connected by a closed walkway. To the left of the museum was a long building that housed some kind of yacht service, I seemed to remember, and a second, similar building used by a fibreglass company.

At the southern end of the yard was a larger, three-storey building, the windows on the ground floor boarded up, the windows on the other levels obscured by wire screens, where Billy Purdue had said he was hiding. There was no doorway on the harbour side but the northern end had a wooden, shedlike structure that housed the main door. A roadway wound past the doorway and sloped upwards to the visitor entrance to the complex on Fore Street. The whole place appeared deserted and the rain fell hard and unforgiving upon it. The drops sounded like stones beating on the roof of the museum, where a side door stood open. Silently, I indicated it and Louis, Angel and I made our way into the building.

Inside, beneath a vaulted ceiling, deserted railroad cars stood in rows: green Wicasset and Quebec cars, green and red Sandy River cars from Franklin County, a green and yellow Bridgton and Saco, and, to our right, an old Railbus with an REO Speedwagon chassis from the Sandy River line.

Beside the Railbus, a body lay curled, its long dark coat gathered around it like a shroud. I turned it over, steeling myself for the sight of Billy Purdue. It was not him. Instead, the contorted features of Berendt, Mifflin's square-headed sidekick, stared back at me, a dark, ragged exit wound in his forehead. I could smell singed hair. On the floor of the museum, blood and dust congealed.

Louis's shadow fell across me. 'You think Billy Purdue did this?'

I swallowed, and the sound was huge in my ears. I shook my head and he nodded silently to himself.

We made our way left, passing between two Edaville cars on our way to the museum office. There was no one else in the building, but the steel door at the front entrance banged noisily against the frame as the wind blew and the rain continued to fall.

In the darkness beneath the walkway connecting the tool works and the museum building, a black Ford sedan was parked, its windows obscured by the falling rain. I recognised it from the crime scene outside Rita Ferris's apartment.

'It's the feds,' I said. 'They must have found Celli's guys.'

'That, or they were listening in on you as well,' muttered Louis.

'Great,' said Angel. 'Is there anybody who isn't here? Billy Purdue's so fucking popular, he should have his own holiday.'

The rear door of the car opened and a figure in a dark coat stepped out, head down, closing the door softly behind him. He walked quickly in our direction, one hand deep in his pocket, the other holding a black umbrella above his head. A light from the tool works briefly illuminated him as he passed through its beam.

'And this would be . . . ?' said Angel wearily.

'Eldritch, the Canadian cop. Stay here.'

I stepped from the shadows and Eldritch stopped, a puzzled look on his face as he tried to recognise me.

'Parker?' he said at last. 'You want to bring your friends out of the shadows too?'

From behind me, Louis and Angel appeared and stood beside me, Louis regarding Eldritch with relaxed interest.

'Well, you going to get out of this rain?' asked the Canadian.

'After you, officer,' I replied. Something had caught my eye over by the Ford when Eldritch stepped from the car, the interior light casting a faint glow on the ground below. There was a small pool of red beneath the driver's door, which was not fully closed, and, as I watched, something dripped steadily from the crack.

Eldritch stepped by me, one hand still holding the umbrella, exposing a gold cuff-link and a white shirt-sleeve. There was a dark spot spreading on the cuff as he turned to watch my progress towards the car.

I glanced back at Louis but something else had caught his eye.

'You got something on your collar, officer,' he said quietly, as Eldritch stood beneath the light.

Eldritch's shirt collar showed above the lapel of his coat. At its edge, and just above the knot of his tie, there were spots of black, like soot. But as Louis spoke, Eldritch lowered his umbrella, trying to block my view as he made his move, the gun visible to me only briefly as he removed his right hand from his pocket. I could see Louis already raising his own gun as Eldritch began to turn, the umbrella now tumbling in mid air, Angel to one side looking on. But I fired first, the bullet tearing a hole in the umbrella and hitting Eldritch low on the thigh, the gunshot masked by the suppressor and the driving rain. I fired again, this time hitting him in the side. The gun fell from his hand and he tumbled against the wall of the museum, sliding down with his back against it until he sat on the ground, his teeth gritted in pain and his hand clutching at the red stain, spreading across the front of his coat. Beside him, Louis picked up his gun by slipping a pen through the trigger guard and examined the weapon with professional detachment.

'Taurus,' he said. 'Brazilian. Looks like our friend might have vacationed in South America.'

I walked to the car. There were two star-shaped bullet holes in the windshield surrounded by twin sunbursts of blood. I opened the driver's door with a gloved hand and stepped back as Agent Samson fell sideways onto the ground, a dark hole at the bridge of his ruined nose where the bullet had exited. Beside him, Agent Doyle's forehead rested against the dashboard, blood pooling at his feet. Both were still warm.

Carefully, I lifted Samson into the car, closed the door and walked back to where Angel and Louis stood over the bleeding man.

'Abel,' said Louis. Despite his pain, the man on the ground regarded us with dark, hateful eyes, but didn't speak.

'He's not going anywhere,' I said. 'We put him in the trunk of the Ford, call the cops, let them take care of him after we're done.'

But neither Angel nor Louis appeared to be listening to me. Instead, Angel shook his head and tut-tutted: 'A man your age dyeing his hair,' he said to Abel. 'That's just vanity.'

'And you know what they say about vanity,' said Louis softly. Abel looked up at him, his eyes widening.

'Vanity kills,' concluded Louis. Then he shot him once, the Colt jumping in his hand. Abel's head bumped against the wall behind him, his eyes closed tightly, and then his chin slumped forwards onto his chest.

For the first time in my life, I touched Louis in anger. Reaching out, I pushed him hard on the chest. He took a step back, his expression unchanged.

'Why?' I shouted. 'Why did you kill him? Jesus, Louis, do we have to kill everybody?'

'No,' said Louis. 'Just Abel and Stritch.'

And then I understood why Louis and Angel had come here, and the realisation was like a punch in the stomach.

'It's a contract,' I said. 'You took on the hit.' I knew now why Leo Voss had been killed, why Abel and Stritch had chosen this time to recede into the shadows, and it was only partly to do with the opportunity offered by Billy Purdue and the money he had stolen. Abel and Stritch were running, and they were running from Louis.

He nodded once. Beside him, Angel looked at me with a kind of sorrow, but also determination. I knew whose side he was on.

'How much?' I asked.

'A dollar,' said Louis simply. 'I'd have taken fifty cents, but the man didn't have no change.'

'A *dollar*?' It was strange, but I almost smiled despite myself. He had taken a dollar, yet their lives were worth even less than that. I looked back at Abel's body and thought of the two agents in the car and the real Eldritch, who had probably never made it as far as Maine.

'They're that bad, Bird,' said Angel. 'These guys are the fucking worst. Don't let them come between us.'

I shook my head. 'You should have told me, that's all. You should have trusted me.'

Now Louis spoke. 'You're right. It was my call. I called wrong.'

He stood before me, waiting for me to respond, and I knew why he had kept it from me. After all, I was an ex-cop, with cop friends. Maybe Louis still had doubts. I had saved Angel's life while he was in prison and, in return, they had stood by me when Jennifer and Susan were killed, had put their own lives on the line in the hunt for their killer and the killers of others, and asked nothing in return. I had no reason to doubt them; they, on the other hand, a burglar and an assassin, could be forgiven for having concerns about me.

'I understand,' I said at last.

Louis nodded his head once in response, but in that gesture and the look in his eyes he said all that he needed to say.

'Let's go,' I said. 'Time to find Billy Purdue.' And as we walked to the vacant building, the rain falling heavily now, I took a last look at Abel's body and shivered slightly. His huddled form, and the remains of Berendt in the railroad museum, were mute testament to the fact that the squat, grotesque figure of Stritch could not be far away.

There were two cars parked farther up on Fore Street, across from a new development of grey wood houses half clad in red brick. It was too dark to see if anyone remained inside the vehicles. When we reached the main door to the unoccupied building, the lock had already been broken open and the door stood slightly ajar. Staying close to the wall, I peered round the corner to the front of the building. There, the windows on the top floor were boarded up, while a wooden walkway led from the grass border to a locked door on the second storey. Because of the gradient of the slope, the ground floor was actually below the grass, its windows masked with more screens.

I came back to where Angel and Louis were waiting by the door, where we agreed that Angel should leave us and return in the Mercury, so that if we came out with Billy Purdue we could leave quickly.

Inside the door was a flight of stairs, dusty and littered with old newspaper. They led up to the second floor, to a kind of storage bay supported by steel columns. Behind the stairs was a series of empty offices and work areas, all quiet and unlit. The warehouse still smelt faintly of wood, although now the pervading odour was one of dampness and decay. Louis had a flashlight but didn't light it for fear of drawing attention to us.

From where we stood, I could see that mounds of rotted wood still lay in one corner near the stairs. Water dripped from the ceiling as the rain fell through the warehouse roof and gradually leaked through to the floors below. We moved behind the stairway and into the first of the series of workshops, empty apart from some wooden benches and a broken plastic chair. Through the sound of the pouring rain and dripping water I could hear a noise from the other side of the wall as we neared a doorway. I motioned Louis to the left and took up a position at the right wall until I could partially see into the room beyond. Then, slowly, I inched my way forwards, peering in quickly and then carefully progressing when nobody tried to blow my head off.

I was in one of a pair of what were once adjoining offices. There was a faint smell of smoke from the room, which came from a pile of smouldering wood and trash in the far corner. In the corner opposite, something moved.

I spun quickly and tightened my finger on the trigger.

'Don't shoot,' said a raw, cracked voice, and a figure gradually emerged from where it had been crouching in the darkness. It wore plastic bags over its feet, its legs were encased in dirt-encrusted denims and a coat with no elbows was tied around its waist with a length of string. Its hair was long and unkempt, its beard grey but streaked with nicotine yellow. 'Please, don't shoot. I didn't mean no harm by starting the fire.'

'Move to your right. Quickly.' Through a crack in one of the wooden panels on the windows, a weak glow shone from a streetlight. The old man moved until he was caught in its beam. His eyes were small and dull. Even from twelve feet away I could smell the booze, and other things too.

I held him in my sights for a moment longer, then

gestured to my right with the gun as Louis appeared in the doorway. 'Get out of here,' I said. 'It's not safe.'

'Can I collect my stuff?' He pointed at a heap of meagre possessions stacked in a shopping cart.

'Take what you can carry, then go.' The old guy nodded his thanks and began to pick up items from the cart: a pair of boots, some soda cans, a pile of copper wire. Some he put back again, others he seemed to want to think about. As he considered a single Reebok sneaker, a deep voice behind me said: 'Old man, you got five seconds to get your shit out of here, else the coroner be sorting it for you.' Louis's comment seemed to focus the old guy's mind; seconds later he was running past us with a tangled collection of wire, boots and cans in his arms.

'You won't steal anything, will you?' he asked Louis as he prepared to go.

'No,' replied Louis. 'You done took all the good stuff.'

The old guy nodded happily and started to scurry out, Louis shaking his head as he went. The old man paused at the doorway. 'Them other fellas went upstairs,' he said simply, then left.

We moved quickly but carefully through that floor until we reached a pair of parallel staircases at the far end of the building, one at each corner. I heard footsteps above us, moving carefully across the floor. Between the stairs was a set of twin doors to the yard outside. A length of broken chain lay on the floor and a half brick held one of the doors open. Louis took the right-hand stairway, I took the left. As I climbed, I kept to the sides of the stairs to minimise the risk of standing on a weak or rotted step. I needn't have bothered. The rain was falling with a renewed ferocity and the old building echoed and hummed with its sound.

We met at a kind of mezzanine, where a single wide set of steps led up to the second storey. Louis moved ahead, while I stayed a little farther behind. I watched as he pushed open a swinging door, a dirty, wire-mesh window at head level, and began his search of the floor. I had decided to move on to the third storey when there was the sound of movement from below. I looked down over the stair rail and a man stepped into my line of vision, striking a match to light a cigarette. In the flash of illumination I recognised him as one of Tony Celli's crew from the hotel room, left to guard the door from outside, but instead taking shelter from the rain. Above me, a floorboard creaked gently, then another: at least one of Celli's men had progressed to the top floor.

As I watched Tony Clean's man smoke his cigarette, something caught my attention to my left. The windows on the mezzanine, which would once have looked out onto the lot below, were now boarded up and no light shone through them. The only illumination came from a jagged hole in the wall, ringed with damp where the plaster surrounding an old air-conditioning unit had given way and fallen in a heap to the floor below, taking the unit with it. The hole created a kind of murky pool of light between two masses of dark at either side. In one of those unlit areas, I sensed a presence. A pale figure flickered, like a piece of paper gently tumbling. I moved forwards, my heart pounding and the gun heavy in my hand.

From out of the blackness, a face appeared. Its eyes were dark, with no whites showing, and a dark necklace seemed to hang around its neck. Slowly, its mouth became visible, the zigzagging black thread sealing it shut and, beneath it, the mark left by the rope was deeply indented on her skin. She watched me for a moment, then seemed to turn in on herself, and there was only emptiness where she had been. I felt a cold sweat on my back and a feeling of nausea swept over me. I gave one more look at the patch of darkness, then turned away just as a sudden soft cry of pain came from below me.

I paused on the first step, and waited. Around me the rain fell and water dripped. There was the sound of a shoe softly scuffing on the wood below and then a man drifted into view on the right-hand stairway, wearing a tan raincoat from which a bald head emerged at the collar. Stritch raised his strange, melted-wax features and his bleak, colourless eyes regarded me for a moment. Then his too-wide mouth broke into a smile from which all humour was absent and he withdrew back beneath the mezzanine. I wondered if he knew yet that Abel was dead, or how much of a threat he considered me.

The answer came within seconds as the silenced rounds tore through the soft damp wood of the stair rail, splinters spearing the gloom. I sprang up the remaining steps, the bullets following me as Stritch tried to gauge my position from the sounds I made. I felt something tug at the tail of my coat as I reached the top of the steps and knew that he had come close, very close, with at least one of his shots.

I got to the second floor and headed after Louis. There was a kind of lobby inside the door, with an old raised receiving desk to my right behind which lay another storage bay, part of a succession of small bays that led to the back of the building, each connected by a single doorway so that, if the light had permitted, I could have seen straight through to the far wall of the warehouse. Even from where I was standing, I could see that the bays still contained battered desks and broken chairs, rolls of rotting matting and boxes of discarded paperwork. Two corridors stretched away on either side, one directly in front of me and one to the right. I guessed that Louis was already making his way down the right-hand corridor so I moved quickly down the other, casting anxious glances over my shoulder to see if Stritch had appeared yet.

A burst of gunfire came from ahead of me and to my right, answered by two softer shots fired in close succession. I heard voices shouting and running footsteps, the noises echoing around the old building. At a doorway to my right, a figure in a black leather jacket lay slumped on the floor, blood pooling around its head. Louis was already making his mark but he didn't know that Stritch was somewhere behind us, and it was important that he was told. I moved back into the corridor in time to see a flash of tan move behind the receiving desk. I stepped sideways, moving past the prone form of Tony Celli's man until I could see past the top of the desk, but there was no sign of Stritch. I ran quickly to the doorway of the next bay and peered round the door frame in time to receive the muzzle of a silenced pistol in my right temple.

'Shit, Bird, I almost blew your head off,' said Louis. In the semi-darkness he was almost invisible in his black clothes, with only his teeth and the whites of his eyes showing.

'Stritch is here,' I said.

'I know. Caught a glimpse of him, then got distracted by you.'

Our discussion was interrupted by the sound of more firing ahead of us, the same gun shooting each time, loosing off three shots with no return of fire. There was more shouting and then a burst of automatic fire, followed by footsteps running up a flight of stairs. Louis and I exchanged a nod and began to make our way towards the back of the building, one of us at each side of every door frame to give us a clear view of the room beyond and the section of corridor at either side. We kept moving until we reached an open service elevator, in which another of Tony Celli's men lay dead. Alongside the elevator, a single flight of stairs wound up to the top level, where Stritch had presumably gone on ahead of us. We were on the second step when I heard a sound behind me that was chillingly familiar: the twin clicks of a cartridge being jacked into a pump-action shotgun. Louis and I turned slowly, our guns held up and away to our sides, to find Billy Purdue standing before us. His face was streaked with black, his clothes soaked through, and on his back was a black knapsack.

'Put your guns down,' he said. Somehow, he had found a way to hide from his pursuers, and from us, among the old furniture and office waste. We did as we were told, casting cautious looks both at Billy's gun and the staircase above us.

'You brought them here,' he said, his voice shaking with anger. 'You sold me out.' There were tears running down his cheeks.

'No, Billy,' I said. 'We came to get you to safety. You're in a lot of trouble here. Put the gun down and we'll try to get you out of it.'

'No. Fuck you. There's nobody here for me now.' With that, he fired two bursts from the shotgun, spraying the wood and plaster behind us and forcing us to dive to the ground. When we looked up again, splinters and grit in our hair, Billy was nowhere to be seen but I could hear his running footfalls as he headed back in the direction in which we had come. Louis immediately sprang to his feet and moved after him.

More shots came from the floor above as I rose, automatic fire followed by a single shot. I took the steps slowly, my neck craned to one side, my hands slick with sweat. At the top of the stairs, beside the elevator, another of Celli's men lay huddled in a corner. Blood flowed from the bullet wound in his neck. There was something else about him too, something I almost did not see.

His trousers were opened, the zipper pulled down, and his genitals partially exposed.

Before me was a doorway, and beyond the doorway was total darkness. In that darkness, I knew that Stritch waited. I could smell his cheap, sickly cologne and the dark, earthy odour he used it to conceal. I could sense his watchfulness, the tendrils he sent out to test the air around him for prey. And I could feel his desire, the sexual charge he took from hurting and bringing lives to an end, the aberrant sexuality that had led him to touch and expose the young man in the corner as he lay dying.

And I knew with absolute certainty that if I set foot beyond that doorway Stritch would take me and kill me, and that he would touch me as I died. I felt the shadows move around me, and a child laughed in the dim light below. It seemed to summon me back from the brink, or perhaps it was my own fear making me believe that was the case. For whatever reason, I chose to leave Stritch in the darkness and return to the light.

Louis approached as I made my way backwards down the stairs. His pants were torn at the knee, and he was limping slightly. 'I slipped,' he said, spitting the words from his mouth. 'He got away. What about Stritch?'

I indicated the floor above. 'Maybe Tony Celli will do you a favour.'

'You think?' said Louis, in a tone that said he didn't believe it was likely. He looked at me more closely. 'You cool, Bird?'

I moved past him so that he could not see my face. I was ashamed at my weakness, but I knew what I had felt, and what I had seen in the blood-red eyes of a dead woman.

'My concern is Billy Purdue,' I said. 'When Stritch finds out that his buddy is dead, he won't go anywhere until he's settled the score. You'll get another chance.'

'I'd prefer to take this one,' he replied.

'It's pitch black up there. You set foot on that top floor, and he'll kill you.'

Louis remained standing, watching me, but he did not speak. In the distance, I heard the wail of approaching sirens. I saw Louis hesitate, balancing the risk of the police and the shadows on the floor above with the opportunity to try to take out Stritch. Then slowly, with just one glance back to the stairs leading up to the darkness of the third floor, Louis followed me.

We reached the main bay where we had met the old man. 'We go out the front, we may run into Tony Celli's wheelmen, or the cops,' I said. 'And if Billy went out that way, then he's already dead.'

Louis nodded in agreement and we headed down to the door at the back of the warehouse, where the man Stritch had killed lay half in, half out of the doorway, one arm across his eyes as if he had glimpsed the heart of the sun. Across the lot, I could see the Mercury. It growled into life as Angel shot across the lot and turned the car, then stopped to allow us to get in.

'Any sign of Billy?'

'No, at least none that I saw. You two OK?'

'Fine,' I said, although I was still shaken by the fear I had felt on the top floor. 'Stritch was in there. Came from the back of the building.'

'Seems like everybody knows your business except you,' remarked Angel as we tore out of the lot and followed the tracks back in the direction of India Street. Just before they ended, he swung the wheel to the right and sped through the gap in the wire fence to bring us into the parking lot at One India. He killed the lights as sirens wailed and two black-and-white police cars raced up Fore Street. Then we waited to see if Billy Purdue might show.

While we sat in silence, I tried to piece together what had happened. The feds had either been monitoring my phone or had managed to find some trace of Tony Celli's crew. When they moved, Abel contacted Stritch and told him where to go, with the intention of joining him after taking care of the feds. With three different groups of people after him in one enclosed space, Billy Purdue had still managed to get away.

And I thought too of that half-imagined figure I had glimpsed in the shadows. Rita Ferris was dead and, soon, the snow would be falling on her grave. My mind was playing tricks on me, or perhaps I hoped that was the case.

No one came towards us on foot from the direction of the complex. If any of Tony Celli's men had survived, I figured that they would head north instead of coming straight back into town and risk meeting the cops.

'You think he's still in there?' I asked Louis.

'Who? Stritch? If he is, it's because he's dead, and I don't believe Tony Celli has anyone that good on his side, assuming anyone was left alive in there,' replied Louis.

Again, I caught that thoughtful look in his eyes as he examined my face in the rear-view mirror.

'I tell you this,' he said. 'He knows now that Abel is dead, and he's gonna be real pissed.'

# Chapter Fifteen

Louis and Angel dropped me at my Mustang, and then followed me to Java Joe's. I felt drained, and sick inside: I thought of the look in Abel's eyes before he died, and the sight of the young gunman violated at the moment of his death, and an old man loaded with sneakers and copper wiring running into the cold, wet night.

At the coffee shop, Louis and Angel decided to stay outside in the Mercury drinking take-out mochas. Lee Cole was seated by the window, her jeans tucked into shin-high fur-lined boots, a white wool top buttoned to the neck. As she stood to greet me, the light caught the streaks of silver in her hair. She kissed me softly on the cheek and held me tightly. Her body started to shake and I could hear her sobbing into my shoulder. I pushed her gently away, my hands on her shoulders, and watched as she shook her head in embarrassment and searched through her pockets for a tissue. She was still beautiful. Walter was a lucky man.

'She's gone, Bird,' she said, as she sat. 'We can't find her. Help me.'

'But she was with me only a few days ago,' I said. 'She stopped off here for a few hours with her boyfriend.'

She nodded. 'I know. She called us from Portland, told

us she was heading on with Ricky. Then she rang us one more time on the way to some place farther north and that was the last we heard from her. She was under strict instructions to call us each day, but when we didn't hear . . .'

'Have you been in touch with the police?'

'Walter has. They think she may have run off with Ricky. Walter argued with her about him last month, about how she should be concentrating on her study and not on chasing boys. You know how Walter can be, and retirement hasn't made him any more tolerant.'

I nodded. I knew how he could be. 'When you get back, call Special Agent Ross in the FBI's Manhattan office. Mention my name. He'll make sure that Ellen's name is in the NCIC database.' The National Crime Information Center kept records of all missing persons, adults and juveniles, reported to the police. 'If it isn't, it means that the police aren't doing what they should be doing, and Ross may be able to help you with that as well.'

She brightened up a little. 'I'll ask Walter to do it.'

'Does he know you're here?'

'No. When I asked him to contact you, he refused. He's already been up there, trying to put pressure on the local police. They told him that the best thing to do would be to wait, but that's not Walter. He drove around, asking in the other towns, but there was no sign. He got back yesterday, but I don't think he's going to stay. I told him I had to get out of the house for a while. I had the flight already booked. I'd tried calling you on the cell phone, but I could never get through. I don't know . . .' She trailed off, then began again. 'I don't know all that happened between you two. I know some of it and I can guess at more, but it has nothing to do with my daughter. I left him a note on the refrigerator. He'll have found it by now.' She stared out the window, as if visualising the discovery of the note and Walter's response to its contents.

'Is there any chance that the police might be right, that she has run away?' I asked. 'She never seemed like that kind of kid and she didn't seem troubled at all when I met her, but they get funny when you introduce sex into the equation. I know I always did.'

She smiled for the first time. 'I remember sex, Bird. I may be older than you, but I'm not dead yet.' The smile disappeared as her words set off a chain reaction in her head, and I knew she was trying not to picture what might have happened to Ellen. 'She didn't run away. I know her and she would never do that to us, no matter how badly we had fought with her.'

'What about the kid – Ricky? I get the impression that their eyes met from opposite sides of the track.'

Lee didn't seem to know much about Ricky beyond the fact that his mother had left the family when he was three and his father had raised him and his three sisters by holding down two dead-end jobs. He was a scholarship student – a little rough and ready, she admitted, but she didn't believe that there was any malice in him or that he would have been party to some elopement.

'Will you look for her, Bird? I keep thinking that she's in trouble somewhere. Maybe they went hiking and something went wrong, or somebody . . .' She stopped abruptly and reached out to take my hand. 'Will you find her for me?' she repeated.

I thought of Billy Purdue and of the men hunting him, of Rita and Donald, of Cheryl Lansing's granddaughter emerging from a mass of wet, rotting leaves. I felt a duty to the dead, to the troubled young woman who had wanted to create a better life for herself and her child, but she was gone and Billy Purdue was drifting towards some kind of reckoning from which I couldn't save him. Maybe my duty now was to the living, to Ellen, who had looked after my little girl for the brief span of her life.

'I'll look for her,' I said. 'You want to tell me where she was going when she made the call?'

As she spoke, the world seemed to shift on its axis, throwing strange shadows across familiar scenes, turning everything into an off-kilter version of its former self. And I cursed Billy Purdue because, somehow, in some way that I couldn't yet recognise, he was responsible for what had happened. In Lee's words, once-distant worlds eclipsed one another and indistinct shapes, like plates moving beneath the earth, came together to form a new, dark continent.

'She said she was heading for a place called Dark Hollow.'

I brought her to Portland Airport in time to catch her flight to New York, then drove back to the house. Angel and Louis were in the front room, watching a sleazy talk show marathon on cable.

'It's *I Can't Marry You, You're Not A Virgin*,' said Angel. 'At least they're not claiming to be virgins, else it'd be *I Can't Marry You, You're A Liar*.'

'Or *I Can't Marry You, You're Ugly*,' offered Louis, sipping a bottle of Katahdin ale, his feet stretched out before him on a chair. 'Man, how they get the audience for this show? They drag dollar bills through the trailer parks?' He hit the remote, muting the sound on the TV.

'How's Lee doing?' asked Angel, suddenly serious.

'She's holding together, but only just.'

'So what's the deal?'

'I've got to head north again, and I think I'm going to need you two to come with me. Ellen Cole was last heard from on the way to Dark Hollow, the same place Billy Purdue grew up, for a time, and the place I think he's heading back to now.'

Louis shrugged. 'Then that's where we going,'

I sat down in an easy chair beside him. 'There may be a problem.'

'Jeez, Bird,' said Angel, 'we're not exactly starved for problems as it is.'

'This problem have a name?' asked Louis.

'Rand Jennings.'

'And he would be?'

'Chief of police in Dark Hollow.'

'And he doesn't like you because?' said Angel, taking up the baton from Louis.

'I had an affair with his wife.'

'You the man,' said Louis. 'You could fall over and make hitting the ground look complicated.'

'It was a long time ago.'

'Long enough for Rand Jennings to forgive and forget?' asked Angel.

'Probably not.'

'Maybe you could write him a note,' he suggested. 'Or send him flowers.'

'You're not being helpful.'

'I didn't sleep with his wife. In the helpful stakes, that puts me a full length clear of you.'

'You see him last time you were up there?' asked Louis.

'No.'

'You see the woman?'

'Yes.'

Angel laughed. 'You're some piece of work, Bird. Any chance you might keep the mouse in its hole while we're up there, or you planning to renew old acquaintances?'

'We met by accident. It wasn't intentional.'

'Uh-huh. Tell that to Rand Jennings. "Hi Rand, it was an accident. I tripped and fell into your wife".' I could still hear him laughing as he headed for his bedroom.

Louis finished his beer, then lifted his feet from the chair and prepared to follow Angel. 'We screwed up tonight,' he said.

'Things got screwed up. We did what we could.'

'Tony Celli ain't gonna give up on this thing. Stritch neither.'

'I know.'

'You want to tell me what happened on the top floor?'

'I felt him waiting, Louis. I felt him waiting and I knew for sure that if I went in after him, I'd die. Despite evidence to the contrary, I don't have a death wish. I wasn't going to die at his hands, not there, not anywhere.'

Louis remained at the door, considering what I had told him. 'If you felt it, then that's the way it was,' he said at last. 'Sometimes, that's all the difference there is between living and dying. But if I see him again, I'm taking him down.'

'Not if I see him first.' I meant it, regardless of all that had taken place and the fear that I had felt.

His mouth twitched in one of his trademark semismiles.

'Bet you a dollar you don't.'

'Fifty cents,' I replied. 'You've already earned half your fee.'

'I guess I have,' he said. 'I guess I have.'

Louis and Angel left early the next morning, Louis for the airport and Angel to scout around Billy Purdue's trailer to see if he could find anything that the cops might have missed. I was about to lock up the house when Ellis Howard's car bumped into my drive and then Ellis himself stepped heavily from the car. He took a look at my bag and gestured at it with a thumb.

'Going somewhere?'

'Yep.'

'You mind telling me where?'

'Yep.'

He slapped his hand gently on the hood of the Mustang, as if to transfer his frustration into the metal of the car. 'Where were you yesterday evening?'

'On my way back from Greenville.'

'What time'd you get back into town?'

'About six. Should I call a lawyer?'

'You come straight home?'

'No, I parked up and met someone in Java Joe's. Like I said: should I call a lawyer?'

'Not unless you want to confess to something. I was going to tell you what happened out at the Portland Company complex last night, but maybe you already know, seeing as how your Mustang was down by the harbour yesterday evening.'

So that was it. Ellis was fishing. He had nothing, and I wasn't about to break down and beg for mercy.

'I told you. I was meeting someone.'

'This person still in town?'

'No.'

'And you don't know anything about what happened at the complex last night?'

'I try to avoid the news. It affects my karma.'

'If I thought it would help, your karma would be kicking its heels in a cell. We found four bodies in that complex, all of them associates of Tony Celli, plus two dead feds and a mystery caller.'

'Mystery caller?' I asked, but I was thinking of something else. There should have been five bodies in the complex: one of Tony's men had survived and escaped, which meant there was a good chance that Tony Celli knew Louis and I had been in the building.

Ellis looked closely at me, trying to assess how much I knew. As he spoke, he waited for a reaction. He was disappointed.

'We found the Toronto cop, Eldritch, dead. Three bullets, two different guns. The one to the head was an execution shot.'

'I'm waiting for the "but".'

'The "but" is that this guy wasn't Eldritch. His ID says he was, his prints and his face say he wasn't. Now I've got the Toronto Police Department howling at me to find their missing man, I've got a bunch of feds who are very interested in the John Doe who killed two of their agents, and I have four members of Boston's finest crew using up morgue space that I can't afford to give them. The ME is considering relocating here permanently, seeing as how we're such good customers and all. Plus Tony Celli hasn't been seen since his night at the Regency.'

'He stiff on the bill?'

'Don't, Bird. I'm not in the mood. Don't forget that Willeford is still missing and, until you came along, he knew as much about Billy Purdue as anyone.'

I let it pass without comment. I didn't want to think of

what I might have brought down on Willeford. Instead, I said: 'Bangor turn up anything on Cheryl Lansing?'

'No, and we're no further on the killing of Rita Ferris and her son. Which brings me to my second reason for calling. You want to tell me again what you were doing in Bangor? And then Greenville?'

'Like I told Bangor, Billy Purdue hired someone to trace his parents. I thought that maybe he might try to follow that trail now that he's in trouble.'

'And is he following that trail?'

'Someone is.'

Ellis moved towards me, his bulk menacing, his eyes more so. 'You tell me where you're going, Bird, or I swear to God I'll arrest you here and now and take a close look at that gun of yours.'

I knew that Ellis wasn't kidding. Even though the silenced guns now lay at the bottom of Casco Bay beside Mifflin, I couldn't afford to delay the search for Ellen Cole. 'I'm heading north to a place called Dark Hollow. The daughter of a friend of mine has gone missing. I'm going to try to find her. Her mother was the person I met at Java Joe's last night.'

Some of the anger went out of his face. 'Is it a coincidence that Dark Hollow is Billy Purdue's country?'

'I don't believe in coincidences.'

He patted the hood one more time, and seemed to reach a decision. 'Neither do I. You stay in touch now, Bird, y'hear?'

He turned and walked back to his car.

'Is that it?' I said. I was surprised to see him let it go so easily.

'No, I guess it isn't, but I don't see what more I can do.' He stood at the open door of the car, and watched me.

'Frankly, Bird, I'm balancing the benefits of hauling you in and grilling you, assuming you'd tell us anything, against the benefits of having you wandering around and looking under rocks. So far, the scales are tipping in favour of the second option, but only just. You remember that.'

I waited a heartbeat.

'Does this mean you've decided against recruiting me, Ellis?'

He didn't reply. Instead, he shook his head and drove away, leaving me to think about Tony Celli and Stritch and an old man in a harbour bar, drinking beers and waiting for the new world to sweep him away.

I had told Ellis some of the truth, but not all. I was going to Dark Hollow, and would be there by nightfall, but first Louis and I would pay a visit to Boston. There was a slight possibility that Tony Celli might have taken Ellen Cole, perhaps in the hope of using her as leverage if I found Billy Purdue before he did. Even if that was not the case, there were some things to be clarified before we went up against Celli again. Tony was a made guy. It was important that everybody knew where they stood on Tony's future.

Before I left to meet Louis at the airport, I stopped off at the Kraft Mini-Storage. There, in three adjoining units, was what I had retained of my grandfather's possessions: some furniture; a small library of books; some silver plates and a brass screen for a fireplace; and a series of boxes filled with old paperwork and files. It took me fifteen minutes to locate what I was looking for and take it back to the car: a manilla expanding file, held closed by a piece of red ribbon. On the index tab, written in my grandfather's ornate script, were the words 'Caleb Kyle'.

# Chapter Sixteen

Al Z operated out of an office above a comic-book store on Newbury Street. It was an odd location, but it suited him to be in a place where tourists browsed among chichi clothes stores, sipped exotic teas or browsed in galleries. It was busy, there were too many people around for anyone to cause trouble and he could send out for flavoured coffees or scented candles any time he wanted.

Louis and I sat outside a Ben & Jerry's ice cream parlour across from Al Z's brownstone office, eating chocolate-chip-cookie-dough ice cream and drinking large coffees. We were the only people sitting outside, mainly because it was so cold that my ice cream hadn't even begun to melt yet.

'You think he's noticed us?' I asked, as my fingers gave up their efforts to hold the spoon without shaking.

Louis sipped thoughtfully at his coffee. 'Tall, handsome black male and his white boy sittin' outside eatin' ice cream in the fuckin' winter? I think someone must have noticed us by now.'

'I'm not sure I like being called "boy",' I mused.

'Get in line, whitey. We got a three-hundred year start on that particular grievance.'

At a window above the comic-book store, a shadow moved.

'Let's go,' said Louis. 'It wasn't for the damn cold, brothers be running the world by now.'

At the top of a flight of steps, next to the window of the store, there was a buzzer beside a wooden, windowless door. I pressed the buzzer and a voice answered simply: 'Yes?'

'I'm looking for Al Z,' I said.

'No Al Z here,' replied the voice, all in a fast flow of heavily accented English so that it came out as 'Noalseeher'. It was followed by a click and the intercom went silent.

Louis hit the buzzer again.

'Yes,' said the same voice.

'Man, just open the damn door.'

The intercom clicked off, then buzzed, and we passed through, the reinforced door springing shut behind us. We walked up four flights of stairs to where a plain, unvarnished door stood open. A figure leaned against the window beyond, small and bulky, its hand resting midway between its neck and its belt, ready to move for the gun if necessary. The only ornamentation on the wall was a cheap-looking, black-and-white clock, which softly ticked away the seconds. I figured the surveillance camera was probably hidden behind it. When we entered the room and saw the television screen on Al Z's desk showing only an empty stairwell, I realised I was right.

There were four men in the room. One was the short bulky guy, his skin yellow as a beeswax candle, who had watched us from the doorway. An older man, his flesh heavy at the jowls like a basset hound's, sat on a worn leather sofa to the left of the doorway, his legs crossed, a white shirt and red silk tie beneath his black suit. His eyes were hidden by small, round-framed sunglasses. Against the wall, a young buck leaned with his thumbs hooked into the empty belt loops of his pants, holding his silver-grey jacket away from his sides to reveal the butt of a H & K semi-automatic at his waist. His grey suit pants were baggy, narrowing to pipecleaner thinness where they met his silver-tooled cowboy boots. The eighties revival was obviously still in full flow where he came from.

Louis was looking straight ahead, as if the room were empty apart from the fourth man who sat behind a teak desk topped with green leather, the desktop empty apart from a black telephone, a pen and notebook and the TV screen, which kept up its unceasing vigil on the stairs.

Al Z looked like a well-groomed undertaker on vacation. His thin silver hair was swept back from the broad expanse of his forehead and slicked tightly to his skull. His face was craggy and wrinkled, the eyes dark like opals, the lips thin and dry, the nostrils on his long nose slim and strangely elongated, as if he had been bred specifically for his powers of smell. He wore a three-piece suit of autumn hues, the fabric a mix of reds and oranges and yellows, finely interwoven. His white shirt was open at the neck, the collars narrow pinpoint, and there was no tie. In his right hand he held a cigarette; his left lay flat on the desk, the nails short and clean, but not manicured. Al Z acted as the buffer between the upper reaches of the organisation and the lower. He solved problems, when they arose. It was his gift to be a problem solver, but there was no point in a manicure if your hands were always going to be dirty.

There were no chairs in front of his desk, and the man in the dark suit remained spread across the sofa, so we stayed standing. Al Z nodded at Louis, then looked long and appraisingly at me.

'Well, well, the famous Charlie Parker,' he said at last. 'If I knew you were coming, I'd have worn a tie.'

'Everybody knows you, how you gonna make any money as a private dick?' muttered Louis. 'Hiring you for undercover work be like hiring Jay Leno.'

Al Z waited for him to finish before turning his attention from me to Louis. 'If I knew you were bringing equally distinguished company, Mr Parker, I'd have made everybody else wear a tie too.'

'Long time no see,' said Louis.

Al Z nodded. 'I got bad lungs.' He waved the cigarette gently as he spoke. 'The New York air don't agree with me. I prefer it up here.'

But there was more to it than that: the mob was no longer what it once had been. The world of *The Godfather* was history before the film ever hit the screen, the image of the Italians already sullied by their involvement in the heroin epidemic of the seventies, and since then walking disaster areas like John Gotti Jr had debased it even further. RICO – the racketeer-influenced and corrupt organisation laws – had put an end to the construction shakedowns, the garbage collection monopolies, and the mob control of the Fulton Street Fish Market in New York. The heroin-smuggling business that had operated out of pizza parlours was gone, busted by the FBI in 1987. The old bosses were dead, or in jail.

Meanwhile, the Asians had spread from Chinatown, crossing the divide of Canal Street into Little Italy, and the blacks and the Latinos now controlled operations in Harlem. Al Z had smelt death in the air, and had receded even further into the background, eventually moving north. Now he sat in a bare office above a comic-book store in Boston, and tried to maintain some element of stability in what little remained. That was why Tony Clean was so dangerous: he believed the myths and still saw the potential for personal glory in the tattered remnants of the old order. His actions threatened to bring down heat on his associates at a time when the organisation was in a weakened position. His continued existence threatened the survival of everyone around him.

To our left, the young gun eased himself from the wall. 'They're carrying, Al,' he said. 'You want me to lighten their load?'

From the corner of my eye, I saw Louis's eyebrow raise itself about a quarter of an inch. Al Z caught the gesture, and smiled gently.

'I wish you luck,' he said. 'I don't think either of our guests are the kind to give up their toys so easily.'

The young gun's glow of confidence flickered, as if he were unsure whether or not he was being tested. 'They don't look so tough,' he said.

'Look harder,' said Al Z.

The gunslinger looked but his powers of perception left a lot to be desired. He glanced once again at Al Z, then made a move towards Louis.

'I wouldn't, if I were you,' said Louis softly.

'You ain't me,' said the younger man, but there was a hint of wariness in his voice.

'That's true,' said Louis. 'I was you, I wouldn't be dressed like no crack pimp.'

A bright light flashed in the young man's eyes. 'You talk to me like that, you fuckin' nig . . .' The word died in a kind of gasp in his throat as Louis's body twisted, his left hand closing tightly on the man's neck and propelling him backwards, his right quickly slipping the gun from the Italian's belt holster and tossing it to the floor. The young man gurgled once as he hit the wall, spittle flying from his lips as the air was forced from his body. Then slowly, his feet began to lift from the floor; first his heels, then his toes, until the only thing holding him upright was Louis's unyielding left hand. His face turned pink, then deep red. Louis did not release his grip until a hint of blue began creeping into his lips and ears, then the fingers of his hand opened suddenly and the gunman sank to the ground, his hands fumbling at the collar of his shirt as he struggled to draw painful, choking breaths into his parched lungs.

During the whole incident, nobody else in the room had moved, because Al Z hadn't given any indication that they should. He looked at his struggling soldier the way he might have looked at a one-clawed crab dying on a beach, then returned his attention to Louis.

'You'll have to excuse him,' he said. 'Some of these boys, they learn their manners and their speech patterns in the gutter.' He turned his attention to the bulky man at the door, waving his cigarette at the figure on the floor, who now lay with his back against the wall, his eyes dazed and his mouth open. 'Take him to the bathroom, get him a glass of water. Then try to explain to him where he went wrong.'

The bulky guy helped the younger man to his feet, and accompanied him outside. The big man on the sofa didn't move. Al Z got to his feet and walked over to the window where he stood for a moment, watching the street below, before turning and resting against the windowsill. The three of us were now on the same level, and I recognised the gesture of good manners after what had taken place.

'Now, what can I do for you gentlemen?' he asked.

'A girl came to visit me a few days ago,' I began.

'Lucky you. The last time a girl came to visit me, it cost me five hundred dollars.' He smiled at his joke.

'This girl is the daughter of a friend of mine, an ex-cop.'

Al Z shrugged. 'Forgive me, but I don't understand how this concerns me.'

'I had an encounter with Tony Clean after the girl's visit. It kind of hurt, but I don't think Tony got much more satisfaction out of it than I did.'

Al Z took a long drag on his cigarette, then exhaled the smoke in a noisy sigh through his nose. 'Go on,' he said, wearily.

'I want to know if Tony took the girl, as leverage maybe. If he has her, he should hand her back. He doesn't need cop trouble. Not on top of everything else,' I added.

Al Z rubbed the corners of his eyes and nodded without speaking. He looked to the fat man on the sofa. The fat man's head moved slightly, the eyes impossible to see behind his shades.

'Let me get this straight,' said Al Z at last. 'You want me to ask Tony Clean if he has kidnapped an ex-cop's daughter and, if he has, you want me to tell him to hand her back?'

'If you don't,' said Louis quietly, 'we have to make him do it ourselves.'

'You know where he is?' replied Al Z. I was aware of the air in the room quickly becoming charged.

'No,' I said. 'If we knew that, maybe we wouldn't be here. We figured you might.' But something in the way Al Z had asked that last question told me that he didn't know, that Tony Clean was operating in some place beyond Al Z's control, and I guessed that Al Z was weighing up his position even before we arrived. That was the purpose of the fat man on the sofa. That was why he had not been asked to leave, because he wasn't the kind of man anyone asked to leave a room. He was the kind who did the asking. Things were coming apart for Tony Clean, a fact that Al Z seemed to confirm with his next words.

'Under the circumstances, it would be unwise for you to involve yourselves in this matter,' he said softly.

'Under what circumstances?' I replied.

He puffed out some smoke. 'Private business matters, the kind you should leave private. If you don't back off, we might have to push you.'

'We might push back.'

'You can't push back if you're dead.'

I shrugged. 'Getting us there might be the difficult part.'

It was handbags at ten paces, but the underlying threat in Al Z's voice was coming through loud and clear. I watched as he stubbed out his butt in a cut-glass ashtray with more force than was strictly necessary.

'So you're not going to keep out of our affairs?' he asked.

'I'm not interested in your affairs. I have other concerns.'

'The girl? Or Billy Purdue?'

He surprised me for a moment, but not for long. If there was a pulse, then Al Z had his finger on it and he would only remove his finger when the pulse stopped.

'Because if it's Billy Purdue,' he continued, 'then we may have the seeds of a difficulty.'

'The missing girl is a friend, but Rita Ferris, Billy's ex-wife, was my client.'

'Your client's dead.'

'It goes beyond that.'

Al Z pinched his lips. To his right, the fat man on the sofa remained as impassive as a buddha.

'So you're a man of principle,' said Al Z. He tackled the word 'principle' like it was a peanut shell he was crushing beneath his heel. 'Well, I'm a man of principle too.'

I didn't think so. Principles are expensive things to maintain and Al Z didn't look like he had the moral resources to support any. In fact, Al Z didn't look like he could work up the moral resources to piss on a burning orphanage.

'I don't think your principles and mine would qualify for the same definition,' I said at last.

He smiled. 'Maybe not.' He turned to Louis. 'And where do you stand on all this?'

'Beside him,' said Louis, inclining his head gently in my direction.

'Then we have to reach an accommodation,' Al Z concluded. 'I'm a pragmatist. You step lightly in this matter, and I won't kill you unless I have to.'

'Likewise,' I said. 'Seeing as how you've been so hospitable and all.' Then we left.

Outside, it was cold and overcast.

'What do you think?' asked Louis.

'I think Tony's out there on his own, and maybe he hopes he can sort this mess out before Al Z loses his patience. You think he has Ellen?'

Louis didn't reply immediately. When he did, his eyes were hard. 'He does or he doesn't, somehow it all ties in with Billy Purdue. Means it's gonna end bad for some-one.'

We walked around to Boylston and hailed a cab. As it pulled up, Louis slid in and said 'Logan', but I raised a hand.

'Can we take a detour?'

Louis shrugged. The cab driver shrugged too. It was like bad mime.

'Harvard,' I said. I looked at Louis. 'You don't have to come. I can meet you at the airport.'

Louis's eyebrow rose half an inch. 'Nah, I'll tag along, 'less you think I'm going to cramp your style.'

The cab dropped us off at the monolithic William James Hall, close by Quincy and Kirkland. I left Louis in the lobby and took the elevator to Room 232, where the psychology department had its office. My stomach felt tight, and there was sweat on my palms. At the office, a polite secretary told me where Rachel Wolfe's office was located, but she also told me that Rachel wouldn't be in that day. She was at a seminar out of town, and wouldn't be back until the following morning.

'Can I take a message?' she asked.

I considered turning round and walking away, but I didn't. Instead, I reached into my wallet and took out one of my cards. On the back, I wrote the new telephone number for the Scarborough house and handed the card to the secretary. 'Just give her this, please.'

She smiled. I thanked her, and I left.

Louis and I walked back to Harvard Square to catch a cab. He didn't speak until we were on our way to Logan.

'You do that before?' he asked, with just the faintest hint of a smile.

'Once. I never got that far, though.'

'So, you, like, stalking her, right?'

'It's not stalking if you know the person well.'

'*Oh.*' He nodded deeply. 'Thanks for clearing that one up. Never really understood the distinction before.'

He paused before he spoke again. 'And what you trying to do?'

'I'm trying to say I'm sorry.'

'You want to get back with her?'

I tapped my fingers on the window. 'I don't want it to be the way it is between us, that's all. Frankly, I don't know *what* I'm doing and, like I told your significant other, I'm not even sure that I'm ready yet.'

'But you love her?'

'Yes.'

'Then life will decide when you're ready.' He didn't speak again.

# Chapter Seventeen

Angel met us at the airport, and we drove to the food court at the Maine Mall to eat before we headed north.

'Shit,' said Angel, as we drove down Maine Mall Road. 'Look at this place. You got your Burger King, your International House of Pancakes, your Dunkin' Donuts, your pizza parlours. You got your four main food groups right here on your doorstep. Live here too long and they'll be rolling you from one place to the next.'

We ate Chinese in the food court of the mall and told Angel about our encounter with Al Z. In return, he produced a crumpled letter addressed to Billy Purdue, care of Ronald Straydeer.

'Cops and the feds did a pretty good job, but they didn't deal with your buddy Ronald the right way,' he said.

'You talked to him about his dog?' I asked.

'Talked about his dog, then ate some stew.' He looked a little queasy.

'Roadkill?' I knew that Ronald wasn't above scavenging, despite the state's laws on taking roadkill. Myself, I couldn't see the harm in using a deer or squirrel for food instead of letting it rot by the side of the road. Ronald did a pretty mean venison steak, served with beets and carrots preserved by burying them in sand.

'He told me it was squirrel,' said Angel, 'but it smelt like skunk. It didn't seem polite to ask. Seems this letter came for Billy about a week back, but Ronald hadn't seen him to give it to him.'

The letter was postmarked Greenville. It was short, little more than an extension of good wishes, some details of renovations to the house and some stuff about an old dog that the writer still had around the place and with which Billy Purdue seemed to have been familiar when it was a pup. It was signed, in his old man's scrawl: 'Meade Payne.'

'So they stayed in touch all these years,' I remarked. It seemed to confirm what I had thought: if Billy Purdue was going to seek help from anyone, it would be Meade Payne.

We drove nonstop to Dark Hollow, Angel and Louis shooting ahead in the Mercury. The mists gathered as I went farther north, so that journeying from Portland to Dark Hollow was like moving into a strange, spectral world, where house lights glowed dimly and the beams of headlights assumed their own, lance-like solidity, where road signs announced towns that existed only as scattered dwellings without any hub or centre. There was more snow forecast, I knew, and soon the snowmobilers would arrive in numbers to hurtle along the Interstate Trail system. But, for now, Greenville was still quiet as I drove through, sand mixed with snow by the side of the road, and I passed only two cars on the uneven, pitted surface of Lily Bay Road on the way to Dark Hollow.

When I arrived at the motel, Angel and Louis were

already checking in. The same woman with the blue-rinse hair who had greeted me earlier in the week stood behind the desk, examining their details on a single registration card. Beside her, a brown cat slept on the counter, curled in on itself with its nose almost touching its tail. Angel was doing the talking while Louis examined a series of battered tourist booklets in a rack. He glanced at me when I came in, but didn't acknowledge my presence further.

'You gentlemen sharing a room?' asked the blue-rinse woman. 'Yes ma'am,' replied Angel, with a look of homely wisdom on his face. 'A dollar spared is a dollar made.'

The woman glanced at Louis, resplendent in a black suit, black coat and white shirt. 'Your friend a preacher?' she said.

'Kind of, ma'am,' said Angel. 'He's strictly Old Testament, though. An eye for an eye, and stuff like that.'

'That's nice. We don't get many religious folks staying here.'

Louis's face had the long-suffering look of a saint who has just heard that the rack is to be tightened.

'If you're interested,' the woman continued, 'we got a Baptist service tonight. You're welcome to join us.'

'Thank you, ma'am,' said Angel, 'but we prefer to engage in our own forms of worship.'

She smiled understandingly. 'Long as it's quiet and doesn't disturb the other guests.'

'We'll do our best,' intervened Louis, taking the key.

The woman recognised me as I approached the desk. 'Back again? You must like it here in Dark Hollow.'

'I hope to get to know it better,' I replied. 'Maybe you can help me with something.'

She smiled. 'Sure, if I can.'

I handed her a photo of Ellen Cole, the small, ID kind taken in a photo booth. I'd had it blown up on a colour copier so that the picture was now eight-by-ten size. 'You recognise this girl?'

The woman looked at the picture, squinting her eyes behind the thick lenses of her spectacles. 'Yes, I do. She in some kind of trouble?'

'I hope not, but she's missing and her parents have asked me to help find her.'

The woman turned her attention back to the picture, nodding as she did so. 'Yes, I recall her. Chief Jennings was asking about her. She stayed here with a young man for one night. I can get you the date, if you like.'

'Would you, please?'

She took a registration card from a green metal card box and examined the details. 'December fifth,' she said. 'Paid by credit card made out in the name of Ellen C. Cole.'

'Do you recall anything that happened, anything out of the ordinary?'

'No, nothing important. Someone had suggested to them that they visit here, someone they gave a ride to from Portland. That's about all. She was nice, I remember. He was kind of a surly kid, but they can be that way at that age. I should know: raised four of my own and they were meaner than wharf rats until they were twenty-five.'

'Did they give any indication of where they might be heading after they left here?'

'North, I guess. Maybe up to Katahdin. I don't know, for sure, but I told them that, if they had some time to spare, they should drive out and watch the sun set on the lake. They seemed to like the idea. It's a pretty sight. Romantic, too, for a young couple like that. I let them check out late in the afternoon, just so they wouldn't have to be rushing to pack.'

'And they didn't say who recommended that they see Dark Hollow?' It seemed an odd thing to suggest. Dark Hollow didn't have too much going for it.

'Sure they did. It was some old guy they met along the way. They gave him a ride up here, and I think maybe he met up with them before they left.'

I felt my stomach turn a little. 'Did they mention his name?'

'No. Didn't sound like anybody from around here, though,' she said. Her brow furrowed a little. 'They didn't seem concerned about him or nothing. I mean, what harm could an old man do?' I think she meant the question to be rhetorical when she started out, but by the end I don't think it sounded that way to either of us.

She apologised, told me she didn't know any more, then gave me directions to the lake, about a mile or two outside the town, on a tourist map. I thanked her, left my bag in my room and knocked on the door of the room next door, now occupied by Angel and Louis. Angel opened the door and let me in. Louis was hanging up his suits in the battered brown closet. I put the old man to the back of my mind. I wasn't about to leap to conclusions, not yet.

'What do people do for fun around here?' asked Angel, sitting down heavily on one of the two double beds in the room. 'This place sees less action than the pope.'

'Wrap up warm for the winter,' I said. 'Wait for the summer.'

'And what happens when the summer comes?'

'Sometimes it doesn't.'

'So how can they tell the difference?'

'The rain turns to snow in winter.'

'Fulfilling existence, if you're a tree.'

Louis finished arranging his clothes and turned to us. 'Find out anything?'

'The manager remembers Ellen and her boyfriend. She told them to go watch the sun set out of town, then reckons they went north.'

'Maybe they did go north,' said Louis.

'Rangers up in Baxter State Park have no record of them, according to Lee Cole. Apart from that, the options up north are limited. Plus, the woman at the desk says they gave some old guy a ride up here, and it was this old man who suggested that they stay in Dark Hollow.'

'Is that a bad thing?'

'I don't know. Depends on who he was. It could be nothing.' But I thought of the old man who had tried to take Rita Ferris at the hotel, and the figure of the old man Billy Purdue claimed to have seen shortly before his family was taken from him. And I thought too of something Ronald Straydeer had said when he misheard my comment as we stood before Billy Purdue's trailer, discussing a man he might or might not have seen on his property.

'*You're getting old.*'

'*Yuh, he could have been old.*'

'So what now?'

I shrugged glumly. 'I'm going to have to talk to Rand Jennings.'

'You want us to come along?'

'No, I have other plans for you two. Take a ride out to the Payne place, see what's going on.'

'See if Billy Purdue's turned up, you mean,' said Angel.

'Whatever.'

'And if he has?'

'Then we go and get him.'

'And if he hasn't?'

'We wait, until I'm certain that Ellen Cole isn't in some kind of trouble here. Then . . .' I shrugged.

'We wait some more,' finished Angel.

'I guess,' I replied.

'That's good to know,' he said. 'At least I can plan what to wear.'

The Dark Hollow Police Department lay about half a mile beyond the northern end of the town. It was a single-storey brick building with its own generator in a concrete bunker at its eastern side. The building itself was quite new, a consequence of a fire a couple of years back, which had destroyed the original structure just off the main street.

Inside it was warm and brightly lit, and a sergeant in shirt sleeves stood behind a wooden desk filling in some forms. His shiny name badge said 'Ressler', so I figured he was the same Ressler who had watched Emily Watts die. I introduced myself and asked to see the chief.

'Can I ask what it's in connection with, sir?'

'Ellen Cole,' I replied.

His brow furrowed a little as he picked up the phone and dialled an extension number. 'There's a guy here wants to talk to you about Ellen Cole, chief,' he said, then put his hand over the receiver and turned back to me. 'What did you say your name was again?'

I gave it to him again and he repeated it into the phone. 'That's right, chief. Parker. Charlie Parker.' He listened for a moment, then looked at me closely, sizing me up. 'Yeah, that sounds about right. Sure, sure.' He put the phone down then reappraised me without saying anything.

'So, does he remember me?' I asked.

Ressler didn't reply, but I got the feeling that the sergeant knew his chief well and had detected something in his voice that put him on his guard. 'Follow me,' he said, unlocking a dividing door to one side of the desk and holding it to one side to let me pass. I waited while he relocked it, then followed him between a pair of desks and into a small, glass-walled cubicle. Behind a metal desk, on which lay trays of papers and a computer, sat Randall Jennings.

He hadn't changed too much. True, he was greyer and had put on a little weight, his face now slightly puffy and the beginnings of a double chin hanging down below his jawline, but he was still a good-looking man, with sharp brown eyes and wide, strong shoulders. It must have hurt his ego, I thought, when his wife had commenced an affair with me.

He waited for Ressler to leave and close the door of the office before he spoke. He didn't ask me to sit down and didn't seem troubled by the fact that, standing, I could look down on him.

'I never thought I'd see your face again,' he said at last.

'I guessed by the way you said goodbye. I'm surprised you didn't ask your sergeant to stay in here and guard the door.'

He didn't respond, just rearranged some papers on his desk. I wasn't sure if the gesture was meant to distract him, or me. 'You're here about Ellen Cole?'

'That's right.'

'We don't know anything about it. She came, she left.' He raised his hands in a gesture of helplessness.

'That's not what her mother thinks.'

'I don't care what her mother thinks. What I'm telling you is what we know, same thing I told her father when he was up here.'

It struck me that I must just have missed Walter Cole, that we might even have been in town at the same time. I felt a twinge of sorrow that he had been forced to come up here alone, fearing for his daughter's safety. I would have helped him, had I known.

'The family's filed a missing person report.'

'I'm aware of that. I had a federal agent chewing my ear over a non-existent NCIC filing.' He looked hard at me. 'I told him it was a long way from New York to Dark Hollow. We do things our own way up here.'

I didn't respond to his bout of territorial spraying. 'Are you going to act on the report?' I persisted.

Jennings stood up, the knuckles of his large hands resting on his desk. I had almost forgotten what a big man he was. There was a gun in a holster at his belt, a Coonan .357 Magnum out of St. Paul, Minnesota. It looked shiny and new. I guessed that Rand Jennings didn't have much cause to use it way up here, unless he sat on his porch and took potshots at rabbits.

'Am I having trouble making myself understood?' he said softly, but with a hint of suppressed anger. 'We've done what we can. We have responded to the missing person report. Our view is that the girl and her boyfriend may have run away together and, so far, we have no reason to suspect otherwise.'

'The manager of the motel said they were heading north.'

'Maybe they were.'

'All that's north is Baxter and Katahdin. They never made it there.'

'Then they went someplace else.'

'There may have been someone else with them.'

'Maybe there was. All I know is that they left town.'

'I can see now why you never made detective.'

He flinched, and his face flushed red. 'You don't know the first damn thing about me,' he said. The anger was distinct now as he pronounced his next words slowly and with deliberate emphasis. 'Now, if you'll excuse me, we have some real crimes to deal with.'

'Really. Somone stealing Christmas trees? Maybe trying to screw a moose?'

He walked around the side of the desk and came close to me as he passed by to open the door of his office. I think he half expected me to take a step back from him, but I didn't.

'I hope you're not planning on looking for trouble here,' he said. He could have been talking about Ellen Cole, but his eyes said he was talking about someone else.

'I don't have to look for trouble,' I replied. 'I stay still long enough, trouble finds me.'

'That's because you're dumb,' he said, still holding the door open. 'You don't pay attention to the lessons life teaches you.'

'You'd be surprised how much I've learned.'

I prepared to leave his office, but his left hand shot out to block me. 'Remember one thing, Parker: this is my town and you're a guest. Don't abuse the privilege.'

'So it's not a case of "what's mine is yours"?'

'No,' he said, with menace. 'No, it isn't.'

★  ★  ★

I left the building and walked to my car, the wind now howling through the trees and biting at my bare fingers. Above me, the sky was dark. As I reached the Mustang, an old green Datsun Sunny pulled into the lot and Lorna Jennings stepped from the car. She was wearing a black leather jacket with a big fur collar and blue jeans tucked into the same boots she had been wearing the last time we met. She didn't see me until she had begun to walk towards the main entrance. When she did spot me, she stopped short for a moment before coming over, casting an anxious glance at the illuminated doorway as she did so.

'What are you doing here?' she asked.

'Talking to your husband. He wasn't very helpful.'

She raised an eyebrow at me. 'Are you surprised?'

'No, not really, but it's not about me. A girl and a young man are missing and I think somebody here may know what happened to them. Until I find out who that might be, I'm going to be around for a while.'

'Who are they?'

'The daughter of a friend, and the girl's boyfriend. Her name is Ellen Cole. You ever hear Rand mention her?'

She nodded. 'He said he'd done what he could. He thinks they may have eloped.'

'Young love,' I said. 'It's a beautiful thing.'

Lorna swallowed and ran a hand through her hair. 'He hates you, Bird, for what you did. For what we did.'

'That was a long time ago.'

'Not for him,' she said. 'Or me.'

I was sorry I'd mentioned young love. I didn't like the look in her eyes. It made me nervous. But I surprised myself by asking the next question.

'Why are you still with him, Lorna?'

'Because he's my husband. Because I have nowhere else to go.'

'That's not true, Lorna. There's always somewhere else.'

'Is that an offer?'

'Nope, it's just an observation. You take care.' I began to walk away, but she reached out and stopped me by placing her hand on my arm.

'No, you be careful, Bird,' she said. 'Like I said, he hasn't forgiven you, and he won't.'

'Has he forgiven you?' I asked.

There was something in her face as she spoke, something that reminded me of that first afternoon we spent together and the warmth of her skin against mine. 'I didn't want his forgiveness,' she said. Then she smiled sadly and left me.

I spent the next hour wandering around the stores in Dark Hollow, showing Ellen Cole's photograph to anyone who'd take the time to look. They recalled her at the diner, and in the drugstore, but nobody had seen Ellen and Ricky leave and no one could confirm whether or not they were with another man, or speculate as to who that person might have been. It grew colder and colder as I walked, my coat wrapped tightly around me, the lights of the stores casting a yellow glow on the snow.

When I had exhausted every avenue of inquiry, at least for the present, I went back to my room, showered, and changed into a pair of denims and a shirt and sweater before pulling on my overcoat and preparing to meet Angel and Louis for dinner. Angel was already outside the room, drinking coffee and blowing puffs of white breath into the air like an unhealthy steam engine.

'You know, it's warmer out here than it is in that room,' he said. 'I lost a layer of skin from my feet, the tiles in the bathroom are so cold.'

'You're too sensitive. It must be a gay thing.'

'Yeah, and I play the violin and write great works of literature while I'm on the can. You know, it's stereotyping like that that's stopped gays from . . .'

'From what? What exactly have you not done that you really, desperately want to do?'

'Go back to New York?'

'And being gay is stopping you from doing that?'

'No, I guess not. You're stopping me from doing that.'

'See? So being gay has nothing to do with it. You could be straight and you'd still be stuck up here.'

Angel snorted unhappily and stamped his feet while alternating the coffee cup from hand to hand, each time putting his free hand under the opposite armpit.

'Stop,' I said. 'You're going to make it rain. Any sign of activity out at Meade Payne's place?'

He came to a relative standstill. 'None that we could see without knocking on the door and asking for cookies and a glass of milk. Caught a sight of the young guy and Payne eating supper, but they were alone, far as we could see. You have any luck with Jennings?'

'No.'

'You surprised?'

'Yes and no. He's got no reason to help me, but this isn't about me. It's about Ellen and her boyfriend, but I could see in his eyes that he would use them to get at me, if he could. I don't understand him. He's suffered. I know he has. His wife took up with another man behind his back, a man a good ten years younger than him, but he's still with her, and it's hell for both of them. It wasn't as if

Rand was old, or cruel, or impotent. He had what it took; or, maybe, he had it according to his own definition of it. I took something away from him, and he won't ever forgive me for it. But how can he not feel for Ellen Cole, for Ricky, for their families? No matter how much he hates me, they have to matter.' I kicked idly at the dirt on the ground. 'Sorry, Angel. I'm thinking out loud.'

Angel tossed the remains of his coffee into a mound of frozen, compacted snow. I could hear the soft hiss as it landed, as the coffee corrupted the whiteness of its crystals one by one.

'Suffering isn't enough, Bird,' said Angel softly. 'So he's suffered: big fuckin' deal. Get in line with the rest of us suckers. It's not enough to suffer, and you know that. What matters is that you understand that others suffer, and some of them suffer worse than you could ever do. And if you can do something about that, then you do it, and you do it without whining or waving your own fuckin' cross for the world to see. You do it because it's the right thing to do.

'From what you say, this Rand Jennings doesn't have a compassionate bone in his body. All he feels is self-pity, and he doesn't understand any suffering but his own. I mean, look at his marriage. There are two of them in it, Bird; whatever you may have felt for her, she's stayed with him this long and if you hadn't turned up like a fire in February then everything would be just the way it was. He'd be unhappy and she'd be unhappy and they'd be unhappy together, and it seems like they've set their own boundaries on what is and is not going to happen to change that situation.

'But he's selfish, Bird. He only thinks of his own hurt, his own pain, and he blames her for it, and you, and, by

extension, the world. He doesn't care about Ellen Cole, or
Walter, or Lee. He's all full up pissing and cursing at the
bum hand he thinks life has dealt him, and that hand ain't
never gonna change.'

I looked at him, at his unshaven profile, the wisps of
dark hair curling out from under his dark wool hat, the
empty coffee cup forgotten in his hand. He was a mass of
contradictions. It struck me that I was taking life lessons
from a five-six semi-retired burglar whose boyfriend, not
twenty-four hours earlier, had executed a man against a
brick wall. My life, I reflected, was taking some strange
turns.

Angel seemed to sense what I was thinking, because he
turned to me before he spoke again. 'We've been friends
for a long time, you and me, maybe even without either
of us realising it. I know you and, for a time, you weren't
far off becoming like Jennings and a million others like
him, but I know now that's not going to happen. I'm not
sure how things changed and I don't think I want to
know most of it. All I know is that you're becoming a
compassionate man, Bird. That's not the same as pity, or
guilt, or trying to pay off some debt to fortune or to God.
It's feeling other people's pain as your own, and acting to
take that pain away. And maybe, sometimes, you have to
do bad things to do that, but life doesn't balance easy.
You can be a good man and perform bad actions, because
that's the nature of things. People who believe otherwise,
well, they're just timeservers, because they spend so much
time wrestling with their consciences that nothing gets
done, and nothing changes, and the innocent and the
defenceless, they just keep getting hurt. In the end you do
what you can, maybe what you have to do, to make
things better. Your heart isn't going to be weighed

against a feather in the next life, Bird. My guess is they do a comparative study, otherwise we'll all end up in hell.'

He smiled at me, a small, wintry smile that said he knew the cost of following that philosophy. He knew, because he was following it himself: sometimes with me, sometimes with Louis, but always, always according to what he believed was right. I wasn't sure that what he said could be applied to me. I made moral judgments in what I did, but I didn't believe that I was always entitled to do so and I knew that I had not yet managed to purge myself of the guilt and grief I felt. I acted to ease my own pain and, in doing so, I sometimes managed to ease the pain of others. That was as close to compassion as I thought I could get, for the present.

From the far end of town came the sound of sirens, gradually drawing nearer. Red and blue lights flashed across the buildings on the main street as a cruiser tore around the corner and headed in our direction at high speed. It screeched a hard left at the intersection and drove by. In the front seat of the car I could see the figure of Randall Jennings.

'Must be a doughnut sale on,' remarked Angel.

A second unmarked car came down the main street, spun on its rear tyres as it made the turn, then headed after the first vehicle.

'With free coffee,' he added.

I tossed my keys in my hand, then nudged Angel off the hood of the Mustang, where he had just taken up a position. 'I'm going to take a look. You want to come along?'

'Nah. I'm a-waitin' for Black Narcissus to finish making himself lovely for us. We'll hang on for you, burn some furniture to keep warm.'

I followed the lights of the lead cars as they glanced against the trees, the branches like hands outstretched over the road. After a mile I caught up with them as they headed up into the forest through a private logging company road, the wooden barrier thrown to one side to enable the cars to pass. Beside the barrier stood a man wearing a wool hat and a parka. A path wound down behind him to a small house on the edge of the company land. I figured that maybe it was he who had made the call to the police.

I stayed close behind the rear car, watching its taillights as it swerved and dipped along the narrow, rutted track. Eventually the cruiser came to a halt beside a Ford truck with a ski-doo in back, a huge bearded man with a belly like a pregnant woman's standing beside it. Jennings emerged from the lead car, Ressler stepping out of the car behind at the same time accompanied by another patrolman. Flashlights blinked into life and the line of three cops headed over to the back of the truck and peered inside. I took my own Maglite from the trunk and walked over to them. As I went, I heard the bearded man say:

'I didn't want to leave him out there. There's snow coming on, means he might have been lost till the thaw.'

Faces turned towards me as I approached, one of them that of Rand Jennings.

'The fuck are you doing here?' he said.

'Collecting berries. What you got?'

I shone my flashlight beam into the bed of the truck, although what was there didn't need the extra illumination. It needed darkness and dirt and a headstone six feet above it.

It was a man's body, laid out on a sheet of tarpaulin, his

mouth wide open and filled with leaves. His eyes were closed and his head was twisted at an unnatural angle. He lay, crumpled and broken, amid the tools and plastic containers in the truck, his hair touching the empty gun rack.

'Who is he?'

For a moment, I didn't think Jennings was going to answer. Then he sighed and said:

'It looks like Gary Chute. He was a surveyor for the timber company. Daryl here found him when he was out checking some traps. Came upon his truck back a ways as well, couple of miles from the body.'

Daryl looked like he was about to deny the traps part of the statement. His mouth opened briefly then closed again at a look from Jennings. Daryl looked kind of slow, I thought. His eyes were dull and his brow low, and his mouth, though closed, was in continual motion, as if he was worrying at the inside of his bottom lip with his teeth.

Beside him, Ressler was flicking through the dead man's wallet.

'It's Chute all right,' he said. 'No cash in the wallet, though. Credit cards are still here. You take it, Daryl?'

Daryl shook his head wildly from side to side. 'No, I didn't touch nothin'.'

'You sure?'

Daryl nodded his assent. 'Sure,' he said. 'I'm sure.' Ressler didn't look like he believed him, but he didn't say anything more.

I turned to Daryl. 'How did you find him?'

'Huh?'

'I mean, what position was he in?'

'Lying at the bottom of a ridge, near buried by the snow and the leaves,' replied Daryl. 'Looked like he just slipped, hit some stones and trees on the way down, then caught his neck on a root. Must have snapped like a twig.' Daryl smiled uneasily, unsure that he had said the right thing.

It didn't sound very likely, especially with the money missing from his wallet. 'You say there was snow *and* leaves on him, Daryl?'

'Yessir,' said Daryl eagerly. 'Branches too.'

I nodded, and shone my flashlight on the body once again. Something caught my attention at his wrists and I let the light linger for a moment before flicking it off. 'It's a shame he was moved,' I said.

Even Jennings had to agree. 'Shit, Daryl, you should have left him as he was, then let the wardens go and get him.'

'I couldn't leave him out there,' said Daryl. 'It weren't right.'

'Maybe Daryl's right. If it snows, and it will, we could have lost him until the spring,' said Ressler. 'Daryl says he found the body at Island Pond, wrapped it in the tarp and hauled it back ten miles to his truck with his ski-doo. Island Pond's quite a ways from here and, according to Daryl, the road already turns into one big snowdrift way before you reach the pond.'

I glanced at Daryl with respect; there weren't many men who'd haul the body of a stranger for miles. 'No way anyone can head out there in the dark, assuming we could even find the place,' concluded Jennings. 'Anyway, this is a matter for the wardens, maybe the sheriff's department, but not us. We'll arrange to have him taken to Augusta in the morning, let the ME take a look at him.'

I looked up, beyond the trees and into the black night sky. There was a sense of heaviness, as of a weight above us about to fall. Ressler followed my gaze.

'Like I said, Daryl was right. Snow's coming.'

Jennings gave Ressler a look that said he didn't want any more details of the discovery spoken of in front of Daryl and, especially, me. He slapped his hands together sharply. 'OK, let's go.' He leaned into the bed of the truck and covered Gary Chute's body with the tarp, using pieces of scrap metal, a wheel iron and the butt of a shotgun to hold it in place. He crooked a finger at the patrolman.

'Stevie, you ride in the bed here, make sure that tarp doesn't come off.' Stevie, who looked about eleven, shook his head unhappily then climbed carefully into the truck, squatting down beside the body. Ressler went back to his car, leaving only Jennings and me.

'I'm sure we all appreciate your assistance, Parker.'

'Funny, but I don't think you mean that.'

'You're right, I don't. Stay out of my way, and out of my business. I don't want to have to tell you that again.' He tapped me once on the chest with a gloved finger, then turned and walked away. The cars started almost in unison and formed a convoy with the truck – one ahead, one behind – as Gary Chute was brought back to Dark Hollow.

Leaves and branches, as well as snow, had covered Chute's body, according to Daryl. If his death was accidental, and Daryl had taken the money from his wallet, then that didn't make too much sense. The trees were bare, and it had been snowing pretty regularly over the last week or so. Snow would have covered the body, but not leaves and branches. Their presence indicated that someone could have been trying to hide Gary Chute's body.

I walked back to my car and thought of what I had seen in the flashlight's glow: red marks on the dead man's wrists. Those marks weren't made by a fall, or by animals, or frost.

They were rope burns.

When I got back to the motel, Angel and Louis were gone. There was a note under my door, written in Angel's strangely neat hand, telling me that they had gone to the diner and would see me there. I didn't follow them. Instead, I went down to the motel reception desk, filled two foam containers with coffee and returned to my room.

Chute's death continued to bother me. It was unfortunate that it had been Daryl who found the body, even if he had acted with the best of intentions. Chute's truck could probably have served as a rough marker for the crime scene but now its integrity had been fatally compromised by Daryl's removal of the body.

Maybe it was nothing, but on a map I marked roughly where Gary Chute's body had been found at Island Pond. Island Pond was to the north-east of Dark Hollow. The only way to reach that area was along a private road, which required a permit for use. If someone had killed Gary Chute, they'd have to have taken that road to get to him, following him into the wilderness. The other possibility was that whoever killed him was in the wilderness already, waiting for him. Or . . .

Or maybe Chute was unlucky enough to see someone, or something, that he shouldn't have. Maybe whoever killed him didn't go into the wilderness after him, but was coming back out again. And, if that was the case, then the first place that person would arrive at was Dark Hollow.

But this was all speculation. I needed to get my thoughts in order. On a page of my notebook, I noted all that had happened since the night that Billy Purdue had stuck his knife in my cheek. Where there were links, I formed dotted lines between the names. Most of them came back to Billy Purdue, except Ellen Cole's disappearance and the death of Gary Chute.

And in the centre of the list was a white space, empty and clean as new-fallen snow. The other names and incidents circled around it, like planets around a sun. I felt the old instinct, the desire to impose some pattern on incidents that I did not yet fully understand, some form of explanation that might begin to lead me to an ultimate truth. When I was a detective in New York, dealing with the deaths of those whom I had not known, with whom I had no direct connection, to whom I had no duty beyond that of the policeman whose task it is to find out what happened and to ensure that someone answers for the crime, I would follow the threads of the investigation as I had laid them out and when they led nowhere, or proved simply to be false assumptions, I would shrug and return to the core to follow another thread. I was prepared to make mistakes in the hope that I would eventually find something that was not an error.

That luxury, the luxury of detachment, was taken away from me when Susan and Jennifer died. Now they all mattered, all of the lost, all of the gone, but Ellen Cole mattered more than most. If she was in trouble, then there was no room for error, no time to make mistakes in the hope that they would lead to some final reckoning.

Neither could I forget Rita Ferris and her son, and at the thought of her I looked instinctively over my shoulder and towards the dark rectangle of the window, and I recalled a weight on my shoulder, cold but not unyielding, the touch of a familiar hand.

There was too much happening, too many deaths revolving around the white space at the centre of the page. And in that space, I put a question mark, dotted it carefully, then extended the dots down to the bottom of the page.

And there I wrote the name 'Caleb Kyle'.

I should have gone out to eat then. I should have found Angel and Louis and gone to a bar where I could have watched them drink and flirt oddly with each other. I might even have had a drink, just one drink . . . Women would have gone by, swaying gently as the alcohol took hold of their bodies and minds. Perhaps one of them might have smiled at me, and I might have smiled back and felt the spark that ignites when a beautiful woman focuses her attention on a man. I could have had another drink, then another, and soon I would have forgotten everything and descended into oblivion forever.

The anniversary was approaching. I was aware of it as a dark cloud on the horizon, moving inexorably to engulf me in memories of loss and pain. I wanted normality, yet it continued to hang beyond my reach. I wasn't even sure why I had gone to Rachel's office, except that I knew that I wanted to be with her even though my feelings for her made me feel sick and guilty, as if I were somehow betraying Susan's memory. With these thoughts, after all that had happened over the past few days, and after allowing my mind to explore the nature of the killings that had occurred in both the recent and distant pasts, I should not have remained alone.

Tired and so hungry that my appetite had faded entirely away to be replaced by a deeper, gnawing unease, I undressed and climbed into my bed, pulling the sheets over my head and wondering how long it would take me to fall asleep. Just long enough, it emerged, to get that thought out.

I awoke to a noise, and a faint, unpleasant odour that took me a few moments to identify. It was the smell of rotting vegetation, of leaves and mulch and standing water. I rose from my pillow and wiped the sleep from my eyes, my nose wrinkling as the smell of decay grew stronger. There was a clock-radio on the nightstand – the time read 12.33 a.m. – and I checked it in case the alarm might somehow have switched itself on during the night, but the radio was silent. I looked around the room, conscious now of a strangeness to the light, a tinge of unfamiliar colour that should not have been present.

There was singing coming from my bathroom.

It was low but sweet, the sound of two voices combining to sing the same song, a song that sounded like a nursery rhyme, the words muffled by the closed bathroom door.

And from beneath the door, a green light seeped, its form rippling across the cheap carpet. I pushed back the covers and stood naked on the floor, but felt no cold, no chill, and began to walk towards the bathroom. As I did so, the smell grew stronger. I could feel it adhering to my skin and hair, as if I was bathing in its source. The singing rose in volume, the words now clear, the same three syllables repeated over and over again in high, girlish tones.

*Caleb Kyle, Caleb Kyle*

I was almost at the point where the tendrils of light from beneath the door reached their farthest extension. From behind the door came the sound of water softly lapping.

*Caleb Kyle, Caleb Kyle*

I stood for a second at the periphery of the green light, then placed one bare foot in its pool.

The singing stopped as soon as my foot touched the floor, but the light remained, moving slowly, viscously, across my bare toes. I reached forward and carefully turned the handle of the door. I pulled it open and stepped onto the tiles.

The room was empty. There were only the white surfaces, the neat pile of towels above the toilet, the sink with its low-grade soaps still wrapped, the glasses with their paper covers, the flower-speckled curtain on the bath pulled almost completely across . . .

The light came from the behind the curtain, a sickly, green glow that shone with only a vestige of the power of its original source, as if it had fought its way through layers and layers of obstacles to offer what little illumination it could. And in the quiet of the room, broken only by the soft lapping of water from behind the curtain, it seemed as if something held its breath. I heard a soft giggle, smothered by a hand, the laugh echoed by another, and the water behind the curtain lapped more loudly.

I reached out a hand, gripped the plastic and began to pull it quickly across. There was some resistance, but I continued to open the curtain until the interior of the bath was completely exposed.

The water was full of leaves, so many that they reached up to the faucets. They were green and red, brown and yellow, black and gold. There was aspen and birch, cedar and cherry, maple and basswood, beech and fir, their shapes twisted and overlapping, the ferocity of their decay polluting the water and creating a stench that was almost visible as it rose.

A shape moved beneath the leaves, and bubbles broke upwards. The vegetation separated and something white began to rise to the surface, a long, slow ascent as if the water was far deeper than it could possibly be. As it neared, it seemed to separate into two figures, their hands held as they rose, their long hair spreading and flowing as they came, their mouths open, their eyes blind.

I let the curtain fall and tried to move, but the tiles betrayed me, just as they had betrayed me on the day that I first found the little girls. And as I fell, their shades moved behind the curtain and I backed away on my hands and heels, my fingers and toes scrabbling for purchase until I awoke once again, the sheets in a pile at the end of the bed, the mattress exposed and a bloody hole in its fabric where I had torn through it with my nails.

A hammering came at the door.

'Bird! Bird!' It was Louis's voice.

I crawled from my bed and realised I was shivering uncontrollably. I struggled with the chain on the door, my fingers fumbling at the catch, and then, at last, it was open and Louis was standing there before me in a pair of grey sweatpants and a white T-shirt, his gun in his hand.

'Bird?' he repeated. There was concern in his eyes, and a kind of love. 'What's the matter?'

Something bubbled in my throat, and I tasted bile and coffee.

'I see them,' I said. 'I see them all.'

# Chapter Eighteen

I sat on the edge of my bed, my head in my hands, and waited while Louis went to the office and poured two cups of coffee from the eternally brewing pot. As he passed by his own room I heard him exchange words with Angel, although he was still alone when he closed the door behind him, shutting out the cold night air. He handed me the foam cup, and I thanked him before sipping from it silently. From outside came the soft tapping of snow falling on my window. He didn't talk for a time, and I felt him considering something in his mind.

'I ever tell you about my Grandma Lucy?' he said at last.

I looked at him in surprise. 'Louis, I don't even know your surname,' I replied.

He smiled dimly, as if it were all he could do to recollect what it might have been himself. 'Anyways,' he continued, and the smile faded, 'Lucy, she was my gran'momma, my mamma's momma, not much older than I am now. She was a beautiful woman: tall, skin like day fading into night. She wore her hair down, always. I never recall her wearing it no other way but down, it tumbling over her shoulders in dark curls. She lived with us until the day she died, and she died young. The pneumonia took her, and she faded away in shakes and sweats.

'There was a man who lived in the town, and his name was Errol Rich. Ever since I knew him, he just wasn't a man to turn the other cheek. When you were black, and you lived in that kind of town, that's the first thing you learned. You always, always, turned the other cheek, 'cause if you didn't, weren't no white sheriff, no white jury, no bunch of redneck assholes with ropes ready to tie you to the axle of a truck and drag you along dirt roads till your skin came off, weren't none of them going to see it no other way but a nigger gettin' above himself, and settin' a bad example to all the other niggers, maybe gettin' them all riled up so's that white folks with better things to do would have to go out some dark night and teach them all a lesson. Put some manners on them, maybe.

'But Errol, he didn't see things that way. He was a huge mother. He walked down the street and the sun wasn't big enough to shine around his shoulders. He fixed things – engines, mowers, anything that had a moving part and the hand of man could find a way to save. Lived in a big shack out on one of the old county roads, 'long with his momma and his sisters, and he looked them white boys in the eye, and he knew they was afraid.

'Except, this one time, he was driving by a bar out by Route 5 and he heard someone call out "Hey, Nigger!" and the cracked old windshield of his truck, it just exploded in. They threw a big old bottle through it, full of all the piss those assholes could work up between 'em. And Errol, he pulled over, and he sat there for a time, covered in blood and glass and piss, then he climbed out of the cab, took him a length of timber maybe three feet long from the bed of his truck, and he walked over to where them good ol' boys were sitting on the stoop. There was four of 'em, including the owner, a pig of a man called Little Tom Rudge, and he could see them freeze up as he came.

' "Who threw that?" says Errol. "You throw that, Little Tom? 'Cos if you did, you better tell me now, else I'm gonna burn your shit-heap down to the ground."

'But nobody answered. Them boys, they was just struck dumb. Even together in a bunch and all liquored up, they knew better than to mess with Errol. And Errol, he just looked at them for a time, then he spat on the ground and he took that length of timber and threw it through the window of the bar, and Little Tom, there wasn't nothing he could do. Least of all, not then.

'They came for him the next night, three truckloads of 'em. They took him in front of his momma and his sisters and brought him to a place called Ada's Field, where there was a chestnut tree that was maybe a century old. And when they got there, half the town was waitin' for 'em. There was women there, even some of the older children. Folks ate chicken and biscuits, and drank soda pop from glass bottles, and talked about the weather, and the coming harvest, and maybe the baseball season, like they was at the county fair and they was waitin' for the show to start. All told, there was more than a hundred people there, sittin' on the hoods of their cars, waitin'.

'And when Errol came, his legs and hands were tied and they hauled him up onto the roof of an old Lincoln that was parked under the tree. And they put a rope around his neck, and tightened it. Then someone came up and poured a can of gasoline over him, and Errol looked up, and he spoke the only words he said since they took him, and the only words he would ever say again on this earth.

' "Don't burn me", he said. He wasn't asking them to spare him, or not to hang him. He wasn't afraid of that. But he didn't want to burn. Then I guess maybe he looked up into their eyes and saw that what was to be would be, and he bowed his head and he started to pray.

'Well, they tightened the rope around his neck and they pulled it so that Errol was balancing on the tips of his toes on the roof of the car, and then the car started and Errol hung in the air, twisting and thrashing. And someone came forward with a burning torch in his hand and they burned Errol Rich as he hung, and those people, they listened to him scream until his lungs burned and he couldn't scream no more. And then he died.

'That was at ten after nine, on a July night, maybe three miles away from our house, right on the other side of town. And at ten after nine, my Grandma Lucy, she rose from her chair by the radio. I was sittin' at her feet. The others, they was in the kitchen or in bed asleep, but I was still with her. Grandma Lucy, she walked to the door and stepped out into the night, wearin' nothin' but her nightdress and a shawl, and she looked out into the woods. I followed her, and I said: "Miss Lucy, what's the matter?" but she didn't say nothin', just kept on walkin' until she was about ten feet away from the edge of the trees, and there she stopped.

'And out in the darkness, among the trees, there was a light. It didn't look like no more than a patch of moonlight but, when I tried to find it, there was no moon, and the rest of the woods was dark.

'I turned to Grandma Lucy and I looked at her eyes.'

Louis stopped, and his own eyes flickered closed briefly, like a man recalling a pain that has been forgotten for a long time. 'Her eyes were on fire. In her pupils, right in the blackness at the centre, I could see flames. I could see a man burning, like he was standing before us, sheltered by the trees. But when I looked into the darkness, there was only that patch of light, nothin' more.

'And Lucy, she said: "You poor boy, you poor, poor boy", and she started to cry. When she cried, it was like her grief put out the flames, because the burning man in her eyes started to fade until, in the end, he was gone, and the patch of light in the woods, that was gone too.

'She never spoke about what happened to nobody else, and she told me not to tell either. But I think my momma knew. Least, she knew that her momma had some kind of gift that nobody else had. She could find the dark places, the places nobody else could find, the places where nobody else would look. And the things that moved through the shadows, the folks passing on their way, she saw them too.'

He stopped. 'Is that what you see, Bird?' he asked softly. 'The shades?'

I felt cold at my fingertips and in my toes. 'I don't know,' I replied.

'Because I recall what happened back in Louisiana, Bird,' he continued. 'You saw things back there that nobody else saw. I know that. I could sense it from you, and it scared you.'

I shook my head slowly. I couldn't admit to what I didn't want to believe myself. I sometimes thought – maybe even hoped – that I had been unhinged by grief, that the loss of my wife and child had made me mentally ill, emotionally and psychologically disturbed, so troubled by guilt that I was haunted by images of the dead conjured up by my sick mind. Yet I had seen Jennifer and Susan first of all, after meeting Tante Marie Aguillard in Louisiana, after she had told me what had happened to them when she could not possibly have known. The others came later, and they spoke to me in my dreams.

Now, as I saw Rita and Donald, my own Jennifer, felt my Susan's hand upon me, I half hoped that it was the fact that the anniversary was almost on me, that remembered grief had wormed its way into the recesses of my mind and had started to unhinge me again. Or maybe it was a product of guilt, the guilt I felt at wanting Rachel Wolfe, the guilt I felt at wanting the chance to start over again.

There is a form of narcolepsy in which sufferers literally daydream, the dreams of REM sleep coming upon them in the course of their daily lives, so that the real and the imagined become one and the worlds of sleeping and waking collide. For a time, I thought I might have been a victim of something similar but I knew, deep down inside, that this was not the case. Two worlds came together for me, but they were not the worlds of sleeping and waking. No one slept in these worlds, and no one rested.

I told some of this to Louis, as he watched me quietly from a chair in the corner. I now felt a little ashamed at my outburst, at bringing him in here to listen to my ravings. 'Maybe I just have bad dreams, that's all. But I'll be okay, Louis. I think I'll be okay. Thank you.'

He looked me hard in the eyes, then stood and walked to the door. 'Anytime.' He opened the lock, then paused.

'I'm not the superstitious kind, Bird. Don't go makin' that mistake about me. But I know what happened that night. I could smell burning, Bird. I could smell the leaves on fire.'

And with that he returned to his room.

Still the snow fell, the crystals turning to ice on my window. I watched them form, and thought of Cheryl Lansing's granddaughters, and Rita Ferris, and Gary Chute. I didn't want Ellen Cole to join them, or Billy Purdue either. I wanted to save those who remained.

In an effort to distract myself, I tried to read. I had just about finished a biography of the Earl of Rochester, an English dandy who had boozed and whored his way to an early grave in the time of Charles II, writing some great poetry while he did so. I read the final pages lying on my bed beneath the yellow light from the wall lamp, warm air humming into the room. It seemed that in 1676, Rochester had been involved in the slaying of a constable and had gone into hiding, disguising himself as a quack physician named Dr Alexander Bendo who sold medicines made out of clay, soot, soap and pieces of old wall to the suckers of London, none of whom ever guessed the true identity of the man they trusted with their most intimate secrets, and with the most private parts of their wives' bodies.

Old Saul Mann would have liked Rochester, I thought. He would have appreciated the element of disguise, the possibility of one man taking on the identity of another in order to protect himself, then conning the very people who were searching for him. I fell asleep to the soft patter of snow on glass and dreamed of Saul Mann, wrapped in a cloak of moons and stars, his cards spread on a table before him, waiting quietly for the great game to begin.

# Chapter Nineteen

The snows that came that night were the first heavy falls of the winter. They fell on Dark Hollow and Beaver Cove, on Moosehead Lake and Rockwood and Tarratine. They sugar-coated Big Squaw Mountain and Mount Kineo, Baker Mountain and Elephant Mountain. They turned the Longfellows into a white scar that ran across the back of Piscataquis. Some of the smaller ponds froze, creating a layer of ice as thin and treacherous as a traitor's blade. The snow sat heavy on the evergreens and the ground below lay silent and undisturbed, save for the sound of branches giving way reluctantly beneath the weight they carried, the compressed flakes falling heavily to the drifts below as snow welcomed back snow. In my disordered, disturbed sleep, I felt the snow falling, sensed the change in the atmosphere as the world was shrouded in white and the night waited for the exquisite perfection of winter's work to be revealed in the slow dawning light of day.

Quite early, I heard a snowplough moving down the main street of the town and the slow, careful progress of the first cars, their chains making a distinctive noise on the road. The room was so cold that beads of moisture turned the windows to shattered glass, miraculously restored by the sweep of a hand. I looked out on the world, at the tracks of the cars, at the first people walking on the streets, their hands deep in their pockets or by their sides, the bulk of their layers of sweaters and shirts, thermals and scarves, forcing them to move with a comical unfamiliarity, like children thrust into new clothes.

I approached the bathroom with unease, but all was quiet and clean within. I showered, keeping the water as hot and powerful as I could stand, then dried myself quickly, my teeth already chattering as the temperature cooled the drops on my body. I pulled on jeans, boots, a thick cotton shirt and a dark wool sweater, added a coat and gloves, and stepped out into the crisp, cold morning air. Beneath my feet, the snow crunched and shifted, my progress marked by the impressions of my footsteps behind me. I knocked twice, sharply, on the door of the next room down.

'Go away,' said Angel's voice, the force of his words undiminished by the fact that they came through about four layers of blankets. I felt a moment of guilt at having woken them the night before, and tried to keep my mind off the conversation I had had with Louis.

'It's Bird,' I replied.

'I know. Go away.'

'I'm heading over to the diner. I'll see you there.'

'I'll see you in hell first. It's cold outside.'

'It's colder in there.'

'I'll take my chances.'

'Twenty minutes.'

'Whatever. Just go away.'

I was about to head for the diner when something about my car distracted me. From the window of my room it had seemed that its red lines were only partially obscured by the snow, for flashes of colour showed through as if a hand had wiped away some of the snowfall. But that wasn't why the snow on my car was streaked with red.

There was blood on the windshield. There was blood also on the hood, and a long line of it ran from the front of the car, across the driver's door and the rear window, before pooling below the trunk. I walked through the snow, feeling it crunch beneath my feet. At the back of the car, beside the right rear wheel, lay a pile of mangled brown fur. The cat's mouth was open, and its tongue hung over its small white teeth. A red wound ran across its belly, but most of its blood seemed to be on my car.

To my left, I heard the office door slam and watched as the manager walked over to me. Her eyes were red from crying.

'I already called the police,' she said. 'I thought, when I saw her first, that you'd hit her with your car, but then I saw the blood and realised that couldn't be. Who'd do something like that to an animal? What kind of a person could take pleasure in hurting it so?' She began to cry again.

'I don't know,' I said.

But I did know.

It took me three knocks to get Angel to the door. He stood shivering as I told him about the cat, Louis behind him listening silently.

'He's here,' said Louis, finally.

'We don't know that for sure,' I replied, but I knew he was right. Somewhere close by, Stritch was waiting.

I left them and walked across to the diner. It was ten after eight, and the diner was already almost full, warm air circulating with the smell of fresh coffee and bacon, voices raised at the counter and in the kitchen. For the first time, I noticed the Christmas decorations, the Coca-Cola Father Christmas, the tinsel and the stars. It would be my second season without them. I felt almost grateful for Billy Purdue, maybe even for Ellen Cole, for giving me something on which to concentrate my mind. All of the energy I might have poured into grieving, into anger and guilt, into fearing the anniversary, I now put into the search for these two people. But that gratitude was a brief, passing thing, an ugly betrayal of the people involved, and I quickly felt disgusted with myself for using someone else's sufferings to alleviate my own.

I took a booth and watched the people passing by. When the waitress came, I ordered only coffee. The sight of the cat and the thought of Stritch trailing us had ruined my appetite. I found myself closely examining the faces of the people in the diner, as if Stritch might somehow have mutated himself, or stolen their form. There were a couple of timber company men across from me, eating plates of ham and eggs and already talking about Gary Chute.

I listened and learned, for the world of the northern wilderness was on the verge of change. An area of almost one hundred thousand acres of forest, owned by a European paper company, was about to be harvested. The area had last been logged in the thirties and forties and now it had matured again. For the last decade, the company had been restoring roads and bridges in preparation for the big lumber trucks with their claw-shaped hydraulic lifts that would move into the wilderness, enabling the transportation of the pine, spruce and fir, the oak, maple and birch, to begin. Chute, a graduate of the University of Maine at Orono, was one of those responsible for checking the roads, the tree growth and the likely boundaries for the logging.

The laws relating to forestry had changed since the last cutting. Then, the companies had cleared all of the land, causing silting that killed fish, displaced animals and led to serious erosion. Now they were obliged to cut in a checker-board pattern, leaving half the forest for another twenty to thirty years so that the habitats could grow again. Already there were signs of early cuts, where the deer and moose would feed on the raspberries, willow and alders that sprang up to fight for the new light. And so the days of the undisturbed northern wilderness were now numbered, and soon men and machines would be making their way into its vastness. Gary Chute had been the first of many, and it struck me that his job must have taken him into areas where few people had set foot in decades.

Across the street, Lorna Jennings stepped from her green Nissan, wearing a white padded jacket buttoned and tied over black denims and black, calf-length boots. I wondered how long she had been there: there were no exhaust fumes around the car and, despite the fact that there was little traffic on the street, the tracks of her tyres had been crossed by a number of other vehicles.

She stood at the curb, her hands in the pockets of her jacket, and looked over at the diner. Her eyes moved along the windows until they came to where I sat, a mug of coffee in my hand. She seemed to consider me for a moment, then walked across the road, entered the diner and took a seat opposite me, unbuttoning her jacket as she sat. Beneath it, she wore a red, turtleneck sweater that tightly followed the sweep of her breasts. One or two people looked over at her as she sat, and words were exchanged.

'You're attracting attention,' I said.

She blushed slightly. 'The hell with them,' she said. She wore a trace of pink lipstick and her hair hung loose to the nape of her neck, strands falling gently near her left eye like dark feathers from a bird's wing. 'Some of them know you were out there last night, when they found the body. People have been asking why you're here.'

She ordered, and a waitress brought her coffee and a bagel, with some thin slices of bacon on a separate plate, then gave each of us a sly look before stepping away. Lorna ate the bagel unbuttered, holding it in her left hand while her right picked up pieces of bacon that she nibbled at daintily.

'And what answer have they got?'

'They've heard that you're looking for a girl. Now they're trying to figure out if you had any reason to be interested in the disappearance of the timber company man.' She stopped and took a sip of coffee. 'Well, have you?'

'Is that you asking, or Rand?'

She grimaced. 'You know that's a low blow,' she said quietly. 'Rand can ask his own questions.'

I shrugged. 'I don't think Chute's death was accidental, but that's for the ME to confirm. I don't see any connection between him and Ellen Cole.' That wasn't completely true. They were connected by Dark Hollow and the dark line of a road drawn through the wilderness upon which Chute's death hung like a single red bead.

'But there have been other deaths as well, some of them tied up with a guy called Billy Purdue. He was one of Meade Payne's boys, once upon a time.'

'You think he might be here?'

'I think he might try to get to Payne. There are people after him, bad people. He took money that didn't belong to him and now he's running scared. I think Meade Payne is one of the only people left whom he can trust.'

'And where do you fit in?'

'I was doing some work for his wife. Ex-wife. Her name was Rita Ferris. She had a son.'

Lorna's brow furrowed and then her eyes closed briefly and she nodded as she remembered the name. 'The woman and child who died in Portland, that was them, wasn't it? And this Billy Purdue, he was her ex-husband?'

'Uh-huh, that's them.'

'They say he killed his own family.'

'They say wrong.'

She was silent for a time, then said: 'You seem very sure of that.'

'He wasn't the kind.'

'And do you know "the kind"?' She was watching me carefully now. There were conflicting emotions in her eyes. I could sense them coming from her, just as I had sensed the snow falling softly in the night. There was curiosity, and pity, and something else, too, something that had lain dormant for many years, a feeling repressed and now gradually being exposed. It made me want to draw back from her. Some things were best left in the past.

'Yes, I do. I know the kind.'

'You know, because you've killed them.'

I waited a heartbeat before I answered. 'Yes.'

'Is that what you do now?'

I smiled emptily. 'It seems to be part of it.'

'Did they deserve to die?'

'They didn't deserve to live.'

'That's not the same thing.'

'I know that.'

'Rand knows all about you,' she said, pushing away the remains of her food. 'He spoke about you last night. Actually, he shouted about you, and I shouted back.' She sipped her coffee. 'I think he's afraid of you.' She looked out on to the street, refusing to look directly at me and instead staring at my reflection in the glass. 'I know what he did to you, in that men's room. I always knew. I'm sorry.'

'I was young. I healed.'

She turned back to me. 'I didn't,' she said. 'But I couldn't leave him, not then. I still loved him, or thought I did. And I was young enough to believe that we had a chance together. We tried to have children. We thought it might make things better. I lost two, Bird, the last one three years ago. I don't think I can carry to term. I was so useless, I couldn't even give him a child.' She tensed her lips, and brushed her hair back from her forehead. There was a deadness about her eyes.

'Now I dream about walking away, but if I leave, I leave with nothing. That's the understanding we have, and maybe that's the way it'll have to be. He wants me to stay, or so he says, but I've learned a lot too these last few years. I've learned that men hunger. They hunger and they want, but after a while they stop feeling that hunger for what they have so they look elsewhere. I've seen the way he stares at other women, at the girls in their tight dresses when they come through town. He thinks that one of them will fill whatever he aches for, but they can't and then he comes back and says that he's sorry, that he knows now. But he only knows for as long as the guilt is sharp and alive, and then it passes and he starts to want again.

'Men are so stupid, so self-absorbed. Each of them thinks he's different, that this ache, this emptiness inside him, is unique to him and him alone, and that it somehow excuses whatever he may do. But it doesn't, and then he blames the woman for somehow holding him back, as if, without her, he would be better than he is, more than he is. And the hunger grows and, sooner or later, it starts to feed on itself and the whole sorry mess falls apart like muscle and tendon separated from the bone.'

'And don't women hunger too?' I asked.

'Oh, we hunger all right. And, most of the time, we starve. At least, we do around these parts. You hunger too, Charlie Parker. And you want, maybe more than most. You wanted me, once, because I was different, because I was older and because you shouldn't have been able to have me, but you could. You wanted me because I seemed unobtainable.'

'I wanted you because I loved you.'

Lorna smiled at the memory. 'You'd have left me. Maybe not immediately – it might have taken years – but you'd have left me. As I got older, as the wrinkles started to appear, when I dried up and couldn't have children, when some pretty thing came along and flashed you a smile and you started to think, "I'm still young, I can do better than this." Then you'd have gone, or strayed and come back with your tail between your legs and your dick in your hand. And I couldn't have taken that pain, Charlie, not from you. I'd have died. I'd have curled up and died inside.'

'That shouldn't have been the reason that you stayed with him.' I stopped myself, because no good could come of this. 'Anyway, that was in the past. What's done is done.'

She looked away, and there were furrows of hurt at her brow. 'Were you ever unfaithful to your wife?' she asked.

'Only with a bottle.'

She laughed softly, and looked up at me from beneath her hair. 'I don't know whether that's better or worse than a woman. Worse, I think.' The smile disappeared but a kind of tenderness stayed in her eyes. 'You were full of pain, Bird, even then. How much more pain have you taken on since?'

'It wasn't of my choosing, but I was to blame for what led to it.'

It seemed as if all of the other people around us had faded away, had become mere shadows, and the small circle of daylight around the table represented the boundary of the world, with darkness beyond in which faded figures drifted and flickered like the ghosts of stars.

'And what did you do, Bird?' And softly, so softly, I felt her hand touch my own.

'Like you say, I hurt people. And now I'm trying to make up for what I've done.'

And in the gloom around us, the figures seemed to draw closer, but they were not the folks eating in a small-town diner, filled with gossip and the tiny tendernesses of a close-knit community. They were the figures of the lost and the damned, and there were those among them whom I had once called friend, lover, child.

Lorna stood and around us the diner came into focus again, and the spectres of the past became the substance of the present. She looked down upon me and my hand burned gently where she had touched me.

' "What's done is done",' she said, repeating my words. 'Is that how you feel about us?'

The lines between our past and our present had become blurred, somehow, and we were digging at old wounds that should have healed long before. I didn't reply, so she shrugged on her jacket, took five bucks from her purse and left them on the table. Then she turned and walked away, leaving me with the memory of her touch and the faint lingering of her scent, like a promise made but not yet fulfilled. She knew that Rand would hear that we had been seen together, that we had spoken at length in the diner. I think, even then, she was pushing him. She was pushing us both. I could almost hear the clock ticking, counting down the hours and minutes until her marriage finally self-destructed.

In front of her, the door opened and Angel and Louis stepped into the diner. They glanced at me, and I nodded back. Lorna caught the gesture as she left and, as she passed, she acknowledged them with a small smile. They sat opposite me as I watched her cross the street and head north in her white jacket, her head low like a swan.

Angel called for two coffees and whistled softly as he waited for them to arrive. He was whistling 'The Way We Were'.

After they had eaten breakfast, I went over with them in detail the discovery of Chute's body the night before and we divided out what we were going to do that day. Louis would head up to the lake and try to find a vantage point from which to continue watching the Payne house, since the previous night's scouting party had proved unproductive. Before heading out, he would drop Angel in Greenville, where we arranged for him to rent an ancient Plymouth at a gas station. From Greenville, he would head out to Rockwood, Seboomook, Pittston Farm and Jackman, West Forks and Bingham, all of the towns to the west and south-west of Moosehead Lake. I would take Monson, Abbot Village, Guilford and Dover-Foxcroft to the south and south-east. In each town, we would show photographs of Ellen Cole, checking stores and motels, coffee shops and diners, bars and tourist information offices. Wherever possible, we would talk to local law enforcement and the old-timers who occupied their favourite booths in the bars and diners, the ones who would be sure to notice strangers in town. It would be tiring, frustrating work, but it had to be done.

I noticed Louis was edgy as we spoke, his eyes moving swiftly around the diner and out onto the street beyond.

'He won't come at us in daylight,' I said.

'Could have taken us last night,' he replied.

'But he didn't.'

'He wants us to know he's here. He likes the fear.'

We said nothing more about him.

Before heading down to my assigned towns, I decided to follow the route Ellen and her boyfriend might have taken on the day they left town. On the way, I stopped off at a service station and got a mechanic to fit the Mustang with chains. I wasn't sure how bad the roads might get as I headed north.

I kept glancing in my rear-view mirror as I drove, conscious now that Stritch might be somewhere in the area, but no cars followed me and I passed no other vehicle on the road. A couple of miles outside the town was a sign for the scenic ridge. The road up to it was steep and the Mustang struggled a little on some of the bends. Two minor roads snaked east and west at one point but I stuck with the main route until it came to a small parking lot that looked out over an expanse of hill and mountain, with Ragged Lake shimmering to the west and Baxter State Park and Katahdin to the north-east. The parking lot marked the end of the public access road. After that, the roads were for the use of the timber company, and would have played hell with the shocks of most cars. The land was startling in its whiteness, cold and beautiful. I could see why the woman at the motel had sent them up here, could imagine how wonderful the lake looked when it was bathed in gold.

I came back down to the intersection, where the minor road to the east was thick with snow. It went on for about a mile before ending in fallen trees and thick scrub. The land at either side was heavily wooded, the trees dark against the snow. I drove back and took the western road, which gradually veered north-west to skirt the edge of a pond. The pond was maybe a mile long and half a mile wide, its banks surrounded by skeletal beech and thick pine. By its western bank, a small trail wended its way through the trees. I left the car and followed it on foot, the ends of my jeans quickly becoming heavy and wet.

I had walked for maybe ten minutes when I smelt smoke and heard a dog barking. I left the trail and climbed an incline through the trees, which revealed, at its peak, a small house, maybe no more than two rooms wide. It had an overhanging roof and a narrow porch and square, four-pane windows from which old paint flaked. The house itself might have been white once but most of the paint had now disappeared, leaving only patches below the eaves and on the window frames. Three or four large rubber garbage cans, the kind used for recycling by businesses, stood to one side of the house. On the other was an old yellow Ford truck. The rusting hulk of a blue Oldsmobile, its tyres long gone, its windows thick with dirt, stood about five feet from the Ford. I caught some movement inside, and then a small black mongrel dog, its tail docked and its teeth bared, sprang through the open window from the backseat and moved quickly towards me. It stopped two or three feet from me and barked loudly.

The door of the house opened and an old man with a thin beard appeared. He wore blue overalls and a long, red raincoat. His hair was long and matted and his hands were almost black with dirt. I could see the hands clearly, because they were clutching a Remington A-70 pump-action shotgun, which was pointing in my direction. When the dog saw the old man emerge, its barking increased in volume and ferocity and its stumpy tail wagged frenziedly from side to side.

'What do you want here?' said the old man, in a voice that was slightly slurred. One side of his mouth remained immobile when he talked, and I figured he had some kind of nerve or muscle damage to his face.

'I'm looking for someone, a young woman who may have been around here a couple of days back.'

The old man almost grinned, exposing a mouthful of yellow-stained teeth, broken, on both the top and bottom rows, by gaps. 'Don't get young women around here no more,' he said, the gun not moving from me. 'Don't got the looks.'

'She was blonde, about five-five. Her name was Ellen Cole.'

'Didn't see 'em,' said the old man, and he waved the gun at me. 'Now get off my property.'

I didn't move. Beside me, the dog lashed out and nipped at the end of my pants. I was tempted to kick it, but I figured it would latch on to my leg in an instant. I didn't take my eyes from the old man as I considered what he had just said.

'What do you mean "them"? I only mentioned the girl.'

The old man's eyes narrowed as he realised his mistake. He jacked a shell into the shotgun, driving the small dog wild. It gripped the wet end of my jeans and tugged with its sharp white teeth.

'I mean it, mister,' he said. 'You just take your leave and don't come back, else I'll shoot you now and take my chances with the law.' He whistled to the dog. 'Come away now, boy, I don't want you gettin' hurt.' The dog instantly turned and ran back to the Plymouth, its powerful back legs propelling it through the open window. It watched me from the front seat, still barking.

'Don't make me come back, old man,' I said quietly.

'I didn't make you come here to begin with, and I sure ain't makin' you come back. I got nothing to say to you. Now I'm tellin' you for the last time: get off my land.'

I shrugged, turned and walked away. There was nothing more to be done, not without the risk of getting my head shot off. I looked back once to find him still standing on the porch, the shotgun in his hands. I had other people to talk to, but I figured I'd be back out to see that old man again.

That was my first mistake.

# Chapter Twenty

After I left the old man I drove south. His words bothered me. It could have been nothing, I supposed; after all, he might have seen Ricky and Ellen together in town, and the news that someone was concerned that they were missing would have spread pretty quickly, even as far as the boondocks where the old man lived. If it turned out there was more to it than that then I knew where to find him, if I needed to.

I made my tour of the towns, Guilford and Dover-Foxcroft taking more time than the others, but I came up with nothing. I stopped at a pay phone to call Dave Martel in Greenville and he agreed to meet me at St Martha's in order to pave the way with Dr Ryley, the director. I wanted to talk to him about Emily Watts.

And Caleb Kyle.

'I hear you've been asking about the Cole girl,' he said, as I prepared to hang up.

I paused. I hadn't been in contact with him since I arrived back in Dark Hollow. He seemed to detect my puzzlement.

'Hey, it's a small place. News gets around. I had a call from New York early this morning, asking about her.'

'Who was it?'

'It was her father,' continued Martel. 'He's on his way back up here. Seems he got into a shouting match with Rand Jennings, and Jennings told him to keep away from Dark Hollow if he wanted to help his daughter. Cole called me to see if I could tell him anything that Jennings wouldn't. Probably called the county sheriff as well.'

I sighed. Giving Walter Cole an ultimatum was like telling the rain to fall up instead of down.

'He say when he was going to arrive?'

'Tomorrow, I guess. I think he's going to stay here, instead of in the Hollow. You want me to give you a call when he gets here?'

'No,' I said. 'I'll find out soon enough.' I told him a little about the background to the case, and how I had become involved at Lee's instigation, not Walter's. Martel gave a small laugh.

'Hear you were out there when they found Gary Chute as well. You sure lead a complicated life.'

'You hear anything more about it?'

'Daryl brought the wardens out to where he thinks he found Chute – hell of a trip, from what I hear – and the truck's being brought back for examination, soon as they can clear a road through the snow. The body's on its way to Augusta. According to one of the part-timers who was down here this morning, Jennings seemed to think there was some bruising to the body, like he'd been beaten before he died. They're going to question the wife, see if she might have run out of patience with him and sent someone to take care of him.'

'Pretty lame.'

'Pretty,' he agreed. 'I'll see you at the home.'

★　　　★　　　★

Martel's car was already pulled up outside the main entrance to St Martha's when I arrived, and he and Dr Ryley were waiting for me by the reception desk.

Dr Ryley was a middle-aged man with good teeth, a well-cut suit and the oily manner of a casket salesman. His hand was soft and moist when I shook it. I had to resist the temptation to dry my palm on my jeans when he had detached himself from me. It wasn't hard to see why Emily Watts had taken a shot at him.

He told us how much he regretted what had happened and advised us on the new security measures that had been introduced as a result, which seemed to consist of nothing more than locking the doors and hiding anything that could be used to knock out the guard. After some to-ing and fro-ing with Martel, he agreed to let me speak to Mrs Schneider, the woman who occupied the room next to that of the late Emily Watts. Martel decided to wait in the lobby, in case we spooked the old lady by arriving as a team. He sat, drew a second chair in front of him with the tip of his shoe, then put his feet up and seemed to fall asleep.

Mrs Erica Schneider was a German Jew who fled to America with her husband in 1938. He was a jeweller and brought enough gems with him to enable him to set up business in Bangor. They had been comfortable too, she told me, at least until he died and the bills that he had been hiding from her for the best part of five years resurfaced. She was forced to sell their house and most of her possessions, then fell ill from stress. Her children had put her up in the home, arguing that most of them were within visiting distance anyway, although this didn't mean that any of them actually bothered to visit her, she said. She spent most of her time watching TV or reading. When it was warm enough, she walked in the grounds.

I sat beside her in her small, neat room with its carefully made bed, its single closet filled with old, dark dresses, its dressing table covered with a limited selection of cosmetics that the old woman still carefully applied each morning, as she turned to me and said: 'I hope I die soon. I want to leave this place.'

I didn't reply. After all, what could I say? Instead, I said: 'Mrs Schneider, I'll try to keep what's said here today between us, but I need to know something: did you call a man named Willeford in Portland and talk to him about Emily Watts?'

She said nothing. I thought for a moment that she might start to cry, because she looked away and appeared to be having trouble with her eyes. I spoke again. 'Mrs Schneider, I really need you to help me. Some people have been killed, and a young girl is missing, and I think that maybe these things are connected to Miss Emily in some way. If there's anything at all you can tell me, anything that might assist me in bringing this thing to a close, I would appreciate it, I truly would.'

She gripped and twisted the cord of her dressing gown in her hands, wincing. 'Yes,' she replied, at last. 'I thought it might help her.' The cord drew tighter and there was fear in her voice, as if the rope was tightening not around her hands, but around her neck. 'She was so sad.'

'Why, Mrs Schneider? Why was she sad?'

The hands still worked at the cord as she replied. 'One night, perhaps a year ago, I found her crying. I came to her, and I held her, and then she spoke to me. She told me that it was her child's birthday – a boy, she said, but she had not kept him, because she was afraid.'

'Afraid of what, Mrs Schneider?'

'Afraid of the man who fathered the child,' she said. She swallowed and looked to the window. 'What harm can it do to talk of these things now?' she whispered softly, more to herself than to me, then turned her face to mine. 'She told me that, when she was young, her father . . . Her father was a very bad man, Mr Parker. He beat her and forced her to do things, you understand? Sex, *ja*? Even when she was older, he would not let her leave him, because he wanted her near him.'

I nodded, but stayed silent as the words tumbled out of her like rats from a sack.

'Then another man came to her town, and this man made love to her, and took her to his bed. She did not tell him about the sex, but, in the end, she told him about the beatings. And this man, he found her father in a bar and he beat him, and told him that he must never touch his daughter again.' She emphasised each word with a wag of her finger, carefully spacing each syllable for maximum emphasis. 'He told her father that if anything happened to his daughter, he would kill him. And because of this, Miss Emily fell in love with this man.

'But there was something wrong with him, Mr Parker, in here –' She touched her head '– and in here.' Her finger moved to her heart. 'She did not know where he lived, or where he came from. He found her when he wanted her. He went missing for days, sometimes weeks. He smelt of wood and sap and once, when he came back to her, there was blood on his clothes and under his nails. He told her that he hit a deer in his truck. Another time, he told her that he was hunting. Two different reasons he gave, and she started to feel afraid.

'That was when the young girls began to disappear, Mr

Parker: two girls. And once, when she was with him, she smelt something on him, the smell of another woman. His neck, it was scratched, torn, as if by a hand. They argued, and he told her that she was imagining things, that he had cut himself on a branch.

'But she knew it was him, Mr Parker. She knew it was him who was taking the girls, but she could not tell why. And now, now she was pregnant by him, and he knew this. She had been so scared to tell him, but when he learned about it he was so pleased. He wanted a son, Mr Parker. This he told her: "I want a son".

'But she would not hand over a child to such a man, she told me. She grew more and more afraid. And he wanted the child, Mr Parker, he wanted it *so* badly. Always, always he was asking her about it, warning her against doing anything that might damage it. But there was no love in him or, if there was, it was a strange love, a bad love. She knew that he would take the child, if he could, and she would never see it again. She knew he was a bad man, worse even than her father.

'One night, when she was with him, in his truck by her father's house, she told him that she was in pain. In the toilet outside, she had a newspaper, and in the newspaper was – ' She struggled for the words. 'Guts, blood, waste. Again, you understand? And she cried and smeared the blood on herself and put it in the bowl and called for him and told him, told him that she had lost his baby.'

Mrs Schneider stopped again, and took a blanket from her bed, which she wrapped round her shoulders to ward off the cold. 'When she told him this,' she continued, 'she thought that he would kill her. He howled, Mr Parker, like an animal, and he raised her by the hair, and he hit her, again and again and again. He called her "weak" and

332

"worthless". He told her that she had killed his child. Then he turned and walked away and she heard him in the woodshed, moving among the tools her father kept there. And when she heard the sound of the blade, she ran away from the house and into the woods. But he followed her, and she could hear him coming through the trees. She stayed quiet, not even breathing, and he went past her, and he did not come back again, not ever.

'Later, they found the girls hanging from the tree, and she knew that he had left them there. But she never saw him again and she went to the sisters here, at St Martha's, and I think that perhaps she told them why she was afraid. They sheltered her until she had the boy, and then they took the child away from her. After that, she was never the same and she came back here, after many years, and the sisters, they took care of her. When the home was sold, she used what little money she had to stay here. It is not an expensive place, this, Mr Parker. This you can see.' She raised her hand to show the dull little room. Her skin was thin as paper. Sunlight dripped like honey through her fingers.

'Mrs Schneider, did Miss Emily tell you the name of the man, the man who fathered her child?'

'I do not know,' she replied.

I sighed softly but, as I did so, I realised that I had not given her time to finish, that she had more to say.

'I know only his first name,' she continued. She moved her hand gently in the air before me, as if conjuring up the name from the past.

'He was called Caleb.'

Snow falling, inside and out; a blizzard of memories. Young girls turning in the breeze, my grandfather watching them, rage and grief welling up inside him, the smell of their decay wrapped around him like a rotting cloak. He looked at them, a father and husband himself, and he thought of all the young men they would not kiss, the lovers whose breath they would not feel against their cheeks in the dead of night and whom they would never comfort with the warmth of their bodies. He thought of the children they would never have, the potential within them for the creation of new life now stilled forever, the gaping holes at their bellies where their wombs had been torn apart inside them. Within each one, there had existed possibilities beyond imagining. With their deaths, an infinite number of existences had come to an end, potential universes lost forever, and the world shrank a little at their passing.

I stood and walked to the window. The snowfall made the grounds look less forbidding, the trees less bare, but it was all an illusion. Things are what they are, and changes in nature can only hide their true essence for a time. And I thought of Caleb, moving into the comforting darkness of the forest as he raged at the death of his child unborn, betrayed by the too-thin, too-weak body of the woman he had protected and then inseminated. He took three after her in rapid succession, fuelling his fury until it was spent, then hung them like trimmings on a tree to be found by a man who was not like him, a man who was so far removed from him that he felt the deaths of each of these young women as a personal loss. For Caleb's was a world in which things mutated into their opposites: creation into destruction, love into hate, life into death.

Five deaths, but six girls missing; one remained unaccounted for. In my grandfather's file, her name had been marked on a sheaf of pages, upon which her movements on the day she disappeared had been minutely reconstructed. A picture of her was stapled to the corner of the bundle: plump, homely Judith Mundy, a hardness to her passed down by generations of people who had worked thin, unforgiving soil to create a foothold and scratch a living from this land. Judith Mundy, lost and now forgotten, except by the parents who would always feel her absence like an abyss into which they shouted her name without even an echo in reply.

'Why would this man do such a thing to these girls?' I heard Mrs Schneider ask, but I had no answer for her. I had stared into the faces of people who had killed with impunity for decades, and still I did not know the reasons for what they did. I felt a pang of regret at the loss of Walter Cole as a colleague. This was what Walter could do: he could look inside himself and, secure in his sense of his own innate rightness, he could create an image of that which was not right, a tiny tumour of viciousness and ill will, like the first cell colonised by a cancer from which he could construct the progress of the entire disease. He was like a mathematician who, when faced with a simple square on a page, plots its progress into other dimensions, other spheres of being beyond the plane of its current existence, while remaining ultimately detached from the problem at hand.

This was his strength and also, I thought, his weakness. Ultimately, he did not look deeply enough because he was afraid of what he might find within himself: his own capacity for evil. He resisted the impulse to understand himself fully that he might understand others better. To understand is to come to terms with one's potential for evil as well as good, and I did not think that Walter Cole wanted to believe himself capable, at whatever level, of doing acts of great wrong. When I had performed deeds that he found morally unacceptable, when I had hunted down those who had done wrong and, by doing so, had done wrong myself, Walter had cut me adrift, even though he had used me to find those individuals and knew what I would do when I found them. That was why we were no longer friends: I recognised my culpability, the deep flaws within myself – the pain, the hurt, the anger, the guilt, the desire for revenge – and all of these things I took and used. Maybe I killed a little of myself each time I did so; maybe that was the price that had to be paid. But Walter was a good man and, like many good men, his flaw was that he believed himself to be a better one.

Mrs Schneider spoke again. 'It was the mother, I think,' she said, softly.

I leaned against the windowpane and waited for her to continue.

'Once, when this man, this "Caleb", was drunk, he told Miss Emily of his mother. She was a hard woman, Mr Parker. The father, he had left them out of fear of her, then died in the war. She beat her boy, beat him with sticks and chains, and she did worse things, too. At night, Mr Parker, she would come to him, to her own boy, and she would touch him, and take him inside her. And later, when she was done, she would hurt him. She would drag him by the legs, or the hair, and kick him until he coughed blood. She chained him outside, like a dog, naked, in rain, and snow. All this, he told Miss Emily.'

'Did he tell her where this took place?'

She shook her head. 'Maybe south. I don't know. I think . . .'

I didn't interrupt as her brow furrowed and the fingers of her right hand danced in the air before me.

'*Medina*,' she said at last, her eyes ablaze in triumph. 'He said something to Miss Emily about a Medina.'

I noted down the name. 'And what happened to his mother?'

Mrs Schneider twisted in her chair to look at me. 'He killed her,' she said simply.

Behind me, the door opened as a nurse brought in a pot of coffee and two cups, along with a tray of cookies, presumably at the instigation of Dr Ryley. Mrs Schneider looked a little surprised, then took on the role of hostess, pouring my coffee, offering sugar, creamer. She pressed cookies on me, which I refused, since I figured she might be grateful for them later. I was right. She took one for herself, carefully put the rest in two napkins from the tray and placed them in the bottom drawer of her dressing table. Then, as the snow clouds gathered once again in the skies above and the afternoon grew dark, she told me more about Emily Watts.

'She was not a woman who talked very much, Mr Parker, only that one time,' she said in her carefully-pronounced English which still carried traces of her roots in her 'w's – 'vas', 'voman' – and in some of her vowels. 'She said "hello", or "good-night", or spoke of the weather, but no more. She never again talked of the boy. The others here, if you ask them, even if you step into their rooms for a moment, they will talk of their children, their grandchildren, their husbands, their wives.' She smiled. 'Just as I did to you, Mr Parker.'

I was about to say something, to tell her that I didn't mind, that it was interesting, the least I could do, something half meant and well intended, when she raised a hand to stop me. 'Don't even begin to tell me that you enjoyed it. I am not a young girl who needs to be

337

humoured.' The smile remained as she said it. There was something in her, some relic of old beauty, which told me that in her youth many men had humoured her, and had been glad to do so.

'So she did not talk of such things,' she went on. 'There were no photographs in her room, no pictures and since I have been here, five years, all she has ever said to me is "Hello, Mrs Schneider", "Gutt Morning, Mrs Schneider", "Is a fine day, Mrs Schneider". That was all, nothing else, except for that one time, and I think she was ashamed of it later, or perhaps afraid. She had no visitors, and never spoke of it again, until the young man came.'

I leaned forward, and she imitated the movement, so that we were only inches apart. 'He came some days after I made the call to Mr Willeford, after I saw his notice in the newspaper. The first we knew, there was shouting from downstairs and then the sound of running. A young man, a big man, with large, wild eyes, came past my door and burst into Miss Emily's room. Well, I was afraid for her, and for me, but I took my stick –' she pointed to a walking stick with a head carved into the shape of a bird and a metal tip at the end '– and I followed him.

'When I came to the room, Miss Emily was sitting at her window, just as I am now, but her hands were like, *ach*, like this.' Mrs Schneider put her hands flat on her cheeks and opened her mouth wide in an expression of shock. 'And the young man, he looked at her and he said only one word. He said to her: "Momma?" Like that, like a question. But she only shook her head and said, "No, no, no," again and again. The boy, he reached out for her, but already she was moving away from him, back, back, until she was in the corner of her room, down on the floor.

'Then I heard from behind me the sound of the nurses. They came with the fat guard, the one Miss Emily hit on the night she ran off, and I was bundled out of the room while they took the boy away. I watched him as they took him, Mr Parker, and his face . . . Oh, his face was like he had seen someone die, someone he loved. He cried and called out again, "Momma, momma",' but she did not reply.

'The police came, and they took the boy away. The nurse, she came to Miss Emily and she asked her if it was true, what the boy had said. And she told her "No", that she does not know what he is talking about, that she has no son, no child.

'But that night, I heard her crying for so long that I thought she would never stop. I went to her and held her. I told her that she should not be afraid, that she was safe, but she said only one thing.'

She paused and I saw that her hands were shaking. I reached out and stilled them and she moved her right hand, slipping it over mine and holding it tightly, her eyes closed. And I think, for a moment, I became her son, her child, one of those who never visited and who had left her to die in the cold north as surely as if they had hauled her into the forests of Piscataquis or Aroostock and abandoned her there. Her eyes reopened and she released my hand. Her own hands were still once again when she did so.

'Mrs Schneider,' I said gently. 'What did she say?'

'She said: "Now he will kill me".'

'Who did she mean? Billy, the young man who came to her?' But I think I already knew the real answer.

Mrs Schneider shook her head. 'No, the other. The one she was always afraid would find her, and nobody could help her, or save her from him.

'It was the one who came later,' concluded the old woman. 'He learned of what had happened, and he came.'

I waited. Something brushed softly against the window and I watched a snowflake drift down the pane, melting as it went. 'It was the night before she ran away. It was cold that night. I remember, I had to ask for an extra blanket, it was so cold. When I woke, it was dark, black, with no moon. And I heard a noise, a scraping from outside.

'I climbed from my bed and the floor was so chilly that I – ah! – I gasped. I went to the window and drew the curtain a little, but I could see nothing. Then the sound came again, and I looked straight down and . . .'

She was terrified. I could feel it coming off her in waves, a deep abiding fear that had shaken her to her core.

'There was a man, Mr Parker, and he was climbing up the pipe, hand over hand. His head was down, and turned away from me, so I could not see him. And, anyway, it was so dark that he was only a shadow. But the shadow reached the window of Miss Emily's room and I could see him pushing at it with one hand, trying to force it up. I heard Miss Emily scream, and I screamed too, and ran into the hallway calling for a nurse. And all the time, I can hear Miss Emily screaming and screaming. But when they came, the man was gone and they could find no trace of him in the grounds.'

'What kind of man was he, Mrs Schneider? Tall? Short? Big? Small?'

'I told you: it was dark. I could not see clearly.' She shook her head in distress as she tried to remember.

'Could it have been Billy?'

'No.' She was definite about that. 'It was the wrong

shape. It was not as big as him.' She lifted her hands in imitation of Billy's large shoulders. 'When I told the nurse about the man, I think she believed that I was imagining things, that we were two old women frightening each other. But we were not. Mr Parker, I could not see this man clearly, but I could *feel* him. He was no thief come to steal from old women. He wanted something else. He wanted to hurt Miss Emily, to punish her for something she did long ago. The boy Billy, the boy who called her "Momma", he started something by coming here. Perhaps, Mr Parker, I started it, by calling this man Willeford. Perhaps it is all my fault.'

'No, Mrs Schneider,' I said. 'Whatever happened to cause this started a long time ago.'

She looked at me then with a kind of tenderness before she reached out and laid a hand softly on my knee to emphasise what she said next. 'She was afraid, Mr Parker,' she whispered. 'She was so afraid that she wanted to die.'

I left her, alone with her memories and her guilt. Winter, the thief of daylight, caused lights to twinkle in the distance as Martel and I walked to our cars.

'Did you learn anything?' he asked.

I didn't reply immediately. Instead, I looked north, to the forest, to the wilderness. 'Could a man survive out there?' I asked.

Martel's brow furrowed. 'Depends on how long he's out there, what kind of clothing and supplies—'

'That's not what I mean,' I interrupted. 'Could he survive for a long time, for years, maybe?'

Martel thought for a moment. When he spoke, he didn't mock the question but answered it seriously, and he rose in my estimation by doing so. 'I don't see why not. People have been surviving out there since the country was settled. There are still the remains of farmhouses to prove it. It wouldn't be an easy existence, and I guess he'd have to go back to civilisation once in a while, but it could be done.'

'And no one would disturb him out there?'

'Most of it hasn't been touched in the best part of fifty years. Go far enough into the forest and not even hunters or wardens are likely to bother you. You think someone went in there?'

'Yes, I do.' I shook his hand and opened the door of the Mustang. 'Trouble is, I think he's come out again.'

# Chapter Twenty One

I had the scent of him then, had begun to feel the
knowledge of him creep over me, but I needed more
if I was to understand him, if I was to hunt him down
before he found Billy Purdue, before he killed again. I
was so close to making the connection: it hung just
beyond my reach like the name of a half-remembered
melody. I needed someone who could take my own semi-
formed suspicions and mould them into a coherent
whole, and I knew of only one person I trusted that much.

I needed to talk to Rachel Wolfe.

I drove back to Dark Hollow, packed an overnight bag
and placed the file on Caleb Kyle at the top. Louis and
Angel returned in their separate cars as I was leaving. I
explained what I was doing then started to drive to
Bangor to catch the flight to Boston.

I was just outside Guilford when, three cars ahead of
me, I spotted a yellow Ford truck, its exhaust belching
dirty fumes onto the road. I accelerated past it, glancing
idly at the driver as I did so. In the cab sat the old man
who had threatened me with his shotgun. I stayed ahead
of him for a time, then pulled into a gas station at Dover-
Foxcroft to let him pass. I stayed four or five cars behind

him all the way to Orono, where he drove into the parking lot of a run-down mall and stopped outside a store called 'Stuckey Trading'. I checked my watch. If I delayed any longer, I'd miss my flight. I watched the old man as he removed a couple of black sacks from the bed of his truck and headed into the store, then I slapped the steering wheel once in frustration and accelerated towards Bangor and the airport.

I knew that Rachel Wolfe was holding tutorials at Harvard while the college funded research she was conducting into the link between abnormal brain structures and criminal behaviour. She no longer engaged in private practice and, as far as I knew, was no longer assisting with criminal profiling.

Rachel had acted as an unofficial adviser on a number of cases for the NYPD, including the Travelling Man killings. That was how I met her, how we became lovers, and it was what eventually tore us apart. Rachel, whose policeman brother had died at the hands of a disturbed gunman, believed that by exploring the criminal mind she could prevent similar tragedies from happening to others. But the Travelling Man's mind had been unlike any other, and the hunt for him had almost cost Rachel her life. She had made it known that she did not wish to see me and, until recently, I had respected that wish. I did not want to cause her any more pain, yet now I felt that I had nowhere else to turn.

But there was more to it than that, I knew. Twice in the last three months I had gone to Boston with the intention of finding her, or trying to reestablish what we had lost, but each time I had turned back without talking to her. Leaving my card on that last visit, with Louis waiting downstairs in the lobby, was as close as I had come to contacting her. Perhaps, in some way, Caleb Kyle would provide a bridge between us, a professional conduit that might also allow the personal to run alongside it.

On the flight, I added what I had learned from Mrs Schneider to my grandfather's file, writing carefully in block capitals. I scanned the photos as I went, noting the details of these young women now long dead, their lives more carefully documented by my grandfather after they were gone than by anyone while they were alive. In many ways, he knew them and cared about them as much as their own parents. In some cases, he cared about them more. He outlived his own wife by thirteen years, and outlived his daughter by twelve. He had lived to mourn a lot of women, I thought.

I remembered something he said to me once, after I became a policeman. I sat beside him in the Scarborough house, matching coffee mugs on the table, and watched as he examined my shield, the light reflecting on his spectacles as he twisted and turned it in his hand. Outside, the sun shone, but the house was cool and dark.

'It's a strange vocation,' he said at last. 'These rapists, and murderers, thieves and drug peddlers, we need them to exist. Without them, we'd have no purpose. They give our professional lives meaning.

'And that's the danger, Charlie. Because, somewhere down the line, you'll meet one who threatens to cross over, one you can't leave behind when you take off your badge at the end of the day. You have to fight it, or else your friends, your family, they all become tainted by his shadow. A man like that, he makes you his creature. Your life becomes an extension of his life, and if you don't find him, if you don't bring him to an end, he'll haunt you for the rest of your days. You understand me, Charlie?'

I understood, or thought I did. Even then, as he came to the end of his life, he was still tainted by his contact with Caleb Kyle. He hoped that it would never happen to me, but it did. It happened with the Travelling Man and, now, it was happening again. I had inherited the monkey on my grandfather's back, his ghost, his demon.

After I made my additions, I went through the file again, trying to feel my way into my grandfather's mind and, through his efforts, into the mind of Caleb Kyle. At the end of the file was a folded sheet of newspaper. It was a page from the *Maine Sunday Telegram* dating from 1977, twelve years after the man my grandfather knew as Caleb Kyle had blinked out of existence. On the page was a photograph taken in Greenville of a representative of the Scott Paper Company, which owned most of the forest north of Greenville, presenting the steamboat *Katahdin* to the Moosehead Marine Museum for restoration. In the background people grinned and waved, but farther back a figure had been caught, his face turned to the camera, a box containing what might have been supplies held in his arms. Even from a distance, he appeared tall and wiry, the arms holding the boxes long and thin, the legs slim but strong. The face was nothing more than a blur, ringed carefully in red felt-tip.

But my grandfather had enlarged it, then enlarged it again, and again, and again, each enlargement placed behind the preceding picture. And from the page a face grew, bigger and bigger until it took on the size and dimensions of a skull, the ink turning the eyes into dark pits, the face a construct of tiny black and white dots. The man in the picture had become a spectre, his features indistinguishable, unrecognisable to anyone except my grandfather. For my grandfather had sat beside him in that bar, had smelt him, had listened as this man directed him to a tree where dead girls twisted in the breeze.

This, my grandfather believed, was Caleb Kyle.

At the airport, I called the psychology department at Harvard, gave them my ID number and asked them if Rachel Wolfe was due to teach that day. I was informed that Ms Wolfe was due to give a tutorial to psychology students at 6 p.m.. It was now 5.15 p.m. If I missed Rachel on-campus, there were people who could get a residential address for me but it would take time and time, I was rapidly coming to realise, was something I just didn't have. I hailed a cab and, after actively encouraging the driver to take the Ted Williams Tunnel to avoid the worst of the traffic, arrived in Cambridge.

A UC election banner hung outside the Grafton pub and a lot of the kids on the streets wore student election badges on their bags and coats as I headed across the campus to the junction of Quincy and Kirkland. I sat in the shadow of the Church of the New Jerusalem, across from the William James Hall, and waited.

At 5.59 p.m. a figure dressed in a black wool overcoat, ankle-length boots and black trousers, her red hair tied back with a black and white ribbon, walked down Quincy and entered the Hall. Even at a distance, Rachel still looked beautiful and I caught one or two male students sneaking looks at her as she passed. I kept a short distance behind her as I followed her into the entrance hall and watched her take the stairs to Seminar Room 6 on the lower ground floor, just to make sure that she wasn't going to cancel and leave. I followed her as she entered the seminar room and closed the door, then I took a seat in a plastic chair with a view of the room and waited.

After an hour, the door opened and students began to stream out, most with large-format, wire-bound notebooks clutched to their chests or poking out of their bags: wire-bound notebooks were a weakness of Rachel's. I moved aside to let the last student leave, then stepped into a small classroom dominated by a single big table, with chairs arranged around it and against the walls. At the head of the table, beneath a blackboard, sat Rachel Wolfe. She was dressed in a dark green sweater with a man's white shirt beneath it, the collar turned up around her neck. As always, she wore some light make-up, carefully applied, and a dark red lipstick.

She looked up expectantly, a half smile on her face that froze as soon as she saw me. I closed the door gently behind me and took the first vacant seat at the table, which was just about as far away from her as I could get.

'Hi,' I said.

She very deliberately put her pens and notes away in a leather attaché case, then she stood and started to shrug on her coat. 'I asked that you not try to contact me,' she said, as she struggled to find her left sleeve. I stood and walked over to her, and held the sleeve out so she could get her arm in. I felt kind of sleazy intruding on her space that way, but I also felt a momentary twinge of resentment: Rachel had not been the only one hurt in Louisiana in the hunt for the Travelling Man. The resentment quickly passed, to be replaced by guilt as I recalled the feel of her in my arms, her body racked by sobs after she was forced to kill a man in the Metairie cemetery. Once again, I saw her raising the gun, her finger tightening on the trigger, fire leaping from the muzzle as the gun bucked in her hands. Some deep, unquenchable instinct for survival had kicked in on that awful summer day, fuelling her actions. I think that now, when she looked at me, she recalled what she had done, and she felt a fear of what I represented: the capacity for violence that had briefly exploded into existence within her and whose embers still glowed redly in her dark places.

'Don't worry,' I said, lying a little. 'I'm here for professional reasons, not personal ones.'

'Then I certainly don't want to hear about it.' She turned, her case beneath her arm. 'Excuse me, I have work to do.'

I put out a hand to touch her arm, and she glared at me. I withdrew it. 'Rachel, wait. I need your help.'

'Please, let me leave. You're blocking my way.'

I moved back and she shuffled past me, her head down. She had the door open when I spoke again. 'Rachel, listen to me, just for a moment. If not for me, then for Walter Cole.'

She stopped at the door, but didn't turn around. 'What about Walter?'

'His daughter Ellen is missing. I'm not sure, but it may have something to do with a case I'm working on. It may also be connected somehow to Thani Pho, the student who was killed.'

Rachel paused, then took a deep breath, closed the door and sat down in the seat I had previously occupied. Just to keep things equal, I sat down in her seat.

'You have two minutes,' she said.

'I need you to read a file, and give me an opinion on it.'

'I don't do that anymore.'

'I hear you're working on a study about the connection

349

between violent crime and brain disorders, something involving brain scans.'

I knew a little more than that. Rachel was involved in research into dysfunctions in two areas of the brain, the amygdala and the frontal lobe. As I understood it from reading a copy of an article she had contributed to a psychology journal, the amygdala, a tiny area of tissue in the unconscious brain, generates feelings of alarm and emotion, allowing us to respond to the distress of others. The frontal lobe is where emotions are registered, where self-consciousness emerges and plans are constructed. It is also the part of the brain that controls our impulses.

In psychopaths, it was now believed, the frontal lobe failed to respond when confronted with an emotional situation, possibly due to a failure in the amygdala itself or in the processes used to send its signals to the cortex. Rachel, and others like her, were pressing for a huge brain-scan survey on convicted criminals, arguing that they could reveal a connection between brain damage and psychopathic criminal behaviour.

She frowned. 'You seem to know a lot about me. I'm not sure that I like the idea of you keeping tabs on me.'

I felt that twinge of resentment again. I felt it so strongly that my mouth twitched involuntarily. 'It's not like that, but I see your ego is still strong and healthy.'

Rachel smiled slightly, a tiny, fleeting thing. 'The rest of me isn't quite so robust. I'm going to be scarred for life, Bird. I'm in therapy twice weekly and I've had to give up my own practice. I still think of you, and you still frighten me. Sometimes.'

'I'm sorry.' Maybe it was my imagination, but there was something in that pause, in that 'sometimes', that implied she thought of me in other ways too.

'I know. Tell me about this file.'

And I did, giving her a brief run through the history of the killings, adding some of what Mrs Schneider had told me and some of what I suspected, or had guessed, myself. 'Most of it is in here.' I raised the battered manilla file. 'I'd like you to take a look, see what you can come up with.'

She reached out and I slid the file to her across the row of tables. She flicked quickly through the handwritten notes, the carbon copies, the photographs. One of them was a crime scene photo taken by the banks of the Little Wilson. 'Oh my God,' she whispered, and closed her eyes. When she opened them again, there was a new light in them, the spark of professional curiosity but also something else, something that had attracted me to her in the first place.

It was empathy.

'It could take a couple of days,' she said.

'I don't have a couple of days. I need it tonight.'

'Not possible. I'm sorry, but I couldn't even begin to do it in that time.'

'Rachel, no one believes me. No one will accept that this man could ever have existed or, worse, could still be alive now. But he's out there. I can *feel* him, Rachel. I need to understand him, in however small a way. I need something, anything, to make him real, to bring him out of that file and to form a recognisable picture of him. Please. I've got this jumble of details in my head, and I need someone to help me make sense of it. There's no one else I can turn to and, anyway, you're the best criminal psychologist I know.'

'I'm the *only* criminal psychologist you know,' she said, and that smile came again.

'There's that as well.'

She stood. 'There's no way I'll have anything for you tonight, but meet me tomorrow at the Co-op bookstore, at, say, eleven o'clock. I'll give you what I have then.'

'Thank you,' I said.

'You're welcome.' And with that she was gone.

I stayed where I always stayed when I was in Boston, in the Nolan House over on G Street in south Boston. It was a quiet bed-and-breakfast, with antique furniture and a couple of restaurants close by. I checked in with Angel and Louis, but there was no movement in Dark Hollow.

'You see Rachel?' asked Angel.

'Yes, I saw her.'

'How'd she take it?'

'She didn't seem too pleased to see me.'

'You bring back bad memories.'

'Story of my life. Maybe, someday, someone will see me and think happy thoughts.'

'Never happen,' he said. 'Hang loose, and tell her we were asking after her.'

'I will. Any move out at the Payne house?'

'The younger guy went into town to buy milk and groceries, that's about all. No sign of Billy Purdue, or Tony Celli, or Stritch, but Louis is still acting funny. Stritch is around here somewhere, that much we can be sure of. Sooner you're back here, the better.'

I showered, put on a clean T-shirt and jeans, and found a copy of the Gousha deluxe road atlas from 1995 among the guidebooks and magazines in the hallway of the Nolan House. The Gousha listed eight Medinas – Texas, Tennessee, Washington, Wisconsin, New York, North Dakota, Michigan and Ohio – and one Medinah, in Illinois. I ruled out all of the northern towns in the hope that my grandfather was right about Caleb's southern roots, which left Tennessee and Texas. I tried Tennessee first, but no one in the Gibson County sheriff's office recalled a Caleb Kyle who might or might not have killed his mother on a farm sometime in the 1940s but, as a deputy told me helpfully, that didn't mean it didn't happen, it just meant that nobody around could *recall* it happening. I made a call to the state police, just on the off chance, but got the same reply: no Caleb Kyle.

It was approaching eight-thirty when I started calling Texas. Medina, it emerged, was in Bandera County, not Medina County, so my first call to the Medina County Sheriff didn't get me very far. But I hit lucky on the second call, real lucky, and I couldn't help wondering how my grandfather would have felt had he got this far and learned the truth about Caleb Kyle.

# Chapter Twenty Two

The sheriff's name was Dan Tannen, a deputy told me. I waited to be transferred to the sheriff's own office. After a couple of clicks on the line, a female voice said: 'Hello?'

'Sheriff Tannen?' I asked. It was a good guess.

'That's me,' she said. 'You don't sound surprised.'

'Should I be?'

'I've been mistaken for the secretary a couple of times. Pisses me off to hell, I tell you. The Dan is short for Danielle, for what it's worth. I hear you're asking about Caleb Kyle?'

'That's right,' I said. 'I'm a private investigator, working out of Portland, Maine. I'm—'

She interrupted me to ask: 'Where did you hear that name?'

'Caleb?'

'Uh-huh. Well, more particularly Caleb *Kyle*. Where'd you hear *that* name?'

That was a good question. Where should I begin? With Mrs Schneider? With Emily Watts? With my grandfather? With Ruth Dickinson and Lauren Trulock and the three other girls who ended up dangling from a tree by the banks of the Little Wilson?

'Mr Parker, I asked you a question.' I got the feeling

that Sheriff Tannen was likely to be holding on to her post for some time.

'I'm sorry,' I said. 'It's complicated. I heard it for the first time when I was a boy, from my grandfather, and now I've heard it twice in the last week.' And then I told her what I knew. She listened without making any comment, and when I had finished telling my story there was a long pause before she spoke.

'It was before my time,' she said, at last. 'Well, some of it was. The boy lived out in the Hill Country, maybe four miles south-east of here – him and his momma. He was born, best as I can recall without looking up a file, in nineteen twenty-eight or twenty-nine, but he was born Caleb Brewster. His pappa was a Lyall Brewster who went off to fight Hitler and ended up dying in North Africa and the two of them, Caleb and his mother, were left to fend for themselves. Plus, Lyall Brewster never got around to marrying Bonnie Kyle, Bonnie Kyle being his mother's name. You see, that was why I was interested in hearing you say *Caleb Kyle*. There aren't many people who'd know him by that name. Fact is, I ain't never heard him called by that name. He was always Caleb Brewster here, right up until the time he killed his mother.

'She was the devil's own bitch, according to those that knew her. Kept herself to herself, and the boy beside her. But the boy was smart, Mr Parker: at school, he raced ahead in math, reading, just about anything he put his mind to. Then his mother decided that she didn't like the fact that he was attracting attention to himself and took him out of school. Claimed she was teaching him herself.'

'You think there was abuse?'

'I think there were stories. I recall someone telling me that they once found him wandering naked on the road between here and Kerrville, covered in dirt and hog-shit. Police brought him home to his momma in a blanket. Boy couldn't have been more than fourteen or fifteen. They heard him yelpin' as soon as the door closed behind 'em. She sure took the stick to him, I reckon, but as for anything else . . .'

She paused again, and I heard her gulping liquid at the other end of the line. 'Water,' she said, ''case you're wondering.'

'I wasn't.'

'Well, whatever. Anyway, I don't know about sexual abuse. It came up at the trial, but it came up at the Menendez brothers' trial as well, and look where it got them. Like I said, Mr Parker, Caleb was smart. Even at sixteen, seventeen, he was smarter than most of the people in this town.'

'You think he made it up?'

She didn't answer for a time. 'I don't know, but he was smart enough to try to use it as mitigation. You have to remember, Mr Parker, that people didn't talk about it so much in those days. The fact of someone bringing it up was unusual. In the end, I guess we'll never know for certain what happened in that house.

'But there was more to Caleb Brewster than intelligence. People around here recall that he was mean, or worse than mean. He tortured animals, Mr Parker, and hung their remains from trees: squirrels, rabbits, even dogs. There was no evidence to tie him to it, you understand, but folks knew it was him. Maybe he got tired of killing animals, and decided to move up a step. There was other stuff too.'

'What do you mean?'

'Well, let's take this in the order it happened. We know

he killed his mother and fed her to the hogs. Two or three days after that incident on the road, Sheriff Garrett and another deputy came up to check on the boy. They found him sitting on the porch, drinking sour milk from a jug. There was blood in the kitchen: on the walls, on the floor. The floorboards were soaked with it. Boy still had the knife beside him. Bonnie Kyle's clothing was in the hog pen, along with some bones, which was pretty much all that the hogs had left. That, and her wedding ring. One of the hogs had passed it out in its stool. I think they got it in the Frontier Museum over in Banderas now, alongside two-headed lambs and Indian arrowheads.'

'What happened to Caleb?'

'He was tried as an adult, then sent down.'

'For life?'

'Twenty years. He got out in sixty-three or sixty-four, I think.'

'Was he rehabilitated?'

'*Rehabilitated*? Hell, no. I reckon he was off the scale before he ever killed her, and he never got back on it again. But someone saw fit to release him, taking into account the extenuating circumstances. He'd served his time and they couldn't keep him locked up forever, no matter how good an idea that might have been. And, like I said, he was smart. He kept his nose clean in prison. They thought he was getting better. Myself, I think he was waiting.'

'He came back to the hill country?' I asked.

Again, there came that pause. This time, it remained unbroken for what seemed like a long time.

'The house was still standing,' began Tannen. 'I remember him coming back into town on the Greyhound – I was maybe ten or eleven – and Caleb walking out towards the old house, and folks stepping onto the other side of the street and then watching him as he passed. I don't know how long he spent there. Couldn't have been more than a couple of nights, but . . .'

'But?'

She sighed. 'A girl died. Lillian Boyce. They reckon she was the prettiest girl in the county, and they were probably right. They found her down by the Hondo Creek, near Tarpley. She'd been cut up pretty bad. That wasn't the worst of it, though.'

I waited, and it seemed to me that I knew what was coming, even before she said it.

'She was hung from a tree,' she said. 'Like someone wanted her to be found. Like she was a warning to us all.'

The line seemed to hum, and the cell phone was hot in my hand, as Sheriff Tannen concluded her story. 'When we found her, Caleb Brewster had gone again. There's still a warrant outstanding, far as I know, but I didn't think anyone would ever get to serve it.

'At least, I didn't until now.'

After I hung up, I sat on my bed for a time. There was a deck of playing cards on a bookshelf in the room and I found myself shuffling the deck, the edges of the cards blurring before my eyes. I saw the queen of hearts and drew her from the deck. 'Hanky-poo', that was what Saul Mann used to call 'Find The Queen'. He would stand at his felt-covered trestle-table, seemingly talking to himself as he arranged the cards before him, flipping one card over with the rim of another. 'Five gets you ten, ten gets you twenty.' He didn't even seem to notice the punters slowly gathering, attracted by the sure movement of his hands and the promise of easy money, but he was always watching. He watched and he waited, and slowly, surely, they came to him. The old man was like a hunter who knows that, at some point, the deer must surely cross his path.

And I thought too of Caleb Kyle, staring at the remains of the girls he had torn apart and hung from trees. A memory came to me, a recollection of a legend told of the Emperor Nero. It was said that after Nero killed his own mother, Agrippina the Younger, he ordered that her body be opened, so that he could see the place from which he had come. What motivated this action is unclear: morbid obsession, perhaps, or even the incestuous feelings that the ancient chroniclers ascribed to him. It may even have been the case that he hoped to understand something of himself, of his own nature, by revealing to himself the site of his own origin. He must have loved her once, I thought, before it all turned to fury and rage and hate, before he found it in himself to take her life and rend her remains to pieces. For a brief moment, I felt a kind of pity for Caleb: a sorrow for the boy he once was, and a hatred for the man that he became.

I saw shadows falling from trees, and a figure moving north, ever north, like the needle on a compass. Of course he would have headed north. North was as far away from Texas as he could get after avenging himself on the community that had seen fit to jail him for what he had done to his mother.

But there was more to it than that, it seemed. When my grandfather was a boy, he told me that the priest would read the gospels at the north side of the church because north had always been perceived as an area that had not yet seen God's light. It was the same reason why they buried the unbaptised, the suicides and the murderers on northern ground, outside the boundaries of the church walls.

Because north was black territory.

North was the darklands.

The next morning, the bookstore was crowded with students and tourists. I ordered coffee and read a copy of *Rolling Stone*, which someone had left on a chair until Rachel arrived, late as usual. She still wore her black coat, this time with blue denims and a sky-blue V-neck sweater. Beneath it, her blue-and-white-striped Oxford shirt was buttoned to the neck. Her hair hung loose on her shoulders.

'Are you ever early?' I asked, as I ordered her a coffee and a muffin.

'I was up until five a.m. working on your damned file,' she replied. 'If I was charging you for my time, you couldn't afford me.'

'Sorry,' I said. 'I can barely afford the coffee and muffin.'

'You're breaking my heart,' she said, but it seemed that her attitude had softened a little since the day before, although it could have been wishful thinking on my part.

'You ready for this?' she asked.

I nodded, but before she went on I told her what I had learned from the sheriff in Medina and how Caleb had taken his mother's name to escape his past.

She nodded to herself. 'It fits,' she said. 'It all fits.'

The coffee arrived and she added sugar, then unwrapped the muffin, tore it into bite-sized pieces and began to talk.

'Most of this is guesswork and supposition. Any decent law enforcement officer would laugh me out of the building, but since you're neither decent nor a law enforcement officer, you'll take what you can get. Plus, everything you've given me is also based on guesswork and supposition, with a little superstition and paranoia thrown in.' She shook her head in bemusement, then grew serious as she opened her wire-bound notebook. Line upon line of closely-written text lay before her, dotted here and there with yellow Post-its. 'Most of what I'm going to tell you, I think you know already. All I can do is to clarify it for you, maybe put it into some kind of order.

'Bird, if this man does exist – at least, if the same man, Caleb Kyle, is responsible for all of these killings – then you're dealing with a textbook psychopathic sadist. Actually, you're dealing with worse than that, because I've never encountered anything like this in the literature, or in clinical work; at least, not all in one package. By the way, this file doesn't record any killing after 1965. Even allowing for the newspaper photograph, have you taken into account the possibility that he might be dead, or maybe imprisoned again for other crimes? Either could explain the sudden cessation of killing.'

'He could be dead,' I admitted, 'in which case this is all a waste of time and we're dealing with something else entirely. But let's assume that he wasn't imprisoned: if the sheriff was right, and Caleb was as smart as she believed, then he wasn't going back to prison again. Plus my grandfather checked at the time – it's in the file – and I know that he consulted on a random basis in the intervening years, although he would have been looking for Caleb Kyle, not Caleb Brewster.'

She shrugged. 'Then you have two further possibilities:

either he continued to kill, but his victims are all listed as missing persons if they've been missed at all or . . .'

'Or?'

Rachel tapped the top of her pen on her notebook, beside a word encircled in a red ring. 'Or else he's been dormant. The possibility that some serial killers enter periods of dormancy is one that's being considered by the FBI's Investigative Support Unit, the folks in the Criminal Profiling and Consultation Program. You know this, because I've told you about it before. It's a theory, but it might explain why some killings just cease without anyone ever being apprehended. For some reason, the killer reaches a point where the need to find a victim isn't so strong, and the killings stop.'

'If he's been dormant until now, then something just woke him up,' I said. I thought of the timber company surveyor, heading into the wilderness to pave the way for the forest's destruction, and what he might have encountered in the forest. I recalled too Mrs Schneider's story, followed up by a piece in the newspaper, and Willeford's old-style investigation, where you knocked on doors and pinned up notices and put the word around until it filtered down to the person you were trying to reach; and the newspaper story about Billy Purdue's arrest at St Martha's. If you put out honey, you shouldn't be surprised when the wasps come.

'It's tenuous, but those are the possibilities you have to consider,' Rachel continued. 'Let's look at the original killings. First, although it may only be a minor point, the location where the bodies were found was important. This Caleb Kyle determined how soon they would be found, where they would be found and by whom. It was his way of controlling and participating in the search. The original killings may have been disorganised – we'll never know for sure, since we don't know where they were killed – but the display of the bodies was very organised. He wanted to be part of some element of the discovery. My guess is that he was watching your grandfather right up to the moment when he found the women.

'As for the killings themselves, then if what the Schneider woman told you is true, which depends in turn on the truth of what Emily Watts told her, Kyle was already killing during their relationship. The extent of decay on each of the five bodies differed: Judy Giffen and Ruth Dickinson were killed first, with a gap of almost one month between them. But Laurel Trulock, Louise Moore and Sarah Raines were killed in rapid succession: the ME's report indicated that Trulock and Moore could have been killed in the same twenty-four-hour period, with Raines killed no more than twenty-four hours later again.

'My guess is that each of these girls – or certainly the last three – were physically similar to Emily Watts. They were slim, delicate girls: more passive than Emily, maybe, who was strong when the need arose, but still of a type. You encountered revenge rapes when you were a policeman, didn't you?'

I nodded. I knew what they were.

'A man argues with his wife, or his girlfriend, storms out of the house and takes out his anger on a complete stranger,' continued Rachel. 'In his mind, all women bear collective responsibility for the perceived faults of one woman, and therefore any woman can be disciplined and punished for the real or imagined slight or insult or overstepping of whatever boundaries the rapist has established in his mind as acceptable behaviour for a woman.

'Well, Caleb Kyle is like those men, but this time it went much further. The ME found no evidence of actual sexual assault on the three later victims, but — and here we're into classic morbid fear of female sexuality territory — there was some damage to the sexual organs, presumably inflicted by the same instrument that was used to make stab wounds to the belly and to destroy the womb of each victim. In fact, what's interesting is that, in the cases of Giffen and Dickinson, he stabbed them *after* they had been dead for almost one month, probably after he killed the other three girls, or shortly before.'

'He went back to them after he thought she had lost the baby.'

'*Exactly*. He was punishing them because Emily Watts's body had betrayed him by losing his child: many women being punished for the faults of one. My guess would be that he had punished other women before, perhaps for different reasons.'

She fed herself a piece of muffin and sipped her coffee. 'Now, when we go back to the ME's report, we find evidence that each of the girls was tortured before death. There were fingernails missing, toes and fingers broken, teeth removed, cigarette burns, bruising inflicted by a coat hanger. That might be significant, but not for now. In the case of the last three victims, the torture inflicted is significantly more extreme. These girls suffered a lot before they died, Bird.' Rachel looked at me solemnly, and I could see the pain in her eyes: pain for them and the memory of her own pain.

'According to the victim profiles collated by your grandfather, these young women were gentle, from good homes. Most of them were shy, sexually inexperienced. Judy Giffen appeared to have had some sexual experience.

My guess is they probably pleaded with him before they died, thinking they could save themselves. But that was what he wanted: he wanted them to cry and to scream. There may be a connection there between aggression and fulfilment: he experienced a sexual excitement from their pleas, but he also hated them for pleading, and so they died.'

Her eyes were bright now, her excitement at trying to worm her way into this man's consciousness obvious in the movement of her hands, the speed with which she spoke, her intellectual pleasure in making startling, unexpected connections, yet balanced by her abhorrence of the acts she was discussing. 'God,' said Rachel, 'I can almost see his PET scan: temporal lobe abnormalities associated with sexual deviancy; distortion in the frontal lobe leading to violent activity; low activity between the limbic system and the frontal lobes, leading to a virtual absence of guilt or conscience.' She shook her head, as if she was marvelling at the behaviour of a particularly nasty bug. 'He's not asocial, though. These girls may have been shy, but they weren't stupid. He would have to be skilled enough to gain their trust, so the intelligence fits.

'As for Kyle's social background, if what he told Emily Watts is true, he was abused physically and possibly sexually in childhood by a mother figure who told him that she loved him during or after the abuse, and then punished him afterwards. He had little nurture or protection and was probably taught self-sufficiency the hard way. When he was old enough, he turned on his abuser and killed her, before moving on to others. With Emily Watts, something different happened. She was herself a victim of abuse, then she became pregnant. My guess is that he would have killed her anyway, as soon as she had the child. From what she said, he wanted the child.'

She took a sip of coffee and I used it as an opportunity to interrupt.

'What about Rita Ferris and Cheryl Lansing? Could he have been responsible for their deaths?'

'It's possible,' said Rachel. She regarded me quietly, waiting for me to find a connection.

'I'm missing something,' I said at last. 'That's why you look like the cat that got the cream.'

'You're forgetting the mutilation of the mouths. The damage inflicted on the wombs of those girls in 1965 was meant to convey a message. The mutilations were a signifier. We've seen damage to victims used in that way before, Bird.' The smile went away, and I nodded: the Travelling Man.

'So, once again, three decades later, we have mutilations, in this case directed to the mouths of victims and in each case meant to signify something different. Rita Ferris's mouth was sewn shut. What does that mean?'

'That she should have kept her mouth shut?'

'Probably,' said Rachel. 'It's not subtle, but whoever killed her wasn't interested in subtlety.'

I considered what Rachel had said for a moment before I figured out what it might mean. 'She called the cops on Billy Purdue and they took him away.' That could have meant that he had been watching the house the night Billy was arrested, making him the old man whom Billy claimed to have seen before Rita and Donald were killed, maybe even the same old man who had attacked Rita at the hotel.

'In Cheryl Lansing's case,' continued Rachel, 'her jaw was broken and her tongue torn out. I'm pushing the envelope a little here, but my guess is that she was being punished for *not* speaking.'

'Because she was party to the concealment of the child's birth.'

'That would seem to be a plausible explanation. In the end, regardless of what made Caleb Kyle this way, and regardless of signifiers and whatever grievances he may feel, he's a killing machine, completely without remorse.'

'But he felt something for the loss of his child.'

Rachel almost leapt from her chair. '*Yes!*' She beamed at me the way a teacher might beam at a particularly bright pupil. 'The problem, or the key, is the sixth girl, the one who was never found. For a whole lot of reasons, most of which would probably result in me being ostracised by my peers if I stated them in print, I think your grandfather was right when he suspected that she was also a victim, but he was wrong in the *type* of victim.'

'I don't understand.'

'Your grandfather assumed that she had also been killed but had not been displayed for some reason.'

'And you don't.' But I could see where she was going, and my stomach tightened at the possibility. It had been at the back of my mind for some time and, maybe, at the back of my grandfather's. I think he hoped that she was dead, because the other option was worse.

'No, I don't assume she was killed, and it comes back to the torture inflicted on those girls. This wasn't simply a means of gaining satisfaction and fulfilment for this man: it was a test. He was testing their strength, knowing at the same time, but perhaps not admitting it to himself, that they would fail his test because they simply weren't strong enough.

'But look at the profile of Judith Mundy. She's strong,

well built, a dominant personality. She didn't cry easily, could handle herself in a fight. She would pass that kind of test, to the extent that he probably didn't have to hurt her very much to realise that she was different.'

Rachel leaned forwards and the expression on her face changed to one of deep abiding sorrow. 'She wasn't taken because she was weak, Bird. She was taken because she was strong.'

I closed my eyes. I knew now what had happened to Judith Mundy, why she had not been found, and Rachel knew that I had understood.

'She was taken as breeding stock, Bird,' she said quietly. 'He took her to breed on.'

Rachel offered to drive me to Logan, but I declined. She had done enough for me, more even than I felt I had a right to ask. As I walked alongside her across Harvard Square, I felt a love for her made all the more intense by the fact that I believed she was slipping further and further away from me.

'You think this man Caleb may be connected to the disappearance of Ellen Cole?' she asked. Her arm brushed against mine and, for the first time since I had come to Boston, she did not pull away from the contact.

'I don't know for sure,' I replied. 'Maybe the police are right: maybe her hormones got to her and she did run away, in which case I'm not sure what I'm doing. But an old man found her and drew her to Dark Hollow and, like I keep telling people, I don't believe in coincidences.

'I have a feeling about this man, Rachel. He's come back, and I think he's returned for Billy Purdue and to avenge himself on everyone who helped to hide him. I think he killed Rita Ferris and her son. It may have been out of jealousy, or to cut Billy off so that he'd have no other ties, or because she was going to leave him and take the boy with her. I don't think the boy was meant to die. It just got out of control.'

I put out my hand when we reached the square. I didn't kiss her because I didn't feel that I had the right. She took my hand and held it tightly.

'Bird, this man feels he has some dispensation to avenge himself on anyone who crosses him because he believes that he's been wronged. I've just labelled him as psychopathic.' In her eyes, there was concern, and more.

'In other words, what's my excuse?' I smiled, but it went no deeper than my mouth.

'They're gone, Bird. Susan and Jennifer are dead, and what happened to them and to you was a terrible, terrible thing. But every time you make someone pay for what was done to you, you hurt yourself and you risk becoming the thing you hate. Do you understand, Bird?'

'It's not about me, Rachel,' I replied softly. 'At least, not entirely. Someone has to stop these people. Someone has to take responsibility.' There was that echo again: *they are all your responsibility*.

Her hand moved gently over mine, her fingers on my fingers, her thumb rubbing lightly on my palm, then she touched my face with her free hand. 'Why did you come here? Most of what I told you, you could have figured out for yourself.'

'I'm not that smart.'

'Don't bullshit a bullshitter.'

'So it's true what they say about psychologists.'

'Only the New Age ones. You're avoiding the question.'

'I know. You're right: some of it I had guessed, or half-guessed, but I needed to hear it back from someone else, otherwise I was afraid that I was going crazy. But I'm also here because I still care about you, because when you walked away you took something from me. I thought that this might be a way of getting closer to you. I wanted to see you again. Maybe, deep down, that's all it was.' I looked away from her.

Her grip tightened on my hand. 'I saw what you did, back in Louisiana. You didn't go there to find the Travelling Man. You went there to kill him, and anyone who stood in your way got hurt, and got hurt badly. Your capacity for inflicting violence scared me. You scared me.'

'I didn't know what else to do, not then.'

'And now?'

I was about to answer when her finger touched the scar on my cheek, the mark left by Billy Purdue's blade. 'How did this happen?' she asked.

'A man stuck a knife blade in me.'

'And what did you do?'

I paused before answering. 'I walked away.'

'Who was he?'

'Billy Purdue.'

Her eyes widened, and it was as if something that had been curled inside her to protect itself gradually began to unfurl. I could see it in her, could feel it in her touch.

'He never had a chance, Rachel. The odds were stacked against him from the start.'

'If I ask you a question, will you answer me honestly?' she said.

'I've always tried to be honest with you,' I replied.

She nodded. 'I know, but this is important. I need to be sure of this.'

'Ask.'

'Do you need the violence, Bird?'

I thought about the question. In the past, I had been motivated by personal revenge. I had hurt people, had killed people, because of what had been done to Susan, and to Jennifer, and to me. Now that desire for revenge had dwindled, easing a little every day, and the spaces it left as it receded were filled with the potential for reparation. I bore some responsibility for what happened to Susan and Jennifer. I didn't think that I would ever come to terms with that knowledge, but I could try to make up for it in some small way, to acknowledge my failings in the past by using them to make the present better.

'I did, for a time,' I admitted.

'And now?'

'I don't need it, but I will use it if I have to. I won't stand by and watch innocent people being hurt.'

Rachel leaned over and kissed me gently on the cheek. Her eyes were soft when she pulled away.

'So you're the avenging angel,' she said.

'Something like that,' I replied.

'Good-bye, then, avenging angel,' Rachel whispered softly.

She turned and walked away, back to the library and her work. She didn't look back, but her head was down and I could feel the weight of her thoughts as she surrendered herself to the embrace of the crowd.

The plane rose from Logan, heading upward and north through the cold air, heavy cloud surrounding it like the breath of God. I thought of Sheriff Tannen, who had promised to hunt up the most recent pictures available of

Caleb Kyle. They would be thirty years old, but at least they would be something. I took the blurred newspaper photo of Caleb from my grandfather's folder and looked at it again and again. He was like a skeleton slowly being fleshed out, as if the process of decay were being gradually, irrevocably reversed. A figure that had been little more than a name, a shape glimpsed in the shadows, was assuming an objective reality.

I know you, I thought. I *know* you.

# Chapter Twenty Three

I arrived in Bangor early that afternoon, picked up my car in the airport parking lot and started back for Dark Hollow. I felt like I was being pulled in ten different directions, yet somehow each one seemed to lead me back to the same place, to the same conclusion by different routes: Caleb Kyle had come back. He had killed a girl in Texas shortly after his release from prison, probably as an act of revenge against a whole community. Then he had assumed his mother's name and headed north, far north, eventually losing himself in the wilderness.

If Emily Watts had told the truth to Mrs Schneider, and there was no reason to doubt her, then she had given birth to a child and hidden it because she believed its father to be a killer of young women, and sensed that this man wanted the child for his own purposes. The leap required was to accept that this child might be Billy Purdue, and that his father could be Caleb Kyle.

Meanwhile, Ellen Cole and her boyfriend were still missing, as was Willeford. Tony Celli had gone to ground, but was undoubtedly still searching for some trace of Billy. He had no choice: if he did not find Billy, he would be unable to replace the money he had lost and he would be killed as an example to others. I had a suspicion that it was already too late for Tony Clean, that it had been too late from the very moment that he had purchased the securities, maybe even from the time when the thought of using someone else's money to secure his future first crossed his mind. Tony would do whatever he had to do to track Billy down, but everything he did, all of the violence he inflicted and all of the attention it drew to himself and his masters, made it less and less likely that he would be allowed to live. He was like a man who, trapped in the darkness of a tunnel, focuses his mind on the only illumination he sees before him, unaware that what he believes to be the light of salvation is, in reality, the fire that will consume him.

There were other reasons, too, to be fearful. Somewhere in the darkness, Stritch waited. I imagined that he still wanted the money but, more than that, he wanted revenge for the death of his partner. I thought of the dead man in the Portland complex, violated in his last moments by Stritch's foulness, and I thought too of the fear that I had felt, the certainty that I could have allowed death to enfold me in those shadows if I had chosen to do so.

There remained also the old man in the forest. There was still the chance that he knew something more than he had told me, that his remark about the two young people was based on more than gossip he had overheard in the town. For that reason, there was one stop to be made before I returned to Dark Hollow.

At Orono, the store was still open. On the sign above the door, the words 'Stuckey Trading' were illuminated from below, the name written in script. Inside, it smelt musty and felt oppressively warm, the AC making a noise as if glass were grinding in its works as it pumped stale air through its vents. Some guys in biker jackets were examining second-hand shotguns while a woman in a dress that was new when Woodstock convened flicked through a box of eight-tracks. Display cases held old watches and gold chains, while hunting bows stood upright on a rack beside the counter.

I wasn't sure what I was looking for, so I browsed from shelf to shelf, from old furniture to almost-new car-seat covers, until something caught my eye. In one corner, beside a rack of foul-weather clothing – old slickers mainly, and some faded yellow oilskins – stood two rows of shoes and boots. Most of them were ragged and worn, but the Zamberlains stood out immediately. They were men's boots, relatively new and considerably more expensive than the pairs surrounding them, and some care had obviously been lavished on them recently. Someone, probably the store owner, had cleaned and waxed them before putting them out for sale. I lifted one and sniffed the interior. I smelt Lysol, and something else: earth, and rotting meat. I lifted the second boot and caught the same faint odour from it. Ricky had been wearing Zamberlains on the day they came to visit me, I recalled, and it wasn't often that boots so fine turned up in an out-of-the-way second-hand goods store. I brought the pair of boots to the counter.

The man behind the register was small with thick, dark artificial hair that seemed to have come from the head of a department store mannequin. Beneath the wig, at the back of his neck, wisps of his own mousy-coloured strands peered out like mad relatives consigned to the attic. A pair of round eyeglasses hung from a string around his neck and lost themselves in the hairs of his chest. His bright red shirt was half unbuttoned and I could see scarring on his upper body. His hands were thin and strong looking, with the little finger and ring finger of his left hand missing from just above the first joint. The nails on the fingers that remained were neatly clipped.

He caught me looking at his mutilated left hand and raised it in front of his face, the twin stumps of the lost fingers making his hand look as if he was trying to form a gun with it, the way little kids do in the school yard.

'Lost them in a sawmill,' he explained.

'Careless,' I replied.

He shrugged. 'Blade damn near took the rest of my fingers as well. You ever work in a sawmill?'

'No. I always thought my fingers looked good on my hands. I like them that way.'

He looked at the stumps thoughtfully. 'It's strange, but I can still feel them, y'know, like they're still there. Maybe you don't know how that feels.'

'I think I do,' I said. 'You Stuckey?'

'Yessir. This is my place.'

I put the boots down on the counter.

'They're good boots,' he said, picking up one with his unmutilated hand. 'Won't take less than sixty bucks for them. Just waxed them, buffed them and put them out for sale myself not two hours ago.'

'Smell them.'

Stuckey narrowed his eyes and put his head to one side. 'Say what?'

'I said, *Smell them.*'

He looked at me oddly for a few moments, then took one boot and sniffed the inside tentatively, his nostrils twitching like a rabbit's before the snare.

'I don't smell nothin',' he said.

'Lysol. You smell Lysol, don't you?'

'Well, sure. I always disinfect them before I sell them. Don't nobody want to wear boots that stink.'

I leaned forwards and raised the second boot in front of him. 'You see,' I said softly, 'that's my question. What did they smell of *before* you cleaned them?'

He wasn't a man who was easily intimidated. He thrust his body forward in turn, six knuckles on the counter, and arched an eyebrow at me. 'Are you some kind of nut?'

In a mirror behind the counter, I saw that the bikers had turned around to watch the show. I kept my voice low. 'These boots, they had earth on them when you bought them, didn't they? And they smelt of decay, human decay?'

He took a step back. 'Who are you?'

'Just a guy.'

'You was just a guy, you'd have bought the durned boots and been gone by now.'

'Who sold you the boots?'

He was becoming belligerent now. 'That's none of your goddamned business, mister. Now get out of my store.'

I didn't move. 'Listen, friend, you can talk to me, or you can talk to the cops, but you will talk, understand? I don't want to make trouble for you, but if I have to, I will.'

Stuckey stared at me, and he knew that I meant what I said. A voice interrupted before he could respond. 'Hey, Stuck,' said one of the bikers. 'You okay back there?'

He raised his battered left hand to indicate that there wasn't a problem, then returned his attention to me. There was no trace of bitterness when he spoke. Stuckey was a pragmatist – in his line of business, you had to be – and he knew when to back down.

'It was an old fella from up north,' he sighed. 'He comes in here maybe once a month, brings stuff that he's found. Most of it's junk, but I give him a few bucks for it and he goes away again. Sometimes, he brings in something good.'

'He bring these in recently?'

'Sure, pretty recent. Yesterday. Gave him thirty bucks for them. Brought in a backpack too, Lowe Alpine. I sold it straight off. That was about it. He didn't have nothin' else to offer.'

'This old guy from up Dark Hollow way?'

'Yeah, that's right, Dark Hollow.'

'You got a name?'

His eyes narrowed again. 'Just tell me, mister, what are you? Some kind of private cop?'

'Like I said, I'm just a guy.'

'You got a lot of questions for someone who's just a guy.' I could sense Stuckey digging his heels in again.

'I'm naturally curious,' I said, but I showed him my ID anyway. 'The name?'

'Barley. John Barley.'

'That his real name?'

'The hell do I know?'

'He show you any identification?'

Stuckey almost laughed. 'You seen him, you'd know he wasn't the kind of fella carries no ID.'

I nodded once, took out my wallet and counted six ten-dollar bills onto the counter. 'I'll need a receipt,' I said. Stuckey filled one out quickly in sloped capitals, stamped it, then paused before handing it to me.

'Like I told you, I don't want no trouble,' he said.

'If you've told me the truth, there won't be any.'

He folded the receipt once and put it in a plastic bag

with the boots. 'I hope you won't take this personal, mister, but I reckon you make friends 'bout as easy as a scorpion.'

I took the bag and put my wallet back in my coat. 'Why?' I asked. 'You sell friendship here too?'

'No, mister, I sure don't,' he said, and there was a finality in his tone. 'But I don't reckon you'd be buying any even if I did.'

# Chapter Twenty Four

It was already dark when I began the journey back to Dark Hollow. Snow was drifting across the road to Beaver Cove and beyond, where the narrow, winding, tree-lined road led to the Hollow. The snow seemed to glow in the headlights, small golden fragments of light tumbling down, as if heaven itself was disintegrating and falling to earth. I tried to call Angel and Louis on the cellphone, but it was a useless effort. As it turned out, they were already at the motel when I got back. Louis answered the door dressed in black pants with a razor sharp crease and a cream-coloured shirt. I could never figure out how Louis kept his clothes so neat. I had shirts that had more creases than Louis's while they were still in the box.

'Angel's in the shower,' he said, as I stepped past him into their room. On the television screen, Wolf Blitzer mouthed silently on the White House lawn.

'What's seldom is wonderful.'

'Amen to that. If it was summer, he'd be attracting flies.'

It wasn't true, of course. Angel may have looked like someone who was barely on nodding terms with soap and hot water, but he was, all things considered, remarkably clean. He just looked more crumpled than most people. In fact, he looked more crumpled than just about anyone I knew.

'Any movement over at the Payne place?'

'Nothing. The old man came out, went back in again. The boy came out, went back in again. After the fourth or fifth time, the novelty started to wear off. No sign of Billy Purdue, though, or anyone else.'

'You think they knew you were out there?'

'Maybe. Didn't act like it, which could go either way. You got anything?'

I showed him the boots and told him of my conversation with Stuckey. Angel came out of the shower at that moment, wrapped in four towels.

'Shit, Angel,' said Louis. 'The fuck are you, Mahatma Gandhi? What you use all the towels for?'

'It's cold,' he whined. 'And I got marks on my ass from that car seat.'

'You gonna get marks on your ass from the toe of my shoe, you don't get me some towels. You just dry your scrawny white ass and haul it down to the desk, ask the lady for more towels. And you better make damn sure they fluffy, Angel. I ain't rubbin' my back with no sandpaper.'

While Angel dried himself and dressed, muttering softly as he did so, I told them in detail about my encounters with Rachel, Sheriff Tannen and Erica Schneider, and what I had learned of Billy Purdue's visit to St Martha's.

'Seems like we accumulatin' a whole lot of information, but we don't know what it means,' remarked Louis, when I was done.

'We know what some of it means,' I said.

'You think this guy Caleb really exists?' he asked.

'He was real enough to kill his mother, and maybe another local girl the best part of two decades later. Plus, those girls who died in sixty-five weren't killed by a mentally handicapped man. The display of the bodies was a lot of things – a gesture of contempt, a means to shock – but it was also an attempt at an act of madness. I think it was designed to make people think that only a madman could have done it, and the planting of an item of clothing at Fletcher's house gave them the madman they were looking for.'

'So where did he go?'

I sat down heavily on one of the beds. 'I don't know,' I said, 'but I think he went north, into the wilderness.'

'And why didn't he kill again?' added Angel.

'I don't know that either. Maybe he did, and we just never found them.' I knew that hikers had been murdered on the Appalachian Trail, and I'd heard that others had gone missing and never been found. I wondered if, somehow, they might have left the trail, hoping for a shortcut, and encountered something much worse than they could ever have imagined.

'Or it could be he was killing before he ever arrived in Maine, but nobody ever traced the deaths back to him,' I continued. 'Rachel thought that he might have entered a period of dormancy, but recent events may have conspired to change that.'

Angel took one of the Zamberlains and held it in his hands. 'Well, we know what this means, assuming these once belonged to Ellen Cole's boyfriend.' He looked at me, and there was a sadness in his eyes. I didn't want to answer him, or to acknowledge the possibility that if Ricky was dead, then Ellen could be dead too.

'Any sign of Stritch?' I asked.

Louis bristled. 'I can almost smell him,' he said. 'The woman at the desk is still pretty cut up about her cat, no pun intended. Cops are blaming it on kids.'

'What now?' said Angel.

'I go see John Barley,' I replied, but Louis shook his head.

'That's a bad idea, Bird,' he said. 'It's dark, and he knows the woods better than you do. You could lose him, and then any way of finding out how he came by these boots. Plus, there's his damn dog: it'll warn the old man, and then he'll start shooting, and could be you'll have to shoot back. He's no good to us dead.'

He was right, of course, but it didn't make me feel any better. 'First light, then,' I said, but reluctantly. Unspoken between us was the possibility that I had already encountered Caleb Kyle, and had turned away from him because he had threatened me with a gun.

'First light,' Louis agreed.

I left them and went back to my own room, where I dialled Walter and Lee Cole's house in Queen's. Lee picked up on the third ring, and in her voice was that mixture of hope and fear that I had heard in the voice of hundreds of parents, friends and relatives, all waiting for word of a missing person.

'Lee, it's Bird.'

She said nothing for a moment but I could hear her footsteps, as if she was moving the phone out of earshot of someone. I guessed it was Lauren. 'Bird? Have you found her?'

'No. We're in Dark Hollow, and we're looking, but there's nothing yet.' I didn't tell her about Ricky's boots. If I was wrong about what might have happened to him, or mistaken about the ownership of the boots, it would only be worrying her unnecessarily. If I was right, then we would know the rest soon enough.

'Have you seen Walter?'

I told her I hadn't. I figured he was probably in Greenville by now, but I didn't want to see him. He would only complicate matters, and I was finding it hard enough to keep my emotions in check as it was.

'Bird, he was so angry when he found out what I'd done.' Lee started to cry, her voice breaking as she spoke. 'He said that people get hurt when you get involved. They get killed. Please, Bird, please don't let anything happen to her. Please.'

'I won't, Lee. I'll be in touch. Goodbye.'

I hung up and ran my hands over my face and through my hair, letting them come to rest eventually at the knots in my shoulders. Walter was right. People had been hurt in the past when I became involved in situations, but they got hurt mainly because those people also chose to involve themselves. Sometimes you can push folks one way or the other, but they take the most important steps on their own initiative.

Walter had principles, but he had never been put in a position where those principles might have to be compromised to safeguard those he loved, or to avenge them when they were taken from him. And now he was close to Dark Hollow, and a situation that was already difficult and complicated was likely to get worse. I sat with my face in my hands for a time, then undressed and showered, my head down and my shoulders exposed to allow the water to work like fingers on my tired, tense muscles.

The phone rang as I was drying myself. It was Angel. They were waiting for me so that we could head off and eat together. I wasn't hungry, and my concerns for Ellen were muddling my thought processes, but I agreed to join them. When we arrived at the diner, there was a sign on the door announcing that it had closed early. There was some kind of charity event in the Roadside Bar that night to raise funds for the high school band and everyone and anyone was going to be in attendance. Angel and Louis exchanged a look of profound unhappiness.

'We got to help the band if we want to eat?' asked Louis. 'What kind of peckerwood town is this? Who we got to pay off if we want to buy a beer? The PTA?' He examined the sign a little more closely. 'Hey, a country band: "Larry Fulcher and the Gamblers". Maybe this town ain't such a dump after all.'

'Lord, no,' said Angel, 'not more shit-kicker music. Why can't you listen to soul music like anyone else of your particular ethnic persuasion? You know, Curtis Mayfield, maybe a little Wilson Pickett. They're your people, man, not the Louvin Brothers and Kathy Mattea. Besides, not so long ago people used that country shit as background music when they were hanging your people.'

'Angel,' said Louis patiently, 'nobody ever hung no brother to a Johnny Cash record.'

There was nothing for it but to head down to the Roadside. We went back to the motel and I got my car keys. When I came out of my room, Louis had added a black cowboy hat with a band of silver suns to his ensemble. Angel put his hands on his head and swore loudly.

'You got the rest of the Village People in there too?' I asked. I couldn't help but smile. 'You know, you and Charley Pride are ploughing a pretty lonely furrow with that black country and western act. The brothers see you dressed like that and they may have words to say.'

'Brothers helped to build this great country, and that "shit-kicker music", as our resident cultural theorist put it, was the sound-track to generations of workers. Wasn't all Negro spirituals and Paul Robeson, y'know. Plus, I like this hat.' He gave the brim a little flick with his fingers.

'I was kind of hoping you two could maintain a low profile while we were here, unless it's absolutely necessary that you do otherwise,' I said, as we got into the Mustang.

Louis sighed loudly. 'Bird, I'm the only brother from here to Toronto. 'Less I contract vitiligo between this motel and the high-school band scam, ain't no way that I can be low profile. So shut up and drive.'

'Yeah, Bird, drive,' said Angel from the backseat, "else Cleavon Little here will get his posse on your ass. The Cowpokes with Attitude, maybe, or Prairie Enemy . . .'

'Angel,' came the voice from the passenger seat. '*Shut up*.'


The Roadside was a big old place done in dark wood. It was long, windowed and single storeyed at the front with a gabled entrance in the centre which rose up above the rest like the steeple of a church. There were plenty of cars parked in the lot, with more around the sides stacked up almost to the treeline. The Roadside was at the western edge of town; beyond it was dark forest.

We paid our five-dollar cover charge at the door – 'Five dollars!' hissed Angel. 'This a mob place?' – and made our way into the bar itself. It was a long cavernous room, almost as dark inside as it was outside. Dim lights hung on the walls and the bar was lit sufficiently so that drinkers could see the labels on the bottles, but not the sell-by date. The Roadside was a lot bigger than it looked from the outside and the light died just beyond the limits of the bar and the center of the dance floor. It stretched maybe three hundred feet from the door to the stage at the far end, with the bar on a raised platform at the centre. Tables radiated from it into the dimness at the walls, which were lined in turn by booths. At the edges, the Roadside was so dark that only pale-moon faces were visible, and then only when their owners stepped into a pool of light. Otherwise, they were only vague shapes moving against the walls, like wraiths.

'It's a Stevie Wonder bar,' said Angel. 'The menu's probably in braille.'

'It's pretty dark,' I agreed. 'Drop a quarter here, it'll be worth ten cents by the time you find it.'

'Yeah, like Reaganomics in miniature,' said Angel.

'Don't say nothing bad about Reagan,' warned Louis. 'I have good memories of Ron.'

'Which is probably more than Ron has,' smirked Angel.

Louis led the way to a booth over by the right-hand wall, close to one of the emergency doors that stood halfway down each of the Roadside's walls. There was probably at least one other door at the back, behind the stage. At present, that stage was occupied by what seemed to be Larry Fulcher and the Gamblers. Louis was already tapping his feet and nodding his head in time to the music.

In fact, Larry Fulcher and his band were pretty good. There were six of them, Fulcher leading on the mandolin, guitar and banjo. They played 'Bonaparte's Retreat' and a couple of Bob Wills songs, 'Get With It' and 'Texas Playboy Rag'. They moved on to the Carter Family with

'Wabash Cannonball' and 'Worried Man Blues', 'You're Learning' by the Louvin Brothers and then did a neat version of 'One Piece at a Time' by Johnny Cash. It was an eclectic selection, but they played well and with obvious enthusiasm. Even Louis was impressed; the last time I saw him looking that impressed was when Angel opened fire on Joe Bones's lawn back in New Orleans without hitting either of us while he was doing it.

We ordered burgers and fries. They came in red plastic baskets with a liner on the bottom to hold in the grease. I felt my arteries hardening as soon as I smelled the food. Angel and Louis drank some Pete's Wicked. I had bottled water.

The band took a break and people flooded towards the bar and the bathrooms. I sipped some water and scanned the crowd. There was no sign of Rand Jennings, or his wife, which was probably a good thing.

'We should be out at Meade Payne's place now,' said Louis. 'Billy Purdue arrives, he ain't gonna do it in a parade float in daylight.'

'If you were out there now, you'd be freezing and you wouldn't be able to see a thing,' I said. 'We do what we can.' I felt like the whole situation was slipping away from me. Maybe it had always been slipping away, right from the time I took five hundred dollars from Billy Purdue without ever questioning where he might have found it. I still felt certain that Billy would make his way to Dark Hollow, sooner or later. Without Meade Payne's cooperation there was always the chance that he could slip past us, but my guess was that Billy would hole up with Meade for a time, maybe even try to make for Canada with his help. Billy's arrival would disturb the routine out at the Payne place, and I had faith in the ability of Angel and Louis to spot any such disturbance.

But Billy was still a comparatively minor concern next to Ellen Cole, although, in some way that I hadn't yet figured out, there had to be a connection between them. An old man had guided them up here, perhaps the same old man who had shadowed Rita Ferris in the days before her death, maybe even the same old man who had once been known as Caleb Brewster by the people of a small Texan town. Dark Hollow was just too small a place for those kinds of unconnected occurrences to take place.

As if on cue, a woman pushed her way through the throng at the bar and ordered a drink. It was Lorna Jennings, her bright red sweater like a beacon in the crowd. Beside her stood two other women, a slim brunette in a green shirt and an older woman with black hair, wearing a white cotton top decorated with pink roses. It seemed to be a girls' night out. Lorna didn't see me, or didn't want to see me.

There was a burst of applause and Larry Fulcher and his band came back onstage. They burst into 'Blue Moon of Kentucky' and the dance-floor instantly became a mass of movement, couples swinging each other across the floor, smiles on their faces, the women spinning on their toes, the men twisting them expertly. There was laughter in the air. Groups of friends and neighbours stood talking, beers in hand, enjoying a night of community and kin-ship. Above the bar, a banner thanked everyone for supporting the Dark Hollow High School Band. In the shadows, younger couples kissed discreetly while their parents practised foreplay on the dance floor. The music seemed to grow in volume; the crowd began to move faster; the sound of glass breaking came from the bar, accompanied by a burst of embarrassed laughter. Lorna stood beside a pillar, the two women on either side silent now as they listened to the music. In the shadows at the walls, figures moved, some barely more than indistinct shapes: couples talking, young people joshing, a community relaxing. Here and there, I heard talk of the discovery of Gary Chute's body but it wasn't personal and it didn't interfere with the night's festivities. I watched a man and woman seated at the bar across from Lorna as they kissed hard, their tongues visible where their mouths met, the woman's hand snaking down her partner's side, down, down . . .

Down to where a child stood before them, lit by a circle of light that seemed to come from nowhere but within himself. While couples moved close by, and groups of men walked through the crowds carrying trays of beer, the child still held a space to itself and no one came close or broke the shell of light surrounding him. It lit his blonde hair, brought up the colour of his purple rompers, made the nails of his tiny hands shine as he raised his left hand and pointed into the shadows.

'Donnie?' I heard myself whisper.

And from the darkness at the far side of the bar, a white shape appeared. Stritch's mouth was open in a smile, the thick, soft lips splitting his face from side to side, and his bald head gleamed in the dim light. He turned in the direction of Lorna Jennings, looked back at me, and drew his right index finger across his neck as he moved through the crowd towards her.

'Stritch,' I hissed, springing from my seat. Louis scanned the crowd, already rising, his hand reaching for his SIG.

'I don't see him. You sure?'

'He's on the other side of the bar. He's after Lorna.'

Louis went right, his hand inside his black jacket, his

fingers on his gun. I moved left, but the crowd was thick and unyielding. I pushed my way through, people stepping back and yelling as their beer spilled. ('Buddy, hey buddy, where's the fire?') I tried to keep Lorna's red sweater in view, but I lost it as people passed into my line of vision. To my right, I could just make out Louis moving through the couples at the edge of the dance floor, his progress attracting curious glances. To my left, Angel was making his way around the bar in a wide arc.

As I neared the counter, the men and women were packed tightly, calling for drinks, waving money, laughing, caressing. I pushed through, spilling a tray of drinks and sending a thin, acned young man tumbling to his knees. Hands reached for me and angry voices were raised, but I ignored them. A barman, a fat, dark-skinned man with a thick beard, raised a hand as I climbed onto the bar, my feet slipping on the wet floor.

'Hey, get down from there,' he called, then stopped as he saw the Smith & Wesson in my hand. He backed off, making for a phone by the register.

Now I could see Lorna clearly. Her head turned as I rose above her, other heads turning too, their eyes wide. I spun to see Louis fighting his way through the pack at the bar, scanning the crowd, trying to catch a glimpse of that white, domed head.

I saw him first. He was maybe twenty people back from Lorna, still moving in her direction. Once or twice people looked his way, but they were distracted by the sight of me on the bar, the gun hanging from my right hand. Stritch smiled at me again, and something flashed in his hand: a short, curved blade, its point wickedly sharp. I made a jump from the bar to the central section where the cash register and bottles stood, then a second jump, which put me almost beside Lorna, glasses flying from my feet and shattering on the floor. People moved away from me and I heard screaming. I stepped from the bar and pushed my way to her.

'Move back,' I said. 'You're in danger here.'

She was almost smiling, her brow furrowed, until she saw the gun in my hand. 'What? What do you mean?'

I looked past her to where I had last seen Stritch, but he was receding from sight, losing himself once again in the crowd. Then a head appeared as Louis stood on a table, trying to keep low enough to avoid making himself a target for a shot. He turned to me and gestured to the centre exit. On the stage, the band kept playing, but I could see them exchanging worried looks.

To my left, burly men in T-shirts were moving towards us. I grabbed Lorna by the shoulders. 'Take your friends and stay close to the bar. I mean it. I'll explain later.' She nodded once, the smile no longer on her face. I think I knew why. I think she had caught a glimpse of Stritch and had seen in his eyes what he had intended to do to her.

Using my shoulders, I started to make my way to the centre exit. A small flight of steps led up to it and I could see a waitress at the door, a pretty girl with long, dark hair, frowning uncertainly as she watched what was happening at the bar. Then a figure appeared beside her, and the white, domed head broke into a smile. A pale hand lost itself in her hair and the blade flashed beside her head. The waitress tried to tear herself away and fell to her knees as she did so. I tried to raise my gun but people were jostling me, heads and arms obscuring my vision. Someone, a young man with a football player's build, tried to grab my right arm, but I struck him in the face with my elbow and he moved back. Just as it seemed that we were powerless to prevent the girl from getting her throat cut, a dark object spun through the air and shattered as it struck Stritch's head. To my left, Angel stood on a chair, his hand still raised from where he had released the bottle. I saw Stritch stumble backwards, blood already pouring from the multiple cuts in his face and head, as the waitress tore herself away and tumbled down the steps, leaving a garland of hair in her attacker's hand. The door behind Stritch swung open and, in a blur of movement, he disappeared into the night.

Louis and I were only seconds behind him. We reached the steps at almost the same instant. Behind us, blue uniforms appeared at the main door and I could hear shouting and screams.

Outside, beer kegs stood stacked to one side of the door, a green trash can at the other. Ahead of us was the edge of the forest, illuminated by the big lamps that lit the side of the bar. Something white moved into the darkness beyond, and we moved after it.

# Chapter Twenty Five

The silence of the woods was startling, as if the snow had muted nature, stifling all life. There was no wind, no night-bird sounds, only the crunch of our shoes and the soft snap of unseen twigs buried beneath our feet.

I closed my eyes hard, willing them to adjust to the dark light of the forest, my hand supporting me against a tree trunk. Around us, mostly hidden by the snowdrifts, tree roots snaked over the thin soil. Louis had already fallen once, and the front of his coat was speckled with white.

Behind us, noises and shouting came from the direction of the bar, but no one followed as yet. After all, it was still unclear what had happened: a man had waved a gun; another man had thrown a bottle and injured a third; some people thought they had seen a knife, a fact that the waitress would surely confirm. It would take them a while to find flashlights and for the police to organise a pursuit. Occasionally, a weak beam of light flashed yellow behind us, but soon the thickening trees blocked its path. Only a sickly moonlight that fell wearily through the branches over our heads provided any illumination.

Louis was close by me, close enough so that we

remained in each other's sight. I raised a hand and we stopped. There was no sound ahead of us, which meant that Stritch was either picking his steps carefully or had stopped and was waiting for us in the shadows. I thought again of that doorway in the Portland complex, that certainty I had that he was there and that, if I went after him, he would kill me. This time, I resolved, I would not back down.

Then, from my left, I heard something. It was soft, like the sound of evergreen leaves brushing against clothing, followed by the compression of snow beneath a footfall, but I had heard it. From Louis's expression, I could tell that he had noticed it too. A second footfall came, then a third, moving not towards us, but away from us.

'Could we have gotten ahead of him?' I whispered.

'Doubt it. Could be someone from the bar.'

'No flashlight, and it's one person, not a group.'

But there was something else about it: the noise was careless, almost deliberately so. It was as if someone wanted us to know that he or she was out there.

I heard myself swallow loudly. Beside me, Louis's breath briefly threw a thin mist across his features. He looked at me and shrugged.

'Keep listening, but we best get moving.'

He stepped out from behind the trunk of a fir and the sound of a shot shattered the silence of the forest, sending bark and sap shooting into the air beside his face. He dived for the ground and rolled hard to his right until he was shielded by a natural depression, in front of which the blunt edge of a rock nosed its way out of the snow.

'That was close,' I heard him say. 'Fuck these professionals.'

'You're supposed to be a professional,' I reminded him. 'That's why you're here.'

'Keep forgetting,' he replied, 'what with being surrounded by amateurs and all.'

I wondered how long Stritch had been watching us, waiting to make his move. Long enough to see me with Lorna, and to understand that some kind of bond existed between us. 'Why did he try to take her in such a public place?' I wondered aloud.

Louis risked a look round the edge of the stone, but no shots came. 'He wanted to hurt the woman, and for you to know it was him. More than that, he wanted to draw us out.'

'And we followed him?'

'Wouldn't want to disappoint him,' replied Louis. 'I tell you, Bird: I don't think the man gives a fuck about that money anymore.'

I was getting tired of hugging the big fir. 'I'm going to make a move, see how far I can get. You want to take another peep out of your hole and cover me?'

'You the man. Get going.'

I took a deep breath and, staying low, began to zigzag forwards, tripping on two concealed roots but managing to keep my feet as Stritch's gun barked twice, kicking up snow and dirt by my right heel. It was followed by a burst of fire from Louis's SIG that shattered branches and bounced off rocks but also seemed to force Stritch to keep his head down.

'You see him?' I yelled, as I squatted down, my back to a spruce and my breath pluming before me in huge clouds. I was starting to warm up at last, although, even in the darkness, my fingers and hands appeared to be a raw, vivid red. Before Louis could reply, something off-

white whirled in a copse of bushes ahead and I opened
fire. The figure retreated into the darkness. 'Never mind,'
I added. 'He's about thirty feet north-east of you, heading
farther in.'

Louis was already moving. I could see his dark shape
against the snow. I sighted, aimed and fired four shots
into the area where I had last seen Stritch. There was no
return fire and Louis was soon level with me but about
ten feet away.

And then, again to my left but this time farther ahead,
there came the sound of movement in the woods. Someone was moving quickly and surefootedly towards
Stritch.

'Bird?' said Louis. I raised a hand quickly and indicated
the source of the noise. He went silent, and we waited.
For maybe thirty seconds nothing happened. There was
no noise, not even a footstep or the falling of snow from
the trees. There was nothing but the sound of my heart
beating and the blood pumping in my ears.

Then two shots came in close succession followed by
what sounded like two bodies impacting. Louis and I
moved at the same instant, our feet freezing, our legs held
high so that they would not drag in the snow. We ran
hard until we burst through the copse, our hands raised to
ward off the branches, and there we found Stritch.

He stood in a small, stony clearing doused in silver
moonlight, his back to us, his toes barely touching the
ground, his hands braced against the trunk of a big spruce.
From the back of his tan raincoat, something thick and
red had erupted which glistened darkly in the light. As we
approached him, Stritch shuddered and seemed to grip
the tree harder, as if to force himself off the sharp stump
of branch on which he had been impaled. A fine spray of

blood shot from his mouth and he groaned as his grip weakened. He turned his head at the sound of our footsteps and his eyes were large with shock, his thick, moist lips spread wide against gritted teeth as he tried to hold himself upright. Blood coursed from the wounds in his head, dark rivers of it flowing over his pale features.

As we were almost upon him, his mouth opened and he cried out as his body shuddered hard for the last time, his grip failing, his head falling forward and coming to rest against the bark of the tree.

And as he died, I scanned the glade, conscious that Louis was doing the same, both of us acutely aware that beyond our line of sight someone was watching us, and that there was a kind of joy in what he saw, and in what he had done.

# Chapter Twenty Six

I sat in Rand Jennings's office in the Dark Hollow police department and watched the snow falling on the windowpane against the early morning darkness. Jennings sat across from me, his hands steepled together, the fingertips resting in the small roll of fat that now hung beneath his chin. Behind me stood Ressler, while outside the office uniformed patrolmen, mostly part-timers called in for the occasion, ran back and forth down the hallway, bumping into one another like ants whose chemical signallers had been interfered with.

'Tell me who he was,' said Jennings.

'I already told you,' I said.

'Tell me again.'

'He called himself Stritch. He was a freelance operator – murder, torture, assassination, whatever.'

'What's he doing attacking waitresses in Dark Hollow, Maine?'

'I don't know.' That was a lie, but if I told him it was an attempt to gain revenge for the death of his partner then Jennings would have wanted to know who killed the partner and what part I had played in the whole affair. If I told him that then the chances were that I would be locked up in a cell.

'Ask him about the nigra,' said Ressler. Instinctively, the muscles on my shoulders and neck tightened and I heard Ressler snicker behind me. 'You got a problem with that word, Mr Big Shot? Don't like to hear a man being called a buck nigra, especially if he's your friend?'

I took a deep breath and brought my rising temper under control. 'I don't know what you're talking about. And I'd like to see you talk like that in Harlem.'

Jennings unsteepled his hands and jabbed an index finger at me. 'Again, I'm calling you a liar, Parker. I got witnesses saw a coloured follow you out that door, same coloured checked into the motel with a skinny white guy in tow the day you arrived, same coloured who paid cash in advance on the room, the room he shared with the same skinny white guy who hit this man Stritch with a bottle and the same coloured . . .' His voice rose to a shout. 'The same fucking coloured who has now left his motel and disappeared into the fucking ether with his buddy. Do you hear me?'

I knew where Angel and Louis had gone. They were at the India Hill Motel on Route 6 outside Greenville. Angel had checked in and Louis was lying low. They would eat out of the McDonald's nearby and wait for me to call.

'Like I said, I don't know what you're talking about. I was alone when I found Stritch. Maybe someone else followed me out, thought that I might need some help catching this guy but, if he did, then I didn't see him.'

'You're full of shit, Parker. We got three, maybe four, sets of prints running in the direction of that clearing. Now I'm going to ask you again: why is this guy attacking waitresses in my town?'

'I don't know,' I lied, again. If the conversation had been a horse, someone would have shot it by now.

'Don't give me that. You spotted the guy. You were moving after him before he even went for the girl.' He paused. 'Assuming it was Carlene Simmons he was after to begin with.' His face took on a thoughtful expression, and his eyes never left my face. I didn't like him. I never had, and what had passed between us gave neither of us any particular reason to mend our fences, but he wasn't dumb. He stood and went to the window, where he stared out into the blackness for a time. 'Sergeant,' he said at last, 'will you excuse us?'

Behind me, I heard Ressler shift his weight and the soft, deliberate tread of his footsteps as he walked to the door and closed it quietly behind him. Jennings turned to me then and cracked the knuckles of his right hand by crushing them in his left.

'I took a swing at you now, not one man outside this room would try to stop me, even if he wanted to. Not one man would interfere.' His voice was calm, but his eyes burned.

'You take a swing at me, Rand, you better hope someone tries to interfere. You might be glad of the help.'

He sat on the edge of his desk, facing me, his right hand still cupped in his left and resting on his thighs. 'I hear you been seen around town with my wife.' He wasn't looking at me now. Instead, all his attention seemed to be focused on his hands, his eyes examining every scar and wrinkle, every vein and pore. They were old man's hands, I thought, older than they should have been. There was a tiredness about Jennings, a weariness. Being with someone who doesn't love you just so no one else can have her takes its toll on a man. It takes its toll on the woman too.

I didn't respond to his statement, but I could tell what he was thinking. Things come around sometimes. Call it fate, destiny, God's will. Call it bad luck if you're trying to keep a dying marriage frozen so that it doesn't decay any further, like those egomaniacs who keep their bodies frozen in nitrogen after death in the hope that, centuries later, medical technology will have advanced and they can be revivified, as if somehow the world will want an old corpse from the past wandering through the present. I think Rand's marriage had been like that, something that he willed to be the way it was, frozen in some neverworld waiting for the miracle that would bring it back to life. And then I had arrived like the April thaw and he had felt the whole construct start to melt around his ears. I had nothing to offer his wife, at least nothing that I was prepared to give. What she saw in me, I wasn't sure. Maybe it was less to do with me than with what I represented: lost opportunities, paths untaken, second chances.

'You hear what I said?' he asked.

'I heard.'

'Is it true?' He looked at me then, and he was scared. He wouldn't have called it that, wouldn't even have admitted it to himself, but it was fear. Maybe, somewhere deep inside, he did still love his wife, although in such a strange way, in a manner that was so disengaged from ordinary life, that it had ceased to have any meaning for either of them.

'If you're asking, then you already know.'

'You trying to take her away from me again?'

I almost felt pity for him. 'I'm not here to take anyone away from anyone else. If she leaves you, she does so for her own reasons, not because a man from her past bundles her off against her will. You got a problem with your wife, you deal with it. I'm not your marriage counsellor.'

He shifted himself off the desk and his hands went to his sides, forming fists as they did so. 'Don't talk smart to me, boy. I'll . . .'

I rose and moved forwards, so that we were face-to-face. Even if he tried to hit me now, there would be no space for him to give the swing momentum. I spoke softly and distinctly. 'You won't do anything. You get in my way here and I'll take you down. As for Lorna, it's probably best that we don't even talk about her, because, like as not, it'll get ugly and one of us will get hurt. Years ago, that was me taking your kicks on a piss-covered floor while your buddy looked on. But I've killed men since then, and I'll take you down if you cross my path. You got any more questions, chief, or you want to charge me, you know where to find me.'

I left him, collected my gun from the desk, and walked out to the Mustang. I felt raw and filthy, my feet still cold and damp in my shoes. I thought of Stritch, writhing and struggling against the tree, raised up on his toes in a vain, futile effort to survive. And I thought of the strength it had taken to force him onto the stump. Stritch had been a squat, powerful man, with a low centre of gravity. People like that are hard to move. The collar of his raincoat had been torn where his killer had gripped him, using his own body weight against him, building up the momentum necessary to impale him on the tree. We were looking for someone strong and fast, someone who perceived Stritch as a threat to himself.

Or to someone else.

A cold wind rippled the main street of Dark Hollow and sprinkled the car with snow as the motel drew into view. I walked to my room, put my key in the lock and turned it, but the door was already unlocked. I stepped to the right, unholstered my gun, and gently eased the door fully open.

Lorna Jennings sat on my bed, her shoes off and her knees pulled up to her chin, the main illumination in the room coming from the lamp by the bedside. Her hands were clasped around her shins, the fingers intertwined. The television was on, tuned to a talk show, but the volume was down to near zero.

She looked at me with something that was almost love, and nearly hate. The world that she had created for herself there – a cocoon of indifference surrounding buried feelings and the dying heart of a poor marriage – was falling apart around her. She shook her head, her eyes still fixed on me, and seemed on the verge of tears. Then she turned away, towards the window that would soon be shedding bleak winter light into the room.

'Who was he?' she said.

'His name was Stritch.'

Near her bare feet, her thumb and index finger pushed her wedding ring almost to the end of her finger and spun it there, back and forth, before it eventually slipped off, to be held instead between her fingertips. I didn't think it was a good sign.

'He was going to kill me, wasn't he?' Her voice was matter-of-fact, but something trembled beneath it.

'Yes.'

'Why? I'd never seen him before. What had I ever done to him?' She rested her left cheek on her knee, waiting for my response. There were tears running down her face.

'He wanted to kill you because he thought you meant something to me. He was looking for revenge, and he saw his chance to take it.'

'And do I mean something to you?' Her voice was almost a whisper now.

'I loved you once,' I said simply.

'And now?'

'I still care enough about you not to let anyone hurt you.'

She shook her head, lifted it from her knees and put the heel of her right hand to her face. She was crying openly now.

'Did you kill him?'

'No. Someone else got to him first.'

'But you would have killed him, wouldn't you?'

'Yes.'

Her mouth was curled down in pain and misery, tears falling from her face and gently sprinkling the sheets. I took a tissue from the box on the dresser and handed it to her, then sat beside her on the edge of the bed.

'Jesus, why did you have to come here?' she said. Her body was racked by sobs. They came from so deep inside her that they interrupted the flow of her words, like little caesuras of hurt. 'Sometimes, whole weeks went by when I didn't think about you. When I heard you got married, I burned inside, but I thought that it might help, that it might cauterise the wound. And it did, Bird, it really did. But now . . .'

I reached out to her and touched her shoulder, but she pulled away. 'No,' she said. 'No, don't.' But I didn't listen. I moved fully onto the bed, kneeling beside her now, and drew her to me. She struggled, and slapped me open-handed on my body, my face, my arms. And then her face was against my chest, and the struggling eased. She wrapped her arms around me, her cheek hard against me, and a sound came through her gritted teeth that was almost a howl. I moved my hands across her back, my fingertips brushing the strap of her bra beneath her sweater. It rose up slightly at the end, exposing a moon-sliver of skin above her jeans and the lace decoration of her underwear beneath the blue denim.

Her head moved slightly beneath my chin, her cheek rubbing against the skin on my neck and progressing upwards, never losing contact, until it was against my own cheek. I felt a surge of lust. My hands were shaking, as much a delayed reaction from the pursuit of Stritch as her closeness to me. It would have been so easy to go with the moment, to re-create, however briefly, a memory of my youth.

I kissed her softly on the temple, then drew away.

'I'm sorry,' I said. I stood and moved to the window. Behind me, I heard her move to the bathroom and the door closing, the hiss of the faucets. For a brief instant I had been a young man again, consumed with desire for something I had no right to have. But that young man was gone, and the one who had taken his place no longer had the same intensity of feeling for Lorna Jennings. Outside, the snow fell like years, blanketing the past with the unblemished whiteness of possibilities untold.

I heard the bathroom door reopen. When I turned around, Lorna was standing naked before me.

I looked at her for a moment before I spoke. 'I think you left something in the bathroom,' I said. I made no move towards her.

'Don't you want to be with me?' she asked.

'I can't, Lorna. If I did, it would be for the wrong reasons and, frankly, I'm not sure I could deal with the consequences.'

'No, it's not that,' she said. A tear trickled down her

cheek. 'I've grown old. I'm not like I was when you knew me first.'

It was true: she was not as I remembered her. There were dimples on her upper thighs and buttocks, and small folds of fat at her belly. Her breasts were less firm and there was soft flesh beginning to hang on her upper arm. The faint trace of a varicose vein wormed its way across the upper part of her left leg. On her face, there were fine wrinkles around the mouth and a triad of lines snaked away from the corner of each eye.

And yet, while the years had transformed her, were changing her even now, they had not made her any less beautiful. Instead, as she grew older, her femininity, the sense of her as a woman, seemed to have been enhanced. The fragile beauty of her youth had withstood the harsh winters of the north and the difficulties of her marriage by adapting, not fading, and that strength had found expression in her face, in her body, lending her looks a dignity and maturity that had been buried before, that had only occasionally displayed itself in her features. As I looked into her eyes and her gaze met mine, I knew that the woman I had loved, for whom I still felt something that was almost love, remained untouched within.

'You're still beautiful,' I said. She watched me carefully, trying to be certain that I was not trying to blind her with kind lies. When she saw that I was telling the truth, her eyes closed softly as if she had just been touched deep inside but could not tell whether she felt pain or pleasure.

She covered her face with her hands and shook her head. 'This is kind of embarrassing.'

'Kind of,' I agreed.

She nodded and went back into the bathroom. When

she emerged, she walked straight to the door. I followed her, reaching it as she touched the handle. She turned before opening it, and rested her hand against my cheek. 'I don't know, Bird,' she said, her forehead resting gently against my shoulder for a moment. 'I just don't know.'

Then she slipped out of the room and into the morning light.

I slept for a time, then showered and dressed. I looked at my watch as I strapped it to my wrist, and a pain lanced through my stomach unlike anything I had felt in months. I curled up, dropped to the floor and softly began to cry, my arms wrapped around me, my body still racked by huge slashes of agony. In all that had happened – the hunt for traces of Caleb Kyle, the encounter with Rachel, the death of Stritch – I had lost track of the days.

It was December eleventh. The anniversary was one day away.

It was past three when I ate dry toast and coffee at the diner, and thought of Susan, and the rage I felt at the world for allowing her and my daughter to be taken from me. And I wondered how, with all of this pain and grief coiled inside me, I could ever begin again.

But I wanted Rachel, I knew, and the depth of my *need* for her surprised me. I had felt it as I sat opposite her in Harvard Square, listening to her voice and watching the movements of her hands. How many times had we been together? Twice? Yet, with her, I had felt a peace that had been denied me for so long.

I wondered too at what I might bring upon her, and upon myself, if the relationship was allowed to develop. I was a man moon-haunted by the ghost of his wife. I had mourned for her, and I still mourned for her. I felt guilt at my feelings for Rachel, at what we had done together. Was it a betrayal of Susan's memory to want to start over? So many feelings, so many emotions, so many acts of revenge, of attempted recompense, had been concentrated into the last twelve months. I felt drained by them, and tormented by the images that crept unbidden into my dreams, and into my waking moments. I had seen Donald Purdue in the bar. I had seen him as clearly as I had seen Lorna naked before me, as clearly as I had seen Stritch impaled on a tree.

I wanted to start again, but I didn't know how. All I knew was that I was moving closer and closer to the edge, and that I had to find some way to anchor myself before I fell.

I left the diner then drove down to Greenville. The Mercury was parked at the back of the motel beneath a copse of trees, making it almost invisible from the road. I didn't think Rand would come after Angel and Louis, not as long as he had me, but it didn't hurt to take precautions. As I parked, Angel opened the door to room six, moved aside to let me in, then closed the door behind him.

'Well, look at you,' he said, a wide grin on his face.

Louis lay on one of the room's two double beds, reading the latest issue of *Time*. 'He right, Bird,' he said. 'You the man. Pretty soon, you and Michael Douglas both be in one o' them sex clinics and we be reading about you in *People* magazine.'

'We saw her arriving as we left,' said Angel. 'She was in kind of a state. I didn't see there was anything else I could do but let her in.' He sat alongside Louis. 'Now I just know you're going to tell us that you and the chief sat down and talked this thing out and he said, "Sure, you can sleep with my wife, because she really loves you, not me". Because, if you didn't, then, pretty soon, you're going to be even less welcome there than you are already. And, frankly, you're currently about as welcome as a dead man's feet in summertime.'

'I didn't sleep with her,' I said.

'She come on to you?'

'You ever hear of sensitivity?'

'It's overrated, but I'll take that as a "yes" and assume that you didn't respond. Jeez, Bird, you got the self-restraint of a saint.'

'Let it go, Angel. Please.'

I sat on the edge of the second bed, and put my head in my hands. I breathed deeply and closed my eyes tightly. When I looked up again, Angel was almost beside me. I lifted my hand to let him know that I was OK. I went to the bathroom and soaked my face with cold water before returning to them.

'As for the chief, I haven't been run out of town yet,' I said, picking up the conversation where we had left off. 'I'm a witness-cum-suspect in the unsolved murder of an unidentified man in the Maine woods. Jennings asked me to stick around, shoot the breeze. He did tell me something else as well: the ME hasn't officially delivered his report yet, but it's likely to confirm that Chute was beaten badly before he was killed. From the marks on his wrists, it looked like someone hung him from a tree to do it.' Added to the death of Stritch, it meant that Dark Hollow was likely to be crawling with media and even more cops by the following morning.

'Louis made some calls, touched base with a few of his associates,' said Angel. 'He found out that Al Z and a contingent of Palermo irregulars flew into Bangor last night. Seems like Tony Celli just ran out of time.'

So they were closing in. There was a reckoning coming. I could feel it. I went to the door and looked out on the quietness of the India Hill Mall, with its gun shop and tourist information office, its deserted parking lot. Louis came over and stood beside me.

'You called that boy's name in the bar last night, just before you saw Stritch,' he said.

I nodded. 'I saw something, but I don't even know what it was.' I opened the door and stepped outside. He didn't pursue the subject.

'So what now?' said Louis. 'You dressed up like you ready for an Arctic adventure.'

'I'm still going after the old man to find out how he came to sell Ricky's boots to Stuckey.'

'You want us to tag along?'

'No. I don't want to spook him any more than I have to, and it's better if you stay out of Dark Hollow for a while. After I've spoken to him, maybe then we can decide how to progress. I can handle this one on my own.'

I was wrong.

# Part Three

Midway in our life's journey, I went astray from the straight path and woke to find myself in a dark wood.

Dante, *Inferno*

# Chapter Twenty Seven

As I drove to the house of the old man known as John Barley, the image of Stritch impaled on a tree returned to me. He couldn't have known about Caleb Kyle, couldn't have suspected that he was being hunted on two sides. He had reckoned on killing Louis and me, avenging his partner while simultaneously ending the contract on his life, but he had no inkling of Caleb.

It seemed certain to me that Caleb had killed Stritch, although how he had learned of his existence I didn't know; I guessed that he might have encountered Stritch when both of them were closing in on Billy Purdue. In the end, maybe it came down to the fact that Caleb Kyle was a predator, and predators are attuned not only to the nature of their prey but also to the nature of those who might prey upon them in turn. Caleb hadn't survived for over three decades without a highly developed ability to sense impending danger. In this case, Stritch had posed a potentially lethal threat to Billy Purdue, and Caleb had sniffed him out. Billy was the key to Caleb Kyle, the only one who had seen him and survived, the only one left who could describe what he looked like. But as I approached the road to John Barley's shack, I knew that Billy's description might prove unnecessary. When I stepped from the car, my gun was already in my hand.

It was already dark when I reached the old man's house. There was a light burning in one of the windows as I ascended the hill which sloped gently upwards to his yard. I came from the west, against the wind, keeping the house between me and the dog in its makeshift automobile kennel. I was almost at the door when a sharp yelp came from the car and a blur moved fast across the snow as the dog at last caught my scent and tried to intercept me. Immediately, the door of the house swung open and the barrel of a shotgun appeared. I grabbed the gun and yanked the old man through the gap. Beside me, the dog became frenzied, alternately leaping at my face and nipping at the cuffs of my pants. The old man lay on the ground, winded by his fall, his hand still on the gun. I lashed out at the dog and put my gun to the old man's ear.

'Ease off the shotgun, or I swear to God I'll kill you where you lie,' I said. His finger lifted from the trigger guard and his hand moved slowly from the stock of the shotgun. He whistled softly and said: 'Easy, Jess, easy. Good boy.' The dog whined a little then moved away a distance, contenting itself with circling us repeatedly and growling as I hauled the old man to his feet. I gestured at a chair on the porch and he sat down heavily, rubbing his left elbow where he had barked it painfully as he landed.

'What do you want?' asked John Barley. He didn't look at me, but kept his gaze on the dog. It moved cautiously over to its master, giving me a low growl as it did so, before sitting down beside him where he could rub it gently behind the ear.

I had my Timberland pack over my shoulder and I

threw it at him. He caught it and looked dumbly at me for the first time.

'Open it,' I said.

He waited a moment, then unzipped the pack and peered in.

'You recognise them?'

He shook his head. 'No, I don't believe I do.'

I cocked the pistol. The dog's growling rose an octave.

'Old man, this is personal. You don't want to cross me on this thing. I know you sold the boots to Stuckey over in Bangor. He gave you thirty dollars for them. Now you want to tell me how you came by them?'

He shrugged. 'Found 'em, I guess.'

I moved forward and the dog rose up, the hairs on its neck high and tight. It bared its teeth at me. I kept the gun on the old man then, slowly, moved it down to his dog.

'No,' said Barley, his hand reaching down to hold the dog back and to cover its bared breast. 'Please, not my dog.'

I felt bad threatening his dog, and the feeling made me wonder if this old man could possibly be Caleb Kyle. I thought that I would know Caleb when I found him, that I would sense his true nature. All I got from John Barley was fear: fear of me and, I suspected, fear of something else.

'Tell me the truth,' I said softly. 'Tell me where you got those boots. You tried to get rid of them after we spoke. I want to know why.'

He blinked hard and swallowed once, his teeth worrying his bottom lip until he seemed to reach a decision within himself, and spoke.

'I took 'em from the boy's body. I dug him up, took the boots, then covered him again.' He shrugged once more. 'Took me his pack too. He didn't have no need for 'em anyways.'

I resisted pistol-whipping him, but only just. 'And the girl?'

The old man twice shook his head, as if trying to dislodge an insect from his hair. 'I didn't kill 'em,' he said, and I thought for a moment that he might cry. 'I wouldn't hurt nobody. I just wanted the boots.'

I felt sick inside. I thought of Lee and Walter, of times spent with them, with Ellen. I did not want to have to tell them that their daughter was dead. I once again doubted that this raggedy old man, this scavenger, could be Caleb Kyle.

'Where is she?' I asked.

He was rubbing the dog's body methodically now, hard sweeps from the head almost to its rump. 'I only know where the boy is. The girl, I don't rightly know where she might be.'

In the light from the window, the old man's face glowed a dim yellow. It made him look sickly and ill. His eyes were damp, the pupils barely pinholes. He was trembling gently as the fear took over his body. I lowered the gun and said: 'I'm not going to hurt you.'

The old man shook his head and what he said next made my skin crawl. 'Mister,' he whispered, 'it ain't you I'm afraid of.'

He saw them near the Little Briar Creek, he said, the girl and the boy in front and a figure, almost a shadow, in the backseat. He was walking with his dog, on his way home from hunting rabbits, when he saw the car pull in below him, harsh noises like stones grinding coming from the engine. It was not yet evening, but darkness had already fallen. He caught a glimpse of the two young people as they passed before the headlights of the car, the girl in blue jeans and a bright red parka, the boy in black, wearing a leather jacket that hung open despite the cold.

The boy lifted the hood of the car and peered inside, using a pocket flashlight to illuminate the engine. He could see him shake his head, heard him say something indistinguishable to the girl, then swear loudly in the silence of the forest.

The rear door of the car opened and the third passenger stepped out. He was tall, and something told John Barley that he was old, older even than Barley himself. And for reasons that, even now, he did not fully understand, he felt a chill cross him and, from close by, he heard the dog give a low whine. Beside the car, the figure stopped and seemed to scan the woods, as if to ascertain the source of the unexpected noise. Barley patted the dog lightly: 'Hush, boy, hush.' But he could see the dog's nostrils working quickly, and felt the animal shivering beside him. Whatever he scented, it had spooked him badly and the dog's unease communicated itself to his owner.

The tall man leaned into the driver's side of the car and the headlights died. 'Hey,' said the boy. 'What're you doing? You killed the lights.' His flashlight beam moved and illuminated first the face of the man approaching and then the gleam of something in his hand.

'Hey,' said the boy again, softer now. He moved in front of the girl, forcing her back, protecting her from the blade. 'Don't do this,' he said.

The knife slashed and the flashlight fell. The boy stumbled back and Barley heard him say, 'Run, Ellen, run.' Then the old man was upon him like a long, dark cloud and Barley saw the knife rise and fall, rise and fall, and heard the sound of its cutting against the noise of the trees gently swaying.

And then the figure moved after the girl. He could hear her stumbling, awkward progress through the woods. She did not get far. There was a scream, followed by a sound, as of a blow heavily falling, and then all was silent. Beside him, the dog shifted on the ground, and gave a low, soft keen.

It was some time before the tall figure returned. The girl was not with him. He lifted the boy beneath the arms and hauled him to the rear of the car, where he bundled him into the trunk. He opened the driver's door and slowly, surely, began to push the car down the dirt road that led to Ragged Lake.

Barley tied his dog to a tree and gently wrapped his pocket handkerchief around its muzzle, patting it once and assuring it that he would be back. Then he followed the sound of the car as its wheels crunched on the trail ahead.

About half a mile down the road, just before Ragged Lake, he came upon a clearing next to a patch of beaver bog, dead trees fallen and twisted in the dark water. In the clearing, a pit had been dug and newly excavated earth lay in piles like funeral mounds. There was a slope at one end of the pit, and the old man used it to push the car into the earth. It came to rest almost level, the right rear wheel slightly raised. Then the figure climbed onto the roof and, from there, made its way to the lip of the hole. There was the sound of a spade being removed from the earth and then the soft shifting as it plunged deep once again, followed by a scraping as the first load hit the roof of the car.

It took the old man almost an hour, all told, to bury the

car. Soon, snow would cover the ground and the drifts would hide any subsidence in the earth beneath. He lifted and threw methodically, his pace never varying, never once stopping to take a breath, and, despite all that he had seen, John Barley envied him his strength.

But just as the old man had finished circling the area to make sure that he had done his job well, Barley heard a bark from nearby followed by a long howl and he knew that Jess had managed to remove the binding from his muzzle. Below him, the figure stopped and cocked its head, then swung the spade hard into the beaver bog and began to move, his long legs eating up the incline, heading towards the sound of the dog.

But Barley was already moving, quickly and silently. He picked his way over fallen logs, following deer paths and moose trails so that he might avoid alerting the man behind by breaking new branches. He reached the dog to find it pulling from the rope, its tail wagging, emitting gentle yips of joy and relief. It struggled a little as he restored the binding, then he untied it, took it in his arms, and ran for home. He stopped once to look back, certain almost that he had heard sounds of pursuit from close behind, but he could see nothing. When he got back to his cabin, he locked his door, reloaded his shotgun with lethal Number One shot and sat in a chair, never resting until dawn broke, when he fell into a bad, fitful sleep, punctuated by dreams of earth falling into his open mouth.

'Why didn't you tell someone what you saw?' I asked him. Even then, I was not sure whether or not to believe him. How could I believe that he was who he said he was, that such a story could be true? But when I looked in his eyes there was no trace of guile, only an old man's fear of approaching death. The dog now lay beside him, not asleep, its eyes open, sometimes casting glances at me to make sure that I had not moved during the telling of the old man's tale.

'I didn't want no trouble,' he replied. 'But I went back to see if there was any trace of the girl, and for those boots. They were fine boots and maybe, maybe I wanted to be sure that I hadn't imagined what I saw. I'm an old man, and the mind plays tricks. But I didn't imagine nothing, even though the girl was gone and there wasn't even blood on the ground to tell where she might have been. I knew that I hadn't imagined it as soon as I saw the dip in the ground and the spade hit metal. I was going to keep the boots and the pack, maybe had half a notion to take them to the police so they wouldn't think I was crazy when I told them the story. But . . .' He stopped. I waited.

'The next night, after what happened, I was sitting here on the porch with Jess and I felt him trembling. He didn't bark or nothing, just began to shake and whine. He was staring out into the woods, just there.'

He raised a finger and pointed to a place where the branches of two striped maples almost touched, like lovers reaching out to each other in the dark. 'And there was someone standing there, watching us. Didn't move or nothing, didn't speak, just stood watching. And I knew it was him. I could feel it deep in me, and I could sense it in the dog. Then he just seemed to fade into the woods, and I didn't see him again.

'But I knew what it was he wanted. It was a warning. I don't think he knew for certain what I might have seen, and he wasn't going to kill me unless he knew, but right then and there I wished I'd never gone back for them boots. And if I said anything, he'd find out and he'd come for me. I knew that. Then you came around asking questions and I knew for sure I had to get rid of them. I emptied the pack and sold it and the boots to Stuckey and I was glad for what he gave me. I burned the boy's clothes out back. There was nothing else for it.'

'You ever see this man before?' I asked.

Barley shook his head. 'Never. He wasn't from around these parts, else I'd have recognised him.' He leaned forward. 'You didn't ought to have come here, mister.' There was a tone almost of resignation in his voice. 'He'll know, and he'll come for me. He'll come for us both.'

I looked out into the gathering night, into the shadows of the trees. There were no stars visible in the sky and the moon was obscured by cloud. The forecast was for more snow; twelve inches were promised over the next week, maybe more. And suddenly I was seized with a fearful regret that my car was back down the road, and that we would have to walk through the darkness of the woods to get to it.

'You ever hear the name Caleb Kyle?' I asked him.

He blinked once, as if I had struck him on the cheek, but there was no real surprise in it. 'Sure I heard it. He's a myth. There was never a man by that name, least not around these parts.' But just by asking him I had sown doubts in his mind, and I could almost hear the tumblers falling into place, and I watched as his eyes widened in realisation.

So Caleb had tracked Ellen and Ricky, had wormed his way into their trust. He was the one who had advised them to visit Dark Hollow, just as the hotel manager had told me, and I didn't doubt that it was Caleb who had sabotaged the engine of their car and then told them where to pull in, close by Ragged Lake where there was a grave already waiting. What I couldn't understand was why he had done this. It made no sense, unless . . .

Unless he had been watching me all along, ever since I began helping Rita Ferris. Anyone who sided with Rita would automatically be perceived as taking a stand against Billy. Did he take Ellen Cole, maybe even kill her as he killed her boyfriend, to punish me for interfering in the affairs of a man whom he believed to be his son? If Ellen was still alive, then any hope of finding her now rested on understanding the mind of Caleb Kyle, and perhaps finding Billy Purdue. I thought of Caleb watching me as I slept, after he had killed Rita and Donald, after he had placed the child's toy on my kitchen table. What was he thinking then? And why didn't he kill me when he had the chance? Somewhere, just beyond my reach, lay an answer to these questions. I tightened my fists in frustration at my inability to grasp it, and then it came to me.

He knew who I was, or, more importantly, he knew whose grandson I was. It would appeal to him, I thought, to torment the grandson as he had tortured the grandfather. Thirty years later, he was beginning the game again.

I motioned to John Barley. 'Come on, we're leaving.'

He stood slowly and looked out at the trees, as if in expectation of seeing that figure once again. 'Where are we going?'

'You're going to show me where that car is buried, and then you're going to tell Rand Jennings what you told me.'

He did not move, but remained looking fearfully into the trees. 'Mister, I don't want to go back there,' he said.

I ignored him, picked up his shotgun, unloaded it and

tossed the empty gun back into the house. I motioned him to go ahead of me, my gun still in my hand. After a moment's hesitation, he moved.

'You can bring your dog,' I said, as he passed by me. 'If there's something out there, he'll sense it before we will.'

# Chapter Twenty Eight

The first snow began to fall almost as soon as we lost sight of the old man's house, thick, heavy concentrations of crystal that covered the road and added their weight to the earlier falls. By the time we reached the Mustang our shoulders and hair were white, and the dog gambolled beside us, trying to catch snowflakes in its jaws. I sat the old man in the passenger seat, took a pair of cuffs from the trunk, and cuffed his left hand across his body to the armrest on the door. I didn't trust him not to take a swing at me in the car, or to run off into the woods as soon as he had a chance. The dog sat on the back seat, leaving muddy pawprints on my upholstery.

Visibility was poor as I drove and the windshield wipers struggled to remove the snow. I stayed at thirty at first, then slowed to twenty-five, then twenty. Soon, there was only a veil of white before me and the tall shapes of the trees at either side, pine and fir standing like the spires of churches in the snow. The old man said nothing as he sat awkwardly beside me, his right hand holding on to the dashboard for support.

'You'd better not be lying to me, John Barley,' I said.

His eyes were blank, their gaze directed inward, like

those of a man who has just heard his death sentence pronounced and knows that it is fixed and inalterable.

'It don't matter,' he said, and behind him the dog began to whine. 'When he finds us, won't matter what you believe.'

Then, perhaps fifty feet ahead of us, the driving snow playing games with perspective, I saw what looked like headlights. As we drew closer, the shapes of two cars appeared as they pulled fully into the road, blocking our path. Behind us, more headlights gleamed, but farther back, and when I continued to move forwards, they seemed to recede, then disappeared, their glare reflected now from the trees to my right, and I realised the car behind had turned sideways and stopped, boxing us in.

I slowed about twenty feet from the cars ahead. 'What's going on?' said the old man. 'Maybe there's been an accident.'

'Maybe,' I said.

Three figures, dark against the snow and the lights, moved towards us. There was something familiar about the one in the centre and the way he moved. He was small. An overcoat hung loose over his shoulders and, from beneath it, his right arm protruded in a sling. As he moved into the glare of the car's lights, I saw the dark threads of stitching in the wounds on his forehead, and the ugly twisting of his harelip.

Mifflin smiled crookedly. I was already reaching for the keys to the cuffs with one hand while with the other I removed my Smith & Wesson from its holster. Beside me, the old man sensed we were in trouble and began yanking at the cuffs.

'Cut me loose!' he screamed. 'Cut me loose!'

From behind came the barking of the dog. I tossed the

keys to the old man and he reached down to free his hand as I slapped the car into reverse and hit the accelerator, my gun against the wheel, hoping to knock the rear car out of the path. We slammed into it with the sound of crunching metal and breaking glass, the impact straining the belts as we jerked towards the windshield. The dog tumbled forwards into the space between the seats and yelped as it hit the dash.

Ahead of us, five figures now moved through the snow in our direction, and I heard the sound of a door opening behind us. I moved the car into drive and prepared to hit the accelerator again, but the Mustang cut out, leaving us in silence. I leaned down to turn the key in the ignition, but the old man was already opening his door, the dog on his lap nosing at the gap. I reached out to stop him – 'No, don't' – and then the windshield exploded and a black and red spray, star studded with glass shards, filled the car, splashing my face and body and blinding my eyes. I blinked them clear in time to see the old man's ruined face sliding towards me, the remains of the dog lying across his thighs, and then I was pushing my door open, staying low as I hurled myself from the car, more shots tearing into the hood and the interior, the rear window shattering as I tumbled onto the road. I sensed movement behind and to my left, spun and fired. A man in a dark aviator's jacket, a stunned look on his face and blood on his cheek, twisted in the snow and fell to the ground ten feet away from me. I glanced at the point of collision where the Mustang had hit their Neon and saw the body of a second man forced upright between the driver door and the shell of the Dodge, crushed by the impact as he tried to get out of the car.

I turned and broke for the side of the road, sliding

down the slope and into the woods, bullets striking the road above me and the snow and dirt around me, shouts and cries following me as I found myself among the trees, twigs snapping beneath my feet, branches scraping my face, twisted roots pulling at my legs. Flashlight beams tore through the night and there came the staccato rattle of an automatic weapon, ripping through the leaves and branches above me and to my right. The old man's blood was still warm on me as I ran. I could feel it dripping down my face, could taste it in my mouth.

I kept running, my gun in my hand, my breath sounding harsh and ragged in my throat. I tried to change direction, to work my way back to the road, but flashlights shone almost level with me to my right and left as they moved to cut me off. Still the snow fell, trapping itself on my lashes and melting on my lips. It froze my hands and almost blinded me as it billowed into my eyes.

And then the terrain changed and I stumbled on a rock, wrenching my ankle painfully, and half slid, half ran down a final incline until my feet splashed in icy cold water and I found myself looking out on the dark expanse of a pond, the winter light drowning in its blackness. I turned, trying to find a way back, but the flashlights and cries drew nearer. I saw a light to my far left, another approaching through the trees to the right, and realised that I was surrounded. I took a deep breath, wincing at the pain as I tested my ankle. I drew a bead on the beam to my right, aimed low and fired. There was a cry of pain and the thrashing of a body falling. I fired twice more, straight ahead at the men approaching through the darkness, and heard a call to 'Kill the lights, kill the lights'.

Automatic fire raked the bank as I plunged into the water, keeping the gun extended at shoulder level. The pond was not deep, I figured: even in the darkness, I could see a chain of rocks breaking the water about half a mile out, midway across its width at its narrowest point. But those rocks were deceptive; I was maybe twenty-five feet out from the bank, cutting diagonally across to the far shore, when the bed sloped and I lost my footing with a splash. I surfaced, gasping, and a flashlight scanned across me, then returned, freezing me in its beam. I took another deep breath and dived as shots dashed the surface of the water like raindrops. I could feel the slugs tearing by me as I descended, deeper and deeper, into the black waters, my lungs bursting and the cold so intense that it felt like a burning.

And then something tugged at my side and a numbness began to spread, slowly mutating into a new, bright red pain that spread fingers of hurt through my body. I twisted like a fish caught on a line as warm blood spilled from my side into the water. My mouth opened in agony, precious oxygen bubbling to the surface, and my gun slipped from my fingers. I panicked, scrambling madly upwards, only barely calming myself enough so as not to make a noise when I broke the water. I took a deep breath, keeping my face almost level with the surface, as the pain swept over me. There was numbness in my legs, in my arms and at the tips of my fingers. The gunshot wound burned, but not as badly as it would out of the water.

On the banks, figures moved, but only one light was visible now. They were waiting for me to appear, still fearful of the gun I no longer had. I took a breath and dived again, keeping barely below the surface as I swam, one handed, away from them. I did not rise again until my hand brushed the bottom of the pond in the shallows by the bank. Keeping my injured side raised, I dragged myself through the shallows, looking for a point where I could safely climb onto land. The automatic spoke again, but this time the bullets struck far behind me. Other shots came, but they were random, unfocused, hoping for a lucky hit. I kept moving onwards, my eyes on the deeper darkness ahead where the woods lay.

To my right, I saw a break in the bank and water falling over stones: the river. And that river, I knew, flowed through Dark Hollow. I could have headed for the farthest shore and the woods beyond, but if I fell down among the trees or lost my sense of direction, the best I could hope for would be death from freezing, because no one would know I was there except for Tony Celli's men. If they found me, I would not have to worry about the cold for long.

I found a footing at the mouth of the river, where it flowed from the lake, but I did not stand, preferring instead to keep pulling myself along until an outcrop of trees masked me enough from the men behind to enable me to rise and move into the river itself. My side ached badly now, and every movement sent a fresh surge of pain through me. Water tumbled over a small bank of stones and it took me two attempts to gain a foothold. I pulled myself up and lay, once again, in the water as a flashlight beam moved by and shone in my direction before continuing on past the mouth. I counted to ten, then stumbled for the bank.

The snow had eased a little as the wind dropped. It was less driving now but still falling thickly, and the ground around me was completely white. The pain in my left side grew as I struggled through the deep snow, and I stopped against the trunk of a tree to examine the wound. There was a ragged hole in the back of my jacket, and the sweater and shirt beneath, with a small entry hole around the tenth rib, and a larger exit hole at the front at more or less the same level. The pain was bad but the wound was shallow: the distance between the entry and exit holes was little more than an inch. Blood dripped through my fingers and pooled on the snow below. That should have warned me, but I was scared and hurt and was not as careful as I should have been. I reached down, gasping at the pain it caused, and took two handfuls of snow. I packed the snow into the wounds and moved on, slipping and sliding on the bank but remaining close to the water so I would not lose my way. My teeth were chattering uncontrollably and my clothes clung damply to my body. My fingers burned from the icy water. I was nauseous with shock.

It was only when I had travelled some distance, stopping occasionally to rest against a tree, that I recalled where I was in relation to the town. Ahead of me and to my right, perhaps two hundred yards away, I could see the lights of a house. I heard the noise of a set of falls, saw before me the steel skeleton of a bridge and I knew where I was, and where I could go.

A light burned at the kitchen window of the Jennings house as I fell against the back door. I heard a noise from inside and Lorna's voice, panicked, saying: 'Who's there?' The curtains at the door parted a little and her eyes widened as she saw my face.

'Bird?' There came the sound of a key turning in the lock and then the support of the door was taken away from me and I fell forwards. As she helped me to a chair, I told her to call room six at the India Hill Motel and no one else, and then I closed my eyes and let the pain wash over me in waves.

\*    \*    \*

437

Blood bubbled from the exit hole as Lorna cleaned the wound; the skin around it had been wiped down and she had removed some tattered pieces of cloth from within with a pair of sterilised tweezers. She passed a swab over the wound and the burning sensation came again, causing me to twist in the chair.

'Hold still,' she said, so I did. When she was done, she made me turn so that she could get at the entry hole. She looked a little queasy, but she kept going.

'Are you sure you want me to do this?' Lorna asked when she was done.

I nodded.

She took a needle and poured boiling water on it.

'This will hurt a little,' she said.

She was being optimistic. It hurt a lot. I felt tears spring from my eye at the sharpness of the pain as she put two stitches in each wound. It wasn't textbook medical care, but I just needed something to get me through the next few hours. When she had finished, she took a pressure bandage and applied it, then took a longer roll and wound it around my abdomen.

'It'll hold until we can get you to a hospital,' she said. She gave me a small, nervous smile. 'Red Cross first-aid classes. You should be grateful I paid attention.'

I nodded to let her know that I understood. It was a clean wound. That was about the only good thing that could be said for high-velocity bullets: they didn't deform on impact, tearing up the flesh, but continued on their merry way with most of their energy, and their jacket, intact.

'You want to tell me what happened?' asked Lorna. I stood up slowly and it was only then that I noticed the blood on the tiles.

'Damn,' I said. A wave of nausea swept over me, but I held on to the table and closed my eyes until it had passed. Lorna's arm curled around my upper body.

'You've got to sit down, Bird. You're weak, and you've lost blood.'

'Yeah,' I said, as I pushed myself away from the table and walked unsteadily to the back door. 'That's what I'm worried about.' I lifted the curtain and looked outside. It was still snowing but in the light from the kitchen I could see the telltale trail of red leading from the direction of the river to the door of the kitchen, the blood so thick and dark that it simply absorbed the falling snow.

I turned to Lorna. 'I'm sorry, I shouldn't have come here.'

Her face was solemn, her lips pinched, and then she gave another small smile. 'Where else could you have gone?' she said. 'I called your friends. They're on their way.'

'Where's Rand?'

'In town. They found that man, Billy Purdue, the one they've been looking for. Rand's holding him until the morning. Then the FBI and a whole lot of other people will arrive to talk to him.'

That was why Tony Celli's men were here. Word of Billy Purdue's capture would have spread like wildfire through the agencies and police departments involved, and Tony Celli would have been listening. I wondered how quickly they had spotted me when they arrived. As soon as they saw the Mustang, they must have known and decided that it would be less trouble to kill me than to risk my interference.

'The men who shot me, they want Billy Purdue,' I said

quietly. 'And they'll kill Rand and his men if they won't hand him over.'

Something flickered on the window, like a falling star reflected. It took me a second to figure out what it was: a flashlight beam. I grabbed Lorna by the hand and pulled her to the front of the house. 'We've got to get out of here,' I said. The hallway was dark, with a dining room leading off to the right. I stayed low, despite the pain in my side, and peered through the space beneath the window blinds into the front yard.

Two figures stood at the end of the yard. One held a shotgun. The other had his arm in a sling.

I came back to the hallway. Lorna took one look at my face and said: 'They're out front as well, aren't they?'

I nodded.

'Why do they want you dead?'

'They think I'll interfere, and they owe me for something that happened back in Portland. You must have a gun in the house. Where is it?'

'Upstairs. Rand keeps one in the dresser.'

She led the way up the stairs and into their bedroom. It contained a large, country pine bed, with a yellow bed-spread and yellow pillows. A matching country pine dresser stood across from a large closet. In one corner was a small bookshelf packed with books. A radio played softly in another corner, The Band singing 'Evangeline', with Emmylou Harris's vocals snaking in and out of the verse and chorus. Lorna pulled socks, men's underwear and T-shirts from a drawer and threw them on the floor until she found the revolver. It was a Charter Arms Undercover .38, with a three-inch barrel, a real lawman's weapon. The five chambers were loaded, and there was a speed loader beside it, also fully packed. Close by, in a

Propex holster, was a second gun, a Ruger Mark 2 with a tapered barrel. 'Rand sometimes uses it for target shooting,' said Lorna, pointing to an almost empty box of .22 Long Rifle rimfire cartridges in the corner of the drawer.

'God bless the paranoid,' I said. On the bedside cabinet stood a large plastic bottle of water, almost empty now. I steadied myself against the dresser. In the mirror facing me, my skin appeared deathly pale. There were smudges of hurt and exhaustion under my eyes and my face was pockmarked by glass cuts and smeared with sap and the old man's blood. I could smell him on me. I could smell his dog.

'Do you have tape, adhesive tape?'

'Maybe downstairs, but there's a roll of adhesive bandage in the bathroom cabinet. Will that do?'

I nodded, took the plastic bottle and followed her into the yellow-and-white tiled bathroom, loading the Ruger as I walked. She opened the cabinet and handed me the roll of inch-wide bandage. I emptied the last of the mineral water into the sink, inserted the slim barrel of the Ruger into the bottle and held it in place by wrapping the bandage repeatedly around it.

'What are you doing?' asked Lorna.

'Making a suppressor,' I replied. I figured that, if Celli's men searched the house, I could take one of them out with the suppressed .22 if I had to and buy us five, maybe ten seconds of time. In a gunfight at close quarters, ten seconds is an eternity.

From below came the sound of the back door being kicked in, followed by the shattering of glass and the sound of the front door being opened. I tucked the .38 into my pants and slid the Ruger's safety down.

'Get in the tub and keep your head down,' I whispered.

She slipped off her sandals and climbed silently into the bathtub. I removed my shoes and left them on the tiled floor, then moved softly onto the landing and back into the bedroom. The radio was still playing, but The Band had now been replaced by Neil Young, his high, plaintive tones echoing around the room.

*'Don't let it bring you down . . .'*

I took up a position in the shadows by the window. The Ruger felt awkward in my hand after the Smith & Wesson, but at least it was a gun. I cocked it, and waited.

*'It's only castles burning . . .'*

I heard him on the stairs, watched his shadow moving ahead of him, saw it stop and then begin to move into the room, following the music. I tightened my grip on the trigger, and took a deep breath.

*'Just find someone who's turning . . .'*

He pushed the door open with his foot, waited a moment, then darted fully into the bedroom, his shotgun raised. I swallowed once, then exhaled.

*'. . . And you will come around.'*

I pulled the trigger on the .22 and the top of the bottle exploded dully with a sound like a paper bag bursting. It was a clean shot, straight through the heart. I advanced and fired again as he stumbled back against the wall, then slid slowly down, leaving a dark, red trail across the cream paint. I caught the shotgun, a pistol-grip Mossberg, as it slipped from his grasp. Dropping the .22, I stepped over his body, my stocking feet soundless on the floor, and moved back into the hallway.

'Terry?' called a voice from below, and I saw a man's hand, a .44 Magnum held in its grip, then his arm, his body, his face. He looked up and I took him in the head, the noise of the shotgun like a cannon's roar. His features disappeared in a red haze and he tumbled backwards. I pumped and was already moving onto the stairs when a bullet struck the wall close to my left ear, a muzzle flashing in the darkness of the dining room. I fired, pumped, fired, pumped: two rounds into the darkness. Glass broke and plaster disintegrated, and no more shots came. The front door now stood ajar. What remained of its glass burst and wood splinters flew as more shots came from the kitchen. I stayed on the stairs, jammed the shotgun between the supports of the bannisters, turned it and fired the last round.

In the kitchen, a shadow detached itself from the wall and moved to the edge of the long hallway, firing a barrage of shots, sending wood singing from the bannisters and yellow dust clouding from the wall beside me, as his aim gradually grew closer and closer. I reached for the .38, yanked it from my belt and fired three shots. There was a cry of pain as, from the corner of my eye, I saw movement at the front door. It distracted me and, as I turned, the wounded gunman in the kitchen exposed himself fully and moved into the hall, his gun hand raised, the other hand holding onto his shoulder. He bared his teeth and then a noise came, louder than any gunshot I had ever heard before, and a hole appeared in his torso, big enough for a man to put his fists through if he chose. I thought I could see the kitchen through it, the glass on the floor, the sink unit, the edge of a chair. The gunman remained upright for a split second longer then tumbled to the ground like a puppet with its strings cut.

At the door stood Louis, a huge Ithaca Mag-10 Road-blocker shotgun in his hands, the rubber stock still fast against his shoulder. 'Man just had himself a 10-gauge handshake,' he said. From the back of the house came more shots and the sound of a car accelerating fast. Louis jumped the corpse, with me close behind, and we headed through the ruined kitchen and into the yard. Angel stood at the gate, a Glock 9mm in his hand, and shrugged at us.

'He got away, the ugly fuck. I didn't even see him until he was in the car.'

'Mifflin,' I said, wearily.

Louis looked at me. 'That freak still alive?' He shook his head in wonder.

'Maybe we could blast him into space and hope he burns up on re-entry,' mused Angel.

I shivered in the cold, with only the bandages to cover my upper body. They were already soaked with red. My ears rang from the noise of the gunfire in the enclosed space of the house. Louis slipped off his overcoat and put it over my shoulders. Despite the cold, I felt like I was burning.

'You know,' said Angel. 'You oughta be more careful. You're gonna catch your death like that.'

The three of us started at a noise from behind, but only Lorna stood at the door. I walked up to her and placed a hand on her shoulder.

She wrapped her arms around herself, keeping her eyes on me and away from the bodies on the floor behind her. 'What are you going to do now?'

'We're going back to Dark Hollow. I need Billy Purdue alive.'

'And Rand?'

'I'll do what I can. You better call him, tell him what's happened.'

'I tried. Our phone is dead. They must have cut the wires before they came in.'

'Go to a neighbour's house and make the call. With a little luck, we'll get to Dark Hollow shortly after.' All of which assumed that the lines hadn't been cut from outside town, in which case Dark Hollow itself would be cut off.

It was time to go, but Lorna raised a hand. 'Wait,' she said, and went back upstairs. When she returned, she had a thick cotton shirt, a sweater and a padded jacket from LL Bean, along with a box of cartridges for the .38. She helped me to put on the clothes, then touched my hand gently.

'You take care, Bird.'

'You too.'

Behind me, Angel started up the Mercury, Louis in the front seat. I climbed in back and we moved off. I looked back to see Lorna standing in her yard, watching us until we were gone from her sight.

# Chapter Twenty Nine

The roads were deserted as we drove, the silence around us broken only by the purr of the Mercury's engine and the soft thud of snowflakes impacting on the windshield. The pain in my side burned fiercely and, once or twice, I closed my eyes and seemed to lose a couple of seconds. There was blood on my fingers and an ochre stain on my pants from my groin to my lower thigh. I caught Louis taking careful looks back at me in the rear-view mirror, and I raised a hand to let him know that I was still with them. It might have looked more convincing if the hand hadn't been covered in blood.

When we pulled into the parking lot in front of the police department there were two cruisers parked ahead of us, along with an orange '74 Trans-Am that looked like it would take a miracle to start it and a couple of other vehicles that had remained stationary long enough for the snow to blur their lines, including a rental Toyota out of Bangor. There was no sign of Tony Celli, or any of his men.

We entered through the front door. Ressler stood behind the desk, examining the jack on the telephone. Behind him was a second, younger patrolman whom I didn't recognise, probably another part-timer, and farther back again, standing across from the station house's two holding cells, was Jennings himself. In a chair beside the desk sat Walter Cole. He looked shocked at my appearance. I was kind of unhappy about it myself.

'The fuck do you want?' said Jennings, causing Ressler to rise from his position and cast a wary eye first over Louis and Angel, then me. He didn't look too pleased at the sight of our guns and his hand hovered near his own side arm. His eyes widened a little as he saw the marks on my face, and the blood on my clothing.

'What's wrong with the phones?' I returned.

'They're out,' Ressler said, after a moment's pause. 'All communications are down. Could be the weather.'

I moved past him to the cells. One was empty. In the other, Billy Purdue sat with his head in his hands. His clothes were filthy and his boots were stained with mud. He had the haunted, desperate look of an animal caught in a snare. He was humming to himself, like a little boy trying to block out the world around him. I didn't ask Rand Jennings's permission to talk to him. I wanted answers, and he was the only one who could provide them.

'Billy,' I said sharply.

He looked up at me. 'I fucked up,' he said, 'didn't I?' Then he went back to humming his song.

'I don't know, Billy. I need you to tell me about the man you saw, the old man. Describe him to me.'

Jennings's voice came from behind me. 'Parker, get away from the prisoner.'

I ignored him. 'You listening to me, Billy?'

He was rocking back and forth, still humming, his hands wrapped around his body 'Yeah, I hear you.' He screwed his face up in concentration. 'It's hard. I didn't but hardly see him. He was . . . *old.*'

'Try harder, Billy. Short? Tall?'

The humming started again, then stopped. 'Tall,' he said, during the pause. 'Maybe as tall as me.'

'Slim? Stocky?'

'Thin. He was a thin guy, but lean, y'know?' He stood, interested now, trying hard to picture the figure he had seen.

'What about his hair?'

'Shit, I don't know from hair . . .' He went back to his song, but now he added the words, only half forming some of them as if he were not entirely familiar with them.

*'Come all you fair and tender ladies*
*Take warning how you court your man . . .'*

And I recognised the song at last: 'Fair and Tender Ladies'. Gene Clark had sung it, with Carla Olson, although the song itself was much older. With the recognition came the remembrance of where I had heard it before: Meade Payne had been humming it as he walked back to his house.

'Billy,' I said. 'Have you been out at Meade Payne's place?'

He shook his head. 'I don't know no Meade Payne.'

I clutched the bars of the cell. 'Billy, this is important. I know you were heading out to Meade. You won't get him into trouble by admitting it.'

He looked at me and sighed. 'I didn't get out there. They picked me up before I even got into town.'

I spoke softly and distinctly, trying to keep the tension out of my voice. 'Then where did you hear that song, Billy?'

'What song?'

'The song you're humming, "Fair and Tender Ladies".
Where did you hear it?'

'I don't recall.' He looked away, and I knew that he did
recall it.

'Try.'

He ran his hands through his hair, gripping the tangled
locks at the back as if afraid of what his hands might do if
he didn't find some way to occupy them, and began to
rock back and forth again. 'The old man, the one I saw at
Rita's place, I think he might have been singing it, soft-
like, to himself. I can't get the damned thing out of my
head.' He started to cry.

I felt my throat go dry. 'Billy, what does Meade Payne
look like?'

'What?' he asked. He looked genuinely puzzled. From
behind me, I heard Jennings say: 'I'm warning you for the
last time, Parker. Get away from the prisoner.' His
footsteps sounded as he walked toward me.

'That's Meade over there, in that picture on the wall,'
said Billy, standing up as he spoke. He pointed to the
framed photograph of three men which hung on the
wall near the front desk, a similar version of the picture
that hung in the diner but with only two faces instead of
three. I walked over to it, nudging Rand Jennings out
of my way as I went. In the middle of the group was a
young man in a US Marines uniform, his right arm
around Rand Jennings, his left arm around an elderly
man who grinned back with pride at the lens. A plaque
below the photograph read 'Patrolman Daniel Payne,
1967–1991'.

Rand Jennings. Daniel Payne. Meade Payne. Except
the old man in the picture was short, about five-six,
stooped and gentle-eyed, with a crown of white hair

surrounding a bald head marked with liver spots. His face was mapped with a hundred lines.

He was not the man that I had met at the Payne house. And slowly, tumblers began to fall in my mind.

Everybody had a dog. Meade Payne had mentioned it in his letter to Billy, but I had seen no dog when I was out there. I thought of the figure Elsa Schneider had seen climbing the drainpipe. An old man couldn't climb a drainpipe, but a young man could. And I recalled what Rachel had said about Judith Mundy, about her being used as breeding stock.

Breeding stock.

*Breeding a boy.*

And I remembered old Saul Mann, his hands moving over the cards, swiftly palming the lady, or slipping the pea from under a soda pop cap to take five bucks from a sucker. He never pushed them, never hailed them or tried to force them to come, because he knew.

Caleb knew Billy would come back to Meade Payne. Maybe he got Meade's name from Cheryl Lansing before he killed her, or it could have come up during Willeford's investigations. However he found out, Caleb knew that if he took away all of the obstacles and all of the options, Billy would have to turn to Meade Payne.

Because Caleb understood what con men and hunters all understood: that, sometimes, it's best to lay the bait, wait, and let the prey come to you.

I turned to find Jennings with his Coonan in his hand, pointing in my direction. I guessed that I had ignored him for just that little too long. 'I'm tired of your shit, Parker. You and your buddies just drop your weapons and get on the ground,' he said. '*Now.*'

Ressler, too, drew his weapon and, in the rear office,

451

the younger policeman was already holding a Remington pump to his shoulder.

'Looks like we just crashed a nervous cops' convention,' said Angel.

'Jennings, I don't have time for this,' I said. 'You have to listen to me – '

'Shut up,' said Jennings. 'I'm telling you for the last time, Parker, put . . .' Then he stopped suddenly and looked at the gun in my belt.

'Where did you get that gun?' he asked, and menace stepped softly into his voice like a gunman at a funeral. He eased back the hammer on his pistol and took three steps towards me, his gun now inches from my face. He had now recognised the jacket and sweater as well. Behind me, I heard Angel sigh loudly.

'You tell me where you got that gun, dammit, or I'll kill you.'

There was no good way to tell him what had taken place, so I didn't even try. 'I was ambushed on the road. The old man who lived out by the lake, John Barley, he's dead. He died in my car. I was chased, I got to your house and Lorna gave me a gun. You may find some bodies in your living room when you get back but Lorna's safe. Listen to me, Rand, the girl – '

Rand Jennings let the hammer fall gently, hit the safety and then pistol-whipped me with the barrel of the gun, catching me a hard blow on the left temple. I staggered backwards as he drew his arm back to hit me again, but Ressler intervened and caught his arm.

'I'll kill you, you fuck. I'll kill you.' His face was purple with rage, but there was grief there too, and the knowledge that things could never be the same again after this, that the shell had finally been broken and the life he had lived up to then was escaping even as we spoke, dissipating into the air like so much gas.

I felt blood running down my cheek and my head ached badly. In fact, I ached all over, but I figured that was the kind of day it was. 'You may not get the chance to kill me. The men who ambushed me work for Tony Celli. He wants Billy Purdue.'

Jennings's breathing slowed, and he nodded at Ressler, who cautiously released his hold on Jennings's arm. 'Nobody is taking my prisoner,' said Jennings.

Then the lights went out, and all hell broke loose.

For a few moments, the station house was in total darkness. Then the emergency lighting kicked in, casting a dim glow from four fluorescents on the walls. From the cells, I heard Billy Purdue shouting: 'Hey! Hey in there, what's happening? Tell me what's going on. What happened to the lights?'

From the rear of the station came the sound of three loud bangs, like hammer blows, followed by the sound of a door hitting a wall. But Louis was already moving, the huge Roadblocker still in his hand. I saw him pass Billy Purdue's cell and wait at the corner, where the corridor leading down to the back door began. I felt him count three in his head, then he turned, stood to one side and fired two shots down the corridor. He moved out of sight, fired one more shot, then moved back into our line of vision. Jennings, Ressler and I ran to join him, while the young cop and Angel bolted the front door, Walter beside them.

In the corridor, two men lay dead, their faces concealed beneath black ski masks, both wearing black denims and short black jackets.

'They picked the wrong camouflage gear,' said Louis. 'Ought to have checked the weather forecast.' He pulled up one of the masks and turned to me: 'Anyone you know?'

I shook my head and Louis released his hold on the mask. 'Probably not worth knowing anyways,' he said.

We advanced cautiously to the open door. Wisps of snow flew into the corridor, blown by the wind outside. Louis took a broom and used it to nudge the door closed, its lock splintered by the impact of the blows it had received. No more shots came. He then helped Ressler to carry a desk down the corridor from the office and they used it to block the door. We left Louis to watch the door and returned to the main office, where Angel and the young cop were each at one side of a window, trying to catch a glimpse of the men moving outside. There couldn't have been many of them left, I figured, although Tony Celli was still among them.

Walter stood farther back. I noticed he had his old .38 in his hand. I was certain now that I knew where Ellen was, assuming she was still alive, but if I told Walter he would run hell-for-leather into Tony Celli's men in an effort to get to her, and that would serve no purpose at all, apart from getting him killed.

A voice came. 'Hey, inside. We don't want nobody to get hurt. Just send Purdue out and we'll be gone.' It sounded like Mifflin.

Angel looked at me and grinned. 'Just promise me, whatever happens, that you'll finish off that gimpy fuck for good this time.'

I took up a position beside him and looked out into the darkness. 'He is kind of irritating,' I agreed. I turned around to find Louis beside me.

'The door should hold. They try to come in again, we'll hear 'em before they can do any damage.' He took a quick look out of the window. 'Man, never thought I'd hear myself say this, but I feel like John Wayne.'

'*Rio Bravo*,' I said.

'Whatever. That the one with James Caan?'

'No, Ricky Nelson.'

'Shit.'

Behind us, Jennings and Ressler seemed to be attemping to come up with a game plan. It was like watching two children trying to hold chopsticks with their toes.

'You got a radio?' I asked.

It was Ressler who acknowledged the question. 'We're getting white noise, nothing else.'

'They're blocking you.'

Jennings spoke. 'We stay here, they'll give up. This isn't the frontier. They can't just attack a police station and take a prisoner.'

'Oh, but this is the frontier,' I said. 'And they can do what they want. They're not going to leave without him, chief. Celli wants the money Purdue took from him, or his own people will kill him.' I paused. 'Then again, you could always give them the money.'

'He didn't have any money when we found him,' said Ressler. 'Didn't even have a bag.'

'You could ask him where it is,' I suggested. I could see Billy Purdue looking at me curiously. Ressler looked at Jennings, shrugged and moved across to the cell. As he did so, Angel dived sideways while Louis pushed me to the floor. I cried out as my injured side hit the carpet.

'Heads up!' shouted Angel

The front window of the station house exploded inwards and bullets tore into the walls, the desks, the filing cabinets, the light fittings. They shattered glass partitions, blew up the watercooler and turned reports and files to confetti. Ressler fell to the ground, the back of his leg already ragged and red. Beside me, Angel rose and opened fire with the Glock. Louis's Roadblocker thundered as he took up a position beside him.

'We're going to be torn apart here,' shouted Angel. The firing from outside ceased. Behind us, there was only the sound of paper settling, glass crunching and water still dripping from the remains of the ruined cooler. I looked at Louis. 'We could bring the fight to them,' I said.

'Could do,' he said. 'You up to it?'

'Just about,' I lied. On the floor, Jennings was cutting the leg of Ressler's pants to get at the wound. 'You got a window that leads out into somewhere dark, maybe concealed by a tree or something?' I asked.

Jennings looked up at us and nodded. 'Window of the men's john, down that corridor. It's right beside the wall, too narrow for anyone to fit through the space but someone could get onto the surrounding wall itself from there.'

'Sounds good,' said Louis.

'What about me?' said Angel.

'You doing a bang-up job with that Glock,' replied Louis.

'You think?'

'Yeah. You actually hit anybody I'll start believing in God, but you sure scaring the hell out of Tony's boys.'

'You want help?' said Walter. They were the first words he had spoken to me since the funeral in Queens.

'Stay here,' I said. 'I think I've figured something out.'

'About Ellen?' The pain in his eyes made me wince.

'It's no good to any of us while Tony Celli's men are out there. When this is done with, we'll talk.'

We turned to leave, but it seemed like it was going to be one obstacle after another. Rand Jennings was still kneeling by Ressler. His gun was still in his hand. It was still pointing at me.

'You're not going anywhere, Parker.'

I looked at him, but continued walking. The muzzle of the gun followed me as I moved past him.

'Parker . . .'

'Rand,' I said. 'Shut up.'

Surprisingly, he did.

With that, we left them and headed to the men's toilet. The window was frosted and opened out above a pair of sinks. We listened carefully for movement outside, then slipped the latch, pulled the window open and stepped back. There were no shots, and within seconds we were hauling ourselves over the wall and into a patch of waste ground behind the north wall of the station, the shells in Louis's coat pockets jangling dully as he hit the ground. My side hurt, but by now I was past caring. I reached out for Louis as he prepared to move away.

'Louis, the old man out at Meade Payne's house is Caleb Kyle.'

He almost looked surprised. 'What you say?'

'He was waiting for Billy. If something happens to me, you take care of it.'

He nodded, then added. 'Man, you be takin' care of it yourself. They ain't killed you yet, then they ain't never gonna kill you.'

I smiled and we separated, slowly making our way in a pincer movement to the front of the station house, and Tony Celli's men.

# Chapter Thirty

I do not remember clearly much of what happened after I stumbled into the darkness. I recall that I was shivering constantly, but my skin was hot to the touch and my face was shiny with sweat. I had Jennings's gun but it still felt strange and unfamiliar in my hand. I vaguely regretted the loss of the Smith & Wesson. I had killed with it and, in doing so, had killed something inside me, but it was my gun and its history over the previous twelve months had mirrored my own. Perhaps it was for the best that it now lay deep in the water.

Snow was falling and the world was mute, its mouth stifled with flakes. My feet sank deep as I followed the wall, the station house to my left, cold piercing my boots and numbing my toes. On the other side of the station, I knew, Louis was moving steadily, the big shotgun in his hands.

I stopped where the wall fell suddenly at the edge of the building, becoming instead a three-foot high surround for the parking lot. I glanced into the lot, saw no movement, and made for the cover of a late-model Ford, but my responses were sluggish and I made more noise than I should have. My hands now shook continuously, so much so that I had to reach up with my left and still the barrel of my gun as I went. The pain in my side was unrelenting. When I looked down, I saw fresh bloodstains on the sweater.

The snow was being urged on by a wind that seemed to have gathered renewed vigour as the night drew on. Great swaths of white were swept into my face, and flakes crowded on my tongue. I tried to find Louis's dark form, but could see nothing beyond the lot. I knelt down, breathing heavily, sick to my stomach. For a moment, I thought that I might faint. I took a handful of snow and, crouching down carefully, rubbed it into my face. It didn't make me feel much better, but the gesture saved my life.

Above me, and to my left, a shape moved behind one of the cruisers. I saw a black, patent leather shoe rise from the snow, flakes still clinging to the cuff of the dark pants above it, the tail of a blue overcoat dancing and waving in the wind. I rose, and the gun rose with me, up, up, until my head and the gun were above the hood of the Ford. And as the figure turned, registering the movement, I fired a single shot into his chest and watched dispassionately as he fell back into the drift that had built up against the wall. There he remained slumped, his chin resting on his breast, his blood turning the snow black.

And in that instant, something happened inside me. My world turned dark as the blood-drenched snow and my mind began to lose its general focus. The universe blurred at its edges, leaving me with only a pinhole of perspective. And as the world shifted and tilted I seemed to both feel and hear the sound of a blade entering flesh and then a noise like a melon being halved with a single blow. I followed the tiny lens of clarity across the wall and over the road, where a small bank sloped down to the trees. In the snow a man lay in a heap, his body split from chest to navel and snowflakes gathering in his ruined head. There were footprints around his body, deep and firm. The footsteps veered away from the body and headed towards town, following a second trail of prints whose footfalls were distorted by a limp. There was blood between the marks of Mifflin's shoes. As I followed the tracks, more shots came from the direction of the station house, among them the sound of Louis's gun.

I walked south for five, ten minutes, maybe a little more, before I found myself at the end of a residential street. A woman and a man, both elderly, wrapped tightly in overcoats and blankets, stood on their porch, the old man with one arm around the woman's shoulders. There were no more shots now, but still they waited, and still they looked. Then they caught sight of me and both drew away instinctively, the man pulling his wife, or perhaps his sister, back through the open door and closing it behind them, all the time never taking his eyes from me. There were lights on in some of the other houses, and here and there curtains moved. I could see faces haloed with dim light, but no one else appeared.

I reached the corner of Spring Street and Maybury. Spring Street led on into the centre of town, but there was darkness at the end of Maybury, and the twin trails of prints moved in that direction. About halfway down the street, they separated, the distorted set moving on into the shadows, the second set veering north-west through the boundary between two properties. I guessed that Mifflin had got there first and found himself a position in the darkness from which he could view the street below him, and his pursuer had veered off to circle him when he guessed what was happening. I turned south and made my way around the backs of the houses until I came to the edge of a copse of trees where the western verge of the forest began. There I halted.

Perhaps thirty feet from me, at the edge of a pool of light shed by the last street lamp on the road, a cloud formed and then disappeared. Something moved in a startled, frightened gesture. A face scanned to the left, then to the right, and a figure peered from behind a tree. It was Mifflin, one arm still shrouded in a sling. As I drew nearer, shielded by the shadows and my footfalls silenced by the snow, I saw blood drip thickly from his fingers and join a growing pool at his feet. I was almost upon him when some small sound caused him to turn. His eyes grew wide and he rose swiftly, a knife flashing in his good hand. I shot him in the right shoulder and he spun, his feet twisting beneath him, falling on his back and loosing a loud cry of pain as he landed. I moved forwards quickly with the gun trained on him. He blinked hard and tried to focus as the light illuminated my features fully.

'You,' he said at last. He tried to rise but he had no strength. Only his head moved before the effort proved too much and it fell back into the snow. As I looked at him, I saw that a long gash had been torn across the front of his coat. Something shone wetly within.

'Who did this?' I said.

He tried to laugh, but it came out as a cough and blood sprayed from his mouth and flecked his teeth with red. 'An old man,' he said. 'A fucking old man. He came out of nowhere, slashed me, then took Contorno before we even knew what was happening. I fucking ran, man. Fuck Contorno.' He tried to move his head, to look back to the town. 'He's out there now, watching us. I can tell.'

Maybury was quiet, and nothing moved on the street,

but he was right: there was a watchfulness about the darkness as if, somewhere in its depths, someone held his breath, and waited.

'There'll be help here soon,' I said, although I was unsure even as I spoke that things had gone our way back at the police department. At least we had Louis, I thought, otherwise we'd all be dead. 'We'll get you to a doctor.'

He shook his head once. 'No, no doctor,' he said. He glared at me. 'It ends here. Do it, you fuck, do it!'

'No,' I said softly. 'No more.'

But he was not going to be denied. With all the strength left in his body, he reached into the breast of his coat, his teeth gritted with the effort. I reacted without thinking and killed him where he lay, but when I drew his hand from his coat it was empty. How could it be otherwise, when he had only a knife to defend himself?

And as I stood back something seemed to flicker in the darkness across the street, and then was gone.

I headed back to the police department and had almost reached it when a figure appeared to my right. I twisted towards it, but a voice said: 'Bird, it's me.' Louis appeared from the shadows, his shotgun cradled in his arms like a sleeping child. There was blood spray on his face, and his coat was torn at the left shoulder.

'You tore your coat,' I said. 'Your tailor's going to shed a tear.'

'It was last season's anyways,' said Louis. 'Made me feel like a bum wearing it.' He stepped closer to me. 'You don't look so good.'

'You are aware that somebody shot me?' I asked, in a pained tone.

'Somebody always shooting you,' he replied. 'Weren't somebody shooting at you, beating up on you or electrocuting you, you'd be listless. Think you can hold it together?' His tone had changed, and I guessed there was bad news coming.

'Go on,' I said.

'Billy Purdue's gone. Looks like Ressler collapsed from his wounds and Billy dragged him by the cuff of his pants over to the cell while Angel and the others were distracted. Took his keys from his belt and a shotgun from the rack, then let himself out. Probably left the same way we did.'

'Where was Angel? He OK?'

'Yeah, Angel and Walter both. They was helping Jennings to reinforce the back door. Seems like the last of Tony's guys made a second attempt on it after we left. Billy just walked out.'

'After we'd helped him by clearing the way.' I swore viciously, then told him about Mifflin and the dead man in the snow.

'Caleb?' asked Louis.

'It's him,' I said. 'He's come for his boy, and he's killing anyone who threatens him or his son. Mifflin saw him, but Mifflin's dead.'

'You kill him?'

'Yes,' I said. Mifflin had given me no choice but to kill him, yet there had been a kind of dignity to him in his last moments. 'I have to get out to Meade Payne's place.'

'We got more immediate problems,' said Louis.

'Tony Celli.'

'Uh-huh. It's got to end here, Bird. His car's parked maybe half a mile east, just on the edge of town.'

'How do you know?' I said, as we began walking in that direction.

'I asked.'

'You must have a very persuasive manner.'

'I use kind words.'

'That, and a big gun.'

His mouth twitched. 'A big gun always helps.'

A black Lincoln Towncar stood on a side road, its lights dimmed, as we approached. Behind it were two other cars, big Fords, also with their lights dimmed, and a pair of black Chevy vans. In front of the Lincoln, a figure knelt in the snow, its head down, its hands tied behind its back. Before we could get any closer a gun cocked behind us and a voice said: 'Put them down, boys.'

We did as we were told, but didn't turn around.

'Now walk on.'

The driver's door of one of the Fords opened, and Al Z stepped out. As the interior light came on I saw another figure, fat and silver haired, dark glasses on his eyes and a cigarette in his hand. Then he faded into the gloom again as Al Z closed the door. He walked to the kneeling figure as three other men appeared from the second Ford and stood, waiting. The kneeling figure raised its head, and Tony Celli looked at us with dead eyes.

Al Z kept his hands stuffed firmly in the pockets of his grey overcoat and watched us as we approached. When we were ten feet from Tony Celli he raised a hand, and we stopped. Al Z looked almost amused.

Almost.

'I asked you to stay out of our business,' he said.

'Like I told you, it was the "our business" part that I had a problem with,' I replied. I felt myself swaying, and willed my body to remain still.

'It's your hearing you have a problem with. You

should have picked somewhere else to start your moral crusade.'

He withdrew his right hand to reveal a Heckler & Koch 9mm, shook his head gently once or twice, said, 'You fucking guys,' in his soft, clipped tones, then shot Tony Celli in the back of the head. Tony slumped face first on the ground, his left eye still open and a hole where his right eye used to be. Then two men came forwards, one with a plastic sheet over his arms, and they wrapped Tony Celli and placed his body in the trunk of one of the cars. A third man ran a gloved hand through the snow until he found the bullet, then slipped it into his pocket along with the ejected case, and followed his comrades.

'He didn't have the girl,' said Al Z. 'I asked him.'

'I know,' I said. 'There's someone else. He took a blade to two of Tony's men.'

Al Z shrugged. The money was now his primary concern, not the ultimate fate of those who had chosen to follow Tony Celli. 'The way I figure it, you've done worse than that,' he said.

I didn't respond. If Al Z decided to kill us for what we'd done to Tony Clean's machine, there wasn't a whole lot I could say that would make him change his mind.

'We want Billy Purdue,' he went on. 'You hand him over, we'll forget what happened here. We'll forget that you killed men you shouldn't have killed.'

'You don't want Billy,' I replied. 'You want your money, to replace what Tony lost.'

Al Z took his left hand from his pocket and moved it in a gesture that indicated: 'Whatever'. Discussing the circumstances of the money's retrieval was just an exercise in semantics as far as he was concerned.

'Billy's gone. He got away in the confusion, but I'll find him,' I said. 'You'll get your money, but I won't hand him over to you.'

Al Z considered this, then looked to the figure in the car. The cigarette moved in a gesture of disregard, and Al Z turned back to us.

'You have twenty-four hours. After that, even your friend here won't be able to save you.' Then he walked back to the car, the men around him dispersing into the various vehicles as he did so, and they drove away into the night, leaving only tyre tracks and a smear of blood and grey matter on the snow.

# Chapter Thirty One

The station house looked like it had been attacked by a small army. Its front windows were almost entirely shattered. The door was pitted with bullet holes. Angel opened it as we arrived, and glass tinkled to the floor. Walter stood behind him. Behind us, some of the braver locals were approaching from the northern end of the town.

'Now we go find Caleb,' said Louis, but I shook my head.

'There are going to be feds on their way here soon. I don't want you or Angel here when they arrive.'

'Bullshit,' said Louis.

'No, it isn't, and you know it. If they find you here, no amount of explaining is going to get you out of trouble. Anyway, this part is personal – for me and for Walter. Please, get going.'

Louis paused for a moment, as if he were going to say more, then nodded. 'Tonto,' he called. 'We leavin'.' Angel joined him and they headed for the Mercury together. Walter stood beside me as we watched them go. I reckoned I had about an hour left in me, maybe an hour and a half, before I collapsed.

'I think I know where Ellen is,' I said. 'You ready to go get her?'

He nodded.

'If she's still alive, we're going to have to kill to get her back.'

'If that's what it takes,' he said.

I looked at him. I think he meant it.

'Fine. You'd better drive. It hasn't been my best day behind the wheel.'

We left the car a quarter of a mile beyond the Payne house and approached it from the rear, using the trees as cover. Two lights burned inside, one in a front room, the other in an upper bedroom. There was still no sign of life when we reached the verge of the property, where a small hut, its roof fitted with a sheet of corrugated iron, stood decaying slowly. There were footsteps in the snow that were not entirely obscured by the snowfall. Someone had been moving about recently, and the engine of the truck parked close by was still warm.

A smell came from the hut, the desolate odour of decaying meat. I moved to the corner, reached around and carefully slipped the bolt. It made a little noise, but not much. I opened the door and the smell became stronger. I looked at Walter, and saw hope die in his eyes.

'Stay there,' I said, and I slipped inside.

The smell was so strong now that it made my eyes water, and the stink was already clinging to my clothes. In one corner stood a long chest freezer, its corners eaten by rust which had left holes in its structure, its unconnected lead twisted around one support like a tail. I covered my mouth and lifted the lid.

Inside, a body lay curled. It was dressed in blue overalls, its feet bare, one hand behind its back with the rotting fingers splayed, the other obscured by the body. The face was bloated and the eyes were white. They were an old man's eyes. The cold had preserved him somewhat, and despite the ravages that had been visited on his body I recognised him as Meade Payne, the man in the photo back at the diner, the man who died so Caleb Kyle could take his place and wait for Billy Purdue to come to him. Beneath his body, I saw a tail and black fur: the remains of his dog.

Behind me, I heard the door creak on its hinges and Walter entered slowly and fearfully, his eyes following my stare into the freezer. He could not keep the relief from his features when he saw the body of the old man.

'This the guy in the picture?' he asked.

'That's him.'

'Then she's still alive.'

I nodded, but I didn't say anything. There were worse things than being killed and I think, in the dark, shuttered places of his mind, Walter knew that.

'Front or back?' I said.

'Front,' he replied.

I followed him outside and took a deep breath 'Let's do it.'

The house smelt sour when I opened the back door quietly and stepped into the large kitchen. There was a pine table with four matching chairs, the surface of the table covered with bread, some of it days out of date, and opened cartons of milk which even the temperature in the room had not prevented from going off. There were also some cold cuts, their edges curling and hard, and a dozen empty Mickey's Big Mouths, along with half a bottle of cheap, grain whiskey. In one corner stood a black trash bag, from which the worst smells of all came. I reckoned it contained over a week's worth of rotting food.

Through the open kitchen door I saw Walter enter the house, his nose wrinkling at the smell. He moved to his right, his back to the wall and his gun scanning the front dining room, which was connected to the kitchen by a closed door. I moved forwards and did the same with the TV room on the left side of the house. Both rooms were littered with discarded potato chip bags, more beer bottles and cans, and half-eaten food on dirty plates. The TV room also contained a green knapsack, all strapped up and ready to be taken away. I gestured to the stairs and Walter led, keeping to the wall to avoid any creaking steps, his gun high in a two-handed hold.

On the first landing was a bathroom that stank of urine and excrement, with damp, filthy towels lying across the toilet or piled on the floor by the door. Up two steps was the first bedroom, the bed unmade and more scattered food on the floor and dresser, but with no other indication that it had recently been occupied. There were no clothes, no shoes, no bags. It was in this bedroom that the light still burned.

Ellen Cole lay on the bed in the second bedroom, her hands tied to the bed-frame with ropes. There was a black rag tied over her eyes and ears, cotton padding stuffed beneath the band to muffle her hearing. Her mouth was taped, with a small hole torn in its centre. Two blankets covered her body. On a small bedside table sat a plastic water bottle.

Ellen didn't move as we entered the room although, as we drew closer, she seemed to sense us. Walter reached out to touch her, but she drew away with a small whine of fear. I pulled back the blankets gently. She had been stripped to her underwear, but she didn't appear to be hurt. I left them there as I searched the third bedroom. It, too, was empty, but the bed had obviously been slept in. When I returned to the second bedroom, Walter was gently holding Ellen's head and working the blindfold free. She blinked, her eyes narrowed even in the comparative darkness of the room. Then she saw him and started to cry.

'All empty,' I said.

I walked to the bed and cut the ropes holding her hands with my pocketknife while Walter stripped away the tape. He held her in his arms as she cried, her body heaving against him. I found her clothes in a pile by the window.

'Help her to get dressed,' I told him. Ellen still had not spoken, but while Walter slipped her feet into her jeans I took her hand and drew her attention to me.

'Ellen, there are just two of them, right?'

I took her a moment or two to respond, then she nodded. 'Two,' she said. Her voice was strained from lack of use, and her throat was dry. I gave her the water bottle and she took a small sip from the straw.

'Did they hurt you?'

She shook her head, then began to cry again. I held her, then moved away as Walter put her sweater over her arms and drew it down. He put an arm around her shoulders and helped her from the bed, but her legs collapsed almost immediately.

'It's okay, honey,' he said. 'We'll get you down.'

We were about to make our way down the stairs when, from below, there came the sound of the front door opening.

My stomach tightened. We listened for a moment or two, but no sound came from the stairs. I indicated to Walter that he should leave Ellen. If we tried to move her again, we would alert whoever was downstairs. She made a tiny, mewing sound as he drew away from her and tried to hold him back, but he kissed her gently on the cheek to reassure her, then followed me. The front door hung open, and snow billowed in from the darkness beyond. As we approached the final steps, a shadow moved in the kitchen to my right. I turned and put a finger to my lips.

A figure moved across the doorway, not looking in our direction. It was the young man I had met on my first visit to the house: Caspar, the man I believed to be Caleb's son. I swallowed hard and moved forwards, my hand up to let Walter know that he should hang back near the front door. I counted three and stepped into the kitchen, my gun raised and pointing to my left.

The kitchen was empty, but the connecting door into the dining room was now open. I sprang back to warn Walter, just in time to see a shape move behind him and a knife gleam in the dimness. He saw the look on my face and was already moving when the knife came down and caught him in the left shoulder, causing his back to arch and his mouth to contort in pain. He brought his gun across his body and fired beneath his left arm, but the knife rose and caught him again, this time in a slashing movement across his back as he fell. Caspar pushed Walter hard from behind, and his head impacted with a loud smack on the end of the bannisters. He fell to his hands and knees, blood running down his face and his eyes heavy and dazed.

The young man turned to me now, with the knife held blade down in his right hand. There was a fresh bullet wound at his hip, staining his filthy chinos a deep red, but he did not seem to notice the pain. Instead, he curled himself and hurled his body down the hallway towards me. His mouth was open, his teeth were bared, and the knife was ready to strike.

I shot him in the chest as he ran and he stopped hard, his body teetering on the soles of his shoes. He put a hand to the wound and examined the blood, as if only then would he believe that he had been shot. He looked at me one more time, cocked his head to one side, and then made as if to move at me again. I fired a second shot. This time, the bullet took him straight through the heart and he fell back onto the bare floor, his head coming to rest close to where Walter was trying to raise himself onto his hands and knees. I think he was dead before he hit the ground. Above me, I heard Ellen cry out, 'Daddy,' and saw her appear at the top of the stairs, dragging herself across the steps towards him.

Ellen's cry saved my life. As I turned to look at her, I heard a whistling sound at my back and saw a shadow move on the floor ahead of me. Something caught me a painful glancing blow to the shoulder, missing my head by inches, then the blade end of a spade swept by me. I grabbed at the wooden handle with my left hand, striking back with my right hand at the same time. I felt it connect with a jaw, then used the momentum of the spade to pull the man behind me forwards, using my right foot to trip him as he moved. He stumbled ahead of me, then fell to his knees. He stayed on all fours for a couple of seconds, then rose up and turned to face me, framed against the night by the open door behind him.

And I knew that this, at last, was Caleb Kyle. He was no longer posing as twisted and arthritic but stood tall and straight, his thin, wiry limbs encased in blue denims and a blue shirt. He was an old man, but I felt his strength, his rage, his capacity to inflict pain and hurt, as almost a physical thing. It seemed to radiate from him like heat and the gun in my hand wavered with the impact. His eyes were fierce and glowed with a deep, red fire, and I thought instinctively of Billy Purdue. I thought too of the young women left dangling from a tree and the pain they had endured at his hands, and of my grandfather, forever haunted by his dream of this man. Whatever pain Caleb himself had endured, he had returned it a hundredfold on the world around him.

Caleb looked at his dead boy lying close by his feet, then at me, and the intensity of his hatred rocked me on my heels. His eyes shone with a deep, malevolent intelligence. He had manipulated us all, evading capture for decades, and had almost succeeded in evading us again, but it had cost his son his life. Whatever happened after, some small measure of justice had been achieved for those girls left hanging from a tree, and for Judith Mundy, who had died, brutalised and alone, somewhere in the Great North Woods.

'No,' said Caleb. 'No.'

It was only then that I began to realise why he had wanted so badly to beget a boy. I think if Judith Mundy had given birth to a daughter then his hatred would have led him to kill the child, and try again for a son. He wanted what so many men wanted: to see himself replicated upon the earth, to see the best part of himself live on beyond him. Except, in Caleb's case, that which he desired to see continue was foul and vicious and would have consumed lives just as its father had before it.

Caleb moved forwards a step and I cocked the pistol. 'Back up,' I said. 'Keep your hands where I can see them.'

He shook his head, but moved back a few steps, his hands held out from his sides. He didn't look at me but kept his eyes fixed on his dead son. I advanced and stood beside Walter, who had raised himself to a sitting position, his uninjured right shoulder against the wall and blood streaking his face. He held his gun loosely in his right hand, but he was unable to focus and was obviously in severe pain. I wasn't doing so good myself. By now, Ellen was halfway down the stairs, but I held up a hand and told her to stay back. I didn't want her anywhere near this man. She stopped moving, but I could hear her crying.

In front of me, Caleb spoke again. 'You'll die for what you did to him,' he spat. His attention was now fully directed at me. 'I'll tear you apart with my bare hands, then I'll fuck the slut to death and leave the body in the woods for winter feed.'

I didn't reply to his taunt. 'Keep moving back, old man,' I said. I didn't want to be with him in an enclosed space; not in the hallway, not on the porch. He was dangerous. I knew that, even with the gun in my hand.

He retreated back again, then slowly moved down the steps until he stood in the yard, snow falling on his exposed head and his outstretched arms, light from the front roòm gilding him slightly. His hands were held two feet away from his side and I could see the butt of a gun protruding from the belt of his pants.

'Turn around,' I said.

He didn't move.

'Turn around or I'll shoot you in the legs.' I couldn't kill him, not yet.

He glared at me, then turned to his right.

'Reach around. Use your thumb and forefinger to take the butt of the gun, then throw it on the ground.'

He did as I told him, tossing the gun into some pruned rosebushes below the porch.

'Now turn back again.'

He turned.

'You're him, aren't you?' I said. 'You're Caleb Kyle.'

He smiled, a grey, wintry thing like a blight on the living organisms around him. 'It's just a name, boy. Caleb Kyle is as good as any other.' He spat again. 'You afeared yet?'

'You're an old man,' I replied. 'It's you who should be afraid. This world will judge you harshly, but not as harshly as the next.'

He opened his mouth, and the saliva made a clicking sound at the back of his teeth. 'Your granddaddy was afeared of me,' he said. 'You look the spit of him. You look afeared.'

I didn't reply. Instead, I tossed my head in the direction of the dead man on the floor behind me. 'Your dead boy, was his mother Judith Mundy?'

He bared his teeth at me and made as if to move in my direction, and I fired a shot into the ground in front of him. It kicked up a flurry of dirt and snow, and brought him to a halt.

'Don't,' I said. 'Answer me: did you take Judith Mundy?'

'I swear I'll see you dead,' he hissed. He stared beyond me to where his son lay, the muscles in his jaw tightening as he gritted his teeth against the pain he felt. He looked like some strange, ancient demon, the tendons on his neck standing out like cables, his teeth long and yellowed. 'I took it to breed on, after I thought my other boy was lost to me, lost down a shithouse sewer.'

'It'. 'Is she dead?'

'Don't see how it's any of your business, but it bled to death after it had the boy. I let it bleed. It weren't of no account anyhow.'

'Now you're back.'

'I came back for my boy, the boy I thought was lost to me, the boy that bitch kept from me, the boy all them bitches and sonsofbitches kept from me.'

'And you killed them all.'

He nodded proudly. 'Them as I could find.'

'And Gary Chute, the forestry worker?'

'He had no business being there,' he said. 'I don't spare them that cross my path.'

'And your own grandson?'

His eyes flickered for a moment, and there was something close to regret in them. 'It was a mistake. He got in the way.' Then: 'He was a sickly one. He wouldn't have survived anyhow, not where we were going.'

'You've got nowhere to go, old man. They're taking back their forest. You can't kill every man who comes in.'

'I know places. There are always places a man can go.'

'No, not anymore. There's only one place you're going.'

Behind me, I heard a movement on the stairs. Ellen had ignored me and gone to Walter. I guess I knew she would.

Caleb looked over my shoulder at her. 'She your'n?'

'No.'

'Shit,' he drawled. 'I saw you, and I saw your granddaddy in you, but my eyes must have deceived me when I saw you in her.'

'And were you going to "breed on her" too?'

He shook his head. 'She was for the boy. For both my

boys. Fuck you, mister. Fuck you for what you did to my boy.'

'No,' I said. 'To hell with you.' I raised the gun and pointed it at his head.

Behind me, I heard Walter groan and Ellen shouted 'Bird' in her strange, cracked voice. Something cold touched the back of my head. Billy Purdue's voice said: 'Your finger moves on that trigger, and it'll be the last thing you ever do.'

I hesitated for an instant, then released my grip on the trigger and moved my finger away from the guard, raising the gun to show him that I had done so.

'You know what to do with it,' he said.

I slipped the safety and threw the gun onto the porch.

'Down on your knees,' he said.

The pain in my side was almost unbearable, but I knelt and he moved around me, Walter's gun tucked into the waistband of his pants and a Remington shotgun in his hands. He stepped back so that he could keep us both in view.

Caleb Kyle looked upon him with admiration. After all that had happened, after all that he had done, his son had come back to him.

'Kill him, boy,' said Caleb. 'He killed your half-brother, shot him like a dog. He was kin to you. Blood calls for blood, you know that.'

Billy's face was a mass of confusion and harsh, conflicting emotions. The shotgun moved towards me. 'Is that true? Was he kin to me?' he said, unconsciously adopting the phrasing of the older man.

I didn't reply. His nostrils flared and he brought the butt of the gun down in a glancing blow across my head. I fell forwards and from in front of me I heard Caleb laugh.

'That's it boy, kill the sonofabitch.' Then his laughter subsided and, dazed as I was, I could see him move forwards a step.

'I came back for you, son. Me and your brother, we came back to find you. We heard you was lookin'. We heard about the man that you hired to find me. Your momma hid you away from me, but I came lookin' for you and now the lamb that was lost is found again.'

'You?' said Billy, in a soft, bewildered tone I had never heard from him before. 'You're my daddy?'

'I'm your daddy,' said Caleb, and he smiled. 'Now you finish him off for what he did to your brother, the brother you never got to meet. You kill him for what he did to Caspar.'

I rose to my knees, my knuckles supporting my weight, and spoke: 'Ask him what *he* did, Billy. Ask him what happened to Rita and Donald.'

Caleb Kyle's eyes glittered brightly, and spittle shot from his mouth. 'You shut up, mister. Your lies ain't going to keep me from my boy.'

'Ask him, Billy. Ask him where Meade Payne is. Ask him how Cheryl Lansing died, and her daughter-in-law, and her little granddaughters. You ask him, Billy.'

Caleb sprang onto the steps and his right foot kicked me hard in the mouth. I felt teeth break, and my mouth filled with pain and blood. I saw the foot come forward again.

'Stop,' said Billy. 'Stop it. Let him be.' I looked up and the pain in my mouth seemed as nothing to the agony etched in Billy Purdue's face. A lifetime's hurt burned in his eyes; a lifetime of abandonment, of loss, of fighting against a world that was always going to beat him in the end, of trying to live a life that had no past and no future, only a grinding, painful present. Now a veil had been pulled back, giving him a glimpse of what might have been, of what might still be. His father had come back for him, and all of the things he had done, all of the hurt this man had inflicted, he had done for love of his son.

'Kill him, Billy, and be done with it,' said Caleb, but Billy did not move, did not look at either of us, but stared into a place deep inside himself, where all that he had ever feared and all that he had ever wanted to be now twisted and coiled over each other.

'*Kill him*,' hissed the old man, and Billy raised his gun. 'You do as you're told, boy. You listen to me. I'm your daddy.'

And in Billy Purdue's eyes, something died. 'No,' he said. 'You ain't nothin' to me.'

The shotgun roared and the barrel bucked in his hands. Caleb Kyle hunched over and tumbled back as if he had been struck hard in the pit of his stomach, except now there was only a dark, spreading stain in which viscera shone and intestines protruded like hydra heads. He fell over and lay on his back, his hands raised to try to cover the hole at the centre of his being, and then, slowly and agonisingly, he hauled himself to his knees and stared at Billy Purdue. His mouth hung open and blood bubbled over his lips. His face was filled with hurt and incomprehension. After all that he had done, after all that he had endured, his own boy had turned on him.

I heard the sound of another shell being jacked into the gun, saw Caleb Kyle's eyes widen, and then his face disappeared and a warm, red hand obscured my vision, winter light dancing through it like thoughts through the mind of God.

From Dark Hollow the sound of sirens came, carrying on the cold air like the howls of wounded animals. It was 12.05 a.m., on December twelfth.

My wife and child had been dead for exactly one year.

# Epilogue

It is December twentieth, and soon Christmas will be here. Scarborough is a place of ice cream fields and sugar-frosted trees, with coloured illuminations at the windows of the houses and holly wreaths on the doors. I have cut a fir in the yard, one of a crop my grandfather had planted in the year that he died, and have placed it in the front room of the house. I will add small white lights to it on Christmas Eve, as an act of remembrance for my child, so that if she is watching from the darkness among the trees she may see the lights and know that I am thinking of her.

Above the fireplace, there is a card from Walter and Lee and a small, gift-wrapped box from Ellen. Next to it is a postcard from the Dominican Republic, unsigned but with a message written by two different hands: 'This communicating of a man's self to his friends works two contrary effects; for it redoubleth joys, and cutteth griefs in halves.' The quotation is not attributed. I will call them when they return, when the interest in the events that took place in Dark Hollow has begun to recede.

Finally, there is a notelet. I recognised the handwriting on the envelope when it arrived, and felt a kind of wrench in my heart as I opened it. The message said only: 'Call me when you can.' Beneath this line, she had written her home number and the number of her parents' house. She had signed it. 'Love, Rachel.'

I sit by my window and I think again of the winter dead, and of Willeford. He had been found two days before, and I felt the news of his loss with a sharp, savage pain. For a time, after he disappeared, I had half suspected the old detective. I had done him an injustice, and I think, in a way, I may have brought death upon him. His body had been buried in a shallow grave at the back of his property. According to Ellis Howard, he had been tortured before he died, but they had no indication of who might have been responsible. It could have been Stritch, I thought, or it could have been some of Tony Celli's crew, but I think, deep down, that he died because of the old man, Caleb Kyle, and I guessed that maybe it was Caleb's son Caspar who had killed him.

Willeford's name had been attached to the search for Billy Purdue's parents. It was his number that the old woman, Mrs Schneider, had called. If she could find him, then so could Caleb, and Caleb would have wanted to know all that Willeford knew. I hoped that the alcohol had dulled the pain, had made him a little less frightened as the end came. I hoped that he had told all that he knew as quickly as he could, but I knew that was probably a false hope. There had been something of the old honour, the old courage, about Willeford. He would not have given up the boy so easily. I had a vision of him, sitting in the Sail Loft, his whiskey and his beer chaser before him, an old man adrift in the present. He thought that it was progress that would spell his end, not some demon from the past that he had raised by doing a good turn for a lost, troubled young man.

And I think of Ricky, and the grinding noise that the trunk of the car made as it was opened, and the sight of him huddled beside the spare tyre, and how he had tried to save Ellen in the last moments before he died. I wish him peace.

Lorna Jennings had left Dark Hollow, and Rand. She called me to tell me she was leaving for Illinois to spend Christmas with her parents before looking for a new place to live. The machine took the message, although I was in the house when she called and could hear her voice against the soft whirring of the tape. I didn't pick up. It was better that way, I thought.

And the man known as Caleb Kyle had been buried in a pauper's grave to the north of a churchyard outside Augusta, alongside the boy he called Caspar, and prayers were said for their souls. A few days later, a man was seen at the graveside, a big man with pain in his eyes. He stood in the snow and looked at the shape of the newly disturbed earth beneath it. To his left, the sun faded from the sky, leaving streaks of red across the clouds. The man had a small pack on his back, and a piece of paper with the date of his court appearance written upon it by his bail bondsman. It was an appearance he would never make, and the bondsman knew it. Some of Al Z's money had bought his complicity, and his silence. Al Z could take the loss, I thought.

This was the second cemetery that Billy Purdue had visited that day, and he would never be seen in it again. Billy Purdue would never be seen anywhere again. He would disappear, and no trace of him would ever be found.

But I think I knew where Billy was going.

He was going north.

\* \* \*

Two days after the anniversary, I attended mass at St Maximilian Kolbe and listened as the names of Susan and Jennifer Parker were read out from the altar. The next day, the fifteenth, I visited the grave. There were fresh flowers laid upon it – from Susan's parents, I supposed. We had not spoken since her death, and I think they still blamed me for what had happened. I blamed myself, but I was making reparation. That was all that I could do. That was all any of us could do.

On the night of the fifteenth, they came to me. I awoke to the noise of them in the woods, sounds that were not sounds, but the slow joining of worlds within worlds, and I walked to my porch and stood, but I did not descend to them.

Among the shadows, behind the trees, a host of figures moved. At first, they might have been the light shifting as the wind stirred the branches, phantasms of hands and faces, for they were silent as they came forward for me to bear witness. They were young girls, and their dresses, once torn and stained with blood and dirt, were now intact and glowed from within, clinging to soft, slightly rounded stomachs that might, once before and long ago, have caused the young men to twist in the seats of their bright red cars, to whistle at them from their vinyl booths, to lean across and whisper to them, to playfully block their escape as they basked in the light from their eyes. The moonlight shone on the soft down of their arms, the gentle movement of their hair, the soft glistening at their lips; the girls in their summer dresses, gathered together in the new-fallen snow.

And farther behind them, others gathered: old women and old men, nightdresses fluttering like moths, stained dungarees war-painted with flecks and dashes of enamel, their gnarled hands traced with thick veins like the roots of the trees clinging to the earth beneath their feet. Young men stood aside for them, their hands joined with those of their women; there were husbands and wives, and young lovers, once violently separated, now together once more. Children moved between their legs, solemn and watchful, carefully making their way to the boundary of the woods; children with the broken bones in their fingers now miraculously restored, children who had been wrenched apart in dark, pain-filled cellars now restored to beauty, their eyes bright and knowing in the winter darkness.

A whole host of the dead gathered before me, their numbers stretching back into the shadows, back into the past. They did not speak but only watched me, and a kind of peace came over me, as if the hand of a young woman had touched me gently in the night, whispering to me that I should sleep.

*for now*

And beside the rail, where the old man had sat with his dog, where my mother had leaned, still beautiful despite the years, I stood and felt their eyes upon me. A small hand gripped mine and when I looked down I could almost see her, radiant and new, a small beauty revealed against the gentle luminosity of the snow.

And a hand touched my cheek and soft lips met mine, and a voice said:

*sleep*

And I slept.

JOHN CONNOLLY

THE KILLING KIND

A Mass Grave. A Suspicious Suicide.
A Tangled Web of Ageless Evil.

Grace Peltier is dead. But before she died, she stole
something. A relic capable of linking a sinister
organisation known as the Fellowship to decades of
violence and murder.

Now someone has been sent to recover it.

And someone has to stop him . . .

Charlie Parker's shocking confrontation with demonic
Mr Pudd will force Maine's maverick detective to
descend into a honeycomb world of lost souls and
dark angels, where he must do battle with a terrifying
evil as old as time itself:

The Killing Kind.

'The unrivalled master of Maine noir.
Menace has never been so seductive.'
Maxim Jakubowski, GUARDIAN

JOHN CONNOLLY

THE WHITE ROAD

New Atrocities.
Old Evil.

A young South Carolina black man faces the death
penalty for rape and murder. But for private detective
Charlie Parker, the roots of this case stretch much further.
Tracing them will mean a descent into the abyss; a
journey through a living nightmare peopled by the
strange instruments of a fanatic's revenge.

And truth lies buried in the darkest places . . .

It lies in the outcome of the terrible reckoning that
threatens Parker's lover, his unborn child and his
very soul.

It lies on the path where the living and the dead converge.

It lies on the White Road.

'One of the most distinguished practitioners of US
crime-writing. The book synthesises literate, poetic
writing with scarifying grue.' INDEPENDENT

# JOHN CONNOLLY

## BAD MEN

In 1963, the settlers on the small Maine island of Sanctuary were betrayed to their enemies and slaughtered. Since then, the island has known three hundred years of peace.

Until now. For men are descending on Sanctuary, their purpose to hunt down and kill the wife of their leader and retrieve the money that she stole from him. All that stands in their way are a young rookie officer, Sharon Macy, and the island's strange, troubled policeman, the giant known as Melancholy Joe Dupree. But Joe Dupree is no ordinary policeman. He is the guardian of the island's secrets, the repository of its memories. He knows that Sanctuary has been steeped in blood once; it will tolerate the shedding of innocent blood no longer. Now a band of killers is set to desecrate Sanctuary and unleash the fury of its ghosts upon themselves and all who stand by them.

On Sanctuary, all hell is about to break loose . . .

'One of the most distinguished practitioners of US crime-writing.' INDEPENDENT